THE
SHALLOW
SEA

Books by Neil Ruzic

For Adults:

THE SHALLOW SEA
WHERE THE WINDS SLEEP* *(Doubleday)*
SPINOFF (NASA)

For Teenagers

THERE'S ADVENTURE IN CIVIL ENGINEERING
THERE'S ADVENTURE IN METEOROLOGY
    (Popular Mechanics Press)

For Scientists and Engineers

THE CASE FOR GOING TO THE MOON *(Putnam)*
STIMULUS (ed.) *(Scientific Research)*
OPEN-OCEAN POLYCULTURE SYSTEM
A BLUEPRINT FOR AN ISLAND FOR SCIENCE
TECHNOLOGIES EMERGED (ed.)
    (Technical Publishing)

* *A Literary Guild selection*

THE
SHALLOW
SEA

Neil Ruzic

ST. CLAIR PRESS

Copyright © 1992 by Neil Ruzic

Manufactured in the United States of America
10   9   8   7   6   5   4   3   2   1

This book has been typeset completely in 12 pt. Times Roman
using Ventura Publisher® software.

Ventura Publisher® is a registered trademark of Ventura Software, Inc.

Jacket design Don Lewis

Distributed to the trade by:
Lifetime Books, Inc.
Hollywood, Florida

Cataloging-in-Publication Data

Ruzic, Neil
The shallow sea
1. Bahamas—Bahamian culture—Bahamian Government.
2. Drug smuggling. 3. Reverse race predjudice. 4. Fiction
92-061197

ISBN 0-9632357-0-2

To: Carol, forever

Acknowledgements

WHEN YOU HAVE LIVED in the locale of a novel, there's a tendency to include too much. For help in choosing scenes and for plot strategy I am indebted to my son, Dr. David N. Ruzic, and for editing and plot tactics to Dr. Bruce Michelson. David and Bruce are among the world's great teachers. University of Illinois professors of nuclear physics and American literature, respectively, they occasionally join together to teach a seminar combining technology and the humanities. Both have helped immeasurably with this book through a dozen rewrites.

Others who have made constructive suggestions include author Norbert Hansen and editors Eric Tobias of Pocket Books and John Douglas of Avon Books. My former allies in magazine publishing, Terry Sinclair, Tim Burkholder, and Thérèse Harbart, were of immense help, as was Bob Warnke of St. Clair Press.

Technical experts who helped add realism to the text include: my scuba buddy, the private detective Joe Mahr, a weapons authority; Andy Raymond, my advisor on Bahamian jails; Alfred Weisbrich, inventor of the remarkable wind-augmentation design described in the book; NASA Langley's chief pyrotechnics engineer Lawrence Bement, and Joe Gowdey, head of Langley's electrical systems section, who helped me design the miniature torpedoes; Robert Multer, president of Aidco Maine Corp., solar pond expert; Dr. Tom Corbin, station manager of Pioneer Hi-Bred International Inc., who furnished ideas for genetic engineering of drugs; Dr. Sam Gruber, University of Miami shark authority; and vascular surgeon Dr. Rade Pejic, who guided me through both the bloodstream and the Serbo-Croatian language.

Among my Bahamian friends who lent attitudes and ideas are, on the island of Great Harbour Cay, Harry Rolle, Fuzzy Adderley, Chris Roberts, and Val Dean (proprietor of the Grave Yard Inn). Also Tony Robinson of Harbour Island, Ray Pinder of Freeport, and Magistrate Ian Bethell of Nassau. Dr. Gail Saunders, director of archives in Nassau, located often-obscure historical references.

Don Lewis, art director of my former magazine company, is the artist who did the jacket cover, not once but three times. And Scott Carpenter, astronaut, aquanaut, novelist, and friend, offered editorial advice. —nr

PROLOGUE

The Horse Latitudes, March 16

SINCE early summer Grant North and his workers had lived on the Island, sending their supply ship, the *Half Fast*, back and forth to the Florida coast a hundred and fifty miles away. The Island and the thousand other Bahama Islands that flit like sandflies over the map of Cuba had stayed hot and restless all winter. Now the storms came, cooling their fever.

Tonight the waves clawed the *Half Fast*, a war-surplus "landing craft motorized" or LCM. To Captain Evan Symes, she was long and ghostly, her bow dissolved in fog. The waves smashing into her square bow made piloting like plowing a field with a cement block. The rollers were liquid metal, and when one broke over the ship the ocean closed in leaving no wake, no mark on the planet, as if the ship were already dead. Symes and his crew had been making these runs every week. And now they were lost.

Basil Campbell came in from the forward deck in his yellow slicker and climbed the four steps to the wheelhouse. "It's 'orrendous out there, Captain Evan."

"Happens every March," said Evan Symes. What did this white foreigner expect when the seasons changed, a blue lagoon?

"We should be seein' lights by now," Campbell said. "Palm Beach, Lauderdale, Miami . . . Some bloody thing!"

"We been blown all over the damn ocean," said Symes. "For all I know, we still on the Bimini side."

"Want I should wake the boys?"

Symes shook his head wearily. They were *his* sons, and he resented the white man's interference as he resented everything this Scotsman did or said.

Symes lit a cigarette and wished that his party, the party of the black majority, had thrown out *all* the white men in 1973 when the blacks took over the country. The spray soaked his cigarette. In disgust he flicked it out the window he kept open to prevent fogging of the glass, and of his brain. He unbuttoned the neck of his military-cut jacket, revealing the gold chain and shark's tooth that had come from a big one he'd speared himself. The red binnacle light turned Symes's brown skin black and made his eyes appear even redder than they were, as raw as those who had once endured sleepless voyages in galleons. Native to the island of Abaco, Symes and his teenage sons, Kenny and Keith, were descended from the slaves of the loyal colonists who fled the American Revolution.

Basil Campbell was a "Belonger," a uniquely Bahamian term that designates second-class citizenship for U.K. subjects who were residents before Independence and are allowed to work but not vote. Symes relished that second-class bit: it fit Campbell with his short stature and dirty blond hair as much as it did the white Bahamians on Abaco whose faces were pushed in from inbreeding, they being too proud to intermarry after two hundred years of living alongside the blacks. Campbell, one of Dr. North's hiring mistakes, irritated Symes the way he always tried to butter up the kids and pretended to ignore their racial difference.

Campbell rumbled around in the galley located on the well deck and returned with steaming mugs of tea.

"Worried about yer monster from the black lagoon?" said Symes as he took the mug.

"I'm worried about getting lost, I am."

"Think you could pilot dis barge better'n me?"

Campbell said nothing, which suited Symes fine. He was edgy. Out here above the vast seagirt plateau, gnawed by waves into islands and breached by unfathomed canyons called the Tongue of the Ocean, a man could imagine the edge of a flat earth, and dwell on the abyss of fear.

Nothing could be seen ahead, so Symes kept watch to his rear, swiveling his head around every few seconds to check the compass. The anemic light from the binnacle hardly made it to the afterdeck, but whenever the moon broke through the clouds he could see his wake drawn irregularly over the ocean like the path of a frantic snake.

The *Half Fast* broached again and a maverick wave slammed into her steel beam with a noise like a cannon blast. The wheelhouse flashed with intermittent lightning, popping like flashbulbs and ruining their night vision. Symes kept the throttles open and the compass as close as he could to two-eight-zero. The bloated half moon, tilted like a crucible, emerged from its nimbus shroud and dripped metallic light into the cabin.

At least they weren't carrying this time. Last week, with a half ton of cocaine hidden between the steel plates of the hull, Symes had shaken like a fern as he faced the little men with matching mustaches and machine-gun Spanish on the Florida shore, while their scout plane tracked the Coast Guard that might be vectoring the area. Symes had taken the gamble offered to private captains in these waters, and vowed never to do it again. He had delivered without incident three hundred bricks of compressed white crystals weighing two kilos each, with a wholesale value of nine-million dollars. His ten-percent cut, wrapped in waterproofing within the double hull, would buy a freighter several times larger than this LCM.

The Cubans didn't seem to care whether Symes quit or continued. During the nine months he had been working for Grant North's Island for Science, the art of smuggling had undergone a transformation. You didn't have to risk your ass when you could catapult drone aircraft from a mothership. Or make air drops into a mangrove jungle with the cocaine and a beeper stuffed inside automobile tires. Or sew the dope inside a dead jewfish and tow it behind a Cigarette boat. The truly big shipments these days use ordinary cargo containers aboard unsuspecting freighters, and when even one of a dozen consignments gets through, the Cubans are money ahead. And of course nearly every shipment makes it these days.

Symes's searchlight did nothing except bounce off the fog, and he prayed for more lightning so he could see what lay ahead. He closed the side window all but an inch. "This be some kinda night," he said to no one in particular. "Damn waves are Sevens, at least."

Evan Symes hated waves of any kind, except Ones which according to his private rating system meant ripples on a flat ocean. His repugnance grew number by number until it crested for the hurricane-driven Tens, the towering cliffs of water which few ships could survive. The rollers surrounding him now were as high as the wheelhouse, but he saw them only sporadically, for the fog was thickening in the first black hours of the new day.

"Here come a *real* bastard," Campbell said, bracing himself as the little ship lifted to a crest and plunged like an elevator in free fall. He laughed. "That'll uncurl yer kinky hair!"

"Piss ant," Symes muttered. Straining his eyes through the pie-sliced shape made by the windshield wipers, he steered aimlessly through the fog that was settling above the sea like a lethal gas.

The bow took a force-eight wave head-on, slashing water like iron across the windshield and rattling the side panes. Campbell lurched. "Bloody 'ell . . . Let there be lights soon!" He pulled himself erect to look out the window. A giant breaker, capped in froth, slid beneath the hull and out again.

"Forget the lights. We ain't nowheres near the coast."

Sixes and sevens cascaded over the square bow, rushed down the length of the upper deck that kept the well deck dry, and assaulted the windshield. When he had his own freighter, Symes thought, he'd head south. In his years at sea he had come to hate this latitude twenty-five degrees north where the winds varied from banshee screams to an ocean so flat that mosquitos could walk on the surface. The horse latitudes were named three centuries ago when captains of becalmed square riggers killed their horses to conserve dwindling supplies of fresh water. Symes could imagine grim, bearded sailors in their filthy brigs and barks staring at a sea where the winds slept, slaughtering a horse a day on their wooden decks, drinking the blood for the water in it and for the red courage in it, saving what little of the meat they could eat before it spoiled, and throwing the majority of the carcass to the sharks.

Symes understood such men. Years ago after his divorce, he and his brother William deliberately sank a heavily insured hundred-tonner they'd bought cheap. With the insurance payoff, the brothers left the island of Abaco for Nassau, where they tried to ooze into the white shipping aristocracy like shark repellent in ocean water and with the same lack of effectiveness. Instead, William bought a fast-boat distributorship, and Evan piloted other people's freighters.

As much as Symes hated heavy seas and white men, he loved ships, even this little LCM *Half Fast*. Designed to land an M-60 tank or fifty troops on an enemy beach, the landing craft now brought bulldozers, cement mixers, and building materials to Grant North on the Island. With the removable deck in place, you could keep cement dry in the well deck, and haul lumber above. Aft of the cargo area on the well deck were crew lockers, a small stateroom, head, and galley. Mounted above the lockers were the ship's two stainless-steel Winchester shotguns. Inside a locker behind a false wall was Symes own 9-mm Uzi submachine gun.

Symes liked to imagine himself the *capitán* and the LCM a galleon. Both were about sixty feet on the water line and both could carry enormous cargos for their size. Like those early explorers, Symes sailed west on the tradewinds, picked up the bounty of the New World, and returned northeast across the Straits of Florida where the Gulf Stream gave him a boost, then east across the shallow sea back to the Island. On the Spanish galleons, the highest part of the ship lay astern in an elevated deck called the poop. Sixteen feet above the water line, the *Half Fast's* poop grew out of the roof of the cabin into a wheelhouse accessible from inside.

This morning Symes had been in the wheelhouse preparing to depart from the Island, the bow door yawning open on the beach like the mouth of a whale, when he heard Grant North squabbling with his daughter Coby. A moment later the girl ran inside with her suitcase and crumpled sobbing against the steel hull. North ran after her, eating up the distance from his villa to the LCM, face red, eyes fixed like a battle steed. Their voices carried through the empty well deck and up through the cabin to the wheelhouse.

"*All* my friends—"

"*Never again!*" North's words reverberated in the steel hull. "*. . . again, gain, gain, gain, gain . . .*"

When Symes called down to North and asked, "You want I should throw her off?" the scientist had wavered for a moment.

Then he said, "Forget it. Maybe she'll come to her senses in Florida."

SYMES DISCOVERED the bottom of the ocean not where it was supposed to be, and he felt in his stomach the terror of sudden foam swirling around an unseen mass of coral. Switching his gaze from fathometer to chart and back again, he sent Campbell to a-waken the boys and post them with lifelines forward and aft. As soon as he reached the bow, Kenny shouted something to Campbell who was holding open the starboard door.

"Evan!" said Campbell, relaying the message, flinging the words up to the wheelhouse. "*Rock dead ahead! Full astern, quick!*"

"Holy shit!" whispered Symes, a prayer as heartfelt as an Ave Maria from the *conquistadores* he emulated.

A giant, something black and sinister, hung in the fog off their starboard bow. Symes slammed both engines into reverse, then idled, letting the *Half Fast* creep closer until the spray and mist thinned.

"Jesus, that ain't no rock!" shouted Campbell. "She's a Defender!"

And Symes could see her eight-foot Oerlikon 20-mm cannon aiming down his throat. He knew that patrol boat: Her Majesty's Bahamas Ship, the *HMBS Munnings*. The radio sputtered with a voice as deep as the Tongue of the Ocean, a voice he recognized. "Heave to, *Mister Symes*. This is St. Gregory. I'm gonna board you."

Symes stared at the radio, rubbing his temples and trying to supress rage born of contempt for Carlos St. Gregory. A captain in the Royal Bahamian Defence Force, the man was about as far as you can get from being a saint.

"Go on, Evan, ignore the bastard. Maybe you 'urt 'is feelings enough, 'e'll go away."

St. Gregory's voice over the radio had the sound of a pred-ator concealing its appetite. "You copy, Mister?" The gunboat's arclight snapped on, boiling through the fog into the windshield of the *Half Fast*.

Symes picked up the mike. "I hear yuh, mon! Turn thot damn light off."

"Then heave to."

"The hell I will, you Bay Street asshole! These seas'll swamp me." If there was anyone Evan Symes hated more than a white Belonger, it was a white Bahamian who had been born into the Nassauvian aristocracy.

"Turn to course one-zero-five. There is a cay ten minutes ahead. We will board in her lee. Out."

A cay? Here? How could a cay sprout in the middle of the Gulf Stream? Then he realized he must have been blown clear to one of the islands south of Bimini. Symes swung the wheel to port until his compass came up on one-zero-five. The *Half Fast* plodded ahead, drenched in the beam of the arclight that St. Gregory waved back and forth like a pointer.

"D'ya think they bloody know?" Campbell said from the shad-ows of the wheelhouse.

Easily twice as long as the LCM, the sleek gunboat closed the distance between them. The uneven pair plowed evenly toward the invisible shore, the diesel exhaust making Symes sick. Two of the Defence Force crewmen, one forward, one aft, readied lines thick as wrists, balancing themselves to board the smaller craft and lash her to the patrol boat. The moonlight made their blue uniforms fluoresce, but their black faces and hands melted into the night as if headless sailor suits had been stuck on the stanchions for a joke. The rain had subsided to a drizzle and now the moon rode brighter behind purple clouds, spilling more of its silver light. They could hear the rumble of the gunboat's power-plant over their own. Keith and Kenny waited at the door in their slickers.

Campbell tried again. "You think the Defenders found out?"

The Defence Force was the Bahamian version of a Coast Guard, and everyone called them "Defenders" except the troops themselves who liked to be known as "marines."

"Who cares?" said Symes. "We be clean now. He jus' mad cuz he told me to clear this trip wid him."

"Weeping Jesus!" Campbell's streetface, outraged and unrelenting, supplanted his patronize-the-blacks face. "Why 'adn't you called the bugger?"

Symes fell silent. He was trying to shake his own voices out of his head, let alone Campbell's, and they lashed his brain like the roar of the wind.

"We must a been seen in Bimini," Campbell persisted, "and been blabbed about to the bleedin' Defenders."

In Alice Town they had paraded like tourists in and out of the shops along King's Highway, while Keith and Kenny had shown off over the beaches and parkways, climbing coconut palms, hanging like monkeys from the top fronds—fooling around like that all over town. Coby kept to herself along the docks where she talked to some of the charter captains. Campbell, though, seemed intent on increasing his profile and had flirted with every young woman in sight, wanting nothing more than to take back to the States a hold full of girls.

"If we was seen it was your fault," said Symes.

"Maybe North found out about last time and tipped the Defenders, eh?"

"Naw," said Symes, "he'd never let his little gal go aboard a ship he'd set up."

Every time the two ships closed the gap, the wind gusted and created eddies in the sea that caused one or the other to broach or slam their hulls together. But here in the comparative lee of the unseen cay, a ship *could* be boarded. It was only a matter of time.

Campbell came up from the well deck with a fierce look on his face and the Uzi in one hand.

"Jesus, Basil! That ain't no play boat out dere. These be *Defenders!*"

For a moment Symes felt the security that had washed over him like a force-one wavelet when he'd bought that nine-pound protector in Miami, with its cyclical firing rate of six hundred fifty rounds per minute and its velocity of thirteen hundred feet per second. But he knew it would only make things worse. "Get rid a thot gun—" He wrenched the Uzi out of the Scotsman's hands, and shoved it under the seat cushion.

BaaaMmmm! ScrRRReeeeee! Steel against steel, a fingernail across the blackboard of the night, a plangent groan over the noise of wind, waves, and diesels. A dozen Defenders vaulted across the gap and dropped to the deck of the smaller vessel. Like viruses spreading a deadly disease, they swarmed over the *Half Fast* brandishing submachine guns.

In the next downswell the vessels parted, then yawed toward each other. The *Munnings*' steel superstructure became a giant sabre that sliced off the aft starboard corner of the LCM's wheelhouse. Raising his arms against flying debris, Symes moved away from the gaping hole. His ship's radio had been shattered, yet he could hear St. Gregory talking. Looking down into the cabin, where Kenny and Keith were trying to make themselves invisible, Symes saw that the voice was coming from the Defenders' hand-held radios.

"Everything under control?" squawked Captain St. Gregory.

The heavier Defender, a force chief with an armful of stripes and hashmarks, spoke into the portable VHF. "Yessuh. Two here in de cabin, two more up in de wheelhouse."

"All right, keep them covered and send the squad home, now. I'm coming across."

One of the two Defenders in the cabin snapped his submachine gun on safety, vaulted out the starboard door, and clambered with the other troops back to the *Munnings*. Captain St. Gregory arrived in a surreal haze, his bulk filling the cabin, his brown beret brushing the ceiling, his 9-mm NATO submachine gun held in one massive hand.

In a strobelight of slow-motion horror, Evan Symes witnessed the inexorable chain of events. His sons wearing expressions of disbelief that a Defender would shoot children. A burst of ear-shattering SMG explosions at ten rounds per second. The boys slumping into heaps against the bulkhead. Spent cartridges flopping around the cabin deck like caught herring.

The sound of the force chief spraying another submachine gun elsewhere in the vessel shocked Symes back to reality. He saw Captain St. Gregory aiming impassively into the wheelhouse, but he couldn't take his eyes off the bodies of his sons and the blood that ran down their chests like spilled paint. He entertained a rabid thought of reaching under the seat for the Uzi, but he was frozen where he stood.

The smell of the night turned from salt to fear, ebbed like the tide, deepened, then flowed again. The screaming was monstrous and he wished whoever it was would stop. It turned out to be Campbell standing next to him, arms overhead, mouth wide. Not screams of terror, screams of reason. Symes hung on every word, knowing that *only* loud talk could possibly save them now.

Campbell was shrieking over and over again, "I'll *show* you w'ere the money's 'idden! Almost *a million!* I'll show you . . ." Campbell, who never in his life had pronounced an "H," now said, *"The money is HHHHHHHHHHHHHhidden in the—"*

Evan Symes's hands were pressed so tight over his head they were numb and seemed detached as if praying on their own. Mustering strength, he wrenched his eyes away from the horror and turned to face the foaming ocean, drinking in the night, filling his mind with the shattered geography of the Spanish Main. The ocean had become a seething wall between life and death, and he could feel it yielding. The last sounds he heard were the 9-mm shots that found Basil Campbell, then riddled his own body with a pain that spread on the waves across the chaotic sea.

1 *Island of Dreams*

THE ISLAND is a daylight world so ablaze with promise that the air tastes like strong wine, the tides breathe new life, and you can feel the sovereign pulse of the jungle. The men who came to shape the Island for Science left behind a weary, indifferent world where they seldom noticed when it rained or snowed. Grant K. North, who once had tried to go to the moon, arrived here nine months ago with a dream and the tenacity of a mako shark. Now there was a settlement of sorts, though no larger yet than one of his proposed lunar colonies. And in the surrounding jungles, savannas, and beaches the echoes of the buccaneers still rang and the curses of Blackbeard and Calico Jack still tortured the air.

At the east end were the stone villas, the lodge, and the dock. Down-island, the wind tower and the shrimp-breeding laboratory faced the seafarm on the shallow side of the Island. Beyond these buildings the jungle forest with its cave-like holes winding into the earth, the waiting scorpions, and strange poisonberries whispered dark thoughts to the Bahamians. Out on the flats a head-on crash of two speeding boats was blamed on the local ghost, or Chickcharney, who fed the broken bodies of the speeders to the sunning sharks. Another malevolent spirit stopped a girl's heart in the village on Great Snake Cay, from where North's forty workers commuted daily. In that world across eight miles of shallow sea, where huge rays glide like the shadows of clouds, and in this new world of Grant North's making, a man might think about nature's purpose for himself.

These could be savage islands when the sharks or the breakbone fever appears, and desolate islands when night descends like a shroud, the desolation allayed by a drink at the Grave Yard Inn in the village, or for those staying on the Island, by the "Cleary Coladas" drunk at the hammocks between coconut palms. For Grant North and his daughter Coby, for Jack Cleary, North's best friend, and for Andy Angelo, their young helper, the rocky coast was a barrier that divided past from future. Like all pioneers, they had come to build a better life for themselves, and were proud that their technology would benefit every tropical region of the world. They struggled, innovated, and entertained themselves here surrounded by the magnificent tumult of the ocean. They lived in this Island. And they were finding that the Island lived in them too.

Today at dawn, waiting for the workers to arrive in the company jollyboat, Grant North realized his intuition had been calling him all day. Something was not right with Coby, something beyond their fight. Like most intuitives, North had been told in childhood that intuition is second-best and notoriously unreliable. He grew up suspecting that those who deny their hunches were making excuses for not strengthening this parallel but different kind of thinking, and he saw it as a grave fault of Western "rational" education. Like his left-handedness, intuition was as compelling for him as a planet fixed by gravity to a star. And now it was sounding an alarm.

North and his daughter had fought now and then after her mother's tragic death, but nothing like yesterday's quarrel. He had entered her side of their duplex villa to borrow a portable radio. It was dead, so he opened the battery compartment. And a compact fell into his hand, white inside with the powder that was claiming the planet. For all of her eighteen years he had stressed but one rule, "Don't follow the crowd," only to discover that she was following the worst of crowds. As if in a cloud, he watched Coby return and become startled at his presence in her room, and fix her gaze on the dismantled radio. She touched the cocaine compact lightly, pulling back her hand as if from fire, and sank onto the bed.

"It's only a couple of grams," she'd said between tears. "Far less than an ounce."

He felt as if he had wandered too far and had landed on a planet of awful vastness where nothing seemed familiar. She sounded so hopeless, her body quivering as it tried to disappear, hands over ears to shut out the expected outburst. She had thrown a few things into an overnight bag, and then run from her humiliation, blonde hair flying, shirt tail streaming. And North had raced after her down the beach, thundering, *"Never again will I trust you. Never again. . . !"*

As a biophysicist, North understood that conflict is the way of the species; from the moment of birth, we are geared to action first, thought second. Yet knowing this had done nothing to stop him from hurting her. He felt as you do in the last game of a long tournament when you realize your blunder but your hand is glued to the wrong chess piece and it's too late to call it back. But this was no game.

Jack Cleary trudged over the rocks to the dock carrying a canvas overnight bag, and made a show of looking at his watch. "Back in New York, I'd just be getting in about now."

"Breathe that sky," said North, postponing anxiety over Coby. "Feels like a martini before breakfast."

"The only thing that feels like a martini before breakfast is illegal," said Cleary.

The two friends were opposites in many ways. Where Grant North was physically hard as when he had served in Vietnam, Jack Cleary had grown slack. North, with unruly hair silvered at the sides, looked the classical Island man: rugged, brown, matted chest, strong chin. His eyes, hazel like the coral seen through a fathom of sea, were committed to his dream. Cleary had the kind of eyes you noticed, brisk and bright blue. Though he was four years older than North's forty-five, there were no gray hairs in his sandy mop, and the few lines that furrowed his open face came by way of alcohol, not stress. North's craggier face was both young and old, a face you suspected could hide things when necessary, the way the Island hid things in the crevices and gullies of its jungle. The parents of both men had been immigrants: Cleary's from Ireland, North's from Croatia, whose family name *"Sever"* meant "North."

The jollyboat's antique diesel rumbled in the distance, and a minute later she chugged around the corner of Harbour Rock. A fat workboat of lapped mahogany and doubled ends, the jollyboat rolled with the waves until she entered Slaughter Harbour and bumped up against the dock. Wet from the splashy crossing, the workers clambered over the gunwales. They were of all ages, even a few in their sixties, which in the out-islands is old to have a job or even to be alive. There was one woman, the cook. North felt an affinity for these people; they had become his family of Family Islanders, the term the government promoted to replace Out-Islanders and its outcast connotation. You could read the history of Caribbean slavery in these faces: the habit the older men had of turning their eyes downward in the presence of whites, the dark African pigment mixed over the generations with the blood of former masters and Carib cannibals.

The older men yawed doggedly, the sun drying their clothes and depositing salt like ashes on mahogany arms and legs. The youths rolled and pitched to an inner beat that Cleary had named the "Goombay Shuffle" after the slow Bahama rhythm performed on goatskin drums. Goombay originally meant slaves brought here from Gambia, but no slave ever walked like that. To perform the Shuffle, you twist your upper body opposite from the lower like a skier turning, shoulders straight and into the hill, legs limp. There is always an audience when you do the Goombay; otherwise there is no point, and you traverse the streets and beaches of the Bahamas as conventionally as Members of Parliament. Shuffling along in the sunshine, the men were animated and talked in that staccato, uniquely Caribbean collision of seventeenth-century English and modern black American.

"Christ Almighty, that's an ugly dialect," Cleary said. "Sounds like orangutans fucking."

When North didn't react, Cleary said, "How does it feel to be king of the Island, Grant? Bossing forty blacks and all?"

"That's not even slightly funny in these parts, Jack."

"As long as we're stuck on this godforsaken rock, we might as well start a monarchy, issue currency, apply for American aid, impose slavery—"

"You turning into some kind of racist?"

"Me? You know I do my part to improve race relations."

It was an in-joke, a reference to Cleary's prowess with women, which indeed was color blind. North remembered Delilah Mae, the foxy *café noir* singer in dyed blonde hair, breasts straining against her green lamé dress, belting out a husky "Down by the Riverside," and how Cleary had clung to her like a white second skin.

Decidedly non-regal, North went around on the Island unshaven, shirtless, in frayed khaki work pants and an old Panama hat that Gauguin might have worn to paint. A tiny crescent moon was tattooed on his left wrist, a remnant of Army days that had nothing to do with having later become a NASA scientist. One day years ago Cleary had covered North's eyes and questioned him about the color and pattern of his own clothes; North couldn't even guess.

Cleary dropped his bag into the jollyboat that Shark would pilot to the village to deliver the rest of the workers. From Great Snake, Cleary would catch the morning flight to Nassau for another day of wall-bashing at various ministries, trying to convince the government to bestow upon them the permits they needed to operate. He wore a deep-blue linen blazer with a crest on the outside pocket, a buttoned-down shirt faintly striped in blue, slacks sharply pressed, and soft Italian loafers. North knew that when the sun rose higher, Cleary would spend the day carrying the blazer over his shoulder.

"Good luck," North said.

"Luck nothing. Everything in this life has to be sold. The guy who said, 'Build a better mousetrap and the world will beat a path to your door,' was full of . . . mouse shit!" He climbed into the boat. "Worry not," he said smiling, "subterfuge overcomes reluctance!"

But North wondered whether he should be worrying. It would be a year soon and they had no operating permits—surprising in the face of Cleary's legendary salesmanship. The Islanders were call it Cleary's Enigma.

orget," said Cleary, "my girlfriends are coming from
r the St. Patrick's Day weekend."

That's a switch. I'm going to New York right after that for
the United Nations thing."

"That's right! I almost forgot. Make damn certain you meet
the Prime Minister and his buddies."

"You sure they'll be there?"

"Positive. The Prime Minister's secretary told me."

North didn't really have the time for this trip but he had promised
the U.N. coordinator. And he thought of another reason to go to
the States—to call Coby's friends and make amends for yesterday's
quarrel. Sometimes it's hard to make radiophone calls from an
island, waiting for traffic to clear, for the ionosphere to cooperate,
and for people returning calls to struggle through the process all
over again.

Shark started the engine as Cleary jumped in the jollyboat,
waving his version of a Mussolini war salute. The way he clasped
his left hand over his right upper arm and aimed his middle finger
toward the sky instead of making a fist was funny. Everything
Cleary did was funny.

NORTHERNMOST in the Wracking Island chain, the Island lies on
the ocean like a sleeping whale. It stretches an exact mile from
tail to nose, its flukes define a tiny beach at the west end, its blunt
head faces east, and its long narwhal tusk of a dock reaches southeast
into Slaughter Harbour toward the prevailing wind.

At the rocky base of the dock overlooking the harbor, North's
two Bahamian foremen—Godfrey Knowles for building on land and
Sidney Rolle for seafarm construction—assigned those of the men
who were new or hadn't worked for a while. Every Snake Cay
worker not strung out on smoke or crack or swamp juice showed
up here sooner or later, and North hired every man who would work.

God Knowles, a master mason in his fifties, had thick, almost-
black arms as hard as the stone he laid. He was one of those
foremen who say little, look at no one, and yet know each man's
capability, the first names of his wife and children, the depths of

his hangover, and which bush tea he uses as an antidote.

Sidney Rolle, some ten years younger than Knowles, was several shades lighter. A man of the sea and an ex-fisherman with a surprising linguistic ability, Rolle pondered the world out of intelligent, irreverent eyes punctuated by a three-inch scar on his right cheek that might have been made in a sword fight. Whereas the wool on Knowles's head was half white, Rolle's hair and his Van Dyke beard black with only a trace of gray at the edges. Where Knowles jumped into a project with an abundance of energy and little forethought, Rolle would search alternatives first—which was fortunate because the construction of the seafarm required ingenuity.

Knowles's dozen apprentice masons already were laying stone at their walls as laborers carted the native rock in wheelbarrows they called "buggies," emulating their former British rulers. Burly men in baseball caps climbed onto their earthmovers and roared their engines, puffing smoke over the medley. The two elderly mechanics gossiped with some carpenters: the wreckage of a yacht and parts of human bodies had washed up on a nearby island. *"Mus' be de Bermuda Triangle!"* was the consensus, although the mechanics blamed the druggies.

Knowles hurried over to break up the group. "Doan be gabbin' on me, boys. Get yo'selves straight now!"

The men respected Knowles, no matter their complaints. "Now Godfrey, we ain't no slavy-time peoples! Doan mash us none, God boy. We git usselves straight soon 'nough."

When North first came to these islands he wondered, like Cleary, if the language he heard could possibly be English. Now the curiously inflected, Dickensian words bouncing from worker to worker in the sunshine seemed as ordinary as the occasional report from the drug war going on around them, subliminal battles like those between the scorpions in the Island caves.

Without waiting for Sidney Rolle, his seafarm workers, protected by shoes and work pants, waded out to their waists into the urchin-strewn flats where they were jetting pilings to build the seafarm corrals. They folded around themselves the ragged ends of their shirts—not the white ones their women starched for them to wear in the bars of the village, but coarse wool sweatshirts worn to retain body heat, bleached by salt and left each night to dry on the Island. The corrals took priority over other construction; the first crops of shrimp and seaweed were essential to replenish their dwindling funds.

Now and then Rolle grabbed an arm to assign the new men to the watery corrals, his eyes dilating as he plucked a thin arm from among the crowd. "Unnn-uhh! Jus' one small minute dere, brudder." Rolle had the unique ability to talk either like the rest of the family islanders or in standard English as desired.

Rolle's target had his shoulders up and his cap down, but his light-brown anemic face shone from behind a beard stringy as an Apostle's.

"This here's no worker! This here's a Rasta!" said Rolle.

"A Rasta?" said North.

"Rastafarian! Besides which, the little gold brick owes me money!"

"Who is he, Sidney?" asked North.

"This fucker? Why, he's my brother-in-law, Louis Rahming. A Nassauvian. From Nassau, that is." It was not clear which of these Rolle regarded as the worst sin.

North didn't interfere. Rolle could be vindictive at times, but when you put a man in charge of something, you lived with the consequences.

"*Peeeace!*" demanded the Rastafarian. "Jah Rastafari! Peace and love, mon," said the brother-in-law, his words out of sync with his body. "You cain't sen' me bok, Sidney. I ain't got no bread!"

Rastafarians abound in the Bahamas, having started as a black Jamaican religious cult whose members worshiped Haile Selassie Ras Tafari Mahonnen, the deceased Ethiopian emperor. This Rastafarian, thin as a sapodilla sapling, must have forsaken eating along with cleanliness, and he showed a string of crumbling teeth like a neglected picket fence. Under his martyr's beard he wore a turtle-neck wool sweater in the eighty-degree sunshine. One hand clasped the empty bowl of a pipe with the tenacity of a child clutching his blanket.

"You *got* bread, Louie. The dough I give my sister fer de kids' food." Rolle thought it over, and added, "Keep outa de way today an' when de boat go back tonight, you stays on de udder side. You do dot an' I give yuh a leetle more money. Unerstan'?"

At the mention of money, Rahming let out a dab of foam at the corners of his mouth and nodded his head in agreement. As Rolle left for work Rahming peered up at North, but on finding no sympathy there he wandered off under the climbing sun. Those who had stayed to watch the argument Goombay-shuffled or otherwise trudged to their jobs.

"OOOOOOW-WAA-EEESSHHH. . . !" The shriek came from the roof of the double-circle lodge, loud as a siren, its pitch rising due to the Doppler shift and Louie Rahming's skid across the shingles as he careened down the slope of the roof. Cuda, who was on the roof installing a radio antenna, lunged after the sliding body. North ran out of the lodge where he'd been making an engineering drawing. Men on the ground were pointing up, yelling:

"Ma Lord, here he come!"

"Lookadot muddafucka. . . !"

"Oh my Jesus God!"

Rahming's foot wedged into the gutter and flipped his frail body over the edge. You could hear the bone-wrenching double thump of flesh and head meeting concrete. Rahming lay conscious on the walk, his left leg perpendicular to the rest of his body. Miraculously he still clenched the pipe between his teeth; the mouthpiece, bitten through, dangled from its severed stem like his leg from his pelvis. Any moment the pain will arrive and he'll start bellowing, thought North, but Rahming only whimpered like an abandoned puppy.

Kneeling beside him, North eased back the leg parallel to the other. His femur was broken and had punctured his flesh, which was swelling rapidly. A thin plum of milky smoke wafted from the pipe bowl, a caustic odor not of tobacco. North put the bowl to his nose and identified the unmistakable smell of phencyclidine, the cheap, highly hallucinogenic PCP developed as an animal tranquilizer and outlawed for humans.

The workers knew that odor too. *"He some member o' de Holy Smoke Church? Jus' looka dem eyes!"*

19

"Dot mon sho be at peace wid his peace *pills!*"

"Jus' go to show, even a Rastafari cain't fly like de angel on de angel dust."

"Father Josh done blessed dot roof too. Some blessin'!" Father Joshua Christie was the wise old Anglican priest from the Snake Cay village.

"Go get Sidney Rolle," North said to one of the teenagers who stood there paralyzed.

"Sid-ney. . . ?" said the boy. Standard out-island delay, not a question.

"He's in the water at the seafarm. Tell him to meet us at the dock."

Cuda, who had come down from the roof, said, "Sidney ain't at de seafarm, Mistuh Grant. He was on de roof wid me."

What had Rolle been doing up there? He was supposed to be supervising his crew jetting pilings for the seafarm, extending it westward from the head of the Island toward the tail. North scanned the area and saw Rolle slinking away from the building toward the dock.

"Sidney! Wait a minute!" North caught up to him, and out of earshot of the others said, "Sid, did you push Rahming?"

Rolle returned a cryptic grin. "Does it matter?"

North would think back to that answer often. Could this man he thought of as a friend be capable of mayhem, or even murder? "Yes," he said. "Of course it matters."

"If it eases your mind any, I climbed the roof looking for him, but he slipped all by himself. Now I've got to take the asshole to the hospital in Nassau."

Rolle turned on his heel and continued toward the dock where he met the stretcher bearers. By the time they lifted Rahming off the sheet of plywood and onto a pile of blankets in the bottom of the Mako, Rolle had the boat's first-aid kit out and was filling a syringe from an ampule of penicillin. "Oh, the black man's burden," he said, smiling to the men on the dock as he plunged the hypodermic needle into his brother-in-law's arm. "Our perpetual burden!"

2 *Wracking*

AT CORAL HARBOUR, headquarters of the Royal Bahamas Defence Force, the LCM *Half Fast* limped like a crippled dog tethered to the *HMBS Munnings*. On the deck of the wheelhouse, like the broken toys of hostile giants, splintered mullions and pieces of fathometer, radio, binnacle, and compass, lay twisted with the soggy pulp that had been navigation charts. Windows were shattered, and shards of glass reflected the coppery sunlight in a moment of gold. The LCM looked like an exhausted creature driven to its death. No angry voices throbbed in those steel hulls, no engines plowed her through reluctant waves, her secret places no longer held secrets. Death had set her afloat like a drifting cloud.

In tow, and indentured to Capt. Carlos St. Gregory, the vessel seemed the victim of "wracking," from which the chain of North's Island derived its name. Wracking had been the primary industry of the Bahamas for hundreds of years beginning when the Jolly Roger flew over countless ships and whole villages lapsed into anarchy. Wracking was legal then, even when at night you placed a lantern on the back of your mule to simulate the motion of a ship at sea, and so lured your victim into the reefs. The only rule, as St. Gregory well knew, was that you had to ramble, or wait, until a hull hit the rocks before you salvaged her.

When you didn't wait for a ship to get into trouble, wracking was called piracy.

3 *The Appointment*

IT SEEMED to Jack Cleary these days that he no longer "carried the sun in his pocket," an old Croatian saying he'd heard North use often enough over the years. He had expected the Island for Science to follow the pattern of the instrument company, where he sold what North innovated. Instead, "sales" were made only to the various government ministries and the effort went unfocused. Ever since North bought the Island, Cleary had spent most of his time here in Nassau basking in the smiles of the bureaucrats as once he had with corporate purchasing agents. Whereas he formerly invested in martini lunches, now there were "Cleary Coladas" made specially for him by bartenders in dark lounges, where the bands played Calypso and the girls wriggled low under the limbo bars, their black hair brushing the floor. Cleary was a firm believer that wining and dining paid off eventually, but now spring had arrived and he realized that Cleary's Enigma was real: they had none of the dozen or so licenses and permits the government required.

He had found the Bahamas to be more socialistic, more bureaucratic, and therefore less efficient than the U.S. Did the government actually intend to let them build their buildings only to deny them permission to operate? "Permits? No problem!" said the bureaucrats. "The government looks kindly upon scientists, since, you see, we have none of our own here!" And they would laugh and sip their coladas or their goombay passion punches, while Cleary discovered new dimensions of frustration. The act of worrying came new to him. Before, he had managed to transfer that assignment to Grant North or to St. Jude, the patron saint of impossible dreams. Slavs and saints make the best worriers, Cleary maintained.

Today being St. Patrick's Day, he decided to try some Irish initiative. Spurning the usual waiting in ministerial offices, he sought out Sterling Hanna, the Island for Science attorney whose legal firm belonged to the party in power, and whose senior partner had come to the end of his term as ambassador to the U.S. and the U.N. In the law offices of Franklin, Albury & Dawkins Ltd., he found Hanna working in short sleeves. Against his white shirt, his skin shone with a bluish black luster, and he wore a cigar in the corner of his mouth. Cleary liked him because he was earthy and accessible.

"Sterling, I'm tired of trying to sell every monkey in this government. I've got to see the organ grinder."

Hanna laughed. The American Irishman and the Bahamian African were much alike under their skins. Both seemed to swing from one side of the room to the other on vines of sacrilege.

"I assume you mean our illustrious Prime Minister."

"Yeah, Mr. Handsome himself. Prime Minister Transom."

"'Transom?' Ah . . . Mr. T. Ransom," Hanna said slowly. "Clever."

"He's my only hope. You know as well as I that no one gets permission for *anything* in this country without his okay."

"There are channels for—"

"Screw channels. The only things I've got to show for a year spent going through channels are building permits."

"What else do you need, man?"

Cleary had run into this lack of understanding, even by local lawyers, of what a foreigner needs to start a business in the Bahamas, and he found it curious. "Work permits. Permits to import rare shrimp and seaweed. Permits to export the stuff after we grow it. Duty-free permit under the Industries Encouragements Act. Exchange-control permit to take U.S. dollars out of the country. Ninety-nine year lease of the seabed. Business license. Environmental permit. . . . Christ Almighty, Sterling, we're like Israel when it became a new state: we need permission to exist!"

Hanna's cigar died and he relinquished it to the ashtray. "You might not realize it, Jack my friend, but you're asking a lot. The seabed lease will be especially troublesome. You see, we Bahamian monkeys are capitalists on the land and socialists on the water. 'It is as it was and still is everywhere and always amongst us,'" he quoted from something. "The seas belong to Bahamian citizens."

"If Transom knew *the good* the Island for Science can bring to Bahamian citizens, he'd welcome it," Cleary said.

"Maybe Franklin can help. He is *our* organ grinder. And he's in town checking up on the firm for a few weeks until he goes to a United Nations meeting, after which he starts his new assignment."

"Which is?"

"The Cabinet job he had before—Minister of Fisheries."

"Fantastic, Sterling! He'll cream all over when he hears about our seafarm!"

Hanna chuckled, showing he loved the way Cleary talked. "The goal of self-sufficiency by the end of the decade," Hanna explained, "faltered during the year Franklin was at the United Nations. Mr. . . . Transom . . . needs him back in Fisheries. The job requires a loyal S.O.B., one who will carry out the boss's orders without question and who won't be swayed by anyone."

"Hardly a description of a diplomat."

"It is, however, a precise description of Mr. Franklin," Hanna said with a wry grin. "Come on, I'll introduce you."

Hanna entered Franklin's office alone, abandoning Cleary at the door jamb where the vinyl tile ended and a thick carpet began. Lined with books and framed photographs, the office was over-stuffed with easy chairs, cocktail table, even a well-stocked bar under ornate windows overlooking the bustle of Providence Street. Hanna whispered a few words to Franklin, who hastened to meet Cleary at the door jamb.

"How good to see you, Mr. Cleary. I have met your Dr. North, and of course he's well-known to us through his drug detector."

Trim and erect, Franklin had a nervous tic under his right eye and a habit of moving his head and shoulders horizontally as if sowing seeds—or forever saying no. Cleary typed him as one of those invisible little men who seem to thrive in nationalistic little nations. Mediocre and flatulent as a British lord, he tried to emulate his cosmopolitan namesake by wearing wire-frame half-glasses.

"Mr. Franklin, we're trying to start a large-scale seafarm, along with developing other technologies to benefit the Baham—"

Franklin interrupted. "It's true we're emphasizing fish to decrease imports of food. But we don't have to *raise* fish, man!" He removed his half-glasses and polished them vigorously.

"Shrimp," said Cleary.

"The ocean's full of fish *and* shrimp. We only need better ways of capturing them!"

"Well, *our* shrimp come already captured," Cleary said, wishing the former diplomat would show some diplomacy and invite him in for a drink. "Mr. Franklin, there's a lot more to the Island for Science than just the seaweed-shrimp farm. It's an interdisciplinary research center, a think tank, an engine of technology. Leading scientists and engineers from all over the world, from different fields will work together here to solve the problems of the Bahamas—"

"Problems? What problems?"

"Fresh water, expensive energy, dependence on other countries for food, a one-industry economy." Cleary was wound up, talking fast. "We can harness the sun to desalinate seawater. We can replace diesel generators with solar cells for cheap electricity. We can mine the sea for useful drugs. Listen, Mr. Franklin, this is no minor venture. Shallow-water seafarms like ours all over the out-islands will employ thousands of Bahamians, create a new industry. So will the windmill and other developments. You can have all of our proprietary discoveries—for nothing. We'll teach your people new skills, make them something more than bus boys and caretakers for rich foreigners."

"Excuse me, Mr. Cleary, but just what is it you want?"

"I want you to arrange an appointment for Dr. North to see the Prime Minister."

Franklin's mouth moved slowly as if he were mulling over a response, trying it out in his mind. "Why doesn't Dr. North just call him?"

Surely Franklin knew you don't *just call* the Prime Minister. "He has tried. The P.M.'s always too busy to talk to him."

"Well, Mr. Cleary, the P.M. *is* always busy. In fact, right now, we're all very busy getting ready for the United Nations conference in New York. . . ." The two continued to stand, Franklin guarding his office by keeping Cleary halfway in the hall.

"It's important we talk to him before we go any further with—"

"It's important *to you*," Franklin interrupted. He pressed the long fingers of both hands together and poked the steeple into his central incisors. It wasn't a natural gesture, as if he'd copied if from someone else. "I could try. But please understand, Mr. Cleary, that the Prime Minister has a longstanding policy of avoiding sup-plicants—"

"Supplicants!"

"Well, yes, I assume Dr. North wants something, doesn't he?"

"Sure, he wants to bring jobs to the Family Islands, taxes to the government, and knowledge of how to live in the Twentieth Century to the Bahamas in general—"

"Excuse my saying so, Mr. Cleary. But it is precisely that kind of . . . arrogance, if you'll excuse the word, which I have to worry about when I arrange appointments for the Prime Minister. If anything like that were ever said . . ." He swayed his head slowly from side to side. "Well, you see, I am a Cabinet member, which of course is why you came to me, but being in the Cabinet carries a definite responsibility. If the meeting were to go badly—"

"Mr. Franklin," Cleary said in exasperation, "how could it go badly? I know Mr. Ransom would want to see Dr. North if he understood what the Island for Science could do for the country."

Franklin swung his head again, and Cleary pictured him making that irritating gesture while kneeling before a guillotine. Franklin said, "I will try, though I am afraid it will take time, a lot of time."

As long as you orbit the planet in your private satellite, you can make believe that governments are there to help you. The problem comes, Cleary was finding out, when you land on an earth corrupted.

CLEARY wandered away from the side streets of office buildings to Bay Street where the stores and lounges catered to tourists. To look at the main street of Nassau with the eye of a familiar foreigner is to see wavy lines of picturesque shops along both sides of a path paved in the eighteenth century, now hopelessly congested with automobiles too large for any island smaller than Australia. Here you can buy emeralds from Brazil, flowered dresses from Taiwan, ice cream Bahama-flavored with rum raisin or sapodilla from Florida, and in the semi-open-air straw market, purses from Borneo and wood carvings from Jamaica. Cleary realized that nothing sold in the Bahamas is made or grown here, despite what barrister Hanna once had called "the depressing ubiquity" of import duties that ranged from thirty-two to a hundred percent.

At the Churchill Building, Cleary made his way to the third floor where the Prime Minister and his Deputy kept their offices. He passed a vacated receptionist's desk, and stood before another where a discrete nameplate identified, MISS EFFIE FERGUSON, SECRETARY.

"Hello, Mr. Cleary. What can I do for you today?"

"Hi, Effie." He had been here before trying to see the P.M. or the D.P.M, and had graduated to a first-name basis with this middle-aged lady, who returned his wide smile. He said, "It seems our colleague, Benjamin Franklin, has promised to arrange a meeting between the Prime Minister and Dr. Grant North, president of Island for Science Ltd. Benjamin hasn't had confirmation of the meeting yet and, well, I wonder whether we might shortcut the procedure."

"You mean will I schedule the appointment?"

Cleary watched her large brown eyes and made himself think how beautiful they were. "Well, yes, if you would," he said.

"What's it about? The meeting?"

"Dr. North wants to offer his help to the government on desalination, self-sufficiency in food, solar energy . . . science in the cause of humanity." Cleary smiled.

Miss Ferguson smiled back. "The P.M. is certainly concerned about desalination. Both our seawater-conversion units are down again."

Cleary had seen the huge water barges bringing the million-gallon a day lifeblood of the city from Andros, and knew that Ransom had to be concerned about the cost.

"The problem is that the P.M. usually decides himself whom he'll see," she said pensively, even while reaching for her calendar.

"I'm sure he will want to see Dr. North." Cleary pressed gently, wanting not to offend her, only to deceive her.

She hesitated, obviously eager to help him, then said, "The P.M. is so busy he's been making appointments on Saturdays. Will that do?"

"Certainly!"

She read aloud as she wrote in her appointment book. "Saturday, April first, three o'clock."

"Thank you, Miss Ferguson. Thank you very much."

WHEN CLEARY was about to enter a bar off Bay Street, a familiar figure cut across his path. It was Sidney Rolle, who offered him a ride to the Island in the company Mako. Cleary accepted readily since he had to be back for the weekend, and bought a pint of gin, which he emptied in the three hours it took to get to the Island. It was dark when they arrived at the dock, and the workers had gone home to the Great Snake village. They found North in the lodge.

Beaming as though he'd found a pile of gold coins on the beach, Cleary strode over to the bar and made himself a martini.

"How goes it?" North asked.

"It's a dog's life. I've been lapping at the bureaucracy now for nine months—that's four years in human life." Cleary's blue eyes crinkled, prematurely drunk on victory and gin. "But, finally I've got something!"

"What have you got?"

"An appointment for you with Transom."

"Ransom?"

"Charles T. himself. Transom the Magnificent."

"When?"

"Saturday, the first."

"Saturday? *April* first?"

"Fuck superstition," he said, tie askew, his wrinkled blue blazer slung over one shoulder. "It'sss good a day as any. You butter up Transom in New York and then when you meet again in his office, you tie it all up."

North, wearing his Gauguin hat, work pants, and no shirt, poured himself and Rolle a drink. Like Cleary, Rolle wore his Nassau clothes, but for Rolle that meant tight leather pants and a white tailored shirt-jacket that appeared incandescent against his brown skin.

"Tell me about Charles T. Ransom," said North.

"Never met the guy," said Cleary.

"I have," said Rolle.

"Whass he look like?" Cleary said. He had a theory that a face revealed character.

"Like a prime minister."

"How are prime ministers supposed to look?"

"They have a certain rare expression of inner power," Rolle said. "If Ransom's head appeared behind glass in the Nassau Museum alongside a Bahamian parrot and a leatherback turtle, you'd look at it and say, 'Now dot be a classic specimen of a P.M. all right.'" He affected the creole of his countrymen. "Jus' look a dot jutting chin, looka dem piercing eyes—"

"Piercing eyes, hey? What makes the guy tick?" Cleary wanted to know.

"Ego, what else?," Rolle said in standard English. "The entire Cabinet and Parliament are afraid to shit until he says squat. But in his speeches he says he's receptive to new ideas."

North said, "So far he's been as 'receptive' as, say, Fidel is to the global wave of capitalism."

"Maybe he's holding out for a bribe," Cleary said, too loud.

"Forget it," North said.

"Jack," said Rolle, lean and as efficiently designed as an owl-fish, "You give a bureaucrat the slightest inkling you're thinking bribe, and he'll hold out forever. Bahamians have been extracting money from Americans for two hundred years and they're damn good at it."

Cleary said, "Well, they seem to be holding out for something."

"Hey look, these government turds make less than your secretary back home. Some Colombian comes around with fifty G's and says, '¿Plata o plomo?' 'silver or lead?' What'd you suppose the turd will do?"

"Call the Defence Force?"

"The head turd is the Prime Minister, and he gives not a shit for anybody but himself," said Rolle. "But don't ever try to bribe him. He's rumored to have a hundred million stashed away."

Rolle revered nothing man-made or supernatural, not the gods of his fellow men, certainly not the government nor the voice of any authority that hadn't proved itself to him personally. He believed in the sea, the coral reefs, and the islands where he cherished wild jungles, half vinegar, half champagne.

"Maybe he earned his money," said Cleary, a twinkle in his eye.

"How can a politician earn a hundred mil?"

"I hear he works hard for his money. Studying those applications for permits, traveling to oversee his bank accounts in Switzerland. Passing out crack to school kids so they'll vote for him when they grow up."

Sneering at the government was in the air, a kind of Bahamian ozone. Of course Cleary had considered greasing a palm here and there to get things lubricated, but it wouldn't be necessary now that he'd arranged for North to see the Prime Minister. He drained his drink.

"No bribes," North said.

"Okay, we'll leave it up to St. Jude. Patron saint of—"

"We know."

"All right, no bribes. Not counting three-martini lunches, of course."

"Dots de spirit," said Rolle. "Yuh ain't too awful bad, Mistuh Cleary. For a Cauc, dot is. Yuh be a credit to yo race, mon!"

4 *A Bother*

CAPTAIN Carlos St. Gregory, carrying his seabag from the *Munnings,* stepped onto one of five narrow docks that reached like the fingers of a hand into Nassau's Coral Harbour. The sky hovered low over a row of gray gunboats and a dozen pleasure yachts of various sizes that had been confiscated. Two dope dogs strained at their leashes, pulling toward the LCM a gray-haired man wearing the stripes of a chief petty officer.

St. Gregory stopped to have a word with the chief, after which they boarded the LCM and made their way to the well deck. The dogs stopped near the galley to sniff at a manhole that led to the double hull, then moved on to the cargo area.

"We can open dot manhole, suh," Chief Lightbourne said, "but what dope be in dere long gone. Otherwise dese pooches woulda barked up a storm."

St. Gregory dismissed the chief and walked with him a little way as he lead the dogs toward the kennels. The captain turned into the drab quonset hut that served as the Royal Bahamian Defence Force headquarters, where he adjusted his eyes to the low light and strode down the hallway, returning the salutes of young Defenders in blue fatigues and Wehrmacht-style caps. He knocked once on the open door of Commodore Bridgewater's office, stood before his desk, and squared his shoulders.

The commodore peered up over half-glasses. "I hear you had a bit of a bother the other night." He was English, one of the last remnants of the British officer corps that had trained the Defence Force.

"Yes sir."

"How much dope did you confiscate this time?"

Tie off, uniform wrinkled, the commodore looked burnt out and lethargic. They'd be getting rid of him soon, thought St. Gregory.

"Not a damn thing." He knew Bridgewater would check with the dog handler, so he stuck close to the truth. "The dogs sniffed the vessel and acted as though there *had* been dope stowed in the false hull. The crew must have dumped it over the side while we were trying to board."

"What happened out there?"

St. Gregory stayed at attention, although the commodore gave every indication that the gesture was wasted. The captain's white jacket was as crisp as starch could make it, his face a mask of military ambiguity as he answered:

"The barge captain refused to heave to, and opened fire with an Uzi. Everyone on board was killed."

5 *A Place to Live for*

JACK CLEARY, his Irish eyes twinkling, introduced the girls to North at the Great Snake airport in precise order: Steve, born Mary Stephens in Ireland; Eve O'Malley, dubbed "Evil Malley" by Cleary; and Xaviera. Cleary had met Xaviera at the nearby beach bar earlier that morning before Steve and Eve landed, and when he found her name started with an *X*, couldn't resist talking her into joining them. She was a yacht-hiker from Amsterdam who bartered crew work for rides, jumping ship at whatever port appealed to her sense of freedom.

The five of them hitched a ride in the back of a truck and made it to the village saloon before the rain started. They passed under a sign of driftwood and letters of broken glass:

COME ALIVE AT THE GRAVE YARD INN

Steve, Eve, and Xaviera, in minidresses and flowing hair of diverse colors, thought the place charming. Actually the Inn was one of those unbridled free ports you still find in dingy corners of the planet, wide-open like Port Royale before it sank into the sea, where pirates from the Spanish Main could down their rum and draw their cutlasses across the throats of Englishmen and other fools in the noonday sun.

At the horseshoe bar Cleary shouted over the jukebox noise

to introduce the girls to Rolle. No quiet Calypso for this place. Rock music synchronized to a flashing strobe revealed in quick takes three dozen villagers staring at a television screen above the bar and swilling rum at two in the afternoon. Being here made you feel you had infiltrated not the Third World but the Lower World, a place very different from the one you left an hour ago. The Sunday afternoon drinkers seemed so surly, you could see why guns weren't allowed in the Bahamas. From the back room the odor of marijuana wafted over a game of high-stakes pool.

Thunder clapped and the clouds emptied in bucketfuls on the galvanized roof, silvering the asphalt street and flooding the graveled path outside. Rolle left to put the top up on the Mako.

"It rains here like it did at home when I was a kid," Cleary said, ordering his second martini. The others were drinking whiskey and coffee.

"You're still a kid," Eve said with a little laugh.

"I know what he means," Steve said. "The rain you remember from your childhood seems stronger than any of your modern rain."

Standing behind the girls perched on the barstools, Cleary said to Xaviera, "Grant here possesses hundred-volt humanity. The problem is, he doesn't know how to live."

Xaviera turned to North. "Well, how *do* you live?" she said in her Dutch accent, with a naive innocence designed to coax a man to find its opposite.

North tried to change the subject. "What do you do back in Amsterdam?"

"About what?"

He laughed. "About making a living."

A ruminative pause ensued while Evil, in her Irish rendition of a Bahamian accent, ordered a second Gin Grin. Steve said no to another drink and removed a scraggly joint from a leather container in her purse. She lit it casually.

"What I do, there and here, is *experience* things," Xaviera said in a husky voice no longer camouflaged in naiveté. Then she opened a compact, pinched a little powder, and snorted it. "Here, try some." She offered the compact to North, but he pushed it away.

"Don't you want to try *just everything*? At least *once*?" She reached over and stroked the stubble on his chin.

"No, not *everything*," he said. "Not Russian roulette. Not leaping off tall buildings. And certainly not cocaine."

She looked at him as if he were a Martian breathing through his spiracles and wiggling his mandible.

The rock melted into one sentence repeated endlessly: *"Down by the sea, I want you with me. . . ."* which caused Xaviera to rise, glide a few steps to the dance platform, and writhe to the music. She whacked the air with one arm held high like a drill sergeant and tossed her golden mane, beckoning North to dance with her. It reminded him of an art movie he'd seen of the making of a milkshake, in which the music stopped, a long-haired girl froze, and a section of her scull hinged open to receive two scoops of ice cream and a measure of milk, after which the music and the head-shaking resumed. Xaviera sang along with the juke. *"want you with me—eee!"*

North stepped onto the platform, reaching her seconds after someone else got there. Reeking of rum and tobacco, a surly two-hundred-fifty-pounder with half-closed steely eyes bared Xaviera from North. Except for the leather vest and big silver buckle on his belt, he looked like a Mau Mau who uses aluminum plates so he can eat the metal.

He seized North's arm and swung him around. "Bug off, white-ass, Ah got here first!"

Xaviera stopped gyrating to the music, and pressed close to North. *"Grant!"*

North's hazel eyes flashed with ambiguous feelings. On the one hand, he cared nothing for dancing and little for this cokehead. On the other, the village was the sole source of his labor supply; he and Rolle had come not so much to meet Cleary's girls as to recruit laborers not already employed at the Island. He could hardly back down in front of them.

"Beat it, *muddafucka!*" the Mau Mau said, poking a finger into North's chest.

When North didn't leave, the man lunged. North ducked and grabbed his belt buckle, pulling him in the direction he was going. The maneuver would gain, say, six seconds. The villagers gathered in a circle, stepping back to make room for the fight. The drunk attacked again, aiming too high.

North bent low and threw his total strength into a punch to the solar plexus, his only chance to prevent disaster. But the big man simply belched and reached two huge hands out for North.

A fist solid as a cannon ball jackhammered past North's skull into the man's neck, sending him crashing to the floor. The fist was attached to the wet arm of Sidney Rolle. The drunk rubbed his neck and rose, subdued and sorrowful. "Sidney, you got no cause ta do dot. You knows I doan mean nutin' by it."

"It be okay now, Buddy. Youse jus' in yer cups. All's forgiven."

Cleary slid off his stool and chuckled. "That's real white of you, Sid, to forgive the man for running into your fist like that."

Rolle understood Cleary well enough to know he made these racial slurs only because he thought they were funny, and Rolle laughed so his countrymen would not take offense. Barechested and dripping wet from the rain, he looked jaded, as though some Sidney Rolle essence had leaked away through the wide scar on his right cheek. Even in the semidarkness, his face was curiously handsome, enhanced by wide eyes and the scar itself that spoke more of mystery than menace, the face of a populist gangster who steals for the poor. The girls couldn't keep their eyes off him.

Rolle turned on the lights and began to introduce the men who lingered on the dance floor. As he did so the cutthroats of Port Royale were miraculously transfigured into amiable neighbors.

". . . and this here prize fight*er* is Buddy Martin," Rolle was saying with his hand on the humbled man's shoulder.

"Buddy Martin," said Cleary. "They ought to call you Purple Martin. Or maybe Black and Blue."

Laughter, slaps on the back, and for the rest of his life the big man would be known as Purple or Black and Blue. Cleary made jokes of the other nicknames like Digger or Fuzzy, or Garlic or Shark who already worked at the Island.

A half hour later North could remember barely half their names, and yet Cleary had committed them all to memory. The ability sprang from his affinity for people and cryptology, which he maintained were one and the same; he had spent the Vietnam war years as a message coder aboard merchant ships.

"If anyone wants to work, meet our boat tomorrow at daybreak," North said in a deep voice, "and we'll try you out. Right now have a drink on us."

The room brightened with animated talk and anecdotes: how the government screwed them out of their national health insurance benefits when they were sick, or how they never got their last paychecks the last time the Snake Cay resort went bankrupt.

Cleary, smiling but serious, stood on a chair and raised his glass. The room quieted. "You never have to worry about getting paid when you work at the Island for Science. As far as Grant North is concerned there's only one reason for not keeping your word, and that's if you're dead." He added with no smile, "Of course, that works both ways."

THE LAST of the water had drained from the sky, and the sun resumed its steady monochrome as they sped toward the Island in the Mako. North and Xaviera were in the bow, Steve and Eve amidships, and Cleary in between. Rolle was aft at the helm. Xaviera lifted her face to the sky and let the wind ruffle her long hair.

"Let me ask *you* a question now, Grant," she said over the sound of the engine, as if they'd been in conversation all along. "What's your sign?"

"My what?"

"Your *sign*. You know, what *are* you?"

North pretended he didn't know.

"Well, when were you born?"

"April twentieth," he said with reluctance.

"No *kid*ding! You barely made Taurus. Fantastic! I'm a Virgo. Tauruses and Virgos get along wonderfully. My last boyfriend was a Leo and we fought like cats and dogs."

"You mean like lions and virgins."

"What?"

"Listen, Xaviera, Newton erased astrology three centuries ago."

"No *way!* Lots of people believe in astrology."

"Why don't they learn how the universe really works?"

Cleary had been listening, and he answered, "It's simple, Grant.

They've been taught that God moves in mysterious ways, so anything mysterious or illogical is close to God."

Xaviera closed her eyes and pointed her face toward the sun.

If Cleary thought he was being funny, North thought maybe he was being right. The more absurd their cosmic calendars, the more outlandish their crystal rocks, or the more their flying saucers look like soft ripened cheese, the closer the believers feel they are to God. No proof, no argument ever changed anything with the astro folks, and there was no point in trying with Xaviera. If he were to find a woman to love and marry, she would have to be rooted in this century. No longer, as occasionally when he was younger, could he find ignorance endearing or cute. Or even safe.

ROLLE steered wide of shoals, weaving across the flats to the Island. He kept in "white water," the Bahamian term for the white-sand shallows where no mounds of turtle grass protrude to seize a speeding hull and stop it dead. Already halfway up the eight-mile run, Rolle curved gracefully around tidal banks.

Xaviera, miffed with a man who couldn't swap astrological traits with her, turned to Rolle. "Sidney, where did you get that exotic scar on your face? Makes you look like a pirate."

"I met a drug-crazed white man one dark night in an alley."

"Oh, Sidney!"

Finding deeper water, Rolle rammed the throttle forward and headed for the tail of the Island, soaring over a deep sea whose surface was inlaid with effervescent plankton. Three miles off, the Island floated alone in the infinite sea like a sleeping whale casting a turquoise shadow. From somewhere deep in the interior, North heard a thin music like the refrain of a violin or the pure monotone of a conch horn, delicate and plaintive, fading away, the Island whispering. Was this his own astrology? His own irrational belief filling some deep need within himself?

As they drew closer, the jungle became a green blanket and you could distinguish yellowed grass, wispy palms, and the chartreuse fur of pines blending at the beach. At the ends of the Island the shallow water darkened into the deep ocean, and the sun tinged whitecaps in golden shadow. It's impossible to capture such a scene in a painting or photograph, thought North. You can't show the wind adding life to the chlorophyll or water molecules to the air. You can't depict the lace that bands the atmosphere, or trap the green mist of the forest that builds it, transmuting oxygen into the breathing biocolors of living sky. As they entered the flats, the bottom bloomed in reds and browns where coral mounds lived their millions of lives in immobile silence. There might be poverty on these islands, he thought, but there was always color on the sea.

Everyone on the boat felt these liquid colors, but none so much as Eve's quiet friend Steve. Overwhelmed by the colors of sea and Island, she breathed them into the depths of her spirit, overdosing on rapture.

"Oh," Steve said simply. Tears of anguished joy flooded her eyes, rising like a wave, and crashed in a laugh of zany hysteria. *"Oh!"* Pleasure and pain mingled in her mind like too-violent sex or the ecstatic terror of leaping from an airplane. She whipped off her white dress, under which she wore nothing, and straightened her perfectly formed figure into an arrow. She sprang from the boat into the exotic brilliance, sacrificing herself to the god of life, inviting him in one long second to take her . . . before crashing into the churning wake.

Rolle had guessed Steve was going to dive, and eased back the throttle beforehand. Other girls had leapt from his speeding boat the first time they'd savored the living pastels of the Bahamas—uninhibited, impressionable, modern girls finding an excuse to go naked in the sunshine. The first time it happened, the girl collided with a bottom more solid than her daydream, and fractured her arm. That wasn't so bad. Rolle had known a veteran skydiver who, mellowed by friendly clouds and jaded by hundreds of jumps, swooped from his last airplane before remembering he wore no parachute.

Rolle backed a little, threw out the anchor, and waited. A still-intact Mary Stephens, her chromo-craze diluted in the water, swam to catch up. At the boat she treaded water while waving at the others, and called in her liquid Irish singsong:

"I missed the sky, that's the laugh! Come on in. This water is delicious!"

Cleary peeled off his swim suit and dove into the crystal ocean.

Eve followed. Xaviera scrutinized North, formed a demure little smile, and climbed the steps to the rigid canopy over the driver's station. Removing her necklace and waist sash, wrapping the first in the second, she unfastened her minidress, which slid to her feet and slithered over the edge of the canopy onto the deck. She stood there a moment in a glow of golden honey, then executed a perfect swan dive.

North looked at Rolle, and Rolle looked at North. Stoicism has its limits.

They stripped and were ready to follow the others into the water when North felt something at his back.

"What's the matter?" said Rolle.

North turned and saw a military vessel patrolling a mile off the west end of the Island. Shrouded in haze, it appeared to hover above the glassy sea like some malignant mirage. North grabbed a pair of field glasses and saw a uniformed, bearded officer standing at the rail and staring back at him through his own binoculars. "Someone's watching us," North said, naked in the sunshine.

"So what?" laughed Rolle. "You some tight-assed honky?"

"I can't make out the name of the ship, but she's a gunboat with a long cannon on deck."

"They got it pointed toward us?"

"No."

"Then don't worry about it. They just the Defence Force, and there ain't no law against nudity in the Bahamas." Rolle laughed and dove overboard.

North returned the binoculars to the console, thinking of his own ship, and of Coby. He'd left radiophone messages for Symes at several suppliers in Ft. Lauderdale, but Symes had yet to return the calls.

North tried to shrug off his apprehension as he followed the others into the water. Soon they were six porpoises frolicking in seltzer surrounding the mystic land, making their way to the tail of the whale where, narrowing, it flared into rocky flukes enclosing a pure-white beach. This was North's favorite place on the Island, and he had named it Scuba Beach because you could swim out wearing a tank and find deep water around the corner of the Island.

Rolle dove for crawfish, or clawless spiny lobster. The others waded to the anchored boat for their clothes and provisions, holding bundles on heads like safari porters and rising together from the water, glorious and gleaming in the sun. The girls drowsily drank beer and flopped onto the warm sand around a pile of rocks that Cleary had fashioned into a barbecue pit.

North threaded through the rock-strewn water to the deeper, sandy bottom and began a slow stroke, feeling his muscles tighten. Dark-ened by the sun, he was stronger, healthier than he'd been at North Scientific where he had spent too many years at drawing boards and conference tables. His triceps and leg muscles had hardened on the Island to their former army firmness. Pressing his left ear into the pillow of ocean, he pumped a steady beat, welcoming the strain of thighs and arms. At the first coconut grove he stopped to turn back, and scanned the sea for sight of the ominous gunboat. It was gone.

He looked toward shore, where the only thing resembling human shapes was a cluster of three palms, like his former family: the first two of Coby and her mother Heather, billowing feminine fronds like long hair, their trunks smooth and tan like legs pressed together; the third a taller, thicker tree representing himself. Steps had been carved in it by Great Snake villagers to gather coconuts. The voices on the wind seemed to come from there, whispering a song like the one the whales sing.

CLEARY AND NORTH left the others at the campfire, and made their way through the boulders of the landscape to the deep side where they meandered like ants along the royal headlands that tumbled into the sea. They felt a different freedom here, unencumbered by the forest, kin to the racing clouds. They leapt from one boulder to another, around jagged spires and wide bays, past Lake Michigan and the water tower to the villas at the east end, and then they were on the shallow, southern side with Slaughter Harbour behind them. Their zigzag path now generally followed the sun until it sank beneath the rim of the ocean. They skirted the laboratory building and returned in the dark to Scuba Beach from the other direction, feeling like astronauts circumnavigating the moon, filled with the joy of the land.

Rolle had a bonfire going, and the girls were basking in its blaze, passing a bottle back and forth.

"I like your Island," said Xaviera privately, moving close to the fire, snuggling against North.

Phantoms of dreams floated over the coals. *I am in this Island, he thought, and this Island is in me.* The words flashed an alien image in his mind, a preview of a dream so exotic, so bizarre he feared even then it might recur, that the Island and Grant North would merge, that its green blood like that of some gigantic arthropod would enter his body and flow secretly through his own veins and arteries.

"Sometimes I imagine the world flat with an Island in the middle," Xaviera said, "a place where no one can find you and you can do anything you want."

Xaviera said it with a dimension North hadn't seen before, a depth he hoped she possessed. But then he heard something else.

"Did you hear it?" he said.

Cleary came over, listening too, not speaking.

"Hear what?" she asked.

"Did you hear it whispering?"

"What's 'it?'" she said.

"The Island," he said softly. Cleary smiled silently.

"Oh sure," said Xaviera. "It's whispering sweet nothings."

Cleary said, "I know what you mean, Grant. I heard something too. It's as though the jungle is alive, it kind of . . . talks to you."

"You guys are crazy," Xaviera decided.

And yet it seemed natural enough. The Island whispered to you through the dusk in a harmony of tamarind and casuarinas. It possessed an intimacy that transformed the trees and grasses and spiders and creeping crabs into one great living organism, like a colony of coral programmed by a single individual. You could see its sleeping boulders as monumental muscles to be released in the next hurricane. You could feel its seawater, the bloodstream of a pagan eucharist, seeping into the interior, filtered by renal sand to nourish verdant limbs. Men used to believe in such things. A storm at sea meant that the sea-god was angry, that some inherent property of stone made one pebble fall faster than another. Or that the pulse of an Island could beat in the heart of a man.

From the bonfire the sweet pungent odor of pigeon-plumb coals tossed sparks to a steady breeze. Cleary sat on a boulder and began roasting crawfish tails. Rolle hacked away at a coconut. The girls knelt at the fire, their long hair silhouetted against the sky. The night had darkened so fast and was so clear a man could get drunk just by looking at the stars.

By his actions, Cleary tried to involve Rolle with Steve, who seemed willing enough. But this man of the sea, showing a quiet resolve, sat a little apart during the barbecue. After dinner Cleary looked at Rolle with eyebrows raised, received no response, and shrugged his shoulders. He wrapped an arm around each girl and pretended to do the Goombay Shuffle as he led them toward his torrid trigonometry.

The moon plunged out of a cloud and shimmered the Island with rays so luminous that North could discern individual trees in the jungle. The longing he used to feel when he thought of stepping foot on another world and discovering mountains and valleys, alien caves and untouched mysteries, had been transferred from moon to Island. Where once the moon lit the path to uncounted worlds in space, each a new chance for mankind, now the Island represented a dawn, if not for all men then at least for North and his colleagues, a place to innovate, to rebuild paradise in their own image. Subtle passions flew back and forth over the bonfire like wraiths, eager to take shape as lush truths, sweet science, technology applied.

From down the beach North could heard Cleary and the two girls, their laughs merging oddly in his mind like nucleons forming a tritium atom. A last streak of sunlight tinged the edge of the ocean and died. Xaviera inched closer to him, her body pulling him as the moon pulls the ocean. They moved to the fluke of the whale and sat on a smooth shelf of rock forged by the sea into a low cliff. Night insects began to call, and under the silver light of the moon the jungle settled like a snoring beast.

Xaviera's short white dress had filled again in her spirited shape. She cupped fingers of both hands around the bottom of her skirt and lifted it slightly, no more than an inch. An image of

Heather, North's deceased wife, entered his mind, unwilled, unwanted, stained in guilt. Rejecting the feeling, he found Xaviera's lips, and slipped out of his trunks, holding her against his bare body. He ran his hand downward over her thigh, then upward under her skirt. She was wet and he was hard, and there was no time for thoughts of commitment or love or Heather who was dead. They lay on a slab of sand-strewn rock, cool and deep, and merged in rhythm with the wind and the cricket songs and the singing sands.

Afterwards he laughed a sustained laugh: at his counterfeit love, no more than a biological need, and at Cleary's absurd duet. Men's souls are debased, he realized, not by their hopes of greatness but by what they do. Yet most actions in life, such as this one, deserve no introspection. They're neutral, like a bowel movement.

"A penny for your thoughts," said Xaviera.

You don't want this thought, he said to himself, looking at the attractive young woman who sat beside him. She could do an excellent swan dive; perhaps in Europe she lives with five cats, skis, and cooks gourmet shrimp—or for that matter, knows how to grow them in a polyculture system. But he didn't want to ask, didn't want to know her or what she cared about or even learn her last name. It had been four years since Heather died, and although he could march through the motions of love, he could not love anyone. Not yet.

"Why the laugh?" she persisted.

"I guess I laughed because I'm happy," he said, thinking not of her, but of the Island.

IN THE MORNING, North watched Xaviera's easy slumber and the seabirds hunting their breakfast, and rejected this promiscuous life. It might be okay for Cleary. If Jack could survive it emotionally intact and forget about love and children, moving in the world unfettered like the creatures of the sea, maybe he needed no greater bonds. But Grant North was not Jack Cleary.

He roused Xaviera so he could pack in time to take the jollyboat to Great Snake and begin his trip to New York. Cleary was going with him as far as Nassau, and on the way they would discard these girls as you might a poker hand that could not possibly win.

6 ORIGINS: the Island

THE BAHAMA ISLANDS, like the Great Lakes of Grant North's former life, are remnants of the last massive glacier that had come nowhere near the tropics, yet had drawn into its mountains of ice so much of the Atlantic that the sea level fell. The lower water allowed the coral heads and other high areas of the ocean floor to break the surface and lie exposed to air, permitting plants to root. The first trees able to survive long ocean voyages were the red mangrove seedlings that set their roots in salt water. Birds and ocean currents brought the seeds of other plants while waves at the water's edge ground the rocks into sand, forming beaches. Some seventy thousand years later man arrived, and many millennia after that, the islands were stumbled upon by Columbus.

During the five hundredth year anniversary, Sidney Rolle was fond of saying that Columbus didn't discover America in 1492. He discovered the Bahamas. Weary and sick, he and his captains repeatedly grounded their ships on the shoals around the easternmost of these islands, and so Columbus called the region "the Shallow Sea," which in Spanish is *Bajamar*. Grant North kept a satellite photograph from NASA in his quarters that revealed both the extent of Columbus's shallow-water problem and the beauty of his discovery. From space the Bahama island groups look like strings of jade strung between variegated patches of white and pastel shallows on the inside and the indigo of the depths on the outside. In the Wracking Island chain, the expanse of convoluted shoals and flats less than a fathom deep connect its thirty cays in the shape of a conch shell, their lee sides flaring into exotic blue and white whorls, which are rippling flats of white sand.

The Bahamas does not touch the Caribbean Sea, so it is not part of the Caribbean geographically. But socially and politically, even before the Spanish Invasion, it is referred to as the "northern Caribbean" and is part of the West Indies. The original Indians of the Bahamas consisted of peaceful Lucayans and a branch of them called Arawaks, who for centuries had been paddling up from South America in ornate dugout canoes, some as long as sixty feet and carrying more than a hundred men. They wore no clothes and lay around on woven vines slung between the palms; for beauty they flattened their heads. A completely different tribe, fierce cannibals called Caribs, came on raiding missions from as far as the Windward Islands. But the Carib devastation was minuscule compared to that of the fortune hunters from Spain, who replaced cannibalism with murderous labor in the mines of Hispaniola. Before the papal bull of 1537, Americans were believed to be subhuman like orangutans or gorillas, and even after the decree the Spaniards tortured, en-slaved, and now tried to convert every native they encountered. In chains there was nothing to live for, no green mornings spearing bonefish on the flats, no nights of laughter. Only those brief twilights that painted their bronze bodies in fire and promised to burn their Christian souls forever.

By the mid-sixteenth century the three American tribes, perhaps as many as a million people, had relinquished their last coral reef, their last feathered palm. Although a few survived long enough to mate with the hardier Africans brought there to replace them, as a race they abandoned this earth forever, leaving no heritage or culture and only one invention, the hammock.

With the slave trade, the Island saw its first slaughter. After crossing the Atlantic in the filth of airless holds, the Negroes were brought up on deck and examined like cattle for commercially acceptable health. Those too sick to be marketable in Nassau or the Carolinas were put to the knife, and the turquoise water of Slaughter Harbour ran purple with their blood.

When Grant North bought the Island, he had the feeling that he and Cleary were the first men since the days of the buccaneers to tread this virgin land, Crusoes unstranded. As if exploring another planet, each step was hot revelation, pure excitement, fiery infatuation. Skiers know that feeling when they awaken early after a night's heavy snowfall and are the first to bequeath their tracks to the mountain powder. Magellan must have known it when he struggled around the straits that bear his name and beheld the Pacific. It isn't just being first; after all, Balboa preceded Magellan. It is the knowledge that no one lives here now, that your pristine world sweeps untouched before you. You name the places you discover. You explore them. You savor them. Godlike, you believe your Island is alive, that you can create its future.

7   *Money in the Bank*

THE OVERHEAD joists of the LCM's covered well deck reminded St. Gregory of his basement, and he had to crouch to avoid bumping his head. He flicked on the lights and saw the galley and large plywood crew lockers toward the stern, and forward, the cargo bay. The steel deck was crossed every yard by reinforcement ribs that tripped you if you didn't watch your step. He stopped at one of the two manholes that led to the crawl space under the deck. The double hull provided flotation, housed auxiliary fuel tanks—and furnished hiding places. Using a socket wrench he'd brought with him, he began loosening twenty-four short bolts that secured the manhole. The possibility that Symes might have given the money to North for safekeeping entered his mind.

After removing the last bolt, St. Gregory slid the manhole aside and aimed his flashlight into the crawl space. He squeezed his enormous frame inside head first, and wriggled on his belly toward the portside tanks. It made him remember how his father had locked him in small closets when he was a child, how as an adolescent he had said no to exploring the caves and potholes of Nassau, afraid his arms might cling to his sides in a passage too narrow to advance, too steep to retreat. Eventually he had forced himself to enter tight tunnels to experience the fear, and had learned to control it as he controlled the other aspects of his life.

Arms in front, he held the light and wriggled farther into the spaces between the decks. Despite his bulk there was little danger of being trapped *unless someone closed the manhole!* He wished he could wipe the sweat from his face. He was already a rich man, and for a moment he wondered why he rejected the simple rules and instead sought unremitting conflict.

Something was stuffed in the spaces between the aluminum fuel tanks. Inching his way closer he made out dozens of packages wrapped in waterproof plastic. Pulling the bundles toward him, he backed toward the manhole, listening to the amplified sounds of harbor water a half inch away. Only when he had gotten out and bolted the manhole again did he allow himself to examine his find.

Opening the first bundle, he ran his hand over hundred-dollar U.S. bills, and felt a surge through his groin. He knew from experience that hundreds weigh sixty thousand dollars a pound, and estimated the packages weighed a total of fifteen pounds. Each hundred was a discrete unit of energy transmutable into power, like bullets into death. He stuffed his printed energy into a duffelbag and strode outside onto the dock, breathing the sparkle of the night air.

The duffel safe in the trunk of his big bulletproof Mercedes, he headed toward his farmhouse. The rest of the night and all day Sunday he did push-ups, lifted weights, and thought intermittently about Grant North and the surprise he had for him. The guy had guts for a scientist, he had to admit.

At eight Monday morning, St. Gregory drove to downtown Nassau where he pulled into a no-parking space in front of the bank on Shirley Street. He sat there waiting for the bank to open and looking through his polycarbonate windshield, considering what he would do if the scientist tried to get Symes's money back.

The S.F.E. Bank & Trust Company, a subsidiary of Société Financiere Europeenne Luxembourg, opened at nine. St. Gregory took the fifteen-pound duffelbag from the Mercedes' trunk, hugged it against his thigh, and entered. Like priests and lawyers, Bahamian banks are stable and are sworn to secrecy, but to make sure of both, St. Gregory had the nine hundred thousand dollar deposit wired to his numbered account in Luxembourg.

8 *The Drug Warriors*

UNITED NATIONS building, New York. Implacable March fog, bleak and oppressive like something out of a Dickens novel—the more so because North had been unsuccessful in locating Symes by phone at any of their suppliers in Ft. Lauderdale. Nor could he find Coby after spending an hour calling her friends in Florida and Chicago. She had wanted to go to college in France. Imagining her on the Left Bank living on cannabis and cornbread, he threaded his way through crowds of grim-faced tourists into the conference building, down the stairs, and through doors marked, DELEGATES ONLY.

Conference Room Four held five hundred delegates to the U.N. Economic & Development Council and their aides seated in a semicircle. North sat in the speakers' row at the front.

Months ago when the invitation had come to address the council, North had accepted for an unusual reason. He wanted to make amends for an invention he had come to regret. The invention, for which his name had found its way into the dictionary, was the North Detector, a device that measured the involuntary movement of the eyeball, called "nystagmus." Instead of time-consuming lab tests to determine whether a person took drugs, the North Detector measured inebriation optically at a glance. All you had to do was *look* at the device for a fraction of a second.

It was too easy. Soon North Detectors were attached to myriad lenses of surveillance cameras hidden above mirrors in the lavatories of corporate buildings, and sometimes illegally over ticket coun-ters and other public places. Wholesale body searches at airports became commonplace, as were seizures of yachts found with a few grains of marijuana aboard. Drug police confiscated thousands of acres because persons unknown had cultivated illegal plants in hidden areas. Zero tolerance at work—courtesy of the North Detector.

Fully half the U.N. delegates were thin dark men in crisp suits who represented the developing nations, places like the Bahamas that offered tax breaks and cheap labor. The cocaine epidemic as they saw it was a United States problem, and they wanted the U.S. to leave them out of it, to take action instead against its own popula-tion.

Finally it was North's turn at the podium. Cleanly shaved, he wore an expensive brown suit, snow-white shirt with small stone cuff links, and a rust-colored tie. He began talking as if to one person, perhaps Heather. "Even if you beheaded drug dealers, the Plague would continue," he said, "because the risk-reward ratio is so skewed. The lifetime wages of an ordinary person living in Latin America can be earned in a single night."

A few delegates nodded.

"Worldwide, drug users spend *four hundred billion dollars* a year, illegal billions that ought to be deployed to teach kids not to get started on drugs in the first place, illegal billions going to criminals instead of rehabilitation centers. Ninety-two percent of their drug shipments evade detection. The pushers are getting away with murder."

North felt a strange sensation of being alone in the great hall, talking to himself. Most of the audience wore headsets, so he couldn't tell which delegates were listening to his voice and which to trans-lations of it in Chinese, Arabic, French, Russian, or Spanish.

"Prohibition is the problem, not the solution. Unlimited num-bers of soldiers are recruited by the drug lords we keep in business with our laws against drugs. The courts struggle with these minor players, whose appeals average six years and who usually go free.

We jail mostly freelancers in the U.S. In at least one state, Michigan, a first offender gets a mandatory life sentence for possession of less than a pound and a half of cocaine. We've got more than a million people in prison, and half of them are drug offenders."

That's your problem, the audience seemed to say. *Your country consumes sixty percent of cocaine, angel dust, speed, and all the rest. Shifting the burden to us is North American arrogance.*

"There are at least another fifty million abusers *outside of the United States*—and that makes our Plague your Plague too. How can a small government with corruptible authorities fight a 'drug government' with billions of dollars and private armies?"

He paused to see if he had the attention of the delegates from the producer countries, whose customs officers are being corrupted, whose police are being killed, whose national economies are being devastated. He had their attention, all right, but not their agreement. They admitted no paradox.

"Limiting the supply of dangerous substances doesn't work, can't work, has never worked. Even if you could wipe out eighty percent of the world supply of cocaine—an enormous, impossible task—you would have done nothing except increase the price and therefore the numbers of crimes required to pay for the drugs. Even if you could do the impossible and eliminate *all* drugs at their source, superdrugs would be developed using the billions at stake—designer drugs like the sernyls or derivatives of belladonna, internasel gels, or gene-spliced dope we haven't even heard of yet.

"The concept of zero tolerance, or harassing the users, is worse than absurd. How many millions can we arrest? Even if we had a place to put them, taking them out of society would collapse our economies."

North plunged into an alternative policy he called an "urgent experiment." He could tell by the rustling in the hall that they had guessed where he was going and would not hear the distinctions, the sharp clarifications upon which every idea worth having depends. North called for gradual legalization with close government control. Most important, he wanted the immense proceeds to be spent on rehabilitation and anti-drug education—not the spiritless ten-second television ads and newspaper slogans that proved no match against cartel money.

"The billions earned from taxing drugs can be added to the billions you save as the result of no-longer-needed interdictions, trials, and prisons. In the U.S., we spend a hundred and twenty billion dollars a year on prosecuting and jailing drug users. The massive education program so funded would use every means available to halt drug use: negative advertising, skull-and-crossbone labeling, classes in schools, tax incentives for company anti-drug programs. The movie industry, for example, would be asked to show villains doing the snorting, smoking, or injecting, while the heroes disdain dope as obsolete, obscene, out of fashion—the exact opposite habits the movies once emphasized to help hook people on cig—"

A vaguely female voice suddenly blared from the loudspeakers: *"No way! You legalize dope, you increase the number of addicts! Pure and simple."*

A sea of faces turned to the left side of the room where an almost-spherical black woman stood beside her desk holding a microphone. Thick legs stuck out below an enormous tent of a dress like some evolutionary error in biophysics.

"My name is Senator Doctor Dame Cora Carstairs from the Commonwealth of the Bahamas. I see dope-crazed pushers enticing our chil—"

Her words stabbed North like a stiletto. *Please, not the Bahamas!* The audience was on her side, the applause monstrous. "Senator Carstairs," he said when the room quieted, "don't you believe people can govern themselves?"

"Not when it comes to drugs."

"Even if legalization resulted in an increase, it would be temporary. The use of marijuana declined after it was virtually decriminalized in the U.S."

"Crack is different!"

"Not in its availability."

Other voices fought to be heard.

"It's a hell of a lot easier to say no to drugs when you have to drive into some crime-ridden slum than simply buy the stuff in a government drugstore!"

"It's the poor who will suffer. The blacks—"

The delegates were standing, scurrying, clenching fists, talking at once. Aides, secretaries, visitors jammed the aisles. The fat lady had been the catalyst, precipitating a chemical reaction without consuming herself. Now she sat down.

"Clear the aisles! Please be seated!" The sergeant-at-arms banged a gavel, then threw a switch somewhere that killed the microphones other than his own. *"Order in the hall. Clear the aisles!"*

The riot of words had gone too far. Ushers wove their way through each row, encouraging the most vociferous of the arguers to sit down or leave. A trickle of delegates broadened into a steady stream that flowed into the General Assembly lobby where a cocktail party had been scheduled. The sergeant-at-arms announced euphemistically that there was "insufficient time for questions.

North saw himself as he imagined the delegates saw him: a craggy, suntanned inventor disguised in a banker's suit trying clumsily to save the world. Was he really doing that? Or, having invented the civil liberties violator called the North Detector, was he simply assuaging his guilt? Even the best of plans, he thought, can sour into pessimism, depositing scars on the ego.

There are moments in history when ideas catch fire. This was not one of them. What little genuine applause came to him before he left the podium he wanted to preserve like rare champagne and take back to the Island for Coby. But you can't save partial acceptance. Like wine, it turns too easily to vinegar.

9 *Prime Engine*

WHEN NORTH ascended to the vast cocktail party, he
appeared as a visionary to some and to others a demon who would
sell their children heroin at the candy store. Everyone involved in
the Great Drug War knew of the North Detector but few knew its
inventor. Now his anonymity had been shattered and a dozen delegates mustered to get at him.

North strained to hear their questions against a background of
social noise and a busy stairway that rose from the lobby to the
General Assembly. At least there were no cat-calls here. Reality
lived in that other room, pretense in this one, and the reality of
his rejection had left pretense far behind. He accepted congratulations and skepticism with patience, answering questions tactfully.
Clawed by doubt, bolstered by righteousness, he told himself that
tonight on this question of legalization he was a squid, shooting
his essence over anything that came along and then getting away
in the confusion. After twenty minutes the crowd around him had
not perceptibly thinned. Pleading that his voice was giving out, he
grabbed a glass of champagne from the nearest bar, escaped from
the questioners, and roamed the enormous lobby searching for the
Bahamian delegation.

North avoided reefs of people, searching faces for the wire-framed glasses of the Bahamian ambassador, who curiously was named Benjamin Franklin. A year ago North had gone to see the ambassador in Washington and had found him noncommittal about the Island for Science, implying that everything was up to North, that the government routinely approved worthy projects. Franklin would be of even more importance to the Island now, for his new job was Minister of Fisheries.

A young woman sat down to a piano and played a Chopin etude. She was too beautiful, too talented for a delegate, thought North, but too nervous for a professional pianist. On the opposite side of an immense glass wall, the trees of a patio garden swayed somewhat with the music, the farther ones lost in a misty rain. North spotted Franklin holding a drink and gazing outside with a sad look as if he were about to blend into the fog.

Franklin saw him approaching. "Dr. North, good to see you again," he said with failed enthusiasm. A nerve under his right eye pulsed irregularly as he extended his hand.

It was like shaking hands with a noodle.

"Before I introduce you to the P.M.," he said, "tell me why you started your science island in the Bahamas instead of the States."

"I needed tropical waters for the seafarm. The ocean's too deep in Hawaii, and the Florida coast is reserved for recreation. The shallow water of the Bahamas is *made* for mariculture, and since the country's a democracy—"

"It certainly is," interrupted Franklin.

North recalled the evaluation of Freedom House, which every year groups the more than two hundred nations into seven ranks. Year after year the Bahamas falls into the first rank for political rights and rank two or three for civil liberties, right under Barbados as the freest of West Indian nations.

"Well," said Franklin, "let's go meet the P.M.," and without waiting for an answer he led the way to a group near the center of the room.

"Mr. Prime Minister," Franklin said, "I would like to present Dr. Grant North."

Prime Minister Charles T. Ransom, a heavyweight in his late fifties, wore a charcoal tussah suit that looked as if it had been tailored for him in Savile Row. But under that suit he seemed to possess the rugged physique of a cowboy, and he clasped North's hand firmly. A cinnamon-colored mulatto with aloof lips, Clark Gable mustache, and narrow nose, he was ageless, like the men who ride horses through the cigarette ads and manufacture their metabolites at a gallop.

Rumor had it that Ransom's father, a U.S. Navy noncom, had been married to someone other than his mother when Ransom was born. North detected a spark in the Prime Minister's brown eyes, an attitude of defiance that said he played his games of power only for himself. The eyes were framed by caterpillar brows, heavy with fur, that enhanced his regal position. At second glance he appeared not so much a cowhand as a well-tanned rancher, an aristocrat whose money earns money while he hunts wild boar or attends United Nations conferences. North had read that he once had been married to a Haitian voodoo priestess.

"And this is Malcolm Pyfrom, the Prime Minister's deputy," Franklin announced. Pyfrom's title was Deputy Prime Minister, but the way Franklin turned it around, the newcomer might have been the P.M.'s bookkeeper.

"Dr. North," said Pyfrom. The long thin hand he offered felt cool and limp, even damp. After the handshake, Pyfrom flexed his fingers in a strangely reptilian gesture, as if he were regenerating them.

North expected to be introduced to the other two men but they looked away, apparently finding more excitement in scanning the field. One, a burly black six-footer, weighed in at something over two-fifty. The other, a lighter-skinned welterweight, might have started working out at age thirteen as an antidote to being called a feather merchant. You could see the pectoral muscles ripple under their shirts when they moved. Franklin leaned close to North and whispered, "They don't want to be introduced. They're like the Secret Service men who protect your President. The big man is Wright, the little one is Wilson."

"Well-lll, Dr. North," said Prime Minister Ransom in a voice liquid as oil, causing Franklin to melt into the ambience of clinking ice and tobacco smoke. "Too bad half the delegates missed your conclusions."

"Thank you, Mr. Prime Minister," North said.

"Your ideas certainly are . . . interesting. For a scientist, that is. Less so for a chessplayer willing to make sacrifices."

North was astonished. How had the Prime Minister known he played chess?

Lighting a pipe, Ransom contracted the caterpillars over his eyes, making them writhe as he exhaled a tobacco cloud of rainless nimbus. "It would seem at first glance that legalizing drugs might fit that general philosophical idea of freedom. But this drug business is so devastating, sacrificing people with their free use could be dangerous, don't you think?"

"Somebody," North answered, "once said that 'an idea not dangerous is unworthy of being called an idea at all—'"

"Oscar Wilde," said a voice behind him in a soft contralto.

"What?" he said, turning around.

"Oscar Wilde said that."

The voice, a low melody, belonged to the young woman he had noticed playing the piano. Her hair, luxurious and dark-brown, flowed close to her left eye, cascaded over a bare shoulder and a perfect breast, and ended majestically at her waist. A single earring hung like an icicle, and her eyebrows, arched high in mystery, were almost as thick as the Prime Minister's. She had strong cheek bones, pure green eyes, and lips abundant but not thick that neither wore nor required lipstick. Here stood a stunning Eurafrican who blended the genes of her ancestry in a racial harmony that spoke well for the future of mankind, for in the end, thought North, we'll all be golden brown.

"Dr. North, may I present my daughter, Marianne Price." Ransom was proprietary, as if it were important that he distinguish "present" from "bestowing a gift."

She said simply, "Dr. North." Her smile formed far back in the crystal of her eyes, perhaps as far back as her childhood that spoke of summers spent in sunshine and love in a tropic land. Magnificent in a low-cut white dress, she appeared to be uneasy with herself and yet eager for life. As she moved next to North, her radiance struck him with the energy of a wave washing a swimmer.

". . . she's a concert pianist," Ransom was saying with an odd smirk on his face. "And a Marxist. Post-*perestroika*, of course."

North looked straight into Marianne's emerald eyes and said, "Man can't live by capital alone."

She laughed. "Even entrepreneurs can be for the underdog."

It was a strange interlude, as though father, daughter, and intruder had glimpsed the future and were trying to alter it. An errant thought emerged from his subconscious: *too bad she's black.* Ashamed of the notion, he wondered where it had sprung from. Never had he been close to a girl of another race, and yet he had defended the concept of mixed blood in arguments with his sister Jo, arguing that the races strengthened each other like metals in an alloy. Chicago kids grew up wearing their prejudices like uniforms, but he liked to think he had outgrown all that. Did it make any difference that Marianne's skin wasn't even black? A better comment would be: *too bad she's married.* Or was she? She wore no wedding ring.

Senator Carstairs waddled toward the group, muddying North's speculations and reminding him that the Island project came first. The space between Marianne and her father filled with the senator's bulk.

"I didn't mean to kick over the anthill in there," she said, in deep baritone, smiling. She held a furiously smoking, unfiltered cigarette between pudgy fingers and sported the largest most-amorphous breasts North had ever seen on any species of mammal. On her blazer a six-inch badge proclaimed, MOTHERHOOD AND GOD.

Was she kidding with that sign?

"I think you already have met Senator Doctor Dame Cora Carstairs," Ransom said, flicking her multiple titles with a twinkle of his rancher's eyes. "Dr. Carstairs is president of the Bahamian Senate. She is the person responsible for achieving women's suffrage in our country."

She was not kidding. The woman had been knighted, and North could imagine the Queen's sword pressing that varicose flesh.

"Oh? When was that?" North asked dutifully. He would rather talk to Marianne, but knew he was on display.

"A mere quarter century ago," Senator Carstairs said. "More

than fifty years after suffrage came to the United States." She chang-ed the subject. "Dr. North, the law serves to express society's moral repugnance to drug abuse—"

The others in the group were assiduously elsewhere. Malcolm Pyfrom, occupied with the complexities of getting drunk, was olive-fishing between the ice cubes of his third or fourth martini. Benjamin Franklin had wandered off and returned now with a waitress who carried fresh drinks on a tray. When he saw the drinks, Pyfrom drained his old one and seized another, peering through lizard eyes at a world that seemed to weary him. Marianne studied North like a schoolgirl on her first date. Prime Minister Ransom beamed in the sunshine of his daughter's luster, of his importance to the world, and of the martinis he drank with a relish uncommon to diplomats in public.

Senator Carstairs went on in her heavy voice about how her people needed protection, about how Bahamian law prudently pro-hibits citizens from gambling in the Nassau casinos.

Ransom interrupted. "The question seems to be: would the lives wasted by those who would take drugs, if they were legal, be outweighed by the lives saved as the educational effort decreases demand for drugs? In other words, does the end in this case justify the means?"

Marianne was shaking her head no.

"If the end can't justify the means, what the hell else can?" Ransom responded.

It was a singular remark from the head of a western democracy. North changed the subject. "I wouldn't use cocaine simply because it was legal or even free," he said to Marianne. "Would you?"

"No," said Marianne quietly. Her father stared at her strangely.

North tried another tack. "There are only two ways to fight drugs. One is to execute the pushers as they do in Malaysia. For-tunately the western world isn't ready for that. Yet. The other way is to legalize and thereby control the stuff. Cigarettes are legal in the U.S. and three-quarters of our adults *don't* smoke, even though inhaling nicotine is known now to be more addictive than cocaine or heroin."

"More addictive?" Marianne said.

"For some people apparently. I think it depends on how fast a person's dopamine is catalyzed by the cocaine; that is, how fast it converts to norepinephrin—"

"Of course it is these neurotransmitters that provide the pleasure," she said. "Or at least my doctor brother thinks so."

"No biophysicist could state it better. The point is that tolerance to cocaine is vastly different in different people."

"Well, if smoking is anywhere near as addictive as cocaine in even a small number of people—and since it is known to kill millions—why does your government subsidize tobacco growing?" Marianne said brightly, and went on to show her socialist leanings in denigrating Uncle Sam. "The same government, incidentally, that thinks nothing of shutting down a Third World nation's economy when it discovers some miniscule trace of insecticide in imported fruit."

"Stupid policies," said North, noticing that Ransom, concealed by his pipe, had an amused look on his face. "The U.S. did manage to reduce cigarette consumption by teaching the public about the health hazard. Now it's public pressure that makes the difference, not laws of prohibition or armies of enforcers."

Marianne steered the conversation as though it were her duty, "The issue is drugs, not cigarettes, Dr. North. Rehabilitation in the face of cheap and legal dope could be a nightmare. The only thing keeping coke addicts from their habit is the cost. If smokable White Lady were freely available, addicts would be so strung out they'd keep taking it day and night until they dropped dead. Like lab rats."

North stretched his heavy frame, stifling a yawn. It had been a long day and he was tired of standing so long in one spot, tired of talking, tired of rich women like Marianne and the Senator showing off their Biochemistry-101 or their Nassau street slang. They wouldn't recognize a crack addict if they stepped on one.

"You may be right," he said, worn but vigilant. "I don't claim to have all the answers. The Island for Science I'm trying to establish will double as a think tank to address such problems, to see whether there are any technological answers to the social problems of the region."

"Technical answers to dope?"

"Well, you could make drugs non-addicting."

Benjamin Franklin paused in rocking from one wooden foot to another. North readied himself for Ransom, who had been listening intently, to say something like, "How is your island project coming along?" in which case North would tell him about the dead-ends they were encountering in getting government permits. Instead, a strange thing happened. While the Prime Minister's right eye continued to scrutinize North, the left skipped out of its parallel track and, on its own, focused on the group next to theirs. Immediately, as if to hide his walleyes, Ransom refueled his pipe, filling, tapping, lighting, and finally issuing smoke like a dragon at rest between battles. The conversation ebbed.

Marianne gave North one of her warm smiles, and it fell across his heart like a sunbeam from a southern shore.

"Like Goethe," she said, "I find it best to be on the side of the minority, since it is always the most intelligent." She handed him her card, which read:

REHAB
Rehabilitation, Education & Health
Association of the Bahamas
Marianne Price,
Director

North suffered a flash of embarrassment for having wrongly assumed that Marianne knew nothing about the drug scene. Or was her job insulated and cushy, the result of tropical nepotism. . . ?

Senator Carstairs spoke out of the corner of her mouth opposite the cigarette. "During your speech, I couldn't help but think what would happen in the Bahamas should your plan for legalization take place."

"We would never allow that," the Prime Minister said.

"Just suppose—"

"It's unthinkable," Ransom said with mild finality.

"Of course, Mr. Prime Minister," she said, shifting gears with-out missing a cog. "If the United States ended drug prohibition, wouldn't that send a message of unrestricted hedonism to Americans—and from them, via tourism, to the Bahamas and the Caribbean?"

Ransom nodded, as did Franklin in robotic agreement. Pyfrom looked wound up and ready to strike. Poor guy, thought North. He must be having a day as bad as his own.

"As someone in the auditorium pointed out," the senator said, "legalizing drugs would hurt American blacks more than whites. They're the ones in the lower socioeconomic class."

North recognized the justness of her accusation and it irritated him. As repulsive as she was, she had a way of putting her finger concisely on the difficult questions. He could counter the other objections: millions of innocents rushing to try drugs *(unenforced laws don't stop them anyway)*; professionals too doped to drive or do surgery and so forth *(performing critical work under the influence would remain as illegal as it is now)*; the devastation of drug-growing nations' economies *(substitute other crops, export technology)*; and so on. But the charge that his plan was essentially racist vexed him, because even though it had been his very concern for civil rights that had led him to advocate legalization, the lower classes *would* suffer the most. They were the ones who embraced synthetic oblivion the hardest.

"Senator Carstairs—"

"You may call me Dame Cora," she said, justifiably proud of her knighthood.

"Please call me Grant. Dame Cora, the heart of the argument is that people confuse legalizing drugs with condoning them. If we spend the vast sums we save on teaching that drugs are *not* acceptable, we'll have *less* addiction, less crime in the ghetto, fewer prisons—more money for education and habitation, as well as for *re*habilitation."

"Unlikely," said the president of the Senate.

"In the long run—"

"It doesn't work that way," said Ransom.

"Father. Dr. North," said Marianne Price with a cheery smile, "the enormous sums of money that legalization in the United States would generate could be harnessed right here. We could make the Bahamas the world's focal point for the rehabilitation of addicts. People might combine a cure with a vacation—as they do now to lose weight."

Her father clung to a majestic silence, but North saw something smoldering beneath those caterpillar eyebrows. Was the P.M. being proprietary toward his daughter, or had North sniffed out some hidden truculence? He decided to probe it.

"Sure," said North, smiling at this alluring, audacious girl who apparently had joined his side of the argument. "At first the wealthy addicts from the U.S. and Europe would come to Nassau for help. Gradually, as you built a therapy industry, Bahamian citizens also would benefit."

"You seem to know a lot about the Bahamas," Marianne said. "Did you know we have twice the alcoholism and drug-addiction rate of your country?"

"I'm afraid I do know that. Twice the per-capita consumption of alcohol, cigarettes, marijuana, cocaine, and heroin. Twice the suicide rate. Fifty-eight percent illegitimate births. These are drug-related problems, fertile ground for—"

He stopped suddenly and looked around like a cat who has dropped his mouse. Their eyes—all but Marianne's—had glazed over. The others focused not on his eyes but somewhere nearby, the way you look at the guy who tells you he talks to God. Had he offended them by reciting their country's ills? No, they were too realistic, too tough. He'd seen that look before. They were impassive scientists peering into the lenses of their microscopes, discovering in him a paramecium who couldn't divide, a peculiar Dreamer Organism—something like their own Marianne perhaps. Here he was, edging into his Island for Science, wanting to sell the benefits of it to the most important people in this government, and he came off like some smart-ass do-gooder. Or worse. The corrupt American hiding his true mission behind an Island for Evil. North's introspection dissolved into a puddle of perplexity.

"Father," explored Marianne, "isn't it exciting that Grant is building his Island for Science in our country?"

Ransom gave a politician's answer. "Dr. North appears to have done his homework on the Bahamas quite carefully. Surely he knows it's a free country."

It may be free but if its leaders were any indication, it was also aloof, inflexible, and noncommittal. North shrugged off the thought, luxuriating in the warmth of Marianne's wide and hopeful eyes.

The Prime Minister furrowed his forehead, and his eyebrows resumed their crawl. "In spite of our comments, Dr. North, your ideas have interest, and we shall ponder them. . . . I enjoyed your peroration immensely."

Peroration? It was an odd way to say something; North supposed it meant speech or "oration."

The P.M. reverted to his former role as cultured diplomat. The mistrust North had read earlier in his eyes might have been shock that an outsider saw so much to be done in the Bahamas.

Ransom shook hands with North and then stood aside, extending his right arm like a sword and holding his pipe in the other like a dagger, so that Marianne, smiling her radiant goodbyes, could lead the way out under the protection of his weaponry. The P.M.'s body language didn't exactly give the impression he was ready to relinquish control of his daughter. With his entourage winding behind him through clusters of delegates, Ransom was the locomotive of a train winding around obstacles. The train meandered through the lobby seeking other people who would voice other topics, the prime engine of the Bahamian government periodically letting loose a puff of pipe smoke, the savory smoke of status. The scene was ridiculous yet somehow ominous, flashing images to North of tiny cancer cells, like submarines navigating the bloodstream. Or armies marching in goosestep.

10 *Needlefish*

SEVEN P.M., Tuesday. The workers comfortable on their Snake Cay barstools, the government's permits safe from Jack Cleary, and Grant North back on the Island from New York, the night descended like purple velvet and the moon trembled on the water. Sidney Rolle sprinkled diesel fuel over the near end of the six-foot barbecue pit in the lodge, igniting thick sapodilla branches.

"Cold or somethin', Sid?" asked Cleary.

North came over to the bar wearing Levi's and an unbuttoned long-sleeved shirt that revealed strong pectorals and a profusion of body hair. "This is your night, Jack. For your hard work braving the air-conditioned offices in Nassau and drinking all those Cleary Coladas, we are going to do something just for you."

"You're moving the shrimp farm to New York?"

"We are taking you needlefishing!"

"Aw shit," said Cleary, lifting his iced gin. "I'd rather drink."

Nighttime needlefishing, invented by Rolle and North, was becoming a tradition of the Island, but Cleary had never done it.

"Yo bring de bot*tle*," Rolle said to Cleary.

He filled a giant pot a third full of water, placed it over the charcoal, and left it there to boil. They went outside, took a storage battery from a shed, and carried it with an automobile spotlight to the fiberglass whaler. North looked up at the stars. The moon had not yet risen but Orion hunted the heavens, dagger blazing in belt.

The stellar flux from a billion suns lit their way to the dock. They climbed into the whaler and motored slowly toward the center of the harbor, North at the outboard, Rolle in the bow, Cleary scanning the stars whose scintillating light had been traveling for eternity. Slaughter Harbour is bordered by the Island and by Harbour Rock, a storm-washed thousand-foot appendage where not a blade of grass can live. Legend has it that the barren appendage, in guarding the approach to the Island, was cursed with no soil because it had been an indifferent witness to unspeakable slaughters. But Grant North imagined Harbour Rock a captured satellite of the Island. Like the moon, the islet is scarred, pockmarked, and barren of life, except for the sea crabs that scurry sideways up its jagged slopes.

"'Tis a holy night," said Cleary, intensely off-planet. He took a swig on a new quart of gin he'd brought with him, and handed it to North who drank some and passed it to Rolle.

"Ugghhh!" said Rolle.

"Quiet," said Cleary, "I'm meditating."

"With your clothes on?"

"If we had a sky like that in Manhattan," the meditator mused, "we New Yorkers wouldn't need our clothes off for recreation."

North and Rolle drank in silence, searching a universe so vast it invalidated humanity. A heron flapped across the breadth of the Great Bear and lit on Harbour Rock, oblivious of the curse men had placed on it. The Islanders trolled slowly and passed the gin bottle while Rolle held the spotlight over the black surface. North cut the engine, and the stillness became so thick you could almost hear the fish swim. The night air tasted organic and salty, caviar on the tongue.

Soon dark shadows like giant darning needles darted in and out of the pool of light.

"Here come dem houndies!" announced Rolle, calling them by their creole name. He was excited as a stallion hearing the trumpet call to battle.

"What the hell do I do?" said Cleary, back from the stars.

"Grab a machete," North said, sliding beside him on the center thwart. "Port side. I'll take starboard."

Cleary waited, steadily drinking gin.

A four footer darted into the light. North swung his machete and cut off the head, but the fish swam away as he and Rolle lunged after it, splashing water. They laughed and gulped more raw gin. Rolle swung the light to the other side.

Emboldened by alcohol and watching how North had lost his, Cleary lashed out and cut off a tail. "Grab it! Somebody grab it!"

"Watch the teeth!" North said, as Rolle lunged to port and came up with a two-foot fish that might weigh five pounds.

"Christ Almighty, the damn thing's got more molars than a horse!"

North hacked indiscriminately at the shapes in the black liquid, sending heads and tails flying, pulling in two- and three-foot headless or tailless fish. Rolle worked the light, laughing, drinking, helping Cleary, shoving fish with snapping jaws away from arms and legs. In a quarter of an hour, two dozen snapping or headless needlefish slithered over the floorboards.

Cleary slashed the tail off a four footer. "Grab him, Sid!"

Rolle chuckled. "*You* grab the son of a bitch!"

Cleary made a weak attempt to get the fish, which was sinking slowly below the pool of light on the water. Rolle laid down the light, leaned over the gunwale after it, and slipped on the fishy boat boards. In the process, he snatched the tailless needlefish in the water too close to its mouth. Needlefish have no scales, making them hard to hold onto. The fish clamped its jaw around Rolle's hand.

"Help! The fucker's got me!"

Cleary laughed.

North shone the spotlight on Rolle's hand. The head of the fish was clamped over the palm and upper portions of the first three fingers of Rolle's right hand. The night smelled of blood, fish and human.

"Hold the spotlight, Jack," said North, instantly sober. Producing an awl from his pocket knife, he grasped the fish firmly behind its head, and thrust the steel point between the fish's eyes into its brain until the jaws relaxed in death.

His hand dripping blood, Rolle glared at Cleary under the

spotlight. "If you weren't so chicken, this wouldn't have happened. We ever get in a fight, you go fuckin' help somebody else."

As Cleary lifted the gin bottle, Rolle tore it out of his mouth, banging the end against his teeth.

"Ouch!" said Cleary. "What the hell are you doing?"

What Rolle was doing was pouring gin over his wound, slowly emptying the bottle while North steered to shore. From the grimace on his face, it must have hurt a lot.

CLEAN AND HUNGRY, the Islanders gathered around the lodge fire pit watching Rolle cook with one hand, assisted by God Knowles. The glow of charcoal was like a campfire.

Face pink from the shower, Cleary wore a pastel-blue oxford shirt with button-down collar, trousers of a soft expensive material, and imported loafers, the picture of casual wealth. The others wore dungarees or shorts. Pound-size hunks of needlefish dropped from Rolle's left, unbandaged hand into the boiling water. Knowles sliced tomatoes, breadfruit, onions, and peppers into the pot and added a quarter of a small bottle of Louisiana hot sauce. The fish turned red with liquefied tomatoes. Peas and rice steamed in an army-sized cookpot. Only the rice came from Florida by LCM; everything else grew on the Island, most of it wild. While he waited, North cut some raw fish and gave it to the cats.

A bronze fragrance filled the room as the odor of fish stew blended with the charcoal of sweet-burning sapodilla. Knowles inhaled deeply and sipped a spoonful. "Plenty hot pepper. But we needs more hoan*yuns* in dere, Mistuh Sidney." Rolle nodded.

When they sat down to eat, Cleary watched the veteran needlefish eaters cut along the outside of the spine and remove the skeleton intact. The bones, thick and bright, were kelly green. He raised his martini glass, and said, "A bit of the green, I see. A belated happy St. Patrick's Day to one and all!"

"Fuck you," said Rolle.

"Ah, Sid. Don't make me feel guilty. I'm Catholic enough, born in original sin."

"Bullshit. You replaced original sin with Methuselum gin."

"I told you I was no fisherman."

"You forgot to mention you had no guts."

"That's enough, Sid," said North. "It was an accident." He'd heard this kind of thing from Rolle before. If Jack Cleary's output of courage wasn't great at times, at least you never had to worry about being pushed off a roof.

Andy Angelo and Bruiser came in, following their noses. Andy, tall and thin with a mild case of acne, made a show of sniffing the odors, wearing the bittersweet look of the primate who knows there is only one banana remaining in the jungle and that he alone has found it.

"Fry or souse?" he asked, enjoying the roll of the Bahamas-learned words on his tongue.

"Souse," said Rolle. "Grab up a dish."

You could hear the ceramic plunk of fish slabs landing on two plates. Andy removed the bones, ladled the viscous red gravy over the "soused" fish, and set it on the floor for Bruiser. "He likes this stuff. He be Bahamian."

Andy placed a frying pan on the fireplace grill, and added a quarter pound of butter, hot sauce, and slices of raw breadfruit. When the breadfruit was as brown and crisp as a French fry, he shredded a pound of boiled needlefish into it, and stirred.

"Where did you learn to cook?" said Cleary.

"I never did. I only learned to eat." He glared at Cleary's third or fourth martini. "The way you learned to drink."

"I love these breakfasts," said Andy, eating voraciously.

" Dinner for us, breakfast for you," Knowles said smiling.

Andy operated his loader at night because he lacked a work permit. Cleary had no work permit either, but what he did in Nassau wasn't considered "work" by the Bahamian bureaucracy. Running the heavy machines was another story. There were workers on the Island who would gallop to the Immigration Office on Great Snake Cay like miscreant Paul Reveres sounding the warning, "Americans be wor*kin'!*"a sin sufficiently grave to warrant deportation. Such transgressions were punished in spite of the fact that the government granted work permits only after an overall project license was issued, which according to the rules could not be awarded until the project had been approved, and approval not given until an enterprise proved itself beneficial to the Bahamas. It was a circle North had not yet discovered how to square.

Before Coby left—it had been five days already, North realized—she and Andy had worked together every night. They would climb a tire as high as their heads, sling themselves onto the steel carapace, and pretend they were explorers on another planet taming some alien arthropod. Completion of the dock was North's first priority so that cargo could be delivered at the east end of the Island instead of a mile away at Scuba Beach, the only beach deep enough to land the LCM without getting stuck.

Along the northern coast where the Island grayed into barren coral remnants of a reef dead these million years, Coby had chosen which boulders to remove. She would leave intact those rocks clustered in galleries and parapets like torn parts of an ancient castle, and take instead the shapeless hulks, big as belfries. Gifts of the ocean over centuries of hurricanes, they lay loose on the coast where they formed a bastion against the sea. Andy loved riding with Coby under the stars, articulating the segments of the beast to dump load after load into the ocean, extending the dock deeper into Slaughter Harbour. Returning by way of the jungle road, they would stop every time their spotlight stunned a land crab, climb down, and twist off a single claw for the freezer, letting the animal live to regenerate another claw. North realized he wasn't the only one who missed Coby. Andy still worked at night, but alone.

"Ridin' dot pay*load*ina away from de tings what live in de sun*light*, you'll be startin' ta see duppies soon, Mr. Andy," said Knowles with a smile.

Knowles called those he liked "Mr. First Name." His stomach stuck out over his belt, and he thrust both hands into the pockets of worn work pants, widening the gap left by a broken fly. No one on the Island laughed or called attention to it; they respected his considerable dignity too much for that, and besides, he looked like he could bend steel rebars with his bare hands. Knowles opened the backgammon board for a game with Rolle.

"No duppies yet, Mr. God," said Andy. The affection was mutual. Lanky and eighteen, with an impish grin and a younger boy's fuzz on his chin, Andy resisted college, seeing himself as an adventurer.

North waited until Andy finished eating, and followed him out to the payloader. North reached into the young man's shirt pocket for a cigarette.

"Nervous or somethin'?" Andy asked. North rarely smoked, constantly trying to quit for good.

"I revert under stress. I'm worried about Coby." He smelled the cigarette and returned it unlit.

"Typical father. She's the bad guy, and you do the worrying."

"Bad guy is right. I found two grams of coke in her room. She says her friends use the stuff. That include you?"

"Aw shit, Grant, two grams ain't nothin'. Everybody does it once in a while."

"That's a dandy reason. Who was your Sunday school teacher, Hermann Goering?"

"Okay, I tried it once or twice a long time ago. That don't make me an addict."

"Coby too?" North's eyes penetrated Andy's skull.

"We never did it much, and we only snorted it. We didn't shoot it or smoke crack. Where'd you find the stuff, in the radio?"

"Yeah."

"She probably forgot she'd hidden it there. That was eight, nine months ago, when we first got here. She never liked it much, said it made her queen of the shit heap. I guess it was too lonesome for her way up there. If anything, she'd be more likely to crash on grass than coke."

"Did she?"

"I don't know. I doubt it. Look, Grant, she's no doper."

Andy raised his eyes to the stars as if longing to go there. After a moment he saw the skepticism on North's face and broke the silence. "That's the God's honest truth, Grant."

North said goodnight and headed for his side of one of the villas facing Slaughter Harbour. The square duplexes looked like the little green houses you use in monopoly games, except their sides were stone and their roofs were dazzling white to reflect the heat. North heard the loader's starter whine, and then the low growl of the big diesel as Andy moved the machine toward the coast.

The naked emotions of the young moved North to compassion; neither Andy nor Coby had any sense of the velocity of life, he thought, or of its dangers. But Andy had spoken the truth, and that meant North's fight with Coby had been even more foolish than he'd first thought.

NORTH LAY AWAKE in bed thinking of the Island and of a single parent's responsibility. The Island was a unique and sovereign undertaking, an adventure more important to him than had been the moon. The argument with Coby, the problem of the permits, the background of violence in these islands were small things, mere upsets he had to learn to ignore. The light from the Little Snake Cay lighthouse flashed through his insomnia at thirty-second intervals, and he closed his eyes against it, practicing blank thinking, trying to absorb the darkness into his brain. Coby crept in there too, lighting the space with a flame. Coby crying as a little girl. Coby tonight—where?

The thick glass of the sliding door, coated in mist, gathered moonbeams into its prisms and splashed a spectrum of color on the wall next to his bed. He rose and slid open the door, stepping into the silver night. The moon etched a path across the sea, and pulled him as it does the home planet. Reaching into the room for a pair of binoculars, he traced on the moon a curving line from the greenish gray Ocean of Storms in the north to the magnificent Crater Copernicus on the equator. The plateaus and peaks glistened like sapphires and emeralds; the rays streaked from the floor of the crater like spokes on a wheel, and he followed the great walls rising from a valley vast enough for eight terrestrial Grand Canyons. It was here that he had advised NASA to establish a permanent base, wanting desperately to go to that world, but the politicians had turned off the manned lunar program. He was aware that he had come to the Island in substitute.

He was aware too that his intuition had been nudging him all night. Beware the middle days of March, the ides of Caesar's soothsayer. Absurd. The *Half Fast* would return tomorrow or the next day with its load of building materials. Then he could stop worrying about Coby.

11 *The Bottom of the Sky*

IN THE MORNING North waded in chest-deep waters collecting various species of *Gracilaria* and *Hypnea* so his University of Miami phycologist could measure their carrageenan and agar content. These gels are in demand by processors who use them to thicken ice cream, smooth evaporated milk, whiten bread, stabilize dog food, and otherwise improve some ten thousand different foods. In the corrals the seaweed soon would provide the shrimp with oxygen, shade, and a natural antibiotic to keep them healthy, while ingesting shrimp waste as fertilizer—a true symbiosis.

Rolle, who had been supervising his crew in building the corral fences, came over wearing a wet-suit jacket.

"Ready?" North said.

"I wanted to talk to you about Cleary before we go diving. He's a rummy."

"I know."

"Look, a rummy can't get our permits—"

"Drop it, Sid." North started wading toward shore, towing his tote bags filled with various species of seaweeds. "I'll worry about the permits. You worry about getting the seafarm ready."

Rolle tightened his jaw, his scar vivid in the low sun. He glanced at the bandage on his right hand. "Don't you sometimes wonder what the hell Cleary does in Nassau? That place is a cesspool of intrigue."

"What are you getting at? I thought he was such 'a credit to his race'"

"When I was in Nassau I heard rumors about Evan Symes smuggling—"

North had heard nothing of such rumors. "What the hell has that got to do with Cleary?"

"I dunno, but every smuggling ring needs a point man to deal with the government. That's common knowledge. You trust Cleary?"

"With my life."

Rolle said no more. He relieved North of one of the bags of seaweed, and followed him to the beach and down-Island to the laboratory. The seafarm here was in full view. While the others had been working on the land all winter, Rolle and his crew had been jetting hundreds of pilings with their raft-mounted diesel pump, and attaching mesh screens between them. The resulting corrals now formed parallelograms each the size of a large house, a twisted checkerboard laid on the ocean like giant tic-tac-toe games.

Everything in the universe has an optimum size: stars, humans, governments, and seafarms. The most profitable size for the seafarm, North had determined, was the length of the Island squared. When finished, the square-mile seaweed-shrimp farm would be the largest marifarm in the world. Some of the corrals already were populated with hatchlings reared in the laboratory tanks, and now they browned the emerald water in gushes of fertility. Prevented from importing hardier species from South America, North and Rolle dove several times a week for mother shrimp, each of which bears a hundred thousand eggs. They had captured a mere dozen spawners so far, which now lived here in big cisterns, safe from the myriad sea predators who find them as delectable as do *Homo sapiens.*

North and Rolle placed the seaweed in a tank, took scuba gear, and made their way to the deep side. It was quiet for March, and they dove straight to the fringing fertile reef, halting motionless at the base of a coral head. In their masks they looked like raccoons, and they breathed evenly to conserve air. North peered up. The silver ceiling of the ocean sky refracted the watery light like a sheet of glass. Slowly they worked their way outward from the shore, generally staying above thirty-three feet so they didn't have to decompress.

The ocean, an electric blue, remained transparent over an extraordinary distance. A school of yellowtails flapped up to investigate a ripple on the surface, jumped, and dove to circle each other. Tiny reefers in black and white stripes like miniature prisoners darted in and out of rock dungeons under balustrades of coral castles. It isn't only mammals who play when their stomachs are full. Foot-long needlefish and their fat opposites, the parrotfish, whose teeth are fused into a cutting plate like a beak, are the jet airplanes and dirigibles of this world. Above these lesser creatures, a single angelfish swam in silent royalty, her fins like veils. It reminded North of Marianne and of the idyllic days that lay ahead. Hovering near the bottom, he wanted to cultivate that sensation of rapture, to think about the girl with the emerald eyes and ready smile, feeling a tinge of the narcosis that told him he could smell the ocean flowers and remain here forever. He supposed it was enchantment for the underwater world and not, at this depth, an overdose of nitrogen.

Rolle pointed to the short lengths of plastic pipe they carried to hold the shrimp, extending and closing a forefinger to indicate he already had two gravid females. He didn't hold up two fingers because that was the signal for shark.

A dozen shrimp burrowed in the sand at their feet. Their transparent snouts and antennas waved, and their outboard eyes bulged and swiveled independently of each other. The divers scooped them up with aquarium nets and examined them close to their masks. Those that bulged between carapace and abdomen with eggs—the mother shrimp—they pressed gently into the pipe containers. Now they had five for the obstetrics ward. Spring had arrived underwater.

Rolle swam away into an ocean so still that the coral heads and ledges evaporated in haze as though receding into prehistory. Suddenly, as if emerging from a primeval planet, an extraterrestrial stared into North's alien eyes with what seemed to be curiosity. Oscar. On recent dives North had been allowed to come a little closer, and now he could almost touch the shy animal before it backed away.

Oscar's was not the glass-eyed stare of an insentient fish or shrimp. He actually made eye contact with North like a dog, but differently. A dog knows you are the friend who feeds him, whereas the intelligence of an octopus is alien to mammalian thought. Octopi are mollusks like conch, clams, or snails. Yet Oscar is as far evolved from those soft-bodied invertebrates who live in their shells as a man is from the reptiles, with which he shares a backbone, red blood, and little else.

We don't really live on the land, North decided. We live at the bottom of the sky, and climb stairs or mountains. The octopus lives at the bottom of the ocean, and climbs rocks or coral mounds. Just as man sometimes rises above his ocean of air, the octopus journeys a short distance onto the land. What a staggering thought had North, that a simple invertebrate mollusk could evolve to dominate the seabed as we evolved to dominate the land. What was the next step in the evolution of this not-so-simple mollusk of the ocean sky?

Only three feet long from the tip of one arm to the farthest of his other seven, Oscar periscoped both huge eyes, swiveling them in a full circle to inspect North from his flippers to the possibly-intelligent eyes behind his mask. Then the octopus scurried off.

North followed, inadvertently disturbing the animal's home of shells and small rocks. A silent rage played out on his skin as browns rippled into yellows and reds, and then into white. Leaving no doubt about his message, Oscar threw small stones at the alien invader, using several of his pitching arms.

North quickly replaced the stone walls of the dwelling. As he worked, the animal's colors settled into their normal state of brown. Forgiveness? Oscar piled up his own rocks as if to say, "Thanks, man, but I'll do it better. I got more arms."

North watched in awe, hovering there and pondering the allegory he was living. If the dwelling that was his Island suddenly became devastated, would his own eight arms—those of Cleary, Knowles, Rolle, and his own—be able to put it back together again?

THOUGH HUSBANDING their air as much as they could without actually holding their breath, an inefficient practice at best, North and Rolle had only ten minutes left for this glorious world on this magnificent day. They moved toward the shore where the water lightened into exotic pastels in the short end of the spectrum: emerald, cyan, turquoise, violet, and colors they couldn't even name. Rising five feet above the seafloor where they were anchored to the coral by thin cables, a series of domes made of plexiglass a meter wide stretched along Harbour Rock like a field of giant mushrooms.

Passing from dome to dome, North and Rolle pressed the buttons of their regulators to charge them with air. The air stations were a kind of insurance. You never knew when another few breaths could get you one more gravid shrimp, or when you might need to talk to your partner. Or evade a shark.

Rolle ran out of air first, surfaced, and breathed through his snorkel. Gliding under him like a reflection of a dolphin, North headed for the dock. Suddenly his pulse surged as he made out the hull of a ship.

Was it the LCM—and Coby?

Drawing closer he saw the hull was round, not flat like the landing craft's. And it was twice as long.

North climbed the ladder to the platform at the end of the dock and removed his mask, squinting through the bright sunlight at a pair of long legs clad in a crisp camouflage material. His eyes followed the legs up to the holstered 9-mm Colt automatic, khaki shirt, Lucifer beard, and brown beret of an officer of the Royal Bahamian Defence Force. The man was a giant, easily six foot six and weighing a lean two hundred fifty pounds.

As North came to his feet, the Defender officer leaned against the side of his vessel, the way you do when someone is taking your picture. The gunboat, battle-gray, was berthed across the width of the dock, extending beyond it on both sides like a big fish hanging over a dinner plate. The bow read *HMBS Munnings*, and she wore amidships a British Oerlikon cannon, an ugly though considerably smaller gun than the 90-millimeters North had known in Vietnam.

12 *Dissidents*

NORTH REMOVED his tanks while studying the camouflage-uniformed officer bearing the insignia of captain. He had no doubt that the bearded Defender was the same man who had watched them with binoculars when they were swimming with the girls last Sunday.

"I am Captain Carlos St. Gregory of the Military Operations Platoon," he announced in a deep voice.

St. Gregory wore mirrored sunglasses, an affectation North thought had vanished with the Tontons Macoutes when Baby Doc quit in Haiti. Two enlisted men holding automatic weapons at port arms were dressed in ordinary camouflage that looked cheap compared to the starched designer jungle fatigues of their captain. North resented their arrogance. The Defenders had shoved the company's new Mako down to the rocky portion of the unfinished dock to make room for their gunboat, and had tied its painter so short it banged against the boulders.

Rolle swam up, lashed the shrimp containers to the bottom of the platform, and climbed the ladder. He acted less surprised at the presence of the gunboat than at finding a white Defender in charge.

"Come aboard, both of you," St. Gregory commanded, removing his mirrors. "I've something to tell you."

If his black beard had not been trimmed so precisely, had it been greasy and curled in ringlets, or had he been wearing a felt hat instead of a beret, this giant martinet with his ferocious countenance might have doubled for Edward Teach, the pirate Blackbeard. For all that, he had a dead man's face immobile from the mouth up, and his amber eyes heightened the English-pirate look. North half expected to see him light sulfur matches and stick them in his beard in a reincarnation of the seventeenth-century pirate, and yet his hair was jet black and shiny. Blood from the Holy Inquisition flowed in those veins, thought North, and indeed his slightly accented speech suggested a Hispanic parent. He wondered how this white man had become a captain, the second-highest rank in the Royal Bahamian Defence Force.

He waved them into the forward cabin and immediately left through an internal door. The room was the gunboat's bridge, stacked high with loran, radar, and very-high and high-frequency radios. North made a mental note of the frequency to which the HF was tuned in case he ever had to call them.

A scuffling noise sprang from beyond the inner cabin door, and St. Gregory walked in followed by a two-stripe enlisted man. The able seaman saluted and said, "As requested, suh!"

The item requested came next: a sheepish Andy Angelo.

North was incredulous. Andy's hands were cuffed and extended as if holding a beggar's cup. Barefooted, hair mussed, Andy had become a captive of the people he so often had ridiculed.

Over the past nine months, a Hatteras or Chris Craft had entered Slaughter Harbour every other week or so and transfer garbage bags to a pack of thunderboats from Great Snake Cay. After the smaller boats depart at highway speed, heading west with their running lights extinguished, the Defenders arrive in their shiny black boots, leap off the bows of inflatable boats in knee-deep water, and doubletime to the villas, holding their weapons imperiously and seeking someone in authority. Usually that meant Andy, barely awake from his morning's sleep after working the payloader all night. Oblivious to the requirement for work permits, the Defender noncom would halt his squad under the vine-covered trellis on Andy's porch where the blossoms struggle against the grimness of the weaponed men. You had to be eighteen to join the RBDF but most of them looked younger than Andy. The non-com would ask in formal, memorized words, "We inquire in de name of de Royal Bahama Defence Force whether you seen anything 'spicious in dis here harbor." And Andy would answer as if discussing the latest Bears' game, "Suspicious? Nothin' out of the ordinary, Mack. Just the usual mother ship transferring a couple tons of Smoke to five Cigarillos, which are halfway to Florida by now." The Defender petty officer would nod his head, cracking not a hint of a smile, and march his troops out from under the flowers down to their dinghies and back to the anchored gunboat.

Now in handcuffs, Andy tried to manage a grin of defiance against the armed Defenders he thought of as clowns.

"Mr. Angelo here is accused of possession of firearms," St. Gregory said. "We found a sawed-off shotgun and two other guns when we searched your buildings at this end of the Island."

"What buildings?" said North.

"Your bungalows. Mr. Angelo was asleep in one of them."

"You've got the wrong man, Captain," North said. "I'm in charge here, no one else. Besides, we have permits for those guns."

"No one has a permit for a sawed-off shotgun in the Bahamas, mister."

Andy said, "It's over eighteen inches, isn't it?"

"That may be the legal length in your country. In ours it is twenty-two inches."

Sidney Rolle started to say something but the officer raised a hand heavy as Blackbeard's, commanding silence. "Forget that for the moment. There is a more serious charge. We received a tip that you've got White Lady here. *And* a marijuana farm."

"White Lady?" That was the second time North had heard that term. Stunned by the enormity of the charge, he felt himself digesting data like a scientist whose experiment has done awry.

"Yes, North, White Lady. *Cocaine,* if you prefer. It's an expression here as common as Smoke for marijuana. You ought to learn the vernacular for the shit you peddle."

Rolle leaned toward the captain, their beards short waterfalls of hair. "You can't talk to Dr. North that way. He's a scientist, for crysake? Whoever tipped you off is either stupid or a liar."

"Your name please?"

"Sidney Rolle."

"This doesn't concern you, Rolle. This is Mr. North's island, and the guns were found in Mr. Angelo's room. If the accusation is false, I'm sure you people won't mind giving me a tour of the place."

North might have laughed at the charge if his permits and the Island itself weren't at stake. The marijuana nonsense was nothing in itself, and yet in the real world one groundless rumor could ruin plans and even lives. North had seen it happen before: you work for years on a NASA project, write reports and meet with endless committees until the day some slob in authority with a cigar and a brainful of misinformation strolls into a conference room, muttering, "It won't work," and a whole project gets dumped in the soup. The mere rumor of illegal drugs in connection with the Island for Science could result in their permits being denied. It brought home to North their terrible vulnerability.

St. Gregory had his sunglasses off and North tried to penetrate those strange amber eyes, seeking a weak spot, feeling that the officer didn't believe the marijuana story any more than he did. Like many officious men who live in a hierarchy, maybe St. Gregory made a habit of lying because truth had too much value to be given away free. But then he wondered whether the lie was more substantive, perhaps to transfer attention away from St. Gregory himself. From what? About what?

An elderly chief petty officer, jacket unbuttoned, tie askew, was being pulled onto the dock by two young German shepherds straining at their leashes. St. Gregory and his captives were joined on the dock by a one-stripe seaman, a teenager with a loose manner who carried an ugly 9-mm Colt submachine gun. It was the standard NATO weapon that North knew could fire thirty rounds in three seconds and kill a man at three hundred yards.

Under guard, St. Gregory led North, Rolle, and Andy around the curve of the harbor where North had left his plantation hat to go diving. He put it on against the sun.

Where Harbour Rock almost touched the Island, a narrow spit of water led the way through the thick jungle and widened beyond a tangle of mangrove roots into the eastern lake that North had named Lake Superior. They trudged back through history around the shore of the lake on flagstones that rang like iron. Ten generations ago pirates had come to islands like this and found hidden places behind hills of green fronds where you could slice a throat with no one to hear the screams, or dig deep holes the size of a treasure chest at the edge of the lake. North's crew had deepened the three-acre lake, lined it with black plastic sheet, and transformed it into a salt-gradient solar pond that glistened black in the sun. Nearby a seawater-evaporation area was encrusted in salt, its pipes wide enough to pass coconuts.

"This where you process your dope, North?"

North ignored the taunt and attempted an explanation. "It's a solar pond, a heat collector and energy storehouse in one. Sunlight is absorbed as it disperses through eight feet of clear water that's increasingly salty from top to bottom. Solar heat gets trapped because there's no convective flow upward. At each level the brine, even when it's near the boiling point, is denser than the cooler water above it. We're going to install low-pressure turbines that will be driven by steam from the bottom—"

St. Gregory had been half listening while cutting a swagger stick from a limb, and now he started down the road. He ignored the warehouse where the steam turbines and generators were stored, acting as if he knew exactly where he was going. Could the anonymous tip have come complete with directions? As they walked, coral rock jutted through the sandy road and gnawed at North's and Andy's bare feet.

"Can't we stop at the villas and get some shoes?" Andy said.

"No," said St. Gregory, and picked up the pace until they came to a crest of a hill. On the shallow side, platinum beaches curved one after the other, bordered by coconut groves, seagrape, thatch palm, and wispy pines. On the ocean side, a series of spheres bobbed with the waves a dozen yards offshore.

"Those are wave generators, Captain."

"What for?"

"For electricity. Inside each sphere a magnetized ball is connected to the ends of copper windings. The waves move the spheres, and the ball magnets mounted inside roll around, cutting the flux lines and sending current through a rectifier. Small quantities of power go to the Island by cable."

St. Gregory shook his head and plunged on. The dogs took the lead, dragging their elderly trainer whose name, North found out, was Chief Lightbourne. Andy tried to hang back but the captain herded him forward. North, also barefooted and still in his swim suit, glanced uncertainly at Rolle who lagged behind.

St. Gregory saw Rolle and yelled, "Get lost, boy!"

"You can't order me around!" Rolle bellowed. You could see the purple of his scar swelling in the afternoon sun. But he left the road and slipped into the jungle, casting a meaningful look toward North before disappearing.

As they progressed down-Island, the forest gave way to glades of tall grass and wild flowers, and the low stone of the "Slave Walls" streaked into the jungle where they formed rectangular corrals for pigs or goats. The walls had been laid two centuries ago with great effort and no mortar by the slaves of Spanish plantations owners. Near the center of the Island, the road skirted the ruins of an ancient plantation house whose first floor of foot-thick stone still remained, a huge cactus filling an entire room. The upper floor, most likely of wood, had long since rotted away.

They came to Lake Michigan, the freshwater pond that was as useful to the Island for Science as the saltwater Lake Superior. Fresh water from the lake was pumped to the laboratory building across the road to adjust salinity in the shrimp-spawning tanks.

Except where the two lakes or the small savannas broke the jungle, the area between the north-shore boulders and the south beaches grew a thick mass of trees and ferns: low thatch palm; the shiny-leaved pigeon plum; straight-trunked sapodilla that bleeds latex when broken; poisonwood eager to leave blisters (or tattoos when its sap is drawn deliberately over a black youth's arm); the fernlike fronds and hanging cigar pods of tamarind; thick red-barked gum elemis, the "oaks" of the Indies; seven-year apples which never ripen (not even in seven years); and lignum vitae whose wood is the color and hardness of bronze.

St. Gregory stopped at the wind tower and peered up at the strange shapes against a turquoise sky. He turned to North, who saw his own strained and creviced face reflected in the sunglass mirrors. "What in the name of God is *this* supposed to be, North?"

"It's to generate electricity. A way to speed up the wind."

"*More* electricity?" he said in a flicker of interest. "Don't you have enough?"

"We do research here, Captain. On lots of energy systems."

"Explain this one."

North didn't know how much explanation the captain could take. "The power in the wind is proportionate to the cube of the velocity, but only to the square of the rotor diameter," he began, "so you see we can get more wind energy from a faster wind than from bigger windmills, or rotors. These toroidal housings act like funnels to speed up the wind and spin the rotors faster—"

"I don't give a mouse's fart for your squares and cubes, man! But I admit one thing. You sound like a scientist." He fondled his swagger stick like a living creature.

"Was there any doubt?"

"Not that you are a scientist. I have considerable doubt, however, about what's going on here. What happens if a bird or some other piece o' crap gets sucked into one of those funnel things? Does the whole tower fall apart?"

North indicated an impressive series of switches and dials under the tower. "Not unless you deliberately skew these synchronizers. Otherwise, if anything flies in there, the rotors will yaw, park, and stop."

"This really is an 'island for science' I suppose."

"Of course. . . !" North seized the moment. "And we do have a permit for the shotguns, Captain. Someone—not Andy Angelo—*probably sawed off the barrel because it was bent.*"

"And the Uzi?"

"What Uzi?"

"We'll get into that later," the captain said, and started hiking again. His pirate's nose was screwed up over his black moustache as though smelling excrement.

North glanced around to see if the dogs were relieving themselves. They were not. Content to sniff at the edges of the jungle, they had shown no urge to leave the road. Nor did they seem aware of Rolle who, if he was following, must be beyond the limits of their olfactory range. Failing to discover a marijuana farm, St. Gregory may have been smelling other subjective alternatives he found odoriferously foul.

"And this over here?" He pointed to a large building nestled under the reddish branches of a huge gum elemi tree.

"That's the lab. We're doing shrimp-breeding experiments and some spawning, for when the corrals are finished. We also screen ocean organisms here for drugs."

St. Gregory stopped cold. "Drugs?"

"Yes, drugs. The kind you use for headaches or to thin your blood. Or to relieve your psychoses."

At the mention of "psychoses," St. Gregory gave a start, making North wonder whether the man had been in therapy some time in his life.

St. Gregory recovered, and raised his eyebrows in question. "Eighty percent of animal life lives in the water. We're screening thousands of ocean organisms to see if they have potential for . . . pharmaceuticals."

Inside the lab, the dogs sniffed the fifty-pound bags piled high along one wall.

"Ammonium nitrate," St. Gregory read on the labels. "That's an explosive, isn't it?"

"It's fertilizer, for seaweed. We grow seaweed with the shrimp," North added tentatively, trying to prove the legitimacy of his projects without coming across as sounding too scientific.

St. Gregory looked around.

The laboratory consisted of an open gallery as big as a small house, a row of cubicles for offices, a lavatory, and off the open area a small infirmary, into which St. Gregory strode. He pointed past a bed, kept here for injured workers, to a closet door marked PHARMACY.

"This where you keep the drugs?"

"Pharmaceuticals, Captain."

North opened the closet, revealing shelves of bottles, bandages, tape, tongue depressors, and a physician's stethoscope that the Bahamian workers referred to as the "sounding rod."

St. Gregory opened a few bottles impassively and turned into the gallery. The room echoed with the interrupted voices of technicians taking water samples from a pair of low circular tanks open at the top and each stretching thirty feet across. These were above-ground swimming pools, the least expensive way North had found to contain water on the land. Aerators bubbled seawater to keep alive the postlarval shrimp swimming near the bottom. Vinyl cords, thinner than clothes lines, ran in rows at the top to support sprigs of seaweed dangling like tentacles beneath the surface. The mother shrimp had been removed to a series of smaller tanks the size of home aquariums, so that they couldn't eat their offspring; mankind is not the only species that kills its own.

North sent one of the technicians to retrieve the gravid shrimp in the containers Rolle had tied under the dock. Anticipating by two months the completion of each corral of the seafarm, North was stockpiling mother shrimp in a tank of seawater slightly warmer than the ocean, for water only a few degrees colder would cause them to spawn immediately.

The four lab technicians gaped at the Defender officer examining the room with an expressionless face, at the adolescent enlisted man in the doorway cradling a submachine gun, and at the sight of Andy Angelo in handcuffs. North told them to go back to work.

The captain peered into the bubbling shrimp tank and frowned as if smelling a gigantic cauldron of cocaine. The technician in charge, Lionel Sweeting, emerged from his office cubicle with his hand extended affably, the way he welcomed visiting scientists. Like St. Gregory, Sweeting was a "Conchy Joe" or white Bahamian, a descendant of the loyalists who came here from America during the Revolution. Unlike the Defender captain, he wore his frizzy yellow hair in an Afro, as did his black colleagues at the culture tanks. St. Gregory ignored the hand, and stared into the shrimp pool.

"What're these tanks for, man?"

Those were words of ecstasy to Sweeting, who loved to demonstrate his mariculture jargon, which he melded uniquely into his own brand of Bahamian creole. "We doin' de eyestalk ablation here, Cap'n."

"The what?"

"You see suh, like a lotta Bahama gals, penaeid shrimp jus' love ta fuck wid dere eyes open. So some smart-ass marine biologist decides one day to cut off an eyestalk to see what partial blindness would do to de sex process. Surprise, surprise! It turns out dot cuttin' de eye decreases de flow of a certain hormone dots been keepin' de ovaries from for*ming*—'cept at certain seasons—an' de female den be fertile whenever *we wants her fertile.* Trouble is, Cap'n suh, de shrimp like all de crusta*ceans* be canni*bals* and de act of sex truly whets dere appe*tite.* Wid only one eye, de female she be de los*er.* Jus' when de bliss arrive an' she 'bout to come, de male gobbles up her head. Dot mekes for bigger males, but plays hell wid our breedin' pro*gram.*"

The young Defender seaman stifled a laugh.

"He pulling my leg?" St. Gregory asked North without the slightest smile.

"Only a little. Eyestalk ablation really is used in breeding experiments."

The captain moved to the opposite wall in a spasm of suspicion. Living bioscreens in glass aquariums—brine shrimp in one and sea urchins, mosquito fish, plant seeds, or molds in others—were interacting furiously with sea organisms chosen at random that could have useful properties to fight viruses and cancer, coagulate blood, or control blood pressure or human fertility. The bioscreens themselves did the work; they were miniature, tireless, and unpaid laboratory workers. Next to them on a long chemist's bench bulged glass and metal caricatures of sea creatures: an oven, a centrifuge, and at the end next to a medicine closet, the small pumps and column of an experimental solar desalinator. The distillation column rose in a maze of convoluted glass tubing that penetrated the ceiling and led to a solar collector on the roof, in which seawater boiled by the sun returned as saltless steam through the glass pipes and into a heat exchanger inside. It was large enough to process salable quantities of moonshine. Or crack cocaine.

Yet St. Gregory, who questioned every other research project, seemed as ignorant of the machinery's potential use as those brain-less bioscreens. Anyone who can't at least smile at a Lionel Sweeting joke, thought North, must be sick as well as ignorant.

The captain examined the objects on another bench that stretched along the wall perpendicular to the drug-bioscreening counter. With eyebrows raised, he looked accusingly at North as he pointed to a lathe and three metallic cylinders on the bench. "These look like the barrels of firearms to me, mister."

Sweeting chuckled in an insolent way as if the idea of firearms was hilarious. "They won't go off!" he said, rocking on his heels.

"They're experimental," North said. "Aquadarts."

The narrow projectiles, eight inches long and no heavier than hand grenades, looked like expensive flashlights with stainless-steel barrels and propellers at the rear.

"You mean underwater hand grenades? You can't be serious."

"One of our research projects, North said evenly. "As defense against sharks. Or to blast small, controlled craters at archaeological or treasure sites. Divers trapped in a wreck could use them to blast free. In northern climates you could blow a hole in the ice from beneath if you're diving and can't find your way out."

"You have a permit for these weapons?"

"As far as I know, Captain, we don't need a permit until we have explosives. We've applied for a license to bring in nitro-dynamite so we can test them."

"The government doesn't issue permits for explosives. *Any* explosives. It's our way of isolating potential agitators."

Instead of isolating the agitators, North wondered why the government didn't agitate the isolates, that is, induce his dissidents to emigrate to Miami the way Castro purged Cuba.

Then the thought occurred to him that this was precisely what was going on.

13 *Son of a Bay Street Boy*

THE CURVING road stretched along the spine of the whale-shaped Island like a beige ribbon over hills and valleys thick with palmetto and thatch. West of the wind tower, except for the road itself, the Island remained as virgin as in the days when the Arawaks came here to hunt iguanas. Less a modern thoroughfare than a wide Indian trail, the road parted the jungle, showing on both sides thatch palm, casuarinas, seagrape, and poisonwood. Where the land narrowed below the belly of the whale, the forest thinned into patches of savanna studded with aloe waving green fronds like tongues of reptiles. The terrain was more open here, and North hoped for a glimpse of Sidney Rolle.

Jutting bones of coral tormented North's and Andy's bare feet. Low beach dunes drenched in the sun and covered with sea oats shimmered through gaps in big-leafed seagrape trees that lined the south side of the Island. The dogs worried an occasional chameleon, ignoring the slower hermit crabs who dragged their shell homes in search of larger quarters.

Having conserved for some distance his imperious, guttural voice, St. Gregory called a halt. On a flat smooth surface, the top of a boulder, he turned to North with the low sun mirrored in his glasses so that it hurt to look into his eyes. "Vile," he began. "Vile.

90

All this is truly vile." He pronounced it halfway to "bile," and with as much bitterness. His beard bobbed as he talked in a brooding monotone, denouncing North as a hypocrite and an impostor, accusing him of the vilest act he said anyone could imagine: operating a dope ring under the noble guise of science.

"The Bahamas has had enough of cover-ups with the veneer of honest work. Drugs from the sea! *Shark grenades!* Who you think you're fooling, man?"

Disheartened yet somehow unsurprised, North listened patiently, remembering his father's Croatian adage: *"Kada se ništa ne može reći, ćutanje je najbolje.* When nothing need be said, silence is the eloquence of discretion." Of course, now something did need to be said, but nothing came.

St. Gregory trudged along the opposite side of the road, recoiling from living men and dogs. The white Island owl chose that moment to vault out of the jungle and glide straight down the road on its four-foot wingspan. It was in this area that North first encountered in the crook of a tree an owl pellet, the regurgitated remains of mouse fur and bones, and learned thereby the presence of the night marauder. Whenever North had occasion to be in the forest he looked for the owl's nest, its mournful cry reminding him of how an owl once had saved his life in Vietnam. The sad group watched the great bird fly, its flapping muffled by flight feathers of velvet. If the Defender captain believed in omens, here came one from the primeval Islander himself, silent in wisdom and stealth, stalking prey.

Between the laboratory and the Island's west end, Bruiser caught up with the group, questioning the dope dogs with yelps and tail waggings as the three took the lead together. The incident warmed the already genial Chief Lightbourne, who treated North civilly. Hiking alongside the captives, smelling of dog and disinfectant, he declared that he had joined the Defence Force because he loved dogs. When St. Gregory was out of earshot, he said, "Ah tells you right now, Ah don't give no goddamn about capturin' de smugglers." He was in charge of all the dogs, he said, and this was the first time he'd been asked to bring any of them to an out-island. They'd never before been aboard a ship, yet they had ridden the decks well, enjoyed the wind and the spray, and found their four sea legs as young animals usually do. North liked the man and they exchanged dog stories. North bragged how Bruiser could corral, beach, and kill a stingray, or catch his own fish for dinner like any self-sufficient out-islander. Lightbourne boasted how the male of this very pair of sibling shepherds won an impromptu race and a hundred dollars for him in the barracks at Coral Harbour.

By the time they arrived at the west end, the orange top of the sun was sinking below the ocean and dark boulders of the whale's flukes secluded Scuba Beach. Transparent ghost crabs were digging new homes in new land created by slack low tide. Seagrape trees and coconut palms swayed in the breeze. Dangers are few on the land, but the edge of the sea is another story—especially when you are barefooted. The sharp coral can gash your flesh like a sword; turtle grass conceals the black spines of sea urchins; sand-colored skates, cousins to sharks, lie camouflaged on the bottom, their secret spears jutting in ambush. St. Gregory herded his captives off Scuba Beach onto the sharp spikes of coral where the south side of the Island began. North and Andy had to search with their toes for smooth rock at each step.

The captain chose that instant to turn as ugly as Blackbeard. "Okay, North, we found no Smoke growin' here, but I got plenty of reason to suspect this Island is a front for coke transfers."

He tugged at his mustache. Like the archfiend who gassed people by the millions, St. Gregory would have been incomplete without facial hair, uniform, and swagger stick to define his authority.

North shot him a piercing look. "Captain, this thing is insane. You don't really believe there's a marijuana farm here. Why would we endanger our whole project with dope smuggling?"

"Why indeed!"

St. Gregory turned to Andy, smelling that rotten something that wasn't there, and bared his teeth in the manner of Edward Teach. "Come on, Andy Angelo. Where is it? Where is the goddamn Smoke, boy?" His refrain, a deep whisper, came from the guttural regions in back of his beard, and without the slightest warning he shoved Andy forward.

Andy took a giant step, splaying, flailing, swinging his cuffed arms together for balance in an attempt to avoid the razor-sharp rocks. The boy with the NATO 9-mm SMG moved anxiously.

"Go fuck yourself, asshole!" Andy said when he recovered his balance.

Andy had his own ingenious ways of screwing things up, thought North as St. Gregory unholstered his Colt automatic, presumably to scare the boy. North couldn't take the chance. With both hands, he grabbed the thick wrist of the hand that held the weapon and cracked it across his raised knee. An assault like that on any other arm would have broken or sprained it or at least caused him to drop the gun, but St. Gregory freed himself with a flick of his wrist, then pressed the Colt flat against North's right ear, bending the brim of his straw hat. He squeezed the trigger.

North had known temporary deafness from his days in a Patton tank, but this explosion was worse. It sent him staggering. St. Gregory caught him and began shaking his upper body the way Bruiser flicks stingrays, losing control, shouting, *Tell me where you're growing the stuff? Tell—"*

Suddenly Sidney Rolle leapt out of the woods like a Carib after a wild boar. The motion startled the Defender captain, who released his grip. Seeing the enlisted man tracking the charging Rolle with his submachine gun, North threw his body at the seaman's legs, causing him to jerk his trigger, sending bullets flying high. His mistake gave Rolle the split-second he needed. He rammed the seaman with his head, seized the SMG by its barrel, and tore it away from him. Before either Defender realized what had happened, Rolle, in a fluid motion like a batter aiming at left field, swung it across St. Gregory's spine. You could hear the *CRRAAACK!* of the stock as it connected with enough force to make a paraplegic of a lesser man.

St. Gregory started at Rolle with his passionless face registering surprise, the way you do when you're bitten by a bee. Using his pistol as a hammer, the captain creased the right side of Rolle's head, above his scar. Rolle went down unconscious.

After a moment, with North and Andy supporting him against the rising coagulation of blood and flesh, Rolle came to and turned to St. Gregory. "You slimy pigfucker, I'll have your Bay Street ass for this. . . ."

So he was that St. Gregory? It was common knowledge that a Sir Thomas St. Gregory, doubtless this St. Gregory's father, had been a member of the former minority ruling class, the white professionals. Because they had their shops and offices along the main street of Nassau, they had come to be known as the "Bay Street Boys." Sir Thomas was remembered best for his introduction in Parliament of anti-miscegenation legislation.

"Cuff him," St. Gregory said to the seaman, who had regained his SMG and was nervously awaiting the captain's wrath for having yielded his weapon so easily.

As the young Defender pinioned Rolle's arms, the son of the Bay Street white man and the black out-islander stood glaring at each other from different heights, their beards punctuating their words like exclamation points. Rolle rattled off a string of invective, *"Su madre es una puta, usted hijo de un Muchacho Calle Bayu—"*

"Cool it, Sid," whispered North, knowing enough Spanish to translate "you son of a Bay Street Boy." The incident, he thought, was too peripheral in the larger scheme of the threat to the Island.

But Rolle didn't cool it. *"Su padre es un cabrón, su—"*

"That did it, you shit," said St. Gregory, making the word sound more like "sheet." He removed a handkerchief from his pocket and stuffed it into Rolle's mouth, while the seaman pulled a length of rope from his pocket and tied it between Rolle's open jaws and around the back of his head, like the bit of a bridle.

St. Gregory started back along the southern shore, his boots clanging on the iron stone. The moon shone in a pencil-thin crescent and raced nimbus clouds against a mauve sky. You could feel the rain in the air and you could imagine the Island feeling it, touching low clouds pregnant with unrained rain and unfulfilled promise.

North and Andy were permitted to wade around the rocks in the low-tide water. Rolle, wearing shoes, was restricted to the shore. The seaman stayed close to him, apparently afraid that anyone so reckless as to charge the giant St. Gregory might decide to burst his handcuffs, rip the gag from his mouth, and swim off through ten inches of ocean. St. Gregory picked his way around the spires of the rocks well ahead of the others, elevating aloofness to a form of communication.

The coral gave way to beach where a dozen sandpipers picked at microorganisms on the run. The little birds fled like ballet dancers before each wavelet, and when the water drained back into the sea, the troop ventured out again. Out on the flats, the parallelograms of the unfinished seafarm blended into the darkening sky. Sea oats rippled low dunes all the way to the coconut grove. Somewhere in a different era, as the time before the raid now seemed to North, the Islanders had triumphed here like those coconut palms standing alone, staunch yet flexible, bending only to benign forces of nature. They came to the second grove, where once they had spent their evenings lying on hammocks tied between the trunks, or climbed on each other's shoulders to reach the coconuts. In that earlier innocent time when the coconuts were green, they would hack off an end of the husk with a single swing of a machete, drink the water and spoon out the pudding that would have matured into coconut meat. It was Cleary who first added rum to the coconut water, and many a night they had drunk their Cleary Coladas from those green shells, spilling the sweet raw mixture down the shirts or the dresses of their visiting guests. It was a long time ago.

As they approached the dock at the east end, the last of the red and violet sunset blinked out and it was night. St. Gregory took North and Rolle aside and peered down at them with the arrogance bred in the white sons of Nassau since the days the wrackers clubbed drowning sailors on their way to shore. His eyes burned with a yellow flame.

"All right. I'll let the boy go," he said in his guttural voice. "But you two—you're coming to Nassau for a long dose of Bahamian hospitality. I've got all the evidence I need now."

Rolle had his scar screwed up like a buccaneer getting ready to spit in the eye of the hangman.

"Evidence!" North said, his voice easy, contemptuous. "One sawed-off shotgun?"

"One saw-off shotgun—and other guns. One Island full of drug apparatus. One LCM full of White Lady . . ."

"White Lady?"

"Yeah, before your crew dumped it overboard. The dogs found

the cocaine residue hidden in the false hull of your LCM when we towed her to Nassau—which explains why your drug-runners opened fire on us."

"What?"

"They're all dead, North. Your accomplices. Your nigger captain, Symes. His two worthless, retarded sons. Your insolent Conchy Joe. Everybody on board."

"Good God, man, *my daughter was on that boat. . . !*" Fear stabbed his heart. "What about Coby?"

St. Gregory planted his feet farther apart in the soft beach, and narrowed his eyes. "You can read the report when I file it. Now move!"

North lunged at the Defender captain. He was a wild animal going for the throat, knowing only retaliation, craving grouts of human meat.

A rifle butt crashed into the back of North's head, cushioned only slightly by the straw of his hat, and he sank unconscious onto the sand.

14 *Welcome to Nassau*

A BARRAGE of photons streaming through the bars of a tiny high window burned North's eyes. He sat up with a throbbing head, thinking for a moment he was looking out from under his tank near Long Binh. If he had been killed, his resurrection was incomplete. Head throbbing, tongue furry, his body felt like it was dissolving in the urine that puddled on the floor of the cell. He still had his Gauguin hat, caked with blood, and the hair on his chin was longer than stubble.

Coby!

North tried to clear his brain, remembering last night, Wednesday, and the *Munnings* bouncing at twenty knots over man-high seas, in whose lightless lazarette he had come awake to Sidney Rolle and the roar of the pounding hull. The *HMBS Munnings* had docked at the massive Nassau wharf where a police van swallowed them up and brought them to the Central Police Station. An antique building of coral stucco and white trim, it looked more like the Ladies' Aid Society than the prison of paradise. Policemen talked and smoked and leaned on the wrought-iron railing of the balcony over the entrance. Most of them wore sunglasses even at night in some macho police tradition. North and Rolle were kept at the porticoed door while the guards bantered up at their colleagues on the balcony. North slumped against Rolle's boots where he remembered the five-foot ceramic mural over the door that looked like a Disney duck wearing diving flippers and a helmet. He had come to when they wre being fingerprinted, and again when a steel door clanged behind them and they circumvented a mound of garbage on the way to this crowded cell, where they had spent the night.

Rolle was still asleep on the wet concrete, breathing heavily as a doctor fly lighted on his face. The walls, stuccoed in a dark coral aggregate, flaked into powdery dust. Beyond the bars, the decayed food of fifty men formed the elongated mound they had circumnavigated the night before. North tried not to breathe. At the near end of the corridor, a hole had been kicked through the plasterboard, and two rats peered in twitching their noses. One huge, the other a small albino, they acted as if they were testing whether the odor exceeded their tolerance. Opposite the garbage mound in each of three cells identical to those on North's side, six to ten prisoners were snoring or moaning. In the cell next to his own, an old man hung on the bars to steady his shaking hands, lighting one cigarette after another. He watched him for a long time but the man wouldn't meet his eyes. The man was no older than himself, North decided; he just looked old.

North dwelled on Coby, going over the words she had spoken in the anguish of youth, *"I'm not a Renaissance person like you. I can't do anything!"?* She wanted to press the accelerator of her own life, he knew, and it was that more than any great desire for cocaine that had led to her departure.

Was Coby missing. *Or was she dead?* The startling possibility plucked the heart out of his chest and carried it beating across the length of his nightmare. He tasted again the bitterness of the fight, her stunned look as she ran down the beach and fled into the closing bow ramp of the LCM. Maybe she had left the ship somewhere before the raid. She could be in Chicago by now or even in Europe visiting her friends. Hope bolstered him with the means, reminding him that she had access to money; on her eighteenth birthday a bank account had become hers, the result of a trust inherited from her grandparents. He kept seeing the hurt look on her face. Did she think he meant to disown her? A vast sea like the Ocean of Storms on the moon separates the generations, and a vacuum as hard as space boils the blood of those who try to cross it.

He turned his mind from Coby to catalog his resources. The money left from the sale of North Scientific would hardly be enough to see them through construction without using it to fight these preposterous charges. Godfrey Knowles and Andy would have to keep things moving on the Island without Rolle's help. That left Jack Cleary, a flaming alcoholic but also a staunch friend in an era when loyalty seemed to be something that only dogs had.

What North really needed was a detective.

He knew of none, but his sister Jo was an investigator of sorts, a broadcast journalist who railed against the dictatorships of the region from a sparsely populated island in the Turks & Caicos. She worked there at a maverick anti-Castro, pro-democracy station called Radio Free Caribbean. Coby had been proselytizing to go to college in Paris. He would ask Cleary to call Jo and tell her Coby was missing so she could ask friends at the collaborating agency, Radio Free Europe, to find out whether Coby was some-where in France. Jo flew her own plane, and would be a tremendous asset if only . . . if only she would overlook the disagreements that had driven them apart. They hadn't spoken to each other in four years.

Rolle awoke with an aching yawn, saw the stuffed toilet and the sleeping bodies, and covered his nose with a handkerchief. "It's broken in the Bahamas," he said in a muffled voice and closed his eyes again.

North could stand the place only by looking out the high win-dow where puffy white clouds scudded across the bars. Under those far-flung formations lay New Providence, almost synonymous with Nassau, where more than half the Bahamian people lived out their colorful rhythms. Somewhere south of Bay Street a woman's voice would be calling a child to breakfast from the porch of a cracker-box house the size of a Chicago garage but painted yellow and fuchsia or orange and purple.

North may not have known New Providence as well as Rolle, but he loved the busy harbor filled with conch boats, the Nassauvians who make strangers feel wanted, the seventeenth-century flavor of the city founded in the days of Blackbeard. The woman in the cracker box would smile and say, *Welcome to Nassau.* Along an empty beach off West Bay where children pick seagrapes and wild almonds from the trees, an old man would be caulking a boat canted to the receding tide, its hull striped black between white laps like rows of decayed teeth. *Welcome to Nassau?* On the spit of land under the concrete bridge that flows over the river-like narrows between New Providence and Paradise Island, the fishermen bait crawfish traps or clean enormous piles of conch. Bevies of buyers, brown housewives in white blouses and skirts like parachutes billowing over hips, watch to make sure no hidden thumb presses against the scale. The women gossip and plan dinner: cracked conch with peas and rice, or gogglefish fried whole, the bulging eyes to be eaten first, or spiced crawfish swimming in lime butter. *Welcome to Nassau!*

"Fuckin' Nassau," said Rolle, stretching. "I'm starved." Neither of them had eaten since yesterday's breakfast. He took a pack of Rothman's from his shirt pocket and offered one to North, who was tempted but shook his head no.

Rolle lit his cigarette and pointed it toward the rats at the end of the hall. "Bahamian hamsters."

"Hamsters?" repeated a skeptical voice from the upper bunk. It belonged to a man with blue-black skin, bushy hair, and the heft and frame normally associated with rhinoceroses. He looked to North like a more-intelligent version of Purple Martin, the Mau Mau he'd run into on Great Snake . . . could it have been only a week ago?

"Where dese hamsters you talkin' bout?"

"Just a joke," Rolle said. "We call rats that on our Island."

The albino rat came halfway inside, then scurried back into the fresh air where it sat on its haunches looking unconcerned.

"I be J.D.," he said from his bunk, Bahamian-polite and smiling. "On de floor, dot be Miguel, not too con*scious*. You want to stay upwind of him. An' dis here be Mike Morgan," pointing to the body in the lower bunk and adding with enthusiasm, "He da kil-*ler!*"

North introduced himself and Rolle. Morgan, a small light-skinned Negro with dark splotches on his face, had a face like a ferret's. He was dressed in a wrinkled but expensive suit with snakeskin loafers. "Welcome to Nassau," Mike Morgan said in his ferret voice that squeaked while at the same time managing to sound menacing.

"When do we eat?" Rolle said.

"You cain' eat de slop dey gives you here," J.D. said.

"I could eat a rat."

"Rat be okay. It dot slop you cain't eat," J.D. said, pointing to the mound in the corridor.

They learned from J.D. that the prisoners grew the mound from the food they couldn't eat, and that the police allowed them to shovel it out every few weeks when the maggot crawl became a frenzy, just before the eggs hatched. J.D. slapped at a pair of flies noisily conceiving next week's maggots.

Rolle moved casually across the room and addressed Morgan quietly. "American?"

"Yeah."

"Why're you here?"

"I like it here."

"You really kill someone?"

"She-*et!*" he muttered through clenched teeth. He filled his cheeks with air, metamorphosing from ferret to hamster. "I don't kill nobody."

Morgan was the palest Negro that North had ever seen. When he wasn't posing, he resembled more a body killed than a killer. Like the albino rat at the peephole, he was as anemic and seemed as harmless as any deskbound accountant who visited Nassau on his annual vacation. He couldn't be more than two or three years older than Coby.

"Dot's cuz yo missed!" said J.D., gloating.

"I. Never. Miss . . . asshole," Morgan said, enunciating each word through bloodless lips. "How the hell can I miss with an infrared detector on a Kalashnikov M76 sniper rifle? Fact was, I didn't get to do no aiming. I jus' look through the scope in the daytime and the fucking cop gets a reflection off the lens."

"Casing the setup?" asked Rolle.

"You might say that."

"Who you trying to kill?"

"None of your fucking business, friend."

But J.D., less reticent, pupils dilated with whatever animated him, said, "It ain't no secret. He gettin' ready to kill de new ambass*ador* soon as he come!" He added with something like pride. "De American ambas*sador!*"

Morgan shot a look of contempt at J.D. and glanced around to make sure no Defender was concealed in the cracks of the concrete.

"Why?" asked North. The U.S. ambassador to the Bahamas quit suddenly, giving no reason, and it would take a few months before his successor would be appointed and confirmed.

J.D. laughed. "It pays, dot's why. Pays real good."

Mike Morgan smirked and shook his head.

The Islanders didn't know what to make of the assassination yarn, but J.D. acted as though it were hilarious for someone to "pay real good" just to have an ambassador killed. Why *he* might do it with his bare hands, his expression said, for most nothin' at all. He lifted a big thigh and slapped it against the concrete bunk.

The jailer arrived at their cell carrying a basket of biscuits and a bucket of something wet. Between the bars J.D. and Rolle shoved two contoured aluminum cups like the kind in an army mess kit. Behind the guard with the food appeared another policeman escorting a young lady in dungarees and a sweatshirt, her hair tied in a ponytail. Probably a social worker, North thought, as the cop unlocked the door of the cell to their right. The man North had watched chain-smoking edged away from the others in his cell to talk to the woman, who turned her smudged face to profile. North recognized her!

"Are we supposed to use the broken toilets?" Rolle was asking the guard.

The cop ignored him, ladling a viscous yellow liquid to those who extended their cups.

North moved casually behind Rolle and whispered. "That's the P.M.'s daughter Marianne, a rehab worker. She didn't see me."

"Let's keep it that way," Rolle said quietly, positioning his body between North and the next cell, which Marianne had entered. She wore no earring and no smile.

While their cellmates were talking or flinging food into the hall, North and Rolle listened to the conversation in the next cell.

"You helped me real good, Miss Price, when Ah catch de drug Plague," the chain smoker said quietly. "So you de only one I could think of, and Ah right happy you come. I ain't done no drugs since, but if I doan tell someone what Ah got to tell, I will. I know I will."

"It's okay, Johnny," said Marianne. "What did you want to tell me?"

"Well, if you go on and tell yer daddy, though, you gotta promise you doan use ma name."

"I promise, Johnny."

"Look, Miss. It 'bout dot white Defender officer, Mistuh St. Gregory."

At the mention of St. Gregory, North and Rolle moved as close to the bars separating the cells as they dared, straining to hear. In whispered tones and with only a little urging, the middle-aged old man told Marianne a story as implausible as it seemed pertinent:

Johnny and a friend have a good thing, running dope from Barranquilla, until last month when St. Gregory intercepts them near Cat Island, south of Nassau. At first they think the approaching cutter, shrouded in fog, is a pirate ship. "Dere be pirates in dese here waters," Johnny tells Marianne, his junkie eyes dilating like those of a small nocturnal animal. As the cutter draws close, the smugglers see she is a patrol boat, and they let their vessel be boarded.

"Dis stuff tastes like catshit," J.D. said to Morgan, oblivious of the conversation in the next cell.

"Tastes like the usual yellow crud to me," Morgan said. "Course, I never tasted catshit."

The Defenders search but find nothing. The two dopers refuse to tell St. Gregory where on the boat they stashed the coke. Furious, he orders his chief petty officer to bring the offenders to St. Gregory's house in the scrubby forests south of Nassau. The captain and the chief call Johnny their "Insurance Policy" and his partner "the Premium."

"I been here a week," Morgan said. "Had my arraignment already. Monday I go out on bail. Five hundred big ones."

"Fifty thousand?" said J.D.

"Five *hundred* thousand, man!"

When St. Gregory goes out on patrol, the chief stays behind on guard duty. Every day he asks them to reveal the hiding place of the dope, warning that St. Gregory will kill them otherwise. They refuse to tell. On St. Gregory's return to the house, he drags his captives out to sea on their own boat and has the chief pry open the Premium's mouth. The Defender captain then pours gasoline down the victim's throat until he swallows and gags and swallows some more, finally vomiting blood and turning gray like a boated marlin. While the man convulses, St. Gregory heaves him overboard. Johnny is forced to watch the sharks tear apart his partner's still-living body. Docilely he leads St. Gregory to the contraband. At his hearing yesterday he reveals not a word of the murder, and he's slated to be freed tomorrow.

"*Ah keeps seeing dem sharks and thinkin'* bout takin' de drugs, Miss Price. You gotta help me."

North tried to read the reaction on Marianne's face, but it was too dark to see from a distance and he didn't want to reveal his presence. He shrunk back into the shadows as Marianne rose to leave. She touched Johnny lightly on the shoulder and made him promise to come to the REHAB clinic as soon as he was released, day or night.

After Marianne left, North noticed for the first time that J.D. and Morgan were silent. They had been listening as intently as had he and Rolle. Miguel still was strung out under the lower bunk.

"Dot mon be the *devil* hisself," J.D. said quietly, out of earshot of Johnny in the next cell.

"You know St. Gregory?" said North.

"No, mon. But Ah hears o' him in Fox Hill."

"That's the prison, right?"

"Indeed it be. Worse than dis place," J.D. said. "Dis place merely de city jail."

North looked incredulous.

J.D. repeated, "Lot worse. Least here you doan get yo pos-ses*sions* stole. You doan git gang-*raped*. You doan git zombified by dem Haitian voodoo mons wid dere cocks in yo mout. Lotta place worse dan dis!" He chuckled at their relatively beneficent surroundings.

"J.D. won't go to Fox Hill," Mike predicted to North. "After all, he don't do nothin' much, just breaks a man's back and rapes a couple, three women. He's livin' proof the early Bahamians fuck-ed the wild pigs—"

It was irrational but North felt guilty for the black American's slurs. J.D., though, only laughed as if it were the funniest thing he'd heard all day.

"J.D.," said North in a low voice, "tell me more about this St. Gregory."

"Well, as Ah say," said J.D., "Ah never actually meets de mon, but he be de son of a powerful person." How this white son of the hated former ruling class had become an officer in the De-fence Force under the current black regime, J.D. could only guess. Maybe he hailed from the old days and Ransom owed him or his father a favor. Maybe— But what the hell, a Defender he was, and the most vicious in the force.

ON SATURDAY a guard dropped by to tell Mike Morgan in a casual tone that although his bail money had arrived the magistrate had decided to sit on it for a while. "She ponderin' de sum," the guard said, chuckling. The news made Morgan petulant, and J.D. acted as if he knew enough to stay out of his way.

Later North inadvertently bumped Morgan's arm, and the would-be assassin shoved him against the bars. North let it pass because the guards had come into the cell block, this time to take Rolle upstairs for "questioning."?

The frustration of inaction, like false dawn, had drained North of hope. The last few days were like watching your parachute Roman-candle, or sucking the last breath from your scuba tank as the sharks circle. He had St. Gregory to worry about now, he couldn't help Rolle, he couldn't escape, he couldn't search for Coby. He could only worry. He began straining over memories like an old man, seeking clues in the past. An animated Coby stood up in his mind. At eighteen she sought righteousness and humanity, having written and starred in a high-school play called "Purrs," a comic parody of "Cats," for which she had spent hours practicing with microphones pressed to cats' throats. North had been proud of her independence, her leadership, her love of animals.

An hour later Rolle returned.

"What happened?"

"Zilch," Rolle said. "They asked me a lot of questions about the shotguns. And about you."

"What about me?"

"Whether you were some kind of drug lord." Rolle lay down on the floor. "I'm tired," he said, and closed his eyes.

Rolle had been through as much yesterday and today as himself. *But what if Rolle is on the other side?* Then North thought, *what side is that?* He leaned against the cell wall, commanding himself to remain calm.

Gradually the pain in his head subsided. Across the barred window raced a fingernail moon so crisp the tops of its craters were lighted along the nightside edge. For the first time in his life the moon seemed ominous, an airless orb cratered by cosmic bombs. He had to get out by next Saturday, to keep his April Fool's Day appointment with the Prime Minister. He could hardly ask his jailors to release him for the meeting; they'd call the P.M.'s office and reveal that the distinguished scientist was in the jug on a drug charge. He decided to say nothing. If the left hand of the bureaucracy was as unaware of the right as usual, Ransom might never learn of his arrest. How fragile seem your hopes when you examine them from the shadows of a dungeon.

During alpha sleep as he listened to the moans of men in misery that night, North clung to a boulder beyond the orbit of the moon: barren, airless, battered by meteors, too tiny to bind him by gravity. If he let go he would crumble to dust, lost in infinity. Worst of all he could see from space the green plains and valleys of earth, the continents and islands where he searched for Coby in countless coves and dark streets of the cities . . . while clutching to his asteroid of sanity.

When at last the sky filled again with color, and the cacophony of metal cups against steel bars began, North put away the fears of the night and made himself a soldier as once he had been—and had never wanted to be again. To stay healthy, they covered the toilet, stripped to the catcalls and jeers of the prisoners across the hall, and washed themselves and their clothes in the running sink. Rolle shaved off his beard.

"This the new Sidney Rolle?" North said.

"I guess I don't want to be mistaken for Captain Blackbeard of the RBDF. To say nothing of the ambient lice problem."

In the days that followed, North could feel himself adapting, regaining the vigilance, distrust, and suspicion learned in Vietnam, while at the same time loading those places in his mind where solutions could incubate. He had to give answers a chance to materialize. Consciously he freed his instincts and his creativity, letting the ideas flow unchecked. Plato, Spinoza, and Eastern mystics believed intuition to be a power beyond reason, a higher form of knowing; unlike them, North saw nothing incompatible between intuition and science. Intuition for him, like algebra or calculus, simply served to shortcut the conclusion. The hell with understanding the microsynapses and mental jumps that made it possible.

Now his intuition whispered that something was slithering before the attack, and that Coby might be hurt or held hostage. Leaning against the wall, he felt the stucco crumble, as if from the pain of his thoughts, or from the agony of thousands before him. He made himself search for Coby in the only place accessible to him, his own mind. It is a misconception that hypotheses arise among scientists to confirm the evidence. Almost always, a scientist gets a sudden intuition and then seeks evidence to sustain it.

One: St. Gregory's psychodrama over the marijuana farm had been staged to get rid of North and the Island for Science Ltd. Why? He could picture the arrogant son of a Bay Street Boy, endorphins sizzling as he readied the gasoline can over the victim's mouth. . . . But was that picture true? If St. Gregory actually had murdered the man, would he have left this Johnny alive?

Two: If St. Gregory thought North was dealing drugs, why had he hung off shore watching and then waited five days before landing on the Island to accuse him? Because it was common knowledge within the government that North was in New York.

Three: The Prime Minister and colleagues did not know about the raid, for they surely would have said something at the U.N. reception.

Four: St. Gregory had lied when he said the dogs had sniffed the cocaine residue aboard the *Half Fast* the night of the raid. None of his dogs had been to sea except the two young ones that had not yet learned to sniff dope, according to Chief Lightbourne. That meant the residual odor of cocaine had not been detected, if at all, until the vessel reached Nassau. Why had St. Gregory said otherwise?

To explain his killing the LCM crew?

Could Symes and Basil actually have been so stupid as to start a battle against overwhelming odds? Maybe so, if they really had a fortune in dope aboard. They had shotguns. And Symes was a hothead, having flown off the handle with North often enough. He pictured Symes creeping below, slipping the stainless-steel Winchesters out of a crew locker, the four of them waiting until the gunboat drew close, then letting loose a barrage while breaking away from the cutter, trying to lose it in the fog. Lousy thinking, but people did lousy things in a crisis.

Where might that have left Coby? His intuition had never failed him before—almost never. If he could trust it now in his hour of need, then Coby was alive. She could have made Symes put her off in Bimini before the raid. For once North prayed for his daughter's continued impulsiveness.

The moon, a sliver the size of his freedom, rose into view again, clove by the metal bars. He remembered teaching Coby at age four that if placed on the earth, the moon's width would reach only from the Caribbean to Chicago, and yet it was an entire world, a sister planet to earth. Her Croatian grandfather Nonich, however, had told her the moon was a person, a grandfather in the sky: *Nonich mesec.* The old man had grown up in Croatia when that republic first became melded into Yugoslavia, a federation of alienated nationalities, languages, and religions where myths multiplied like children, and he had carried them like baggage to the new country. Yet even at four, Coby's math was too good to admit the existence of triple fathers of her two parents, and she had solved it by rejecting the myth of grandfather moon. As a child, Coby would sit on North's lap and turn the pages of the biggest book in the house, the unabridged Webster's dictionary. And North would read the page corners of the bedtime story she wanted most to hear, always similar yet different, ". . . one thousand and eighty, one thousand and eighty-one . . ." until, tired of the relentless plot but loving the characters, she would fall blissfully asleep in his arms.

"I can't do anything!" she had lamented last week, this girl who had been recognized as a gifted child in math, who had earned A's in every subject.

ROCK biscuits and rotten stew, the din of voices and clanking bars became the chorus of a noisy song. They had survived eight days of stench, lice, disease, and hunger; eight days of inactive hell for North who imagined Coby hurt and bleeding from severed arteries; eight days of hearing the seconds tick on a clock as colossal as the cosmos. Twice they had been permitted to phone their barrister Sterling Hanna, but he was out of the country, and now the police would allow no more calls.

To ease the worry, they played chess. With a chunk of stucco from the wall, North had drawn an eight-by-eight square board on the concrete floor, and for chessmen they'd sculpted rough shapes by chipping away at rock biscuits. During one opening, Rolle picked up his queen and captured North's unguarded queen knight's pawn.

Only humor could dispel the ghosts of jail. In a mix of compassion and mirth that Rolle had come to appreciate, North said, "Have you ever heard 'North's three rules of moderation?'"

"I guess I can always use another three," said Rolle.

"*One:* never drink more than a gallon of booze during the day. *Two:* never sleep with more than two girls at the same time. And *three:* by far the most important of these rules against gluttony and greed: never, *ever*, take the queen knight's pawn with your queen." Laughing his first laugh since their incarceration, North bent over to move his rook to knight one and launch an attack on Rolle's queenside that soon would end in checkmate.

But he never got to make the move. A foot in an expensive loafer scattered the chessmen across the cell. The foot belonged to Mike Morgan. "You cocksuckers!" he said, "what's so fuckin' funny?"

North had enough. He grabbed Morgan's foot and twisted it, sending him to the floor. North scrambled to his feet a second ahead of him, and had time to deflect Morgan's charge. The escape maneuver bent him low, and he came up with hands clenched in a double fist that hammered the pale ferret face. After eight days of forced inaction, the exertion released North's emotions, the adrenalin flowed, and his head no longer ached.

Something told him to guard his rear, but before he could twist around, J.D. jumped from the top bunk and landed on his spine. North felt like he'd been gored by a rhino, but he managed to counter with a savage kick to J.D.'s groin.

The fight had begun so fast, Rolle was still on his way over when J.D., doubled over in pain, yelled to *Rolle* as though he were his ally? *"Get dot whitey, brudder!"*

It was a surreal moment, the words understood but unaccepted by an incredulous North and, he hoped, by Rolle.

Morgan, his nose spurting blood, came up from behind and slid his arms under North's armpits and up around the back of his head, forcing it forward in a stranglehold. J.D., still struggling to his feet, kept shouting at Rolle, *"Pound dot whitey!"*

If you've ever bumped your shin on the sharp edge of a coffee table, you know a tenth of the pain a kick below the knee can produce. Rolle aimed a fierce kick to J.D.'s shin. And missed. He

110

sledgehammered instead the place J.D. would least have chosen for the landing of a flying combat boot.

As J.D. screamed in pain and outrage, the prisoners in the other cells bellowed and banged their metal cups. North rammed an elbow into Morgan's side, twisted out of the stranglehold, and hurled the assassin's head as if he were putting a shot, sending it crashing into the steel bars. The fight had taken less than a minute.

A squad of police came doubletiming around the garbage mound and stopped in front of the cell with their rifles at port arms. North and Rolle were sitting quietly on the lower concrete bunk; Mike Morgan had slumped unconscious on the floor alongside Miguel in his usual trance. J.D. whimpered and cursed, holding his bruised and bloody balls.

"Whot hoppen in heah?" the guard with the keys asked.

Rolle glanced up at him with a nonchalant look on his face. "Dese three mon try to start de race riot. Doan worry none dough, Mistuh Guard, we be right 'nough."

AFTER the police brought the three to the hospital, the Islanders were alone in the cell. Rolle said to North, "Not too bad for a biophysicist. Where'd you learn to fight like that?"

North laughed. "From playing chess."

Rolle shaped his eyebrows into a question mark.

"The novice in chess or any other battle sees only the one way he can win and ignores the dozens of ways he can lose." North's eyes twinkled. "Chess taught me to calculate my chances ahead of time."

"Grabbing an assassin's foot," Rolle said. "Seems to me that qualifies for losing."

"Well, there's another rule in chess that overrides all the others."

"What's that?"

"The only good defense is an offense."?

North had put that rule to the test twice in the past week, and on both occasions Rolle had come to his aid. . . .

Suddenly the result of his idea incubation lay on the chessboard of his mind. He, Grant North, had been guilty of playing like an amateur—not because he defended instead of attacked but because he had utterly underutilized his king, himself, to attack these minor chessmen. If they were pawns, St. Gregory was the most minor of officers. Forget Morgan and J.D. Forget the knight St. Gregory. With the care of a combat soldier, he planned a coordinated attack against the enemy king, the master of the board whose men dared not make the slightest move without his explicit permission. Charles T. Ransom.

THAT NIGHT a guard rounded the rotting mound of garbage and stopped at their cell, looking compassionate. "Someone bring dis for you," he said to North, and shoved a Bible through the bars.

By the light of the crescent moon, he could make out the inscription on the flyleaf, scrawled in expansive Jack Cleary handwriting:

Jesus Christ is working for you.
He moves in mysterious ways.
Look to the original Sabbath for thy salvation.

North understood at once the cryptogram and the reason behind it. Since bureaucratic police rules prohibited visitors or messages except for those from an accused's lawyer, Cleary must have been unable to find their barrister, Sterling Hanna, and had used the religiosity of the Bahamas to deliver his message. "Jesus Christ" was Jack Cleary, who often referred to himself as J.C. Somehow, even without Hanna, he had arranged for them to be released two days hence, on Saturday, the "original Sabbath."

15 *ORIGINS: the Scientist*

DURING the Vietnam War, Grant North had learned that survival in combat, as in chess, consisted of taking the first shot. The M-48 Patton tank he commanded rumbled through villages, crunching rocks or fallen enemies, erupting fast with fire from cannon, rockets, and machine guns. As members of the First Cav Squadron, they took their motto seriously: *Attack.*

One foggy night, the air thick with humidity, thier tank was hidden in a tiny glade partially surrounded by greenish black walls of jungle. Smitty, Petros, and North slept beneath the forty-seven-ton steel steed. Ginovich, the driver who had been assigned guard duty, had been dozing too and was forward of the tank. At false dawn, the slow hooting of an owl off the starboard beam awakened North. Owls locate their prey as much through sound as sight, and Grant North had an overwhelming hunch that he ought to do the same.

He placed a hand on Smitty's neck. "You and Petros get inside," he whispered. "Where's Gino?"

"Don't know."

Bow gunner and loader clambered up into the tank through the bottom hatch. North searched the perimeter for his driver, but saw nothing in the foggy darkness. Something told him he had only seconds.

He never let his crew sleep until the big gun had been cleaned and loaded, and the xenon searchlight mounted above it had been checked and its drive mechanism oiled. So as soon as they were at their stations, they were ready. Smitty knelt under the breach, his hands already on the second shell; in the bow, Petros trained his machine gun on the invisible enemy where North had pointed. North guided the unlit searchlight with his left hand while his right trigger finger tensed, waiting. He poked his head out of the turret, at the same time activating the battery-operated motor that turned the 90-mm gun in the direction of the hooting. The radar showed only a wide swath of jungle. He switched on the monster-beacon and blasted the area with xenon light. Petros, the bow gunner, opened up with 7.62-mm fire, and North poured round after round of HEAT—high-explosive antitank—shells into the jungle. Spent shell casings and acrid fumes filled the bucking tank until all but one round remained. In a tank, you never fire your last shell until you're safe behind your lines. North and Smitty converted the gun into a flamethrower in little more than a minute—one of North's innovations—and washed the jungle with a blood-red tongue. The night filled with screams and living torches.

"Hot damn!"

"It's enough to wake a man up!"

"Where's Gino?"

They discovered they had destroyed a company of NVAs armed with Soviet rocket-propelled antitank grenades. The enemy troops hadn't had time to launch more than a few grenades, but their small-arms fire had found Ginovich. Most likely, he had never awakened.

THE MOST significant event of Grant North's tour of Vietnam had been neither that battle nor others like it, but the blossoming of his intuitive sense. Normally your intuition appears in infancy along- side sight, hearing-balance, smell-taste, and touch, but by the time you leave grade school you learn how notoriously unreliable your "hunches" can be. Instead of developing intuition as you do your sense of balance, you slough it off like dead skin. Sometimes, though, the intuitive sense germinates and survives to adulthood as the focus of imagination and thought beyond logic. North's left-handedness may have contributed to his reliance on his right brain, although not all left-handers are intuitive. Out of a dozen scientists, eleven think digitally and one makes analogs of seemingly unrelated events. It is the analog thinkers who make the unexpected inventions.

It may have been North's intuitive sense that brought him, after his discharge and before his physics courses started at Yale, to the psychology experiments then in progress. It was where North met Jack Cleary. The researcher introduced the two, then attached electrodes to Cleary's arm, saying with a worried tone of voice, "This is going to be a kind of trial by fire."

Cleary fidgeted. He was about to have his memory tested by suffering increasingly strong electric shocks each time he made a mistake in matching word pairs. It was North's job to administer the shocks.

"School," began North.

"College."

"No, it's 'University,'" said North, looking at his list and pulling the switch that shot fifteen volts through Cleary's arm.

As the experiment progressed and the shocks passed eighty volts, Cleary cried out in pain. At ninety, a thin sweat glistened his face. North had seen enough unnecessary pain in his life. Even if the higher voltage wouldn't do real damage, it would cause suffering—all for some damn report that would wind up in somebody's filing cabinet.

"Ohhhhhhhhhhhh, my *arm!*" said Cleary, his face red.

North hesitated.

"Go *on?* Pull the hundred-volt switch, North. It's your duty to do it." The researcher, wearing an expression of faintly amused boredom, was the epitome of the anonymous, uniformed commander North had learned to hate.

A bystander, a grad student, was watching. "Go on, pull! It's only fun and games!"

North ignored the taunts, hearing instead the screams from the jungle as flaming gasoline whooshed out of his tank gun to engulf the souls of the damned.

"Listen, Mister," the researcher said in exasperation. "I *order* you to pull that switch!"

That did it. "Fuck off, sadist!" North ran into the next room and yanked the electrodes from Cleary's arm.

Suddenly Cleary stopped moaning and let out a belly laugh.

The researcher came into the room, smiling. "Grant, welcome to the Obedience Experiments," he said. "The electrical apparatus was a stage prop. It wasn't Cleary or his learning ability we were testing, it was you! You and a few hundred other students are being tested to see how far you'd go in following clearly harmful instructions."

Since then, everyone in the field of psychology has heard of the "Eichmann Experiments" that sought to determine whether ordinary Americans would behave as had ordinary Germans under Hitler. When ordered to administer shocks by a person in authority, two-thirds of the Yale subjects continued beyond three hundred volts, despite the agony and screams of the persons being "tested." In other words, had the experiments been real, two-thirds of the students would have killed their subjects. Nobody ever quit *just because their victims screamed or begged for release.*

"Grant possesses a hundred-volt humanity!" Cleary maintained afterwards.

To a casual observer the friendship of these two seemed founded on disparity. Where North was analytical and tried to be dispassionate, Cleary was a natural actor, an illusionist who could use his deep-blue eyes and ready smile to drain the resolve of his sales prospects. When fall came, Cleary took a job selling yachts, while North reentered the world of ions and the brain's neurotransmitters as he worked on his PhD in biophysics. Through the next five years they kept in constant touch, Cleary making the short trips from Stamford to New Haven. He was the best man at the Grant and Heather wedding, and a year later became the godfather of their daughter, Cobourn North.

North joined the space agency to become a scientist-astronaut, but he was too early or too late. Only twenty Americans went to the moon, and Grant North was not among them. Instead, he became NASA's chief advocate for dramatic missions. Explore the red deserts of Mars, and "terraform" the planet to give it an atmosphere. Build a permanent base on Luna, complete with a convalescent center under one-sixth gravity, perhaps in the Crater Alphonsus where patients could see the earth rising like a blue sun.

North invented a device to extract water from moon rocks by taking advantage of the slow-moving terminator, the line separating the boiling heat of daytime from the ultracold of night. One evening while Heather was at her easel, he was explaining how you could pick up hydrous rocks, crush them, and drive across the terminator, where it is five hundred degrees colder, to condense the water vapor and separate the water into oxygen and hydrogen . . . but he lost her somewhere in the cold shadows. She had been feeding into her creativity the dust-covered rocks, the hostile vacuum, the fierce cold and boiling heat, the implausibly close horizon where the blue-white ball of earth hung in blackness surrounded by millions of diamond stars. She had been imagining the heart-pounding ecstasy of a man detached from the cradle of other men— isolated, independent, resourceful—a special man, a dreamer of practical dreams. She was a realistic Salvador Dali, a surreal Edgar Degas, but her themes emphasized the humanity of adventure and voyagers enduring the adversity of space. Her heros were giants who dared history. "There's something different in the expression of a trailblazer that sets him apart from others," she said. The woman and the artist had found that expression in her husband's face: the restless inner glow, the wrestling with doubt, independence restrained, and the planning, the waiting. It was how she had come to love him.

The scene at her board developed into a portrait and a landscape showing both sides of the lunar terminator. On the darkside, the sun caught the tips of the boulders and the helmet of a man loping out of night toward daylight. On the dayside, flecks of red, brown, orange, and milk-white glass shone like church windows at the bottom of a crater so vast it looked like a walled desert. Seeing her ancient and alien valley of the moon, with its rocks and settled sands, North could sense the violence of the explosions that formed them. He could feel those shards of stained glass crystallizing hundreds of thousands of years ago by the impact of small meteoroids.

"It's eating you up, isn't it?"

"What?"

"Not going there, to the moon. After your NASA proposals, your inventions . . ."

"I'll get over it."

"Don't, Grant. Don't get over it. Make your own moon on earth."

She scrawled the title in the corner of her painting: GRANT. The nighttime moon spilling onto the bleak dayside captured the immensity and loneliness of the lunar landscape, revealing through the faceplate of the explorer the isolation and personality of the man from earth emerging from darkness to brightness, prepared to forsake everything for the exotic unknown.

"How am I supposed to make my own moon on earth?"

"With imagination—and some alien piece of terrestrial real estate."

"You mean like an island?"

"Sure. Like an island."

COBOURN NORTH grew up thinking that what fathers did in this world was invent things, tell men in white lab coats how to build them, and appear occasionally on television talk shows with their creations. The North Detector, launched full-blown on an eager market, was the first of scores of instruments made by his company, North Scientific Inc. Neither Coby nor her mother knew the hazards he encountered in starting the company nor the terror of his doubts, but Heather could feel his insomnia; his heart beat so hard in the middle of the night it rattled the bed. The company, head-quartered at the southern shore of Lake Michigan, prospered and grew stable.

His family life, though, was as vulnerable as the fragile earth viewed from the moon. Heather had developed an emerging melancholia, a depression that robbed her of her vitality. North realized how little time he had spent with wife and daughter as he worked to build the instrument business. In the early years, he and Heather had lived proudly on a few dollars a day, their poverty binding them to a separate togetherness, to the overriding goal of building a dream, and it had nurtured their marriage. They ate soup when they ate at all, in contrast to Cleary investing his inheritance in thousand-dollar business lunches where he would entertain dozens of potential buyers at once. As the company grew, North failed to notice that he was drifting away from his family; it came as a surprise when his sister Josephine admonished him for not spending enough time with Coby.

"With Heather sick, can't you *see* what's happening to her?"

"What do you mean?"

"She's alone too much. I came into her room and found her talking to her cat. She introduced the cat to me as her sister!"

"That's no big deal, Jo. She *is* an only child."

"But she's ten years old!"

That was the year, on her birthday, that her godfather Jack Cleary gave her a tiny medallion on a gold chain bearing the inscription, "J.C. loves you." One day she looked at her father with eyes as hazel as his own, from under the chestnut hair of her mother turned blonde from the summer sun, and said, "Why don't I have *your* medal? Why don't you take me with you on your trips?"

Even then she had the wanderlust of her aunt Jo. All North could think to say was, "Later, Coby. You're in school now."

Like most young couples, the Norths knew nothing of time, treating it as something illimitable that stretched to the farthest star. North sadly and irrevocably let the company spend his time for him. Had he known that Heather was dying, he gladly would have given up his company to be with her.

Heather felt in her artistic way that any destroyer of her body should not have its wild frenzy fertilized by her own anxiety—or Coby's—so she kept her illness a secret, suppressing the concept of cancer even from herself. One day it could be hidden no longer. He looked at her and they both knew, as primitive peoples know, that her "inner light had gone out." Tears streamed down her thin face and she choked on them and dried them and looked at her husband full in his eyes, seeing them for the last time, searching into his soul where she knew she was loved, the intensity of her will erupting like an explosion in the vacuum of the moon, unheard yet much too loud in the middle of the silver night.

Why hadn't he known in time to save her?

For all his knowledge of the imaging devices of medicine, North knew no more about disease than any layman. For all his uncanny powers of intuition, he never once thought of Heather as being physically ill. Blame overwork, preoccupation, or a psychological block where his family was concerned, but one of the two people he cared for most in the world was dying and he'd had no inkling of it. In his pain he grasped for answers. Had he hit some "intuitive block," some hidden fear blockading a feeling that otherwise would have been apparent? How else could his intuition so utterly collapse when he needed it the most?

He carried Heather to the hospital, returning home with her a few days later, putting her to bed in their own room in their own home by the freshwater ocean she loved, where she watched the leaves of oak and sassafras turn brown and yellow, where she smiled weakly at Coby and Grant, and was dead in a month.

Coby wept. Grant wept. And the hallways and rooms of the empty house, where scores of her paintings hung and where her unpainted paintings did not hang, wept too.

16 *How Much Money You Bring?*

JACK CLEARY arrived early for his ten-thirty appointment with Judge Margaret Amin, which had taken U.S. Deputy Chief of Mission Davenport almost a week to arrange. Traffic bleated in the choked streets, straining for release from the narrow alleyways in back of Bay Street. Cleary lit a cigarette, chewed a pair of Gelusils, and cut across the square past a monument whose bronze plaque said REMEMBRANCE, commemorating the fourteen Bahamians who died fighting in World War II. Magistrate's Court Number Five bordered a small square across the street from the Central Police Station in whose basement cells North and Rolle were held. In the center of the square a strangler fig, two centuries old, rose like another monument. Imagining the public hangings that had been conducted here when the tree was a sapling, Cleary entered Court Number Five.

Coming from blinding daylight, it was night inside. Someone cleared a throat and Cleary followed the sound to an elderly bailiff wielding a clipboard and an armload of file folders. The bailiff stood aside a massive judicial desk set on a dais, and by the time Cleary approached it, his eyes had adapted and he could make out rows of benches, a wooden cage for prisoners, and the jury box. Judge Margaret Amin sat at the desk flanked by Bahamian flags wilting in the heat and humidity. Somehow she didn't look Bahamian. Bluish-black, stout, gray-haired, and wearing black robes, she turned her wrinkled forehead to face Cleary. She glanced at her wristwatch and said out of wide and magisterial nostrils:

"You're late, Mr. Cleary."

Cleary was startled; it couldn't be more than thirty seconds after ten-thirty. He offered a smile that lit the darkened room. "I'm truly sorry, your honor."

"You bring the bail?"

"Yes, your honor."

"Why are you alone? Who is the defendant's barrister? Where is he?"

"Our barrister is out of town. Sterling Hanna. He's somewhere in Florida."

"You realize the arraignment must wait until your barrister returns?"

"With respect, Madam, we—"

The old bailiff interrupted him. "Your worship."

"Pardon me?"

"Your worship. Call the magistrate *'your worship.'*"

"Yes, of course," said Cleary to the bailiff and then turned back to the magistrate. "If that's the way it works, your worship, then we elect not to have a lawyer for the arraignment. The defendants will represent themselves." He launched his smile again, more from habit than hope.

"But you already told me you have a lawyer!"

The circle was complete. North and Rolle can't get out of jail without an arraignment, and they can't have an arraignment without a lawyer because they already have a lawyer who isn't here and without whom they can't have an arraignment. Bahamian logic. He had spent the week trying to retain another barrister, but as one of Hanna's colleagues had assured him, Sterling Hanna was the only criminal attorney at Franklin, Albury & Dawkins Ltd., and the only one who mattered in Nassau, since their firm was headed by Minister Franklin, who despite his diminutive stature, threw considerable weight.

"Your worship, Mr. Hanna will return soon. My friends have

been in jail now for over a week. Can't they be released on habeas corpus?"

"Habeas corpus is an American concept. It has no bearing here."

Cleary's lower jaw dropped. You didn't have to be a lawyer to know that the idea of freeing a body under a presumption of innocence *originated* in England, and the Bahamas had been a British colony until 1973. Could the Bahamas somehow have done away with this basic right after Independence?

Forget it. You don't make a sale by arguing with your customer.

"In that case, your worship, how about letting me visit them?"

"You can't do that until the arraignment."

"Isn't there *anything* I can do to get them released?"

The magistrate leaned forward on her arms that stretched across the enormous desk like the necks of two crows gobbling seed. The bailiff placed his folders on a corner of the desk and slunk from the room. When he was out of earshot, she said quietly, "How much bail money you bring?"

Five envelopes containing fifty thousand dollars in hundreds bulged the pockets of Cleary's blazer. Cleary had devastated the company's Nassau bank account, leaving less than four hundred thousand in their Florida bank, down from more than two million and barely sufficient to see them through the construction phase until the first shrimp could be marketed. If he had to, he'd sell his Rubens, the only thing of real value he had left.

"Ten thousand," he said.

She narrowed her dark brown eyes into tight slits, banged her gavel, and shuffled the folders on her desk. "Come back with your lawyer."

"What I meant to say, your worship, was ten thousand for Dr. North, against whom there is not a shred of evidence. And another forty thousand for the bail on Sidney Rolle's assault charge." Sometimes you had to shoot your wad.

"Make it twenty and thirty," she said.

"Yes, your worship."

Staring at him as if he were a urine sample, she leaned over the edge of the massive desk to receive all five of his fat envelopes.

EARLY Saturday, April 1, Grant North and Sidney Rolle, handcuffed and looking out of touch with things that live in sunlight, were escorted from their cell and taken outside where they waited a moment for the police to socialize with their colleagues. North looked at the mural on the front of the station wall he had noticed in the dark ten days ago. Not a duck at all, it was a bouillabaisse of hearts-of-palm fronds and conchs resting under a blazing sun, against which an unboiled marlin and a flamingo stood upright in a bed of whelks. He noticed the "Forward, Upward, Onward" and realized the mural was the Bahamian coat of arms.

The police brought them across the street to the courtroom, and ushered them into a cage made of wooden spindles in the center of pews three and four. The first two pews were reserved for jurors. The police took up guard duty on both sides of the cage, apparently to prevent North and Rolle from ripping their way out with bare teeth and attacking the magistrate. North's freshly shaved face had grown slack from jail like hardwood soaked in brine, but it did nothing to soften his indignation. The restraint of the scientist seeking truth before acting was wearing on him. The sight of St. Gregory sitting in the back near the center isle made things worse.

Hope Arrived in the form of Sterling Hanna who materialized out of the gloom. He approached the bench and mumbled something North couldn't hear. The judge nodded and the police guards unlocked the cage and removed their handcuffs. They were free on bail.

The reprieved prisoners made their way down the isle past St. Gregory sitting at the edge of the last pew. In his crisp white uniform, the Defender officer looked nothing like the unkempt Blackbeard on the Island. He let Rolle pass, then rose and barred North's way with his swagger stick, a new stick, North noticed, lacquered and with a hand grip. North stopped.

St. Gregory tapped the stick against his own palm like a cranky schoolmaster. "How's your Island for Drugs coming along, North? Invented synthetic White Lady yet?"

North ignored him and resumed walking, but St. Gregory followed, jabbing him in the ribs with the swagger stick.

North twisted around, eyes flashing. For a second, he rashly considered breaking the stick in two and shoving them into the Defender's mouth.

St. Gregory kept poking the stick in North's stomach, punctuating each word. "Let me give you a little Bay Street advice, North. If you're going to stay alive and make it in the drug business, you'll need more than dirty looks and shrimp."

North grabbed the end of the stick and held it, reminding himself that St. Gregory was only a minor piece; it was the king he was after.

The Defender officer laughed. That is, he made a sniggering sound without lifting his cheeks or parting his lips, as if he were some animal lower in the evolutionary scale than a primate and had missed the genetic acquisition of facial muscles. His only expression came from around his eyes, and there was no smile in them now.

"I had a visitor yesterday, North. He's only a little out of control, like the thunderboats he sells. He wants to know why his brother got killed."

"What brother?"

"His name is Symes. I told him all about you."

IN A ROOM of the police station reserved for barristers and their clients, the Islanders crowded around Sterling Hanna. The room must have been decorated by a designer on phencyclidine who thought orange drapes accented the radiance of purple chairs. But despite that attempt at psychedelic cheer it was a sad little place, heavy with the smell of mildew and the echoes of catastrophe. Cleary chewed another Gelusil.

"Judge Amin had little choice, so she dropped the drug charges against Dr. North," Hanna was explaining, "since no dope had been found on the Island. But the government in this country doesn't take assault charges lightly." He looked at Rolle. "Your face looks different."

"I shaved off my beard."

Hanna nodded and said, "The government doesn't take firearms lightly either."

"Depends who you are," said Rolle.

"What do you mean?"

"We met an American in jail who got out on bail after trying to kill the ambassador."

"Which ambassador?"

"American."

"The assassin, Mike Morgan," interjected North, "was caught with a sniper rifle he claims he smuggled in to kill the new ambassador when he takes office. He'll probably jump bail, but whoever hired him could hire someone else."

"I shall certainly inform the U.S. Embassy," Hanna said, and he jotted a note. "Now, to return to the case at hand. Dr. North had permits for the shotguns, and there was no proof that the guns on the LCM belonged to him. So the magistrate has dismissed the case against him. But Mr. Rolle has been charged with assault with a deadly weapon, a felony. St. Gregory's report said that Rolle ran out of the jungle and tried to kill him with a submachine gun he seized from the young RBDF guard. Even worse, St. Gregory is claiming that it was Rolle who sawed off the shotgun, which of course indicates premeditation."

"That's ridiculous," North said.

"Nevertheless, the shotgun *was* sawed off. Whoever did it committed a felony. It may sound ridiculous to all of you, but the charge of the sawed-off shotgun against Mr. Rolle is every bit as felonious as if he were caught with a cannon! When coupled with the assault against an RBDF officer, it becomes a very serious matter."

"My 'assault' on St. Gregory was to stop him from killing Grant," Rolle said. "I don't know who sawed off the shotgun."

"Doesn't matter," said Hanna. "Margaret Amin's as mean as her name. Wouldn't surprise me to learn she's related to Idi."

"Where does she come from?" North asked. "She doesn't look Bahamian."

"Guyana. Used to be called British Guyana before independence—a few years before ours. Prime Minister Ransom doesn't believe in having Bahamians sit in judgment of fellow Bahamians, so he imports magistrates from other English-speaking black countries."

"Too bad she didn't keep up with the Joneses," Cleary said.

Hanna didn't smile despite his liking for Cleary comedy. Either he saw no humor in Ms. Amin, or he didn't relate the wisecrack to the Jonestown suicides fifteen years ago.

"Sterling," began Cleary seriously, "what happens to the fifty thousand dollars bail I paid to Ms. Amin?"

Hanna looked at him virtuously. "You get a receipt?"

"No."

"Then your guess is as good as mine."

North was irritated, but there was little he could do. He scratched his chin and glanced at his watch, realizing he needed a haircut. "Sterling, I have an appointment with the Prime Minister this afternoon." He looked out the window toward the morning sun, his hazel eyes dilating painfully. Ten days of jail—coupled with the knowledge that someone, perhaps even the P.M., wanted you there—helps focus your eyes.

"Oh, I'm sorry, Grant. I didn't have a chance to tell you that the meeting has been canceled."

There's only one reason for not keeping your word and that's if you're dead, thought North, but of course that didn't apply to Prime Ministers. "Why was it canceled?"

"Don't know. The P.M. doesn't tell me those things."

"You think he knows I was in jail?"

But Hanna only shrugged as if North had asked why the universe was created. "Look, everybody," the barrister said in a voice hushed but distinct, "we must get something straight here. I'm afraid you are *not* out of the woods yet just because you've been released. You're facing more than an intractable magistrate. Judges here reflect the government view. They're appointed by the Prime Minister one year at a time. If a magistrate does something the party doesn't like, he or she can be *discontinued.* No muss, no fuss."

Hearing Hanna's explanation, it came to North that the mechanisms his own country had installed to insure liberty—freedom of the press, the right to bear arms, and all the rest—didn't mean much without the separation of powers. Without independent judges, a nation could not be considered free, for you couldn't sue the government, and civil liberties would always be in question.

Hanna moved about the room as he talked, focusing alternately on North, on Cleary, and on the progress of his cigar, but never on Rolle. "No matter how ridiculous a weapons charge may seem to you Americans with your country's history of guns and cowboys, it is a serious matter here. When you employ me as Mr. Rolle's defense attorney, you are asking me to come before the magistrate—a Charles Ransom appointee—and vouch for Sidney Rolle, to pretend that he is my ally, an angel who wouldn't swat a sandfly. But for me that is guilt by proximity. Merely being seen *in his company* can be interpreted here as a sin."

Hanna paused and looked outside. Traffic below was snarled, and gaudy tourists, who over the course of a year outnumbered residents eleven to one, oozed between the cars parked along Bay Street.

"Then who protects the accused in this country?" North asked.

Rolle scowled.

"The barristers who got their law degrees in correspondence school. Or solicitors, who aren't even allowed to try a case, may bribe the judges. Normally I spend my days in court pretending I'm a good member of the ruling party. Of course I *am*—don't misunderstand me. The pretending comes when I pose as the mortal enemy of anyone charged with a crime." For the first time he looked directly at Rolle. "You see . . . if I do otherwise, I put my own reputation in jeopardy."

Rolle looked disgusted.

North asked, "Are you saying you won't represent us?"

"I honestly don't know, Grant. I'll have to think about it. What I am doing right now, I guess, is considering the alternative, which is to turn you over to someone else. Trouble is that not one of these Nassau defense attorneys can find their ass with both hands. Except the ones who take and give bribes defending smugglers." He thought for a while, then reignited his cigar, and looked straight at Cleary. "Bribery, of course, is out of the question because Mr. Rolle is a Bahamian citizen."

"What difference does that make?" North asked.

"Only because, in case it backfires, he won't want to leave the country forever." Between cigar puffs he tried to lighten the atmosphere. "If Rolle can act the naive and innocent out-islander," he said, chuckling and producing a cloud worthy of his heft, "I might condescend to testify that he *never once* tried to rape the queen during the annual Goombay parade. At least not on Bay Street."

"Crazy," Cleary said.

North saw Hanna as a Nassauvian Machiavelli, slipping unobtrusively in and out of the back rooms of power in this enigmatic town of inbred politicians. If anyone could retrieve the bail bribe, it would be Hanna.

"Please, folks," Hanna said. "I realize it sounds crazy to you. You get the feeling when you're here in Nassau—it's so close to Florida and the people speak English and all—that you're in your own country. But you are not. Things are different here. Very different."

17 *Home of the Defenders*

ON THE OTHER SIDE of New Providence from Nassau, down Mermaids Boulevard and Jack Fish Drive, the Defender base at Coral Harbour sprawled like a spiderweb. Giant sentries of ancient casuarinas guarded the arrival of North, Cleary, and Rolle, who were questioned in their taxi by an M.P. on a motorcycle and escorted the rest of the way. Young Defenders wearing scraps of uniforms milled around oppressive-looking barracks, or rested in the shade against tree trunks. Headquarters was a steel quonset hut at the harbor where bleak gray gunboats lined wooden piers, and dark clouds occluded the sun.

The LCM *Half Fast* and the Mako were berthed alongside a group of confiscated smuggler yachts. Chris Crafts, Bertrams, and Hatterases that once glistened in brilliant whites trimmed in red or black were uniformly gray now, like butterflies metamorphosing in reverse so they could match the rest of the somber fleet. By contrast, the *Half Fast* still floated proud in white and royal blue, a Monarch among caterpillars.

Cleary and Rolle vanished inside the LCM, while North entered the quonset hut and asked to see Commodore Bridgewater, who was St. Gregory's boss.

"You got de appoin*tment*?" a petty officer said between bites of his lunch sandwich.

"Please tell him Dr. North is here. Tell him it's an emergency."

North sat down on a couch Freud might have used in the last century, and waited. If it weren't for the uncertainty over Coby, he would have reason for optimism. Sterling Hanna had agreed to represent Rolle after learning that the magistrate herself was being investigated for some sort of impropriety.

After a forty-minute wait, the phone on the reception desk rang and the petty officer listened briefly, hung up, and said to North, "De Commodore, he say he release your barge. You free to take her."

"But will he see me?"

The petty officer dialed the phone and after a lengthy conversation, consisting on this side of "yes suhs" and "no suhs," said to North, "He see you now."

"Thank you. Would you please go out to the dock and tell my friends to take the vessel to the Nassau Harbour Club?"

"Yessuh," he said.

North proceeded down a long hall and into an austere office where the air conditioner rattled and a plastic sign on the desk read, COMMODORE BRIDGEWATER. Behind the sign sat an Englishman, whose white dress uniform was soiled and smelled of gin. North guessed his days were numbered. Where the U.S. bureaucracy is long-lived to lend stability to an Administration whose elected leaders change every four or eight years, Third World bureaucrats are transient. It is the leaders who are perpetual.

"What can I do for you, Dr. North?"

"Commodore, my teenage daughter—"

Bridgewater lifted a wobbly hand. "Here is Captain St. Gregory's report."

North sat down and read the one-page report, skimming the stilted language of law enforcement that is the same in any country. "Commodore, my daughter isn't even mentioned in this report. And yet she was aboard—"

"I know nothing of the particulars."

"But Commodore—"

"One second, please." He mumbled something into the phone.

Half a minute later, North felt a jolt of stomach acid as St. Gregory stormed into the office. His white uniform, sharp as a switchblade, gold epaulets, and trimmed beard made him look more commodorish than his boss. Yet he seemed preoccupied in his haughty hatred and his nose was screwed up as it has been on the Island. . . . And then the word for St. Gregory came to North: this son of a Bay Street Boy was a *necrophiliac*, one who preferred those around him to be dead or in captivity so he could control them. St. Gregory's lack of facial muscles was characteristic of that perversion: the mechanical expression, the nose sniffing like a police dog ferreting out not dope but decay.

He narrowed his eyes and nodded at North.

"Captain," North acknowledged.

"What is it now, North?"

"My daughter. She's missing—"

"We know nothing of your daughter," said St. Gregory.

"Tell me straight out. Did you kill her with the rest of them?"

"Now, Dr. North," cautioned Commodore Bridgewater. "We're all doing all we can, don't you see?"

"Look, Commodore, what if the captain here was . . . misinformed? What if she had been hiding on the ship during the battle?"

St. Gregory whispered with a staggering simplicity, "I'm sure she's alive."

Do liars always lie, or do they sometimes speak the truth to mislead? North couldn't tell whether it were the truth, or his intense need, or merely his intuition crying for affirmation, but St. Gregory's words seemed all the more definitive for his having whispered them so concisely.

"If she's alive, where is she?" North asked in the most reasonable tone he could muster.

"I wouldn't know, North. I was only trying to reassure you, to wake up your common sense."

"If Coby had been aboard the LCM during the raid, couldn't your men could have killed her without them even knowing it?"

St. Gregory shrugged and reverted to his usual truculence, his nostrils busy detecting one particle in a million. "You've got your filthy nerve, North. You think we raid boats for fun and kill innocent little girls? We boarded the barge for good reason and only cut loose on those assholes of yours when they opened up with their Uzi."

"What Uzi?"

St. Gregory bolted out of the room and was back in seconds holding a short-barreled submachine gun with a hinged, steel stock. "*This* Uzi!" He threw it horizontally at North, who caught it military style.

North opened the breach, held his thumbnail to reflect the light, and looked into the barrel. Then he held it to his nose and detected the pungent odor of gunpowder solvent. "It hasn't been fired," North said.

"We cleaned it."

"Why?"

"Because it was dirty. Because the RBDF confiscates guns used in felonies. Because it's ours now. Any more questions?"

"Only about my daughter."

"Listen, North. I'm sorry about your daughter. But you should have thought of her when you got into the drug business. You think for one minute this government doesn't know what you're doing on that Island?"

"Only a psychopath like you would ask such a question."

"Now, Dr. North," said Bridgewater. "There's no need for that. The captain may be right or he may be wrong, but as a scientist you certainly must concede his theory is not without merit. An elaborate science center with chemistry apparatus and all *could be* an elaborate charade to hide a drug setup, could it not? Hundreds of millions could be made that way, eh? Your own private harbor for drug transfer, gasoline tanks for refueling fast boats, warehouse for dope storage, laboratory for converting coca to cocaine or coke to crack, solar energy and radios for reliable communications. I'm not saying you are guilty, of course. Only that it looks rather suspicious, don't you see?"

The commodore's patronizing tone angered North, the more so because he knew the man was right. The line between a dreamer and a charlatan is slight. St. Gregory, necrophiliac that he is, murderer that he may be, would simply define a charlatan as the dreamer who failed. Seen through the Defender captain's eyes, North's conspiracy theory flickered and faded above the commodore's desk like heat waves off gasoline. St. Gregory's gasoline.

"We could hardly have missed seeing your daughter if she were aboard," St. Gregory said reasonably. "We went over the whole barge when we towed her back to Nassau."

Commodore Bridgewater nodded sagely, scarcely hiding his desire to end the interview.

"Is there no one else in this government who can help me? Someone who won't throw me in jail for trying to get my daughter back?" As he said it, he remembered Cora Carstairs from the United Nations reception, but she was in the legislative branch and commanded no one who cinduct a search.

Bridgewater composed a careful frown on his face as if he truly cared. "Why don't you go see the Deputy P.M., Malcolm Pyfrom?" He said it as if all North had to do was knock on the deputy's door and walk into his office.

North remembered meeting Pyfrom at the U. N., the thin gray man with the lizard eyes who stood in an alcoholic fog at the right hand of Ransom. He knew Bridgewater was relying on the second rule of bureaucrats: pass problems upward. In the first rule, well along toward fulfillment, you pledged your sincere help even when you intended to withhold it.

"Minister Pyfrom can authorize a more elaborate—a more costly—search of the Bahamas than either the Defence Force or the police could begin on their own," explained Bridgewater prettily. "We have our budget constraints, don't you see?"

"Listen, North," said St. Gregory calmly. "Don't rub Pyfrom the wrong way, the way you did me, or he'll feed you to the sharks."

18 *Think Tank*

THE DIESEL SMELLS of the Harbour Club were rising as
Grant North took a long look at the landing craft he had brought
from Lake Michigan, two thousand meandering miles down the
Mississippi, across the Gulf, through Florida rivers, and here to
the Bahamas. Cleary and Rolle had a ladder against her starboard
flank and were fixing the shattered corner of the wheelhouse. The
stanchions supporting the guardrail were stove in and the deck was
thick with debris and muddy footprints, but otherwise she didn't
look too bad from the outside.

When he entered the door to the cabin, North was hit with
the sinister smell of disinfectant. The cabin, spacious as you would
find on a houseboat, was perforated with bullet holes. Walls, ceiling,
and decks looked like a flock of berserk woodpeckers had been
loosed inside. North propped open port and starboard doors to let
in fresh air, then climbed the four steps to the poop, trying to
ignore the cloying odor—and what it meant.

"Hello, Grant," said a familiar voice he hadn't heard in four
years. It was his sister Jo, her hair blonde as ever, her neck corded
by worry. She was packing what was left of the crew's belongings
in open-top cardboard boxes.

He smiled. "How did you get here?"

135

"When Jack called and told me about Coby, I took a leave of absence. Those . . . Defenders. They really shot up this boat of yours."

"Jo," he said, swallowing his pride, "thanks for coming. I hope we can put our differences behind us and find Coby."

"I flew a detour to Bimini on the way here, and spent a whole day asking the police and everyone I saw whether they'd seen her. No one had."

Jo was two years older than North but didn't look it. Tall and angular, she had the same high Slavic cheekbones and piercing eyes as her brother. But where North's eyes shone hazel-green, hers were ice-blue, and her skin exhibited the pale cast of those who work inside. She had been named after their father, Coby's *Nonich,* and North saw anew some of the Coby in Jo: the blonde hair, purity of eyes, and a hair-trigger smile—or frown.

"I *know* she's alive," said North. "Somewhere."

"That damn smug intuition, again," she said with more of a smile than a frown.

North's overreliance on his intuitive powers had been the root of their estrangement. That and the pursuit of his own business goals to the detriment of Coby who had arrived motherless to a bleak and arid adolescence. Jo had filled the gaps after Heather's death, becoming more of a mother to Coby than he had been a father, attending her school plays, buying her clothes, taking over when North was gone. But when brother and sister were together, their arguments had grown heated. After Jo took the radio job at the Turks & Caicos Islands four years ago, she had seen nothing of him or of Coby.

Now North took care to keep their egos from re-colliding. "Intuition has its place, Jo. Without it, I'd have to conclude that St. Gregory killed her with my boat crew."

"'St. Gregory.' He's the Defence Force captain I've been hearing about."

"Right."

"Not exactly our patron saint, I take it?"

"Right again."

"I've been preaching against the Royal BDF ever since Ransom expanded it from a tiny Coast Guard. What does a country the size of a Chicago suburb need with a military force?"

North nodded. He recognized the pattern of her reproach, launched to hide her embarrassment over being in the same room with him. She didn't have to say that she would do anything possible for Coby. She was here.

"I checked the morgue—"

"Jesus," North said.

"Well, it had to be done. I also placed missing-person's notice in the newspapers and alerted BASRA."

North had heard of BASRA, the Bahamas Air Sea Rescue Association, an organization of a hundred volunteers with forty boats and ten aircraft. "Thanks, Jo."

"I see Jack Cleary's his old cheery self. And I met your man Rolle."

"Where are they?"

"In the basement." She indicated the engine room. "I'm glad you're out of jail, Grant."

"They think I'm a druggie, Jo."

"Of course." She smiled. "Why else would anybody come way out here claiming to do *science?*"

North felt a touch of the warmth he had felt for his older sister when they were children. But it vanished when she said, "Grant, why oh why did you guys ever come here in the first place? All these . . . *people.*"

"People are pretty much the same everywhere, Jo," North said automatically, knowing she meant "black people." They'd had arguments like this in the past and he wasn't in the mood for another. The one thing North disliked about his sister was her prejudice, which on the streets of Chicago had been inoculated in the young routinely, like a vaccine.

He descended to the cabin, knelt to lift the engine-room hatch, and shouted down. "How is it, Sid?"

"Not too bad. Come see for yourself."

Climbing down the rungs on the steel bulkhead that divided the engines from the hold, North stepped along a narrow duckwalk between twin diesels as tall as his shoulders. On both sides of the slippery duckwalk you could see black motor oil floating on the bilge. Cleary was there too.

"We inspected the engines, the pumps, the exhaust system, and the hull," said Cleary. "We were lucky. We only had to replace one battery bank and fix a few holes in the manifolds. Bullets bounced off both engines, but didn't seem to hurt them much."

The six-seventy-one diesels were made of heavy castings that no ordinary round could penetrate after being slowed by the steel bulkheads of the engine room. You could see the dents in the engines made by ricocheting slugs, but there were no leaks. The two battery banks, each consisting of four six-volt batteries wired in series, were re-wired and working again.

North leaned over to retrieve a six-inch red "Cleary paddle" floating on the black bilge. It was used to indicate which bank needed charging, or was being charged. Cleary took the paddle from him, wiped it with a rag, and hooked it over the old bank, which had not been charged sufficiently during the short trip from Coral Harbour around to this side of New Providence.

There was more damage in the open area of the well deck. North saw bullet holes everywhere, in the galley, in the crew cupboards and overhead joists, even in the head. The door to the stateroom had been removed, and Jo was sitting on a bunk examining Coby's last-known habitat. Two footlockers near the bed, in which Symes had stowed his hi-fi, books, clothes, and other possessions, had been emptied and the contents removed by the Defenders.

"No traces of Coby," said Jo.

What had she expected, bits of flesh? "Of course not," he said, smelling the Lysol the Defenders had used. "She would have taken her luggage with her."

"Well, I thought we might see something. A comb. A bottle of shampoo—"

Out of the corner of his eye, a tiny object glistened. He opened his pocket knife and dug it out of the crack between the indoor-outdoor carpeting and the rear bulkhead, and showed it to Jo: a tiny piece of metal with lettering that said, "I ♥ NEW YORK."

"That's a charm," Jo said.

"Coby didn't have a charm bracelet."

"It couldn't be hers anyway. She hated New York."

What did the charm mean? Was it anything more than a lost trinket from one of Basil's or Symes's girlfriends?

"Don't make too much of this, Grant." Big sister had a way of hearing each cog click in the gears of his mind.

North and Jo climbed the steps to the cabin and on up to the wheelhouse where they helped the others replace windows and varnish the new plywood ceiling. Ragged clouds that had blocked the sun finally tore apart at the horizon, spilling an orange light into the little ship.

The four of them came down to the cabin and sat in the booth around the convertible table. North was aware of the pressures of command, aware too of the irony that his scientific think tank finally had been born. On the Island he had hoped to create a new chautauqua, a place where he and his scientists could utilize technology to solve social problems. Too bad the problem before them wasn't something simple, like survival of the planet.

A plan of attack was a fine idea in a chess game. But how do you go on the offensive when your opponents are only vaguely seen? Yet, working with uncertainty was nothing new to him; scientists had made it a Principle, and his own principle was to go after the man at the top.

"First we have to operate on the assumption that Coby is alive," North began. "Otherwise, what's the use . . . of anything? After the argument Coby and I had, she could be hiding, flaunting her independence. The last time she ran away I found her at Jo's place, confused."

"Jesus, she was thirteen then!" Jo said.

"Well, she could be in Europe by now, unaware that anything has happened. She could be kidnapped or isolated on some island where Symes might have put her ashore." He saw blank faces. "Look, *any* problem can be solved, for crysake!" Over a lifetime of management he had come to believe that.

No one had the heart to challenge Grant North's assumption that Coby was alive. Jo became atypically sympathetic, speaking to him alone in Serbo-Croatian, the language they had used as children to say something in secret. "*Dosta sam čud, brate moj, a šta da vradimo.* Say no more, my brother, just tell us what to do."

But he didn't *know* what to do. "We can't let this fucking tyrant steal Coby and kick us out of here."

"Which fucking tyrant?" Cleary said. "St. Greg or Transom?"

North said evenly, "The Prime Minister."

"Transom?" Jo asked.

"A Clearyism," said North.

Cleary said, "I don't stay up all night maneuvering and planning like you. All this time I've been thinking we ought to go and see the head asshole and tell him about St. Blackbeard—ask for his help."

The only intrigue Cleary understood was coaxing people out to lunch so he could sell them something, North knew. He tried to explain. "Jack, when we were in jail we found out that someone else is going to tell Ransom about St. Gregory possibly being a killer. We'll see if he gets fired. And even if Ransom isn't involved, anything we say to him could get back to our saintly Defender."

"You think the P.M.'s part of some conspiracy we've stumbled onto?" Jo asked.

"That's my hunch."

"Oh shit," said Jo. She didn't run her life on hunches.

"Never have I bought the idea," North said, "that the leader of an organization is ignorant of the rotten things that go on under his command. Like Castro pretending he didn't know General Ochoa trafficked in drugs, or Nixon being unaware of Watergate. The Bahamas is a tiny country. You can't even get a work permit without the P.M.'s personal okay."

"Work permit? You can't even blow your nose around here without permission," said Cleary. "I never did get my nose-blowing permit."

North steered the brainstorming. "What do we know for sure about any of these people?"

"We know Ransom's worth mucho millions," Rolle said. "Every time his ex-wife sues him for more alimony, the mansion he's building and his other holdings are plastered all over the *Miami Herald.*"

"Poor guy," said Cleary. "I know how tough things can get. Once I had three ten-dollar bills and I gave one of them to a doorman at Delmonico's, one to my fiancée when she left me, and one to the bank. The doorman wouldn't let me in any more, my girl sued me, and the bank repossessed my car. Transom has to learn that these setbacks are temporary. Today I'm on permanent vacation in the Bahamas and worth well over a hundred and twelve dollars."

They laughed.

"Seriously," said Rolle, "we know that a certain son of a Bay Street Boy holds the rank right under commodore and yet he runs a patrol boat. All the other boats are bossed by lieutenant commanders or less, two ranks below Captain St. Gregory." He paused, but there were no comments. "We also know he speaks Spanish, probably has a Latin mother like me. He'd be the logical one to make drug deals with the spics."

"What country?" asked Jo. "What's his accent?"

"I never heard him *say* anything in Spanish. And he didn't react when I called his mother a whore. But he sure understood my Cuban accent when I called his father a pimp."

"What else?" said the moderator-commander.

"I went over to the Ministry of Works to get a permit to buy a single-sideband to replace the ship radio that was shot up," Rolle said. "Turns out I'm on their shit list, along with you and Cleary and God knows who else. They got all our names."

"Not mine," said Jo. "My last name isn't North. It's Copp, my old married name. Besides, my station has all the radios we could ever need."

"It's not just that," Rolle said. "If they don't want us to have a radio, it follows that by having a radio we can find out things they don't want us to know."

"Takes a Bahamian to think like one," Cleary said, not without admiration. "It could also mean that they actually think we're druggies."

Jo said, "Okay, where do we start?"

"Can you get your station manager to help? Maybe set up a voice-actuated recorder to monitor Defender broadcasts?"

"Of course? The station is in the Turks & Caicos, a British colony. They can't touch us there."

North took from his wallet the HF frequency used on the *Munnings* for long-range transmissions, and he gave the note to Jo. If St. Gregory transmitted on other frequencies as well, her station manager could find them by listening to the first channel and taking note of any switching.

"These *Defenders*," Jo said, as if the word hurt her tongue. "They sound like the DGI in Cuba or the Tonton Macoutes in Haiti."

"This is how it all starts," Rolle said, "Midnight assaults, beatings of families—"

"If I've learned anything in investigating corrupt governments, it's that there's never just *one* secret police. They divide into two or more cliques, one watching the other, like our defending Defenders and St. Gregory's Military Operations Platoon."

"That could make our job easier," North said.

"Yes it could," she said, comprehending immediately.

"Why?" said Rolle.

"Because the more internal dissention, the likelier it is that someone in the Defence Force will say something he shouldn't," Jo answered. "While we're listening to what the Defenders talk about over the air, we ought to find out what they say in the bars they hang out in."

"I volunteer for bar duty," Cleary said.

"You can't do it. As Sidney said, they know who you are. That leaves me." She paused, looking at Cleary. "Trouble is I'm a woman alone and I don't know Nassau very well."

"Maybe we ought to get God Knowles to help Jo," Cleary said, ignoring Jo's look. "He comes from here you know."

"God hates Nassau as much as I do," Rolle said.

"Well, Godfrey does anyway," said Jo with a chuckle.

"Let Godfrey take care of the Island, and the rest of us work on finding Coby," North said. "Sid, how about you going with Jo?"

"Sure, but they know me too."

Jo frowned but recovered fast. "Well, Sidney, you'll . . . blend in better than Cleary."

"You mean I'm black."

"I mean you're Bahamian."

North turned to Cleary. "Jack, I'd like you to penetrate the Wracking Islands, especially the village at Great Snake. Get to know the people. Go to the bars, the church, the two little grocery stores. Attend their picnics. Talk to everybody. See what gossip is floating around about a marijuana farm on the Island; *someone* led St. Gregory to believe we were growing the stuff."

"And what do I say I'm doing there? Learning to be a Bahamian after my latest lobotomy?"

"Do whatever works, Jack. The Mako's faster. We'll take it together and I'll drop you off at Great Snake. Andy can come for the LCM after I get back to the Island."

"And what are you going to do while I'm playing Humphrey Bogart around the Wracking Islands?"

"After I tell Godfrey what's going on, I'm going to Bimini. It's the only place Coby could have gotten off the LCM, voluntarily."

Jo's face flared for a moment, and North knew she was miffed that he didn't trust her findings on Bimini. But she let it pass, and it made hin realize he had a team now.

The think tank broke up as the sky thickened into a dark purple. North and Cleary climbed into the speedboat and untied the painter attached to the LCM.

The Mako strained at harbor speed, her bow held high like a Bahama girl balancing a basket of papayas on her head. At the passage between New Providence and Paradise, they looked back at Rolle and Jo, black and white specks across Third-World water, hard as a corrugated sheet of steel, and knew that never again would they define this nation in terms of liquid colors and soft breezes. Their lives were suddenly afloat.

19 *Ghost Ship*

A MILE OFF their port quarter, a water barge crawled toward Nassau bringing part of the daily freshwater cargo from Andros. Farther off, other water barges hovered in the haze over an ocean of ink.

North hammered the Mako toward the Wracking Islands thinking about how his solar-desalination project could end such absurd effort. One of the research engineers he wanted to bring over as project leader for the freshwater project had spent a lifetime innovating better methods of distilling seawater. His most promising system was a solar still that creates a vacuum by the falling motion of entrapped air bubbles in water, causing the water to flow automatically—and economically. Once North had permits to bring him and the other engineers and scientists he had recruited to the Island, they could adapt the defunct Nassau desalinators as a byproduct, in a matter of months. If only the government would listen. Out of jail, North still felt as imprisoned as the voice of the sea screaming through the convoluted whorls of a conch shell.

But the living sea soon splashed its phosphorescence against the Mako, and the last blaze of feathered fire built fantastic towers in the western sky like the anvils of a mad god. The dipper formed first, then under it Cassiopeia. His former world, two hundred forty thousand miles away, swelled so large and orange as it rose above the horizon he could make out the Mare Tranquillitatis where the first astronauts landed, an alien sea of tranquility. How could you stay angry in the face of such a moon?

North eased back the throttle as far as he could and still maintain the plane, making conversation possible.

"Christ Almighty, this has got to be the world's most idiotic place to start a business," Cleary said, ignoring the sky, the corners of his mouth antacid white. "You import everything because they don't make a friggin thing in this backwater country, but you still have to pay customs forty percent on average. Then you spend all your time and effort getting a dozen separate permissions from a dozen reluctant ministries. After that—if by some wild stretch of the imagination you've got enough money left over to make a go of the business—*then* you pay nothing at all because there's no income tax!"

North had been steering by intuition, but about nine o'clock, the moon reached the top of the sky and they sighted the long narrow shape of Shark Cay off their port beam, feeling the warm land breeze on their faces like a mystical smoke. At high tide they could streak between Shark and Bain Cay, and head straight up the inside curve of the Wrackings. But the tide was out, and North stayed well off the dark shapes of the islands. Venture too close, and the waves would drop you onto reefs or old wrecks that could slice your hull with knife-sharp tentacles. A half hour later and only a few miles off Great Snake, a white mound rose from the black ocean. As they drew closer they saw it was a derelict with no running lights. She was dead in the water.

"Let's take a look," North said, feeling anything but altruism, yet knowing it was a mariner's duty to investigate a stricken ship at sea. He slowed the engine and approached cautiously, circling the hulk.

White and ghostly, her stern pressed heavy into the ocean. There seemed no reason for her to be abandoned: no sign of fire, no gash in the hull, no anchor line, no activity on any of the decks. The lines of the yacht raked forward showing a long row of oval portholes at the waterline, a chrome rail, and above that an enclosed afterdeck, saloon, and pilot house all enveloped in black glass. A radar pylon, still as the night, reared above the flybridge. No name appeared on either bow or stern, only a series of numbers on the forward hull beginning with the "FL" of a Florida registration.

"Hartmann-Palmer," said Cleary, an ex-yacht salesman. "Seventy-eight feet of leading edge. Fiberglass hull of triaxial fiber woven with Kevlar. She'll last forever."

"Unless she sinks." North pointed to the stern that settled slightly lower even as they watched.

They could hear water running into the hull as Cleary examined the sides. "No damage," he said. "Maybe she's being scuttled for the insurance."

At the stern, they found the cabin windows shattered. No one answered their shouts, so they looped the painter of the Mako around a rung of the aft ladder and climbed aboard. The door to the cabin swung back and forth, creaking in the unaccustomed silence of the darkness.

"Insurance, my ass!" said Cleary, entering the cabin. *There are bodies here!*"

North followed with a flashlight, shining it on the corpses and then on the carpet, which sparkled with spent cartridges. The first two, crumpled together, were white men, their hands clinging to AK-47 assault rifles. Thirty-round banana clips jutted from their fatigue-jacket pockets. The cabin smelled oppressive, of blood and mildew.

North pressed a light switch but nothing happened. He found his way to the control console and flicked the main circuit breaker. The lights went on and with them the automatic bilge pumps; at least now the sinking would be slowed. The carpet of the saloon was strewn with two Browning automatics bearing long sound suppressors, a Bellini 12-gage autoloading shotgun, and a dozen boxes of high-penetration sabot slugs—hardly the long-range defensive weapons you would have if you were worried about an attack at sea. A bullet had taken off the corner of one man's head. He and the others looked Hispanic and wore Daniel Ortega mustaches, into which blood and saliva ran from their noses. The bodies had been torn by something distant and fast, probably extra-long 8-mm slugs.

The other corpse was different. A black man, he lay face down on the floor next to the open door at the other side of the saloon, his hand clenched to an automatic Kalashnikov M76 sniper rifle. North saw that the man's shirt was scorched where the bullet had entered the upper back from short range, probably from a pistol.

"Looks like this one was killed up close," North said.

He turned over the body. There was no mistaking that light-skinned ferret face with the brown splotches, no more pale in death than it had been in life, the youth who could never miss, who had jumped bail but who had jumped not far enough.

"The assassin assassinated," said North. "Mike Morgan."

"Christ Almighty, you *know* him?"

"There's nothing like jail to enlarge your circle of acquaintances."

North looked around the saloon. No plastic packages or boxes were there that could contain drugs. Furniture and equipment, relatively untouched, included upholstered chairs, a full-sized bar lined with bottles of liquor, and a console the width of the ship that held the latest in radar, loran, onboard computers, and a high-frequency or HF radio.

"You can count on one hand the number of private yachts that use HF," North said. "Defenders use radios like that."

"The narco-war comes to the Bahamas," said Cleary.

North had heard myriad stories implicating some of the neighboring islands, but this was his first first-hand evidence. Thank God his own Island was clean of trafficking.

"Maybe we should take some of these guns," said Cleary, looking worried.

"That's all we need, for the Defenders to find us with assault weapons."

Suddenly a high-intensity spotlight like an antiaircraft beacon flooded the cabin, burning their eyes.

"That's no damn Defender boat!" North shouted, running out of the cabin.

Cleary followed, the two of them careening over the bodies on the afterdeck, stepping on torsos and legs, flinging themselves down the ladder into the idling Mako. North fell on the throttle and rammed it full forward, the Mako bucking her head like a bronco, her loose rein whipping the bow. After a moment the bow came down a little and the solid ocean hammered the hull like a repeating cannon.

Glancing back, North saw the source of the light, a huge Xenon searchlight much like those on Patton tanks and M-113 armored carriers: million-lumen concentrators whose searing beam could blind you from a thousand feet.

Then came the roar, like Apollo blasting to the moon. A Cigarette, a Fever, a Scarab—one of the overpowered thunderboats with twin 800-horsepower engines that suck air and flaming gasoline through four-barrel, tunnel-ram carburetors. At full power one of these monsters can be heard ten miles away. This one was closer, perhaps only a mile off, and it would be making ninety knots.

"Get down!" North shouted over the roar, and while Cleary squatted between the seat and the console, North crouched as low as could, reaching over his head for the wheel and steering erratically.

Machine-gun fire streamed over their heads—thirty-cals from the sound of them. North pushed Cleary to the floor and crouched beside him, reaching up to steer the boat. He imagined he could see the slugs whizzing by under the promethean spotlight. From his awkward position he turned hard to starboard and back, throwing spray into an giant rooster tail, twisting and plunging the Mako. This was armored-recon evasion, not seamanship. In two minutes the thunderboat would be so close the gunners couldn't miss. He rose to a crouch, leaning against the seat to steer better. As the Mako reared sideways to the crests, he could feel Cleary against his legs on the floorboards. The seas tumbled over them in liquid avalanches. Cleary moaned, and from the smell of him he'd had an involuntary defecation. North felt fear too, but it was mixed with a certain . . . exhilaration. Ten days of rage in the Nassau jail had ignited his competitive fuel and burned away the years since Vietnam.

Less than a thousand feet away, the thunderboat was gaining on them. The Mako strained and pounded in a headlong flight of fear. Nine hundred feet, seven hundred, five hundred. The next salvo could hardly miss.

North felt perversely grateful for the intense light of the pursuing beacon, for it enabled him to make out Flour Beach at the northern end of Great Snake Cay. At the instant the machine guns sounded again, North swung the wheel hard to port and roared into the passage between Great Snake and Little Snake. With the wheel hard over, he waited until the last moment and dipped into a lee roll, rounding the corner into the hidden passageway that the natives called the creek.

This tortuous bayou that divides Water Cay on the west from Great Snake is notoriously unsafe during low tide. At any moment North expected a sandbar to rip the hull and slam them into a bone-crushing halt at fifty miles an hour, but he had no choice. His mind raced. Druggies, especially Cubans, possessed combat equipment. Something would come to hunt them.

North pushed the throttle forward.

"What are you doing?" whispered Cleary.

"Something's coming. A flare. A rocket. Maybe a Phoenix missile."

Cleary sat up and looked at North, whose jaw was set, teeth clenching as if on granite, intent on reading the distant minds of unknown assailants.

North kept the Mako skimming the water with only its propeller submerged, and steered the curves and sharp bends in the creek by moonlight. He imagined a giant log in his path and switched on the spotlight. Seconds later the barrage came, but this was no high-tech assault. Shell after shell old-fashioned mortars flew through the darkness. North wondered whether they were aimed electronically at the miniscule reflection of the spotlight on the water, and doubted that the light, filtered through thousands of trees and vines, would show on a nightscope. Just in case, he dowsed the light and killed the engine, listening to the shells landing ahead of them and onto the eastern shore. The barrage stopped, leaving the creek strangely empty of even the sounds of the nightbirds or the whisper of the wind, as though they had been wrapped in a gigantic blanket.

Cleary straightened up, removed shoes and pants, threw away his shorts in disgust, and dressed again. He didn't have to be told not to smoke. It was slack low tide, and over the stern in the dim moonlight they could see their muddy trail. Dank fingers of branches and the rotting, floating corpses of trees closed around them, making North thankful he had stopped, for he surely would have hit some-thing at the speed he was going. The mangrove leaves turned silvery backs to the concealed men as they pulled on the branches, creeping forward like water moccasins, soundless and as wary. North didn't know how determined were his pursuers, how sophisticated their night-search equipment. If they had infrared sensors, they could locate the Mako by the heat of its engine even now that it was turned off.

Drifting along the Water Cay side of the creek, they wound themselves into a grotto covered at the top with dense arms and coiling tendrils of vegetation. Carnal creepers clogged the grotto, thick assertive vines that dropped from branches like serpents in ambush. The malevolent odor of fungus pervaded the stagnant air, obscenely comforting like the earth surrounding your coffin.

Ten minutes later they heard the thunderboat rumble and roar off, the waning Doppler sound signaling their deliverance.

North pressed the control to raise the outdrive, and with the propeller barely submerged, pushed through the darkness at little more than idle. Fifteen minutes later they emerged into the wide mouth of the village harbor and passed the remains of the rusting freighter that marked the entrance to the ocean. Tying up alongside a dozen other boats attached to moorings, they waded ashore to the Grave Yard Inn, their wet legs unnoticed in the dark barroom. At a small table in the back, Cleary ordered a bottle of gin and two glasses of ice. He lit one cigarette after another and trembled like a sea oat.

Only after gulping his first ultra-dry martini did he speak. "Okay, what the fuck was all that about?"

North shrugged. "Thunderboat. Must be Symes's brother, or at least we're supposed to think so." The Bahamas was turning out to be a bad dream where words like "justice," "government," "magistrate," and "defender" meant their opposites.

"Doesn't all this make you want to go home?" Cleary said.

"How can I go home with Coby missing?"

"Shit Almighty? I get the feeling you're enjoying this, Grant. It's a side of you I've never seen before. Out there on the water, it was like you were playing a game—for fun."

Indeed, North felt himself glowing from the combustion of excitement and drink. "I'd be inhuman if I didn't feel elated. After all, we won—for the moment at least."

Cleary studied North's face, seeing anew the jutting blood vessels and hard sinew of neck and shoulders, and examined the crescent moon tattooed on his wrist, as if measuring the ability of this former combat officer to lead them out of their quagmire. His second drink suspended between table and mouth, Cleary said in an almost-inaudible voice, "Grant, did you ever stop to think that you're becoming an island yourself? An isolated body entirely surrounded by people who want you dead?"

Fleeing from the thunderboat, North had known fear again, but now Cleary's comment made him strangely unafraid. Fear was not only a weapon for the aggressor but a tranquilizer for the victim. And he knew from long experience in combat and in business that if you succumbed to it, fear would give you the feeling that what happens, happens. He could not afford that luxury. He drained his glass and knew he would have to act, not just react, if he were going to get Coby back.

Cleary broke the silence. "I suppose Rolle would say, those guys died of their environment."

"You trust Rolle?" North asked, wary of everything.

"Well, sure. Why not?"

"Just asking."

"Christ, what next? You think Rolle had something to do with this drug war?"

"Who knows?"

Cleary persisted. "Maybe William Symes is in with the druggies who hired the black American—what was his name . . . Mike Morgan?"

North nodded.

"Somebody hired Morgan to kill the drug runners," Cleary

said, "then eliminated him so he wouldn't talk. Maybe they hung around to see who might come to grab the cargo. Then *we* showed up. . . ."

North swallowed the rest of his drink. "Jack, I don't doubt that Mike Morgan was killed by whoever hired him to shoot the druggies on the boat with his long-range rifle. Or that St. Gregory put William Symes or somebody up to chasing us. But the two aren't necessarily related. And I don't buy the idea that they were trying to kill us."

"Somehow I got the distinct impression they wanted us dead. Those fucking mortars weren't exactly firecrackers."

"If they wanted us dead, we'd be dead. You can't miss with machine guns. And mortars are a waste of time against an unseen enemy unless you've got some idea of the range."

"Well, maybe they didn't happen to have an atomic bomb on board."

"But they did have a Xenon searchlight. They could easily have chased us off with just the beacon or the roar of their thunder-boat." North poured another slug of gin over his glass of ice.

"You're saying they wanted to do more that just get us away from the Hartmann-Palmer until she was safe on the ocean floor?"

"Yes."

Cleary thought about that and said, "If all they wanted to do was scare the shit out of us, they did a great job. Maybe they thought we were smugglers too."

"I have a hunch that drugs and smuggling don't drive this country as much as everyone seems to think. I'm getting the idea that drugs have become the national excuse for everything."

"Like what?"

"Like maybe something really simple. Like prejudice, for instance. Third World against First World. Black against white. It's obvious we're no threat to the drug folks or anyone else. And yet someone's trying awfully hard to get us to leave the country."

"Who? Why?"

"I don't know."

20 *ORIGINS: the Salesman*

BEFORE THEY CAME to the Island, chief salesman Jack Cleary peddled North Detectors to state and federal agencies, schools, police departments, corporations that do business with the government, the armed services, airlines, trucklines, buslines . . . And North Scientific prospered in direct proportion to the intensity of the drug war.

Cleary never married. "I can imagine no punishment worse than spending the rest of my life with the same woman," he told North, and proceeded to punctuate his aphorism with show girls. He found humor everywhere: in a man's name, in a girl's hesitancy (or especially her derrière), even in the clop of a horse on the streets of New York, and he had the gift of transferring the amusement he found to those around him. Following a series of sales calls that ended in Miami Beach, he awoke one morning with the nightclub singer Delilah Mae after they had strolled the beaches the night before. The lower half of the bed was streaked with tar from their feet. Glancing at the sheets and then at Delilah, he picked up the phone and dialed North at home. "Grant, I have incontrovertible proof about black girls," and North could hear Delilah giggling as Cleary said, "It does rub off!"

Cleary's womanizing and growing alcoholism prompted lectures from North, but he felt that was envy on North's part, that

North worked too hard and knew not how to live. Zola once said that most people never stop to analyze their lives when they are sailing along successfully; they pause only when something has gone wrong. He was talking about Jack Cleary, not Grant North.

In the winter of Coby's senior year, North told Cleary he was going to sell the company. Cleary was devastated. The company had become his reason for being, as he thought it had been North's.

"Why sell at a time like this?" Cleary said, knowing the question was in vain, that North wouldn't have announced it unless he'd been analyzing his reasons for months.

"I want to do something else while I'm still young enough."

"Young enough for what?"

"To accomplish—" North broke off.

It was a rare moment. Even the closest of male friends rarely find the occasion to spell out their deepest feelings.

"I want to do science."

Through the window of their low-slung office building, Cleary watched a pair of gulls taking turns diving into Lake Michigan, gray and ripe with whitecaps.

"Never could I understand the Slavic mind," he said, but it wasn't true. He felt he understood North better than himself. As far back as Yale, his life had grown inexorably into an adjunct of North's; he had observed his friend through the start of the instrument company, the birth of Coby, the death of Heather, and had come to understand that it wasn't the accomplishment that drove this scientist, but the action itself.

North's feelings came bubbling up from their artesian depths. "Science to me is like religion to you. I believe it is the only way to end war, stop the drug Plague, plug the hole in the ozone layer, prevent overbreeding—solve the problems that threaten humanity. It is our only route to the stars and to the depths of the oceans. I want to be part of those explorations. I want to *do* science, not make instruments for others to do it." He paused for a moment with an expression akin to love. "Science is truth," he said, his face hot with passion. "It is the purest ingredient in our lives, purer than music or art or love or honor. It's the greatest commitment we can render because it alone will empower us to conquer the universe . . . and ourselves."

Outside, the gulls were coasting fast on the wind, heading toward shore. Snow fell softly like rice, and the junipers and pines caught the flakes in the crooks of their arms. Cleary searched the crevices of North's face. He wanted to say something about how all that might be well and good for North, but that he viewed life differently. He felt he should say something. Finally, though, he said nothing.

A few months later, Grant North sold the company.

The first thing Cleary did with the sale of his stock was to buy an original Rubens miniature. The rest of his money evaporated into bouts of drinking and girls and helping North look for the ideal island. Some months later, North found him one morning in a cheap Nassau walk-up where he was nursing a hangover.

"Hi, Grant." A greeting from the gut, but from the wobbliest gut Cleary had ever mustered, weakened in battle against alcohol molecules that bubbled by the billions in his bloodstream and attempted escape through red windows. His war of attrition, being lost by his stomach, sent him reeling for ammunition. He chewed some Tums. Reaching under the bed, he produced a more formidable countermeasure, an open two-liter bottle of cheap wine. One long pull and he drained half a pint.

"Under the bed, for crysake!"

"Yeah, well, this ain't exactly the Twenty-One Club, Grant."

North grabbed the bottle and smelled it. "There're enough polyesters and amines in here to make a three-piece suit. I hope to hell you've got a headache."

Cleary knew what he meant. If you were an alcoholic with hangovers any less painful than pancreatic carcinoma, you were reversely doomed, for there was no hope you'd decline a morning drink. "I would have a headache if I could feel my head."

"That the Rubens?" North said, examining the tiny painting hanging over the dresser. The miniature depicted St. Jude as a trendy long-hair glancing over his left shoulder.

"My heavenly savior," said Cleary. "Maybe you can get to be a saint too."

"By wearing hair shirts and letting my beard grow?"

"It's a start. Jude got to be a saint because he gave up eating, drinking, and screwing to bash the blasphemous and licentious heretics. Only later did he become the patron of those suffering from desperate illnesses."

"And hangovers," said North.

Cleary showered and dressed, while North looked around for something to eat. Inside the refrigerator, the kind with the motor on top that he hadn't seen since childhood, stood three cans of beer and a bottle of gin.

"Let's go out for breakfast," North said.

"The most I can manage now is antacid rain," Cleary said, popping another Tums.

Leaving the apartment, he turned on the stairway and said, "Grant, loan me a fifty."

Automatically North took out his wallet and handed a bill to Cleary, who crouched beside a derelict on the landing. The man was sitting up and nodding his head like a metronome. Cleary tucked the fifty in the man's shirt pocket, moving swiftly to minimize the charity, but the junkie came awake at that instant with a dreamy smile. "Thank you kindly, Mr. Jack. Ah hopes you goes to heaven." Then he nodded off again.

Emerging from the dingy building into the glare of brilliant sunlight was like coming out of a theater in the daytime. Sunday-morning quiet is seductive in cities, where briefcased businessmen give way to families strolling on the grass and you hear church bells instead of automobile screeches. They moved slowly, smelling the city, the salt air wafting from the harbor, the raw fish from the stalls on grassy corners. Only a few vendors had their stands up and were selling conch salad and grouper fingers or sweet ripe mangoes for desert. They shared a mango while watching a pair of gray rats, the squirrels of the Bahamas, hunt across a landscape devoid of acorns but rich in street garbage.

"Nassau," said Cleary with disgust. His tongue showed white. "It's like the government raised the duty on penicillin and the whole city caught the clap."

"What on earth did you do with all your money?"

"Money. . . ?" he said, the last thing usually on Cleary's mind.

"Oh, the usual. It's all gone, except the Rubens. Live fast and make an attractive corpse. When I die I want to be buried in a baseball cap, polo shirt, and a pair of sneakers. Meanwhile, St. Jude will provide."

North had heard it all before, the Cleary penance delivered by a Peter who had disappointed his Christ.

"I've found the perfect island," said North.

"From which to solve the problems of the Third World, right?"

"Think of the Island for Science as a small body of land surrounded by rich blue opportunities. A seafarm, solar desalinators, superfast windmills. . . . Where else except in the Third World do they derive a hundred percent of their energy by burning diesel fuel—while the sun shines all day and the wind blows all night?" Opportunity was half the reason he sought an Island. The other half was to build a memorial to Heather and a refuge for Coby, the home she hadn't known for five years.

"You're an altruistic guy, Grant. You'll always be altruistic. That's why you'll get hurt someday."

But Cleary's grin showed he was pleased. He chewed the last of his Tums, feeling a warm hand on his heart. It was like the last time North started a company. The old Grant North was back, alive with the energy of conception, contagious with enthusiasm, following his dream to its logical and profitable conclusion. A memory flashed into Cleary's mind of North Scientific, of high morale and stunning dedication. We work two shifts, he used to tell potential customers and staff members (never "employees"). Two shifts. Same people.

Grant North too was remembering the instrument company. His focus was on the ideas themselves, how he had grown them and how on the Island he would grow them again like living cells into complex organs that could reproduce and give birth to philosophies, cultural revolutions, renaissances. Before they revolutionize the world, while they are still soft, warm, and pliable, ideas are yours alone. They become your lovers, and you theirs. They embrace you in the night like a gently purling river, working their restless passion, stirring, then rushing in a torrent, and rendering unbearable the long nights, the sleepless waits for tomorrow.

21 *Future Nightmares*

JOSEPHINE COPP and Sidney Rolle headed away from Coral Harbour toward Nassau, their rented Toyota rattling along on the left side of the road. A misty moon broke through a metallic curtain of early-April clouds and shown pale on Jo's face. What was she doing here, a white woman proficient in her prejudices, a radio reporter of death squads and gang rapes by macho secret police, huddled together with a Negro who wore a three-inch knife scar on his right cheek like a testimonial? Yet she had to admit he seemed decent enough with his steady eyes and open manner.

She was nervous not because Rolle was black, she decided, and certainly not because of this foreign city. She had been completely alone in far-worse places: the bowels of Havana, the cesspools of Port au Prince—and the slums of Chicago and Miami. Her anxiety arose from an intuition that differed from her brother's. Coby might not be capering around Europe with a mob of students. Most likely she had been murdered on the LCM along with Campbell and the Symeses. Jo's years of reporting had taught her that the hope of a parent is powerless before the potency of hate and greed. On the other hand, Grant never squandered his or anyone else's energy, and despite their past disagreements she took heart at the fury and conviction with which he led his Islanders.

She turned her examination inward and sank into remorse over her own excuses and postponements through the years that had distanced her from Coby. A reluctance to face her brother, the living in distant places, pressures of the job . . . Clichés, all of them. The truth was that she as well as Grant, and probably everyone else in the world, were amateurs at living.

Rolle stopped at an octagonal HALT sign where a squadron of fruit bats, lit by a street lamp, dive-bombed a field of mangoes. In front of the field, a dormant poinciana shuddered in a gust of wind and pointed hundreds of black claws at Jo. Heavy drops battered the car for a moment and then the rain fell in a torrent. Somewhere a dog howled. If she were in Chicago she would have said a spring frost was on the way. But here the only chill was in her heart.

THE RAINY fields on the outskirts of Nassau reminded Jo of a strange incident often recalled. Grant had come home on leave and they'd attended a Croatian picnic as they had done as children. It was a sprawling festival in a lakefront park where great slabs of lamb called *jagnje* turned on spits over slow fires, and the young people danced a *kola* or round dance. A cloudburst sent them scurrying to a stand of oak trees, and Grant made an astounding prophesy: he alone out of his entire recon company would emerge unhurt. No matter how dangerous the mission, she knew it was extremely rare for an entire company to be annihilated. At the time she dismissed it as guilt on Grant's part because he had been reassigned to the First Cavalry while his former reconnaissance company had been given the mad job of locating enemy troops by drawing their fire.

Incredibly, Grant North was right. Every man died or was wounded in the jungles of Vietnam. In the scientific way he had about him even then, he explained his prediction in terms of the two sides of his brain operating harmoniously in both digital and analog modes. Intuition, faster than step-by-step logic, can be more accurate when it comes to supposedly unsolvable problems—like those that herald technological breakthroughs . . . or future nightmares.

A lazier mind might have sought the answer in the supernatural. The incident started Jo on a lifelong study of how a human brain could process the staggering number of clues required to come to such a prediction. Training routines, casual conversations, troop movements, the weather, insights into soldiers' minds—how they would react in combat, their desires, their idiosyncrasies, their procrastinations—those and thousands of other factors somehow had been analyzed, weighted, and synthesized on both sides of his brain. Birds and fish do something like that when they navigate across the magnetic web of the planet. In proportion to the power of the human brain, Jo came to realize, Grant's prediction was no more exceptional than the flight of an arctic tern to Florida.

But as the years passed, Jo complained to Grant that he thought too much with his thalamus instead of his cortex. Her own intuition, modified by experience and logic, vanished in her brother's shadow. If his hunches were so damn potent, why hadn't it dawned on him that Heather had cancer while something might have been done? Why did he leave Coby alone so much? In her heart Jo carried a lingering resentment, made all the more irritating because in her mind she trusted her brother's instincts more than her own.

The Nassau rain stopped and the water ran off the shoulders of the road and soaked into the earth's sponge. Jo opened the window. Mother Butler's Mission loomed on the right behind a sign explaining the place as a venture in private charity. Then came the Carmichael Holiness Baptist Church, the Gospel Fellowship Church, the Church of God of the Prophecy, and Baccardi & Co. After all that church, she thought, a girl could use a drink.

Slowly the silence fell back on the night breeze.

"You always this quiet?" Rolle said.

"Just thinking."

"Yeah, I guess we all need to do a lot of that." He turned to her in the dim light and said, "Sure is a crazy country, this one, full of illusions."

"Meaning?

"Meaning that crazy things happen here next door to ordinary things. Once or twice a week, right-driving Americans crash their rented cars into left-driving Bahamians. The majority of these island people don't know how to swim. They hate fish. You think Coby's alive?"

A strange progression of thought, but then she realized Rolle had been pondering events as long as had she. If her American thoughts were linear, his Bahamian logic was oblique, like the root of a tree winding through soil. But that soil was fertile, saturated with promise, and if she had learned anything in life, it was that more than one path led to a single goal.

"Coby loved Paris," Jo said, "and when her friends went there to college, she wanted to go too. I'm almost afraid to find out if she's there, because if she's not, there's not much hope."

"Has Grant ever told you how he met Cleary, about the Obedience Experiments an' all?"

"Yes."

"Doesn't it make you think we might be having 'North thoughts' instead of our own? Doing what we're doing for no reason except that we're being obedient to authority?"

She laughed but felt the strength of his question. That very idea had bothered her more than once over a lifetime of being Grant North's sister. But she couldn't encourage dissention. "If there was *any* chance Coby was alive, we'd search for her, wouldn't we?"

"Of course."

"So tell me about the Bahamian craziness, the illusions."

He was quiet for a minute, then said, "These islands are surrounded by calm oceans—which are the most shark-infested waters in the world."

Grant had told her that Sidney Rolle was a modern heretic who believed in coral rock and wet oceans, and hated governments. Now she knew what he meant.

"The Bahama islands are a paradise for the tourists. They come here to make love and recreate themselves. The Bahamians, though . . . well, we don't find it all so damn wonderful. The Plague here is epidemic. We've got the worst drug, alcohol, and robbery rates in the world. The people hide from the government. This business of hiring non-Bahamians for magistrates so we 'don't have to judge each other' is a lot of bullshit thought up by Ransom to keep his judges on a leash. Democracy in this country is nothin' but a delusion. It's one-man rule here."

"Sidney, I've been fighting power like that. It's what I do. I broadcast about the governments in the region—including this one—and how they encroach on personal liberties, their prejudice against minorities, their two classes of citizenship, and so on. I know it's bad, but you make Ransom sound like a generalissimo in a banana republic."

"He's the father of our country, a gem."

"Now, Sid—"

"Maybe I ought to blame the laziness of the people, or the crops that won't grow in rocky soil. Or the guys who flood the place with dope. But isn't it the purpose of government to change all that? They make speeches about becoming self-sufficient in food, and then they won't even give us a permit to raise shrimp. The government says they want the Family Islands developed, but they won't give us permits to operate the Island."

Jo saw why her brother liked this man who could make human logic of rocks and trees, and float his thoughts on the air without trepidation.

"The Defenders raid the Island because a marijuana farm is under cultivation there. A *marijuana farm,* for crysake! Anyone dealing Smoke would be out of his gourd to grow the stuff on his own land. So why do the Defenders make that excuse? Because under the law they don't need a search warrant to hunt for drugs. The truth is they want Grant and the rest of us to go home so we don't penetrate their damn secrets, whatever they are."

They slowed behind the traffic on Baillou Hill Road, one of Nassau's main north-south arteries. The evolution of single-horse carriages into two-hundred horsepower American automobiles had clogged it with fat.

"What bars do the Defenders hang out in?" Jo asked.

"You want to go tonight?"

"Sure."

He smiled at her out of eyes as big as an owl's, eyes that said that any Bahamian, even one from the Family Islands, can find out anything in Nassau by asking. Without a word to her he drew up alongside a parked taxi and conducted a conversation in a dialect that she found totally incomprehensible. He thanked the taxi driver, and told her, "The officers have a club at the base. The enlisted men go Over the Hill."

"AWOL?"

Rolle laughed. "No, that means Grant Town, Delancey Town, or Bain Town—the poor communities south of the original Nassau, now part of it. They were the first areas of New Providence to be settled by freed slaves."

At Herbie's Inn in Bain Town, Herbie had a satellite antenna perched on the roof, and the gray-tiled building matched the drab colors of the RBDF fleet. Inside it was dark and thick with drinkers standing three deep at the bar under the thunder of a jukebox. The men were mostly Defenders in their early twenties, wearing blue uniforms in various stages of disarray that reminded Jo of the Ton-tons Macoutes. One Defender with stripes on his shoulder stared at her, and while never letting his eyes stray, picked up a phone at the bar and dialed a number. The phone call and the staring *could* be unrelated, she told herself, but she couldn't shake the comparison with the Haitian fascists.

Most of the females in the place were black, although a few white coeds on spring break from the States leaned against the juke or the bar, drinking beer from bottles and smiling at cruising Defenders out of cosmeticized faces like Grecian plaster masks. Lanky blacks flowed on the dance floor to exported rock or regional calypso while their North American college girls danced the steps instead of the beat, herons courting flamingoes.

A young man gave Jo his barstool and Rolle stood in back of her. Everyone was yelling at everyone else over the music, using sign language to buy each other beers, or bum a Rothman's, or pass a joint back and forth, and the air was heavy with tobacco and marijuana smoke. A beanpole of a man who wore his hair curled around small sticks like a Carib cannibal smiled at Jo out of a toothless mouth, pointed two fingers at his nose, and waited for her answer.

"No," she said, taken aback. "No . . . thanks."

He raised his eyebrows, evidently surprised. "Den how 'bout

ludes, ma'am? Kay-ludes. Dey cheap."

She shook her head no. A Defender, a quiet drunk, invited her to the dance floor. A four-piece band arrived and the music repeated the seamless rock of the jukebox, rattling the floor like near-miss artillery, then shifted to reggae, to soca, and finally to a sugary tune about a girl who ran nude on beaches washed by moonlight and honeysuckle. Jo could hear her partner's voice now for the first time, but he slurred the language so badly she couldn't understand him. Afterwards she was in demand and danced with others, fluid as water, pretending to be impressed by uniforms and rank, ignoring their barracks odors or the germicidal smells of their cheap cologne. She inquired about their "exciting jobs" and at the right time asked, "By the way, did you know a friend of mine who had been on a drug raid when a barge got shot up?" Most of them had heard about the incident, but no one responded to the bait about the "friend."

A noncom in a starched white uniform strolled up to Jo. His arm was full of oversized stripes in the British style, and his shoulder patch read RBDF MILITARY POLICE. At first she thought he was going to question her, but then she saw the two yellow rum drinks in his hands. They sat away from the bar in a two-place booth the size of a confessional, and talked about Nassau's new status as one of the ten highest-priced cities in the world. The noncom, whose name was Chief Albury, ventured a light handhold on the tabletop between ashtrays and metal chalices of rum drinks. Jo fought down an urge to extract her hand and wipe it on the paper tablecloth. Instead she left it there and encouraged him to boast of his position in the Force. In the bottom of his fourth drink, he said he knew about the raid on the landing craft, but nothing of Jo's mythical acquaintance.

As Jo rose from the booth to return to Rolle, a civilian in work clothes and open shirt with a shark's tooth hanging against his black chest, bumped into her and spilled some of her drink.

"Sorry," he mumbled through the crowd.

She had the impression that the collision was as deliberate as the phone call that had been made when she and Rolle arrived. She sat down again and wet a paper napkin to wipe the spots off her dress.

"Ah knows everybody in the Defence Force," Albury continued, ignoring the civilian. "It ma job ta know. I been in the Force since it started in 1976. Any chance yer frien' be a mopman?"

"Oh, you mean the Military Occupation Platoon? Yes, I believe he is."

His frown said he didn't care much for the elitism of the platoon. She interpreted the halfhearted thumping from his fingers as meaning that the force chief was deciding whether to express his inverted snobbery. Finally he stopped drumming and talked about how the MOP had closed in on themselves over the years until their half-dozen patrol boats and crews had become a separate force within the RBDF. He said a fat noncom had been whimpering around the base, for which he had been granted a "psycho leave." Force Chief Albury knew of the man only from his nickname.

"Which is?"

"What else?"

"I have to guess?"

"His name be Jelly Belly!" He chuckled.

She felt the pulse of the hunt beating in her ear. "Jelly Belly what?"

"Damned if Ah *know*."

"Where's he from?"

"Oh, he from one of de Fambly Islands okay."

"Which one?"

"Doan no. 'Leuthera or somewheres."

"You sure?"

"No."

"But you think it's Eleuthera?"

"Oh, Ah dunno. 'Leuthera, Exuma, Acklins, somewhere out dere. . . . Why?"

Though eager and exhilarated, Jo felt she had asked enough questions. "It doesn't matter," she said. "I'd better be getting back to my date."

"Ah'd sure like to see yuh again sometime, ma'am?"

"Sure," she said with a bright smile, tremendously thankful

for the clue. She drained the rest of her drink, and scribbled on a napkin the three-o-five area code and seven random digits.

At the bar the smoke in the room turned hazy-blue like swirling clouds before a storm, as Jo whispered her findings to Rolle. The band slowed, shifting to a banana calypso:

Daytime come and me wanna go home.
Lift six hand, seven hand, eight hand bunch,
Daytime come and me wanna go home.

Jo and Rolle danced, riding free on the relentless rhythm, separating and merging, in and out like boxers. Suddenly the smoke in the room took on a psychedelic blue mist that made it hard for Jo to breathe. Bending backwards in imitation of a limbo contortion, Rolle's bony knees grew grotesque and pointed like arrows to the ceiling. He advanced beat by beat until those terrible knees, like a skeleton's, straddled her legs. She couldn't move. Her feet were rooted in the dance floor, hardened in concrete. Other dancers pressed closer. She could smell the sweet liquored breath of the angry sons of slaves, the fear in her own perspiration. The guitar player strummed the heart out of his strings, its red liquid surging through the room, and the blood transposed into flames. The smoke thickened. Overwhelming acrid smoke . . .

Jo awakened outside, sitting on the curb with Rolle at her side telling her to inhale. Again. Again.

Finally her head cleared. "I'm sick. All that marijuana smoke in the air—"

"Maybe," said Rolle. "Or maybe someone slipped crank in your drink."

Jo craved logic in her zone of reality, but she was discovering that reality is a step or two beyond logic. She had discovered something else too, the definition of "a bad trip."

The door to Herbie's opened and Chief Albury, solicitous and sympathetic, came out to the curb holding a mostly empty glass in a handkerchief. "Ah believes dis drink—"

The door slammed against the outer wall, hard. The civilian who had bumped into Jo, his eyes wide, shark tooth swinging, was wielding a barstool like a feather and looking here and there. He spotted Jo and lunged.

At the last moment, Jo saw him and bent away fast. The barstool broke apart against the concrete.

In one smooth movement, Rolle picked up a severed leg from the stool and slammed it broadside against the assailant's face, breaking his nose. At the same time, Chief Albury expertly pinned the arms of the man, who snarled at Jo, blood and tears streaming down his face.

"Ah kin smell de meth yuh put in dis gal's drink," Chief Albury said. "Ah'll be keepin' de glass fer de evi*dence*." He held the civilian with one hand while reaching for handcuffs in his rear pocket. "Why yuh do dot, mon? Why yuh wanna hurt dis pretty gal?"

Defenders had been oozing out of Herbie's, and now stood cheering or jeering on the sidewalk, poking each other in the ribs, taking rhythmic sips from their beer bottles to the acid rock of a portable ghetto blaster. Three Defenders, ties off, shirt tails out, Goombay-shuffled down the street, playing catch with empty bottles, keeping three of them in the air like jugglers. A military-police car drove by slowly. The enlisted men who were out of uniform quickly stuffed their shirts into their pants, and the owner of the ghetto blaster turned it off. Rolle could have sworn that the officer sitting next to the driver—bearded, massive, his captain's cap touching the roof of the car—was Carlos St. Gregory.

A squad car pulled up with a short blast of siren.

"Here come de Royal fuzz!"

The driver of the MP car showed palms up to the police as if to say, "this is a civilian problem." Then the MP car seethed off into the night.

"Yuh see dot ape try ta smash dis blondie?"

"Hey, muddafucka! Get yuh ass back to Abaco!"

"Yuh gotta admire de speed of old mon Albury. Look how fast he cuff dot perp, drunk as he be!"

The trio that had been playing catch with beer bottles started up again once the MP car was gone. *"Awwwwrrrrr!"* cried the catcher as a bottle smashed another he already held. The injured Defender lifted his arm high, blood streaming down his uniform.

Two cops threw open the doors of their squad car and ran toward him, guns drawn. The other beer throwers held their sides and laughed. *"Look a dot!* Will yuh *look* at how fast doze fuzz kin *move!"*

The police stopped and headed sheepishly toward Albury, who ignored them and the sideshow, and shoved a knee in the back of his captive. "I said why you *do* dot, mon?"

Handcuffed in back, the civilian was having trouble seeing through the blood in his eyes. In pain, he swiveled his head to Albury and said in a loud voice, "She de sister of Grant North, de drug *lord!* Ma brudder an' his kids are *dead* 'cause of him!"

"Who in de hell yuh be anyways?" asked Albury.

By now the blood had spread over the man's neck and shirt, and was clotting on his hairy face in black welts. Rolle knew how it felt to have your hands locked behind you with a knee in your back, and he almost felt sorry for the guy. Until he heard who he was.

"My name," the man answered through a mouth covered with gore, "is Bill Symes."

22 *The Boat Girls*

TRAVELING by ferry from one Bimini island to another, Grant North examined the backwaters in case Coby had been assaulted and abandoned. Day after day, he returned to the same police, the same street urchins, the same taxi drivers, airport personnel, private pilots, habor masters, and the girls who hang around docks.

Like Xaviera, these ocean hitchhikers are mostly white and in their twenties or thirties; they swab decks, tend lines, and cook for their captains. Scraggly strays, they inhabit every port of the Bahamas, seeking freedom and carrying their life's possessions in backpacks. Most are willing to climb into the captain's bunk if he asks, caring little either way, and they often get bored and leave without notice at some other port. In spite of Jo's reproach, North had expected to find someone here who remembered seeing Coby.

Eventually he did.

On the harbor pier, two American girls were lounging in the shade of a roofed-over display board on which stuffed fish were mounted together with their names and descriptions. Armed with a six-pack, North stopped to talk to them and offered them a beer.

"Never refused a cold beer in my life," one of the girls said. Only a few years older than Coby, she would have been pretty if she took a bath. The other one, equally dirty, was the same age but chubby. She took a can of beer and said nothing.

North fished out his picture of Coby. "This is my daughter," he said. "Have you seen her?"

She glanced at the photograph. "What's the matter, Daddy, your little girl ain't old enough to be on her own?"

"It's not that. We can't find her."

"Of course not," said the boat girl. "Maybe she doesn't want to be found."

North took the photo out of her hands and showed it to the second girl. "Please look carefully. Have you seen her?"

The chubby girl took a long pull on the beer can and examined the picture. "Yeah, I seen her. At least I think I did. I remember that long hair made her look more a tourist than a crew girl." She waved the picture near her friend's face. "Alice, don't you remember her?"

Alice steadied the picture and said, "I think so."

Had she said anything else, North was ready to shake her until her memory improved. But her response made him consider the notion that these two might be trying to set him up, to encourage him with lies so they could ask for money. "When?" he said.

"When did we see her?"

"Yes."

"Oh shit, quite a while ago. A few weeks anyway."

The chubby girl agreed. "That's right. I remember her 'cause it seemed so unusual she would be with the kind of people she was with."

"What was so unusual?"

"You know. She was so clean-cut . . ." She glanced around to make sure no one was listening before she whispered, "to be with a bunch of niggers."

North's heart raced. "What did the black people look like?"

"An older guy in a captain's hat and his shirt open to his goodies, and two light-brown teenagers. And some white people, I think. A stud—maybe an Englishman and maybe a girl. Or maybe they was bystanders. I don't know. I ain't no detective."

"Do you know where they went?"

Alice answered, "Jesus, mister. How would we know that? People around here are like shit. They just happen."

Trudging back to town, North's elation died fast. The fact that the boat girls remembered Coby proved nothing except that she and the *Half Fast* crew had stopped at North Bimini. Whether Coby left the LCM here and hitched a boat ride or bought passage on a plane to the States was still unknown. He questioned others he met on the street until the sun fizzled into the Gulf Stream.

At his hotel he called Visa and other credit-card companies to see whether Coby had bought anything. She had not.

But a cryptic radio message had been left for him:

Tomorrow, early as possible,
Great Snake airport. —Jo

23 *The Eleutherian Adventurers*

AS SOON as North's charter flight landed, he met Jo and Rolle outside the customs-immigration building, where Jo excitedly told him about Jelly Belly. Like most such facilities, there was a wooden box on the wall for people to pick up messages. North left a sealed note in it for Cleary, and the three took off immediately to search for Jelly Belly.

Her twin Cessna-310 was spacious enough for a long flight, and Jo headed down the long Bahama chain toward the southeastern out-islands, planning a stop at the radio station where she worked. Three hours later, east of central Cuba and north of the Dominican Republic, they came to the end of the Bahama chain where the once-Bahamian, still-British Turks & Caicos Islands loomed ahead, parched and brown. They landed, refueled, and took a boat from North Caicos to an area halfway to Providenciales. Here on the leeward side of the reef, mangroves and gumbo-limbos concealed the maverick station of Radio Free Caribbean run by manager-engineer Tomás Rovira. The building was an innocuous concrete cube painted green to blend into the bush. The antenna that poked above the tallest cypresses had been nestled into furry casuarinas and disguised with artificial foliage to make it look like a thin sapling.

172

Radio Free Caribbean—small, underfinanced, unsponsored by any government—was modeled after Radio Martí in Miami, which had been named for the Cuban revolutionary hero Jose Martí in order to infuriate Fidel Castro. When Castro started jamming the Martí broadcasts, a group of exiles established the new transmitter to reach not only Cuba but also the other West Indian dictatorships, which had become as incensed as Castro at the implication of the word "Free" in the name.

Tomás Rovira, thin and tall, was a bachelor with a complexion like Swiss cheese and a ready smile for North and Rolle when Jo introduced them. As dedicated to his job as Jo had been before the crisis over her niece, he rarely saw the sunshine, working alone in the station twelve hours a day, broadcasting political messages written by himself and his confederates throughout the Caribbean. It was clear that he wanted Jo back, but recognized the value of her investigations to their mutual goal of uprooting corruption.

"I have many tapes for you," Rovira said. The spark in his lilting Hispanic voice divulged his affection for her. "You listen to all these tapes?"

"I don't know what else to do."

She finished going through her mail that was brought in every day from North Caicos, put the tapes in her handbag, and motioned her companions toward the door.

"You don't stay?" Rovira looked disappointed.

"I'm afraid not."

Rovira shook North's and Rolle's hands and placed an arm around Jo, obviously hesitant, standing rigid as a priest at a funeral. He tried to force his mouth into a smile but there was no smile in his eyes when he said, "Our allies in Paris at Radio Free Europe send a message that definitely your niece is not in Europe. Through Immigration they check Madagascar as well. She is not there either."

Unknown to each other, Jo, North, and Rolle had been counting on Coby being out of the Bahamas and out of the United States, for no other answer could mean that she was safe. Their futile wish. Their little girl. Their disaster. The message from Europe fell in cold silence like a meteoroid impacting the moon.

ISLAND HOPPING up the Bahama chain, the trio listened to the terse communications of Defender patrols. North's mind wandered, expanding his hope for Coby to include amnesia, sickness, or kidnapping.

The Defender dialog was different from the usual radio banter of locals ordering supplies, freighter captains announcing times of arrival, or cruise passengers calling their brokers. The broadcasts directed patrol captains to locate stranded yachtsmen, interdict smugglers, or deliver government officials to out-island installations. Once in a while North heard a scrambled message, but it didn't matter. The transmissions he wanted would come disguised but in plain language, for the Defenders would know that any coded communication would be entered in Coast Guard records and deciphered at Langley. Despite the screening effected by Rovira's voice-actuated recorder, the sheer number of broadcasts was crushing, and North wondered how they possibly could listen to them all. Somehow they had to narrow the search by knowing what, or whom, to look for.

The late-afternoon sun cast the Cessna's shadow across the cool colors of the shallow sea. North switched off the tape player and slumped down under his Gauguin hat, seeking sleep in the hum of the engines and the fleece of the clouds. He needed sleep to be alert when they landed, but it eluded him as he knew it would. It was action he craved, not these parodies of action: flying here and there like a whirlwind, listening to tapes for clues, taking boats to strange harbors, and talking, talking. . . . With the single exception of the elusive Jelly Belly, there were no leads, no *targets*, nothing tangible to attack. He opened his eyes to Jo, intent on her instruments, and he was thankful she was on his side.

"Well, anyway, it's good to be away from Nassau," Rolle said, leaning over the front seat.

"You hate the place so much?" said Jo cheerfully.

"I guess no out-islander likes it," North interjected, "except maybe me."

Rolle said, "The Bible according to Godfrey Knowles hath it that 'if you die with sin on your soul you skipeth Purgatory and goeth directly to Nassau.' Nassauvians don't care about out-islanders. I doubt if the average guy in the RBDF ever talks to another Defender from a different island."

"Thank God it's a small country," Jo said.

"Small as far as countries go. But it's still a lot of ground to cover," North said.

"We've got more population than Greenland, Bermuda, the Cayman Islands, Aruba, Anguilla, Antigua, Gibraltar, and fifty other countries," Rolle said proudly. "There are a lot of places where Coby could be stranded—seven hundred cays and two thousand islets." He gave the impression that he knew every one of them, and he probably did. "On the other hand, Jelly Belly would most likely be on one of the twenty-nine major islands where a third of the quarter-million Bahamians live. Two-thirds live in Nassau."

The three fell silent. They knew it would be an enormous search, finding a man in all those places from his nickname only. In her mind Jo kept repeating the name Jelly Belly until it crumbled into the reef below, as indifferent to their concerns as to the waves that eroded it. Images of Coby shimmered on the ocean and fluttered Jo's heart as if it would break.

"Sure I'm good in math," Coby had told her a few months after her mother died. She had just started high school and she could hear the pulse of her life ringing in her ear like the surf along a distant shore. "But I'd rather spend my life with animals. I want to be like you, Aunt Jo. You're a woman and yet *you* run around to all kinds of dangerous countries. Maybe I'll go to Africa and study white tigers or ring-tailed lemurs."

"About the only place lemurs live is Madagascar."

"Okay, Madagascar then," she said. "Ever been there?"

"Yes. It's full of Arabs and Indonesians who speak French."

"I'm *taking* French! Maybe I should go there instead of Paris. I want to go *everywhere!*"

Coby had proclaimed it like an explorer finding a new land, as indeed she had, but to Jo flying over the Indies that had suffered the genocides of the *conquistadores*, it was remembered like an epitaph.

OVER THE COURSE of a week they questioned people on a dozen

of the populated islands, which were trisected at Great Exuma by the Tropic of Cancer. They landed on Mayaguana, Acklins, Long Island, Great Exuma, and Rum Cay. In the air between Cat Island and San Salvador, where Columbus first landed five hundred years ago, North heard a simple message on the tape:

> *Munnings* proceed to Governor's Harbour.
> Lend assistance to U.S. Coast Guard.

"Jo, let's skip San Salvador," North said. "The action seems to be in Governor's Town."

"How old is that message?" asked Jo.

North removed the tape and read the date Rovira had written on it. "A week ago," he said.

She nodded agreement, consulted her charts, and changed course. With the sun almost down, Jo was playing it close because out-island runways have no lights. But at dusk, a narrow strip of land sprang from the ocean pastels like a preying mantis in profile. Swooping into Cape Eleuthera at the tail of the mantis, they saw in the harbor a forest of masts over gleaming white yachts: the affluent in eternal fiesta. Eleuthera was more than a hundred miles long and mostly less than a mile wide. It derived its name, according to Rolle, from the Greek word meaning "freedom." The first permanent colony in the Bahamas, the island was settled in 1647 by Englishmen who called themselves "the Eleutherian Adventurers."

They landed at Governor's Harbour where they found the inhabitants still gossiping about last week's U.S.-Bahamian drug bust. The frigates and helicopters and smuggler ships had vanished like the last tide, and there was no sign of the *Munnings.* They made their way by hired boat to the other towns: Upper and Lower Bogues, Gregory Town, Spanish Wells, and finally the jewel of the Eleutherias, Harbour Island, where the beach sand is bright pink and the people are descended from freed slaves.

They visited the bars, whose bartenders laughed and broke into calypso verses without notice, and they drank and talked with the locals, and shot pool or slapped dominos on scarred tables as if they were on vacation. The smoke was thick in these places, but at least it came from burning tobacco. One night they entered the high-priced hotel area on Harbour Island disguised as affluent tourists, North and Rolle in sport jackets, and Jo wearing high heels and a sheer blouse with a silver skirt split in front like two wide petals. No one in any of the hotel lounges had heard of Jelly Belly, and gradually they worked their way to less-pretentious bars, North on one side of the street and Rolle and Jo on the other.

In a native pub, one of those well-lighted and casual places where you get your own drinks and leave the money on the bar, a candyman materialized in front of Jo. Emaciated and grinning out of missing front teeth, he settled alone at the end of the counter and made the familiar parody of the victory sign to his nose. When she nodded no, he pointed to a small coral head decorating the bar. A rock of crack? She shook no again. He extended his two fingers vertically and crossed them midway with a finger from his left hand, forming an unmistakable "H."

A middle-aged derelict, light-skinned and slovenly, watched the miming figure and Jo carefully, while pretending to play a game on a TV monitor in which extraterrestrials fluttered and grunted in Japanese. He shot a glance at Rolle who was shooting pool, and shuffled over to Jo's table.

"Ah doubt dot mon peddlin' Prep-H," he said, laughing at his own joke as the pusher stumbled out the door looking weary. "Dot be medicine fer life's emotional hemor*rhoids!*"

"Why do so many of these pushers have no teeth? Narco-carries?"

"What. . . ?" The drifter kept swiveling his head, watching Rolle, watching the exits.

"Well, he certainly was open about having heroin for sale," said Jo, encouraging this man to talk to her, hoping for anything.

"Dey call it 'smack,' or 'scag.' Dot way it doan seem too bad."

"Whatever they call it, if he's selling, someone's buying."

"You kin buy anything here. Crank, ice, fry daddies, swamp juice."

Jo thought she was up on her subculture slang. Crank was an upper, usually methamphetamine; ice was crystal meth; and fry daddies were crack-laced cigarettes. But swamp juice? Wasn't that gin and fruit punch?

"You wouldn't think they'd need dope on an island as lovely as this," she said.

"Some folks need de stuff. Like Jelly Belly, f'rinstance."

"You know him?" Jo said it as indifferently as possible while trying to keep her heart in her chest.

"Ah hear yuh airin' de name around. Yes'm. Ah think Ah do knows who you means. He a big slob of a mon."

"I'll get my friend and we'll go see him."

"Hole on dere jus' one minute, Miss. Leave yer frien' out of it."

"Why?"

He looked around furtively. "Jus' you come alone." His eyes said that he knew things, but was holding back to test her determination.

"Okay," she said, yielding safety for the hunt. "Any way you want it."

"Meet me out in de bok an' Ah takes you dere. Jus' you, Miss. Ah doan want nobody ta see us leave together." He glanced around some more, and left the building by the front door.

Jo caught Rolle's eye, signalled she was leaving, and ambled out the back door into an unpaved alley. Littered with soggy paper, broken bottles, and splintered wood from a crate, the alley was bordered by rows of casuarinas trees and royal palms. The drifter appeared, smiling furtively. Jo started to say something when suddenly he grabbed her mouth with one powerful hand, forcing her to the ground, and shoved the other hand under the petals of her skirt. He was stronger than he looked. She couldn't breathe, couldn't cry out.

But she could bite.

She clamped her teeth hard onto the base of his middle finger, tasting the blood. He jerked his hand for a brief moment, long enough for her to focus her frustration and outrage into a colossal scream.

Rolle was there in seconds. He came up in back of the assailant, unseen by him and facing Jo, holding an unopened beer bottle by the neck. Without a word, he brought the bottle crashing over the head of the man, who went down fast and crumpled into a mass of foam and brown shards. Rolle turned the body face up, and shoved the jagged bottle into the unconscious face until blood soaked the man's face.

"Sidney, don't. . . !" Jo gasped.

Rolle was about to cut the man again, when Grant North, rushing toward his sister's screams, ran into the alley. He seized Rolle's wrist, and for a long moment the two were frozen in isometric deadlock. North understood Rolle's desire to lash out, but this. . . ?

"*SIDNEY!*" North shouted, as though waking him up. "That's enough."

Slowly, Rolle relaxed his muscles. His eyes came into focus, lingering first on Jo, then on North, and finally on his victim. "Don't worry, I missed his eyes. A face full of scars," he said with no apology, "might warn off the bastard's next victim."

THAT NIGHT the three of them stretched out on their hotel lounge chairs over an ivy lawn. The beach glowed bright pink in the moonlight and the night air was heavy with oleander. Jo watched the traveler palms sway their banana-like leaves in the breeze. North poured milky Gin Grin over ice into three tall glasses, and they clinked glasses, studiously avoiding the topic of Rolle's assault on the would-be rapist.

"I used to think of myself as self-sufficient," she said, "in Cuba, Haiti, Dominica, Jamaica—places with governments worse than the Bahamas."

"There are no worse governments," said Rolle, "because Ransom has the world thinking the Bahamas is so benign."

"Amen," said North. "And nothing's as it seems in the Bahamas, right Sidney?"

"What are you talking about," Jo said.

"I don't believe your rapist acted on his own. I saw St. Gregory in a bar across the street, drinking alone."

"Sure it was him?"

"Is there anyone else on this planet who looks like St. Gregory? I was debating whether to go over to him when I heard you scream."

"The son of a bitch is everywhere!" said Rolle. "I'm sure I saw him in Nassau when Jo had the run-in with William Symes."

"If St. Greg is behind all this," said Jo, "why does he use these people to assault me? Why doesn't he just pour gasoline down our throats and be done with it?"

"Governments exist to cheat, rob, and murder," Rolle said, "but these days everybody is watching and they have to do it with care. Things used to be more direct. Like when the government killed my father."

"Kill your father! Why?" asked Jo with compassion.

Rolle rose from his chair and looked out across the flat-calm sea at the pinpoint lights of boats. "Dad had his own trawler. For years he roamed the Bahamas down to Cuba, which is where he met my mother. One day a Cuban MiG fired rockets at a Bahamian gunboat and a fishing trawler. The trawler was my dad's."

"Me lo siento muchisimo," she said, and her pale-blue eyes said that she truly was sorry. "But why blame the Bahamian government?"

"Because it was the start of the narco-war."

"But that was before Ransom, even before Independence."

"Yes, but not before Castro."

"You think Ransom's in it with Castro?" said North.

"It wouldn't surprise me. They're two rats in a nest. Both viciously competitive, both illegitimate. You know they both cuddled fascism in their youth? It's common knowledge that Ransom was thrown out of law school for committing some sort of felony. And Castro used to walk around campus displaying *La Lucha.*"

"La Lucha?" said Jo, "The Struggle?"

"Yeah, you probably know it better by its German name. *Mein Kampf.*"

For five years Jo had been haranguing on the air about Castro-sponsored drugs without even having heard of the Bahamas connection, and now she had it. Or did she? Rolle had given no evidence of the P.M.'s complicity. Being illegitimate made him a bastard, not a criminal.

She breathed the fragrance of frangipani bordering the porch.

It was the flower they made into leis in Hawaii, and it smelled like honeysuckle, but sweeter, more cloying, more seductive, like Sidney Rolle. Did the analogy hold? The flower was poisonous.

North finished his drink and said goodnight. *To leave us alone?* Jo wondered, amazed at her feelings for this black man. The air drew over them like a blanket, the perfume of the flowers mingling with the caviar of sea organisms abandoned by the ebbing tide. Tamarind fronds whispered like feathers. You could imagine the traveler palms hoarding their quart of water in each hollow stalk and advancing their shoots centimeter by centimeter under the carpet of ivy where she sat looking at Sidney Rolle.

And you could imagine Cigarettes and Scarabs offshore, filled to the gunwales with dope and thundering without running lights toward the Florida shore.

Rolle was leaning on the porch railing, watching the bright diamonds bobbing gently on the sea. She wondered if this pagan, whose life flowed with the sea, who lived among the molecules of the earth, remembered his father as often as she remembered hers, or with the same sense of loss.

Instead, she asked, "You believe in God, Sidney?"

"If I did I'd have to blame Him for murdering my father. . . Unless you think of the ocean and the stars and the coral rock as God. I believe in *them* because they're real."

The clouds had dissolved and a billion stars came out, stars that Rolle could believe in, thought Jo, even though many of them were *not* real, having exploded and died long before man evolved on this planet. She felt his hand on her shoulder, warm and sturdy. He moved closer, reached his other arm around her waist, and examined her face carefully as if memorizing each feature. She tasted his lips, sweet lips with a trace of salt, the same as a white man's lips, durable and carnal like the sea itself. She kept her eyes open so she could see how his nose nestled against hers, how his scar flashed purple and brown on his cheek, how his mouth pressed hungrily against her lips.

She told herself to stop this voyage toward interracial love, a trip she never thought she would begin. Wait until she understood him—and herself—better. What had he been like as a child? Had he ridden his bike no-handed, carried books for his first girl, camped out in the rain with whatever they call the Boy Scouts in this country? How did he get that damn scar on his cheek like some student swordsman in the last century? Why had he never married? This cursed passion-plagued island of freedom with its smiling tourists and singing bartenders, its jasmine and jeweled sky, its frangipani and feathered fronds . . . was enough to make you wither in your resolve, ignore your mission, make mistakes, do things you didn't want to do.

He bent closer for a longer kiss, but she pulled away from him and stood up abruptly.

She said nothing, listening to her heart beat, to the whispering fronds. Finally she found words she felt would be reasonable, if not reasoned. "Sid, what you told me about your father is the first time you've said *anything* personal. . . . It's that—and something else. The way you cut that man's face. There is rage in you, Sidney, and it scares me."

Her soft hair and perceptive eyes, her faint perfume, the whisper of soft flesh under that silver skirt combined to thump his heart like a drum. He struggled against each breath of the sea, each rustle of the tamarind, each twinkle of the stars. He was a traveler palm, he knew, destined to sample love like moist soil, forever moving on to other places in the night.

It had been that way throughout his life, only worse.

24 *ORIGINS: the Pagan*

TWENTY YEARS AGO, before Independence and before the bankruptcies closed the sprawling Great Snake Resort two miles from the village, DC-3s landed tourists twice weekly from Ft. Lauderdale. The eighteen-hole golf course flowed like a green sea around the winter homes of North American businessmen and retirees. Goats from the village roamed freely over the island, getting in the way on the fairways or tailing the British salesmen who pursued the tourists. And Sidney Rolle first embraced his rage. Following his father's murder, the rage ravaged the place inside his body where as a child he had imagined his soul shimmered like a wide fluorescent tube. Now he wasn't sure he had a soul, though he knew the fury inside him had to erupt.

Six girls stepped off the DC-3, sorority girls from northeastern schools coming into heat, eager to prove their non-prejudice to the downtrodden black man. They and others like them had been arriving during spring break and the summer months, dressed in high suede heels and overpriced jeans or fur jackets during the winter holidays. The daughters of the golf-course families, they claimed they were socialists, said "Copen-hah-gen" for "Copenhagen," and bragged to each other about the Danes or the Frenchmen they'd slept with on their last vacation. Rolle held the keys to one of the sixty expensive homes on the other end of the island from the village, a place he looked after when its owner was absent. He drove the girls there in his old Subaru, the seven of them packed so tightly together he had to operate the shift between the legs of one, who cooed over her shoulder to those in the back seat:

"Sidney is a young Poitier under that beard!"

Rolle glanced at himself in the rearview mirror. Maybe he did look like some actor with his green beret, fatigue shirt, and pirate loop in his left ear.

When they got to the house he turned on the well pump, opened the drapes onto a living room wide as a river, and roamed around plugging in three TV sets, refrigerators, and other kitchen appliances he coveted for his mother. The girls tumbled onto a semicircular barge of connected couches where one of them rolled a roach like a steamboat captain. She sucked the first cloud of cannabis from it and passed it with her saliva to the others. They lit dozens of them, using a gold pin for the final drag. Rolle found himself sitting between them on the curved couches, seven equals under the law strung out on Smoke and gin, thanking their gods that there were dope and booze in the world and that they had both. One of the girls ran her hand over his neck. Another fondled him through his pants, announcing to the others each stage of his enlargement, pretending to be a ringmaster announcing the high-wire act: "It walks, it talks, it climbs so high it can almost see her . . . *hole* your seats, folks!" For these girls, the pride of their posh families, it was a circus that held no more meaning than a trapeze stunt. If Rolle had been less high and his passions less confused, he would have been humiliated, as he was in the morning. But the next night he returned and this time took them upstairs one at a time. In a parody of passion he and each girl would fornicate fast like horses. Then the girl would sit on the bed and smoke and drink until the next arrived. Each of them stayed to watch, murmur, caress, and laugh throaty noises until the seven, stoned and spent, sprawled on the bed like a litter of puppies.

The semiweekly air flights became Rolle's personal supply caravan, the pastel sea his bait, the black race his weapon. It wasn't sex that drove Sidney Rolle but smoldering rage. Rage against the

Cuban government for killing his father with no more concern than swatting a sandfly, rage against the Bahamian government for ignoring the murder. The rage burst into flame whenever one of those supercilious white girls used him like a roach, sucking him dry for their thrills so they could smirk at each other and tell their friends back home they'd experienced a real black buck. Rolle pillaged their red lips, their slender ankles in spike heels, their torsos in silks. He saw the skirts they wore as funnels to their vaginas, into which he poured his venom. If what they did to him was exploitation, there was a name for what he did to them too. Rape. Invited rape, non-felonious rape to be sure, but rape nonetheless because he intended vengeance instead of passion. Even then, Rolle understood the difference and marveled at the insensitivity of these girls who could feel lust for him where he felt for them only . . . what? Not aggressive sexuality, but sexual aggression.

Independence brought inflation, bankruptcies, and unemployment to the Bahamas, and understanding to Rolle. He realized he was passing through life plugging his penis like an umbilical cord into white women. He came to see himself as his father might have seen him—worse than a prostitute who did it, at least, for money—and he liked not what he saw.

So he stopped.

He did not substitute a drinking problem. Or snort White Lady. Or spend years in introspection or psychoanalysis. He just stopped plucking flower girls from the Great Snake garden. An abandoned boat, which he re-lapped with native lignum vitae, started him commercial fishing. Working alone, he discovered while cleaning fish that most of the red snapper had shrimp in their stomachs, and he learned to spot the transparent crustaceans concealed among the sprigs of seaweed. There he would stop trolling, toss overboard a sea anchor like a miniature parachute, and lower the hydraulic lines with their multiple hooks to the six-hundred foot bottom where the giant snapper live in cold water.

An exaltation of motion befell him gradually. It came first when he saw a flying fish glide over the surface. It came again as he watched his wire lines, smooth as marlin, hum off their reels in an oiled precision like the earth itself, savoring the thought of an inch of wood separating him from deep water. The first strike of the morning, the snapper coming up two or three at a time, became an erotic pleasure. His arms and shoulders grew hard as he practiced concise movement, working the reels until the fish or the sun quit, whichever happened first. On the way back to Great Snake Cay he would steer with a line tied from wheel to toe so he could clean fish with both hands and throw the entrails to the careening gulls. Manta rays six feet across, like supple flying saucers, glided to the surface and grabbed what the birds missed. Rolle became one with the sea animals, the vast sky, the rolling ocean. Salt air and snapper guts, snappy as vinegar, intoxicating as gin.

When ashore, he stayed in the village and repaired his equipment or read books. And when the white girls came slumming and sidled up to him at his boat, he waited until they spoke first. Then he would stammer in a dull creole filled with "yes mums" and "no mums" and "dese" and "doze" while the boys hanging around snickered and the girls left to seek livelier prey.

One night after drinking too much in the Grave Yard Inn, he lumbered out under a moonless night toward the nearby house he shared with his widowed mother, a seamstress. The other drinkers at the Inn rattled off in their cars, leaving Rolle alone with the stars. Shirtless under a leather vest, the breeze cooled his alcohol-heated body and whispered through the earring in his left ear. The pool of light at the Inn's entrance shrunk like a spit of sand from a moving boat as he made his way down the asphalt road no wider than an alley. The moon had passed its last quarter, making it hard to see the shapes stirring in the buttonwoods at the side of the road. Coming closer he saw two Caucs venting their beer in the brush, tourists from Florida or New York—or Siberia for all he cared. They were the same to Rolle, places where you didn't want to go.

A shuffling sound reached him from beyond the soft boundary of rum. Suddenly there loomed before him a stout man wearing a T-shirt. Rolle heard from behind, *"I got 'im, Red!"* and he took a blow to the center of his back as his arms were wrenched upwards behind him. The stout man, a redhead, snapped open a six-inch switchblade, and stood with his legs apart like a landsman on his first sea voyage.

Half-drunk, Rolle wondered where the illegal blade had come from. Had they bought a switchcomb through a mail-order house and replaced the comb with a razor, the way the village teenagers do? A knee pressed against his back, and those useless thoughts vanished in a confusion of alcohol and adrenaline.

The razor fluttered, flashing an inch from Rolle's eyes, so fast he could hear the *swishhh* and *slashhh* through the air like a barber imitating a mechanical scissors. Red's T-shirt read, ES MEJOR EN LAS BAJAMAS, but he was no Hispanic.

"Nig, Ah jus' want you to know before you depart this hea earth what's fuckin' happenin'. This blade is for Candy Lucas!"

The man's drawl, thick as molasses, savage as the Klan, identified him to Rolle as coming from that stretch of the continent that Sherman blackened. Whenever Rolle used to go to the States, his brother, an educated man, had warned him about the boys with the rabid genes: rednecks, he maintained, have earned their high-blood. But *here*! What on earth were they doing in the Bahamas?

"Candy who?" The sound leapt from Rolle's throat in a barely controlled panic.

"You're Sidney Rolle, ain't ya?"

"There's some mistake—"

"*You're* the mistake!"

With each flash of the blade, Rolle smelled his own fear like a spoiled fish. The anesthetic of alcohol was wearing off, leaving him trembling, breathing loud, racing through his past sins while Satan sat on a coral boulder and grinned. He didn't even know whom his death would avenge, or why these men wanted him to die this way, right here, tonight.

He couldn't bend or turn with the knee in the small of his back. All he could do was watch the knife, knowing he would remember always the silver blade and the T-shirt floating like milk on the black night.

"Candy Lucas had your nigger baby, and you don't even remember."

"I don't *know* her!"

"This'll help you remember."

The blade slashed deep into Rolle's right cheek, cutting through to the teeth and laying open a wide flap. He stuck his tongue right out of the side of his face. In the dim starlight, blood streamed black down his beard and shirt and onto the asphalt like used motor oil.

Red hesitated, perhaps thinking of his own mortality or the penalty for murder in a nation of blacks. He wiped the blade on Rolle's shirt with exaggerated care, folded it into the handle, and returned it to his pocket. Before leaving and while his accomplice strengthened his grip on Rolle's arms, he made hammers of his fleshy paws and slammed them into Rolle's midsection in a rapid punching-bag cadence. Rolle slid to the ground, tasting blood, writhing, finally slumping unconscious, his autonomic nervous system taking over the job of gasping for air.

Rolle didn't remember dragging himself home that night past the chickens that must have squawked and up the porch steps. He came awake hearing his mother's "¡Jesucristo!" She positioned him under the parchment shade of a bright lamp, knelt on the bare floor before him, and began to sew. His only anesthetic was the alcohol he had consumed. She blotted the blood, and when the sandflies interfered with her work, blew on the wound to scatter them, murmuring, "¡No hay que irte al cantina! ¡No irte. . . !" Her tools were soap and water, an ordinary sewing needle, and brown carpet thread. She tied each suture separately, stitching from the outside of the cheek into the mouth and out again across the wound as if mending a baseball. The seamstress worked methodically until the sun rose over the rocks in a jet of fire, then staggered into the early morning, scattering the chickens, and foraged in the bush. In her kitchen, a separate building in the yard, she crushed and boiled aloe sap and jumbie bead over a bottled-gas stove, making a poultice. She came back to her son and taped it to his wound.

The next day, wearing the poultice like an emblem of shame, turning his head often because it hurt to shift his eyes, Sidney Rolle inquired at Immigration about his assailants. No one there remembered a redheaded American and companion leaving the island by air. Could they have departed Great Snake Cay by boat?

Every day Señora Rolle rotated with a tweezers each of eighteen loops of carpet thread, six to the inch, so the sutures wouldn't fester into the flesh. She also removed his earring, which he never wore again. The wound healed with no more of a scar than an out-island doctor might have produced, had one been in residence at the time.

Searching the carnal procession of his memory, Rolle could remember nothing of Candy Lucas or any of the girls' faces, much less their names. He considered at length the concept of "his baby." Would the boy or girl look like Rolle, act like Rolle, develop similar talents, weaknesses? He returned to hauling fish from the purple depths, thinking of the knife attack with biblical profundity, as Elijah's sacrifice that would yield "a little cloud out of the sea like a man's hand."

The snapper that season seemed not to school anymore and each month's fishing became worse than the last. For long hours he would sit idle in the heaving boat, never bored with his gods of sea and wind. Yet he felt the pain of his exile and missed the fellowship of his own kind like any man. When there were no fish, he would stretch out along the hull and look up at the sky, alone as a coral reef or a stalking cat, waiting. Even when he caught an isolated snapper or two, he would search its dead eyes for wisdom or companionship, overpowered by a sense of quarantine.

Rolle was ripe for the offer when it came a few months later from Dr. North, the Cauc everyone talked about who had some science venture going on a nearby cay. Rolle accepted eagerly. He sold his boat, paid his debts, and moved up to the Island for Science. And loved his new job from the start.

LOOKING at Josephine sitting there in her petaled dress, and calling to mind her brother and Andy and Cleary, Sidney Rolle could say honestly that he liked Caucs as well as anyone. If Jo thought he was full of rage these days, she should have known him then. These days when he felt anger, it was focused on some injustice, directed by mind instead of emotion. On the sea, tugging fish from deepwater cliffs, he used to think his life was practice for something that might never happen. Now he had a mission: helping the family of the man he respected. He felt alive, like a child flying down a hill, or a fisherman pulling snapper five at a time, or a diver catching gravid shrimp for the seafarm that would make the Bahamas—and his own life—exceptional. The "little cloud out of the sea" was his reward after all, and he clasped it like a man's hand.

"Sidney?" Jo asked quietly. His mind seemed to have fled his body. Was she whispering into an empty shell?

"Yes, Jo?"

She assumed his long silence was meant to avoid talking about the rage she had questioned in him, so she changed the subject. "I wonder how Cleary is doing looking for Jelly Belly in the Wracking Islands."

Rolle, still pondering the mutability of life that had enrolled him in a crusade on the side of these white people, answered her earlier objection. "The rage I feel is the same rage you feel, Jo. It's directed toward the bastards who killed or kidnapped Grant's daughter. . . . Nothing more."

After his years of hate, of mind-rape and recrimination, of chastisement and ultimate understanding, it was a completely honest statement.

25 *Ebb and Flow*

THE ISLAND ebbs and flows in a rhythm transferred from other places. The Island is a microcosm of the Bahamas, which is a microcosm of the West Indies, which is a microcosm of the Third World, a declination that magnifies the good and the bad of a place, like fish swallowing fish and concentrating in their flesh not only beneficial proteins but toxins as well.

The construction crew, sprinkled like doctor flies over the white roofs of the villas, pounded nails through two-inch decking over cedar beams. Knowing little about Coby's disappearance or North's need to complete the seafarm and bring in a cash crop, they laughed as they worked, told jokes, and made up songs. Some hid Smoke joints or half pints of rum when Godfrey Knowles approached.

The sleek Labrador-like mongrel, named as a puppy after his black fur and blue eyes, bounded through the tidewater corralling a small stingray that tried to flap away. One of the roofers did a slow version of the Goombay Shuffle and pointed to the dog; the others stopped to watch. Bruiser lifted one floppy ear, straining to hear tiny ray squeals. You could see him trying to sniff the ray's intentions while avoiding the barb that got him in the chest the first time he tried this trick, which is why he performed it so often now, to pay back the original manta that stung him. Finally he worried the ray up on the beach and flipped it over and over until the enemy black blob stopped quivering. The only good ray, you could see Bruiser thinking, is a dead ray.

WHEN NORTH first came to the Island and hired his Great Snake crew, Coby worked at the wind tower beside him and Cuda. Tall, trim, muscular, and handsome, Cuda adored Coby. He was uneducated with not even the third-grade average schooling of the other workers, and yet he immediately grasped the intricacies of North's augmented-wind generator system. North said that Cuda had an instinct for electricity, for if he couldn't name a component he found out what it did by taking an electric machine apart and reassembling it. If wiring the buildings was his daily bread, the wind tower and its rotors and regulators were his butter.

The four doughnut-shaped structures on top of the tower are designed to accelerate the wind. The faster the wind, the more electricity can be produced—far more than by increasing the length of the "windmill" blades. The structures look like the rims of four giant automobile wheels stacked on top of each other. Swirling in the deep channels of the rims, a fifteen-knot wind picks up so much speed it becomes almost a gale. Blades that look like airplane propellers are located within the channels, and when they spin in the wind they power electric turbines. The propeller-turbine units with their weather vanes attached are mounted on opposite sides of a round track that turns like a lazy susan to face the wind. The result is the most elegant wind-power machine devised by man. Seen from the side, a unit looks like this:

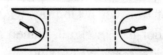

Coby, who was short enough to stand inside a channel without bending, helped North and Cuda wire the voltage regulators, controllers, and safety cutoffs. Cuda sang while he worked, calypso style, making up the words as he went. Coby laughed and hummed the tune, their song entrained in the channel.

Ah don' get no gals, no wine.
But it beat de runnin' jus' fine.

At first North thought he was kidding, but then it became clear to him that Cuda meant it. A couple of years ago the bureaucracy in Nassau decided that electricians would be licensed. Cuda had gone to the expense of taking a plane to Nassau, and arrived at the appointed place and time only to face a *written* test. As simple for Cuda as the test might have been, he had never learned to read, so he flunked. Without a license, no government-sanctioned builder or architect in the Bahamas could hire Cuda, making it impossible for him to support his fourteen children or their various mothers scattered throughout the islands. He entered the only industry open to him, and learned the art of running contraband in fast boats to the Florida coast—until Grant North came along and offered him a chance to be an electrician again. Now Cuda commuted from the village with the other workers, renouncing gold jewelry, limitless gifts to his children, shiny cars, and the glossy girls who had flooded him like the sea in a sunken drug ship.

"Sounds like you miss the adventure," said Coby from inside the propeller channel.

"I dunno, Miss Coby."

"But Cuda," Coby persisted. "The excitement of the race. The *speed!* The pretty girls!"

North wondered whether she expected Cuda to shrug it off, tell her he didn't miss it, and thereby reinforce her adolescent delusion that all men are created honorable.

Cuda stretched under the blue sky, holding a screwdriver like a teacher's pointer. With his other hand, he scratched the area between his legs in the classic, unconscious Bahamian-male gesture. North leaned closer to hear Cuda's answer.

"Yeah, Ah misses de smugglin', Miss Coby." He broke into a broad grin. "But Ah truly loves messin' wid de wires too, an' de onliest ting Ah got to worry 'bout now be gettin' de shock."

Nothing about the damage done by dope to the youth of the Bahamas. Nothing about illegality. And yet North thought the response of his protégé had been noble, for it indicated that Cuda meant to keep his word. Whenever North thought about Cuda he remembered the Croatian inventor Nikola Tesla, the self-taught genius who engineered Niagara Falls. What would Tesla have done with jewelry instead of dynamos to keep his brain alive?

In the afternoons when the heat rose from the exposed beaches at low tide and brought forth rich organic odors, the three of them would take a break by exploring the jungle. The leaves were turning lighter for summer. It was too early for seagrapes, but they gathered the dark-brown fruit of the tamarind for chutney, sapodilla for chewing gum, and breadfruit that could be cooked to resemble anything from potatoes to eggplant. After their jungle break they would climb the spiral staircase through the center holes of the wind structure to the top platform, where North would fill his lungs like a scuba tank. It was not the crisp cool Lake Michigan air of home, but it had a nitrogen narcosis all its own, and he could taste the joy in it. Like Cuda quitting the drug trade, North felt blessed that he had sold his business to come here. Coby entered into that feeling more than he first realized. He delighted in working alongside his daughter, watching the laughter form far back in her eyes and break out at the slightest impetus, her hair a bright tousle as she scurried up and down the wind units like the ten-year-old tomboy she once had been.

One evening before dinner, North and Coby ambled along the coves of the long white beach lined with furry casuarinas that zigzagged like the wrinkles of a whale along the belly of the Island. Bruiser ran with them all the way to Scuba Beach. They swam and waded back, Bruiser paddling beside them. When the faster-moving humans gained on him, Bruiser dashed to shallow water, knee-deep to *his* knees, and once he touched ground, bound and leapt through the ocean with ears flying against his shiny black face well ahead of the family he revered. He reentered deeper water and resumed his paddle until Coby, hair slicked like a golden seal, glowing in her passion for life, grabbed him and romped with him in the surf. As if at a signal, father and daughter stopped swimming and laughed at Bruiser surging toward them, red tongue lolling, tiny bubbles like diamonds glistening on his fur.

"Their lives have as much meaning as ours," Coby said.

"Whose?" North said, suspecting what she meant.

"The *other* animals. Bruiser, the cats, the gulls—even the ghost crabs on the beach. I used to think of them as subplots to our story but now I see that they are parallel. If so, anyone who hunts them is a murderer."

Her discovery warmed North as he stood there in the cool water. If she sometimes exhibited her mother's infuriating fatalism, she had Heather's fine qualities too. She even looked like Heather with the same architecture of cheek and forehead, the erect carriage, the quizzical look in her eyes when lost in thought, the admirable alertness as if ready to emit an electric discharge. In the yellowing light before dusk, golden fuzz colored Coby's arms, and her skin was charged with the seltzer of tropical water. Though her bikini bottom began a full hand below her navel in the center of a perfectly flat abdomen, her smile was one of asexual innocence.

"Murder is a matter of definition," North said to his maturing daughter. "If you killed an evil dictator, let's say Hitler, would that be murder? How about someone who killed Bruiser? Would he be a murderer?"

"I'd like to say no to the first example and yes to the second. But then I'd be justifying the means for the end."

What did success or achievement or wealth matter compared to the stunning melody of your daughter telling you of her affinity for life, even for the most insignificant animal? It is at such times that you understand why you love someone, and can pinpoint the precise moment of such realization. Thinking back to those days only a month ago, North knew that you normally remember the best of times, at least until the remembrance is explored and your mistakes return to haunt you. Then the light of the day goes out between you and the one you hurt, like the earth twisting away from the sun into the abyss of night.

THOSE TIMES seemed long ago to Grant North as spring turned into summer with no news about Coby. While Cleary and Jo spent full time canvassing the out-islands for Jelly Belly, North and Rolle had to divide their days between searching for clues and directing construction on the Island. Not knowing whom to trust, they kept all talk of Coby away from their workers, who went about their labors with that curious mix of Bahamian zeal and dogged routine.

Oris Fisher exemplified the diurnal cycle of Island life. When

Oris stops mixing mortar and readies his skiff, carrying fishlines and his "glass," a wooden bucket with a glass bottom, you know it is sixty minutes to lunchtime. Whatever Oris finds for lunch, he manages to catch and clean within an hour. "De wind be wrong fer de fish," he says, returning. "Conch fer lunch today."

Pressing the "glass" into the ocean surface to spot the pink-shelled queen conch lying all over the shallow-side seafloor is easy. The hard part, for the unpracticed, is cleaning them. Oris brings two dozen conch to the lodge kitchen. He taps a hole in the shell, reaches in with his knife, and severs the muscle anchoring the living mollusk to its swirled chamber. He pulls it out, cuts away the hard foot, and trims the black hood from the pure white meat, slipping into his mouth the slimy, transparent "pissarie" to keep himself virile. Shelled and skinned, he delivers the conch to Naomi the cook, whose breasts hang like breadfruit from a tree. She slices, cracks, and crumbs the meat, then fries it splattering in an iron skillet.

After lunch the tumult resumes. Coral rock powders the air as dozers quake the bony skeleton of the Island, whose flesh of sand and dirt is redistributed by the payloaders. Temporary generators roar as they make their temporary electricity. Men hammer, mix concrete, saw wood, jet pilings in the sea, and curse the machines. Through these workscapes run three contentious boys, the sons of Oris and Velma Fisher, their loud-mouthed mother in hot pursuit, yelling, "*Watch out fer de payloadinas!*" Their fourth son, an adolescent, sits at the end of the dock, his legs streaked with poisonwood sap, watching a bevy of baby sharks swimming in circles. Minutes before, the foot-long sharks had spilled out of their mother's womb as Oris butchered her, too late for lunch, saying as he does when he catches a big one, "Well dere's one less o' dese bastards in de sea now." The Fisher house in the village is rich in seafood and children but little else.

Velma, a tempestuous young woman in short skirt and hair tortured into corn rows, had come here earlier today in the Fisher skiff, as she had been arriving all week with her juvenile belligerents. They hung around the lodge, eating fruit, fidgeting with the single-sideband radio. North had returned to the Island yesterday with

Rolle and Jo, and had ordered Velma and her kids home. Today they were back and Velma was bragging to Oris and Godfrey Knowles that she had a government "posi*tion*" in Nassau, some sort of mysterious job, and she related the latest rumor as if she had firsthand knowledge of it.

". . . and dot whole islan' burn down to de groun'," she was saying. "Buildings, trees, everyting. It be right after de raid fer drugs—you know Defenders doan need no warrant if dey 'spect dope. Dey find one of de biggest hoards ever, tons and tons o' *caine*."

"De whole islan' burn?" said Oris. "How you burn a whole islan'?"

"You kin burn mos' anyting if you knows how."

"Who burn de islan'?" said Godfrey Knowles. "De smug*glers*?"

Instead of answering, Velma just smiled in that secretive way of hers.

If true, thought North, the rumor may be related to whatever conspiracy was driving events. But he didn't want to question Velma about it. Give her information, however minor, and she'll twist it like a conch shell.

"It's your responsibility—and you have the authority," North said to Godfrey Knowles. He had to keep himself free to follow leads that might come up about Coby. On top of everything else, his and Rolle's court hearing would begin the first week in August. That wasn't all bad, for the regular visits would give them an excuse to infiltrate Nassau, seat of clues to Coby.

"Yessuh, Mistuh Grant," Knowles said with the enthusiasm of a cigar-store Indian.

Turning to Velma, North said, "You listen to Godfrey. He's in charge."

She rolled her eyes upward but said nothing. Smoothing the back of her skirt, she sat next to her husband on the dock and wiggled her fishline in the water. Her skin, a dozen shades lighter than Oris's, was drawn tight over her facial bones; combined with eye shadow, it made her eyes big as moons. It's the eyes that get her what she wants, thought North.

Knowles was unaware that anyone knew he was bedding Velma

on his "family-matter" trips to the village, but of course the whole Island knew except Oris Fisher. Finally, like a cat who suddenly stops flicking his tail, Knowles clenched his hands into solid black rocks, squatted down beside Oris, and said to him in front of Velma:

"Mistuh Oris, you comes to work tomorra an' everyday all alone. If you doan do dot, *you* take care of de kids, an Ah hires Missus Oris in your place."

"Velma?"

"Sure, mon. She fish good as you."

Despite the problems of paternalism, indolence, and drugs, North's latent plan for his Island develops, like prints in a darkroom tray. Each afternoon when the sun sizzles into the ocean and casts like a color negative that exotic green reverse blush you find only in these latitudes, and when Shark ambles out of the shop to crank up the jollyboat, Sidney Rolle launches one of his spontaneous smiles, and North scans the Island and the corrals out in the water, and feels a visceral fulfillment.

God Knowles feels it too. "Mistuh Grant, suh," he says as he climbs into the jollyboat for a night on the village, *"Dis here Islan', she comin' straight!"*

Knowles is right. Against all odds, the buildings, the road, the tower, the solar pond, the seafarm are taking the shape of North's dream. He remembers the curious feeling he had when he saw the Island for the first time. Tired from exploring and anticipating a different and better life here for Coby and himself, he had imagined for one brief and dreamy moment that the land and jungle had merged into his own body. Now the sensation of the Island incarnate recurs uninvited, yet welcome, like the first sting of a winter sun. If asked, he would explain the feeling in more rational terms, but emotionally he sees himself metamorphosing into the rock and heart of the Island.

Love.

There is no other word for how he feels about this place. It is important to him, and he no more can separate his thoughts from the Island than can a sculptor from his clay, or a poet from having found at last a theme to repeat.

Dis Islan', she comin' straight!

26 *A Touch of the Brush*

IN THE ETERNITY since Coby's disappearance, Grant North imagined he could feel the earth traveling slower in its orbit, the planet gradually tipping toward the sun as spring slid inconspicuously into summer. The Island still whispered to you if you listened, but no longer in a soft melody that swelled your heart with joy. After three and a half months of searching for Coby, the noise grew clamorous and made you feel restless, as torn and tangled as the sea. You realized Coby was still gone from your life and maybe from hers as well, and that you were nowhere close to being immortal, that if you ever were going to find her, you had to do it now.

No new clues came as to the whereabouts of either Coby or Jelly Belly. Cleary had drawn a blank on Great Snake Cay, and Jo began to doubt the Defender who had injected that name into her brain like a hallucinogenic nightmare.

At six a.m. on the third of July, North awoke to a flood of sunshine. The brown Bahamian, Sugar, sat next to him on the bed, peering at him lovingly out of enormous tawny eyes, as crystal as the dew on a morning flower. Her twin brother, Spice, jumped on North's chest and started kneading it with his paws. Coby's cats— now his. He wondered why most men don't like these affectionate, inquisitive, playful, and feminine animals. What other species purrs?

He climbed out of bed, ready for Nassau. Tomorrow was a holiday only in the States, and Cleary had wrangled another appointment with the Prime Minister that would allow them to probe for information about St. Gregory. Away from the cats, he still heard a rumble, louder than purring, and slid open the glass door. The morning mist wafting in and out like a London fog enshrouded a vessel moving into Slaughter Harbour, which was entered on nautical charts as an anchorage. North's VHF sounded on the bureau.

"G' morning, Island. Happy holiday! This is Victor and Marge Zeller in your harbor," said a pleasant voice. "If you've got a single-sideband, we'd like to use it. Ours is on the blink."

Through the fog the "boat" seemed as big as one of the larger Defence Force vessels, expensive as a mansion. As she moved closer and the mist parted, her mirrored windows reflected the rich hues of coral from the seabed.

"Welcome," said North. "Our SSB is at the lodge—the double-circle building. I'll meet you there in ten minutes."

The boulders of the dock linking the wooden platform to the Island had been completed and paved with crushed stone. Overhead, bougainvillea, trumpet vines, and morning glories swarmed over trellises, forming a tunnel of flowers through which the Zellers passed on their way to meet North. Elderly, aristocratic, and affable, the Zeller faces were full of laugh lines, their heads twin white clouds.

"Our youngest daughter suddenly decided to get married," Marge Zeller said. "We need to talk to her about arrangements since we won't be back until late tonight, and the wedding is tomorrow."

North warmed up the SSB and sat down to transmit. But although he could receive, the mike was dead.

"There some kind of SSB virus going around?" Victor Zeller said with a chuckle.

Rolle came in for breakfast, and North introduced him while unscrewing the casing of the microphone, only half-listening to their conversation. They were tropical-fish hobbyists and had four big aquariums aboard, filled with queen angels, sergeant majors, and other miniature species. In the cottage they were building in

Palm Beach, the fish would swim in lighted water glassed off from the living room. As he was comparing the meaning of "cottage" against the dimensions of their "boat," North located a worn wire in the microphone that no longer made contact. He snipped off a section and reattached it, but still could not broadcast. Removing the steel case, he traced the transmission circuits, discovering that the coils on the relay that keyed the transmitter were damaged. They had been scraped with a pocket knife to resemble normal wear and tear. The relay measured only a cubic inch, but without it you couldn't transmit, unless—

". . . and people on islands always can use a little help," Zeller was saying to Rolle. "Anything we can get for you back in the States?"

"A new relay," interrupted North. "Our radio caught your virus."

"Listen, Grant," whispered Rolle. "These people have aquariums!" He turned to the Zellers and said, "How about taking some live seaweed back in your tanks for us?"

They needed to send live seaweed samples to their University of Miami phycologist to determine which species scored highest in carrageenan and agar. Transporting plants to Florida by air requires prodigious paperwork, since U.S. customs officers are at least as diligent in detecting an occasional coconut or live plant as in ferreting out dope. North would have been eager to have his seaweed samples delivered so easily, but the idea of sabotage preoccupied him. Someone had damaged the relay deliberately. Cuda? Rolle himself? Or one of St. Gregory's men who could have snuck ashore at almost any time?

"Of course we'll smuggle your seaweed for you," Zeller said with a wink. "And why don't you use the relay from our SSB? It's not doing us any good."

Aboard the yacht, Rolle loaded about ten pounds of each of four species of Gracilaria, Hypnea, and other seaweeds from the mariculture tanks into the Zeller's aquariums, while North unscrewed the case of their SSB. Tracing the circuit, he found the problem in the relay of the transmitter circuit board. It was not damaged. It was gone.

"Mr. Zeller, has your yacht been boarded by the Defence Force recently?"

"Why, yes."

"Did they know you were coming here?"

"Sure. They always ask your destination in routine drug in-spections. We've been stopped before."

North told him of his suspicion of sabotage. They returned to the Island, where North tuned his single-sideband, working the defective radio by carefully placing his finger on the relay to trans-mit, then releasing it to receive.

"W-O-M, W-O-M, Whiskey-Oscar-Mike," North broadcast. "This is the motor vessel Islander, India-Sierra-Lima-two-six-three-three off the Wracking Islands, Bahamas. Over." Because it is in violation of U.S. communications regulations to operate a single-sideband radio except from a ship, island inhabitants routinely pre-tend they are aboard some type of vessel.

"High Seas," responded the voice from Pittsburgh, relayed by computer from Ft. Lauderdale.

North handed the mike to Zeller who placed the call to the high-seas operator and talked to his daughter. North then called his phycologist, who said that he would be happy to pick up the seaweed from the Zellers at nine tonight.

After the yacht left, North said to Rolle, "Whoever did this didn't touch the VHF in my villa."

"The lodge is more accessible."

"Someone doesn't want us to communicate long-range," North said.

"Grant, I know you're worried about Coby. But you sure you're not getting a little paranoid?"

"That 'someone' went to a lot of trouble to disguise his sabo-tage."

Rolle sighed and seemed to acquiesce. "Who don't they want us to talk to?"

"Maybe Jo, now that they know she's my sister. Or . . ."

"Or what?"

"The U.S. Coast Guard."

IN NASSAU North started across the soft asphalt street adjoining

Rassin Hospital when Cleary stopped and said, "Get a load of this!"

A 200-mph Ferrari Testarossa convertible, fire-engine red with two animal-carrying cases sticking out of the back, was creeping toward them. The automobile must have cost more than a quarter of a million dollars here, with duty, but the driver ran it up on the curb like it was a bicycle and came to a stop alongside them. Behind the English-style steering wheel on the right side sat a smiling young woman with a café-au-lait complexion for which Caucasians risk skin cancer and endure torture by burning in hot oil.

"Dr. North, I presume!" She opened the door and stood there extending her hand.

Cleary's face couldn't have registered more surprise had St. Jude crystallized out of the sidewalk. Yet in the capital of a country whose population is the size of a single U.S. suburb, you can't walk the streets for long before you meet someone you know.

"*Marianne!*" said North, taking her hand.

She looked nothing like the grubby social worker he'd observed in the Nassau jail. She wore a thin white dress with polka dots indistinguishable from the green buttons that ran from low-cut neck to hem, the last two unbuttoned. High heels matched jade-rimmed sunglasses which matched her eyes. With the heat and humidity in the nineties, her smile was as cool and inviting as water running in a brook, and North found it impossible to picture her with any of ordinary mankind's ordinary afflictions: arthritis, coated tongue, even a hangnail.

Cleary stood looking at her with his mouth open.

"I dropped off my two cats at the vet for their shots," she said. "I'm on my way back to work."

"Something's different," North said, touching her hair. "It's on the other side." As when he first met her in New York, her long brown mane flowed over a single shoulder and on the other side an earring plunged like a raindrop.

"No one ever notices when I go back and forth. Why should you?"

"I don't know. I'm not particularly observant."

Cleary made a guttural sound at the understatement. North remembered Cleary then and introduced them.

A strange thing happened, strange for Nassau. A middle-aged black woman carrying a shopping bag down the street stared at the mulatto girl talking to two white men, and her eyes swept the skirt with the buttons unfastened. The woman flung her words as she hurried by, *"High-yellow bitch! White nigger!"*

Marianne looked stunned. North didn't know what to say.

"For a minute there I thought I was back in New York," Cleary said, trying to make a joke.

"Grant, Jack . . ." Marianne started, "I apologize for what you heard. Nothing like that has ever happened to me in the Bahamas. I never think of myself as black or white—since I'm both."

"Let's all forget it," North said.

"Where are you going?" she asked, changing the subject.

"As a matter of fact, we're on our way to see your father."

"About what?"

"Permits and things. It's a long story."

She looked up at North and raised an eyebrow. "How long have you been in town?" She laughed. "Without calling me?"

"I was . . . tied up. I wanted to call but I didn't know whether you were— Well, I mean, with your last name Price—"

"I'm not married," she said. "I'm a widow. And I'd love to hear that long story."

"How about tomorrow night?"

"Time and place?"

"Seven. The American Independence Day party at the ambassador's house."

"I'll be there." Her palms-up hands, the flex of her breast, the tilt of her nose, the potency of her eyes spoke of an intensity of desire that matched his own. Then she was gone.

Cleary found his tongue. "Christ Almighty, if she doesn't remind me of Delilah Mae!"

"She doesn't remind me of anyone I've ever seen anywhere on this planet," said North.

"Oh-*ho!*" said Cleary. "She seems the right age. I guess even scientists recognize that a ten-thousand-day-old girl is at her sexiest."

Marianne was twenty-eight. Cleary and most of the male population of earth, North suspected, distinguished between women and girls not on the basis of age but of that inner radiance, that lust for life he called a biophile. It doesn't matter what a biophile does or what she says; it is the enthusiasm with which she moves or speaks that sets her apart. It had been a long time since any female had penetrated North's inner self.

"Look, Grant, you know I'm not prejudiced, especially where females are concerned. But there's more than a touch o' the brush in that gal—in case you ever decide to live in Chicago again. I hope you know what you're . . . well, getting into. No pun intended."

"Don't worry about it," North said.

"I'm not worried about it if you're not. The more I think about it, the more I realize you couldn't have found a better girlfriend."

"Why?"

"Because now maybe we'll get somewhere with the head man. We're changing our luck." The cliché meant dating a person of another race, but Cleary meant it both ways.

"Jack, you know I think her father's involved in Coby's disappearance."

"Okay, so here's your chance to test that theory. You get on the good side of the P.M.'s only daughter and you can forget about finding Jello-Stomach or monitoring Defender broadcasts or all that other horseshit. You get the little gal with the long hair and sticky hormones to fall in love with you, and she'll get Daddy to turn these islands upside down until Coby falls out. If he's reluctant—well, that tells you something too. Right?"

Under other circumstances North would have refused to exploit a woman, or any friend. But the quest for Coby took precedence, and he remembered Marianne's talk with the prisoner about St. Gregory. There seemed no other way.

"What the hell. I'll give it a try."

AS THEY TALKED they ambled toward their appointment, moving slowly in the heat to reduce perspiration, rehearsing what they would say to Ransom and how to launch the subject of St. Gregory without revealing their suspicions. They crossed Bay Street onto the paving bricks of what had been Rawson Square, now renamed Ransom Square, where the Churchill building loomed over fiberglass dolphins vomiting water toward passers-by. The seat of government.

Nassau, home to pirates since before its official founding in 1695, had a long history of intrigue and depravity. In squares like this one, Governor Woods Rogers held public hangings in 1718 to induce the pirates to accept pardons and help him against the Spanish. Now cruise-ship tourists wandered around the statues, and a half-dozen sleepy horses wearing hats waited to pull their carriages past historic buildings. A few years ago an enormous straw market had dominated Rawson square where lady vendors lurked like spiders in their stalls to bargain with the tourists. But the stalls had gone the way of the gallows: relocated and out of sight of the government aristocracy.

Two men rose from a shaded bench in the center of the square and hurried into the sunlight. The taller of them supported his still-broken leg with a candy-striped cane he might have won at a carnival.

"Doctuh Nort. Doctuh Nort! You lucky mon dot we fine you heah!" said Louie Rahming in his rabid way, foregoing his usual Rastafarian greeting. About the age of Christ when he died, Rahming's beard reached halfway to his waist.

North knew that whenever Rahming talked fast, the subject was money, but he was curious and early for his appointment, so he stopped.

Rahming's colleague extended a pudgy hand. A short, flamboyant, reddish Negro, his gleaming white-silk shirt stained with tomato sauce fell open to his navel so you could admire the gold against his hairless chest.

"Dis be ma cousin Razor," Rahming said to North, ignoring Cleary. "He does de arrange*ments*!"

The comment made no sense, but then Rahming's comments never made sense even when he wasn't hopped up. It wasn't unusual to encounter Rolle's brother-in-law here, since out-islanders came to Nassau when there were no jobs at home. But North was unprepared for Rahming's utter degeneration. Unwashed as a saint and fifty pounds underweight, he looked like he wanted to sweat but couldn't. Angel dust had turned him into a mangy street dog who wagged his tail so people wouldn't kick him away.

"Dr. Nort, mon, is I glad to meet up wid you!" said Razor. A mass of little red veins streaked the black of his nose. He looked as if he regularly consumed ninety percent of whatever food the cousins might have owned in common. "Louie's tole me all 'bout yer Island. Me and Louie, we got a business proposition to lay on you—"

"You ever hears of *'black coral?'*" Rahming interrupted excitedly. It came out *"Years a black coral."*

"Of course."

Black coral, an extremely rare and valuable substance, grew at depths light enough for coral to grow, yet sufficiently dark to produce an ebony color. Mining black coral was outlawed by all the West Indian nations.

"We knows where dere be *tons* a de stuff! You knows what Ah sayin'?"

"Let me guess," said North. "What you need is a big boat—say a landing craft about the size of the *Half Fast*—and scuba gear, and maybe a small bankroll to get things started."

"Well, sure. . . ," Razor said, saliva beading in the corners of his mouth, "we's hopin' dot—"

"I tells you what, Mistuh Razor," Cleary filled in. "You gets yerselves straight now. You gets Rahming here off the juice or the Lady or whatever he be on these days. Then yous bring us a coral-mining permit from the Ministry of Lands & Surveys, and we talk de busi*ness*. You knows what Ah say-*in'?*"

Before Rahming could decide on how to answer this American madman, Cleary followed North across the street and into the Churchill building.

27 *Polarization*

THE FORTRESS top and pillared front of the Churchill building reminded North of a stolid chess rook. North and Cleary took the elevator to the third floor and entered the executive suite where a photograph of Ransom dominated the wall. His head was profiled so you couldn't see his errant eye, and he was smoking a pipe. A sign next to the portrait proclaimed, SELF-SUFFICIENCY IN FOOD THIS DECADE.

They gave their names to a receptionist busy polishing her fingernails, and sat down hoping the Prime Minister had risen above his bureaucracy's peculiar standard of keeping a petitioner waiting for forty minutes. Cleary leafed through a stack of old magazines. "Interesting," he pretended to read. "Seems Cuba wants to be in-dependent of Spain and we're sending our battleship, the *Maine*."

North, who was browsing through the stack, smiled—until he came to a familiar spiral-bound report with a heavy blue cover. He felt a chill. Holding up the thick document, he poured his eyes into Cleary's, saying nothing, the monstrous insult speaking for itself. The title read, "A Blueprint for an Island for Science." Stamped across the cover in a six-inch red slash:

PROPRIETARY INFORMATION

"Christ Almighty, that's the report we submitted with our application! No wonder we don't have the permits." Cleary slipped the document into his briefcase.

The phone buzzed discretely. The receptionist picked it up on the first ring, said, "Uh-huh," and returned it to its cradle. North looked at his watch. Forty minutes. A moment later Effie Ferguson, the Prime Minister's secretary, tiptoed toward them over the thick carpet as though not to disturb anyone who might be hospitalized on the other side of the wall.

She saw Cleary and smiled. "I'm terribly sorry, gentlemen, but the Prime Minister has been called away. However," she brightened, "Mr. Pyfrom will see you." Responding to the disappointment on their faces, she added, "Mr. Pyfrom, you know, is the *Deputy* Prime Minister. He is an equal Cabinet member with the P.M."

No one is equal to Ransom, North thought, knowing that a Deputy P.M. owes his allegiance to the Prime Minister who appoints him from the ranks of elected Members of Parliament. North remembered how Ransom treated his deputy like a lackey. He followed Miss Ferguson, wondering why his detailed plans for the Island for Science, his confidential "Blueprint," had been treated in such a cavalier manner.

Pyfrom's office was as big as a mortuary chapel. As if to keep bodies from decomposing, the temperature here was at least ten degrees lower and the air conditioner filled the room with a sleepy white noise. Thin drapes obstructed the view of Ransom Square and, across a river of ocean, Paradise Island. A Bahamian flag drooped on a pole beside the deputy's desk, which bore a precise row of pencils next to an orderly stack of papers. Years of pushing a pencil seemed to have left Pyfrom as straight and rigid. He stood behind his desk and peered at his guests through eyes liquefied by thick glasses. When North introduced him to Cleary, he extended a cold hand, withdrawing it a nanosecond later as though he had accidentally touched excrement.

"It is my pleasure to welcome you to the Bahamas, Dr. North." He said it in the damaged voice of one who has been fluent with raw whiskey for four decades or more. Waving them into chairs, he said, "I haven't seen you since your peroration in New York.

What can I do for you?"

North wondered where he'd heard that archaic word before, a symbol of the bureaucracy dredged from the innocent past when the only thing he had to worry about was the war on drugs. He told the story of his daughter's disappearance to the number-two man in the Bahamian government.

"It's been four months!" North said. What do I have to do to get some help? I'd give everything I've got to get her back!" Immediately, he wondered if he'd made a mistake, whether his statement would be mistaken for an offer of a bribe.

"It's really too bad," Pyfrom said, much as if North had told him the lack of rain might dry the grass. "Have you asked BASRA to search?"

"Yes, we did. Right after the raid on the landing craft. But BASRA can search only when someone's lost at sea and they have some idea where to look."

"Well then, we shall do it differently. I'll have the chief of police alert all stations throughout the archipelago. If your daughter is in the Bahamas . . . dead or alive . . . we ought to be able to find her."

North wondered whether he really meant it. Pyfrom's expression was lost behind his thick lenses.

Miss Ferguson knocked once and poked her head inside the opened door. Behind her you could see the receptionist with the red nails. "Anything we can do before we leave, Mr. Pyfrom?"

"Quitting time already? No thank you," he said, and the women left. You could hear the sounds of other employees heading for the exits.

"Won't you have a drink?" Pyfrom asked suddenly, surprising them. "I never drink in the public houses. People come up to me and ask for favors in the most disagreeable ways—because they are drinking, that is. So I have arranged my own cocktail lounge right here."

They moved to the far end of the office where there was an assembly of couches and a bar on wheels. Behind the bar a pale-green wall held pictures, honorary degrees, and a private pilot's license dated fifteen years ago. The abundance of space between the frames, the portable bar, backless couches like those Freud might have used, and vinyl tile on the floor, over which these melancholy objects could be rolled, rendered an ephemeral air to the room as though everything were subject to evacuation should Pyfrom dare leave the office. Except the plants. Ferns, flowering vines, and palmettos grew from pots so massive they seemed part of the floor.

Pyfrom plopped a few ice cubes in a glass and filled it with straight gin. North and Cleary had gin and tonic, and exchanged glances. *Keep him talking!*

"Mr. Deputy Prime Minister," Cleary said over the second round, "we've been trying to get our Island for Science authorized for more than a year. Now, quite by accident," he removed the blue report from his briefcase, "we came across this among the magazines in the reception room."

Pyfrom took it and read the title. "I certainly apologize for your document being misplaced. Quite possibly the receptionist had been given it to file and knew not the meaning of the word *'proprietary.'*"

"Mistakes happen, Mr. Pyfrom. But I wonder whether its being misplaced could account for the fact that we *still* haven't got a lease of the seabed for the shrimp farm, work permits for our scientists, duty-free status, or any of the other permits we need to operate. It's an enigma to me. I've been everywhere, seeing everyone." Cleary had not a Machiavellian bone in his body, but for some reason he added, "We would do *anything* to get those permits!"

Some perverse intrigue drove North to silence instead of making explanations. He was the chessplayer discovering that the mistake might work after all, as a gambit. Pyfrom said nothing, the most eloquent form of acceptance. The deputy excused himself, slithered off the couch, and exited the room, presumably for the lavatory.

"Grant, we've only got a couple of minutes. Come over here." Cleary led North across the room to the wall facing Pyfrom's desk where an oil painting showed St. Joseph sawing a piece of lumber. Adjoining it in a kind of religious harmony were the political saints of the Bahamas, two poster-sized color portraits behind glass and framed in narrow black wood like the borders of newspaper obituaries. They dominated the wall so that whenever Pyfrom glanced up from his work he would see them. One pictured Charles T. Ransom. His profile was turned away from the other, which showed the first governor of the Bahamas, William Sayle.

"Notice anything different about them?" Cleary said. "I mean different *from each other*."

North examined the pictures. Ransom, on the right, faced right. On the left, a distinguished seventeenth-century Governor Sayle faced the print of St. Joseph, so that he looked away from Ransom. Nothing unusual about that. Then he noticed the panes of glass over the pictures: one glared more than the other. North took his polarized sunglasses out of his pocket and twisted his head to examine the pictures again. Both were polarized but in different directions. He thought of Pyfrom's thick glasses, and realized he had discovered a Byzantine crack in the armor of his adversaries. Or was it only another example of how the comic mixes with the tragic in the Bahamas?

They returned to the Freudian couch. "I'm glad you're so damn observant," North said. "The glass of the Sayle print is polarized horizontally in the usual way to eliminate glare. The orientation of the glass over the Ransom photo is vertical. Maybe the framer cut the glass the wrong way on Ransom's picture. Or, maybe not."

"What do you mean?"

"I mean that Pyfrom's eyeglasses may be polarized too, so that when he looks up from his desk he sees a blank picture instead of Ransom's. When Pyfrom comes back, I'll check."

"Signal me," said Cleary.

"Okay. If I place my drink on the cocktail table with my left hand, he's seeing the picture of William Sayle and cancelling out his boss. If I use my right hand, I'm wrong."

Before Cleary could do anything but nod his head, Pyfrom returned across the vinyl floor, smoking a cigarette and exhaling through his nose. In a cordial mood, he made himself another gin over ice, his third, and nodded toward the bottles for them to fix their own drinks. Pyfrom appeared to be a casual alcoholic, one the life he's leading. While Cleary was pouring his drink, North sat on the couch facing Pyfrom. He held up his sunglasses as if to the light while polishing them with his handkerchief, rotating the glasses this way and that, watching as he did for Pyfrom's glasses to go opaque. When Cleary finished at the bar, North made his own drink and set it on the cocktail table. With his left hand.

Pyfrom was saying, ". . . any action required to save human life, and so of course I agreed immediately with Dr. North to institute a search for his daughter. But when it comes to authorizing a business enterprise in the Bahamas, I am afraid that is the province of the board of directors—that is, the Executive Committee. I am pleased to be a member, but only one member."

"Who are the others?" North said, making conversation, covering his former observations, trying to decide whether to defuse any residual memory of a bribe being offered. Or to let it stand. If Pyfrom couldn't tolerate the sight of Ransom's picture while pretending otherwise, he could become an ally. One of the few assets held by invaders of bureaucracies is the knowledge that one hand rarely knows what the other is doing.

"Oh, it varies from time to time. Senior Cabinet members. And of course the Prime Minister."

The inevitable Ransom, the buck-stopper, the hirer and firer, lord of whatever is undertaken by the government. "Will you help us?" North said.

Pyfrom poured himself a fourth drink and sat pensively. After a moment, he said, "Let me think about that. You are, of course, prepared to pay certain fees?"

"I understand that a seabed lease cannot be granted for nothing," said North.

The matter of the bribe hovered unspoken in the ambience of cordiality and good liquor. If Pyfrom drank any more, he might contract loose-tongue disease or even discuss his relationship with the P.M. Pyfrom, though, must have recognized such a peril, for he stood up to adjourn the meeting. His skin, drawn tight against cheek bones, seemed as thin as the paper in the reports he lived by, as if the tools of his trade finally had merged with his complexion. What secrets those books must hold!

"Mr. Deputy Prime Minister, are you coming to the U.S. Independence Day party tomorrow night?" asked North.

"'Independence,'" he said softly, rolling the word around on his tongue as if relishing the thought of it, and North realized the polarized glasses, the drinking in the office, the time he had given them, all these maneuvers constituted the deputy's own personal declaration of independence. "*Our* Independence Day, July Tenth," the D.P.M. said, "was *selected*, not imposed by a bloody revolution. I have been invited to your ambassador's party, of course, but as I mentioned I have an aversion to drinking in public."

The aversion must have evolved since they'd met at the United Nations, thought North. Pyfrom strolled with them across the bare floor to the closed door where he paused, eyes flicking nervously like a hesitant chameleon from North to Cleary to St. Joseph sawing down the wall. Pyfrom loosed a forlorn little laugh that seemed to reveal a vast suspicion of his fellow man. Out of his four-drink voice, cracked and humbled with sincerity and service, he said:

"One last thing, Dr. North. When you do meet with the Prime Minister to ask about your permits, be sure to treat him with deference. Mr. Ransom can hold a grudge, I am sorry to say." He snickered strangely. "Rub him the wrong way and he'll feed you to the sharks."

The same commentary St. Gregory had applied three months ago to Pyfrom. Was this some snide cliché making the rounds of the government? As he turned the remark around in his mind, North knew Pyfrom said it not in enmity, but in envy for anyone powerful enough to hold a man's life in his hands.

28 *ORIGINS: the Number-Two Man*

AS A BOY, Malcolm Pyfrom learned from Preacher the fear of the Lord, and from Charles Ransom how to be an accessory to another person's life. On Andros, the largest Bahamian island and still the most primitive, black magic was practiced alongside Christian fundamentalism even as World War II drew to a close. Malcolm knew the man the boys called Preacher as Charles's father, a tough proxy of the Almighty to the out-islands, combining the strength of an ox, the capricious temper of a Duppie, and the voice of a warden. On Sundays the whole town could hear him intoning the final battle between good and evil, his voice ringing out of the arched opened windows of the tiny church. Androsians had heard the stories of Preacher breaking the arm of more than one man caught blaspheming or failing to acknowledge God before a meal.

Charles and Malcolm had a secret clubhouse, a deceased oarboat in Middle Bight, four miles from their homes in Fresh Creek: dry-rotted, slats missing, beached like a dead sea mammal in white mud. In the bottom of the bow lay the treasure they had stolen from American sportsmen who postured like Ernest Hemingway, or from their women who smoked cigarettes and wore lipstick: dozens of reels, tackle boxes, snorkels, goggles, a small rusty chest containing almost two hundred dollars in ones and fives, and a variety of purses and wallets. Malcolm loved the wallets, the rich smell of leather, the ornate carvings; he longed to be free of Andros where he could carry a wallet like that in his hip pocket. In the bow of the wreck, holding the tobacco pouch with his teeth, Charles snaked a ribbon of Bull Durham into the center of a tissue and rolled a cigarette.

"How we gonna get dis stuff to Nassau?" Malcolm said.

"Boxes with false bottoms. And don't say 'dis,' you ignorant nigger."

"Doan call me no nigger, mon." Malcolm hadn't yet learned to live with the idea of being number two.

"They don't say 'dis' in the city, man."

"Go fuck a knot hole."

Charles handed Malcolm a withered cigarette and rolled another. At fourteen, Malcolm's myopia went uncorrected, giving him the unfocused appearance of a dead fish. Charles, the same age, was robust and handsome except at those odd times when his left eye wandered. On his shoulder, crudely drawn by Malcolm with a pen dipped in poisonwood sap (the painless, economical, out-island method of tattooing dark skin), shone two white stars the size of the gold insignia worn by major generals. On Malcolm's shoulder, Charles had drawn the single star of a brigadier.

"How are we going to get this stuff all the way to Nassau?" Malcolm said precisely, glancing up at the sky and exhaling smoke as he talked. One of the red-hooded black birds that inhabit the skies over Andros rode a thermal on ragged wings, searching for carrion over vast wetlands forty times larger than New Providence. The sight of the buzzard in the immensity of the sky made Malcolm forget his diction again. "It would be somethin' else ta be a buzzard an' drop tings on de countryside. Ah can't wait ta get mah pilot license."

"Haven't you got enough hobbies?"

A skilled gardener, Malcolm collected not only rare plants but match covers, baseball cards, marbles, and metal foil from gum wrappers and cigarette packs that he had rolled into a sphere the size of a cannonball.

"Someday, mon," said Malcolm. "Someday—"

"Jesus. . . !" said Charles, suddenly gasping and struggling against a giant hand that had seized his throat.

It was Preacher, whose reverend knees squeezed a hefty Bible, freeing his talons to seize the boys by their necks. He had the buzzard's movements down pat, the wings of his black-suited shoulder blades rocking from side to side when alighting on something. He yanked the boys out of the wreck, one in each hand.

"Kneel in dis here white mud and pray fer yer souls afore it be too late!"

They knelt.

"Get ye outta dese lads, Lucifer. Get ye an' yer Chickcharneys ahind me." He craned his long neck over the gunwale to examine the loot. "Youse won't be needin' dese stolen goods no more since you ain't goin' to Nassau. Not now, not ever!"

Malcolm was too young to know that similar indignities had shaped heros. But that morning, himself afraid and immobile under Preacher's grasp, he recognized the fact of leadership when, with one unexpected and powerful yank on the cleric's iron grip, Charles broke the hold of tyranny for them both. He stood there defiant, facing Preacher in the white mud. "You can't stop me from going to Nassau, old man. You ain't my pa!" For some time now Charles had been questioning to Malcolm his parentage, noting in the mirror the difference between his own light-brown skin and the buzzard-black of both his mother's and Preacher's.

The Reverend Ransom released his hand from around Malcolm's neck and faced his stepson. "How you know dot, boy?"

"Cuz I know who is!"

"Who?"

"A white man in the American Navy, a surveyor for a submarine base they gonna build here. He comes to see Mama every so often when you're out makin' your rounds—"

Preacher rose and slammed his Bible across Charles Ransom's head. But it was a weak blow from a once-strong, now utterly devastated leader of men, who squatted over the mud, placed his hands over his face, and wept.

They left Preacher there in the Bight and ran four miles to the Fresh Creek Hotel. At the front desk, Ransom grabbed the shirt-front of the aging innkeeper. "My mother, what room?" When the terrified old man told him, they bounded the stairs and banged on the door until it opened a little against a burglar chain. Through the narrow opening, Ransom came nose to nose with a burly red-faced man in khaki underwear. Malcolm could see the resemblance in those faces.

"What the hell. . . ?" the man said, unlatching the door and flinging it open.

Malcolm marveled at how Ransom could stand there unafraid, ignoring his mother who, sitting on the bed in her white slip, turned pale as a ghost. Ransom searched the eyes of his reluctant father, something Preacher had taught them never to do with a white man. Without his uniform, Malcolm saw that he was only a man—less than a man really, bloated and white. More like a grub.

Up from the bed, Mrs. Ransom took a hesitant step toward the door.

"What's your name?" asked Charles Ransom.

"Morgan, chief pett—"

Malcolm supposed that was all Ransom really wanted to know, because he slammed the door and bounded down the stairs. Malcolm followed.

That afternoon there was a DC-3 flight from Fresh Creek to Nassau, forty miles over a glassy sea on a hot June day. The boys were on it, their plunder packed in boxes with no false bottoms, one-way tickets paid, and a fistful of American bills in their wallets. Pyfrom patted his wallet in his hip pocket, thankful for the courage of Charles Ransom, and reflecting that Charles never did find out the first name of his own father.

29 *By the Seaside, Siftin' Sand*

THE TOPS of the cedar trees are chopped off between the fairways at the Cable Beach Golf Course where it borders the U.S. ambassador's residence on Safron Hill, leaving stubby trunks and no place for a sniper to hide. A twelve-foot cyclone fence separates the course from the Colonial mansion. Today the two permanent guards at the sentry post have been supplemented by a dozen plain-clothesmen wandering among the several hundred well-dressed Americans and Bahamians who came here at sunset to toast American Independence. Arnold Armitage had just been confirmed ambassador from the U.S., and North was anxious to talk to him.

North spotted Marianne at the edge of a gigantic party tent. She was wearing a cream-colored evening gown cut low at the bodice and slit up the side, revealing a perfect leg. The low sun sprinkled gold dust on her hair that cascaded over the front of her shoulder. The left ear showed this time, North noticed, and from it hung an amber jewel like an oversize drop of honey. "You do that to save earrings?" He grinned. "Or to make yourself even more alluring?"

"One must be frugal in a small country," she said. "And you—you look as neat as you did at the United Nations!" Clean-shaved, he wore a light-green suit and tie that emphasized the reddish tan of his face, which was darker than Marianne's.

She held his wrist lightly with both of her exquisite hands. Cleary and Rolle were to come to the party later, and for now Grant North was blessedly alone with Marianne. He wondered whether to reveal that he had seen and overheard her when she visited the jail, or whether to tell her about the thunderboat. But her mood changed. She seemed restless, and maneuvered him away from the party tent and around the mansion toward the pool. "Grant, there's something I think you should know before we go any further." She stopped in the passageway between the house and the bushes.

"Further into the party, or into each oth—?"

"Don't make light of it," she said without rancor.

Other couples filed around them on both sides like canoes skirting a shoal in the middle of a river. In tuxedos or dark business suits, the men seemed joined at the hips to their women who swayed on high heels and wore puffy yellows or slim tubes that made them look like giant bumblebees or praying mantises, the light sparkling on their jewels, their voices animated.

It became obvious to Marianne that they couldn't talk here. She led North toward the pool where streamers quivered into red, white, and blue parabolas in the breeze. Long tableclothed bars held champagne buckets, caviar-filled blocks of ice, and a forest of bottles from which white-clad black waiters mixed colorful drinks. On a tiled deck the leader of an eight-piece orchestra was explaining against soft Caribbean music that Calypso was a sea nymph who detained Odysseus on the island of Ogygia for seven years. Why she swam to the West Indies is obscure, he said, but it is curious that many of the verses describe native maidens by the sea. The musicians, wearing wide sashes, mixed conventional with island instruments: the shak-shak or maraca made from the local poinciana trees, a base and two guitars modestly amplified, steel drums hammered into twenty separate convex areas, each section tuned differently, and bamboo tamboo poles of various lengths struck like those of a xylophone.

Beside the pool, Marianne said, "It's really something quite serious, and I must tell you—"

But then a spotlight targeted her in the dying sun, and the

younger Bahamians in the crowd laughed and sang:

All day, all night! Marianne!

It came home to North what a famous person he was courting. The band leader grinned at her and began to sing as his musicians picked up the well-known calypso song:

Marianne, Oh Marianne
Won't you marry me?
We can have a bamboo hut
And brandy in the tea.

"Oh, I should have remembered." She interrupted herself to smile under the spotlight and nod at those she knew. "I used to walk into these dances before . . . well, in the old days, and the band never failed to play *Marianne*. I guess I liked it the first dozen times, but the ego trip is growing a bit thin."

Leave your fat ole mama home.
She never will say yes.

"Do you have a fat ole mama?" North said. He wasn't sure whether the song was a refrain to their conversation, or vice versa.

"Oh no, she's gorgeous, in fact she's far too youthful for a mother! I'd like you to meet her. Will you?"

"I'd love to," he said.

Down by the seaside, siftin' sand.
Even little children love Marianne.
Down by the seaside, siftin' sand.

"Grant, that's what I have to talk to you about. The song. It isn't me . . . it wasn't the kind of life I led." She said it fast, as if events might never allow her to come to the point. Finally the spotlight swept away from her and she blurted it out in one breath, like a diver surfacing. "I'm far from sifting sand and being a role model for children. When I was a teenager I was smoking reefers and popping pills the way normal kids take candy." She looked at him hopefully with tears welling in her eyes.

"It's hard to explain," she said, recovering. "When your father's a preacher, you rebel by getting pregnant. When your father's in the government making speeches against drugs, you do drugs. . . ."

The song continued and the spotlight drifted around the party.

"A man named Gary Price introduced me to cocaine in its worst form: crack. He was my husband. Cocaine killed him fifteen months after we were married."

"When did he die?"

"Last December. I never took the time to find out much about him. Coke does that to people."

North found it hard to visualize this ultra-feminine aristocrat smoking even a cigarette, let alone crack cocaine in a pipe. He couldn't imagine her snorting it either, although that was a better way, he knew, for it ate your nasal septum and your vocal cords before your brain.

"I'm clean now. I haven't had crack—or anything else—since Gary died."

North was astonished, even bewildered, but not chagrinned as he had been when he discovered Coby had taken the stuff. He listened to Marianne's flawless, timeless voice that seemed untouched by corruption, a voice pure as rain falling over a green jungle. He wanted to hold her, to tell her it was all right, that it didn't matter. But maybe it did matter. Not so much that she had been an addict and was still under therapy, but that her story seemed so rehearsed. He'd always hated the idea of rich junkies who haven't even the excuse of poverty for their addiction. And he was wary of confessions that struck just the right note, trembled at exactly the appropriate moment to convince you of the confessor's sincerity. She wanted him to believe that nothing was important except his understanding of her. His intuition told him to be careful.

"Grant?"

She was enticing in her evening gown, earnest and voluptuous. He told his intuition to go to hell. "You could tell me you murdered the queen and I'd still want you," and he realized he meant it. "I'm surprised, that's all."

"It's not easy to live up to a damn song."

"Forget it. Let's dance."

As they moved to the music, she noticed the tiny tattoo on his left wrist. "That a sign of your former occupation, Dr. Moon?"

"It's like all the Dr. Fishers who didn't know they'd someday turn into marine biologists."

The band broke out of an amorphous medley into "Laura," perhaps because someone prominent by that name had arrived. North hadn't danced with anyone since Xaviera almost four months ago, but now held a girl he cared for. In his arms Marianne moved with a natural grace, tight against him as if there were no one else in the courtyard.

Everyone seemed to know her, or at least know who she was, and after their dance she introduced him to laughers and drinkers, the women with their colorful long gowns or wide party skirts, the men in tuxedos or open shirts with gold neck chains. She introduced him as "Grant" or "Dr. North" depending on whether she encoun-tered a friend or a member of government. Some of the women stole glances at North that said they wondered whether he *knew*, then asked Marianne where she'd been all this time, to which she responded, "Oh, around . . . working at the agency."

The sun set, spawning a swift darkness. Tiny holiday lights blinked on in the trees, turning the courtyard into a vast aquarium where colorful fish swam in mating circles, entranced by liquor, music, and an illusory immortality. But the important fish were neither the drinkers nor the dancers. They were the politicians hold-ing court in the centers of little groups: Senator Doctor Dame Cora Carstairs, surrounded by a dozen women, wearing on her gown a smaller version of her "Motherhood and God" badge; Benjamin Franklin, the new Minister of Fisheries, talking to American busi-nessmen; Embassy hosts Arnold Armitage, David Davenport, and their bejeweled wives smiling to a mixed group of partygoers.

North introduced himself and Marianne to Ambassador Ar-mitage. Mustached and deeply tanned, his smile lit the dusk, reeking of prestige and charm as he described the virtues of what might as well have been his private eighteen-hole golf course. A few months ago the American President redeclared war on drugs and announced his choice for the Bahamas post. Last week radio Nassau had been filled with the U.S. Senate confirmation hearings. Asked by reporters why he wanted the job and what he would do with it, Armitage had ignored the drug wars, civil liberties, poverty, illness, and illiteracy, but had spoken in depth of great golf, warm sunshine, and the friendly people of the islands.

While Marianne was busy with someone else, North sidled next to the ambassador.

"Mr. Armitage, I hope you don't find this presumptuous, but my teenage daughter Coby has been missing since March. I don't know what to do about it."

"Of yes, you're the scientist with the island. I had a phone call about that from D.P.M. Pyfrom last night." Armitage, eyes glistening, had grasped North's hand automatically, and now held his arm in the manner of lifelong friends, or expatriates. "I'm awfully sorry," he said, and North had the impression he meant it.

"Is there anything you can do?"

"Sure, sure." Armitage frowned. "We can alert our Coast Guard. I'll get on it first thing in the morning."

A line of well-wishers had been forming in back of the ambassador. He whispered to North, "Try not to worry. We'll see what the Coast Guard turns up." Then he reestablished his bright smile and turned to talk to his guests.

THEIR ARMS linked, Marianne guided North toward her father who was uncharacteristically alone at one of the bar tables, his pipe in one hand and a New York-size martini in the other. "Look who I found!" she said.

Ransom planted his pipe in his mouth and shook North's hand without a trace of a smile. "Ah, the drug-warrior warrior."

You could tell the Prime Minister had been drinking heavily, although he hadn't arrived at the word-slurring stage. From his glance at Marianne's arm entwined in North's, it didn't take an intuitive to understand that Ransom savored not what he saw. Marianne led North away by the hand, as though her father were merely another acquaintance in this sea of citizens to whom she would say hello and little else.

Ransom removed the pipe from his mouth and his voice became a scalpel ready to peel away a person's defenses. "Please, Marianne. Leave Dr. North here for a minute or two."

She shot him a worried look but edged dutifully out of range.

"Dr. North," began the Prime Minister surgically, "I hope you'll forgive me if what I am about to say offends you. We Bahamians live in a modest nation at the doorstep of a superpower." He waved a hand around the grounds at the superpower's exhibition of affluence. "So we may tend toward paranoia at times." He sipped from his glass, wriggling his caterpillar eyebrows as he swallowed. "However, if your plan is to befriend my daughter to get at me— stop it right now, or I'll have you deported. If on the other hand it is a coincidence, then we can be friends. In the latter case, I will expect you to avoid the subject of special favors in securing permits for your project."

North felt he was back in Vietnam where dangers lay in ambush. "There's something more important going on here than permits for my Island for Science. It's my daughter. Are you aware she's missing?"

North watched the P.M.'s eyes as he answered without a trace of guile. "Yes, Mr. Pyfrom told me that and I am truly sorry. There really is very little we can do on that score to help you—other than search the Bahamas for her, which I understand we are doing."

Marianne drifted back toward them, her arms linked in those of Rolle and Cleary who had just arrived. She said, "Father, I'd like you to meet Sidney Rolle and Jack Cleary, two of Grant's Island for Science people."

"Having a good time, men?"

Cleary said yes and shook the P.M.'s hand. Rolle said with a straight face, "I guess it's better than getting chewed by a hammerhead." Too much the earthy fisherman to warm up to a man he despised, Rolle visibly braced himself to shake hands.

Marianne said, "May I have Grant now, for this dance?"

"We were talking about the Plague, Marianne," Ransom lied.

"Again?"

"Well-lll, I took another look last night at Dr. North's book about drug abuse."

Marianne interrupted, "The whole idea of drug abuse is ridiculous. As if anyone can be a user without being an abuser." She said it definitively, as though to preclude further conversation.

"I'd like to invite you and Grant for a longer talk," Ransom said. "Perhaps on my yacht. We could go diving, have dinner. I'll have a surprise set up there."

North wondered whether the P.M. was making the date in apology. Could the surprise be the granting of his permits? No. The choreographed politician would do nothing unrehearsed.

The Prime Minister looked at his watch and said, "This is Friday. Say, Sunday morning? About eight?"

North said yes. The Prime Minister nodded at Rolle and Cleary, then turned to greet a cluster of people who had been waiting discretely to meet him and Marianne.

Rolle whispered to North, "You gonna call your daddy-to-be 'Charlie?' Or 'Chuck'?"

The idea was too incongruous to pursue.

"Seriously, now that I've met Transom," said Cleary, "I think we ought to be wary as hell."

"You reading my mind?" said Rolle.

"I read people, and I don't trust that one."

Rolle nodded with something approaching respect as Cleary drifted off toward the nearest bar. "Uh oh, here come Yin and Yang," Rolle whispered.

In another of those implausible Bahamian transformations, the addict and the hustler approached in crisp tuxedos. The perpetual sweater and long beard that warmed his ravaged body still clung to Rahming, worn now under his white jacket. Razor's tux, a black one, hung limp over flabby flesh that reminded North of pork. Wondering how they'd gotten themselves invited, North considered escape, but he didn't want to miss Marianne in the expanding crowd.

"Jah Rastafari. Love and peace," said Rahming.

"Now see here, Doctuh Nort," said Razor, taking a pack of unfiltered Players from his breast pocket and offering one to North. He ignored Rolle, who took advantage of the situation to sneak off. "You a mon of educa*tion.* Louie Rahming and me, we got a business proposition to negoti*ate.*" That zany Bahamian accenting of the last syllables, the thin red worms of broken blood vessels on Razor's ebony nose, and his emaciated companion cackling like a rooster at every remark made North want to take one of Razor's cigarettes. But he decided he didn't need it.

Rahming took a few labored steps down the long bar to replenish his drink. Returning, he leaned heavily on his cane.

"What's the matter with your legs, Louie?" It had been almost four months since he'd fallen off the roof.

"It de *feet*, not de legs. Could be I gettin' de alcohol*foot*." He snickered and sipped his rum drink. "It doan hurt none."

As if narcotics weren't enough for him, he'd managed to contract the uniquely West Indian disease of the alcoholic male that North had read about, in which the long bones of the foot progressively atrophy, ulcers form, and sensibility to pain diminishes. The afflicted usually quit drinking only after one or both feet are amputated.

Razor said, "We needs yo barge to pull it off, Doctuh—"

"Oh? How unusual."

"Fer de shark fishin' business. Only us Bahamians be 'llowed ta fish commershly. Now dere be somethin' what make dis deal go down real good. . . ." Glancing around for secret police who might be listening, Razor contorted his face into a sly grin. No shirt cuffs showed under his black jacket, and the juncture where suit met skin, imperceptible in the dusk, made him look stuffed in one piece like something intended for scaring birds. His emaciated companion smiled a beati-fic, possibly hallucinogenic daydream over his Jesus beard and degenerating feet.

North stifled a laugh, wanting to encourage their foray into legitimate commerce. He also wanted to hear more about shark fishing, a sound economic proposition when using steel gill nets. Once when he was exploring with Coby the possibility of raising endangered white tigers on the Island, North had thought of shark meat as a way to feed them, and had tried to interest the government in paying a bounty for sharks taken from tourists' beaches. Like the proverbial pig, everything on a shark is usable: white meat, shark-liver oil (sold as cod-liver oil), skin for leather, even the teeth and bones for the macho boys to wear around their necks. The government, however, refused to pay a bounty and insisted that only Bahamian citizens can engage in commercial fishing of any kind. Razor apparently had discovered the gold in sharks.

White gold, as it turned out.

". . . You knows what Ah say*in'*, Doctuh? What we does is meet up on de seas wid de airplane of de Colombians. Dey drops a few sacks a 'caine an' meybe a half ton a de Smoke into yer barge an' we bundle alla dem inside de shark bodies. I got de connec*tions* for de shark *meat*. We mek bread bot ways!" He smiled broadly, revealing a few thousand dollars worth of new gold teeth.

"You're asking me to let you use my boat to smuggle dope?"

"No mon. Heavens no! Not jus' *'use'* yo boat. You be full part*ner* wid us!"

"Tell me you're kidding," said North.

"*Kiddin'? Kiddin'!* Dis be serious proposi*tion*, Doctuh," said Razor, puffing violently on his Rothman and managing to look hurt at the same time.

Rahming beamed at them both with burning eyes.

NORTH ESCAPED to Marianne and they passed through the guarded security gate to the golf course where the sky was wrapped in purple velvet. Out of the sea rose a gibbous moon ripe with hope, and North yearned to take Marianne to that unspoiled world, to show her the craters and mountains and rills and rays, or to bring her to his Island away from her family and her past. He wondered whether junkies were always junkies, like alcoholics.

She answered his half-formed, unspoken questions. "When the decline of western civilization is chronicled, the prominent reason won't be the atomic bomb or the greenhouse effect. It'll be the boiled brains of our youth."

Her voice, low, rich, seductive, a voice meant for love songs in warm places, spoke instead of crack and the black hole of despair and of her doctor brother's therapy. Before her addiction, she had majored in Russian literature at Oxford, afterwards spending a year in what was then the Soviet Union where she became anti-big business, an "original Marxist" in the sense of communes and convents. She loved her father despite his streaks of greed and power. He may not be one of the great men of the world, she said, but he leads the nation efficiently. It turned out that her mother was a part-French voodoo priestess from Haiti, her brother a saintly physician who mixes modern medicine with astrology, numerology, and their mother's rites. Not exactly your everyday family.

Arm in arm they advanced toward a swath of moonlight along the edge of the golf course. Marianne held her shoes and nuzzled the damp grass with bare toes, her perfume mingling with the salt air. At a silent signal they stopped and stared deep into each other's eyes. It is a monumental event when you recognize that first look of love, that arch toward yours of the person you desire, that loud silence full of meaning. They kissed their richest kiss, liquid music to him, melodic water flowing down a mountain stream. He had known Marianne for a total of only a few hours, but they were hours spread over months, amplified by sleepless nights and mornings spent alone, wishing her there to share with him the rapture of the sun climbing the pure wall of sky. On those lonely mornings searching green islands, when the light pours into the sea and the incoming tide lifts his boat, he sees her face in the clouds and knows she is the woman he would love when he can feel love again. When Coby returns. When his private war is over.

Marianne traced the craggy lines of his face with her fingers like a sculptor defining a head, feeling the essence of him, thinking how she had withdrawn from love, comparing him with her former husband. Had she married this man instead of Gary Price, her life would have been . . . what? Painless? Happy? At times Grant seemed so elusive, so mired in alien events, as though he were trapped in an endless maze. Once she had believed that no person could fill the void left by her defection from the Lady, but Grant North had done so. This big man with his youthful enthusiasm, his subtle but decisive mind, his rugged body ready to burst out of his clothes was completely unlike any other man she had ever known. One day she read his "Blueprint for an Island for Science" and came away amazed at the breadth of his ideas and of their utility for her country—relevant, concrete plans ready to inaugurate. Before he had entered her life she had been reinventing herself constantly: as daughter of the Prime Minister, as wife and junkie, finally as director of REHAB, but never as a woman. Her brother's therapy could end now; the love of Grant North would purge the remnant pain from her psychic wounds. She was drawn to him, lured to his strength, to his creativity, to his laugh. And yet, from the man she would love, she demanded understanding. Not forgiveness.

"You deserve to know how I became an addict."

"You don't have to talk about it."

"I think I do." She broke away gently and leaned against a palm trunk. A breeze filled their nostrils with odors originating far out at sea.

"Were you unhappy?"

"No," she said. "I guess I was seeking beauty."

"In drugs?"

"I have a strong imagination," she said not flippantly. "As a student of literature, I convinced myself I was after beauty in an ugly world. I thought I could handle it like one of those three-name authors, Robert Louis Stevenson or Edgar Allen Poe or Arthur Conan Doyle, who took cocaine to improve their imaginations. You're a scientist; did you know Thomas Edison used coke?"

"Thomas Alva Edison?"

She laughed. "'You need imagination to form a notion of beauty at all, and still more to discover your ideal in an unfamiliar shape.' Joseph Conrad said that. He was talking about love for another person, love as Pushkin or Gogol or Dostoevsky perceived it: an overpowering urge to fulfill your fate—to possess and be possessed. Maybe I had too much imagination. I came to feel that way about crack. Imagine experiencing every pleasurable moment of your life all at once in a five-minute blast. That's crack! I fell in love with the stuff."

"And now?"

"Now I try to convince addicts to fall out of love with the most important element in their lives, the White Lady who gives them life and stamina and beauty and the courage to enter the future. . . . I'm new in this job. I guess I'm not too popular sometimes."

"Marianne," he said on impulse, "with your knowledge of the government—with or without your father—I need your help."

"For what, Grant?"

He told her about the murder of his LCM crew, Coby's disappearance, St. Gregory's raid on the Island, and their search for the fat Defender who had been given a psychological furlough.

Saying nothing of jail, he watched her carefully for signs of uncertainty, to see whether she would divulge the St. Gregory gasoline story she had heard. Her face was full of compassion, but she volunteered nothing.

"Don't tell your father about Jelly Belly," North said. "He might inadvertently mention it to someone in the Defence Force."

"Of course I won't. Here I go on and on about myself while you must be completely torn up inside. It's so awful about Coby. I'll do what I can. But how do you . . . ? How do you *feel?*"

The lace of scattered clouds had dissolved in the night breeze. His back to the golf course, North turned toward the ambassador's house, and scanned the Milky Way. In the southwest, Orion hunted his own unknown antagonist.

"How do I feel about Coby?" He knew exactly how he felt, but he had never told anyone, not Cleary, not Rolle, not his sister. As he talked she listened totally, reflecting on all he said, and the fact of her listening lifted the weight from his heart. "Her disappearance is like an open sore that gets worse every day," he said. "It will stay that way until I find her." He paused a long moment under the constellations, wondering whether, like Orion, he was doomed to an eternal, fruitless chase. The stars whispered for him to vent his sorrow.

His disclosure brought Marianne's feelings bubbling up from their artesian hiding place where they had lain through the artificial years of her former life. He told her with complete honesty that he wanted her, that he would love her when he could, that he had loved only one woman before and that she was dead and growing fainter each year like the fading celluloid of an old movie. She kissed him and looped her arms around his neck in a thoroughly feminine, almost feline embrace, and nestled her soft hair under his chin. Lifting her head, he tasted the salt of tears on her cheeks, the first he'd felt since Heather died, but whether they were tears for his grief or tears of happiness that she had found love at last, he could not tell.

"Sometimes I wish I could cry," he said.

"Cry?"

"Yes, real liquid tears. To wash out my feelings. I think about

Coby all the time, when she was a little girl, when her mother died, when she came to the Island to help me build. I think of her lying hurt somewhere, or lost, maybe kidnapped or an amnesiac. Somebody I haven't seen for a while comes up to me and says, 'How are you?' And I have to turn away because I'm choking on dry tears."

The moonlight lodged in the soft luxury of Marianne's hair. The craving in his groin knew no turning back and forced him closer, his thigh between her legs, hers between his. He held her breast. Far from resisting, she placed her palm against the back of his hand and pressed it firmly. Her passion, ripe as his, erupted like the pistils of a flower. She parted her lips, and when he pressed his mouth against them she licked his tongue, softly, fervently. The white moon hung in the sky.

"Oh, no," she said.

"No. . . ?"

"They're paging me." She said it with a soft whimper, wondering whether the moment would ever return.

When they rejoined the party, they found it was only her father retrieving her, using the excuse that he wanted her to see the fireworks. At first, North thought Ransom was being overprotective, perhaps because her therapy was still in progress. But he read on the face of the Prime Minister an alien page of reality.

"Oh, hello, North," Ransom said with reluctance. He was frowning and he held the frown long enough for it to chill the skin of North's neck and turn it to ice.

Never had North experienced a sensation like that. Few white men ever do: the sudden alienation, the frightening intractability. At that moment he knew firsthand the flushed feeling of the black man in the streets of Chicago when someone of another race glares at you for no reason but one. . . .

The barrage of fireworks started, hemorrhaging the night, a toast by the festive Americans to the benevolence of their host government. Rockets ascended and arched, then sprouted into the colors of the Bahamian flag: two rectangles of blue for the water, one of yellow for the sun. And an equilateral triangle bordering the boundless black of the sky. For the people.

30 *ORIGINS: the Lady in White*

WHEN MARIANNE was twenty-six she returned to the Baha-mas with a master's from Oxford, feeling like an alien in her father's country. Her sense of belonging had been stronger under the ano-nymity of Oxfordshire and the Bell Tower, the antique chapel of Christ Church College, the expanse of spires and snowy fields between them, and even in Russia where she had pursued Dostoyevsky, Pushkin, and Gogel. Now she found herself in a strange and snowless winter. No longer were there hills or valleys in her life, no poets of dark souls or abstract socialism, no one to talk to of literature or life, no job to throw herself into.

She met Gary Price in a Nassau bar where people laughed in the dark. An analytical young white man with glasses, his shirt opened halfway to his belt to show gold against a hairless, tanned chest. Recently graduated from the University of London and not yet ready to join the family shipping business, he spent his time sky-diving and partying.

"This is like parachuting onto an unknown island and finding your next-door neighbor," she said. "I was in London too."

"You a sky diver?"

"I tried it once."

"Things too tame in the home town for you?"

"I don't know. I feel . . . peripheral, like a phrase in apposition."

"I can fix that."

He didn't explain what he meant, but a few nights later he invited her to a party. She dressed in black leather: jacket, short skirt, high-heeled boots, the left ankle of which was encircled by silver bullets in a chain. They drove across the causeway to Arawak Cay, stopping before the sprawling Customs complex. At the private warehouse section, he inserted a key into a lock switch inlaid in the brick wall, and an overhead door clanged upward. They entered a freight elevator. At the third floor Gary unlocked the door to his apartment, revealing a single room furnished with zebra-striped couches squeezed against a kitchenette, like the galley in a boat. On an otherwise barren wall, ballerinas danced in a painting by Degas. Gary produced a bottle of gin and two glasses.

"This the party?" she said.

His cheekbones tightened into a grin as he flicked his hair away from his glasses. He raised his drink in toast while pressing a concealed switch. A noise, low and rumbling, grew strident.

Marianne followed the sound with wide eyes. She came to her feet. *"Oh, my God!"*

The wall that contained the Degas was covered on the other side with wedges of acoustical felt, all of which slid smoothly upward and out of sight. An enormous room opened before her in a blaze of color and sound. West Indian paintings splashed the walls in reds and purples. An island melody poured like milk from a five-piece combo. Streams of water shot from a fountain of nymphs over a liquor bar, landing in a copper trough that raced around the perimeter of an oval dance floor where young people of both races were dancing.

Gary ruled this subworld, whose revelers—minor government officials, activists, actors, and oligarchs—seemed to be members of some subterranean army wearing the same uniform: T-shirts with slogans, faded jeans tight on bony bodies, long hair, and pallid faces that smiled at him and his girl. Marianne broke into a musical laugh. "You always surprise your girlfriends like this?"

Gary introduced her to the closest partyers. A man dressed in a London-cut tweed suit, that made him stand out from the rest of them, resumed his argument, speaking in more of an English drawl than an island lilt. "Sure we make profits. If we didn't, the country would go out of business. We'd be like the Soviets before their nation imploded, when they finally realized they had achieved their objective of complete equality in which nobody has anything."

A woman swaying to the music while riding the arm of an art-deco couch looked up at him and chuckled. A man wearing a T-shirt frowned and said, "Christ, I wish I knew as little about it as you."

The man with the profits waved a hand toward the ambient party. "Don't fool yourself that these altruists," he said, "are moved by any compassion for the suffering. They're motivated only by hatred for the successful."

Incredible as it seemed, here was Oxford transported home, except that no one talked about the subconscious. The vogue topic was government in the region: whether Fidel would recognize in time the inherent faults of a command economy, whether Noriega would be released from his forty-year drug-dealing sentence after five years or ten, whether Ransom had stumbled into procedural deadlock in his purge of the whites, whether Dame Cora should have liposuction. . . . Beyond the groups of talkers, men and women paired and headed toward the dance floor.

"The best way to help the poor is to be not one of them. . . ."

Listening, Marianne felt an urge to present the socialist view, to defend the class struggle and define business as greed, but she was too new to these people, too timid. The evening ripened in breathy voices and dense smoke. Marianne and Gary danced to a quiet rhythm.

When they finished, Gary looked at her strangely. Under his glasses he blinked feline eyes that dilated as if they had nictitating membranes.

"Let's get another drink," she said, fearing the alternative.

"Who wants a hangover?"

They came to a narrow cocktail table on which streaked long thin lines of white powder. On hands and knees along both sides of the glass table, two girls were snorting the powder through straws. Barely out of their teens, they had a secondhand look about them, like used cars.

"White Lady?" she said guardedly.

"Ah, you're not a virgin."

But she *was* a cocaine virgin. She'd had Smoke and other soft drugs in high school and a little hash now and then at Oxford, but nothing as serious as coke.

"It looks obscene, kneeling there and ingesting that stuff through your nostrils!"

In the kind of maneuver you remember as slow motion, Gary's fingers opened a drawer in the cocktail table and emerged with a crystal chalice full of soapy white chips. He stuffed some into a glass pipe with a series of fine screens at the bottom of the bowl. "Try it this way."

She held the delicate pipe to Gary's torch and drew on the stem until the rock melted and hot liquid fell from one screen to another. She inhaled.

White Lady doesn't make you wait like alcohol or marijuana. Suddenly Marianne was at the top of the sky where the air turned thin and a brilliant blue-white ball rotated below on its axis. Beyond, the stars burned in kaleidoscopes of infinity. No one could harm Marianne or even touch her here. She could do anything, know everything: rule the little earth below, give orders to her father, denigrate her mother's obeah and her brother's mystic medicine. Her new dimension revolved solely around herself. She was so aware!

Marianne elected to return to the discussion at the front of the room where she was happy to find herself saying to the businessman, "Don't give me that Ayn Rand drivel to avoid your responsibilities to the poor."

"Marxism is dead, honey, thanks to St. Gorbachev—"

"Not Marxism, sugar," she answered, sure of herself. "Marxism defeated fascism, decolonized the world, and has become a force for freedom. It's still with us, under other names."

She *knew* what people were thinking, could *hear* their covert applause. Sauntering to the nook that earlier had appeared to be the whole of the apartment, she saw the Degas on the moving wall that had slid up alongside the ceiling, and wondered how she could have failed to notice that it was an original—and she herself a ballerina, if she so chose. Ethereal harmonies flashed like lightning from the band, unlike any music heard on earth. Too soon, she descended on pillow-soft clouds to the extraordinary nook that was ordinary again with its tacky zebra couches and kitchenette.

Preferring life in the new place, she returned for another drag on the glass pipe. Immediately it floated her to the fountain where ink-blue water cascaded into vertical cliffs, tailing rainbows, dripping frost on trees, falling in soft wings like feathers out of the smoke of the room, and wrapped the din of the party in eternal velvet. Marianne shook off her shoes and stepped regally into the fountain. In her entire life she had never felt so totally in control of her own destiny.

THE TERM "dope fiend" accurately describes crackheads. As soon as the smoke infuses your cilia, it leaps to your brain and the gears of your body mesh together again. You've been weak and lethargic all day, but now you're on fire. Life has meaning. The next day you make yourself stop and your hands flutter like a palmetto frond. Life's purpose drains away. Your soul is a corroded hulk. Your countless worries are replaced by the only one that counts: the fear that you may run out of crack.

But there is no reason for panic, not for the affluent. Not with the glass pipe stretched across the Caribbean and flowing with the bounty of the Andes. Not so long as the Bahama islands lie en route, so long as the feeding frenzy continues in the States, by mouth, by vein, by nose, and since 1986 by lung. Every year the glass pipe moves a hundred billion dollars worth of coke, a dollar amount so vast that if it were denominated in gold it would weigh as much as the population of the Bahamas. You'll never run out.

Three months later Marianne married Gary Price, whom she found to be trendy, creative, and crafty, a doper of genius. Another month of crack parties, and they both were addicted. As other couples might come together in the kitchen to prepare a meal, the newlyweds huddled around the stove cooking their thick soup of 'caine powder and baking soda, nerves quivering, hearing the *crack-crack-CRACK!* from their tabernacle—until the mixture jells and is iced and solidified, then broken with a kitchen knife into soap-like chips. Gary, who had been cooking cocaine paste into freebase long before the smokable form became commercially available, preferred to make his own crack, claiming it insured both purity and avoidance of detection by the police, whom he knew had orders to crack down on crack.

Soon their evening binges swung between moods of elation, depression, and paranoia. Marianne became beleaguered by the idea that Gary had addicted her deliberately and now meant to kill her to inherit her father's money. At other times she feared something worse, that he intended to keep the crack for himself. When they failed to smoke even for a day, her neurons roared with cocaine starvation. She, Marianne Ransom Price, who for the hell of it had parachuted over Nassau without a single lesson, who would jump into a fountain at a wink, had became synonymous with the Lady in White, and she sat slackjawed, comatose. Wasted months dragged on, lived not together but simply in parallel. She cried unbearably.

Gary accelerated into turbocharges, the smoke of crack smoothed and mellowed by marijuana, trying to prolong the increasingly briefer ecstasy. "The first thing you do when you think about how messed up crack has made your life," he says to Marianne, "you take more crack. What else can you do?" His Lady is white, his life synonymous with her benediction. Without ceremony or joy he lights the chips, inhales deeply, hoarding the smoke in his lungs. He gasps for air, letting it out in a rush of euphoria, then smokes a joint fast to calm his shaking hands.

She pleads with him to quit, but he can not, through ten, eleven, twelve—sometimes twenty hits a day. His heart beats in a wild rhythm. A few months later he suffers angina spasms, convulsions, and depression. He talks of suicide. To prevent the murderous coming apart of his mind, he smokes China White, the less-dilute and therefore smokable heroin from Burma that has flooded the streets of Nassau. Each trip becomes a recessional from his altar of despair.

With a heroic act of will, and to show him it can be done, Marianne takes no drugs all day long. But in that secret place where she can be honest with herself she knows that if by some miracle she could abstain for a year and then someone offered her crack, she would take it in a second. Is there any use in trying?

By afternoon Gary is so strung out he lies in bed with his eyes closed listening to the spasms of his shriveled arteries. Sightless in one eye because cocaine has withered the retina, it is only a matter of time before he will be totally blind. She sits aside him on the bed, shipwrecked mates of the horse latitudes. But she can't stay. The blood is too loud in her temples.

Automatically she moves to the sill and stands there looking out the window, knowing she need only torch that pipe for the magic light to explode upon her, to feel the rapture for which it is exquisite to suffer, to weaken, and finally to die. She thinks of those illiterate girls in cheap miniskirts and transparent blouses Goombay-shuffling down Bay Street at two in the morning and she thinks, *Only our clothes are different*. She sees Gary in that dim and dirty apartment, but remembers her brother when they were children in their well-lighted bungalow, and the thought sustains her through the night without a dose. Her first abstinence.

SATURDAY MORNING. The night-long drizzle ended and the air grew gusty with the smells of the drying earth. Marianne forced herself out of the bleak warehouse and wandered across the causeway into the heart of Nassau, past Parliament Square shiny with raindrops, down the sixty-six steps of the Queen's Staircase that slaves had carved from solid rock a century earlier. She trudged over the hill to Bain Town where children play in puddled streets. Edging around three little girls jumping rope, she listened to their rhymes, so like her own childhood, knowing the sadness of a cat grown old and abandoned and wondering whether anyone would feed her.

One of the girls saw Marianne and rushed to her. "I know yer name," the little girl giggled, raven hair falling in a rope across her back, like Marianne's at that age. Light-skinned, eyes wide, stately profile, the girl was a mirror to the past.

"Oh?"

"I seen you afore. I hear somebody call you 'Marianne.' You

the Marianne in the song, ain't you? You sift sand at the beach?"

Marianne gave an embarrassed little laugh, a tortured convulsion of the ego. "No I'm not."

"Yer beautiful! I been lookin' to grow up jus' like you!"

"Oh my God." An image came to her of a cormorant rippling the mirror of a heavenly sea . . . and a shotgun blast sending it screaming to eternity. She searched the face of the girl who smiled at her with the warmth everyone in this town used to show to strangers.

Marianne held the girl's chin. "Now you do somethin' for me, honey. You go back to your jump rope and be glad you are who you are. You see, I've been looking for something too."

"What?"

"I've been looking. . . " She felt the post-rain wind free on her face, damp with the silence of decision. "I've been looking my whole life for a rope like that to jump."

Marianne hurried into the old neighborhood, a zone of shacks and bungalows painted like rainbows. She came to the house she grew up in and saw in the front yard the familiar century plant, so tall now it poked its needle-pointed fronds into the tiled roof. When her brother opened the door to her knock, she stood there looking at him for a long time. Finally she said, "Geedee, cure me."

Through his thick glasses, Dr. Gérard Dean Ransom peered down at her sorrowfully, his beard punctuating his words. "I've been expecting you," he said. "The hospital called. Gary's dead."

31 *Voodoo Therapy*

IF NORTH hadn't known before coming to the bungalow with Marianne the evening after the fourth of July party, he would have thought the three of them were unrelated. Geedee, wearing sandals and beard, was angular and gaunt as Mahatma Gandhi. Their mother, Marie, looked haggard and older than her years, but she carried herself with the complex pride of those who live close to nature, who speak their minds even before the sun sets.

"Drug addicts," said Geedee at dinner, "seem to me the most conscientious of lost souls, more honest than paranoids, more genuine than hystericals, more open than schizophrenics. They at least take their problems in hand and do something about them, even if it's only to anesthetize their pain. Marianne has worked hard at her cure."

It seemed to North that Geedee wanted Marianne to eat herself out of whatever vestige of addiction she might retain. There were three salads of leafy plants marinated in lime juice, and a soup of boiled ginkgo biloba (the tree that lives a thousand years, Geedee explained.) The entrée consisted of steamed legumes that North couldn't identify, and for desert they ate honey-sweetened cassava with baked plantains. Even though Marianne now slept in her father's house, Geedee had continued to decide as he had since her

241

therapy began seven months ago what she should eat, when she would exercise, and in what sequence. His regimen for her included megavitamins, running, piano playing, and potions flavored by Marie's obeah.

To say that Geedee had a colorful background would be like saying Dracula had an interesting habit. Never married, he received his medical degree from the University of Barbados, then spent years investigating the yin and yang of what he called the occult "sciences." His tools became the herbs, the needles in dolls, the strange mixtures of plant and animal parts, the conjurations, the astro-numerologies of their mamaloi mother—"psychic gestalts and paradigms," he called them, that he attempted at every manifestation of their benefit to reconcile with orthodox medicine. In his attempt to merge the old with the new, he regarded himself as a medical Einstein seeking a unified field theory of the human body. His eyes gleamed in the passionless look you see on those who have lived their lives apart from the world of ordinary men and jobs and raising families. Geedee was a witch doctor, but not a rich doctor, believing it evil to profit from the sufferings of others. In payment for his services, the backyard was full of goats, chickens, banana plants, bicycles, antiques, brass pots, and farm bells.

"Marianne is essentially cured," Geedee said as if North were the local health officer. When North didn't respond, he explained, "She worked hard getting to this point. At first she did nothing but eat and sleep, then for months she could do neither. But gradually . . ." He shoved a forkful of green leafy things into his mouth. "Gradually, she struggled out of her addiction and the reasons behind it. Marianne is my greatest success."

Marianne looked embarrassed. "Geedee worked me day and night. I had no time to think about my problems." The black cat jumped on her lap. "This is Prince—Mama's familiar," she said in her musical laugh.

Geedee ignored the comment as if it were the most natural thing in the world for your mother to have a familiar. "As a biophysicist," he said to North, "you know how cocaine activates the neurotransmitters—mostly dopamine—for pleasure. The converse of that, when dopamine is exhausted from the brain, leaves an emptiness, a black pit that can drive you to suicide. I've done a lot of work in treating depression, and that led to my determining certain combinations of foods in conjuction with precisely timed regimens that increase dopamine naturally." He peered at North from around his glasses, seeking approval, apparently glad to be talking to a man of science.

"What do you do to prevent a recurrence?" asked North.

"Addiction is one of mankind's solubles," Geedee said. "Unfed, it dissolves by itself."

"I've seen studies," North said, "that showed nicotine to be more addicting than cocaine."

"Only after the habit's well-established. In the beginning, you have to *force* a laboratory animal to breathe tobacco smoke. You give an animal one dose of cocaine and it's hooked because it wants to be hooked."

This man may be a witch doctor, thought North, but he had a way of getting to the root of a problem. Following conversations with Marianne, North had been thinking that maybe legalization wasn't the best answer to the Plague. Oh, it might be better than prohibition, but why not a technological solution to the drug problem?

"It should be possible," North said, "to gene-splice endopytes of one of the microorganisms that live inside a coca, marijuana, or poppy plant to alter the properties of a drug."

"To remove their hallucinogenic properties?" asked Geedee.

"You *could* do that. But I think we'd be better off if we kept the intoxicant and removed the side-effects."

Marianne widened her eyes. "Why on earth. . . ?"

"Look at it this way. Even if you could spray the planet and wipe out hallucinogenic plants, you haven't wiped out demand. Illegal laboratories would turn out so many different synthetic drugs you couldn't even catalog the ways they'd destroy human brains. The best answer is harmless drugs."

"Not more drugs!" said Marianne.

"Not *more* drugs. *Harmless* drugs," North said. "Genetically engineered, safe drugs for mood enhancement, with built-in antagonists to prevent overuse and no side effects such as addiction or insomnia."

"Would the bad old drugs still be illegal?" Marianne asked.

"Sure, but who would buy expensive, illegal, and addicting crack for a five-minute high when he could buy cheap, legal, non-addicting synthetic cocaine with a high as long as desired and no harmful aftereffects?"

For Marianne and Geedee the concept of perfect drugs was of more than academic interest. "What would happen to the work ethic," she said, "if people could find instant happiness in a pill they knew wouldn't hurt them?"

"Exactly what happens now when people find instant happiness in a lungful of crack. The only difference is that the new drug wouldn't destroy them. Most people would still try to make their lives productive. Besides, if we're building perfect dope, we might as well add a mechanism to make the user want to stop after some level of modest use."

"Well, until you splice the right plant genes, I'm stuck with this," Marianne said, producing a book with a leather cover. "Gee-dee made me write in here everything I felt during my withdrawal—every mood, every craving. Now if I'm tempted, I read it to relive the agony of withdrawal."

"And are you tempted?" North asked. Everything was so overt in this house, he felt he could ask with impunity. He was right.

"Yes," she said. "Even after seven months. But only at night."

Alone in the living room after dinner, Marianne told North her mother's side of the parental divorce. Father had manipulated Marie as he had everyone else, using her as rungs on his ladder to power. Despite her mother's and brother's mix of superstition and modern medicine, Marianne believed they were accomplishing something more substantial than had her father. Her mother lifted the exploited from their complacency; her brother prepared therapies the people believed in, then brainwashed his patients of their afflictions—and their addictions.

Marianne played the piano for North, the same Chopin etude she had rendered at the United Nations, to remind him of when they met. But now she did it with the confidence and poise of a professional. Afterwards she said, "Geedee had me playing twelve hours a day, month after month, until I went to work at the agency."

North imagined Marianne's life in this bungalow. Unable to work, the days must have passed slowly under the watchful eyes of the doctor and the mamaloi, jogging down the streets early in the morning, housewives staring, children waving, then coming home to write her feelings in her diary and being checked for blood pressure and respiration. Her nights had consisted of piano practice, the melodies drifting over Bain Town, halted now and then for Geedee to draw a tube of blood and titrate it while expounding on his theories. And through the ordeal Marianne had been burdened with the fear that dopamine deprivation would renew her despair. No wonder she was nervous when they first met.

North reached for her hand. What do you say to someone you value, who has been to hell and survived, albeit a hell of her own making? "It's over now, Marianne," he said inadequately.

"Geedee keeps saying it may not be. But I *feel* fine, as though it were something that happened to me in a past life, a life before my job at REHAB, even before my time in Europe." She saw him studying her, and said, "What do you think of my family?"

He laughed. "Geedee's doing something right, whatever it is. But *voodoo. . . ?*"

"When I was a little girl I used to read in bed, struggling with the French of Mama's books on Haiti, while the dogs howled in the streets and made me think of werewolves. Voodoo today is different. It's an established religion whose priests are trying to help their congregations instead of turning them into zombies. It doesn't seem so weird when you get used to it."

North didn't know what to say.

"Well, maybe it is weird," she said with a little laugh. "To tell you the truth, I can't get used to it either." She took his hand. "Come on in the kitchen."

Next to a modern gas range, stood her mother boiling something in a huge pot. "What's in it?" Marianne asked.

The answer made North want to laugh—or cry: whole lizards, apricot pits, chicken parts, mashed scorpions, leaves of the horse bush, snake root, cascarilla bark, and rat liver. A few black tail hairs and white whiskers from Prince bounced in the bubbling cauldron like interracial dancers. The curious cat sat like a boat on a rough sea, bewhiskered on the starboard side of his face and listing toward the cauldron. Marie explained evenly, as though describing a recipe for an afternoon bridge party, that the liver of the rat was the catalyst, the cat whiskers the amulet. Yesterday, Marianne explained, Geedee had taken a sample of her blood to determine what trace elements might still be lacking, and hadn't yet given her his prescription.

"That for me, Mama?" North knew she was trying to sound casual.

"Non, ma chérie," said Marie, aware of North but looking at her daughter. "It wouldn't work on *you*. It is for *un pauvre* believer in the parish whose cancer has spread."

Marianne exhaled in visible relief.

North's feelings were mixed. Drawn to Marianne, he wanted to know her better, wanted to love her. If her mother was some kind of witch, at least she was benevolent. It was Charles Ransom, Neanderthal in a business suit, who splattered the entrails of the nation in his rush for power. North was thankful for what her brother had done for Marianne even while deploring his methods, thinking of some poor slob entrusting his life to obeah instead of—to what? What were the options for a metastasized malignancy, like the one that killed Heather? Laetrile? Chemotherapy? And what had been Marianne's alternative? Antidepressants like imipramine? Pyschotalk therapy? You might as well drink lizard-dumpling soup.

The phone rang. It was a radiophone call for Grant North from Anthony Angelo on the Island for Science. North took it at an antique desk in the living room.

Andy wasted no time with preliminaries, and North could picture him pushing in the relay when he talked. "Grant, your seaweed scientist called on the single-sideband. The Zellers never made it to Florida. He went to their home in Palm Beach and found the daughter and her fiancé calling the Coast Guard and her parents' friends. They know something is wrong because her mother and father would *never* miss her wedding. He wants you to alert BASRA. Over."

Was this too part of the central calamity? He looked at his watch. Ten p.m.

"Roger, Andy. I'll do it right now. Anything else?"

"Yes, Grant. Something even worse." He paused, choking the words. "It's Godfrey . . . "

North pictured God Knowles's face for a moment: dark brown, honest, chiseled, like the image on a coin. He had developed a deep affection for his workers and especially for Godfrey. "What happened?"

"God's been murdered. . . . Over."

AFTER NORTH left, the house quieted and Marianne could hear the faint scurrying noises she had known as a child, of mice—or the whispers of the undead. She didn't feel quite right and had asked to stay the night, and now she lay awake in bed thinking she had been right to confide in Grant but worrying that her grotesque life would drive him away. Her insomnia, once chronic, was upon her again. She worried about her job, about Grant's missing daughter, about survival without Geedee in her father's mansion.

Before his "ranch house" was completed and on the second and fourth Thursday of every month, Ransom had used this bungalow which he still owned to conduct the meetings of his inner circle, the "board meetings" he had been holding for as long as Marianne could remember. On such nights Marie and Geedee made their house calls, saying they would rather lie in a zombie grave than inhabit the same space as Charles Ransom.

In March, after she had been under Geedee's care for three months, Ransom had arrived in a blend of good cheer and tobacco smoke, his two bodyguards waiting in the limousine and a flashy convertible. Minutes later three men appeared: Uncle Mal and Ben Franklin who always came, and a member of the Cabinet she didn't recognize. In business suits, carrying briefcases, they spoke in low, cultivated voices. Marianne went to her room, reading, savoring the air that was hers alone to breathe, thankful to be away from the grim patients plodding up the walk, the endless talk of neurotransmitters or the eclectic blend of voodoo and acupuncture.

The meeting over, his associates gone, Ransom beat a tattoo

on her bedroom door and they talked as they always did. "After all those years in construction, the ranch is almost ready," he said. "They're finishing the landscaping this week."

"I'm surprised Uncle Mal didn't do it. Doesn't he still have a green thumb?"

"Green as ever. As a matter of fact, Mal Pyfrom did plan the gardens and even planted some of the shrubs himself." Ransom paused to fill his pipe, visibly preparing to discuss something more important than landscaping. "Live there with me, Marianne," he said suddenly. "In your own wing. The place is so big, you'd have as much privacy as if we lived in the same hotel."

"How would I get around? It's so far from town."

He put down the pipe, made a steeple of his fingers, and smiled. "Merry belated Christmas, Marianne. That little Ferrari Testarossa outside is registered in your name."

"Well . . ." Her eyes misted. "I mean, thank you of course, but what would I do all day?"

"You would go to work. We need someone to run the rehabilitation agency, and I want you to be the director. You can hire Gérard if you like."

It was an enormous compliment, perfectly timed, for she wanted to lose herself in something meaningful, and Geedee had concurred that she needed hard, consuming, mental work. Here was a chance to help herself and others. Eyes lustrous, smiling broadly, she put her arms around her father and kissed him.

They looked over her new red car together, and after he left in his limousine, she whirled under a sky filled with bright stars, the air around her alive and carnal, where the flowers grow in sidewalk cracks and enormous blooms of frangipani and jasmine fill the Bahama night with perfume. A laugh bubbled in her throat that night. She would live in this land she loved, whose sparkling breezes stabbed her insides like champagne and held so much hope she wanted to cry from the joy in it, and from the sorrow of having wasted it for so long, never forgetting the misery of her former slavery.

After her indoctrination of working with addicts, of supporting Geedee and her staff in helping these unfortunates for whom she had perfect empathy, she had moved to her father's mansion and had dared live as a normal person, even bringing Grant North into her life. But now tonight at the final edge of her recovery, she was shaking uncontrollably. Deprived so long of their crystalline dreams, the receptors in her brain sputtered with a deep and burning loss. Her brother had warned her, but nothing could prepare her for reentering that tomb of despair.

She cried out at unspeakable horrors.

The first thing you do when you feel like this is you take more crack! She would not succumb. She would not feed her dopamine starvation the way Gary had fed his. Agony set in, minutes that seemed hours, and against her will she summoned the magic deliverance, for which she would surrender her job, her independence, her family, her love. The blinds of the windows rattled upward and she twisted in bed seeking those translucent crystals on the sill. Instead, the doors of the cupboards sprang open with her mother's memorabilia of Haiti: statuettes and dolls and her *loups-garous* the werewolves that stalk the dreams of the superstitious.

She screamed. Prince leapt from the bed. The air liquefied and flooded her pores, drowning her in sweat. Geedee rushed in, turned on the lights, and held her. Marie came and said the soothing things that even mamaloi mamas say. Marianne wept so hard she shook the bed, finding no words to explain the blown-out parachute of her emotions.

Through his stethoscope Geedee listened to her heart's wild beat. "I was afraid of this. Time we tried something different. Get the needles, Mama."

Rain drummed the metal roof, falling like shards of glass. Marie returned with a handful of long pointed things similar to darning needles but thinner and shorter. She also brought a cup of soursop tea. And something else.

"For Godsake, Geedee! I thought you stuck your pins into dolls!"

Marianne saw her brother smile faintly under his deep-brown beard, saw Mama holding the tea for her to sip, her cheeks shot with tiny veins she'd never noticed before.

"Now Marianne," he said, "this will relieve your anxiety."

While Geedee was inserting needles around Marianne's hairline, Marie's eyes twinkled, sharp as ice picks. She thrust into her daughter's hands a doll the size of a rat with hair long and dark and bunched over one shoulder like Marianne's. Touching the rough texture of the doll, afraid to move her fingers, Marianne felt like the ancient Carib who wrapped a Spanish friar's cloak around her fevered body only to die of superstition, the cloth itself having carried the viruses of that earlier Plague.

Geedee already had three needles stuck in her temple and was inserting a fourth in the lobe of an ear before Marianne fully realized it. She raised a hand as if in a dentist's chair. *"Geraldine. . . !"*

"This isn't obeah," Geedee said, smiling at the epithet he hadn't heard since childhood. "Poking needles in addicts' ears is orthodox medicine. It stimulates production of endorphins, lessens symptoms of withdrawal. They do it in New York . . . *in hospitals.*"

She fought down a sprinkling of claustrophobia as Geedee, wearing a physician's mirror, bent close to look through her pupils. He attached a cuff to her arm and watched as the pressure on her arteries, her pulse, and respiration subsided dramatically. Marie smiled, kissed her daughter lightly, and left the room. The stethoscope still around his neck, Geedee knelt on the floor beside Marianne. Together they prayed, sinner and priest converted by faith and the eerie moonlight that streamed through the narrow blinds of the windows. Marianne wanted to cry out with the passion and hope a girl brings to her faith in an older brother, to suspend belief as in a fairy tale, to tell him she loved him and believed in him and would submit to his arcane therapies. She said nothing like that, though. When Geedee finally stole out of the room, she turned off the light and gazed at the stripes of moonlight on the wall: softer, yellower bands that soothed where once they had threatened. She passed the rest of the night in peace.

In the morning she returned to her father's house.

32 *The Godfrey Mystery*

AT CENTRAL police headquarters the CID detective on the case told North and Rolle that Godfrey Knowles had died at the hands of his weakness, Velma Fisher, and that she planned to plead guilty. The detective, a dark-skinned lean man with a kind face, spoke in a mix of British and American slang. His name was Sergeant Beneby. "We got ourselves a lovely country here, right? But our violence record is shit."

"Compared to where?" North said.

"Everywhere. Your country, f'rinstance."

"I thought we scored last," said North.

"Your frontier heritage or whatever makes for more shootings than anywhere else in the world. But here—where it's a bloody felony merely to possess a gun—the murder rate is three times as high as yours. Right?"

"If you say so," said Rolle. He suspected that Sergeant Beneby like most policemen resented the prohibition of guns. "Where do you get these statistics?"

"We gather them for Interpol. Doubtless the real facts are worse because the out-islands don't do much reporting. Of course, numbers don't tell you much anyway."

"What do you mean?" said Rolle.

"Take the increase in intravenous drug use. There's no AIDS lab in the Bahamas. Combined with our rape rate and free sex with those three-million annual visitors, we're sitting on a bloomin' time bomb."

North asked the detective to check the blotter to see whether the Zeller disappearance had been reported. It had not.

"I understand that Velma Fisher worked for the government," said North carefully.

"That's right. She'll be fired now, she will."

"Do you know what kind of work she did" Rolle asked.

Sergeant Beneby checked his report. "She's listed as a 're-searcher' for the RBDF."

North gave Rolle a look he would feel long after their eyes met and parted.

"What does a Defence Force researcher do?" Rolle said.

"Oh, I suppose she gathers the statistics we were talking about. Crimes, boating accidents, drug interdictions, and so forth. The RBDF has a number of people in the out-islands doing that sort of thing, usually on a part-time basis."

"Who was her boss?"

"Don't know. Why?"

"No particular reason," North said. It was time to back off.

On the veranda of the Nassau Harbour Club, North and Rolle ate a late breakfast. The pelicans that usually stood on the dock pilings were absent, displaced by the Saturday-morning roar of yachts having their engines revved up for absentee owners. The revelation that Velma probably had worked for St. Gregory made them edgy, abetted by the harbor noises and hot sunlight.

"These events are more than your random demons that infest the Bahamas," North said. "What if St. Gregory or Ransom or some other government Medici planted a seed in Velma Fisher's junkie brain?"

"And the seed grew into what?"

"Into the idea that she would be rewarded for doing some mischief to the Island for Science?"

"You mean maybe she wanted to cut Godfrey just a little to scare him," said Rolle, "and then got carried away?"

"Something like that. Or that St. Gregory told her to kill him. You know how prejudiced the bastard is. Beneby said she shoved the knife in under the breastbone and forced it up. How many housewives know how to do that?"

"Aw, I dunno, Grant. She did work for the RBDF and went back and forth to Nassau a lot, but that doesn't mean she even knew St. Greg, much less that he put her up to it. . . . I know Coby bein' missing is terrible for you. But don't let it scramble your brain."

North placed his knife and fork on his egg-smeared plate, and looked out past the harbor to the river of ocean separating New Providence from Paradise Island. Ski boats were bouncing and an amphibious airplane was roaring its takeoff in the morning sun. Puffy clouds inlaid with specks of diamond spilled light into the sea. A normal day in the Bahamas, made abnormal by the mysteries surrounding them.

Deep inside where intuition held reign, North theorized that the murder of Godfrey Knowles, the Zeller piracy, and Coby's disappearance were related. Jo had told him that the bank in Ft. Lauderdale finally revealed the status of Coby's account and reported that not a penny had been withdrawn. North could feel Coby's survival, perhaps on one of the hundreds of Bahamian islands, or held in the dark like a hostage in Beirut, beaten daily, forbidden to talk to anyone. If that were true, wouldn't there be others so detained? Wouldn't there be some hint, some leak? North believed as did Francis Crick, the biophysicist who discovered DNA, that when there is a conflict between theory and unanswered questions, the theory is more likely to be correct.

"They want us to go home," he said quietly.

"Why?" said Rolle.

"Because we're getting close to learning what happened to Coby." He added abruptly. "We've got to find this Jelly Belly."

"Grant, look at it the simple way—like you scientists are supposed to do. Velma stabbed God because he wouldn't marry her. Period. The Zeller's were pirated. Period."

"Out of hundreds of yachts touring the Bahamas, Sid, why does the very one that visits us get pirated?"

"Jesus, why *not* that yacht? It was a three-million-dollar palace!"

"Why is it so easy for me to imagine someone hiring a team of trigger-happy pirates to wipe out the Zellers and letting them keep the boat for their fee? And planting murder in Velma's head. And having her sabotage the radio."

Rolle swallowed the last of his coffee and sulked. "You think those things because you had a run-in with a smuggler's thunderboat. Because scientists think too much. Because it's a fuckin' mystery!"

North fell silent. He would miss God Knowles, both for his craftsmanship and his companionship. Rolle made departure motions; he had to meet Jo at the airport to search more out-islands. North would be alone in Nassau tonight because Marianne had gone to Miami for the day to attend some kind of international drug-rehabilitation meeting, and they were to meet her father in the morning. Facing a bleak night, he felt he was running in place, toning his psychic muscles perhaps, but getting no closer to his destination. If there was one.

"There are secrets and there are mysteries," said North, thinking of God Knowles.

Rolle stood to go. "What the hell is the difference?"

"The difference is crucial. Somebody—maybe Jelly Belly—has the answer to a secret. Nobody knows the answer to a mystery. Except maybe God."

33 *Sunday Outing*

NESTLED in the crook of a mile-long cape appending Nassau, Lyford Cay is where the old Bahamian rich, the new political rich, the expatriate rich, and the retired rich from four continents keep vacation palaces and yachts. At the first slip in the harbor the Prime Minister's sixty-foot custom cruiser glistened, the neck of her superstructure rising like a swan to a flying bridge. Charles Ransom ruled the deck in captain's cap, leisure shirt-jacket, and matching khaki ducks. North had never seen him in anything other than a three-piece suit and tie.

Ransom traversed the polished teak under a cloud of pipe smoke, his friends following close behind. He kissed Marianne and shook North's hand. "This is my friend, Sheila," he said to North. "And Daniel, my mechanic." He used only first names, as you might introduce children.

Sheila, a slender woman in her early forties, had skin the color of anthracite. She smiled sheepishly. Daniel was Ransom's age, lean and weather-beaten like rich old leather. He grinned and shook hands with North vigorously. Two other men, Ransom's ubiquitous bodyguards Wilson and Wright, sat on the foredeck attempting invisibility. The fact that the crew was so small revealed nothing of Ransom's spending habits but only his sense of privacy. No captain, no uniformed staff, no chef for the millionaire Prime Minister who was known in the press as an inveterate do-it-yourselfer and a man suspicious of help.

The cruiser was about as long as North's LCM and powered with the same 671 twin diesels, but there the similarity ended. The Ransom vessel, unnamed for reasons of privacy, splayed antennas for radar, loran, and a variety of radios. Following Ransom inside, North saw at the main control station cellular phones, a fax machine, and gadgets whose function he could only guess, possibly a scrambler and decoder. A floating mansion, the vessel housed an entire kitchen for a galley, staterooms with full-size bathtubs and gold faucets, and a saloon big as a living room. Under the frescoed ceiling of airborne angels afloat in boundless skies, the saloon was furnished in white carpeting and upholstered couches, behind which hung a mixture of paintings from rococo to Victorian, all expensive, all excessive.

Ransom took the cruiser away from the pier past lesser yachts maneuvering around the plush harbor. Safely at sea he turned the controls over to Daniel and asked Marianne to help Sheila in the galley. North followed Ransom onto the afterdeck where a checkered table took the space between two fighting chairs. On it a double clock and thirty-two chessmen shimmered in the sun. So *that* was the surprise!

"I took the liberty of looking up your rating," Ransom said, nodding at the Illinois Chess Federation magazine lying on the table.

Not the U.S. Federation, but *Illinois!* North was from Indiana, but had played most of his tournaments in Chicago.

"We both seem to be rated about the same," continued Ransom, "high expert, not quite master."

"How on earth did you get hold of the Illinois chess magazine?"

"I'm still a member. Didn't you know I went to law school in Chicago?"

"No I didn't." North was astonished.

"How about a martini?" Ransom's voice was supple and oily as it had been at the Embassy party.

"Only if you're having one."

Ransom laughed. Every tournament chessplayer knows that even a small amount of alcohol can ruin his game. Moving to an outdoor bar bolted to the cabin bulkhead, he said, "I'll give us each the same amount of gin." Pouring the clear liquid into two big ship's glasses, he measured as carefully as a chemist filling beakers, then plopped five cubes of ice into each glass.

The smooth slide of the ship over the ocean, the bounce of her bow, the low purr of perfectly tuned powerplants, ice cubes clinking in their martinis, and the prospect of a match with a strong opponent—these tranquilizing forces, natural or contrived, eased the wariness North had adopted since Coby's disappearance. Realizing his guard was down, he nudged it a notch higher as the sun beat hot on the teak and the yacht sped lightly along a golden eastward path.

Ransom took the white pieces and opened pawn to queen four. North responded with the Grünfeld defense. As they played, the last of the land breezes washed over the nameless yacht from a nameless jungle, bearing odors of palm mulch and forsaken safety.

"I understand you and Mr. Cleary offered Mr. Pyfrom a bribe. . . ."

What North valued about chess was that you play according to well-defined rules, but he was finding that the chessboard of the Third World has no rules. At the Embassy party Ransom had said nothing about Pyfrom. Maybe it was just an attempt to throw him off his game, such as advocated by Bishop Ruy Lopez, who in the sixteenth century recommended seating your opponents with the sun in their eyes.

"You don't believe that, Mr. Prime Minister," North said, pushing his Gauguin hat to the back of his head and sitting a little straighter in the canvas chair.

"I hope I don't."

Of course, thought North, a man who would polarize his own glasses rather than remove the boss's portrait would feel compelled to mention such an incident. "Mr. Pyfrom misunderstood us," North said simply. He leaned forward and moved his queen-bishop pawn in gambit, knowing that if there was a real need to explain further, no excuse would suffice. The Island for Science permits lay latent beneath their game like undeveloped photographs.

Ransom declined the Grünfeld gambit and removed his shirt-jacket. July in the Bahamas is no time for decorum even for a Prime Minister. His build was as muscular as North's own, his carriage erect, the weathered body of a worthy adversary. North noticed the two tiny stars tattooed on his right shoulder.

The subject of Pyfrom and bribery evaporated into the silence like a puddle of hazardous fuel. Both players maneuvered to control the center. North saw that Ransom could move his knight to white's fifth rank where, if they exchanged pieces, Ransom's pawn could advance. Ransom restrained a smile and screwed the knight down with a clockwise twist. North had run into players before who screwed their definitive moves into the board, and he had a standard response when warranted. He placed his fingers on the knight and unscrewed it from its imaginary socket. Ransom managed to laugh and frown at the same time. After the exchange, Ransom kept his pawn grip on the center, but North gained a tempo.

Ransom pressed the button halfway down to stop both clocks. "Let's take a break." He began talking about drug legalization as though they'd been discussing it every day since North's U.N. speech. "Your President, your Congress, are strongly committed to prohibition. They draw a picture of future advertising decadence: 'This Angel's for you.' 'Weekends belong to the White Lady.' 'Crack is better than smack!' and so on."

North would rather play chess, but he listened carefully to this man whose words on any subject, he knew, were often disguises for his hatred of whites. North took off his shirt and said, "There's no real reason why you can't deglamorize narcotics and still legalize drugs to deprive traffickers of their profits."

"Don't you feel that an important purpose of the law is to demonstrate society's moral disapproval?" As he spoke he started the chess clock and moved his knight, placing North's queen *en prise*.

These feints, finesses, and artifices on and outside of the board made North realize that Ransom was an experienced actor. His eyes were those of a child as he opened them wide behind the caterpillars of his eyebrows, which he raised now in outrage, now in righteousness, performing at chess—and at government. North moved his queen into the region of the enemy king. In life, as in chess, a threat is often superior to its execution. They both knew that. Why the obsession with legalizing drugs?

"I admit laws often indicate approval or disapproval," said North, castling, a turnabout maneuver that changes the relative positions of king and rook. "But 'legal' doesn't have to mean 'moral.'" He said it with less assurance than he'd felt at the United Nations. "Governments don't approve of tobacco, but they still allow it to be sold—with warnings and so on."

Even as he spoke, North knew he was about to castle his position on the chessboard of the drug issue. You smoke cigarettes and die of cancer forty years later. Meanwhile you've done your job and you've brought up your kids as well as any nonsmoker. Cocaine, on the other hand, corrupts users, enforcers, entire governments in a way the world has never seen. Marianne's experience with crack cocaine weighed heavily on him, made him think in terms more human than when he had written his book. Back then, from the safety of the Lake Michigan dunes, he had looked only at the numbers. Any increase in drug use under fifteen percent had seemed acceptable because it would be balanced by less crime and more money for anti-drug education. But if bright affluent girls like Marianne could get sucked into the drug culture, what hope was there for poor people in the slums? Better to work on safe drugs as he had outlined to Geedee. Meanwhile Ransom's idea to prohibit whatever kills societies may not be so terrible after all.

Ransom castled too. "I have been thinking about your legalization ideas, North. You may be right. The real problem is how to enact such a law when it's still illegal in the U.S. and Europe. We'd be overrun by the world's junkies."

North had the feeling that their black-white pieces were destined to oscillate like a pendulum, reversing roles, changing opinions, swaying with the exotic rhythm of whatever chess game they were playing. Since the Embassy party, North had been seeing racial undertones in the P.M.'s every statement. It was one thing for Ransom to change or pretend to change his position on legalization, and quite another for him to welcome a white man as

Marianne's lover or future husband. He saw himself as Ransom must see him, a white egghead foreigner in bleached dungarees and wrinkled Panama hat, arrogant and naive in the ways of the Bahamas, an interloper come to change his world. He knew then that he no more could change the Prime Minister's opinion of him than he could persuade a shark to close its mouth.

"My ex-wife would have a field day with the two of us," Ransom observed, pointing to their respective tattoos. "A blue moon and a double white star. She'd say we were destined to interact from birth, the moon orbiting an unseen planet, such as these islands."

North studied the chessboard and after ten minutes found a workable knight sacrifice. Mentally he traced several branches of likely moves, concerned that while the sacrifice would shift the attack to his black pieces, he would have to press it one piece down. His resolve weakened, possibly impeded by having drunk half his glass of gin. He looked at Ransom's glass, also half full. Then he saw his opponent staring intently at the black knight.

"Well, it's only a game!" North sighed and sacked the knight. Cat and mouse, half truths, traps, double entendres, a verbal chess game where the rules were known only to one side. Were these to be the basis of his relationship with the father of the girl he would love?

"You don't believe that any more than I do," said Ransom.

"Believe . . . ?"

"That it's only a game."

North smiled. Both men understood that chess is a game only in the sense that music and mathematics are games, boundless crucibles of the real world, abstract and emotional, geometric and revealing.

The Prime Minister had been placed in zugswang, in which any move open to him would damage his position, and was compelled to accept the sacrifice. Six moves later he ended a vicious attack by relinquishing his own knight, then cornered North into a trade of queens. The board was drained of power, an empty battlefield where the kings and a few small survivors limped around without hope. The match came to a draw.

THE CRUISER left placid waters behind and took on the rhythmic thump of freshening seas, plowing up waves that disintegrated into liquid snow along both sides of the bow. Out of sight of land the air smelled of ozone and fish.

Marianne and Sheila joined the men in the forward cabin while Ransom watched the depth finder and Daniel slowly maneuvered over coral heads that appeared gray through the deep water. No one except Ransom seemed to want to eat or drink before diving. He had a cracked-conch sandwich and two beers while examining the reefs below. At a shelf sixty feet down, he told Daniel to stop.

The anchor rumbled out its length of chain. The diesels quit, and a sudden stillness descended upon the cabin, the flawless swells of the sea swallowing sound like a blanket. The moon hung pale in daylight, transparently mottled with the vast craters of the central deserts all the way to the eastern limb. Here on the water planet, a manta quivered above brown coral like a giant bat in a Draculan dream.

By the time the divers donned their gear, a wind had risen that whipped the swells into whitecaps, lowering visibility.

"You and Sheila ride shotgun," Ransom said to his daughter, and without waiting for an answer handed both of them CO_2 bangsticks. In the event of an attack, they could shoot this weapon anywhere into a shark's hulk, and carbon dioxide from a cartridge would expand to fill the body cavity, causing the shark to surface away from the divers. Marianne had carried bangsticks before but never had to use one.

Throughout his life, even after entering politics, Ransom had been at home in the water with a bit in his mouth and a spear in his hand. Now at fifty-eight his only concession to age seemed to be his winking at the law about using a speargun instead of a Hawaiian sling and breathing condensed air from a tank instead of free diving. Ransom and the others sat on the gunwales and splashed backwards, one at a time, heels over heads. They assembled under the hull, then kicked themselves to the bottom. The ocean here, almost as devoid of life as the moon, was murky, signaling a storm. Only a few colorless reef fish worked the coral.

No tropical miniatures in blues or greens or yellows, no transparent shrimp, no angelfish. And no predators except for man.

Hovering above their men, the women resembled Amazons armed with throwing spears. Ransom, his long gun thrust beyond the length of his arms, looked like a monstrous enlargement of a needlefish. As Ransom and Sheila pumped their flippers in search of crawfish or grouper, North moved to a coral head to search the ledges, glancing up occasionally at Marianne. Two big crawfish that had been hiding in the lattices of the coral made a run for it. North grabbed one with his gloved hand. Checking to make sure it wasn't gravid (the season didn't start until August first), he surfaced at the yacht and passed it up to Daniel. Marianne and Sheila stood guard ten feet below.

Ransom broke the surface flaunting a tote bag stuffed with a half dozen jumbo tails. He took the regulator bit out of his mouth. "One crawfish at a time, North? That the scientific method?"

Ransom must have found a colony. Oblivious to the sex of the crawfish his own government sought to protect, Ransom had ripped the tails off the living bodies so he could carry more of them. North was no environmentalist in burlap trunks spouting poetry, and yet . . .

"The bodies of those crawfish you dropped could bring sharks," he said.

Ransom chuckled. "Crawfish? You mean these 'summer crabs'?" using the euphemism of the fisherman who takes crawfish out of season. "Sharks are highly overrated. We are the predators here." He reinserted the regulator in his mouth.

They dove along different diagonals, each woman guarding her hunter. North had seen sharks as big as horses materialize suddenly around a diver, undulating the sensors on their skins, and then in an unpredictable moment gallop in to brush an arm or leg. Such an encounter could flay your skin down to the red muscle, and in a shark's marvelous economy of motion, cause you to be tasted.

At the bottom, Ransom darted from one coral head to another, feeling under the ledges with his spear. Too far away to stop him, North saw Ransom take quick aim and spear an octopus the size of Oscar. Eight arms flailed in pain as the animal activated its pigment sacs, changing its color from placid green to furious red, breaking into frantic white ripples and back again to red. The octopus clouded the water with the orange ink of its life's blood.

Furious, North kicked after them. But Ransom soared upward with the tethered octopus writhing around the spear in a death dance, its ink and blood swirling like veils. The dying animal telescoped one big eye and made contact with North, who knew that even if he could get it away from Ransom and off the spear it would be dead in minutes. The outraged and defiled creature dug his arms into the water against the pull of the man, fought for another minute of life, and perhaps wondered in his remarkable intelligence why this alien was pulling him so relentlessly to the surface. And then knowing . . .

North's saliva thickened behind his regulator bit. Marianne moved close to him, and through her mask he could see her bloodless face. He wanted to stay on the bottom here with her, away from Ransom, but with crawfish bodies and the blood of the octopus in the water, it was too dangerous. The water world, invisible before, came suddenly alive. Barjacks, triggers, crabs, anemones, even the tube sponges seemed electrified, the mobile animals among them racing in terror.

Suddenly a pair of streamlined metal shapes materialized out of the murk. Too lean, too agile for nurse sharks, they were bulls or tigers. They started their wide circle. When sharks come close enough to look you in the eye, thought North, you realize you are part of the food chain.

Marianne was facing a different direction and couldn't see the sharks. North grabbed her, made two fingers into a "V" in front of her mask, and turned her so they were back to back, their tanks clanking together. North braced the airgun against his leg, held the spear guard over the point, and forced the rod down into the barrel. When it was loaded he switched off the safety. Methodically, slowly, trying not to signal distress, they ascended back to back, keeping the enemy in sight while aiming their weapons. They would get only one shot each.

Once in the waters off the Island, a shark far smaller than

these two had gulped an eighteen-inch grouper North had shot and was trailing behind him. The shark had taken the whole grouper, chomping right through the stainless-steel spear, leaving an end cut so clean it appeared to have been sawn off and filed smooth.

The sharks swam faster, tightening their circles. Now you could see their rounded snouts, receding chins, and disconnected stripes. Tigers. A mere hundred people a year are attacked by sharks, North knew, but he found no solace in the rarity. Even allowing for the enlargement underwater, these two had to be twelve feet long and weigh close to a half ton each.

The tigers were restless. Abruptly they dove to the bottom, their long tails pointing up as, heads down, they gobbled the crawfish carcasses. Crunching sounds filled the ocean. North and Marianne continued to rise, each holding his breath. You invite an embolism doing that, but it was essential that their hearing not be diminished by the noise of their bubbles. In the long moments between breaths, there were only the sounds of inner space and fear, a silence so deep it swallowed their bodies.

The sharks reappeared. They circled again, faster now, and suddenly the graceful movement of the closest turned into a tense zigzag. The shark arched its back, pointed its snout up and its pectoral fins down, then rolled a little to the side, opening and closing its mouth. This animal wasn't looking for a meal, North knew; no predator so warns its prey. It was challenging him for supremacy of the territory.

Marianne's bangstick would be more effective than his speargun, which to a shark struck anywhere but in the head was about as damaging as a needle to a man. As she twisted in his direction to face the shark, he saw her masked face had become a mask of terror. There was no hope that she could use her weapon, or that he could get it from her in time.

He fired his single spear—just as Marianne nudged her tank against his. The spear glanced off the shark's head.

In the seconds of the shark's distraction, North and Marianne bobbed to the surface and scrambled onto the rear platform of the yacht, pulling their legs up fast. They climbed onto the afterdeck and moved to the middle of it, as far as possible from the savage sea. He helped her out of her gear and held her while she shuddered like a sea anemone. Her skin was pale.

"Say nothing to father," she said, her eyes greener than the ocean.

"Say nothing? He spearfishes like he has rabies!" North wanted nothing more than to throw Ransom overboard, fully weighted.

But as he embraced Marianne and pressed his face against hers, his body warmth returned with a weary calm, that transitory peace that follows combat, when you know you have no right to be alive or uninjured but that you are.

"You're right," he said at length, thinking of Coby and his need to keep the Prime Minister receptive. "It's not as though we're going to go diving with him every Sunday."

34 *Black Buries the Light*

ICE CLINKED in oversized glasses filled with fresh gin and a spray of vermouth. Daniel was skinning the corpse of the octopus.

"Ah, calamari and crawfish!" Ransom said, lifting his eyes to the angels floating on the saloon ceiling. "Could anything be better?"

Marianne wouldn't meet her father's eyes. They sipped their drinks and looked at the little invertebrate, the admiral of the ocean sky who played the music of color, who made love and had mollusk children and built castles out of pebbles. They watched his boneless body, breaded and fried in oil, basil, and spiced tomato sauce, Bahamian calamari.

Stop it! Forget the octopus, North told himself; animals are killed every minute in the ocean. Remember man's inhumanity to man. The Zellers. Godfrey Knowles.

Rain hammered the windows and flattened the sea into sheets of steel, cleansing North's mind. It turned suddenly cold and the sky darkened, but the cabin was warm and snug in the aura of yellow lights and crystal drinks. In the dining booth Marianne sat at North's side and held his hand as she poked at her dinner, avoiding the calamari.

Ransom, who had been drinking beer since the chess match,

266

switched to straight gin, taking it neat in his giant glass. The more he drank, the more dilated became the nuggets of his eyes, set like ball bearings in the sagging machinery of his face. When she finished eating, Marianne sat like a cat with her bare legs tucked underneath her black knit skirt, whose large white buttons ran up her left side, jumped a bare midriff, and continued their ascent to a matching tank top. The bottom three buttons were unfastened. Ransom grew loud and maudlin, launching provoking questions at Sheila, frowning at the stubble on North's chin, glaring at Marianne's skirt and her hand clasping North's. He lectured them about the black man's plight in the Bahamas before the election of Independence ushered in the majority black government; about the crimes of the Bay Street Boys, who had bartered the casinos to the Mafia; about the effrontery even today of barber shops in Nassau that advertise "Only White Haircuts."

"You're a scientist. Tell me, doctor, how did race come about?"

North decided to ignore the taunt, but wondered how much to say. People ask seemingly simple questions of scientists—such as why the grass is green—then stop listening as the explanation grows more complex than they expected. North assumed that prime ministers, like most of the intelligentsia of the world, are scientific morons by any conceivable measure. "Probably differences in climate," he said. "Then survival of the sexiest."

"The sexiest? Not the fittest?"

"Evolutionists think sexual preference played a greater role. Green frogs mate with other green frogs because they find those with the same characteristics more attractive."

"Then what, may I ask, are you doing with my daughter? You may have noticed she is a *black* woman."

"Father. . . !"

"Merely a scientific question, Marianne," Ransom said, but he was talking so loud that Wilson and Wright edged into the stateroom. Ransom dismissed his bodyguards with a wave of his hand.

"Then I'll answer the question scientifically," North said, taking his beat from a different metronome, rejecting the stock response about accepting people for what they were. "Marianne is not 'black.'"

"Oh? It escaped me."

"What I mean, of course, is that she has Caucasian features."

"There's more to race than that!" He paused. "Marianne and I are both half white. Yet in your country we are denied the ordinary courtesies given to pure whites. Why?"

"Black is the dominant gene," North said, tired of whatever game they were playing. "Even a little Negro blood is noticeable to prejudiced whites." With the Prime Minister as his opponent he could draw but never win.

Having poured its fury into the sea, the thunderstorm was over and the moon floated beneath a sky dulled in metallic clouds. Sheila excused herself and went to Ransom's stateroom. While her father was fixing another drink, apparently in no hurry to have Daniel weigh anchor, Marianne nudged North through the low door and outside up two steps to the wet teak of the afterdeck where they leaned against the rail. The air smelled musty, but the squadrons of sandflies had not yet found them. Lit by a small spotlight, the Bahamian flag flapped wildly on the sternmast. North saw the bold black triangle meant to symbolize the people, and thought about how the word "black" had become synonymous in the language with evil or hopelessness. To the ancients, black meant humiliation and death, because black absorbs all colors and buries the light.

"Don't let father get to you," said Marianne, clasping his hand. But before he could reply, Ransom came out to the afterdeck with the gin bottle in one hand and his glass in the other.

"It's an ugly night," he said, inspecting the clouds scudding across a muddy sky. Seeing the flag, he added, "You know what the black in our flag stands for. You think it's racist?"

An ugly night all right. North pondered his move for a long moment, aware that he was about to sacrifice something more than a knight. But he couldn't help himself. "Yes," he said.

"Why?"

"Because it is. Imagine how American blacks would feel if we said the white in our flag stands for our lily people, the red for our bloody revolution, the blue for . . . how about our 'Mayflower bluebloods?' We'd have riots from Liberty City to Watts."

"It isn't the same!" Ransom said too loudly.

Slurring his words, the Prime Minister told stories of the bad old days of white rule, implying in incident after incident that today's poverty, lack of self-sufficiency in food, the one-industry economy, the majority of babies born to unwed mothers, and the highest crime rate in the world are the fault of the British or Americans. He bragged that his government had turned it all around, refusing work permits to foreigners and the right to vote to Belongers, so that the Bahamas today is only twelve percent white— half the number before Independence and the inverse of the racial mix in the States.

"But you've had two decades of black rule!" said North, knowing he should hold his tongue and at the same time desperate to shake the status quo, to plumb the design of the one man in the world who could help him the most, but would not. North's emotions burst from their depths. "Your administration is black. Your parliament, your judiciary, your police, your Defence Force. . . ." He came to his feet, flaying each of the four branches of Ransom's government, "Black, black, black, *black!*"

Marianne squeezed his arm, hard.

"Dr. North, your remarks are insulting." The Prime Minister's brows arched, showing lines that had not been there before, like lunar rays emanating from the craters of his eyes. Every snub suffered under colonial rule, every white slur endured in the States, every injustice of his life suddenly seemed carved into that face. He staggered and sat on the edge of the chess table, still holding the glass and bottle. "Your very name's an insult!"

"What on earth do you mean?" North was honestly puzzled.

With his right eye out of control and grazing somewhere to the left of North, the Prime Minister answered in a voice no longer liquid, "Grant Kent North. Literally, 'Giver, Whiteman from the North.' Did you think it escaped me?"

Marianne looked ready to cry. If this man weren't so important to him, North would have laughed. Surely when Ransom sobered, he would realize the absurdity of his comment. Or would he? Prejudice was unreasoned as it was unreasonable. He felt the sweat on his neck turning cold, and once again saw himself through the Prime Minister's hardened eyes, this time as a spoiled dilettante trying to foist his ideas and money on an impoverished nation, an exceedingly minor Rockefeller whose white gifts and white face were decidedly unwelcome.

Or was it even worse?

Ransom drained his glass and jumped up, knocking over the chess table. Black and white pieces scattered across the teak.

"It's not jus' your name, North. It's your hypocrisy. All your high-minded ecological and scientific nonsense, your holier-than-thou contempt for our country's drug problem." Questions thundered from him like a repeating cannon. "Don't you think I talk to my Defence Force? Don't you realize I've been told about your Island? Don't you think I know about your bribe to get out of jail? And how you're using Marianne? Are you the one behind her absurd story of St. Gregory pouring gasoline down people's throats?" He paused for a quick breath. "Tell me, is the Island for Science an elaborate front for drugs? Or is it only *bankrolled* by drug money?"

Now North knew why he had been invited to this yacht and why the Prime Minister had launched this charade. He was here to receive his sentence firsthand. Feeling his blood rising, his head began to ache and he knew he would never get the permits to operate the Island for Science. Like those white non-citizens after Independence, he would be allowed to stay until his money or his resolve dried up, his Island a fortress under siege, until at the end he would be forced to desert the Bahamas without Coby, without knowing. Here lay the raw answer to Cleary's Enigma.

Then it came to him that a charade is enacted for an audience, and he knew that Ransom staged his outburst mostly for Marianne's benefit. *Avoid white men bearing gifts!* She had been used, all right. But not by Grant North.

Marianne was arguing vehemently on his behalf, insisting that it was a prisoner under therapy, not North, who had told her the St. Gregory gasoline story. But North could hardly discern a single word. He was frozen as in a nightmare when you're pursued by the shadowy shape of Death who finds you hiding and is ready to strike, and you remain entranced, unable to move your legs.

North remembered saying nothing more that night, not on the yacht as it sped back to Lyford Cay, nor in Marianne's Ferrari coasting down the streets of Nassau, nor when he left her outside the Harbour Club unkissed, both of them lost in contemplation, their passion anesthetized.

In bed like an injured animal in a cave, he indulged his secret emotion, welcoming it like an old friend. The throb in his head mutated from pain to the pulse of the Island jungle. No one could take his Island from him, for he *was* the Island. Grasping his wrist, he felt the heart of an entity larger than man, and it invested in him a strange strength. He must be dreaming. Dreams are bizarre, he told himself, because the cortex receives signals from the brain-stem instead of the outside world, then tries to organize chaos into some sort of coherence. That was happening to him now. Except that he was awake.

North believed he understood his own mind, at least intuitively. He recognized the alien paranoia teetering somewhere beneath his consciousness ready to escape into a new and dangerous version of reality. But how can you fight the dragons of delusion when they are congenial guests? With an act of will, he suppressed the comfort of the Island Incarnate. He lay awake desperately striving to rearrange the pieces of his life.

But as the hours ticked away, he felt only the pain of his Island dream, swiftly severed, the way amputees feel their missing legs.

35 *ORIGINS: the Politician*

WORLD WAR II had turned Nassau into a haven for rich British refugees such as the Duke of Windsor who became governor of the colony. After the war the cocktail society radiated inland from Bay Street, and provided young Charles Ransom and Malcolm Pyfrom a source of income from purse-snatching, while they attended Government High School. In those days the colony had no university. After high school, Ransom, Pyfrom, and the other bright star of the Bahama school system, Cora Carstairs, found acceptance at Roosevelt University, which was located in one of the most racist cities on the planet, Chicago. Carstairs eked out an existence on minor scholarships. The boys paid their way by running the student photolab to provide not only photographs for the school newspaper but also a service for their fellow students.

What did undergraduates want that you could make in the dark, where you were undisturbed and could study your French or economics? Under the dim amber light, the future rulers of the Bahamas memorized the vocabularies of both subjects—*J'acquiers, acquérons, acquérez, acquièrent*—while developing counterfeit drivers' licenses. In those simpler monochromatic days, you manufactured a license as easily as did the State of Illinois, and in the same way: fill out and sign a printed application, paste on the photo, scribble numbers at the edge, and photograph it onto a paper negative, which became the license. Four years later they took the business with them to the John Marshall College of Law, using their own darkroom in their own spacious apartment filled with Pyfrom's potted plants.

Graduation week. Strong sunlight hammered the garbage-strewn lots between the brownstones on South Park Boulevard. No one yet had heard of Martin Luther King, after whom this boulevard would be renamed, but all the people on the street were Negro. A drunk with a live rooster on his shoulder begged coins for drinks. Teenagers jived along the sidewalk as they do in Nassau. In the postwar Bahamas the white minority ran the casinos, the businesses, the government, the press, and comprised the "society" you read about in the *Nassau Guardian.* Ransom would change that someday, but now on this hazy southside-Chicago Saturday he was concerned with his final exams. Wearing the cream-colored summer suit he bought this afternoon for a triumphant return to his country, he parked his convertible and trotted up the steps of the brownstone.

In the vestibule two white men in baggy suits and pockmarked faces accosted him and ridiculed his first name, calling him *"Charlie-girl."* There ain't no *man* in the city of Chicago what calls himself 'Charles,'except a course the ladies' hair dressers and them other fags. You a fag, *Charles?"*

As near as Ransom could tell, he had wandered into someone else's nightmare. In the Bahamas, "Charles" or "William" are names no more effeminate than "Chuck" or "Bill."

"How long you guys been doin' licenses?" one of the detectives said, betraying admiration. "We never would of guessed if the folks at Marshall hadn't tipped us. We got your buddy Pyfrom."

He imagined Pyfrom at the police station, mute, defiant, hiding his fear behind that bloodless expression of his. They had run the license business for so long, they thought themselves immune. Ransom tried arrogance. "Either arrest me or get the hell ou—"

A sledgehammer blow to his belly hurled him to the floor, where he vomited over his new suit. The detectives left and he managed to crawl up the steps. Inside the apartment, he found the contents of drawers and cupboards smashed and boxes of sensitized photo paper opened to the light, ruined. Fortunately Ransom had kept no negatives.

At the college he found the Dean of Students, a white man who unsympathetically pointed out that counterfeiting licenses was both a state and federal felony, each carrying five-year sentences.

"Alleged felony," Ransom said.

They talked, two lawyers citing cases, precedents, witnesses. The dean, knowing that Ransom and Pyfrom had graduated from Roosevelt, already had interviewed Cora Carstairs who was in graduate school at that university. Of course Carstairs knew what her countrymen were doing; more than once she had asked to get in on the lucrative scheme, to sell licenses to the sororities, but Ransom had been afraid of widening their exposure. Despite that, she vouched to the dean for them both. Ransom's legal mind, charging entrapment and prejudice, dredged up the Civil Rights Act of 1866. They negotiated, struck a deal. *Leave tomorrow! No degree. Never practice law in this country.* In return, the Dean would drop charges. Ransom agreed. But first he negotiated for one more day.

He used the time recruiting in the bars. Brothers ready to do what you paid them to do were easy to find, as were men who knew those two cops by sight. The pair who met both of these qualifications accepted Ransom's terms. No killing, no knives, no guns, no bragging afterwards. Baseball bats only. Two hundred cash for each of four broken kneecaps.

At the brownstone, Pyfrom was ungrateful. He had shared the risk at least equally for far less than half the profit—and *he* was the one who got caught! Ransom suggested they go to Canada or England for their degrees, but that missed Pyfrom's point.

"It's not fair, Charles!"

Ransom bristled. "We had an agreement, Mal. Whatever else I did, *I* kept that agreement. That's what's *fair!* You were happy as a pig in shit to earn twenty times what any other job might have paid."

Ransom left for a moment and returned with Pyfrom's Bible. Thumbing it to a place he knew well, he said, "You ever read this book? I mean really *read* it?" He stopped at chapter twenty of the text of Matthew and quoted the parable of the vineyard:

. . . They supposed that they should have received more because they had worked longer . . . they murmured against the goodman of the house, "Friend, I do thee no wrong: didst not thou agree with me for a penny? Is it not lawful for me to do what I will with mine own. . . ?"

For long seconds silence reigned. Then Pyfrom broke out into a high-pitched laugh. He laughed so hard he had to take off his thick glasses to wipe his tears. "Charles, you win. I 'murmured against the goodman of the house!' an' Ah be sorry as shit, mon. With a mind like yours, we'll own the whole fuckin' Bahamas inside a year!"

HERE WAS this white-haired light-skinned woman dressed in a silk gown awash with moonlight, arms raised over her head. Praying wildly in an exotic language, she was surrounded by at least a hundred impoverished blacks chanting something that rhymed.

Ransom and Pyfrom had been welcomed by the white government in Nassau, which in those days was trying to liberalize itself in the face of black agitation. As an inspector in the Ministry of Immigration, Ransom's assignment tonight was to build a case against this woman, a Haitian mulatto named Marie Duvall who had appeared suddenly in New Providence, night-stalking the hinterland. He flowed with the audience that pressed forward up a knoll like Calvary, barren except for a single gnarled fig tree. Some of the people looked like Haitians but most were Bahamian, elderly Nassau Negroes seeking solace, perhaps like Preacher after discovering his wife's betrayal. If Ransom's vanilla leisure suit and brown and white shoes marked him as a government man, he was proud of that signature.

The Haitian priestess, or mamaloi, pulled from a burlap bag a squawking rooster capped red like an Andros buzzard, and chan-ted. *"Osurmy delmusan, atalsloym charusihoa melany bulerator . . ."*

Was she praying to the chicken god? The infernal powers?

He half-expected her to reach into the chicken and pull out frog's feet. Drawing closer, he found to his surprise that she was young, her white hair the work of peroxide, her skin the color of condensed milk, her body under the thin gown sensuous and writhing with emotion. Still holding the rooster, she spun around and stared at him. Something passed through the jade transparency of her eyes to him, touching shapes and places he didn't want to know, and left him traumatized like a minnow in the beak of a gull. Her gaze softened, lingering on his as if to say like that earlier Minister on the mount, I know why you are here and I forgive you for being wrong. Ransom expected lightning to strike then or the heavens to roar, but the winds slept through the electric night and the moon turned her to silver.

The young woman faced her congregation. "Rely on *yourselves!*" Her voice cascaded like water over a fall. "Expect nothing from the white puppet government of the English. . . ."

From beyond the knoll the wail of a conch shell sounded, sorrowful as the black man's descent into slavery. Scores of men and boys circled an enormous drum, wide as a country road, and began a slow pounding like a pulse. The congregation closed in on their mamaloi as the night throbbed with the drum. The faithful swayed on the edge of hypnosis, following her prayer and the sounds of their own beating hearts.

"Pray to the Prince, trust in Him. Offer yourselves as we offer this bird in sacrifice!" Then for the Haitians: *"Priez Le, donnez Lui votre confiance. . . ."* The people were so close to her she changed to a conversational tone. "Remember my friends, your birthright. Vote black! *Votez noir. Noir!"*

So that was her sedition. No wonder the white minority government wanted her deported as an undesirable alien

The mamaloi held the rooster high against the black sky. And at that moment, an ancient cosmic rock slipped out of orbit and incandesced across the heavens, incinerating itself in the lower atmosphere beyond Nassau harbor. People all over the knoll pointed at the trail of the meteor.

The mamaloi dropped her arms hard and wrung the chicken's neck, twisting off its head. *"Ihavala omor, frangam, beldor, dragin. Venite!"* A dollop of blood splashed on her left breast.

Fascinated, Ransom thought the headless rooster might flap toward the congregation, but an old woman snatched the body and shoved it into a shopping bag. The crowd began to disperse in twos and threes. A dozen men rolled the huge drum down the hill.

Ransom, who among the audience had the only car, offered the mamaloi a ride. "Charles Ransom," he said. "How about a cup of coffee somewhere?"

"Marie Duvall," she said. "How about a drink somewhere?"

At the Poinciana, sitting across an oilclothed table drinking white rum, she looked like a tourist in an evening gown and sun-crinkled eyes. Her neck and arms, the intoxicating color of honey wine, emerged bare from the white dress, the material of which gathered at her lap and stretched tight across her bodice. The blood of the slain cock became an exotic brooch, and her hair glimmered like the wax of a burning candle.

"If it wasn't for that white hair—" he began. "You look . . . you seem so normal now. But up there on the hill, you were, well-ll, *tu etais si bizarre!*" he said, demonstrating at one stroke his college French and the intimacy he desired.

"*Ce n'est pas bizarre, ce n'est pas commun,*" she said.

"Well, I wouldn't call voodoo simply 'uncommon.' But what the hell, it's a free country."

"Don't be too sure."

He let that slide. "You really believe in that stuff?"

"What stuff?"

"Animal sacrifices, poking pins in dolls, and all."

"It's a religion. Like yours."

"No ma'am. Not like mine."

She exhaled an exotic plume of smoke from her cigarette. "Aren't you a Christian?"

"I was brought up that way."

"Then you have your sacrifices too. Could anything be more sensational, more hideous than slow death on a cross with iron nails through your hands and a spear in your side? Our sacrifices aren't horrible at all—we turn them into chicken soup!"

Ransom laughed. Forced to memorize the Bible in his youth, he believed in it about as much as he did the Book of the Dead. He glanced at her breast below the brooch. "How did you manage the meteor?"

"I didn't. *Something* happens often enough—a screech owl, a flock of geese seen against the full moon, an eclipse, heat lightning . . . any damn thing."

"And when nothing happens?"

"No one promised anything."

"You make the whole thing sound like a hoax."

"No more than any other religion, Charles. Like all religions, obeah gives order to chaotic lives. The unlearned have something to believe in."

That was the first time she had used the Bahamian word for voodoo, and the first time she called Ransom by his name. Reaching across the oilcloth, he covered her hand with his own. She could be an asset to a man in politics. But . . .

"The god—the *Him*—you invoked on the hill. He's not God, but the Devil."

"God and the Devil, the Holy Ghost and the Prince, Allah and Baron Samedi. It is not necessary to think of them as good-bad pairs. If God created white man in his own image, then who *in hell* should we call the creator of the black man?"

Ransom smiled at the notion of black activism coming from a white person. A mulatto, he corrected himself, the same as he.

"Charles," she said, "how is it that a half-black works for the white government?"

Drinking her drink, composed and smiling, stirring a little under her thin dress, she made him thirst for her. The dark lounge became a crystal sphere inhabited only by themselves

"I want to end white rule," he said. "How better than to work at it from within?"

"Then we're on the same side?"

"Yes, we're on the same side."

Ransom's report to the Minister of Immigration portrayed Marie Duvall as a harmless social worker among the poor, and recommended that she be allowed to stay in the Bahamas. Six months later they were married, the Bahamian and the Haitian. They named their first-born Gérard Dean, their second Marianne. Geedee and his sister grew up in a black-white country that was, with the exception of the white government, essentially devoid of prejudice.

36 *Some Kind of Night*

CAPTAIN Carlos St. Gregory, wearing dress whites despite the July heat, swaggered through the porticoed doorway of the station and demanded to see the suspect, Velma Fisher. The police jumped at his command as if he were S.S. and they mere soldiers. In less than two minutes Velma was in the psychedelic interview room sitting on a purple chair against orange drapes. She nestled her head between her arms on the linoleum table top.

St. Gregory closed the door and hovered over her. "Velma, you dumb cunt! Your assignment was to report what goes on at North's island—not to kill someone. What the hell happened?"

Velma's light-skinned face was raw and red with tears. The braids of her hair, in thin ropes, were beginning to come out of their brass caps. She was wearing a see-through blouse and crossed her legs under a short skirt, but it had absolutely no effect on the taciturn Defender captain whose six-foot-five frame intimidated her.

"Well?" he said, but she just sobbed.

Velma reminded him of his mother when he was a boy, the way she snivelled under his father's questions, her Cuban skin as dark as this light-skinned piece of shit, though his mother had no Negro blood in her, thank God. One of the things he never understood about his father was how he could have married such an inferior being.

Velma was one of a string of *agents provocateurs* the Defender captain had recruited from all over the Bahamas. By appealing to their egos and giving them the title "research assistant," he could control them for almost nothing. Ordinarily he would have let Velma Fisher rot in Fox Hill, but he knew he had to intervene on her behalf in order to transmit a message of paternalism. Another of his agents, Mike Morgan, had screwed up, and the word had gotten around that it was dangerous to work for St. Gregory.

"Now look here . . . Velma," he said, repressing his feelings. "How do you expect me to help you unless you tell me what went on that night?"

She continued to stare at the linoleum.

The odors of the police station were rising with the afternoon, the rotten smell of garbage and unwashed prisoners. Except when he wrinkled his nose against the stench, nothing on the captain's face moved, neither his cheeks, nor lips, nor even the chin under his beard. He seemed to lack facial muscles like a creature lower on the evolutionary scale, relying solely on his eyes and mouth to register emotion.

He sat lightly on the table. *"Look at me, you filthy bitch!"*

Velma lifted her head as if coming up for air, and he could see on her face that look of obstinacy he had come to detest. Never would she admit her crime for fear that he would use it against her. He would have to dig it out of her.

"All right, Velma. If you won't talk here, we'll go somewhere else."

"Somewheres where?" Her voice grated, conditioned by dope and cigarettes.

"To hell, Velma. Straight to hell."

"You ain't goin' ta bring me to dot place of yours, dot evil place. . . ?"

"What do you know about . . . that place?"

"Ah doan know what yuh *do* in dere. But Ah knows what yuh *got* in dere."

"And what do you think it is that I've 'got' in there?"

She peered up at him with slow-rising eyelids like those of a waking cat, but her languor did nothing to conceal her emotions. Her heart thumped visibly under her blouse as she paused to light a cigarette. Suddenly she came alive. "Mistuh St. Gregory sir, now doan go gettin' mad. After all, yuh pays me t'observe tings." She exhaled a plume of smoke. "All Ah knows is yuh got some white gal in dere."

Whatever Velma said, however she said it, made him detest her and her big mouth even more. This latest revelation, that she had been snooping on him, most likely on the day he'd driven the girl to his farmhouse, elevated his rage to a fine art. There is no fear worse than of the unknown, he knew, and the greater the unknown, the greater the fear, which he was about to inflict on Velma. Striding out of the station to his Mercedes, which was parked between two courthouses, he removed a corrugated cardboard box from the trunk, returned to the station, and stopped at the desk for a pair of keys.

Without a word to Velma, he escorted her outside to the rear of the building and down a flight of stairs, her eyes dilating painfully in the brief sunlight. Then they were in the two-cell block reserved for women where she had spent last night alone. A tiny window near the ceiling, more like a slit in the concrete, delivered a thin light from the alley above. The cell was on the same level but at the opposite end of the building from where the men were detained.

St. Gregory shoved her inside the first cell and locked the barred door. While he would rather have performed his procedure farther away from the police, it was fortunate that no other prisoners were in the block. He knelt on the concrete in front of the bars, and removed from his box a brass brazier of the kind used for burning incense. Leaving the top open, he lighted the substance inside and watched with satisfaction as it burned with a pale blue flame. Soon a greenish-yellow smoke poured out of the brazier and filled the cell block.

"What dot stink?" Velma said. "Dot sure ain't no church incense!"

"That, Velma, is fire and brimstone. Sulfur and pitch to be exact."

"You crazy or somethin'?"

"It's the game Edward Teach devised, to see who can last the

longest in the smoke of hell. We played it when we were kids."
He held a handkerchief to his face. "I do it a little differently now,"
he said, and came to his feet.

Huddled in the back corner of her cell, all you could see of
her face were her moonlike eyes imploring him through the chartreuse fog that had begun to eat at her lungs.

"*Ooooooh!*" she said. "De smoke. It hurt ma eyes! Ah cain't
breathe!"

"The game ends when you tell me the truth," he said with his
hand on the outside door. He heard nothing from her, so he left,
locking the door behind him.

After lunch he returned to the cell block, dense with smoke.
"Now suppose you tell me why and how you killed Godfrey
Knowles."

But there was no answer. Velma lay unconscious on the floor.

St. Gregory doused the smokepot, unlocked the cell door, and
carried her through the bright light of day toward his car. The
faces of passersby showed compassion for the injured woman and
admiration for the white Defender officer who carried this small
black person so gently in his arms, doubtless toward the hospital.
At his car, he propped Velma on the front seat and opened the
window. Her arms slumped over the dashboard.

A few minutes later she came to, coughing and crying.

"Doan you never put me back in dot smoke, Mistuh St. Gregory!"

He stared at her with burning eyes.

"It true," she said. "Ah killed Godfrey Knowles, an' Ah be
sorry. Ah takes ma job wid you most serious. But dis here doan
have nuttin' to do wid dot."

"What does it have to do with, lady? You an addict?"

At the mention of the word, Velma broke into a new set of
tears.

He wanted to slap her across the mouth the way Sir Thomas
used to slap him when he failed to answer a question promptly.
But he leaned against the steering wheel and waited. Over the
course of an hour, between sobs and smoky tears, silences, lies,
memory gaps, and failed attempts at flirtation, the story came out
like a rotten tooth.

On one of their nights together in his trailer, a few miles into the woods from the village, Knowles and Velma had fought their usual argument about divorcing their mates and marrying each other. Knowles's "no" apparently had been final, more final than he could have imagined. Velma was frantic with no White Lady, no Smoke, "no nothin'." It was an electric night, the village discharging its mystic darkness, the kind of night in which you anticipate not only riots in the street, but riots steered by the spirits of the departed. Hysteria reigned among the Great Snake junkies, nocturnal creatures who were suffering through one of the government's periodic crackdowns that left the street vendors completely out of drugs. Velma caught a ride "downtown," if you can call it that on an island whose fangs of three or four roads split the jungle and taste the sea. She went to the doctor's office looking for pills—painkillers, tranquilizers, sedatives, anything. The doctor was ministering to inhabitants of another Family Island, and his door had been smashed, the contents of drawers and cabinets dumped on the floor, every pill taken. Of course, the Great Snake village is too small to have its own dentist or pharmacist, but had there been anyone at all on the island who wore a white coat, their offices would have been broken into too.

Velma Fisher came home to find her husband Oris sticking sewing needles into his arm in a frantic, futile attempt to substitute the feeling of the hypodermic for the heroin it once had supplied. The kids were crying. The house was a mess. Disgusted, she returned to the trailer. Tripping over vines and mangrove roots, she brushed spiderwebs from her eyes and smelled the sticky-sweet frangipani that reminded her of Oris's dope. At that point she would have settled for anything, so long as it meant a change from what she had.

Divorce was the only way out she could see, and when she got inside she tried to wake God Knowles and make him listen. But Knowles, tired from the backbreaking work of laying stone while training apprentices, would only shake his head and drift back to sleep. After several hours of waking him and arguing, she waited until he drifted off again. She took a butcher knife from the kitchen, one of those sharp, fat knives Bahamians use to scale fish, and plunged it into his paunch directly under the breastbone. When it was in all the way to the hilt, she envisioned his reluctant heart and twisted the blade upward to meet it.

St. Gregory eyes shone. "That was some night, you piece of nigger shit."

"Yessuh," she said. "It some kinda night." She wiped tears from her eyes. "An' some kinda day today too."

COBY NORTH stopped digging at the rocky earth above her head, annoyed at how her hair kept snagging on coral and roots in the vertical tunnel. She had become as dark-adapted as a mole, spending most of her time working behind the wall where it was black and damp as the bottom of the ocean. Only the smell of it, the smell of the sea, had kept the memory of the Island and of her father intact, dispensing its secret message, luring her toward the surface with its promise of daylight and freedom.

After four months in this basement cell, the hard-packed sand, rocks, and dirt she brought out from behind the wall a cup at a time had become emotions in her mind, strongly evoked. The memories struck without warning, like coming out of a dark theater into blazing sunshine, a recall so sharp it hurt. There was the sand-pain of the beach the last time she had seen her father. He was running along the water's edge yelling that he would never trust her again. There was the rock-piercing pain of the machine guns on the LCM, causing an agony in her thigh so savage she had lost consciousness in the crew cupboard where she had crawled. Finally there was the dirt-pain of St. Gregory's sick mind.

Coby let her lithe frame slide down the shaft into the cell where she slumped against the wall, bone-tired, dejected. She examined the butter knife in her hand that she used for everything from cutting bread to the daily prying of the four loose concrete blocks. With a sigh, she began scraping it on the flat side of one of the blocks, and when it was sharp she sawed at the tangle that once had been her long and comely hair. She watched it fall in wads, feeling no emotion other than boredom. One problem with this place was that you couldn't get yourself or your clothes *clean* with that bar of animal fat they gave her that wouldn't suds.

She swept up the clumps of hair and tossed them through the bars into a trash can that was emptied weekly by the mute old cleaning lady. Reentering the rectangle formed by the removal of the blocks, she wriggled her body inside. Crouching awkwardly, she resumed clawing with her knife at the hard earth above her head. Every quarter hour she emerged back into the cell with a cup full of marl, sand, and bits of coral rock. Trying to forget the past and how she came to be here, she picked rock and marl out of the cup and threw the pieces in the trash can on the other side of the bars, aware that too much weight might be noticed, focusing only on escape.

A transcendental hope rose in her breast as she reached through the bars and flicked the cup, scattering the remaining sand, like a golden mirage, toward the dingy corners of her prison.

37 *ORIGINS: the Defender*

IN THE TIME before Independence, Sir Thomas St. Gregory, suspected of ties with the mafia that ran the casinos, became the first among the Bay Street Boys to introduce miscegenation bills in Parliament. And yet it was he who helped Ransom, the half-breed, ingratiate himself with the white oligarchy of the country. Carlos, twenty years old, noting those times his father had Ransom and his mulatto wife over to the house, watched how Sir Thomas cultivated his new black ally, understanding that he did it only to mute the opposition.

Despite his design, Sir Thomas discovered with Ransom a genuine commonality in hunting. On a lion hunt in Rhodesia, the elder St. Gregory first brought up the idea of a military force for the Bahamas, and Carlos would remember the day. The Negro porters, talking in their tortured singsong, were dressing lion pelts and setting up tents against the insects that swarmed at dusk. Carlos had shot a gazelle for dinner, and admired the animal he was transforming into meat and other useful commodities. Working aside the cooking fire, he inserted the knife at the belly, splattering viscera, enjoying the feeling of tearing the carcass. Watching Ransom drink whiskey with his father, Carlos felt an overpowering urge to tear the black man apart limb by limb. He despised that subhuman pretender, his habit of making a steeple with his fingers in his nostrils, his feigned politeness bordering on insolence, and especially the way he aspired to greatness—all from a nigger no better than these African primates who portered their dead animals for them.

"There's talk of starting an armed service at home," Carlos heard his father say to Ransom.

"To protect ourselves from the North American tourists, no doubt," said Ransom with a chuckle, puffing on his pipe.

Sir Thomas laughed. "Well, that's one way to get foreign aid from the States."

"The reason for military service ordinarily advanced in the halls of Parliament," Ransom said evenly, "is to provide employment and a sense of discipline to our young people."

Carlos finished placing gazelle steaks on the grill, and crept closer. At the folding table that served as a bar, he mixed powdered milk in water for himself. While not above drinking raw rum with his contemporaries, there could be no thought of comradery with these older men, even though they often invited him to have a drink. Besides, he wanted to relax, and liquor left him vulnerable, ruined the control he needed to listen to his knighted father's words. Ransom's pipe had gone out, and in the quiet air Carlos could smell his foul breath. He imagined him pale in death, lying on a marble slab.

"Look, Charles, white control is as doomed in the Bahamas as it is on this continent or anywhere there's a black majority. My kind—well, we're only fighting a delaying action."

Carlos loved the way his father made it come across with the proper mix of sincerity and conspiracy, his voice controlled in a monotone to conceal his motives. Back home, Carlos practiced his own monotone in front of a mirror, toughening and deepening his voice. Now he studied the black man's face to determine whether it was suspicion or plain curiosity he saw. Neither. It was anticipation: Ransom's mustache twitched like the whiskers of a stalking jungle cat.

"Black power is coming. It's written on the sand, Charles."

Ransom nodded.

Animal sounds far away blended into the hot breath of the jungle. The trees here at the edge of the savanna towered overhead, not at all like the Bahama bush. Carlos listened carefully.

"When we return to Nassau," the elder St. Gregory said, "I shall help you get elected to Parliament. The forthcoming election won't put the black majority in power, but it'll be the first step. You will be a part of it."

"And in return. . . ?"

"Nothing for myself. When the armed service gets started, I want you to appoint my son to a position of authority. Of course, that's down the road a ways. First we've got to get you elected, and enroll Carlos into a U.K. military college to correct his overbearing and narcissistic behavior. There was some kids' prank Carlos was involved in; seems they were pretending to hurt one of their schoolmates, and, well, it made things rough for him psychologically."

The story that had been suppressed by the newspapers at Sir Thomas's urging involved Carlos tying a hangman's noose around the neck of a schoolmate and pulling it taut. At first the boys watching had thought it was a great joke.

"Yo, yella eyes! You gonna *hang* de kid, or what?"

"That ain't St. Greg, boys, thot be de pirate-mon!"

"Go ahead, Carlos, *les see how strong ye be.*"

The ridicule had so infuriated Carlos St. Gregory that he'd hoisted the victim halfway up the tree and held him there for long seconds. The boy recovered, but Carlos's mental health did not. His father sent him for psychiatric help to England where he stayed a year, then returned to Nassau, presumably cured.

"Carlos has the bicyclist's mind," Sir Thomas told Ransom with Carlos listening. "He knows how to bow to men above him and kick with his feet at those below." He said it that way in a semblance of frankness, a diplomat's device to yield a lesser derogation and preserve the more-damaging secret. "Charles, you and Carlos ought to be friends. What the hell," he chuckled, "you've both got the same first name, almost. I wanted him to be called Karl, but the boy's Cuban mother kept calling him Carlos, and the name stuck."

Ransom looked attentive.

"Carlos can help you with the white Members of Parliament in the years ahead. He'll make a fine soldier, a fine officer."

The young St. Gregory, incredulous that a life—his life—could turn on such a politician's conversation, remembered it first as an insult and years later as a true gift, the only kindness his father had shown him.

AS SIR THOMAS predicted, the passage of time saw blacks enter the government in droves. With Britain in full retreat, the black majority led the country out of the British Empire in 1973, a month after the U.S. stopped bombing Cambodia, ending twelve years of war in Indochina and as many years of political strife in the Bahamas.

Every election during Ransom's rise to power generated murmurs about the mamaloi wife of the candidate. Wearing a poor, shapeless dress that reached to her ankles, she would trudge Over the Hill like a begging nun, weaving her way between the junked cars and wounded mangroves of the orange and purple shanties into Bain Town and Carmichael and Fox Hill and Sandilands Village, or across the sea to where the out-islanders lived on Grand Bahama, Eleuthera, Andros, or the Abacos. From barren mounts she would preach in favor of Ransom's candidacy, especially when the moon was full and the sun added its influence to the moon to pull the oceans to extremes. These tidal forces influenced all life on earth, she believed, rendering people garrulous and pliable. The press called her "the Voodoo Politician," but the vote she turned out for her husband advanced his career steadily.

During his campaign for Prime Minister, Ransom supporters ran amuck with delight, tearing down the opposition's signs, scrawling black-supremacy graffiti, insulting tourists, ripping out the telephones that didn't work. The crowds that lined Bay Street were his crowds, cheering, pumping placards, waving the flag to the beat of the national anthem: ". . . *march on to glory, march on, Bahamaland!*" Ransomites bulged the cordoning lines. Female "rushers" shrieked, swooned, reached out to kiss the candidate. Ransom hired bodyguards, but he loved those crowds, those nights.

While Marie preached obeah to the superstitious, Ransom took full advantage of his party's incumbency in a religious nation, invoking his stepfather's brand of divinity on the mostly Baptist poor and needy. Often he quoted the apostle Paul in Romans, Chapter Thirteen:

> The powers that be are ordained of God. Whosoever, therefore, resisteth the power, resisteth the ordinance of God. . . . For rulers are not a terror to good works, but to evil . . .

Goombay politics. Yet the voters ignored the slowdown in tourism, the burgeoning unemployment, the telephone strike, widespread labor unrest, bankruptcies, the flight of capital, and specifically the other black party that sought moderation. Ransom won by a landslide.

Inauguration night was hot with trumpets, the fluttering of flags, the passions of bonfires. Euphoria swept Oakes Field in waves. *"Ransom!" "Ransom!"* At the podium the winner acted humble, contrite, modest. Yet there was no doubt who had taken charge of the people, their jobs, their money, their lives.

Like that arch-dictator once had swaggered into the Reichstag, Ransom the day after his triumph marched into Parliament and initiated the process of rendering it harmless. With no one to stop him, he put down the strikes and employed the unemployed. You had to apply for a permit now for any important financial transaction: to import, export, start a business, expatriate dollars, build a building, sell property, install a telephone, buy a boat. White foreigners needed permission to reside in the nation for longer than two months. For his efforts, more precisely for his achievement in rising to the top office of the commonwealth, Ransom was knighted by the queen of England.

As the nation chose Ransom to be the country's chief architect, so Ransom named Pyfrom, who had won a seat in Parliament, to be his number-two man. Overlooking the harbor where cruise ships and freighters gave the impression of a dynamic economy, Deputy P.M. Pyfrom's office was second in size and position only to Ransom's. Yet for all his success, Pyfrom was a small animal in search of shelter. Hair graying, shoulders slightly stooped, skin mottled, he looked like a vampire bat that couldn't find enough blood.

One day after their inauguration, Ransom entered Pyfrom's office, sat down, and placed his feet on his deputy's desk. The office was sparse except for the obligatory photographs on the wall and plants sunk in large terra-cotta pots. From one of these an enormous philodendron snaked up a pole and ran along the tops of the windows.

"Well, old friend," said Ransom, "we've come a long way from the oarboat wreck in Middle Bight." The air was pregnant with ambition. He could sense money flying in the air like green colloids, and wondered whether Pyfrom could feel it too. "You don't even say 'dis' and 'dot' anymore!" Ransom chuckled.

Pyfrom deigned not to smile. His heavily lensed eyes, un-focused like those of a fish on a tray of ice, revealed nothing. If he resented being Ransom's yes man, he was nowhere near the stage where he could say no. The philodendron sagged with the echoes of postponed confidences.

Ransom had grown accustomed to Pyfrom's spells of silence. "There's a whole nation out there to drag out of the last century. The next thing we do, Malcolm, is take all the businesses out of the hands of the foreign—"

"And begin treating the Plague," Pyfrom said, breaking his mood. He had won his seat on a platform of drug prevention.

"Swallowing your own propaganda?"

"No more so than you."

Both men seemed surprised that the other intended to keep his campaign promises.

"Charles, a quarter of the population over the age of thirteen is addicted to cocaine or heroin."

Drug incidents had begun to appear daily in the press. The communist government of neighboring Cuba—abandoned by the Soviets and the rest of the world, desperate for foreign currency and aid, yet hating the colossus on their doorstep—had permeated the drug trade in a big way. *Departmento Z* of the Cuban Ministry of the Interior had started buying cocaine from South American suppliers and was selling it directly to their outlets in Miami.

Ransom knew he was up against the irresistible pressures of Castro's Cuba demanding safe passage across the ninety thousand square miles of the archipelago patrolled by the Royal Bahamian Defence Force. The Cubans were becoming a menace with their secret killings, exportation of rebellion, and terrorisms. Ransom felt that if the Bahamas did nothing to regulate narcotics, criminals would import them in unmanageable quantities. He came to believe the only way to prevent drugs was—paradoxically—to make them legal. "Every head of state in the world," he told Pyfrom, "knows that Prohibition won't work."

"Well, we control the country."

Ransom laughed. "Can you imagine introducing a drug-legalization bill in the House of Assembly?"

"So what do we do? Besides refusing work permits to white foreigners?"

"Maybe we can combine our goals," said Ransom, heralding a plan that would consume his senior Cabinet for years to come. "Maybe we can get rid of the foreigners and control drugs at the same time."

Pyfrom, like number-two men everywhere, had learned to read the mind of his mentor. He glanced out the window at the tourists thronging down Bay Street, smiled, and said, "Sounds like a job for the Defence Force."

"Part of it, anyway. I think we should start a military operations group within the Defence Force. I've got just the man to head it up—to give us an 'out' in case things backfire. . . . He's a white man, the son of a Bay Street Boy."

38 *Sufficiently Guilty*

ALL THROUGH the hottest part of the summer and into October, when the air turned crisp and smelled of salt, North and Rolle had been making weekly trips to Nassau. They came to attend Rolle's trial, ostensibly, but also to seek new paths that might lead to Coby.

The summer had been a bewildering, fruitless campaign on two fronts, to find a lost girl and to build a dream. Repeated visits to Ambassador Armitage had been of no help, and the U.S. Coast Guard had found no clue. Before and after each court hearing, North's quest led them down the path Cleary had begun, into a blur of offices, procedures, evasions. Lands & Surveys, Fisheries, Finance, Immigration, Foreign Affairs, Labour, Works, Customs, National Insurance, even Health—all these ministries had to be convinced that men raising shrimp, distilling fresh water from the ocean, dredging up pharmaceuticals, and harvesting the sun, wind, and waves would not endanger a country whose every island offered poverty, illness, and wasted lives. Gradually a portrait emerged of a Third-World government redistributing wealth: civil servants cutting red tape by falsifying documents; petty officials taking bribes, rising in the ranks by bowing to the power brokers a step above them; or one minister paying another for the privilege of heading a lucrative project. And at the top of the ladder one leader, armed with plenary power, commanding harmony for the masses.

Having heard nothing from Ransom since the night on his cruiser, North felt he was about to receive another lesson from the master, a dark move in the game of anxiety. He and Rolle had docked at the Harbour Club during a brief rainfall, and now they plodded to the courthouse. Over glistening streets, they read the city's unwritten graffiti of traffic jams, rotting garbage, boys snatching purses from tourists, drug venders lurking in hallways, prostitutes getting an early start on the night. At Trinity Place, Rolle pointed to the marquee on Christ's Cathedral that said:

IF YOU DON'T LIKE YOUR LIFE, CHANGE IT.

"Good idea," he said, flicking a thumb at the sign.

"I want to change *their* lives," North said.

Amid the familiar traffic, the functioning churches, the people striding toward their lives, North realized the only life that had really changed was his own, and it was a sea change. The admission made him feel like an amphibious animal coming alive after shedding its exoskeleton on the rocky shore. After the long summer of worry and the hard work of searching, finding Coby no longer was enough; he wanted something else as well. Revenge.

"Well, don't try changing Madam Judge. This is our last day."

Judgment day. As they passed under the giant fig tree and up the courthouse steps, North could feel only outrage, but Rolle seemed weary, as if he already were sentenced and climbing the scaffold.

Inside there were none of the artifacts of courtrooms you find in most countries of British origin where the judiciary is held in high regard. No high ceilings, decorative moldings, balustrades, marble pillars. No tables for opposing barristers, no railings separating jurors. Like a birdhouse in an aviary, there was only that preposterous wooden cage to define the room, and its varnished bars glowed in the amber light.

As she did every week when Rolle arrived under his own volition, Judge Amin nodded to the guard who ushered the defendant inside the cage and locked it. A ritual presumption of guilt.

"Today," said the judge, her white wig floating above black robes, "we shall conclude the examination of the Defence Force witness, Captain St. Gregory."

Mothers brought their children here for a Saturday afternoon's entertainment, and despite the heat the courtroom was packed. Babies cried, noses were blown, housewives fanned themselves waiting for the show. Two girls, three-foot twins wearing red ribbons in their braided hair, peered through the bars with big white eyeballs, wondering why this man sat in a cage. Rolle winked at them.

St. Gregory was sworn by the old bailiff, who had to crane his neck to address the towering figure. The Defender's eyes smoldered in the dim light, but he looked as official as he had in the commodore's office. North decided he resembled Blackbeard only when he was busy pillaging the out-islands.

"Captain St. Gregory," began the judge, "we have heard your testimony that you found a sawed-off shotgun and two other shotguns on the Island for Science when you raided it looking for drugs. Now tell the court how you happened to find hand grenades in the Island workshop."

North shot a look at Sterling Hanna, but the heavyset barrister already was on his feet. "Your worship! I really must object. This is a trial of Sidney Rolle, not Dr. North or his Island for Science—"

"Now, Sterling, don't get excited. I've told you before, this isn't a trial, *per se*. It's a hearing for me to determine whether to send the case to the Supreme Court. To do that, I've got to get the particulars. . . . Go ahead, Captain St. Gregory."

"Well, on our inspection of the island we came to this laboratory building, and there—"

"Slow down, Captain," said the magistrate. She looked predatory in her black shroud.

There is no such thing as a court reporter in the Bahamas; the judge herself wrote in longhand every word of each witness. In this laborious way, over the summer, she had questioned Commodore Bridgewater who authorized the raid, the dog-handler Chief Lightbourne, the young able seaman who had gotten to fire his NATO submachine gun, the Island technician Lionel Sweeting, and Grant North himself.

"Sorry, your worship," St. Gregory said in his slight Spanish accent. He started again, his strident voice unnaturally hobbled as though giving dictation to a novice stenographer, which he was. "There. On the counter. Were. A half-dozen. Of these. Shiny, long grenades. With little. Propellers. In back of . . ."

At this agonizing pace, St. Gregory told how he had questioned North about the weapons, how they could be used in a firefight, how suspicious he found the alleged scientific projects.

Two hours of such testimony, and the charade suddenly was over. Rolle looked hopeful. The magistrate gaveled for silence, and for a moment the room echoed the sounds of breathing.

"I find the defendant Sidney Rolle," she said, "sufficiently guilty to recommend him to stand trial before the Supreme Court!"

North had expected better, considering Cleary's bribe. Rolle groaned, a vortex of hatred threatening to suck him under. Yet he was still free on bail, and the police released him from the cage. As the courtroom emptied, Hanna huddled with them in the pews, explaining their options.

"At the earliest, the Supreme Court trial will not begin until next spring," the barrister said. "It will cost some thirty thousand in legal fees and will take most of a year. It might be better if Mr. Rolle left the Bahamas and forfeited bail." He turned to Rolle. "You've seen the jail, Sidney. You ever see Fox Hill?"

"Not from the inside."

"That's something in life you don't want to experience."

As long as the Supreme Court trial was pending, North decided it would make a good cover for their continued presence in Nassau. He asked Hanna to act as though they planned to go through with the trial, even if they did not.

Hanna nodded. He was used to dealing with devious clients.

DURING the hearings each week, St. Gregory had avoided any further confrontations with North. But now as North followed Rolle toward the bright open doorway of the courthouse, he came out of the shadows and seized North's arm, spinning him around. "I see you're still alive, doctor. No one's fed you to the sharks yet." Ignoring Rolle, he sniffed as though North were carrion.

The curse of parenthood is to find your child in every threat, to see depravity in every man you despise. North tortured himself with the image of a naked St. Gregory, his monstrous body over Coby's, his hairy hand reaching under her bikini, forcing himself into her, beating her. It took a conscious effort of will to refuse to be baited.

Rolle stood ready to launch an attack.

North slid his arm free. "St. Greg," he said in a reasonable tone, "have you ever been treated for necrophilia? Modern medicine might help you."

From the look on the captain's face, St. Gregory's knew more about that perversion than its various definitions. North stared into his eyes, reaching inside with his gaze to touch the living organ where he detected a twinge of the man's pain, or possibly his fear, knowing the chances were good that St. Gregory had been in therapy.

The captain recovered his composure, smirking in his malevolent way. "Good luck, *padrón*," he said, and left.

As they stepped outside to join the others, Rolle turned to North and raised his eyebrows. "What the hell was all that, some kind of chess sacrifice?"

"Not on my part, Sidney. The best idea in chess is to get the other guy to do the sacrificing."

39 *Defeat or Amnesty*

GRANT NORTH felt a burning frustration over his own determination not to strike out blindly at St. Gregory or Ransom. But back on the Island his anger cooled. The wind whispering through the lush jungle, the cobalt ocean where bonefish jump, the gulls floating like cotton against the vault of the sky—this greater gallery of the Island made him feel whole again. He spent October evenings thinking and wandering the tumbled boulders and valleys, so much like the moon under the illimitable sky.

"Just as our ancestors invoked magic to calm the storms and solve the riddles of their lives, we need to use science," he told Cleary and the others, who were tired of thinking, tired of searching for Jelly Belly. The only science that seemed appropriate was radio technology. Every night the men joined Jo in studying the thousands of feet of tapes that her station manager had made of Defence Force radio messages. Jo also had brought eight months of the *Guardian* dating back to March sixteenth, the day St. Gregory's MOPs raided the *Half Fast*. But she found no clues.

With Knowles dead, and money in short supply, construction had ceased on the land. The sea, though, was their financial salvation, and scores of growout corrals had been completed. Rolle and his crew spent the fall days tending the juvenile shrimp and

298

seaweed tied to monolines that streaked the ocean surface like grid lines on a map.

November came caustic and threatening. The seas were rough outside the protected corral area, and the skies, flushed with red at sunrise, turned to iron by midmorning. The pace of Island life turned abruptly faster now. North, Jo, and Cleary came and went, widening their searches to include all the Bahama islands. The trees turned inward, became gnarled, some of them shedding their leaves. No one did the Goombay Shuffle in jest any more; the workers breathed more deeply in the cooler air, talked more solemnly, often of the spirits, and more than usual they were uneasy with the unknown. Each day rushed like a stream before it breaks over the rocks and cascades down a mountain wall.

During crises, North's sensitivity to analog thought could curse him with fantasies. But in transitory times such as now, he was blessed with fresh insights. One morning before dawn, at that time of day when the brain is most receptive, he was awakened by roaring waves and an intuitive thunderbolt. He knew that he had been too long at the microscope, violating his own creed of doing things large-scale. The individual Defender tapes meant nothing. The answer would leap from them if . . .

He dressed and rushed to awaken his sister, who had returned last night to discuss her progress—or lack thereof. Against a strong wind that rustled the trees, they hurried to the lodge where she made coffee and North spread out the newspapers.

"What exactly are we looking for," Jo said, rubbing sleep from her eyes.

"News stories of pleasure craft lost at sea," he said.

A few hours later, they had accumulated four reports of such boats—five counting the Zellers. All were American, all expensive power cruisers, all larger than forty feet—and each of the news reports hinted at some mysterious boating accident or supernatural cause like the Devil's Triangle.

When they correlated the dates with Jo's log of recorded Defence Force messages, the truth stood before them naked. Each missing yacht had undergone a patrol boat search a week or so before vanishing into the devil's own statistics.

As they tried to relate this new clue to Coby's disappearance, the single sideband let out a *Beep-Beep-Beep*. A voice broke suddenly across the radio traffic:

Securité-securité-securité! Hello all stations hello all stations. This is the United States Coast Guard Miami Florida Group Hurricane Warning. Hurricane Henry, Bahamas to Hispaniola. Pressure nine hundred seventy millibars. Wind one hundred ten knots. Eye of hurricane two hundred kilometers northwest of northern coast of Haiti between Great Inagua and Acklins Island, continuing northwest at twenty knots. . . .

"This can't *happen!*" said Jo, suppressing panic. "It's November seventh! Hurricanes *never* come after the last day of October. Well, almost never."

"Jesus, what's next in this crazy country?" North said. "How much time have we got?"

Cleary, Andy, and Rolle, came in for breakfast. North's anxiety, contagious, splashed over the others.

Jo moved over to the radio where a nautical chart lay open on the table. "Henry is moving straight for us. If it doesn't veer, it ought to be here in—" She multiplied quickly. "Twenty-eight hours."

In the upper sky where the last of a broad trail of cirrus was dissipating, a dense cloud bank formed on the horizon. The wind grew noisier, rancorous voices coming closer. On the ocean side of Harbour Rock, long swells moved shoreward, horizontal avalanches that sucked color and liquidity from their path. The sky pulled at the Island the way the moon pulls the sea, making it malleable. North timed the swells at a third their normal frequency.

Hurricanes are fueled by heat transferred to the air when water evaporates from the ocean surface. The higher the volume of warm water and the greater the temperature, the more powerful the hurricane. North knew that east and south of the Bahamas the ocean would be warm to a depth of five hundred feet or more, and the storm wouldn't weaken until it moved over shallow water. That would help the Wracking Islands somewhat, because the miles of shallow water at the most vulnerable side of the Island—the beach side—would prevent damage by tidal wave.

The wind was another story.

"Let's get to work," North said.

"Doing what?" said Cleary, yawning.

"Picking up whatever isn't bolted down—everything a hurricane could hurl through a building."

"What. . . ! Oh, Jeez, *my plane!*" Jo said. With no hangars at the Great Snake Cay airport, even an ordinary gale could wreck an airplane no matter how solidly anchored its wheels, and when Henry approached it would be no mere gale. First the outer wings would rip off, then the engines and tail, then flying debris would demolish what was left of the fuselage. "I've got to take it to Florida, fast. Soon as it's over, I'll fly back—with food."

Within minutes, Jo had packed a bag and was bouncing in the Mako across the comparatively calm flats with Rolle at the wheel. North, Andy, and Cleary began picking up everything they saw. They shoved inside the buildings whole piles of lumber, shingles, PVC pipe, beach furniture, giant flower pots, firepumps, thick jetting hoses, rope, unused pilings, solar stills, oil drums, shrimp tanks, even building stone and bags of concrete—realizing all the while that their drudgery would be wasted if the hurricane veered off course, a fifty-fifty possibility. Atop the tower, North feathered the wind-generator propellers, locked the brakes, and switched off the circuits.

Rolle returned from Great Snake toward evening to find North and Andy working in the rainy wind. Cleary was slumped in a chair and could hardly move. "Great job," Rolle said to his weary friends, "but it's not enough." Although the lodge was equipped with shutters, the sliding-glass walls of the villas were vulnerable, and with Andy's help, Rolle began nailing half-inch plywood to their frames. He'd been in hurricanes before, he explained, where the air pressure dropped so fast it hashed your brains, where flying lumber demolished buildings.

At North's urging, Cleary revived and the Islanders worked through the starless night. By morning, walls of water were pummeling the deepside coast and leaping over Harbour Rock. Reaching gale force, the wind rattled the shutters of the lodge and ripped shingles from roofs.

At that moment, at what might have been the last minute it could be done, a forty-two foot Grand Banks trawler scurried out of the rain into Slaughter Harbour. Pitching and rolling against her steadying sail, she twisted toward the dock like a drunken mouse running from a cat. Across her bow was the incongruous name, *Wind Song*. As North and Andy ran to the dock to help, two middle-aged Americans from the trawler already were fastening lines to cleats, their shirt sleeves fluttering like wings.

"Hope you don't mind if we tie up here," the man shouted over the wind as the woman cleated a line.

"What if I said no?" said North with a laugh, shaking the man's hand. Andy grabbed the other lines.

"Ernie Garbarino," he said, grinning. "Call me Garb. This is my wife Lorraine."

"How many anchors have you got?" North asked.

"Three."

Using the *Wind Song's* dingy, they ran three lines in different directions as far out as they would reach, each tied to its own anchor. On the other side of the dock, similar lines placed earlier radiated from the LCM, the jollyboat, and the Mako. By the time they finished, the skies had drained of color and blended into a malignant ocean that shot waterspouts skyward and produced the near-ultimate waves Evan Symes would have called Nines. On the land, palm fronds and fragments of construction scrap forgotten in the cleanup flew about and careened into trees. The oleander and bougainvillea had lost their leaves and flowers. North led the others through the barren trellis tunnel, their heads bent, leaning into the wind, fighting for each step. The Island moaned like a dying creature and covered itself with a rainy shroud. They could hear boulders on the north coast stirring their twenty-ton masses after centuries of sleep, formerly benign monsters that had protected the shore now awakening to annihilate it.

Inside the library-rec room of the duplex lodge, North looked at his guests the way an Army officer inspects new recruits. Garb was about ten years older than he, and taller, with good muscles, a firm handshake, graying-brown hair, and eyes that smiled through thick lenses. His wife Lorraine, thin and blonde, had strong bones and a no-nonsense manner, a member of that sisterhood of staunch females who go to sea with their husbands and no crew, and prepare gourmet meals on a gimbaled stove.

At the bar Cleary was pouring whiskey into cups of hot coffee. The fireplace crackled, fueled by driftwood and scrap lumber piled waist-high from the floor. The flames, struggling against rain that had seeped through the cupola, lent an aura of cheer to the room, their yellow tongues flickering through smoke into the copper hood. After the introductions, Cleary raised an eyebrow in question as he handed over each cup.

"Sure," said Garb and Lorraine to the whiskey.

"Sure," said Andy.

North handed them towels and they dried their hair.

"Liquid heat," said North, tossing it down and pouring another.

The wind, blowing out of the southeast, lashed the casuarinas and bent the coconut palms so far their fronds thumped the roof. It would be easy to stay here and drink cup after cup of warmth, but a hurricane was no time for that.

Rolle was swilling his third cup. Cleary was ready to begin a binge. "We 'bout to have a hurricane party?" he asked.

"No more, Jack," said North. "We've got to stay alert."

"You're right," said Rolle. He poured the rest of his drink into the sink and opened the refrigerator, taking out food for a late lunch.

Bruiser whimpered. Sugar and Spice huddled so close together in a pool of firelight they seemed to melt into one furred animal with four eyes.

North moved to the single-sideband radio at the rear of the fireplace where channel eight-zero-two barked a U.S. Coast Guard warning. *"PAN-PAN, PAN-PAN, PAN-PAN. Hurricane Henry between Great Exuma and Cuba veering north . . ."*

"Near as I can tell," North said after listening to the coordinates, "the center is heading for the northern tip of Andros. That would mean a direct hit on the Island."

Cleary, his tongue white from four Titralacs, had taken one more drink and now made a show of pouring half of it down the drain. He and the others consumed cold sandwiches in the darkening room, the fire casting yellow cheer on cedar walls lined with books. Heather's paintings filled the spaces between the books and shuttered glass: oils and alkyds of Coby as a pre-teen, the Lake Michigan dunes, alien islands in space, and her favorite painting GRANT, the conquistador emerging into daylight after crossing the lunar terminator.

Rain hammered the roof, striking horizontally and racing through the ventilation grills of the cupola, the water falling like molten metal into the fireplace. Cleary piled on more wood. North shoved the cats inside a floor cupboard along with a bowl of water and a sandbox, and closed it firmly after them. Lightning blued the objects in the room and shimmered anxious faces. The sliding-glass doors, the bookcases between, and even the ceiling started to move, flexing four inches or more under unrelenting gusts.

"This roof going to hold?" Cleary said.

"Sure," said North, clinging to a faith in his own engineering. He'd built these buildings solidly, had set their footings on rodded concrete pilings, bolted each joist to the four sides of each beam, and used steel angles and guy cables to hold down the roofs.

He cranked open a shutter to a mere slit. The air, damp and cold like a slushy Chicago winter, formed a curtain at the edge of the ocean beyond which nothing lived but fear, like the vacuum of space. Time slowed as the storm locked in combat with the buildings. By late afternoon the roar grew so loud you couldn't hear the palm fronds battering the roof.

Rolle looked out and saw the Island screaming in terror. He closed the shutter fast. "Must be over a hundred knots," he yelled over the noise.

Hurricanes could reach a hundred and fifty, North knew, remembering Hugo in 1989 and the year before, Gilbert, which had peaked at one seventy-five. He doubted that Henry was blowing that hard, but the tortured air soured his lungs, and its wild artillery, louder than war, made him wish he had grabbed a pair of ear protectors from the shop.

A series of explosions washed over them, quivering flesh, drowning thought. Jet engines. Jackhammers. Howling devils that clawed the drum of the roof to get at the humans inside. The noise came from all directions at once like sound underwater. During lightning flashes, through the crack of the shutter, you could make out coconut palms bent to the ground. Thatch trees and even gum elemis thick as oaks became uprooted, twisting and tangling around living trunks or smashing into the lodge. Pieces of aluminum shingles shredded the sky.

"Jesus, mie-durt. Meidurts!" yelled Andy.

"What?"

Andy shouted into North's ear, pronouncing each word separately. "My—ead—urts."

"Air pressure dropping fast!"

"What. . . ?"

The six of them—seven counting Bruiser—pressed close to each other around the fire, the Labrador looking like he wanted to hold his ears like everyone else. Clustered as they were, the noise of the wind isolated them, each person retreating into his own fears. An avalanche of water rushed toward the building like a locomotive. North peered out and saw the following waves dissolve the beach and wash away whatever bushes or wild grass that remained.

In these latitudes hurricanes do a fast counter-clockwise swirl as the whole spinning clock moves north or northwest. With the eye of the hurricane somewhere to the southwest, the wind was attacking from the southeast. The only barrier between themselves and the storm was the other circle of the duplex lodge.

A belch of water washed out the fire. Lights dimmed to the current-saving mode, indicating that the solar system had failed. You could see why. Panels of solar cells from the roofs were flying around like kites, their glass covers shattered. Without the panels to charge them, the batteries at the lodge would discharge in three days. Twisted among the panels, like manta rays torn by sharks, were the plywood sheets Rolle had nailed over the villa windows. Rolls of tar paper unravelled in ribbons of black streamers. Coral rocks bowled demented strikes and spares against the pins of the building.

It can't get worse!

But it did. Immediately. The shutters ripped off the sliding door in front of North, cascading glass and water into the room. The portrait of Coby and the moon scene orbited across the floor.

North caught the paintings, bending at the waist to protect them with his bulk, just as a fist of seawater hammered his solar plexus. He couldn't breathe. Thrown to the floor, his body mingled with broken glass, books, and splintered wood. In a final cataclysm, one of the eight walls of the room, the northeast, collapsed onto his left shoulder.

Andy and Rolle fought the deluge to drag North from the building's gaping wound, themselves hydroplaning across the flooded floor in the direction of the wind. Doubled over, North clutched the paintings under his good arm. Together they reached the back of the bar counter and crouched behind it. A few months ago, North had bolted the base of the bar to the concrete floor, but now the vertical slats were cracking.

"Get the pool!" North shouted in pain. "*The pool . . . !*"

No one could hear him. He sat dazed on the floor, one arm still clutching the paintings, feeling the throb of his battered shoulder. In North's imagination the building became a ship, yawing, rolling, broaching, its deck awash with seawater and foam. They should have rigged life lines when they'd had the chance.

He gave up shouting and pointed repeatedly to the pool table until Cleary and then the others understood. Holding on to each other, four desperate men and a woman threw their bodies against Henry's might as wind, water, sand, mud, coral rock, tar paper, and broken glass pelted their legs. Slowly they made their way to the windward side of the table where they managed to turn it on its side and slide it toward North for a barricade.

Between the pool table and the stone fireplace, the Islanders faced the night on soggy mattresses. There are two stages to seasickness, say seafaring Bahamians: first when you know you are going to die, and second when you fear you won't. They had reached stage two. Seasick from the changing air pressure, betrayed by North's dream and their own expectations, they moaned in pain and misery.

To Grant North the storm spoke of more than senseless fury. Like the sun collapsing into itself, the roar of the wind drew him helplessly toward an alien condition of mind, a black hole that drained his senses and reexerted control over the destiny of the Island he foolishly once believed had been his to command. Often during the night he awakened to his damaged shoulder, only to sink back into the primordial soup of rain and sea. In a fever of exhaustion worse than he felt that first night in jail, he saw through the building's gaping wound a strange midnight aurora streaking the sky in arches of color. The scientist, the leader, the visionary—everything he prided himself at being—was terminated now like some paltry role played and forgotten. Had anything of his life really worked? The moon project, his parenthood, this place? All lay scattered out there in the luminous dark. Rubble shifting in the wind.

Then came the alien but welcome rush. His defenses down, the exotic sensation returned, the perception that his body had merged into the Island incarnate. He could feel the hot sap of the jungle pulse in his veins. His skin flayed and streamed down the beaches with the fronds. The cilia of his lungs, filigreed tamarinds, gasped for oxygen. His kidneys became the two Island lakes, fouled by raging seas. His legs metamorphosed into the trunks of gum elemi, his fingers their gnarled twigs. In his dreamy fever he imagined that one of his eyes was blinded like the blown-out glass of the lodge and that two branches, ripped from his upper anatomy, left him helpless with green and oozing arm sockets. In the delirium of his paranoia he lay huddled with the others and waited for defeat or amnesty, caring not which came first.

40 *Lunar Landscape*

AT FIRST LIGHT North came fully conscious under a wet tongue lapping at his face. "You're alive!" Bruiser seemed to be saying, wagging his tail, "And you've still got me!" A shadowless light filled the room, and North could smell the clean odor of ozone in a world vastly different from the one he'd known before. And then he realized what it was. Absolute silence, like the airless moon. No rain, no birds, not even a whisper of the salt breeze.

He looked at his watch. Six o'clock in an alien morning where frothy clouds blanketed a sunless sky and nourished the day as if by some internal light. The Islanders rose on shaky feet, bent at the waists, holding their sides like old people getting out of hospital beds. Even the sounds of moving about seemed smothered as if this peculiar daylight without sun had swallowed vibrations at every frequency. When Cleary lit his first morning cigarette, North imagined he could hear the tobacco burning.

"Well, we're still alive," Cleary said, puffing furiously. "On this fucking Island of yours." The night had given him no fever, only a burning desire to be done with it all.

"Barely," said Garb.

"The quiet," said Andy, patting Bruiser. "It's so . . . thick! Grant, could this be the eye of the hurricane?"

For a moment North thought about his illusory merger into the Island, as you do when you wake from a particularly vivid dream. "I doubt it," he said, coming completely awake. He opened the cupboard to let the cats out. "The hurricane is supposed to be moving north or northwest, not east. Probably won't rain for a couple of hours anyway."

"After which it'll never stop," said Rolle. He looked around. "It doesn't seem funny anymore saying, 'It's broken in the Bahamas.'"

Sugar and Spice stood timidly in the doorway of the opened cupboard, hesitant to discover the rearrangement of their world.

Holding his painful shoulder, North flicked a couple of switches to conserve power in the battery bank, and the lights went out. In the next few days they would have to find a way to recharge them since both the solar panels and the wave-power buoys were gone. The windmills in the center of the island—even if intact—were too far away to power the buildings at this end, and the solar pond was not yet operational.

North looked around. And beheld a scene choreographed by a lunatic. The recreation room had been torn out of the lodge like the entrails of a hook-swallowed fish. On both sides of the ocular cavity that had been the sliding-glass doors lay chairs and tables, broken dishes, bottles, shredded drapes, and playing cards marked with the hearts of hope and the spades of work. Backgammon chips, splintered pool cues, a shiny toaster, a broken blender, a refrigerator dented and doorless—the intact and the mutilated—poked out from mounds of paper and sandy mud all the way to the ocean where a rim of spume divided land from water. In the crooks of tree limbs you could see white metal shingles mired in cloaks of black tar paper. Inside, North spotted a corner of one of Heather's paintings. He retrieved it, an amazingly unscathed picture of frolicking dolphins, and placed it at the overturned pool table alongside the lunar landscape and other scenes rescued last night.

A voice crackled from the cupboard where North had stowed the single-sideband. He took out the radio and placed it on a chair. It was Marianne calling.

"Good to hear your voice, Grant. I was worried. How bad was the hurricane? May I come to help you? Over."

He didn't want her here, not the daughter of his adversary. Not now when his own hope and will lay strewn in the Island rubble. "Thanks, Marianne, but it's a job for a bulldozer. Give me a couple of weeks to work and think. I'll call you when we get things under control. Islander—out."

Better to be abrupt than to try to explain feelings he didn't completely understand. He turned solemn, brooding, trying to discern the significance of the hurricane, or of the Bahamas, or of Coby's disappearance, his view of each wavering as if seen through rain. The storm, the relentless evolution of the islands, the loss of his daughter—the measurement and meaning of these events were uncertain, changed by his observation of them, he knew, not because someone would notice him and therefore behave differently, but simply because of the inseparable and intimate connection in nature between all things, living and inanimate. It was the Heisenberg Uncertainty Principle at work here, and he realized now that the Principle applied not only to random electrons but to the macro-world of storms and prejudice and government intransigence. He found new elegance in the idea of uncertainty itself and in those various subworlds, so stunning in their simple complexities, their individual behaviors capricious, yet accurately predictable when thousands or millions of them interact. If you could predict which way a hurricane was going, why could you not predict where a missing girl might be?

North hung up the microphone and watched Andy pointing his camera at an airplane propeller that must have blown over from another island and was imbedded like a dart in the wood siding. Thank God, Jo had taken her plane to Florida. He climbed over debris through the gaping wound of the lodge. In times of stress you notice the most minute details; his eye caught a page from the ruined library that began:

> By the time the saturated air stream reaches the top of the
> evaporator, its temperature is 63° C . . .

Away from the lodge, thick gum elemis and lignum vitae trunks so hard you had to saw them with carbide blades had been fractured and tossed into heaps of fallen fronds. A handful of sandpipers pecked sluggishly on the beach at their breakfast of diatoms and plankton. Across the shallow sea lay scattered the former tenants of the seafarm. The shark barriers and pilings of the corrals and the bulkheads between the pens had escaped undamaged; the hurricane waves had rolled over them. But the fine-meshed nets and the seaweed tied to monolines were tangled around the pilings like rows of drunken soldiers trying to get dressed. A pair of pelicans stood guard atop the pilings searching the bottom as if on burial duty. The shrimp they sought had been washed away.

The flame of his hatred for Ransom flickered and burned in North's viscera, but he caught himself in time, realizing he couldn't blame *this* on the government. He stayed for a while on the shore, then returned to the others, feeling not the least like an inspirational leader.

"I know it looks hopeless," he made himself say, eyelids rimmed in red, jaws dark with stubble. "But I don't see how we have much choice. Half the company's assets are in this garbage."

"Christ Almighty, Grant, tell me you're kidding!" Cleary's usually cavalier attitude was smothered in stomach acid, his mouth white with antacids. "An army couldn't undo this shitheap. Let's pack our suitcases and go. If at first you don't succeed, there's probably a good goddamn reason."

North looked at him stonily. The idea of *not* repairing the Island was as unthinkable for him as refusing to take an injured friend to the hospital.

"We ought to be glad no one's hurt," Lorraine said, sidestepping the dispute. "I'll see if I can round up some breakfast."

Ignoring the pain in his shoulder, North bent over and grabbed an armful of shingles, paper, and splintered wood. He waded outside and dropped them on a pile of wet rubble. Then he returned for another load. One at a time the Islanders joined in, and after a while they resembled a team. Rolle poured gasoline on piles of soggy muddle brought to the water's edge where the late afternoon tide would carry away the dregs of the fires. The others picked books and utensils from the waste and shoveled the remainder outside. Andy worked the loader, scooping two cubic yards of debris at a time, and brought it to the fires. The sky had been cloudy and dark all morning, and now the rains came in earnest, quenching the fires, making a porridge of the litter.

OVER THE NEXT two days during brief breaks from the cleanup work, North inspected the Island. Fortunately the water in the cisterns and wells hadn't been fouled, but the landscape was a sodden mass. The villas and other buildings were more or less intact as if after a battle. The roofs were damaged and the windows crushed when their protective plywood had been torn away. At the dock, the vines and the tunnel-like trellises had been swept to sea.

The boats had fared better. The water in the cabin and engine room of the *Wind Song* sloshed ankle deep; otherwise the sturdy trawler suffered no injury. Nor had the Mako. The open jollyboat had sunk and it's engine would need cleaning out, but the boat seemed otherwise okay. Only the LCM sustained damage they couldn't fix. Filling with water, she sat listing to port like a floating corpse. During the hurricane the anchors had slipped and sent the stern slamming against the coral boulders of the dock, denting the hull and bending the props and both drive shafts.

North roamed the Island like a shipwrecked sailor, soaked to the skin, shirt tied around his waist, his Panama hat shapeless. The rain had softened to a slow drizzle, too weak to extinguish the bonfires that smoked the beaches.

On the northern coast the massive boulders had rearranged themselves, and where they crashed through the jungle you could see their paths, like rays on the moon. But the wind tower and circular tunnels, as they were designed to do, had let the hurricane whistle through. The laboratory still wore its roof, a wood-brown hat now devoid of shingles and roofing paper.

Concerned that the water table was too high for the septic system that drained waste from the laboratory shrimp tanks, North hiked over to Lake Michigan, where a profusion of narrow caverns wound like intestines into the coral body of the Island. The ground here was too rocky to dig, so the Islanders used these caverns as potholes, to dissipate sewage. North lowered himself into one of them to see whether it might be suitable, careful to find toeholds in the rocky sides. If he fell, he would drop ten feet before coming to the first jagged bottom where the scorpions lived. At the bottom he saw that it flared into a cave, its floor seeded with small boulders. It was quiet down here, cozy even, like those dens in the imagination where we keep our hopes and fears and bring them out only when needed. He rested there for long minutes, enjoying the solitude and the privacy, until the sadness for Coby and for the Island drifted up from the interior and hardened like a fist.

He returned to the lodge. Cleary and Lorraine were hovering over the charcoal barbecue pit where they had started a charcoal fire under the grill. At least a hundred shrimp and thick wads of dough were roasting over glowing embers.

"That's not exactly the hundred-thousand pound harvest I had planned," said North, smiling, "but at least we get to eat some of the critters. Where did you find them?"

"Bruiser found them," Lorraine said. "He came over waging his tail with a mouth full of shrimp. I followed him to the beach, a little west of the tower. They're half-dead, lying all over the sand. All you have to do is fight off the birds."

"Congratulations," North said.

He emptied some cardboard boxes, ran outside, and jumped into the bucket of the loader, Andy at the wheel. Rolle saw them, a hounds-dog grin forming on his face, guessing their mission. He grabbed some broken styrofoam containers, and together they roared off down the beach to a cove thick with squabbling pelicans, sea-gulls, terns, and grebes feasting on the leftovers of the seafarm. The hurricane had swept thousands of lethargic shrimp shoreward where they were knotted in strings of seaweed and monolines. Stunned or dead crawfish were scattered among them, literally a windfall. Working in the drizzle, the three men filled the containers with shrimp and lobster tails. Back at the lodge they packed them into a chest freezer powered by the still-functioning batteries.

The Islanders, including the cats and Bruiser, ate with a dedication known only to those who had assumed they would starve. Smiles of reprieved prisoners formed on their faces.

Afterwards, Garb began awkwardly, "Grant, we talked it over. . . . We're on our first long vacation and we've got a few unplanned weeks. You keep up this fancy cuisine, we might just hang around and make ourselves useful."

Garb was the Samaritan who stopped on the freeway to give you a hand with a flat tire. He had a capable look about him, as if he might put the Island back together before tomorrow's breakfast. Lorraine, tall, bony, robust, already was back at work wielding a broom made of the midribs of coconut fronds, out-island style. The way North felt about his broken Island, he would have accepted help from the devil, let alone from friends, and chances were nil of getting his workers back from Great Snake. They had their own island to repair.

That afternoon North and Garb inspected the eight-foot deep solar pond at Lake Superior, expecting the worst. The pond's various layers of saline water had been mixed by the hurricane's heavy winds and torrents of fresh water. In the absence of saltier and therefore denser layers to trap the heat, the pond no longer was hot enough at the bottom to produce even low-pressure steam to drive the turbines. Normally the salt gradient of solar ponds is so stable that natural formations occur; indeed, it is how such ponds first happened to be discovered. North had read about a solar pond near the Red Sea, hot for three thousand years, and a salt pond called Lake Vanda under ten feet of Antarctic ice that never cools below seventy-seven degrees Fahrenheit.

Until they could reestablish the gradient, the solar pond was of no use for power, so they charged the battery bank with a small diesel generator. They brought mattresses and their personal possessions from the villas to the lodge, which would be their living quarters for an indefinite time.

Rolle came over to North smelling vaguely of smoke and shrimp. He pointed toward the beach and grinned. "Looks like the marines have landed."

A twenty-foot motor skiff ladened to the gunwales with cardboard boxes of provisions floated slowly over the low-tide shallows with outboard motor tilted up, propelled by Cuda pushing against the bottom with a long pole. Amidships in the soft rain sat Josephine Copp, looking like a nineteenth-century aviatrix in her wide-brimmed caffe bianco hat and out-of-Africa cotton shirt. From across the beach Rolle embraced her with his eyes, but Jo wasn't smiling back. She appeared anxious to tell them something.

The men brought the Cessna-sized cargo of food to the lodge, and while Jo stood by impatiently, Cuda told them about Great Snake Cay. The dead were still being tallied, the injured laid out in the churches, the villagers numb after the hurricane had tossed houses into power poles and cars into people. Cuda borrowed some gasoline and sped back to the stricken village.

As soon as he left, Jo said, "Something terrible has happened."

North knew there had to be a reason for her to be gone three days. He closed his eyes, weary of hardship and suffering, and listened to the latest catastrophe.

"Our station in the Caicos—Radio Free Caribbean—was destroyed." Jo's voice, shrill at first, trickled off like rain down a pipe. "I kept calling the station from Miami, but no one answered. So I flew to North Caicos and hired a boatman to take me there. Tomás was lying in the midst of the wreckage, unconscious, his back broken. He died on the way to the hospital."

"Damn hurricane," said Rolle.

"It wasn't the hurricane," Jo said, her eyes mustering the strength to continue. She wiped away a tear and said in a higher than normal voice, "The Turks & Caicos had hardly any damage. Trees and a few powerlines were down and shingles littered the streets, but it was nothing like what happened here. And yet every piece of equipment at the station was smashed. Somebody used a baseball bat." Although her voice returned to its normal range, her body language was militant: she was ready to go after the raiders. "One more thing," she said. "Every tape in the place was gone."

"St. Gregory and his Defenders?" Rolle said.

North's fatigue had stopped at his muscles, leaving his mind smoldering. "Of course the Defenders," he said with increasing adrenaline. "Directed by Ransom."

41 *Fallen Angels*

IN THE AFTERMATH of the hurricane it rained constantly, and the Islanders, working outside during every daylight hour, were dry only at night. But December turned the seas glassy and the air fresh. The sun warmed the bruises of the Island, depositing salt on the buildings, stiff and ashy, scintillating the surviving palms like ghosts and drawing vapor from the steaming jungle, a poultice on a wound. Hurricane Henry had become history like last month's insomnia.

Each morning the Islanders awoke to the splash of reef fish and the cries of gulls. By day they repaired the roofs and windows of the lodge and villas, or floated the jollyboat using air bags. At night with the generator throbbing its lifeblood of electrons to the wounded Island, Jo, North, and Rolle speculated, and planned.

No visitors had landed on the Island these four weeks, but now Cuda started showing up, usually with Lionel Sweeting, to earn money and gasoline. The village was a long way from repair, Cuda said. Bureaucrats from Nassau had flown in to take pictures and ask questions, and then left the job of reconstruction to the local men with the gold necklaces, who paid for funerals, brought food from Florida, and erected temporary housing for the homeless.

At the Island for Science, rain and North's month-long addition

316

of brine from evaporated seawater had restored the salt gradient of the solar pond, and now the bottom layer actually was boiling. North and Garb installed a turbine and coupled to it a fifty-kilowatt generator that had been stored in the warehouse ever since the last Evan Symes shipment, running heavy underground cables from it to the lodge. They hurricane-proofed the pond by installing floating nets and gutters to dampen sloshing, and built spillways to drain off cold rainwater. Noiseless electricity now flowed without the stench of diesel exhaust.

LORRAINE felt it first. By the first week of December, North and the others noticed it too: an inspired renewal, as dramatic for the infrastructure as any that nature herself had achieved in repairing the green mantle of the Island. Through a stroke of luck, for the Island and for himself, a middle-aged man had motored into a strange place that tested his fortitude and restored his life's purpose. After four weeks of rebuilding another man's dream and catching the excitement himself, Ernie Garbarino seemed taller now than his six-foot-two frame, and stronger, as if his molecules had re-formed into an alloy of guts and iron. During this time Garb had said not a word about the obligations that waited for him in the States, but finally the time had come to go home. Together, the scientist and the engineer disappeared into the LCM's engine room, removed the bent eight-foot bronze propeller shafts, and packed the openings. They stowed the shafts in the *Wind Song* for repair in Ft. Lauderdale.

On the eve of their departure they prepared a parting banquet. The moon that night clung close to the horizon, an orange circle filled with promise, filtered so densely by earth's atmosphere that North could make out the Sea of Tranquility, the mile-high Carpathian Mountains below it, and the place where he once had proposed a landing, the Crater Copernicus. The sweet smell of the jungle filled his lungs and made him believe the Island could fulfill its purpose again. Even if they had to abandon the research projects for now, he thought they could grow cash crops of shrimp and seaweed in the repaired corrals.

A long table, striped by pine branches against the moonlight through the open windows of the lodge, held a feast: trays of lobster and shrimp, seagrapes, coconuts, and cassava bread pounded and baked over sweet pigeon-plumb charcoal, the native way. Shimmering in the smoke of the barbecue, the Islanders saw each other in an aura of radiance that pulsed and surged. "To survival," North said, raising his glass. "And friendship."

"You sit around on these islands too much, you ripen, you rot," paraphrased Garb from something.

They laughed and drank to the arduous, pioneering work they had performed.

"To fixing the broken Bahamas," said Rolle.

Cleary frowned as though he'd rather drink to the destruction of Ireland than to the restoration of this country. "To our fearless leader, the man with the crystal ball."

"I guess I proved the adage," said North. "'He who lives by the crystal ball is destined to eat ground glass.' We've made the place livable again, and I thank you from the bottom of my heart."

After dinner, walking alone with Garb where the palm fronds framed a sky full of stars, North told him what they had discovered before the hurricane, that yachts like the *Wind Song* were being pirated after being searched by the crew of the *HMBS Munnings*.

"It's been some time now since the last incident, but that doesn't mean they've stopped. . . . Garb, don't go in your boat. Let Jo fly you two back to Florida."

"But then we can't take the LCM shafts in for repair."

"The hell with the shafts."

From behind his thick glasses, Garb's eyes focused softly on North's. "Grant, I appreciate your concern, but the *Wind Song* belongs to Lorraine's brother. And Lorraine— Well, you know what a skeptic she is."

"Even skeptics can be murdered."

"My brother-in-law needs the boat. He rents it out when no one in the family uses it."

"You heard what they did to Radio Free Caribbean in the Caicos."

"It could have been a freak tail of the storm."

"Look, I'm not trying to scare you, but—"

"Sorry, Grant. I know you're suggesting this for our own good, but the answer has to be no."

With no room for argument, North said, "All right, but I want you to promise that if you're boarded by the Defence Force, you'll turn around and come back."

Garb grinned and extended his hand. "It's a deal. But don't tell Lorraine."

Early the next morning, packed with good wishes and the bronze shafts of the LCM, the Garbarinos took their trawler around Harbour Rock, heading toward Great Isaac and the Florida coast.

The Islanders returned to work. When the sun sank over the whale's tail of the Island and the ionosphere quieted for the night, rendering long-range transmission practical, they turned on the SSB. Months ago North had installed one of several new relays that Jo had brought from Florida, and now he tuned the radio to monitor Defender broadcasts, certain not only that St. Gregory was behind the piracies but that they were related somehow to Coby's disappearance. But how? And why?

"Jo, I know you've searched an awful lot of islands in your Cessna, but what if Coby's marooned on some unpopulated island where she can't be seen from the air?"

"Possible. You can't land on small islands, and God knows there are enough of them. Maybe we should build some sort of a defense against the pirates, Grant. Or get help somehow."

"From whom?" North asked.

"How about advertising over Nassau radio for Jelly Belly?"

"And give away our only clue?"

Random ideas. Desperate thoughts. North fell silent, wondering what Marianne was doing now, his mind sweeping from one subject to another, considering unrelated plans, memories, hypotheses. Idea incubation.

At lunch time the *Wind Song* returned and the Garbarinos entered the lodge. Cleary saw them first and grinned. "Couldn't stand eating alone?"

"We were *boarded!*" said Garb.

North pushed his plate aside.

"I was afraid to try to radio you."

"Good thing you didn't."

Lorraine Garbarino spoke with a weary look on her face, as if explaining a child's nightmare. "Garb thinks that because we were boarded it means we're going to be pirated."

"That's exactly what it means," North asked. "Who boarded you, the Defenders?"

Lorraine smirked.

"Yeah," said Garb, "but I couldn't see the name of their gun-boat."

"You get a look at the captain?"

"The man's a giant."

"With a beard like the devil, right?" asked Andy.

"Yeah, a pointed beard. And those *eyes*, yellow, like a cat's—"

"More like khaki," interrupted Lorraine. "Human beings don't have yellow eyes."

"Did you tell him you were going to return to the Island for Science?" asked North.

"Sure," said Garb. "I thought it might be safer that way."

"Oh, come *on!*" said Lorraine. "Let's get back in the boat and go home."

North paused for a long moment. Thinking of their sea voyage across the shallows and into the Gulf Stream, his analog brain soared over this final ingredient of his idea incubation, and he leapt to a conclusion that astonished him—then and forever later. Beyond these searches of islands and cays, beyond the slow sifting for clues, he knew there was only one good defense in the Bahama game. An offense that would turn things around, alter the status quo, force the illusions of the Bahamas into the open, and possibly reveal the answer to Coby's disappearance.

"You can't leave here now," North said with finality. "Not for two or three weeks—"

"*Weeks!*" said Lorraine Garbarino.

"It'll take that long to prepare. And when we're ready, we'll go with you."

Garb was more amenable now to hearing the whole story of the Zellers. North told the Garbarinos how the elderly couple never made it back to their daughter's wedding, and how Jo had found newspaper reports of four additional piracies since Coby's disappearance eight months ago.

"When the *Munnings*—and it's always the *Munnings*—logs a boarding," Jo explained, "the boarded yacht vanishes within a week. Not always, but sometimes. Maybe some are too hard to catch, or they change course. Did the Defenders ask where you were going?"

"Well, sure," answered Lorraine, eyes wide but recovering her incredulity. "It's a standard question, isn't it? You people can't be serious. You're talking about *pirates!* This is almost the twenty-first century!"

"What do you think happens," said Jo, "to the ten or fifteen yachts that disappear every year in the Bahamas?"

"Accidents, storms at sea . . . the Devil's Triangle?" Lorraine said with a chuckle.

"Unless you believe in triangular devils or the Bad Boat Fairy," North said, "you can assume that most of those yachts were pirated for the drug trade or sold in some other country."

"Isn't ten or fifteen a little high?"

Jo wore her serious reporter's look. "Listen, Lorraine, there are about forty annual highjackings of yachts in the entire West Indies—not counting another couple of hundred boats in the dope trade that are sunk, burned, bombed, or confiscated. We're in the *fin de siècle* Narco-Wars." Jo nodded at Rolle, his term.

"Something happened to the Zellers," Rolle said. "And *something* happened to Coby."

Lorraine stood like a lightning rod, channeling her doubt to a safe grounding. North led the Islanders to the dock where they boarded the *Wind Song*. He switched on the SSB and keyed the transmitter switch. No sound. You could receive on this radio but you could not broadcast. He shot a glance at Lorraine, then opened the radio case and found the relay had been stolen. He inserted a new one he'd brought with him for this purpose. Lorraine sank into silence, her face bloodless, pondering perhaps how the world she had known could have changed so much after one brief hurricane.

Without proof, North could do nothing against Ransom directly. Meanwhile there was the problem of defending themselves against his Defenders. The Islanders were united now—or at least Lorraine's opposition was muted—and North proposed a vastly different kind of work than any of them had done before. They left the *Wind Song* and headed down the wide ribbon of beach to the larger coconut grove and, behind it, to the laboratory.

Great ideas are born in laboratories, thought North. There they rummaged through the inventory of equipment and components, the instrument scientist and the engineer formulating a plan out of what they found. As they talked, the afternoon ebbed into a sky feathered with gold, tinging them with the fire of fallen angels whose souls burn for eternity.

They were a nation preparing for war.

42 *The Fish Works*

THE GARBARINOS were bait. Pirates were waiting for them between here and the Florida coast as once they had waited for the Zellers—ambushed because no hunch had come to the intuitive Dr. North, no inkling of the terrible truth. North berated himself, wondered if he had become a paranoid shadow of himself.

And yet his intuition screamed with a rare tumult. He knew St. Gregory had them in his sights, knew the Islanders had to mobilize fast and move their world out of this stalemate where dreams rotted, where allies like Knowles could be killed at somebody's instigation, where innocent yachtsmen were destroyed, where a man's daughter could disappear because . . . God knows why. Attack was the only practical option, surprise his only advantage.

But aside from some spearguns, there wasn't a real weapon on the Island. The sawed-off shotgun, Symes's Uzi, and the Winchesters from the *Half Fast* were locked up in the Nassau police property room on East Street.

What would work like a tank cannon—from a distance?

North and Garbarino holed up in the laboratory which, with its own solar-power system, was air-conditioned. They designed as they went, sending Andy into the woods to saw the trunks of lignum vitae killed by the hurricane, and Cleary to the utility build-

323

ing to round up five-inch galvanized pipe and thin plate steel. Rolle motored to Great Snake Cay and scrounged for cans of epoxy that the villagers used to repair boats. By evening of the second day, various ideas had solidified into weapons parts spread over the lab benches. Cleary and Rolle worked the metal table saw, cutting the pipe into short sections and the steel plate into fins stronger than any shark's. North patterned clay into trial molds for castings to be made of resin reinforced with fiberglass.

Now and then over the years North would imagine a world devoid of the machines of civilization, the refrigerators and appliances we take for granted. He used to ask himself whether he could build an automobile from scratch? Or even a bicycle? He was about to find out. Without recourse to Tovex or other bounties of Du Pont explosives technology, without commercial propellers, without circuit boards for control, the fabrication of the weapon decided upon by North and Garbarino had become a technical challenge as great as either had faced before.

Their goal: thirty-three small-scale torpedoes, five-inch inside diameter, thirty-two inches long.

Velocity: ten to fifteen knots, half the speed of a full-size torpedo.

Range: two hundred feet.

Time to target: twelve to eight seconds at range.

You could not buy dynamite or nitroglycerin in Nassau, nor could you import any explosives into the Bahamas. Ransom's government seemed terrified that their presence would encourage insurrection. Even industrial explosives were outlawed; harbors had to be deepened with half-ton toothed buckets dropped and dragged over the coral rock of the seafloor.

Among the Island supplies, however, were flash powder for detonators and reloading caps for shotgun shells that could serve as primers. More important, they had one hundred high-efficiency d-c induction motors originally bought for the underwater aquadart program. To power them, North had brought to the Island a hundred lithium-thionyl-chloride batteries containing an exotic electrolyte, a spinoff from the space program. The batteries incorporated a magnesium-oxide separator in addition to a lithium-boron alloy anode, capable of discharging total power to the motors in a thirty-second burst. In that brief period the ten cells of each rechargeable "burst battery," weighing half a pound, could deliver thirty watt-minutes of power. They decided to use three batteries and three motors in each shell.

"The propellers for the aquadarts are way too small," Garb said. "How about torpedo rockets?"

"Too dangerous to launch. Too inaccurate because they get lighter as the rocket fuel is consumed."

"Radio control?"

"No parts."

The final torpedoes would have to be "free-flight" devices propelled by three-bladed props and powered by the motors they already had. Garbarino bent over strips of lignum vitae on the bench, enthusiastic as a kid at his hobby. He grinned up at North. "Well now, you aren't the only guy who spent his youth building model airplanes. Remember those raps on the fingers starting the little gasoline engines? I'm not one of these mechanical engineers who forgets the many uses of wood. Let's use it like this. . . ."

He rambled on as he worked, his voice flying and tumbling, his magnified eyes widening as he positioned the hardwood on a band saw and cut out three half by two-inch strips, tapering and rounding them at one end. He fashioned dowels at the ends of the blades on the shop lathe, drilled three holes in a small steel collar, and forced the dowel ends of the wood into them making a three-bladed prop.

North recognized the merit of the design at once. The pitch of the propeller could be altered during testing. He was grateful for the resourceful engineer. If Lorraine and Jo hadn't yet captured Garb's enthusiasm, they nevertheless had gone to work trimming the hardwood with hand planes, shaving them to the designated shapes. At dinner that night, Lorraine asked the key question. "What good are miniature torpedoes against a Military Operations Platoon armed to the teeth. These guys even have a cannon!"

North considered the Oerlikon 20-mm on the deck of the *Munnings* an insignificant clit of a weapon, but that was bravado from his years in the Army. He knew a direct hit would kill them as dead as a blast from any macho tank cannon.

"St. Gregory wouldn't be crazy enough to use his gunboat," he said with as much conviction as he could muster. "His whole crew would have to know what he was up to."

North didn't like his own answer. St. Gregory *could* be cutting his crew in on the spoils; there would be no one to report them if they failed to take captives. But was there any other real choice? Continue to do nothing, and you continue the murders.

After calculations, they built a trial model of the torpedo. Inside the tip of the warhead, a copper cone pressed its wide side against the outer fiberglass nose. Around the apex of the cone and aft of it, sixty percent of the shell's volume was left empty for packing four pounds or more of explosive—ammonium-nitrate fertilizer. Next came the primer-actuated detonator, made of a mixture of the double-based nitropowder from the shotgun shells and flash powder from fire-crackers. To the rear of the detonator, a percussion cap and firing pin completed the warhead. Next in line, the propulsion unit consisted of three twelve-ounce burst batteries in one compartment and three motors in another, encapsulated in waterproof epoxy. A common drive shaft turned a single high-pitched propeller. Adjustable fins to guide the weapon at the optimum depth flared to the rear, making it look more like a rocket than a torpedo.

In operation, the impact of the torpedo was supposed to drive the nose and its empty copper cone into the explosive behind it and onto the firing pin. The cone-shaped charge, as in an antitank shell, would concentrate the force of the explosion into a high-pressure jet of superheated gas powerful enough to penetrate several inches of steel.

North set up an assembly line to produce the rest of the torpedoes, and Andy hung a cardboard sign on the wall: ROYAL BAHAMIAN FISH WORKS. The Islanders settled under it with the stoic efficiency of factory workers, each with his own job. They put in long hours at their benches littered with multicolored bell wire, hand tools, solder, plastic nose cones, metal scraps, and the carcasses of failed attempts. They were guiding their own destiny. Yesterday's hurricane had been replaced by tomorrow's battle.

EACH DAY North turned more haggard, his eyes more wary, half expecting a pirate ship of old to materialize out of the delicate tints of pink and mauve that colored the sky like the inside of a conch shell. He stood in the open doorway drinking the cool colors of trees and ocean . . . when suddenly out of this idyl stepped Marianne carrying a soft-leather valise.

Her rich brown hair flowed out from under a safari hat, but instead of high heels and designer clothes, she wore faded jeans and a sweatshirt as she had in the Nassau jail. Cuda, in whose boat she had arrived from the Great Snake airport, carried her two matching bags.

Feeling a mix of excitement and trepidation, North strode out to meet them at the beach so that Marianne and Cuda would not see their preparations for war. The electrician and former smuggler handed North the luggage, said goodbye, and hurried back to his still-stricken village.

"I was worried about you," Marianne said, pacing toward the laboratory. "When you didn't call—" Her voice trailed off as she hesitated at the lab entrance and peered inside the open door.

The assembly line came to a halt as if the Islanders were children caught playing with firecrackers.

"It's about time you came to see the Northern elves at work," said Cleary. North stepped inside and introduced her to the others.

"What on earth are you making here?" she asked archly after repeating their names and smiling her vivacious smile. "It looks like an armament factory." Then she saw the sign. "Fish works? What—?"

"You see . . ." North began reluctantly, too late to hide the assemblies, too late for anything but the truth. "We're making torpedoes."

"*Torpedoes. . . ?*" she repeated, her mouth forming a perfect "O" as though she had never spoken the word before in all her twenty-eight years.

"We need to defend ourselves against pirates." It sounded so incredible, so implausible when he said it that way. "So the Garbarinos here can get their boat home to Florida."

"Grant! You can't be serious! Why on earth don't you simply radio the Defence Force?"

"Because they are the pirates."

"You mean you believe that St. Gregory gasoline story?"

He took her outside the building where they wandered down the jungle gash of the road, along which the white owl often flew between stands of buttonwood and seven-year apple. At a path to the beach, bordered by the wide leaves of woman's tongue and sea-grapes, North turned Marianne into the shaded gallery of coconut palms. He told her of Jo's investigation of the Defender broadcasts, of the Zellers, and of his strong intuition that they too would be attacked.

"Even if you're right, can't you stay out of it?"

"No."

She studied his face, and as he was afraid she would, her socialist instinct grabbed for government to solve the problem. "Grant, my father isn't the only person in the Administration. Maybe we could get Malcolm Pyfrom or somebody else with authority to investigate this thing."

How could he answer? That it had to be her father directing St. Gregory, maybe with the help of Pyfrom or the "somebody else." That he *knew* the Garbarino boat would be pirated, as once he had known his recon company would be wiped out in Vietnam? When you pilot your life on intuition, you learn to hide the source of your conviction from those you don't know well. And yet he felt his trust in Marianne deepening, matching his desire for her.

"I guess I just want to be the white chessplayer—"

She felt the need to lighten things. "That some racist comment, Doctor?" she said in her sunny contralto, understanding of course that by "white player" he meant "making the first move."

"You see, if I play it safe and don't do anything myself, I become like everyone else." He stopped, embarrassed to be defining himself, and found words from the milieu of his profession. "Alpha particles, stars, people—we're all inseparable from everything else in the universe whether we like it or not. I am part of whatever has gone wrong here, and my role is to fix it. The only way I have the slightest chance to do that is to be the aggressor, to make first moves instead of trying to defend against a hundred unknowns."

The air was heavy with jungle odors. He put an arm around her shoulders, and her head sank and came to rest on his chest.

". . . Can you understand that?"

She took a deep breath that thrust her breasts forward. "I see things a little differently, Dr. Moon. In this world there are three kinds of people: those who make things happen, watch things happen, and wonder what happened. The first kind is the rarest, and you are one of them. I guess that's what I love about you."

Her words fell on him like liquid tones of a flute. Feeling her ripe femininity, searching deep into the green of her eyes, a dormant part of him sprang into life. His lips traced the cool flesh from her neck to her ear, and he pressed his face against hers. His feelings erupted into those simple words that explain nothing but resolve everything. "I love you," he let himself say, realizing that love is most of life, whereas his separation from her, no matter how pragmatic, was most of death.

"I've loved you since we met," she said.

That voice of hers! Fluid and bright, a voice unbounded like the plains of the moon or the verse of morning birds singing above an island jungle. He found flecks of orchid in her eyes he'd never seen before.

All morning the sun had been baking the Island, lifting from the water a haze that shimmered the seafarm pilings into a mirage of herons standing perfectly still in the shallow sea. In that haze Marianne and North came together, arms entwined, two sleepwalkers awakening to passion and fidelity. Love burned away the pain of psychic bruises, and they lost themselves in their embrace.

When they returned to the laboratory, it was like crossing the lunar terminator from hot to cold. Cleary had shut the door and turned up the air-conditioning.

"She's one of us now," North said to the Islanders, ignoring any reference to her being the P.M.'s daughter.

Jo broke the silence first and smiled at her. "We can use your help, Marianne."

AS THE ISLAND ARMY had grown, so over the following weeks

did their stock of weapons. The day the thirty-three torpedoes were assembled was the day Slaughter Harbour became a test range. The technique North devised for launching the unarmed torpedoes into the sea was similar to releasing a model airplane into the sky, except that you reach down instead of up.

Eight men and women bent under the varnished guardrail of the *Wind Song,* which was anchored near the dock, and steadied their torpedoes, making sure the fins were perfectly horizontal.

They flipped the toggle switches, aimed carefully, timed the waves, and dropped eight unarmed torpedoes horizontally onto the sea. Each torp fell flat and began to sink until its three high-speed motors gripped the water and leveled it off a few feet below the surface. Developing fifteen horsepower, a fish-like silver missile churned across Slaughter Harbour at twenty feet per second or about twelve knots, the peak of their design goal. Those first attempts slammed only a few of each salvo into the practice target, the steel hull of the LCM.

Marianne's eyes followed the wakes of the errant missiles past the *Half Fast* all the way to the barren Harbour Rock. She had heard the local legend about the islet and quoted aloud a line from Conrad, "It has not soil enough to grow a single blade of grass as if it were blighted by a curse."

North, all business, addressed his crew. "Of course we may be doing this at night or in rough seas, or both. We've got to improve our aim." The torpedoes were unimpeded by waist-high waves, but their accuracy was totally dependent upon the precision with which they were launched.

"Maybe we'd improve with a picture of St. Gregory on the target," said Rolle as he and Andy prepared to retrieve the torpedoes and recharge their batteries.

Or Ransom, thought North, but he refused to dwell on that. He needed to cultivate a combat discipline. Army chores like polishing shoes and marching in step have a purpose: to instill the habit of responding without question, so that when your leader says "fire," you fire. North explained this concept to his "troops," who chuckled or shrugged. Aside from Garbarino, who had served in the Navy, the idea was as foreign to them as—well—piracy on the high seas.

Every day after breakfast in seas smooth or rough, and again when the sun slipped almost unnoticed beneath the misty horizon, they rehearsed their movements—launching three salvos, then retrieving the torpedoes and placing their batteries on charge for the next session. Garbarino devised a clip of spring steel to hold the torpedoes firmly onto the deck during heavy seas, and they installed the clips on either side of the *Wind Song*.

When practice became too intense, Cleary would pretend he couldn't wrest his torpedo from his clip, or yell, "Bearing zero-three-five, *fire fish ONE!*" and throw his torp sideways, sending it walloping against the rocky sides of the dock or careening onto the beach in front of the villas. One day when the winds had whipped Slaughter Harbour into low whitecaps and the *Wind Song* was rocking at anchor, he made believe he was going to fall after leaning too far over the rail instead of crouching beneath it as the others did. Rolle came up from behind and pushed, sending him cartwheeling into the water, torpedo and all. Cleary surfaced, sputtering water but still smiling, while the others laughed and the torpedo churned onto the beach. Soaking wet in Bermuda shorts and gartered socks, hair plastered over his eyes, the court jester couldn't have looked funnier had he been wearing a hat with big ears and fuzzy fairy slippers turned up at the toes.

Humor, thought North, shields us from the terrors of the future. If his troops had any idea of the depths of their leader's doubts, they would weep instead of laugh. He didn't know what to make of Rolle, but he was grateful for Cleary's momentary release of their tension.

After one of the practice sessions, Andy came over to North with a quizzical look, and said, "I still don't see how you're going to get these things to explode with seaweed fertilizer."

"Ever heard of the Texas City fire disaster?"

"I have the feeling I'm about to."

"In 1947 a freighter loaded with this same kind of fertilizer—ammonium nitrate—blew up so hard it knocked airplanes out of the sky, set off blasts in a chemical plant, killed hundreds, and injured thousands. It shook the earth as far as the Louisiana border."

"Never again, Dr. Moon, will I underestimate the power of artificial horseshit."

But Andy's smart-aleck words betrayed a maturity that grew with his involvement in the project. He helped North find boron, first in small amounts as boric acid and later in large boxes of borax in the cleaning closet. He mixed borax, ammonium nitrate, and water to North's specifications, then thickened it with seaweed carrageenan to make a slurry impervious to seawater.

The mixture failed to explode in a hole dug on the beach, even using an oversize detonating charge. With the respect due frail exotic flowers, Garbarino dug down to the torpedo shell they were trying to blow up.

"Maybe four pounds of this stuff isn't enough to get hot," Andy said. "Maybe you need tons of it, like they had on the Texas City ship."

Garb looked at North, his eyes widening behind his lenses. "He's right," he said.

"Let's add fuel," North said.

Diesel oil proved insufficiently volatile and gasoline too unstable. What worked was kerosene stirred into the thickened nitrate in a ratio of one to three. The explosion, rewardingly loud, threw sand far into the sky and swirled it toward the clouds. They filled the torpedoes with the explosive slurry.

The next day opened drizzly under a pewter sky, and the raw smell of fish rose out of the sea as they tested eight armed missiles against Harbour Rock. The noise of crashing waves masked the eight explosions, which blasted enough coral loose to make the Islanders confident their torpedoes would breach the hull of a ship.

CHRISTMAS WEEK arrived with jagged seas and a divergence of attitudes. North was methodical, steady. Rolle and Andy were festive, primed for adventure. Garb, apprehensive, kept rechecking propeller alignments in a rig he'd built for that purpose. Jo forever reiterated safety precautions. Marianne and Lorraine were concerned but not distraught, hoping there *were* no pirates.

Only Cleary was unquestionably troubled. He went around smoking furiously, with hair disheveled, shirt tail hanging out, blue eyes flashing. "The pirates are waiting to gobble us up, the Bahamian government is our enemy, the U.S. embassy doesn't give a shit, and the press wouldn't believe us if we tried. What the hell is left?"

"An earthquake?" said Andy.

Cleary frowned and motioned North away from the others. When they were out of earshot, he said, "What happened to your hundred-volt humanity, Grant? I used to think it was science that made you run, but you're a scientist only insofar as you can find something exciting." It was a rare Cleary talking without levity, his lines rehearsed. "I'll never forget that night with the thunderboat. You're an excitement junkie, Grant. You belong in the fifteenth century sailing the edge of the flat ocean to see how long you can totter on the brink. Or in the next century exploring other planets. But here you're out of place, and that's why you're going to get us killed."

Cleary was probably right as far as the danger was concerned. North had no real plan, only a strong hunch and a smoldering lust for something to break the status quo. But it was no mere excitement he sought. It was desperation. He reached down into himself for compassion, for sense, for the discretion the Islanders expected of him, but found there only a cold and overwhelming determination to blast the bizarre Bahamas a few thousand miles out of orbit.

He said nothing to Jack Cleary, but turned and trudged out to Slaughter Harbour, wondering dimly who or what he had become.

43 *More Devil than Man*

IF YOU DISAPPEAR on land there is always someone near-by, always an investigation. But at sea it is assumed that your boat sank in a storm, or that your engine exploded, or that you slipped into the twilight of the Devil's Triangle. Anything except the absurdity of piracy, which was supposed to have ended some centuries ago.

On the afternoon of the shortest day of the year, the sun sank in a sprinkle of fire as the Islanders boarded the Grand Banks trawler *Wind Song*. With so many yachts hastening home to Florida, North suspected that Christmas would be an ideal season for pirates. Doubtless they had radar but probably would consider a night attack unnecessary since they suspected no opposition.

"You can't claim there's little risk and then make me stay out of it," Marianne asserted. The flowers on her T-shirt moved when she talked. Even in grease-smeared dungarees, she was alluring.

North could find no fault with her logic. You anticipate things until you feel you know the future, but the future seldom follows the script. If they were killed, the death of the Prime Minister's daughter would avenge Ransom's complicity. It was a lousy thought, and he shook it off. But after so many months of conjecture and helplessness against an unseen enemy, it felt good to be on the offensive.

Cleary was designated to stay on the Island. If they didn't return, someone had to tell the tale to the press—and continue the search for Coby. Cleary came to the dock to see them off, looking miserable and shaking his head. Behind him, you could hear the Atlantic lapping against Harbour Rock. "I think you guys are crazy. Seven people determined to sample Dr. Guillotine's invention first-hand."

They only smiled in answer.

"Grant," said Cleary futilely, "we're citizens of a superpower. Can't we get the Marines or at least the Coast Guard to help us?"

"Try that," North said, "and the Coast Guard will call the Embassy and someone there will call the Bahamian government."

"Gunboat diplomacy is reserved for getting hostages back," Jo said.

"Or to capture heads of small states out of favor with your government," Marianne said.

"Okay, I give up," said Cleary. He looked North squarely in the eyes, trying to smile. "I guess I haven't watched you give the finger to fate for twenty-three years not to trust your judgment a little."

While the engines warmed up, North had Garb radio the Defence Force in Nassau to ask about the weather and to mention, as if incidental, that the trawler *Wind Song* was departing the Island for Science and heading straight for Ft. Lauderdale. Then they were plowing through black ink, diesels throbbing, the wind at their stern. A spray salted the windshield and left the air inside tangy, like dried fish.

The trawler housed a large saloon, dining area, and galley, as well as an inside control station. Above it rose a flying bridge with auxiliary controls and radio. In the small forward stateroom and down three steps into an aft room, there were plenty of bunks, but of course no one could sleep.

North took stock. The torpedoes worked. They had twenty-five of them, more than enough to keep the enemy at a distance. The crew, while hardly a combat squad, had been honed by the labor of repairing the Island, the barracks-like living conditions, the incessant rehearsal for tonight. Where the hurricane had isolated them, deafening them to each other's needs, the threat of pirates had brought them together. Amateurs yes, but they were a team now, and if not exactly disciplined, at least they were coordinated and motivated.

The moon appeared white and hot as it really is on the dayside, seeming to drip molten silver into a tense boat, but after a few hours it became occluded by rain clouds. At midnight the crew was still too excited to sleep, and huddled around Garb as he steered from the starboard corner of the cabin. Lorraine passed out coffee.

The Grand Banks is a rugged little trawler whose aft steadying sail keeps her from rolling excessively, and the *Wind Song* steadied as she plowed westward. Her compass held at two-eight-zero, undistorted by the metallic mass of the torpedoes which lay like cannon shells on the saloon deck, in the bunks of the forward cabin, and clipped along both sides of the outside bulkheads. For some time now the VHF had sputtered with conversations of unseen islanders or pleasure boaters, but now the shortwave receiver leapt to life.

Jo came immediately alert and scanned the tuning dial. "That's one of the Defender frequencies." The words squawking from the silvered console were low and labored like a tape recorder set at too slow a speed. She adjusted the dial—and lost the broadcast.

"Don't sound much like St. Greg," said Andy.

"Maybe one of his men," said Jo, thinking the Defenders could have them on radar and were announcing their position to a confederate. "It might even be St. Gregory himself. You can't recognize your own father when the radio waves are distorted like that."

"This St. Gregory—" said Garb to no one in particular, steering and sipping his coffee, "if he's really the pirate boss, how do you think he got that way? I mean if the man looks like Blackbeard, maybe—over time—he's unconsciously come to emulate him?"

"I don't know why my father doesn't get rid of him," Marianne said.

No one responded.

Andy said, "The man's simply a necro— What's that word, Grant?"

"St. Gregory is a certain kind of necrophilliac. Not the kind who has sex with corpses; he's like Hitler or Henry Morgan or

Blackbeard." North had read everything he could find about these islands and the pirates who started them on their way. "Necrophilliacs want people around them dead so they can feel alive by contrast—an extreme version of the backbiter who denigrates someone successful to make himself less a failure in his own eyes."

Six faces, lit by the dim red light of the binnacle, were intent on North. An intimacy developed that is possible only in a closed boat at night. "Blackbeard, or Edward Teach," began North, "started out in the Bahamas as a privateer for the British against the French around seventeen hundred. In those days, five-eight was tall, and he stood out like a beanstalk giant at six foot four. He was a bloodthirsty psychopath who convinced himself and his crew that he had come to earth from hell. He did whatever he could to look like a demon, tucking slow-burning sulfur matches in his hat and beard to cloud his face in smoke. People took their devils and hell fires seriously in those days."

"I take 'em seriously *these* days," said Andy. "Sounds to me like you've just described St. Gregory."

"I've never seen eyes like his," said Garb.

It occurred to North that telling pirate tales on the way to battle was like reciting ghost stories in a cemetery, but he couldn't afford to let his crew be seduced by the passing hours into thinking that pirates might not come. He needed to tune his team to a pitch between anticipation and tension, or the plan would self-destruct.

"Teach honed his men into effective assault troops by imposing discipline. A Blackbeard pirate could be killed for letting a prisoner escape, for getting drunk and threatening to defect to a French buccaneer, for burying his own treasure separately, or for raping the girls before the boss got to them. One day after mess, Teach suddenly drew two pistols, blew out the candle, and fired under the table. Israel Hands—the guy Robert Louis Stevenson named his character after in *Treasure Island*—caught a bullet in his knee that lamed him for life.

"'What was that for?' Hands said.

"'Why just for fun, damn you,' said Teach—and when a pirate in those days said *damn you,* he was consigning you straight to the fiery hell they believed in. 'Besides,' Teach said, 'if I didn't shoot one of you now and then, you might forget who I am.'"

"Tell them how Teach used to force his crew down below and light sulfur and pitch," Marianne said.

"When things got slow, when they weren't raping or pillaging or sailing their stolen ships," North said, "Teach would recreate hell with his sulfur smoke. 'Let's see which of us is kin to the devil by staying the longest in it,' he'd announce. One by one, the crew would push up the hatches, gasping for air. Blackbeard always stayed the longest, which is why he and his crew truly believed he was related to the devil."

"Leadership," said Rolle. "Leading by example."

"True," said North. "He was the first over the side to board a ship. He'd wade in firing his Saturday-night specials until his ammo was gone, then switch to throat-slashing or hacking off hands and heads with cutlasses. Gash one of his arms and he'd fight twice as hard with the other. Blind him with his own blood and he'd laugh at you. Surround him with four soldiers and take his weapons away and he'd strangle two men with a hand around each throat, while biting the jugular vein of a third and kicking the fourth in the groin. They all had amoebic dysentery from time to time. If his was especially bad, he'd open a flap in his britches during combat."

In his canvas jacket and dark knit watch cap, North seemed a modern-day Lieutenant Maynard of the Royal Navy—Blackbeard's nemesis who finally decapitated the pirate and hung his bearded head on his bowsprit. To this day, Maynard is a popular name in the Bahamas. Teach is not.

Marianne looked worried, her face ghostly as if forgetting to breathe.

Garb had the opposite reaction. "Pure Hollywood," he said. "Square sails, cutthroats swinging from ship to ship, the flash of sabres, chests of gold . . ."

"Yeah," said Andy, "and the villain with a hole in his pants unleashing the world's first biological warfare."

Marianne frowned, then laughed in spite of herself.

"How could Blackbeard last so long with the Royal Navy after him?" Rolle asked.

"The governors in North Carolina and the Bahamas were his business partners, trading protection for a percentage of the spoils."

"So *that*'s how the tradition got started," Rolle said.

Thinking of Marianne's father, no one pursued the subject, and an ominous silence filled the cabin. North's story was over but the Islanders were bound in that strange indenture of the species where pirates in black beards can jump the centuries to slit living throats.

Marianne wore a troubled look on her face. "There may be a parallel explanation for *our* pirate captain," she said.

"Which is?" said North, watching her closely.

"When was Teach born?" she asked mysteriously.

"No one knows for sure. They didn't keep good records in England back then."

"Could it have been shortly after 1665?"

"Without a doubt. He wasn't old when he was killed in 1718."

"Amsterdam in 1665," Marianne said. "That's when the German Jesuit scientist Athanasius Kircher described the 'unknown unborn' in his *Mundus Subterraneus* or *Underground World*. I did a paper on Father Kircher at Oxford. He portrayed the unknown entity as being born again and again through the ages."

Rolle, the Bahamian, scoffed. Yet Andy, an American who should know better, hung on Marianne's every word. It made North wonder whether these forays into history, designed at first to fine-tune his crew, were backfiring, making them anxious. He remembered the scientist Kircher as the inventor of the slide projector, the original 'magic lantern' and its 'lantern slides,' but had forgotten that the priest Kircher had dabbled in the occult. Did Marianne, despite her intelligence and education, really believe in such drivel? He wanted to tell her—and Andy—that the reincarnationists, the séancers, the flying saucerists, the astrologers, and all the rest are people afraid of life, that their fear makes them feel they can't control their own destinies and so blame God or the void or the stars. It came to him that the daughter of a voodoo priestess growing up in one of the more superstitious countries of the earth could hardly have escaped completely unscathed, and that to change her mind might take a considerable amount of time.

"What did this priest say about the recurring birth?" Andy wanted to know.

"*Surely this monster hybrid comes not from a mother's womb,*'" Marianne quoted, "*but from an ephialtes, an incubus, or some other horrendous demon, as if spawned in a putrid and venomous fungus, son of Fauns and Nymphs, more devil than man.*'"

"What's an 'ephiates' and an 'incubus?'" Andy asked.

"Demons who give you nightmares."

"So you think Kircher was talking about the birth of Teach?"

"And Captain St. Gregory three hundred years later," whispered Marianne.

"You mean . . . ?" said Andy.

"That history repeats its villains? Who knows?"

AN HOUR after midnight they rounded the Great Isaac light, giving the shoals a wide berth by keeping the beacon well to port. Garbarino and North ran the boat from the flying bridge, while Rolle prowled the decks below to search the horizon. The trawler clawed southwest out of the Bahama banks into the deep waters of the Gulf Stream, weaving against the northward current like a tired drunk.

Before daybreak they picked up patches of light scattered low on the horizon. Palm Beach. North knew the glow could not yet be seen from below, where everyone but Rolle was resting and Lorraine may even be sleeping, snug in her disbelief that there were pirates out there. And Marianne? Maybe thinking of devils who pop up again every three centuries.

North cast a glance at Garb and turned the wheel slightly south, then to port a little more, placing the trawler in an unnoticeable shallow turn. Garb looked back at him, raised a hand as if to object, then dropped it, a slow grin forming in back of his thick lenses. No words passed between them, but a fateful agreement had been reached. Both men knew there was no chance of being attacked here in the coastal waters of Florida, and yet they were turning back. Escorting the Garbarinos to safety was only part of North's purpose; his prime motive, shattering the status quo of the Bahamas, would have gone unfulfilled. But how could he explain Garbarino's participation? Probably, thought North, the engineer wanted to try out his torpedo design. A brief but true friend, he had more guts than most men his age and wanted one real adventure before returning to his drawing boards.

The shore lights slipped behind them with Garb at the helm, leaning forward, scanning the seas through binoculars. His forward posture, his Navy pea jacket hunched up around his neck, stocking cap snug on his head, and a hard frown on his face made him look as predacious as North felt.

The compass gradually drifted around to ninety degrees as Rolle climbed the steps bearing mugs of coffee. The red light from the binnacle darkened the scar on his cheek as he glanced at the compass. And then at Garb and North.

"You guys got it bad," he said. He left the coffee and went below.

At false dawn the troposphere reflected the indigo of the deep ocean and made distances seem longer than they really were. The Caribbean Effect. Far off, through air filled with electricity, you could see pinpoints of yachts and the twinkling necklaces of cruise ships timing their voyages in order to reach Miami Harbor before breakfast. Another hour passed and a steam fog crawled over the ocean like smoke. The lighted loops of each cruise ship blinked out one by one as if someone had turned off the separate strings of a Christmas tree. Garb switched on the wipers to no avail; visibility was down to a hundred feet. The trawler labored onward, her twin screws chewing foaming water. North still believed the pirates would show up, but with fog billowing like a blanket, it would be tough to launch torpedoes.

"Faster, Garb." He wanted desperately to make it back out of the rough waters of the Gulf Stream before anything happened.

Garbarino pushed the throttles as far forward as he could without swamping the bow.

Another hour, and they felt the chop of the Stream give way to the calmer, shallow seas of the Bahamas. A misty sun floated on the fog, fed now by the drizzle falling through cooler surface air.

A disembodied voice sounded from the radio:

"Ahoy, blueboat. Any *body* awake in there?" The voice was sticky, mollifying.

"Don't answer, Garb!"

North leapt down the ladder from the flying bridge and plunged wildly toward the duplicate controls at the forward end of the saloon, tripping over furniture and scattering a pile of torpedoes that clanged and rolled into the galley. He needed to be down here to deploy his crew, all of whom were awakened by the commotion. The voice sounded again, tinged in alcohol and Spanish.

"Ahoy there, blueboat, how 'bout loaning ush a cup er two of thee motor oil?"

North grabbed the microphone and keyed the speaker button, forcing himself to pause for a deep breath. In a voice unnaturally passive, he said, "Sorry, *amigo*, but we don't have any motor oil." He faked a yawn into the mike. Then he released the button and said to Rolle who was standing next to him not fully awake, "How do they know the *Wind Song* is blue—in this fog?"

Rolle looked puzzled, then bolted out the cabin door and yelled for the others to join him in a fierce search of the horizon. North bellowed for them to unclip the torpedoes.

"Which side?" Jo shouted through water running down her face.

"Can't tell. *Man both sides!*"

Turmoil. Islanders running, yanking wet torpedoes, frenzied in their rush to stay calm, to remember everything at once. Remove the firing-pin guards, bend under the rail, wait for the command, activate the propellers, then wait again for the crest of a wave before dropping the torpedo flat. Silvered by the diffuse sunlight, the finned steel tubes somehow seemed heavier and slipperier than they had in practice.

The men were aggressive. The women, bent at the knees under the port rail, appeared if not confident, at least ready, steadying their torps against the deck as in rehearsal, awaiting North's signal. Marianne was clearly the most vulnerable. She kept glancing over her shoulder through the open window where North was working the controls only a few feet away.

Garbarino scurried down the ladder, shouting to North. "You can see the boat from above! Southwest! Two-one-five, maybe two-two-zero!"

Seconds later, they saw a dark blotch on the fog, and it was closing on their starboard bow.

"Everyone to starboard!" North yelled.

Jo and Marianne struggled with their slippery torpedoes through the cabin to the other side. Lorraine got there before them and joined her husband farther aft, ready to launch. Andy dashed to the bow in front of the cabin, Rolle to the bowsprit, arming their firing pins on the way.

The Hispanic voice came back on the air, the accent thicker. "Oh, please, you must *hahve* some leetle bit of oil. Every body hahve thee motor oil."

And then North could see her clearly, a forty or fifty-foot dark-gray motor launch steaming straight for them out of the fog. Fast. At least twenty-five knots. That meant turbochargers and most likely gasoline engines, thought North, picturing volatile, aerated fuel pounding the pistons. He figured the closure rate between the vessels at forty knots or more. Easing the throttles, he slid back the front windshield and portside vent. All windows were open now, so his crew could hear him.

"Stand by for a turn. I'm going to veer *left* as soon as they get in range." He increased speed a little to steady the boat.

As the intruder bore down on them, North timed his turn exquisitely, ready to close a narrow triangle of which the *Wind Song* was the base. Four hundred feet, three-fifty, three hundred . . .

Turn!

The sea gurgled through the scuppers as the *Wind Song* healed over in a bank and righted herself. North's tongue felt as metallic as his torpedoes. If the launch did turn out to be a privateer, his own beam would be exposed like a galleon showing her cannons, but his crew of six, spaced apart from each other at the rail, would be in perfect position to launch six perfect shots.

Andy, bent at the starboard bow near the cabin, said quietly, "Here's where we find out if we're cut out to be marines." Then he screamed, "Grant! That ain't no pirate ship! She's a sport fisherman!"

"*Launch!*" North yelled. "*Launch!*"

"No! *Wait!*" shouted Marianne. She straightened at the window, holding her torpedo like a baby. "Grant, listen. They could see us before we could see them because their boat is *gray*! Like the *fog!*"

"*Launch the damn torpedoes!*" He couldn't take the time to explain; their belly was exposed.

Rolle and the Garbarinos already had launched on cue, and their torps were churning at twelve knots through the low-cresting swells of Force-Three waves. You could see their trails streaking toward the inbound launch that ground on like a runaway train. Andy and Jo stood at their rails, stressed, confused, frozen in the indecision North had feared.

"You can't just *destroy* that boat before you know who they are!" Marianne cried, her green eyes flashing in the dim cabin light.

No time to argue. No time to maneuver. No time to run. He had been counting silently . . . *three, four, fi—*

A report like a long thunderbolt leapt from the gray vessel as one of the torpedoes struck her hull near the port bow. The sound of the blast filled air and sea, diffused through bodies, thrust into hearts where it pounded anew. The gray ship, like a bonito ravaged by a shark, jerked toward the trawler. But her momentum kept her coming and she slid alongside them, bow to bow. The boats were so close you could see the men on the gray launch, four of them. Two had been knocked down by the blast and were squirming on the deck, alternately rubbing the afterimage out of their eyes and blindly spraying bullets toward the *Wind Song*.

The others, one black, one white, flung themselves across the narrowing gap with pistols flaring, firing from both pairs of hands like buccaneers as they dropped onto the trawler's bow deck. The black man crumbled where he fell, his head a tangled mass of blood and war paint, a corpse created by his own partners' flying bullets.

The white pirate, in camouflage fatigues, jump boots, and black beret, landed and rolled like a parachutist, bounced up immediately, and grabbed Andy. Wrapping a thick upper arm around the boy's neck, the pirate clutched him head to head. With Andy's cheek against his beard, Andy's body mostly in front of him, he placed his feet wide apart and pumped rounds from his automatic into the cabin as fast as he could pull the trigger. North flung himself under the steering console in time, feeling the windshield collapse over his back, hearing the slugs ripping wood and fiberglass. Rolle, who had been launching from the bowsprit, lunged from behind and bashed a torpedo over the pirate's beret. The pirate slid down Andy's back and collapsed in a mix of blood and hair.

North struggled back to the wheel. Swinging hard to port, he rammed the throttles open, sending the trawler leaping from the pirate ship like an uncaged cougar. *Distance!* He needed distance. When the gap between the boats widened to some three hundred feet, he spun the wheel all the way over, circling back to port and aiming toward the pirate's stern. The trawler's steadying sail strained against the tight circle, and the *Wind Song* came up beam to end in an inverted "T," ready to fire like a man-of-war.

The gray ship lurched as her pilot tried to swing her a hundred and eighty degrees to ram her assailant. But the turn was slowed by water rushing into the hole in her side, and she broached. One of the pirates had regained his bearings after the blast, and opened up with an automatic rifle. Splinters of wood and glass whizzed around the *Wind Song* cabin and tore up the ceiling, but the vessels were bouncing too much in their turbulent wakes for any accuracy.

"More torps! Launch them all!"

This time urging was unnecessary. The Islanders, except North at the wheel and Marianne sitting on the saloon deck with her head in her hands, worked frantically at the port gunwales. They dropped torpedo after torpedo fast, as if Blackbeard himself rampaged on the other ship. When the supply dwindled, Andy and Jo ran back and forth to the cabin, bringing spares. The others stayed at the rail, activating motors, launching torps with each new wave.

Halfway into her turn the pirate boat displayed the tear in her fiberglass hull, a wounded animal lusting to ram her tormentor. Automatic rifle fire kicked in again, falling wide of its mark and sounding to North like a single M-16. It was a race between the AR's scattergun *RRraaaaaattTT* from two hundred feet and the dozen miniature torpedoes that plodded steadily forward, their contrails etching the corrugated steel water.

Ten seconds is forever!

At last the first torpedoes met the oncoming privateer. One after the other, the explosions showered the air with hissing shards of fiberglass. Ripped at the water line, the gray ship trembled like a prisoner before a firing squad. Water rushing into her ragged openings twisted her around again and forced her stern, where the gasoline tanks were located, to face the last of the torpedoes.

Seconds later the gray ship exploded, sending thousands of fragments skyward. Texas City in miniature. The firestorm rocked the *Wind Song,* breaking windows and portholes on the starboard side, singeing hair, numbing eardrums, bloodying faces with flying glass.

Not since Apollo-Seventeen turned the coastal night into broad daylight had North witnessed such a sudden contrast in light and sound. This victory wouldn't get him to the moon, but it was a good explosion as explosions go. At one blast, it vindicated his intuition, avenged the Zellers, and captured an important pawn.

44 *Have Him Put to Sleep*

JO RECOGNIZED the dead man. There was no mistaking that apelike physique, the shark tooth hanging on the gold chain, the deep-brown skin, and the scowl etched into the face even as it turned rigid. He was Bill Symes, Evan's brother. They pushed the corpse overboard where it would join the gray boat that had slipped stern-first beneath the swells. Smoke from the fire already had merged with the fog.

"Now we know why Mr. Symes was in the yacht business," Jo said.

"Thank God, they didn't use one of his thunderboats," Andy said. "We wouldn't of had a chance."

"They could hardly do that," said North. "The whole idea is to creep up on a victim."

Andy and Garb broke into that laughter that comes at the end of violence, when you know the danger is over and you have survived. They couldn't stop chuckling and grinning as they washed off blood and applied adhesive to each other's cuts. "God, what a day. *What a day!*" Garbarino kept saying, pacing back and forth through broken glass scattered everywhere. He was so emotionally intoxicated that the mad decision he had shared with North had turned out all right, he could think of nothing else to say.

Their prisoner was still unconscious. Jo and Rolle wrapped a nylon rope around his wrists in back of his body, looping it under his beard and around his neck the way Jo had seen them do in Haiti—more loosely, though, so he wouldn't choke unless he tried to stand and run.

North crunched through the glass to the console and radioed Jack Cleary that all was well. Lorraine came up to him, laughing and apologizing for her skepticism. ". . . and if Ernie and I had left the Island alone . . . Well, I'm just glad you didn't listen to me. Why Grant, you've saved our lives!"

As North returned the microphone to its clamp, Marianne turned to him, her face a mask of sorrow. "I don't share this levity, these congratulations. You were the most gentle man I've ever known, Grant. But you've changed!"

He had no words for her. A firefight was as foreign to Marianne as an iceberg, and yet her concern was not unfounded; in desperation he had allowed himself to be transformed by events. He knew that, but felt no remorse at having abandoned that earlier, more-compassionate Grant North. The ecstasy of danger, the spice of euphoria spurted through his bloodstream. Cleary had been right when he said that North was born for the attack: it was the way he had survived Vietnam, the way he fought in business or chess. And it was the way he would find Coby.

The pirate, semiconscious on the saloon deck in an area cleared of glass and splinters, groaned and thrashed, pulling on the rope to his neck. Still dazed, he opened both eyes, came to his knees, and glanced upward from face to face.

"What's your name?" said North severely, looking down at him. "Where do you come from?"

The pirate's gaze was blank, a condemned man waiting for the shot. A lump the size of an egg bulged out of clotted black blood on the back of his head. His cheeks and forehead were slashed with red and black body paint, but not the paint commandos use; its purpose had been intimidation, not concealment. He sat back on his haunches, his bloody beret between his legs, and tried to focus his eyes. In his late twenties with long dirty hair and scraggly beard, he combined the wiry Latin look with that of an animal.

The biceps of a gorilla, the small, black, protruding eyes of a craw-fish, his face was so full of hate it made you shudder at the things it must have seen. He smelled like something wild from the sea, and gulped the air as if stealing it. As he struggled toward full consciousness he exhaled a prolonged wail that Blackbeard might have loosed while brachiating on the rigging, decibels louder than any civilized man knows how to make.

Rolle knelt before him, face to face. *"¿Cuál es su nombre?"* When no answer came, he pulled the neck rope. *"¡Dígame su nombre!"*

In the pirate's black eyes North read no plea for mercy. His look seemed to say that piracy is only a job with him, and if it has gone badly then that is in the nature of things, that he would do what he must to survive. To Rolle's further yanks on the rope he looked straight ahead, forlorn and hangdog, and said almost inaudibly, "Juan."

"¿Cuál es su apellido?"

"Doe," he said, spitting the American pseudonym he'd picked up somewhere. *"Juan Doe."*

The answer angered Rolle. He untied the rope binding the pirate's feet, leaving it around his neck, and led him like a dog to the forward cabin.

An hour later they returned to the saloon. The pirate, face bloody and swollen, eyes deadened, had the exhausted look of an animal that has escaped many times before reaching its moment of death.

"What did you do to him?" Marianne asked.

"I beat the shit out of him."

"What did you learn?" asked North.

"I know this is necessary to find out about Coby," Marianne said quietly, "but I don't want to watch." She stepped out to the foredeck and stared straight ahead. The drizzle had ceased and the sun was burning away the fog as the trawler plowed evenly northward.

"As we suspected," Rolle said after Marianne left, "it was St. Gregory and his goons who fucked up our radio. They board an expensive yacht, disable the radio, and get back on their gunboat.

If St. Greg sanctions its capture, the pirates return and kill the owners, take their money, jewels, anything they want. Seems there are two kinds of smugglers operating in the Bahamas. Those un-authorized, like Evan Symes, and the guys condoned by our Saint Sadist. Sometimes they go after the competition, and when they do, they use a sharpshooter to kill as many of the crew as they can from a distance. That explains Mike Morgan and the derelict ship you and Cleary found. St. Greg used Morgan to kill the un-sanctioned smugglers and then wiped out Morgan. They turn these yachts over to the Cubans who apparently pay out the ass."

"St. Gregory and his crew ought to be multimillionaires by now," North said.

Garb was listening. He had come back into the cabin trying to slow his euphoric pacing. "Don't they make enough money smuggling to buy their own?" he said.

"Supply problem. The life of a vessel in the trade is only a year or two, and by that time the boat is usually scuttled or forfeited to the U.S. Coast Guard."

"Who directs St. Gregory?" North said, the crucial question.

"*¿A quién se relata el gigante?*" Rolle asked the subdued pirate.

"*Al Jefe . . . supongo.*"

"St. Gregory reports to his boss, he supposes."

"But who *is* the Boss?" North said, and Rolle asked Juan Doe in Spanish.

"*¿Quién sabe?*"said Juan.

"He doesn't know."

"Ask him why he thinks there *is* a boss," North said.

Juan revealed that after the pirates receive their cryptic orders from St. Gregory, he sometimes hears him talking on the same channel in English to someone farther away, a man with a smooth voice. Doesn't everyone have a *jefe*?

No, not everyone, thought North. Not the Prime Minister.

More likely, Ransom would funnel his orders through someone else, maybe Ben Franklin who cared nothing for the Bahamian goal of self-sufficiency in food. Franklin, though, was such a fright-ened little man, North couldn't picture him giving orders to anyone, let alone St. Gregory. The same for Deputy P.M. Malcolm Pyfrom. And St. Gregory's direct superior, Commander Bridgewater, was an ineffectual weasel with Scotch in his bloodstream.

"Sid," said North quietly, glancing at Marianne on the after-deck. "The boss must be Ransom."

"Why? Because he's got a smooth voice?"

"Just a hunch. Isn't it always the guy at the top?"

"Grant, it doesn't *have* to be *anyone*. Juan doesn't *know* that the person St. Greg talks to is someone in the government. It could be his stockbroker, for crysake!"

"Ask him if he knows anything about St. Gregory ordering Bill Symes to kill Jo—or using Velma to kill Knowles."

There ensued a conversation in fast Spanish, ending with, *". . . para yo ponerlo a dormir?"*

"Rolle said, *"¡Cuidado, hombre!"*

"What was all that about?"

"He knows nothing of Symes or Velma Fisher. He didn't even know Symes's last name. He's got a quaint way about him, this pirate. He said if we were so spooked by St. Gregory, why don't we just pay him a fee to have the captain 'put to sleep?'"

AFTER THEIR adrenaline high, the Islanders were hungry. The sky had turned the milky color of the sea, now coagulating into soft foam against the bow. From the afterdeck Rolle ran long lines from poles held in sockets on the gunwales, and a quarter hour later reeled in two dolphin fish. Gulls patrolled the overcast sky, sentries seeking handouts, chattering in their raucous high-frequency language that required no translation. Rolle gutted the fish and carved yard-long fillets of red meat. As he worked, he threw the waste high in the air, and the gulls multiplied, zigzagging and catching lunch on the fly.

Lorraine broiled the dolphin and served it with breadfruit and beer. While Andy steered from the flying bridge, the shipmates gathered around the saloon table feeling the ocean breeze through the blown-out windows. Marianne fed the bound pirate. North would not agree to freeing his hands for a moment, not even to go to the head. The meal calmed the Islanders, but Marianne was still in shock and went to her bunk after lunch.

By the time the sun tilted into the sea, trailing rainbow dust on the crests of glistening waves, they were cruising off an isolated coast of South Bimini in front of a deciduous forest. Only fifty miles from Florida, it was another world here. The breeze had subsided with the setting sun, which now cast its strange reverse-green blush on the ivory water. A stillness settled over the forest, whose narrow trees, no thicker than a human thigh, would slow but not halt a man's progress.

North and Rolle began to eliminate evidence. North wanted to consign the pirates' automatics and the remaining torpedoes to the deeps.

"Sure you won't need them?" asked Garb. "I'd hate to have to make torps again. And you can't buy guns in Bimini or anywhere in the Bahamas."

"So I've heard," North said. "But our war is over. Even if it wasn't, I wouldn't subject any of you to it again. We were lucky this time. Let's leave it at that."

Juan's guns and then Juan himself, untied and unrepentant, were shoved overboard. The pirate swam underwater, splashing phosphorescence when he rose infrequently for air, as if at any moment expecting a fusillade from the trawler. They watched in the moonlight until he climbed onto the rocky shore. If the pirate made his way back to St. Gregory, that was okay. Let the other side do the worrying for a change.

Night loons took wing over the shallow water as they pulled into Alice Town on North Bimini. Christmas Eve. Marianne awoke refreshed and told North she loved him, that she had resolved to put this day behind her and make what she could of the holiday season. Everyone was eager to go ashore, to walk among ordinary people who did not make their livings by piracy, who cared about things other than ambushes at sea and the firepower of their weapons. Here they could rest for a few days, buy window glass for the trawler, reorder their lives, shop for presents, spend the holidays in human fraternity.

No one in Alice Town did the Goombay Shuffle. Biminians give you the feeling they are more eager than Nassauvians for tourists, and their brown faces were animated with the cheer of the season. While the others went shopping, North and Jo, both having searched Bimini on their own, now rerouted Coby's probable steps, talking to shop owners and restaurateurs along the palm-draped King's Highway. At shops that said, WINE & SPIRITS and THE COMPLEAT ANGLER, HOME OF PAPA HEMINGWAY, at outdoor bars where they ate conch fritters and drank Christmas punch, at Mearil's Book Store and Brown's Hotel, they showed Coby's picture and asked questions, working through Alice Town to Bailey Town and back.

A Salvation Army band relentlessly repeated carols aside a sign that announced, THE BIMINI NATIVE FISHING TOURNAMENT. Furry casuarinas, the closest pines to American-style Christmas trees, were adorned with holly, tinsel, and live white birds who cared not that they had become holiday decorations for another species. The people smiled and talked, oblivious of the search for Coby, and carrying bright packages for Christmas and boxes for Boxing Day, the weekday after Christmas when gifts are given to employees and service people.

One of those package-bearers turned out to be Marianne. Under a bundle of presents for her shipmates and wearing a cheerful Christmas smile, a Navajo sweater, and long suede skirt, she looked as though she had never heard of pirates or torpedoes. North and Jo helped carry the presents, the three of them weaving through thickening street crowds in the general direction of the *Wind Song*.

Every light in North Bimini must have been turned on for Junkanoo Christmas. *Junkanoo!* was scrawled on the sides of buildings, on sidewalks, even on tree trunks. Marianne told them that junkanoo originally meant "something deadly," perhaps corrupted from the Ghanaian sorcerer John Canoe, and West African slaves had brought the word with them to the Bahamas where it eventually came to designate masked dancing at Christmas time. Street dancers called "rushers" in crepe-paper costumes of sea creatures, rushed back and forth to a wizard's oscillations, shaking cowbells and blowing whistles. At the same time bare-chested dark men, their torsos glistening in sweat, pounded goatskin drums to a voodoo rhythm.

Strains of "Silent Night" mixed with the junkanoo beat, and floated the curious medley over the town. North tried to embrace the alien festival, the non-freezing weather, the sugary sentiments written on storefronts. Instead, images stormed his mind of Coby trudging these shining streets, touching the doors of the narrow shops, homeless, sleeping in some passageway. An impenetrable rampart had crossed the dimension of time: the dockmen, the boat girls, the passersby, the shopkeepers were different from those he had talked to before, and all remembrance of Coby in Bimini had vanished like last year's festival.

North evoked Heather and her years spent living while dying, then Coby as a little girl with her legs tucked neatly under her skirt, petting the cat beneath the Christmas tree. She would be attending the Sorbonne by now if only he hadn't sent her away. Perhaps she would have flown home yesterday or today at the end of her first term, making jokes of her French, filling his heart with stories of Paris. It is a myth that time cures all psychic wounds, another myth that the world has shrunk. We live with high-frequency radio and think we've tamed the wilds, that we can communicate with anyone at any place at any time, yet people still become lost in the enormous complexity of the planet. Irretrievably lost.

Marianne, Jo, and North wandered over the island until the junkanoo dancers quit and the carolers quieted inside their bars or homes, releasing the silent night to spread across the village. North tried to imagine Coby carrying her amnesic burden down foreign boulevards, not knowing who she was or why she was there. But he saw ahead only pain. And her blurred shadow on the snowless streets.

45 *Love and Haiti*

"REACH UP under my slip," whispered Marianne in her bedroom suite of her father's mansion.

Seeing her heated face, her breasts, her golden legs backlighted, North entertained the thought that he had created her out of his mind. He pressed his fingers under moist hair, silky soft as the fur of a cat, and the tremor of her body felt like a purr. He had met women who wouldn't plan a tryst but would "let it happen," feeling absolved as might a person who kept a found wallet. He smiled at the idea of Marianne premeditating this episode with all the attention to detail of a spider, and her plot proved more eloquent because of it.

She had wanted him to see where she lived and he had accepted, hoping to find something in Ransom's ten-million-dollar lair that might help him. The Prime Minister's absence—he was in Mexico City—had given North the opportunity, but that was only part of his reason for being here. He loved Marianne and wanted her despite the episode on the *Wind Song* and her lingering superstitions. He was looking for a wife, he reminded himself, not a comrade-in-arms, and given her intelligence and education, he felt he could overcome her obeah heritage.

The bedroom reminded North of the female sex organ, a tight

355

little nook whose pink walls opened into a private study lined with books. A carpet fringed the suite in shaggy black. Breakers crashed at the base of the cliff, the roar muted by the distance from the open French doors, through which a sweet and salty mist permeated the room. North sat on the bed that rose mound-like from the center of the carpet, and Marianne lowered herself onto him. The lace of her hem tickled his thighs, and her breasts brushed his face. Impaled on him, she moved with a rhythm and a sensuousness he hadn't believed possible, while her face radiated heat and love. Every muscle in that glorious anatomy collaborated to draw him deeper into her body. He held her lightly under the skirt of her slip, their hearts hammering like drums, Marianne's long mane flying, earring jangling. When he could stand it no longer, his body exploded into hers. He tasted tears on her mouth but when he inquired into her green eyes he saw a wild happiness, and they both laughed at the same time.

He didn't know precisely why she laughed: a release maybe after those years of denial. But he knew why *he* laughed. He *had* to laugh. Not at the abject absurdity of two animals in rut and heat, nor at his seduction by the Prime Minister's daughter after so many false starts. His laughter sprang from an uncontrollable joy, a zany belief that only by laughing could he detain happiness before reality engulfed him again like a flood tide.

Marianne removed her slip and lay on the white ruffled bedspread under a Winslow Homer painting of a black boy drinking from a coconut against a bluish palm. Nude, they were a study in contrasts. There was skin, the body's largest organ. And then, thought North, there was skin. The color of honey, hers spread before him smooth and stimulating, curved by an inspired architecture. How could he once have felt, no matter how fleetingly, that this magnificent and flawless skin could in any way hinder his attraction?

He tasted her breast and entered her again. They moved together furiously as though this act were a profound discovery, creating love out of their uncertain future. Hour after hour, neither could stop through moans and uninhibited shrieks, until the colloids of the afternoon floated like gold flecks above their spent bodies.

"Love," she said simply, and her wide-apart almond-shaped eyes sparkled like emeralds. "Is this what it really is? Or," she smiled, "are we just a couple of hedonists?"

Her question needed no answer, not for him, not for her. As their passion calmed, his desire expanded like a quiet stream shining in the sun. Her every caress, her every movement lifted pain from his psychic wounds. Leaning on an elbow alongside her, he watched her eyes: bright, mysterious, softened by lovemaking. How small and beautiful she was, stretched nude on the bed, child-sized compared to him, a warm, exotic, feline creature, a femme fatale with a smile like dew on a summer morning.

The low sun penetrated the mist and touched their limbs with a blond flame. They fell asleep in each other's arms, North's harsh insomnia a forgotten relic of the past, replaced by soft slumber in the heart of the tropics. He dreamt strange dreams of saltwater caverns, cool and deep. In the shadows between sleep and consciousness, his mind made the caverns into deep wells of flowing saltwater, and he dreamt that the wells had something to do with his seafarm. The sounds of the well water merged into rollers crashing on the rocks below, and he came fully awake. One of Marianne's two cats, Marx, was purring. The animal made him sad for a moment, thinking of Coby as a child when she had persuaded her cat to allow her to dress it like a doll.

Up close, Marianne's face was softened by love and sleep. She awoke with a laugh, restraining a pair of sharp claws. Gorby had joined Marx. "These cats are in heaven having *two* big bodies to play with."

They took showers, and while Marianne dried her hair, North explored the mansion. It was neo-Spanish, shaped like a crucifix with high ceilings along the long axis and bedroom suites forming the short part of the cross. Soaring at various acute angles, the beams were Brazilian imbuia, richer than walnut, heavy as steel, and rough-sawn like the one Christ died upon. North wondered whether Ransom had planned the cruciform architecture deliberately.

He went to the window and let his eyes roam the compound. Water overflowing evenly out of one long side of a rectangular swimming pool appeared to cascade into the ocean eighty feet below but actually recirculated itself, he reasoned, by means of a hidden gutter. Cypresses and willows like giant black flowers streaked the back wall in branches so thick North doubted whether the mansion ever got wet in the brief Bahamian rains.

The compound was spread across the rocky south coast of New Providence far from the lesser estates of Lyford Cay and Nassau proper, with a guard hut, separate servant's quarters, tennis court, pool, and a nursery, all set on a meadow large enough for a city park. The grounds were bordered on one side by a high fence of steel spikes that grew out of the ocean, and on the others by a wide thicket of dense casuarinas that towered over the landscaping. In the middle of the thicket, North suspected, there would be a barrier of some sort, probably razor wire.

The color of the sky deepened as sodium-vapor yardlights flashed on, bathing the meadow in yellow, another measure of token security. Ransom was not one for having a host of servants around, and Marianne had given the maids and gardeners the New Year's weekend off. Even when Ransom and his bodyguards were home, there were few people in the fifty-acre compound. The two uniformed guards who manned the iron gate and sentry post comprised the first line of defense, and they did a good job of searching cars, Marianne's included. But there were no machine-gun emplacements, no troopers carrying automatic rifles, no armed helicopters. After the guard post, the major defense was the mansion itself. Stone construction and narrow arched windows deterred both the subtropical sun and intruders who would find it impossible to break the bulletproof polycarbonate used instead of glass.

Inside, a time switch blinked on a Christmas tree full of tiny white lights, an obviously imported tree that rose three stories. Behind it, a gigantic stone fireplace whose ornate mantle, a ton of wood that alone must have cost as much as the total furnishings of Marie Ransom's bungalow, held framed photographs of Marianne and her father. Original oil paintings by Copley and Lejuene depicted wars in blood red—ragged American rebels going against the British, Napoleon's troops ladened with gold and pewter invading Italy. The walls were slashed at every turn with plump Venetian nudes, overdressed English kings, baroque seaports in

France, and a profusion of angular angels in gilded frames. North, who detested opulence, could admire any single painting, atom for atom, but the clashing of styles made a mockery of the man whose single criterion for collectibility seemed to be cost. Bric-a-bracs from earlier centuries, gold-plated faucets in the bathrooms, gooey antiques, rococo mirrors, a white grand piano . . . North wouldn't have been surprised to find a throne in one of the rooms, or at least incense and candles oscillating religiously. If you want to know what's important to a man, visit his home. This one shrieked the message that Sir Charles Ransom sought immortality in his possessions.

North wandered through Ransom's trophies, the heads of deer, rhinoceros, elk, and rare tigers staring with frozen expressions. A pair of giant elephant tusks stuck straight up from the floor flanking a pair of double doors. The doors were unlocked so North walked inside. It was a conference room with ornate chairs carved of an exotic wood and, in the corner, a TV with a collection of video tapes. The tape labels marked the P.M.'s political speeches and rallies: INDEPENDENCE DAY, EMANCIPATION DAY, ELECTION CAMPAIGN, and another that said, HAITIAN WATCH. Curious, he inserted the Haitian tape in the video player and watched a beautiful woman appear on the screen wearing a gossamer white gown. She looked familiar. Her arms were raised over an enormous bonfire, and her fists made white orbs against the black sky. She was leading some kind of chant. *"Haiti, Haiti, Haiti. . . !"* No, that wasn't it. The repeated word had but one syllable: *"Hate, hate, hate, hate, hate, hate . . . Hate for the highborn hypocrites. Hate for the hoodlums. Hate for the heathens. Remember Cay Lobos . . ."*

The refrain returned in symbiotic progression, each syllable rising an imperceptible note over the last: *"Hate, hate, hate, hate, hate . . ."*

"Not a pretty picture of one's mother, is it?"

He turned and the sight of Marianne took his breath away. Her silken legs moved in a kind of scarlet fever under the skirt of a red knit dress. Her hair fell to one side, straight and brown, smelling vaguely of flowers, her only jewelry the inevitable single earring. She was ready to greet the New Year.

"In my mother's house you see her side of things; here you see my father's. Mother still does this sort of thing, you know."

"But why—?"

"Why preach hate? She's trying to redirect the natural black hatred of whites against the government. She wants nothing less than to defeat the man she helped elect."

"What do you mean by 'the natural black hatred of whites?'"

Marianne motioned him onto one of the plush conference chairs, then sat down beside him. "I don't think you realize the extent of prejudice against blacks in the Third World."

"Against blacks? The majority is black!"

"There's a world of difference between our black majority and your country's white majority." She poured her eyes into his. "You go back to the States and you're a white man again, part of the accepted class, but a black person is black wherever he goes. No white girl grows up in the Bahamas feeling inferior to her majority black schoolmates. When I was little and noticed I was whiter than most of my friends, I felt *good* about it! Blacks—even a half-breed like me—go through something whites never do. I call it the Revelation."

Marianne's eyes flashed green. "It comes when you're twelve or thirteen years old and someone calls you 'nigger' for the first time. You cry to mama, and mama sits you down with a sad look on her face and tells you the way it is. The Revelation is a coming-of-age event, a black bar mitzvah for Negroes all over the world. I know you were hurt by Father, but it's nonsense to think that a white American in the Third World suffers for his color as much as a black person anywhere."

He remembered the strange feeling of alienation he'd felt last summer at the Embassy party when Ransom slighted him because of his race. But Marianne was right: he was still white. Her sermonizing made him wonder whether this world of prejudice and counter-prejudice onto which he had landed in his naked altruism had anything to do with Coby's disappearance. After all, Ransom hates whites. And St. Gregory hates blacks—and everyone else.

"What's Cay Lobos?" he asked.

"It's a Bahamian island near Haiti. In 1980 a hundred and

two Haitians were stranded there for two months when their boats disintegrated on the rocks. The Defence Force provided a ship, the *Lady Moore*, to take them back to Haiti. They wouldn't go. The Defenders started clubbing them, women and children included— and the networks got it on film. It was broadcast all over the world."

"Is the Defence Force corrupt throughout?" North asked. "Or is it only St. Greg and his MOP?"

"I wish I knew. I never could understand why we need a military service. Grant, maybe we should tell Father about St. Gregory and his pirates. After all, it isn't just hearsay like it was with the addict who told me the gasoline story. Father will listen now. We've got firsthand proof."

"Marianne, what if—" He paused, preparing to test her allegiance. "What if your father *himself* is directing St. Gregory?"

She lifted her arms to fix an earring as a cat might wash its face, gaining time to think out her reply. It was like her to answer with a quotation. "Tolstoy began *Anna Karenina* with the perception that 'Happy families are alike; every unhappy family is unhappy in its own way.' No one can think of one's father as a monster. I suppose even Mafia children feel that way. Mother thinks the entire Defence Force is a vast secret police run by and for my father." She took the tape out of the deck and returned it to its file.

North could see her thinking fast. She was on his side.

"We don't have to confide in Father, or even Uncle Malcolm. There's another alternative."

"Oh?"

"Senator Carstairs. I'm not suggesting you tell her about the pirates. Only that you enlist her help for your Island for Science permits—and in the process try and find out more about Coby. Dame Cora is resourceful. And you can trust her."

"I thought of asking her for help right after Coby disappeared, but I was afraid she was too close to your father and St. Gregory."

"Dame Cora is the most independent person in the government. She's not close to anybody."

The more North thought about Carstairs now, the more he realized he did not have to trust her, that appealing to her for help with the permits could be one more way to shake up the opposition. And without the risk of another sea battle.

They left the conference room, passing the dead animals on their way to the massive fireplace. Marianne looked straight ahead, trying to ignore them. The head of a gazelle stared at her.

"Daddy's idea of trophies?"

"Father used to hunt at least twice a year. He seldom goes these days, but whenever he does he kills these beautiful animals."

Lost in thought and in each other, they watched through the arched windows a full moon rising over the trees, piercing wind-blown clouds. On the lunar surface you could see the scars and craters of ancient meteor wars, lighting earth's night with a message from the past. North heaved a driftwood log into the fireplace, a great black hunk of lignum vitae that might have been a bumper dock graced by a pelican. He listened to the resin of the logs crack and sputter, and watched the embers dance up the chimney. The glow hypnotized him, making him remember serene nights by the frozen shore of his former life by the Great Lake. There can be no warmer hospitality than a fire on the hearth, he thought.

Then he reminded himself that he was not welcome here, not by the master of the house. The flames caressed the black logs, slithering blue at their bases and ran up the chimney in yellow tongues, the three colors of the Bahamian flag. What the hell was he doing here in the Prime Minister's own living room?

The answer came wryly: he was watching the flag burning.

46 *Cold as Hell for Nassau*

ON HIS WAY to see the senator, North was about to cross a side street when he came upon Rahming and Razor. Feeling a rare joy after his night with Marianne, he greeted them with amusement.

Louie Rahming, who always looked out of place above ground, seemed to be searching for a place to vomit. His limp was more pronounced than it had been at the Fourth of July party, while Razor was even more his jolly porcine self than usual. Razor's whiskey nose and dark-sallow skin made North think of the worms that infest pork, but when he flashed a grin, a new gold crown shown on his upper left bicuspid. The gold chain around his neck and matching bracelet were inlaid with some black filigreed substance that gleamed in the winter sun. Rahming unbuttoned the top of his sweater, revealing a clone of Razor's necklace. Both cousins were wearing black coral.

"Peace and love," said Rahming through his Jesus beard.

"Welmasout," said his cousin.

"How's that again, Razor?"

Razor rubbed his pencil mustache and showed blackened teeth. "Ah dunno what dis country be comin' to, you knows what Ah sayin'? *Welma sout!*"

The separation into two words gave North a hint. "Velma's out? Velma Fisher? Out of prison?"

"Yessiree, she done reside at Fox Hill only six monts. Only six monts fer mur*der!* Crime *pays* in dis here country, Doctuh Nort." He fondled his necklace. "Pays real good!"

North could see St. Gregory's hand in Velma's release. In this country the usual sentence for murder is death by hanging. He decided to change the subject. "Well, at least you're not in the drug business, Razor."

"Now dots an idea what bears convers*ation!*"

"Later," said North curtly, leaving Razor's mouth gaping like a grouper's.

He stepped around the pair as if circumventing the garbage mound in jail, and entered the building where Senator Carstairs kept her office. He knocked at the door with her name on it.

"Come in, Dr. North."

It was an old-fashioned office with two rolltop desks open and piled high with papers, her own and that of her secretary who was off for the holiday. Carstairs motioned him to a chair. She took a few short puffs of air and swiveled around, peering at him above the rims of her glasses.

"I should explain, Grant. . . . May I call you Grant?"

He remembered having gone through this back in New York at the United Nation's meeting. "Certainly."

"I want to explain that I must have a fee for helping you. But don't get the idea this is some kind of juice."

North found her choice of words unusual. But then he had thought it unusual for a senator to take consulting contracts.

"The fee is for the hard work I plan to do. Seeing bureaucrats can be time-consuming."

"I know."

"After you called, I took the liberty of preparing this paper." As she ripped a legal-sized sheet out of an ancient Underwood, the rickety stand on which it wobbled gave way. "Son of a *bitch!*" she bellowed, then smiled at him as she picked up the typewriter. She used the machine to brush aside piles of papers on a wooden filing cabinet, and set it down in the cleared space.

North read the contract. In consideration of thirty thousand dollars, it said, Dr. Grant North would be furnished the various permits he needed to operate his Island for Science. A nonrefundable ten thousand-dollar deposit was prerequisite, the remainder payable after the permits were issued.

"This legal?" said North. "I mean, being a senator—"

Carstairs chuckled. "We aren't in the United States. The Senate here is an appointed body established primarily to extend the Prime Minister's influence over Parliament. Since we're paid only a token salary, the P.M. permits us to do outside work. Rest assured that Mr. Ransom will know about it."

"All right," said North. He had little to lose; ten thousand was nothing compared to what was at risk. "I'll sign it and give you a check. But there's something else. I want you to help me find out what happened to my daughter."

"I'll ask around. Actually, I've been doing that since Marianne told me about . . . Coby. Right?"

"Yes."

"You got a picture?"

He gave her a photo of Coby and she looked at it as she took a pint bottle out of a desk drawer, the way detectives do in the old movies when they consummate their agreements. "Drink?" she said, and when he nodded she filled paper cups with Tennessee bourbon. "I know people who know people," she said unnecessarily, and tossed off a healthy slug. "Of course there's no extra charge for inquiries about Coby. You must be worried to death." She emitted a brief sigh and lit a thin corncob pipe.

North had seen out-island crones smoke pipes before, but not the president of the Senate. "I'm worried about Coby. *And* the permits. If we don't start growing shrimp and seaweed, we won't have the money to continue—anything."

"The first thing we do is put it in the newspapers—'Scientist Hires Carstairs as Education Consultant.' Then when I make the rounds, the bureaucrats will be ready for me. We'll start with the Ministry of Fisheries. You can tag along whenever you want."

Having laid out the program for him in such a way as to demolish any lingering fear that her fee was a bribe, she lifted her

bulk with difficulty and propped a 35-mm Nikon against the typewriter on the cabinet. She handed him a rolled-up blueprint left
over from some other project, and activated a timed shutter, hurrying
to get into the picture beside him. She repeated the procedure four
times, finishing the roll.

The phone gave a preparatory chirp before ringing. She picked
it up and listened. Then she frowned, muttered "too bad," and hung
up. "Ambassador Armitage," she said to North. "He was run over
by a car. He's at Princess Margaret."

"How bad is he?"

"Both legs broken and internal injuries."

THE STORY came out in a special edition of the *Guardian*. The
ambassador had been crossing Shirley Street on New Year's Eve
when a hit-and-run driver knocked him down and ran over his
lower legs. His bodyguard immediately looked for the license number and saw that there was no plate. The car was a Toyota, of
which there are thousands in Nassau.

The part about the car having no plate confirmed North's intuition. He hailed a taxi and went to Princess Margaret hospital
where two black American M.P.s were stationed outside the ambassador's fourth-floor room. Showing identification, North explained that he knew the ambassador and had important information for
him.

Arnold Armitage heard North's name from inside the room
and cut through the security. "Let Dr. North in."

The room was full of flowers but no visitors. The ambassador,
propped up against pillows, seemed happy to see North. He had
the face of a retired person: double chin and mustache, mop of
white hair, and a complexion ruddy from sunshine and high blood
pressure. North had never seen him in anything but a tuxedo, but
now he wore a hospital gown and plaster casts from the knees
down.

"Mr. Ambassador," said North, "I have reason to believe your
run-over was a deliberate attempt on your life." North sat on an
old-fashioned radiator under a barred window that faced the hospital courtyard, and the warmth seeped into his body. It was cold in

Nassau, even for January.

"Come on now, Dr. North. You know how narrow Shirley Street is and how fast some of these young people drive. I could never get used to looking the wrong way when I cross streets."

"You know about Morgan, the assassin I met in jail, the black American?"

"Sure, sure, I was told about that. Did you know he was found dead?"

"That's why I'm here," said North. "Having failed the first time with an assassin who was a marksman, I think they've decided to make it look like an accident. That car had no plates."

"Well, lots of cars don't have plates around here. Is that your only reason for suspicion?"

North searched the face of the man who represented the United States of America in this country, the man who had come for great golf and sunshine, the official talker to amiable Bahamians who thought of his job as a reward for past political efforts. Was it a waste of time confiding in him?

"No, there's more to it than that," North said, deciding he had to try. "May I have your word that you won't say anything to the Bahamians about this?"

"Sure . . . if that's what it takes."

"I have firsthand knowledge of piracy by someone in the Royal Bahamian Defence Force."

There was a long and eloquent pause, during which you could sense the ambassador coming to a decision. "You mean Carlos St. Gregory, of course."

North stood up, astonished by the response. The golfer had grown up fast in the realities of the Pan-American Narco War.

"What's going on, Mr. Armitage?" North said.

The ambassador fell into a brooding self-censorship, and stared out the window at the palm trees ruffled by cold gusts. Silence is the most eloquent form of lying, North thought. If the U.S. government with its vast investigatory powers was on to St. Gregory, any contemplated action surely would be filtered first through the ambassador. "Mr. Armitage, you must—"

Armitage interrupted with a look on his face that said he had decided to trust this fellow American. "And who, Dr. North, do you think is behind St. Gregory?"

North was getting the idea that the affability, the golf, the congenial diplomacies he'd witnessed at the July Fourth party constituted a careful front for a mind that knew precisely what was going on in the country of his stewardship. One more example of events and people being not what they seemed.

He decided he would trust this man. "The Prime Minister," North said firmly.

Armitage winced, and not from the pain of his legs. "Okay, Grant, you seem to be an intelligent man who can keep his mouth shut." He paused until North nodded.

The fact that the ambassador had begun using his first name signalled to North that he was being accepted as a player on the American team.

"The Military Operations Platoon of the RBDF has been under our surveillance ever since you told Mr. Hanna about Michael Morgan. We discovered that St. Gregory has a whole string of *agents provocateurs*—not just Morgan, who may have been brought in as a warning for me to let things alone. Before we could question Morgan, St. Gregory got him released, used him once more to assassinate some Cuban smugglers on a yacht, and then killed him. The U.S. Coast Guard found the derelict yacht and the bodies before it sank. The reason we haven't acted against St. Gregory is because of the possibility, no matter how slim, that it is the Prime Minister himself who's in charge of St. Gregory's smuggling and killings." He winced at the thought. "And now you come here to confirm our worst nightmare!"

"In a country where the P.M. decides everything, Arnold, it's unlikely he doesn't know what's going on. I find it equally hard to believe in automobile accidents." It came to North that Arnold Armitage, far from being a dilettante, had been named U.S. ambassador precisely in order to diagnose the Bahamas connection for drugs entering Florida.

Armitage glanced at his legs bound in casts so big they made him look like a goalie in a hockey game. "Of course it occurred to us that this was no accident. I have reason to believe my predecessor resigned because he was threatened. But it serves no purpose to announce our suspicions to the world. Nassau would be so full of newspapermen and CIA agents we'd never discover the extent of St. Gregory's backers. I don't suppose you have any proof against Ransom."

"No."

Armitage sighed the weary sigh of the otherwise-healthy injured. "Jesus God, not the Prime Minister!" he said as if thinking out loud. "Even ironclad proof—which could take years to gather— wouldn't be the end of it. We're not above coming down on the head of the country, and I've already met with State. Ultimately the President will have to weigh any action against such considerations as the continued good will of this government, the status of the AUTEC naval base at Andros, and so on. . . ." He trailed off as his facial muscles knotted. The effort of talking obviously hurt him.

"I realize you must be in pain—" started North.

Armitage raised a fragile hand, cutting him off. "The only thing I can think of doing at the moment is to tell the P.M. about St. Gregory—to see what he does about it."

"Are you going to mention my visit?"

"I already promised you I wouldn't. Besides, there's no point in showing all our cards. I'm being taken by helicopter to Mercy hospital in Miami this afternoon. When I return I'd like to talk to you more about it. Meanwhile, be careful what you say. Let's not start an international incident."

North followed the ambassador's gaze out the window. In back of the swaying palms, a long fence of two-story casuarinas undulated at Elizabeth Avenue, which had been named for Queen Elizabeth II. The hospital itself had been rechristened for the queen's sister who had been called the Calypso Princess, and North marveled at a government that could honor one country's royalty while attempting to assassinate its neighbor's ambassador.

"It's cold as hell for Nassau," Armitage said, looking out the window at the gusting trees, "even if it is New Year's day."

NORTH COULD FEEL his destiny being shaped by forces outside

himself, a condition he detested. Back at the mansion, Marianne touched his neck with a cool hand and said, "Maybe Armitage was run over so he wouldn't tell Father of St. Gregory's smuggling activities."

"Maybe."

There was little more to say and no profit in endless speculation. They turned their talk to themselves, ending by making love in her room. North spent the night in a sound sleep while his subconscious confirmed a decision he had made.

At first light he was awakened by mourning doves sounding four short notes like oboes, the first in E-flat, the next three in the key of F. He leaned over Marianne's face, only inches away. Of the two women in his life, one was passive, the other dynamic. He had loved Heather as much as Marianne, but this love was now, and it was electrifying. He kissed her awake, and when her eyes focused on him, he asked her to marry him.

"Oh, Grant! *Yes!*" And she beamed and cried and kissed him for long moments. She turned thoughtful. "Are you absolutely sure, Grant North, that you can marry a communist?"

"Are you sure you can marry a capitalist?"

Gorby, loose mannered and long-haired, jumped up and Marianne stroked him. She put on a robe and sat on the bed, tucking her knees neatly under the skirt.

"I admit I pity people when I discover they're salesmen or bankers working at something for no reason other than money. But you! You're a scientist first, a businessman second. If money flows from your work, it does so as a matter of course." She smiled at her own rationalization.

He was going to ask whether she believed in reincarnation, then decided he didn't want to know. Not now. When she applauded Marxism, he knew she thought not of government interference reducing exceptional men to the common mold, or the degrading requirement for endless permissions. Marianne was not from the upper earth and had not grown up in the hate-communism culture. To her, communism was socialism, the more precious because it had failed so dramatically. To her, communism was the look in the benign eyes of Karl Marx, a group of nuns living the communal life, or Martin Luther King pleading for lawfulness with a sniper's bullet in his neck. Marianne would be wasted on a society that knew such disparity, one that contained monstrosities like subways, income tax, and the slush of dirty snow. After his quest was finished, no matter what the outcome, they would live in the Caribbean or in the South Pacific, away from injustice, on warm islands where seagulls cry with joy and you can breathe the color in the sky.

MARIANNE dropped him off downtown where he spotted Carstairs's long limousine parked in a no-parking zone and flying on the front fenders two tiny Bahamian flags. Dame Cora's immense buttocks disappeared into the front seat, followed by her bosom badged with the honor of its purpose. Finally the rest of her squeezed between the door and steering wheel where she rested a moment and lit a Player's. When North approached, she smiled and slid the cigarette to the corner of her mouth. "Get in."

Driving your own limo was only one step below having it driven for you, he supposed. He sat next to her in the front seat, smelling her musk and tobacco.

"Heard about Armitage?" she said.

"Something new?"

"He's dead. It's not in the papers yet."

"Dead?" He felt a cold sweat. "From broken legs. . . ?"

"Does seem a strange way to die. I heard it was a stroke. Could one lead to the other?" She placed her butt uncrushed in the crowded ashtray and closed the smoking lid.

North was used to people treating him as though he were a medical doctor. "I suppose the trauma *could* send a clot to the heart or break off a piece of plaque in a blood vessel."

"Unusual, though, right?"

"Unusual," he said.

He believed in Occam's Razor, the scientist's principle that the simplest explanation is almost always the correct one. Every death has a certain logic that can not be denied. If a man's assassination has been incomplete, it is logical to assume its completion. Not only had he genuinely liked Arnold Armitage, but the loss of his American-government ally left him isolated, an alien on a strange planet.

"Auto accidents," she said, "the scourge of left-side driving."

"We lose a few in accidents too."

Carstairs nodded as if tired of the subject, and lit another cigarette. She maneuvered her limo down the narrow streets of Nassau and managed to wedge it into a parking space only inches longer than the car. Wriggling out, she ambled slowly along the concrete walkway to the Ministry of Fisheries building, whose offices were on the ground floor. Cleary had gotten nowhere with Benjamin Franklin, the top man; North would try it now from the bottom up, the Carstairs way.

When the senator entered the stucco building, typewriters stopped clacking and the women in the secretarial pool, a score of them, stood at attention and smiled widely. North wouldn't have been surprised to see them salute. Carstairs's achievement of suffrage for downtrodden Bahamian women in an all-male British colonial government had taken tenacity and intelligence, and she, the feminist hero, had earned the right to her "Motherhood and God" badge.

"Carry on," she said, returning the smile to her acolytes and announcing to the closest woman that they were here to see the Permanent Secretary.

With great deference, they were ushered into the office of the second in command of the ministry, an attractive black woman who leapt to her feet. "Dame Cora! How can I help you?"

The senator sat down laboriously while introducing North. It was not unusual for a woman to hold the office of Permanent Secretary, but it was an exalted position nevertheless. Senator Carstairs asked her whether they had processed Dr. North's application for his science island. Yes, she was told, they had approved it long ago; the file had traveled from here to the Ministry of Lands & Surveys because a lease of the seabed was required; thence to the Ministry of Finance for exchange-control purposes; and from there to the Health Department where she lost track of it. The senator said she would inquire at Health, and then asked the Permanent Secretary to canvass her ministry for information about a certain young white girl who had been missing for almost a year.

"Madame Secretary," North began formally, "in connection

with the search for my daughter, would you also make inquiries about a man—an out-islander—who goes by the nickname 'Jelly Belly?' We have reason to believe he can shed some light on Coby's disappearance."

North knew he was taking a chance revealing to Carstairs their only clue, and he purposely failed to mention the man's Defence Force affiliation. Carstairs grimaced, whether from the exertion of hauling her body out of the chair or from some arcane knowledge of Jelly Belly, North could not tell.

The Permanent Secretary glanced at the senator, whose signal of consent led her to assure North that her ministry would comply. The interview over, Carstairs trundled out through the secretarial pool with North following. Once more, the women stopped typing and came to their feet. Thick or thin, middle-aged or young, in baggy dresses or crisp suits, in hair rollers or knotted tresses, they stood at something between parade rest and present arms, beaming sheepishly at Dame Cora as though expecting her to inspect their typewriters or the polish on their fingernails.

At her limousine she said to North, "I'd like to come and see your Island one day so I know what I'm talking about on these calls."

"You are most welcome, Dame Cora. We're ready to stock the seaweed-shrimp farm; we can't go much longer without a harvest. All we need is permission."

She paused a moment before beginning the ordeal of entering the limo. "Grant," she said, looking him full in the face, "if I were you, I'd go ahead and stock it. Operate your seafarm."

"Without the permits?"

"As long as you're paying full duty on imports, it's doubtful anyone will ever ask to see any permits, and if they do . . . well, we ought to have them by then."

Nothing substantive had happened at the ministry, yet North was impressed by the senator's ability to enter the bureaucracy without preliminaries. Maybe this frank apostle of motherhood could embarrass the Cabinet into action on the permits—or into renewing the search for Coby. He had called Pyfrom's office several times, but had spoken only to his secretary who knew no details of the search, nor even whether it was being conducted.

North roamed the streets thinking over Carstairs's advice while waiting for an hour to pass before he was to meet Marianne. Starting the seafarm was a dire decision. Yet logically there could be but one answer: though he risked the wrath of the government, he had to bring in a crop of shrimp and several of seaweed this spring or they would run out of money. Thinking these thoughts while walking down East Street, he saw something . . . and stopped suddenly as if slamming into a wall.

"Coby. . . !"

Heart pounding, he crossed the street through careening cars, jumped a high curb, and ran toward a narrow alley where he caught the arm of a teenage blonde. Bent at the hips, she was spreading a small rug on the concrete to display costume jewelry for sale. She wore an unbuttoned fawn-colored coat and underneath a long dress the color and texture of a doe. The girl straightened and gazed at him in a haze of cheap perfume and marijuana breath.

"What the hell. . . ?" she said.

Scrawny, weathered, eyes opaque to the world, she had an American accent and three rhinestone studs in each ear. Her face was streaked with dirt.

"Sorry," North said.

The girl turned a vacant gaze back to her trinkets.

He bought a *Tribune*, the opposition paper. Waiting for his pulse to subside, North saw a four-column photo of Ransom leaning over a podium and wearing a beatific smile as he addressed the Organization of American States meeting in Mexico City. Ransom's speech, reprinted in full, related the stern measures his government was taking to reduce drug smuggling. An accompanying story presented the P.M.'s views on his ex-wife's hate campaign. North read it, marveling at a popularity so absolute that you could use even the opposition press to educate the people in your own beliefs. Among the passages he found the most outrageous was one quoting the Prime Minister as if he were a minister of a church:

"It is sinful to speak ill of the Government," Ransom had been reported to say, "or even to think evil thoughts of it."

47 *Career Move*

CORA CARSTAIRS decided she wasn't getting anywhere in life. Sure, she was president of the Senate with a PhD in education, and had been honored many times for her work in the woman's movement. But her stature was measured in girth as well as esteem. By the time she achieved suffrage for women, her circumference had equalled her height. At two hundred fifty pounds she was appointed the first woman senator; at two seventy-five she presided over that assembly; at three hundred she became a knight.

Wearing the jewel once bestowed upon her by the queen of England, she imagined herself in the Middle Ages ensconced in a castle dominating the plain, herself an upstart Medici or freemason working to vanquish serfdom. She tested the order of her titles as she had done after her investiture. "Doctor Senator Dame Cora Carstairs" she said to her mirror.

"Dame Cora Senator Doctor Carstairs," she tried again, separating her names like a Catholic cardinal.

No longer were the honors sufficient. In that private place beyond the eyes where the soul lies bare and whispers bitter masochisms, she said to herself, "The only Middle Ages for you are your own years. Corpulent Cora, sexless, unmarriageable by weight."

If she could not shed pounds, she would emulate the feudal

lords and seek wealth instead. She knew not what Ransom and his colleagues were up to, but there was no denying their pretentious houses, their expensive women, their chauffeured limousines and trips abroad, their yachts and five-hundred-dollar suits, their rumored Swiss bank accounts.

After her meeting with North, she had made an appointment with the Prime Minister. Now she traversed the padded carpeting of Ransom's office, and lowered herself into an oversized chair made from a ship's grating. Smelling of deodorant and ambition, she leaned across the cocktail table toward Ransom.

"Charles, you look as rich as a black boy in new tennis shoes!"

Ransom didn't know quite how to react. She was a supporter, whom he had appointed to the toothless debating society modeled after the House of Lords in England. And she was an old friend. But this—*familiarity*!

She lit a Player's and he noticed it was the raw kind, not the filtered version. She inhaled the sulfur of her match with the smoke, and blew a milky stench toward him. The "Motherhood and God" badge on her breast intimidated him with its reminder of the women's vote.

"*Cora!*" he snapped. But she just sat there and smiled. There was no intimidating the intimidator. "No wonder the British empire fell," he said, rubbing his mustache, "since they began manufacturing cigarettes like that. Well . . . you didn't come here to blow carcinogens across my desk."

"Sir Charles, here I am at this advanced age, nearly as old as you, and forced to take consulting contracts. I've got one now with the American Dr. North, if you have no objection, to push his operating permits through the bureaucracy." She studied his face. "Fees from that sort of thing are peanuts. What I want is—"

She stopped in mid sentence to let Ransom suffer for a moment and to build the illustrious grin that had led her suffrage movement to victory. The grin widened her eye sockets into twin hollows, making Ransom think of her less as a knight than as a virus: mutable, omnivorous, evasive.

"What I want is simple, Sir Charles. I want to attend your secret 'board meetings.' I want *in!*"

Ransom was having trouble keeping his bad eye from wandering. He lit his pipe and blew blue smoke, studying her. "You possess a fifteenth-century mind, Dame Cora. If your idea is to use our friendship to suborn my position—"

"Charles, don't gimme no shit." The Chicago vernacular was a reminder of his debt to her. "I know you too well to think for one blessed minute you didn't get this far without a scheme. In college it was fake drivers' licenses. What is it now, Mr. Borgia? Drugs? The casinos?"

No wonder Parliament fought her feminist audacity, thought Ransom. Over the years she had crashed her umbrella over the skull of more than one dissenting senator. He could annul her appointment to Parliament but she had an enormous following, roughly all the women in the country. Since his divorce he had not done well with women and could use someone like Cora Carstairs to deliver the female vote. Ransom reclined his office chair and examined her, steepling his fingers and aiming the spires at his nostrils. He was undecided.

"Back when the Bahamas was a democracy," she said, "I would not have dreamed of approaching the head of state this way. Now, though, things are screwed up. You need me."

"What do you mean, 'was a democracy?'"

"Face it, Charles. You appoint the judiciary; you choose the Senate; you dissolve the House of Assembly whenever it gets out of hand; the newspapers are in your pocket if not in your wallet; and you pay the out-islanders five dollars per year for their vote. . . . That your idea of 'democracy?'"

"You exaggerate. If this isn't a democracy, what is it?"

"Let's just call it 'Ransomism.'"

"And what is that supposed to mean?"

"Lenin said communism was socialism plus electricity. I suppose Ransomism is capitalism plus graft."

"Cora, what if I invite you to attend our board meetings and you find there is no 'scheme,' as you put it?"

"Invite me, Charles. Make me a member of your Executive Committee. I will turn out the women's vote for you."

She could see Ransom teetering on the edge of indecision, his bad eye roaming her face and the wall in back of it. If she had learned anything in her ascent from poverty to prestige it was that you ruled with the power of your ambition. Head high, breasts steady, she reached across the cocktail table straight into his uncertainty, suspending her hand an inch above his like a queen reassuring a reluctant prince. When at last he grasped it in assent, she drew herself into his inner circle with all the raw strength of her will.

48 *Crime of Initiative*

THE SWIM LADDER at the end of the Island dock gave way with a muffled *thhuuummMPP!* as Senator Carstairs attempted to climb it from Father Christie's small boat. The senator plopped into the ocean, gushing spray like a torpedo, and surfaced face up and spread-eagled.

A crowd gathered to watch. The workers who knew her (those who had wives knew her well) braced for the kind of diction they themselves used when wrestling a rusty bolt. Instead, she shook her varicose flesh and began backstroking in a cavalier way. A smile stretched across her face as she shouted in her sergeant-major's voice, "Takes more than that to sink this ship!"

Hearing the commotion, North and Marianne ran out to the dock to find her bellowing merrily from the water.

"Congratulations on your engagement, you two!"

"Thank you, Dame Cora," Marianne called. "Are you all right?" North was taking off his shoes.

"Stay where you are, Grant. I'm fine. The Reverend Christie will fish me out."

North grinned at Marianne, who winked back. Marianne looked so wholesome, so radiant, it seemed absurd that she had been a coke addict not long ago. The resumption of activity on the Island six weeks ago, its spirited breezes and nights studded with stars, had brought them even closer together. His excitement over their forthcoming marriage would have equalled hers were it not for the frustration that camped in his soul. Coby and "the permits" had become so coupled in his mind, he wondered if they somehow had become linked in reality. Taking Carstairs's advice had led to his rehiring the villagers and stocking the corrals with shrimp and seaweed, but the decision weighed heavily upon him. He was in *zugswang*. Either he produced a crop, or he lost the Island for Science by default.

Strung out along the length of the dock, the workers waved shirts or jackets, cheering the president of the Senate. "She a *floatin'* senator!" "Keep paddlin' hard, Dame Cora!" "Grit an' guts—like how you gots de vote for de womens!"

"She's got grit all right," said North to Marianne.

"You say something, Grant?" whispered Cleary, standing on the other side of him from Marianne. "I was having an orgasm thinking about that floating fragment of femininity."

North elbowed him in the ribs. North saw beyond Dame Cora's physical flaws, and was beginning to like her.

Father Josh Christie, aging ferryboat operator, greengrocer, and Anglican minister, idled his boat alongside the rolling senator. "Kin you swim in, Cora?"

"You above all people, Father Josh, outta know that the good Lord has given each of us a fixed budget of so many heartbeats, and that exercise only squanders them."

"Dot means I gotta tow ya?"

"Please, Father."

Leaning over the gunwale next to the steering column, Christie arranged his thin right hand and both of her wide ones in a clumsy knot. The sight of the Reverend Josh Christie bent over the side and steering with the fingertips of one hand while pulling the senator with the other—her black dress billowing, face beaming, yawing on her back, and wiggling her legs like an enormous loggerhead under tow—provided an indelible topic of gossip for the villagers.

Eventually she made it to shore. With as much dignity as she could muster in her wet clothes, she inspected what was left of the Island for Science after the hurricane. The solar-distillation columns, drugs-from-the-sea aquariums, wave-energy generators —all the projects except the seaweed-shrimp farm—had been postponed. Total emphasis lay on bringing in a cash crop from the seafarm, which now spread from the dock to the wind tower and as far out across the shallow flats.

Working in chest-high water, forty men pulled seaweed from monolines, fed the shrimp from floating rafts, cleaned fouled portions of the netting, and dispersed ammonium-nitrate fertilizer. To handle harvests of the fast-growing, slithery seaweed, North had installed along the ocean bottom wide pipes that angled upwards and opened at the surface of the corrals. Into these manholes, bare-chested men stuffed ton after ton of the reddish weed. The carrageenan-rich plants were sucked through the pipes by diesel pumps to the shore, then pitched like wet hay onto wooden frames to dry before baling. The frames lined the beaches halfway down the Island, looking like giant dress racks in a warehouse—pink and reddish-brown dresses turning gold in the sunshine. The same pipe system would be used two months later to harvest the shrimp.

Silhouetted against the sun, the forty parallelograms of the corrals reflected the light like forty angled mirrors, creating a red mosaic across a meadow of water. Nothing like this in-ocean mari-farm had been built anywhere else in the world, and yet its hundred and sixty acres, an area as large as the Island itself, comprised only a quarter of the plan. The two million juvenile shrimp in the corrals, the offspring of only four dozen mother shrimp that North and Rolle had caught in the wild, would weigh in at half a million pounds and wholesale for three times as many dollars. The seaweed would double that income.

Dry now but sticky from the salt, Dame Cora made rough calculations in her mind. She looked up at North, a lusty smile forming at the corners of her eyes. "This business is as lucrative as smuggling. And it's so . . ." She searched for the right word. ". . . so worthwhile! I can envision these seafarms wherever there's shallow water—and have we ever got *that* in the Bahamas! Why, Grant, you've created a whole new industry. We can employ *thousands!*" Her smile turned into a scowl. "That sonofabitch Ransom must be out of his bloody gourd if he can't see how we need these seafarms!"

IN A RHYTHM rivalling the tides, fourteen times over the past two years, the workers had hoisted the Bahamian tricolors, once for each shingled roof. After mass the Sunday after Senator Carstairs's visit, Father Josh Christie returned to the Island to sanctify the seafarm. And to bless a party.

The workers and their families arrived in both Christie's eighteen-footer and in the jollyboat driven by Shark. The Anglican priest entered Slaughter Harbour like a victorious admiral, his troops waving, yelling, overflowing the gunwales, the women holding babies and umbrellas in case it rained, carrying sweet Bahama bread, conch salad spiced with native hot peppers, and conch fritters still warm in their paper bags.

On the beach between the seaweed racks, they hastened to set up the liquor tables and buckets of ice, and to barbecue the chicken before anyone died of thirst or starvation. Freeport rum and German beer from Christie's store dwindled as fast as the ice in the hot sun. Father Josh, creaking like an old machine deprived of oil, climbed onto one of the picnic tables between cups of rum and plates of fritters to perform his blessing. Holding a hand-scrawled note, he spoke in the singsong lilt of out-islanders who have learned to read in their adulthood.

"Bless dis farm we see here risin' afore us in de yellow rays of de sun oh Lord who be sending us doze rays and dis here flesh an' wine o' His loins which we is about to receive a liddle more of, ah-men."

"Dot ain't no wine, Josh."

"Hell mon, dot be demon rum!"

The workers laughed and the drinking began in earnest. Three parishioners complained to Christie about his sermon in church that morning about the evils of selling their votes. Said one, "Dot's okay fer you, Josh, wid yer grocery and yer boat, but we *needs* dot twenty-five bucks fur de *livin'!*"

"Dot's no God damn reason fer prostitutin' yerself!" Father Josh said with a fierce look on his face.

They contemplated that and drank their rum with a feeling of comfort, touched as they were by the honor of his obstinacy.

MONDAY morning opened in a bleak drizzle as the seafarmers returned to the Island moaning or half-asleep, Sunday's party having continued at the village until daybreak. Moving slowly to the edge of the forest, a middle-aged man weary to the point of exhaustion cut a blue-flowered bough from a lignum vitae evergreen, broke it into pieces for a tiny fire, and began brewing tea. Another worker tossed cuttings from obeah bush and jumbey weed in a pot and boiled the herbs, the obeah smelling like onions. Soon little fires flared on the beach like fireflies. The men huddled around their cook-pots and drank their bitter brews to cure "the party pain." After a time, they trudged to their jobs.

Suddenly a siren pierced the air, stopping the workers in their tracks. They craned their heads in the direction of the harbor where a battle-gray RBDF cruiser condensed out of the mist and bumped up against the end of the dock. The heavy throb of her engines wafted over the Island as the siren ground down like a tired dragon.

"You can't take a shit without the government coming to make sure you flush the toilet," said Rolle as he strode with North to the dock.

"The *Munnings?*" said North.

"Not likely, but—"

To raid the same island twice was unusual harassment even by Defender standards. Yet as they drew closer they saw that it was indeed St. Gregory's gunboat. His uniformed Military Occupation Platoon swarmed about the deck like bacteria, ready to mop something up. A squad carrying placards scurried off the ship and down the beach, submachine guns jiggling on their backs. Every two hundred feet or so, a noncom would stop and point to the ground, and two men would pound a signpost into the sand with the butts of their weapons. The signs read:

PROJECT DISAPPROVED BY GOVERNMENT
NO ACTIVITY ALLOWED
VIOLATORS WILL BE PROSECUTED

Six weeks of seafarming, and the Islanders had almost forgotten St. Gregory. Cleary, Andy, and most of the workers clustered at the dock like fish at the mouth of a stream, glaring at the gunboat. A solitary Defender stared back, his submachine gun at port arms.

"There goes the fucking seafarm," said Rolle. "What are we going to do with two million shrimp too small to harvest? To say nothing of a hundred tons of seaweed."

"I guess Juan Doe got to St. Greg," Andy said.

"Don't be too sure," North said. He called to the guard. "Is the captain here?"

"Yessuh! He expec*tin'* you, suh. In de cabin."

As North stepped onto the deck, the others started to follow.

"Jus' Mistuh Nort, please," the guard said.

Inside the deck-level cabin that served as the patrol boat's bridge, St. Gregory was seated on his high captain's chair, one arm resting sedately over a radar hood. Like his troops, he wore blues, and North knew the absence of camouflage fatigues meant they were not on a raid.

"What the hell is it now, St. Gregory? Looking for more marijuana farms? Or is this just one of your routine missions to kill whatever enterprise is left in the Third World?"

"I don't like your tone, mister." He removed his mirrored sunglasses, eyes blazing.

"And I don't like your surprise parties." North looked toward the Island. "These signs your idea?"

St. Gregory's eyes followed North's and lit on the crowd of workers milling around the dock, clutching pitchforks, machetes, or hammers. He came off his stool and rose above North, his feet planted firmly, torso pitched forward, ready to release something raw within his skull. It was not the behavior of a man who knew his opponent was onto him, and North doubted whether St. Gregory had learned yet about the pirate battle.

"You have no permit to build anything in the ocean," the Defender captain said in his slight Spanish accent. "Your project has *not* been approved."

"You mean it has not been approved *yet.* Your signs say it's been 'disapproved.' Which is it?"

"Same thing. You want to question the signs, man, you know who to see in Nassau."

"We know quite well whom to see, Captain," said a voice, clear as crystal. Unnoticed by North, Marianne had squeezed between the workers onto the gunboat. She was flaming mad. "I assume you're referring to my father."

St. Gregory recognized the Prime Minister's daughter, and put on his mirrors again. "Sorry, ma'am. Those are my orders."

"Orders? Whose orders?"

"Commodore Bridgewater's. He's head of the Royal Defence Force."

"I know who he is. He would—"

Submachine-gun fire sounded. The staccato report from at least a pair of SMGs carried a half mile or so from up the beach.

"What the hell. . . !" said North.

"They're only bringing down a few coconuts," St. Gregory said, his voice venomous. "Close up shop, Mister North. Now. We find you continuing to operate without them, you'll be back in jail."

Marianne's eyes flashed. "We'll be in Nassau in the morning," she said. Turning to go, she flung over her shoulder, "By the way, Captain St. Gregory, my father knows about you and your pirates."

"Speculation," he said, mustering a meager laugh. "What are you people trying to do, make me feel paranoid?"

Marianne pointed toward the dock at the men wielding pitchforks and machetes. "Don't get the idea you're invincible, Captain," and she quoted Winston Churchill. "'Even paranoids have enemies.'"

49 *Full Faith and Cooperation*

ONCE AGAIN North traversed the portico of the Churchill building, this time accompanied by Marianne. At the executive suite the matronly Effie Ferguson, in a tailored suit the color of the walls, ushered Marianne over the carpet, leaving North alone with the portrait of the P.M. and the SELF-SUFFICIENCY sign.

Ransom showed himself as he held open the door to his office for his daughter, who looked up at him with tears welling in her eyes. The P.M. shot a glance at North, his cinnamon face dour, inscrutable. Before the door closed, North caught a glimpse of the room. Spacious and funereal.

The wait began with North thumbing magazines, every few minutes standing up to stare out the window at the tourists flooding Bay Street. Scurrying here and there, seeking shade, eating snacks at vendor's booths, they reminded him of the millions of fingerlings in his shrimp corrals. If Ransom upheld St. Gregory's order, the shrimp would die amid decaying seaweed. Unless . . .

Unless the Islanders erected hundreds of low-cost cisterns like the pair in the lab building, and moved the shrimp from the ocean corrals into them with the seaweed lines stretched across the top. It would require enormous effort and the remainder of their dwindling funds, but if he could pull it off he could save his crop—and wouldn't need Ransom's ocean. The idea that had been incubating in his mind since New Year's Eve came to him now fully formed. *Salt-water wells!* They could become the heart of a seaweed-shrimp farm far from the ocean, perhaps in the middle of south Florida where land is cheap. Harvesting the heavy seaweed would be simplified using small cranes mounted on the backs of jeeps to hoist bottom nets. The state of Florida would welcome a shrimp farm so long as it wasn't located on the shore; who else would buy otherwise-useless acreage whose wells were full of salt?

Why, he asked himself, hadn't he thought of this low-tech alternative before?

Because the mariculture farm had not been enough for him. He had wanted a science-technology center to solve nothing less than the energy, water, and food problems of the Third World. He remembered Cleary's early warning: *You're an altruistic guy, Grant. That's why you'll get hurt someday.*

North glanced at his watch. More than an hour. What were they doing in there?

He saw the receptionist watching him pace, so he sat down. There had been another reason for coming to the Bahamas, he admitted. It wasn't merely a science center he had wanted; it was an *island* for science, an extension of his intimacy with the moon. Maybe it was Heather's legacy, his own image of a haven, or something stronger, but from the beginning the Island had been an ally: friendly, irrational, seductive, a lover cheering you on from the shadows.

Ransom blasted out of his lair, slammed the door behind him without a glance at North, and strode into Pyfrom's office. Minutes later he returned with equal vigor. Had Pyfrom advised the P.M.? Had Marianne implicated St. Gregory to her father?

North hated the thought of leaving the Island, the mammoth job of moving equipment and materials, buying land, and building new facilities, but if Ransom refused to lift the ban on the seafarm, he would have no choice. Damn Ransom. He could hardly be taking that long to say no. But if yes, what price would the father exact from the daughter?

"Dr. North," said the receptionist. "The Prime Minister will see you now."

North walked into the heavily carpeted room and beheld the Prime Minister behind a shiny desk, heavy as a tank. It was a case of contempt breeding familiarity, he thought. Ransom's face was a trifle more desolate than he'd seen it last, but the P.M. still exuded the power of his Marlboro shoulders—and of his office. Marianne sat before him, eyes moist, nose red. From her tears he knew that Ransom had not yet rendered his verdict, that he would give both of them his decision at the same time. Executive efficiency.

Ransom's office made Pyfrom's look like a monk's cell. Packed with nautical furniture made of ship's gratings and planking dipped in acrylic, it fed the P.M.'s passion for possessions. A long row of gilded paintings by Winslow Homer depicted torn and ragged arms jutting from a boiling sea. The arms, frozen in time, were reaching for the gunwales of overfilled lifeboats. Ransom's desk might have resembled a boat, except that it would have sunk; it seemed to be made of a solid block of steel and was ladened with only a telephone and an intercom, a framed photograph of Marianne, and not a single scrap of paper. His swivel seat was a captain's chair. The room looked like it had been designed for a nautical eternity by a tombstone designer. But at least the office, unlike yacht and mansion, had one theme of opulence instead of a medley.

Ransom packed and lit his pipe while he waited for North to take Marianne's hand. The Prime Minister stood up, his furred eyebrows lifting slightly.

Still holding onto North, Marianne rose from the chair and met her father halfway around the perimeter of the desk. He laid down his pipe, placed his left arm around her shoulder, and offered the other hand to North. Ransom forced both of his eyes straight into North's and then into his daughter's, and said:

"Grant, Marianne! Congratulations on your forthcoming marriage!"

Marianne's expression grew hopeful though tentative, like sunglasses that adjust to the changing light. But North didn't trust the politician any more than he would trust a shark to quit its attack once begun. Prejudice dies harder than that, North knew; he would believe nothing this man of greed and opulence would say, now or ever.

"About that other matter. . ." Flashing his eyes back and forth between them, Ransom splashed his oily, "Well-ll—" and said, "I've talked it over with my deputy. Grant, you remember old Mal Pyfrom, Marianne's 'uncle?' He and I feel the Cabinet will ratify our desires. This very afternoon I will call the various ministries concerned and tell them . . ." He paused and forced his mutinous left eye to meet theirs. "That you have the full faith and cooperation of the government of the Bahamas, and as of this moment, *right now*—" He looked at his watch, "three-forty-three on sixteen February—you may call this a wedding present if you wish—your applications are approved. Your island-purchase permit, seabed lease, work permits for scientists, duty-free certificate under the Industries Encouragements Act, import license, export permit, business license, exchange-control document. *Everything!*"

50 *Effects without Cause*

IN THE ATOMIC regions of matter where energy is released in quanta, events can occur without cause, according to theory which describes the impossible. Like Einstein, North thought the quantum theory was spooky, and traces of that feeling lingered now as he mulled over the events that led to his permits. A year, even nine months ago, he might have swallowed the Prime Minister's about-face as a father's acceptance of reality, a wedding gift to a beloved, willful daughter. But not after all that had happened.

Before leaving Nassau for the Island, he asked Marianne, "What did you say to your father to get him to relent?"

The look on Marianne's face said she'd rather just leave things alone.

"Tell me, Marianne."

"I told him that you couldn't be a drug smuggler—that I'd been living on the Island with you off and on for almost two months. That didn't please him at all, so I told him about the pirates. He rushed into Pyfrom's office. When he came back, he seemed changed."

"Talking to Pyfrom made him see the light?

She answered reluctantly. "About St. Gregory, yes. About you? No. He's a complex man and does nothing for only one reason.

Oh, he understood his policy of noncooperation with you could lead to all sorts of problems. But . . . I guess I have to tell you. He feels you'll drop me after you get your permits, so he gave them to you to prove his theory to me."

"Did he say that in so many words?"

There was a ruminative pause as Marianne looked at her betrothed through moist eyes. She said faintly, "Yes."

MARIANNE went to work at REHAB. And North took a commercial flight to Great Snake, where he rounded up his men in the village and told them to report back to work in the morning.

Arriving at the Island, he asked Rolle to look around for suitable savannas where they might place rows of cisterns without having to denude the forest. Just in case. The shrimp were growing, already big enough so that a dozen instead of a hundred made a handful now. Bales of seaweed were piling up on the beaches above the tide mark. Soon they would have enough for their first LCM shipment to Florida and then by rail to the closest carrageenan-processing plant.

At dusk Jo returned to the lodge looking strangely fulfilled and upset at the same time. She settled onto a barstool and uncharacteristically poured herself a stiff drink. Rolle wandered in as she was telling North, "I phoned Mr. Novac in Miami. He's the Serbian arms dealer I told you about, Grant. He's got some assault rifles we can pick up if you want to take a chance on bringing guns into this miserable country."

"Haven't we seen enough of the Bahamian court system?" North said. Rolle's Supreme Court trial had been scheduled for April, two months off, and they would have to make a decision soon whether to fight the charges or have Rolle leave the country and forfeit bail.

"Torpedoes may not be enough, the next time," Jo said. "He *is* a homicidal maniac."

"You mean Blackbeard?" said Rolle.

"He might as well be," she said. She had spent the day at the *Nassau Guardian* office. "I read the papers dated before you landed in jail and I found a clipping of a John Henry and Irwin Stubbs being arraigned for smuggling. I called Marianne at her office the day after you left and she confirmed that John Henry was the "Johnny" who was being treated at REHAB. She said to tell only you, Grant. Well, I know that reporters always follow up their stories, so I went back to the *Guardian*. Sure enough, I found a two-inch story a week later. It said that Irwin Stubbs while out on bail had fallen off his boat and was killed by sharks, and that, without him to testify, the charges against John Henry had been dropped."

"That sort of proves the case against St. Gregory," said Rolle.

North looked pensive. "Marianne told her father about the gasoline story some time ago. If Jo could verify it so easily, certainly Ransom's people could have too. Surely Ransom now believes that St. Gregory is a murderer."

"Surely," said Rolle.

"Then why does he keep him around?"

AT SEVEN on a cool February morning, North attended a meeting of his workers. Following the brief layoff, their "union boss" had convinced them that they needed to be organized to protect their jobs. The union leader turned out to be the ubiquitous Razor, who stood in the center of fifty seafarm laborers squatting in a semicircle on the beach.

Seeing North, he turned to the squatters. "Yous done elect me you lead-*ah*. Now I do de negotia*tions* wi' dis chap."

Razor turned his back toward the men and explained to North that *his* men would not work without "an understan*din'*." When he talked he showed his incisors and cuspids in a mix of gray and gold. "We doan wan' be big-eye but we wants ridin' time round trip. You knows what Ah sayin'?"

"Big-eye" meant "greedy," North had learned. "We had 'riding time' settled a long time ago. We pay *half*."

"Maybe you dids, mehbe you dids not, but now we wan' pay for *alldedime spendaboat*," said the fugleman Razor with great seriousness. "You catch ma mea*nin'?*"

North caught it some seconds later, realizing Razor had said, "for all de time we spend in de boat."

If North's years in management had taught him anything, it was never to let the other side reopen a closed issue, for they would never stop negotiating. "We had an agreement," he said in a loud voice that carried to all the men, thinking of his own contract with Cora Carstairs; he had sent her a check for twenty thousand dollars, regardless of the fact that her efforts had nothing to do with Ransom issuing the permits. "You guys have been told more than once that there is only *one* reason to go back on an agreement, and I can't help but notice that most of you are not quite dead . . . although I can't be absolutely sure until I see you move around a little."

The men laughed too hard, hiding their embarrassment.

"I'm not going to start over again," North said, penetrating each man's eyes with his own. "If you want to work, let's get started. If not, I'll bring anyone back to the village who wants to quit. Right now."

To a man they became intensely interested in their hangnails, or examining the tiny shells glistening in the sand, or watching the sandpipers scurrying at the water's edge.

Razor massaged the wormlike veins of his nose, and suddenly his bloodshot eyes brightened. "I tells you what, Doctuh Nort, in de interest of breakin' dis im*passe*. 'Stead a payin' us half, you pays us de ridin' time *to* dis here key, and we pays our own ridin' time *from* dis here key. Okay?"

North smiled. "Now why hadn't I thought of that?"

North and Razor pumped hands like old friends while their audience beamed and returned to work. North ambled away shaking his head at Razor's next words that fell wasted on the sand. "Now suh, we takes up de matter of comps*ation* fer Louie Rahming who fall off yer negligent roof. . . ."

ROLLE INTERCEPTED Jo as he returned from his tour of the interior. He led her into the storage room of the lodge away from the others who had gone in for lunch.

"You're not going to believe this, Jo. *I found the marijuana farm!* The shit's growing all over a big clearing in the woods."

"Oh my God!"

"Jo, this changes everything. I know you regard your brother as some kind of non-mystic mystic or something with his over-developed intuition—"

"Not really—"

"Look, he's my best friend but he can be wrong. *Anyone* can be wrong."

"Wrong about what?" But she knew "what." She knew that Grant was as hooked on his intuition as an addict on cocaine, sensing the euphoria of Coby being found alive. That belief was his excuse to continue operations on the Island in spite of real dangers.

"Did it ever occur to you that Grant could be wrong about the Defenders, that they might have raided the Island for no reason except the reason they gave—that someone reported a marijuana farm growing here? Symes's smuggling buddies could have killed Coby in Bimini. Or maybe she discovered the coke on the LCM, and Symes threw her overboard. It doesn't make sense to listen to those endless tapes of gunboat broadcasts and search for a Defender named Jelly Belly when—"

Jo looked up to see her brother in the doorway.

"Let's go see this marijuana," he said.

Jo and Rolle sheepishly followed North down-Island. At the wind tower they exited the road with Rolle in the lead. They struggled through pigeon plum and thatch palm, advancing slowly to avoid poisonwood, squeezing against the peeling trunks of gum elemi until they had gone a quarter mile southwest. A wide glade or small savanna opened within the jungle forest. Several hundred marijuana stalks, high as fall corn and as dry and brittle, huddled together like men in a wind storm. The greenish-brown marijuana, surrounded and completely hidden by foliage, would be difficult to detect from the air unless you happened to look straight down at the precise location.

North moved among the stalks, wondering if his Island really was a front for smuggling as St. Gregory and the Commodore claimed. But why did it have to be Rolle who found the 'farm?' North fingered the plants, examining the flowering tops of the females where the cannabis is most concentrated. Marijuana is a lazy man's crop, sprouting like weeds and maturing in only three months. To North, ecology was the understanding of consequences: from the growth of the flowers after a single harvest, he could tell that the plants themselves were less than five months old. The unknown planters of these tall weeds had been lazy, and the recognition made him breath a sigh of relief.

"These are harvest stubs from only one cutting!" North said. "They had to have been planted well after the raid last March."

"I guess that shoots your theory in the ass," Jo whispered to Rolle as they helped North uproot the plants for burning.

Rolle lit a small pile of twigs and threw on some dry stalks. "I guess it does," he whispered back.

The fire smoked furiously as they ripped up more marijuana and piled it on, building a clearing to the west in the direction of the breeze. Marijuana smoke billowed to sea. Ash settled over the glade, flecking the ground.

After the plants were destroyed, they kicked sand on the embers as the sky flamed ruby and dulled quickly to mauve and violet. They followed behind North as he tramped back home, wondering who could have planted this crop, the very presence of which had been capable of shattering their lives. The marijuana farm, the piracies, and related events formed a pattern in his mind, a reverse gestalt where the answer to Coby's disappearance might be derived from the sum of its parts.

The wild grass of the savanna gave way to forest where the setting sun pierced the peeling, paper-like bark of the thickest trunks, those of the reddish gum elemi. Quite a few branches in the tropical forest were barren of leaves, shedding according to their species' own schedule. Along the way, North scanned the trees for the nest of the old white owl, as had become his habit when in the forest. He had seen nothing of his velvet and vigilant friend lately, neither flapping down the road nor skimming the tree tops. He wondered where the owl had gone.

51 *One Family Island*

JACK CLEARY was stuck with taking the whaler for his crossing to Great Snake Cay Wednesday afternoon, because the faster Mako was being used to supplement the jollyboat in shuttling the expanded workforce. By the time he reached the Snake marina his fuel tank was almost empty.

The gasoline truck was parked at the base of the last boat slip, and a handwritten sign wedged next to the fuel nozzle read:

PLENTY PETROL THIS WEEK!

The attendant was gone, but since there was no current fuel shortage he decided he wouldn't wait. He trudged the two miles to the village where he once again would ask about Jelly Belly or try to uncover any other clues to Coby's whereabouts. After ten months of coming here, the broken pavement, the casuarinas bordering the road, the plush vacation homes of retired Americans and Europeans with their hibiscus and bougainvillae were as familiar to him as the streets of Manhattan. The swivel bridge was open, thank God; otherwise he'd have to wind it open by walking in circles while pushing a steel bar.

Past the bridge and over a hill, the village spread before him flanked by two church spires, both built by Father Joshua Christie.

Every time Cleary saw this hamlet in the daytime, the sadder it seemed. In the middle of the harbor an iron freighter, stuck a century ago on a sandbar, lay on its side dissolving in the water, and now only its rusting ribs remained. Legend has it that when the English sea captain went aground, he waded with crew and cargo of indentured blacks to the shore, thereby founding the settlement and awarding it his own name, after which he grew despondent and drank himself to death. The blacks, outnumbering the white crew fifty to one and wanting no longer to remember the captain, called the place simply "the village."

Today the road from the marina snakes between the jailhouse and a boutique for the tourists, mostly Americans, who come across the bridge on Saturday nights. Goats and chickens roam freely over the asphalt. A teenager too old for school does the Goombay Shuffle down the street, tinny music issuing from a little radio he holds at his ear. The men who aren't working on the Island and don't have the money to buy drinks at the bars laze the day drinking from bottles in paper bags, or dozing on the porches of their shacks. You seldom see the women unless you go around to the back yards where they're pounding cassava or hanging the wash so their husbands can wear spotless clothes to the Grave Yard Inn. The older girls help their mothers iron, or hoe little ditches between a row or two of dusty vegetables. At night the girls bloom like the jasmine that grows along the fences, past which they sneak out to the bars.

Nothing is as consistent as the inconsistencies of West Indian communities. Some are happy well-scrubbed little places. Others, like this one, are littered with disemboweled automobiles oxidizing among the banana trees, the seas around them choked with beer cans, rum bottles, the limbs of furniture, and the broken tools of garages. When Father Christie was younger he had energized the villagers to take care of their island and to ignore the drugs that had begun to rain on them like a malignant manna. His church bells tolled on weddings and feast days or for no reason other than to mark high noon. The bells are silent now. One church is closed, the other open only on Sundays. Josh Christie is too old, too tired to wage any vigorous battle against the unrelenting Plague. Except on Sunday mornings, he sits in his store and once a week claims his goods from the mailboat.

At the end of the road where the asphalt merges into the wharf, two boys were butchering a giant green turtle next to an enormous pile of discarded conch shells. They had cut off the turtle's head and were digging the meat out of the shell with long knives. Cleary waved at them and entered the Grave Yard Inn. Inside, only the gold lit the darkness: former carpenters, drifters, or fishermen wore the yellow metal as a badge, signaling their participation in the thriving village industry. He knew them by name but they seemed more and more interchangeable, like empty rum bottles.

Having served in the Merchant Marine, Cleary had gotten over-happy in bars throughout the world. Once he told North that if he died and his molecules recomposed somewhere in a bar, he could determine his location from the drinking styles of the patronage. New Yorkers lean on the counter as they might before a podium, for moral support. Nassauvians use their drinks to communicate, waving beer bottles like an extension of their hands. But Great Snake villagers, except when there's a party, hunch over the bar and drink to get drunk.

Cleary ordered a martini and brought it to a table by the window. Outside, school children were wandering home, the girls in starched red skirts and white blouses, the boys in red pants and white shirts. School is the only hope for the community, the only way the young won't inherit the siege mentality of out-islanders, Cleary was thinking—when out of the corner of his eye he saw . . . something.

At first he wasn't sure of its significance. Then he looked again at the lower half of a barstool, at a pair of shoes pressed against the footrest. Black shiny shoes. No one wore black shiny shoes in the village. His heart thumped as he moved toward the bar, composing his salesman's opening on the way. Coming up behind the owner of the shoes, he gave a shout of unfeigned joy.

"Jelly Belly!"

Startled, the heavyset man bobbed his head and glared at Cleary. "Wha' you want wid Jelly Belly?"

Cleary smiled widely. "You're my role model. I want your

autograph."

"Dot some kinda joke? You a Defender, mon?"

"Not likely. Wrong color."

"We got a few Conchy Joes on de force."

The dark room grew darker as the sun sank below the horizon, and the Defender's eyeballs gleamed in the light of the television set. They had the lifeless look of a glutton after a meal.

"Why they call you Jelly Belly? You're not that fat." Simple flattery. Jelly's swollen belly was the shape of a gourd. Jelly Belly swiveled his head, glancing around to see if anyone was listening. "Doan say dot name in front o' nobody. Dey calls me Cyril here."

Cleary could hardly contain himself. After all the places he and the others had spent looking for Jelly Belly . . . Now if he could manage to lure him to the Island.

Mr. Davis, the proprietor, came over and refilled Cyril's glass with dark rum, splashing a single ice cube into it.

"Martini," said Cleary, "and a tourist's six-pack."

Davis filled his glass with gin and handed across the bar pint bottles of six different rums. Cleary paid both their bills, smiling at Jelly Belly who was perched like a circus elephant on the narrow barstool.

"Why you in here, whitey?" said the fat man. "Why you bother'n me?"

"Oh, I've got a lot of friends in the Defenders—Commodore Bridgewater, a few enlisted men like Farrington, Bethell, Williams, Thompson. . . ." He lied with premeditation. These were names as common in the Bahamas as Gonzalez in Mexico or Johnson in the States.

"You knows Thompson?"

"Yeah, a big guy. Nice guy!"

"He not so big. Ah bigger."

"You're bigger than everybody, Cyril. What's your last name?"

"Christie."

"Not Josh's son?"

"Yep. Him be muh ole dad."

"Cyril, I have the deepest respect for Reverend Christie." He meant it.

Cyril didn't reply, but something close to a tear seemed to form in one eye. Cleary threw some bills on the bar for a tip and grabbed his jacket. "Smells like a gymnasium in here. Let's go outside and see the graveyard."

"Why you wanna see it? Only de dead goes to de grave *yard.*"

"Well, I won't be able to after I'm dead."

Cyril downed his drink and put on his pea jacket. Despite the bulk of the man, he managed to tiptoe toward the door as though leaving his father's church services early.

It was dark but no less humid outside. A breeze had come up, annulling the precision bombing of the mosquito squadrons. Cleary reminded himself that this was no Island for Science where the mosquitos had been bio-seduced into not breeding. They turned right, over a rough dirt road littered with paper, broken bottles, and crumbled cardboard boxes, and circled around the back to the sad little cemetery. Finger streams from the harbor ran between weeds and jumbey bush to lap its scum at the sides of abandoned gravestones. Cleary inspected Cyril Christie in the moonlight, which was brighter than the lights in the bar. A pudding of blubber that must have oozed down the Defender's hairless chest in his youth now clung to thighs the size of hams. His eyes wore a burning sorrow that leapt from his skull, giving him the look of a giant grouper hauled from the depths.

Cyril leaned on his hands against a thick horizontal branch level with his head. The trunk of the tree, a gum elemi, had forced its way between two coral tombstones, and over the years had twisted them so that now they resembled myopic friends craning their heads to see each other.

"Dem be muh little sisters in dere," Cyril said with genuine grief. Chalky inscriptions announced the dates of their deaths ten years ago. "Dey ridin' bikes when dey was eleven and twelve, an' one of 'em run off de end a de wharf when de tide come in. De udder one, she jump in after her. Dey both drown."

Cleary had spent enough time on this family island to know that few Bahamians learn to swim. He looked around at the broken bottles and tin cans containing stagnant rainwater, lush breeding sites for mosquitos. If children here don't drown, they sometimes die of breakbone fever.

An organic smell wafted from the rivulets of harbor water that lapped against the outer row of graves. In the moonlight Cyril shivered violently, either from the thought of his little sisters' deaths or from the alcohol.

"Cold, Cyril?" Cleary uncapped a pint bottle and gave it to him.

Cyril lapped at the liquor and let himself be led slowly out of the cemetery. Now that he had Jelly Belly in his grasp, the next step was to make him comfortable. Meandering back along the dirt path of the inn to the asphalt road, they stopped at the wharf where together they slumped down at the edge and dangled their legs over black water. As Cyril drank from the bottle, the dark sweet rum bobbed his larynx. After a long time without words, he started a quiet but uncontrollable sobbing. Cleary placed a hand lightly on his shoulder.

"Ah jus' got back from England."

Let the client do the talking. And the drinking. For once in his life Cleary only pretended to drink, merely wetting his lips from his bottle. Cyril didn't elaborate, as if the fact that he'd been in England was explanation enough. In front of them, unseen, the Atlantic flowed into the horizonless dark, suspending time.

Cleary withdrew his hand, a subliminal message. "Tell me about England."

"Youse a white mon!" As the tide crawled up the vertical face of the wharf, Cyril removed his Defender shoes and socks, exhibiting toes splayed wide from a childhood spent barefoot. He exuded a mixture of sweet rum and fermented sweat. "Why yuh wanna know 'bout tings?"

Cleary glanced at his own feet clad in Gucci loafers, and realized he and Cyril had been sitting here for half an hour and that he was getting nowhere. He stood up, deciding on shock. "Because, asshole, when I'm not using fat boys for punching bags, I'm not a bad listener. And I hate that son of a Bay Street boy."

Cyril sniffed back his phlegm so hard he almost fell into the water. "Cap'n St. Gregory?"

"He the one."

"How you know dot mon?"

"He raids our Island once in a while. You know, the Island for Science?"

"Den you knows about de *barge*?"

"Of course. We got it back after our crew was killed. Were they really smuggling?"

Cyril took another pull on his bottle and sobbed. He ignored the question but started talking about St. Gregory, telling Cleary how the captain had promoted him through the ranks from able seaman to chief petty officer. "He help muh life make sense! None of dot talk 'bout God an' stuff neither. Ah mon, it hard t'explain. He mek me feel dere's somethin' worth livin' *for*. Ah knows who Ah *be*!" The words rolled off Cyril's tongue in a wail, as if discovering his true identity made him want to die. He lapsed into a dark silence, black as the night.

Cleary knew he couldn't press too hard, but felt the need to keep him talking. "England, Cyril."

Cyril closed his arms around his chest like a pocket knife, and revealed that St. Gregory had arranged for him to be a security officer at the High Commission in London, the equivalent of an Embassy in commonwealth countries. Cyril hated it there and spent his spare time in the Anglican churches and the pubs, thinking of his sins. The day before yesterday he decided to come home and repent. St. Gregory still believed him to be in England.

"Why did St. Gregory send you to London?"

"To be a guard, after—" He stopped, drank from the rum bottle, and lapsed into silence.

"After what?"

"Jus' to be a guard."

Cleary could imagine Cyril, the fat boy far from Nassau, banished in a reverse provincialism, forgotten, insignificant, miserable, left with only his religion and his misdeeds. Cleary felt an urge to reach between the Defender's thick lips and pull out the truth. Why was it so hard for Cyril to talk when he so obviously wanted to unburden himself? Don't Anglicans have confession like Catholics?

The moon had traversed most of the arch of the sky on its way to the graveyard, and you could hear the sounds of the drinkers being turned out of the inn. Somehow Cyril had to be induced to talk before he fell asleep, for he'd be sober in the morning and might never confess.

"You say somethin' mon?"

"No man, it's the wind."

Cyril drained the last of his pint, threw it in the ocean, and reached for another from the six-pack. Cleary grabbed his wrist, forcing the bottle back into its cardboard pack.

"No more rocket fuel. Tell me what's bothering you."

"Ah doan wanna talk 'bout it." He looked up across the harbor into a brooding sky. There was a strong smell of salt in the air, the raw odor of wasted time.

Now or never. Cleary gave a quick punch to Jelly Belly's arm. "Listen, you slob." His voice rose several decibels. "Tell me about the night on the barge! Now!"

"Ah jus' follow de orders!" Cyril said fast, his voice apologetic.

"Then follow *my* orders!"

Cyril hung his head. "Orders all ma life. It alwuys be de or*ders*."

He murmured something about life under the same roof as a clergyman, who dominated his every breath, followed by escape to the "gov'ment" and submission to the absolute authority of Captain Carlos St. Gregory. The Reverend Christie had held Cyril to the straight life, and the captain of the Military Operations Platoon unknowingly had inherited the father's job. By the logic of his own making, Cyril no longer could ignore the LCM raid. At last, he let out a sigh and said, "It be de Ides o' March. Cap'n come an say dis *Half Fast* barge bein' run by de smug*glers*."

"You guys boarded the barge from the gunboat, right?"

"Right on, mon."

"What happened?"

"De Cap'n send everybody back 'cept me and hisself." Remembering, Cyril's body shook in a fit of emotional mayhem. He gushed it out:

"We goes crazy. We kill an' we kill. We kill everybody."

"Everybody? The girl too?"

"We kill everybody. We alwus kill everybody."

IT TOOK another hour for Cleary to extract the story. Evan Symes apparently had failed to pay St. Gregory a commission, so the captain planned the raid to make an example of him. On the LCM, St. Gregory had ordered Cyril below to shoot anyone there, while he himself killed the crew. Cyril plunged down the steps, saw no one, and tried the door to the stateroom. It was locked. Hearing muffled noises, he sprayed the door until the voices stopped and the doorknob assembly fell off. Inside, the room had the feeling of the altar in his father's church—the white sheets on the bed, the blood, the frail, Christlike body—and after years of blindly following his mentor, he suddenly realized what he had done. He bent over the corpse, saw a broken necklace on the bed, and examined the medallion. What he saw sent a chill through his heart. He knew he had offended the Lord, and at that instant suffered a religious experience. The other drug busts had involved unauthorized smugglers, evil men who deserved to die, not innocent girls.

With tears streaming down his face, he brought the dead girl up the stairs and into the cabin, her wounds leaking blood, her blonde head lolling. He heard Captain St. Gregory's order, "Toss that thing overboard," but for the first time in his adult life he didn't hurry to comply. He brought the dead girl out on the after-deck and stood against the rail with the body cradled in his arms, looking up beyond the luminous clouds to the God he had exchanged for the devil of St. Gregory. The clouds bore witness to his contrition as he vowed to atone for his sins. Then he slid the body under the black waves.

Sitting on the village wharf with his bare feet touching the harbor water, Jelly Belly's face gleamed wet in the gluey moonlight. But it was Cleary who was sweating. He heard the wind in the trees, and a shiver began at the base of his spine and ran upward like a jolt from a broken power line. He downed half a pint of rum at one long pull, feeling it turn to acid in his stomach as he heard himself ask, "Cyril, you still got that necklace?"

"Yeah mon. It safe at home."

"What did the medal say?"

"It say 'J.C. Love You.' Cyril blew his nose and whimpered.

"Dot what mek me repent. It tell me 'bout the dead girl, dot she be the special frien' o' Jesus Christ!"

The J.C. medallion lodged in the valves of Cleary's heart, which stopped beating for a moment and sent him reeling to his knees. "J.C." was "Jack Cleary." He had given Coby the medal on her tenth birthday.

"You slime," Cleary said, recovering. "You know who that girl was you murdered?"

Cyril cringed. Every worker on Great Snake had been in Grant North's employ at one time or another, and everyone knew that his daughter was missing. "Yeah, mon. Ah knows."

Cleary fought back an impulse to breathe fresher air away from Cyril, to get back to the Island and tell Grant North . . . what? That Coby was dead? *We alwus kill everybody!* He knew North well enough to know that, given this proof, he would kill everybody too. Or at least bring down the whole damn government. But North was still the cautious scientist and the fiancé of the Prime Minister's daughter, and would need absolute proof that it was Ransom behind St. Gregory. Cleary made himself stay and question Cyril further.

The harbor smelled of dead conch and spilled diesel mixed with the odor of jungle plants and Cyril's rummy breath as the Defender bared his soul. In a recurring dream, the murdered girl's face welled crimson, and her blonde head swayed as he carried her up the stairs to the main deck, then bobbed to his face and asked, *Why was I killed?* That was all there was to the dream, but it haunted him. "Ah tells ma dream to de Cap'n. Yuh knows what he say? Cap'n say de Prime Minister hisself order de raid! It de fault of nobody dot de innocent girl get killed—it like when a civilian be killed in a war, a ac*cident.* De Cap'n, he keep sayin' de raid an important part of de govmunt secret war, de war against dope. De Cap'n tell me dot de 'full faith an veracity of de govmunt stand behin' de raid.'"

"With the PM in back of it—that make you feel better, Cyril?" Cleary made himself ask.

"Yeah. 'Cept at night, Mr. Jack. The night beats on ma temples. De Cap'n sen' me to London and Ah still cain't sleep nohow."

Cleary questioned him further about Ransom. It seemed that St. Gregory, hungry for glory in some Defender bar and rendered articulate by rum and milk, once bragged to Cyril about his relationship with so powerful a person. The way Cleary heard it secondhand was that the Defender captain and the Prime Minister were equal partners in the piracy business, the latter silent. As far as he was concerned, Cleary now had the absolute confirmation he felt he needed for North. He came to his feet feeling hatred. If he had a knife at that moment, he would have cut that blubbery throat and felt no more guilt than the boys who had decapitated the turtle at this very spot. He guzzled the rest of his rum and threw the empty bottle into the water, Bahama-style.

Beyond the wharf, the harbor water was black ice. The wind had strengthened and Cleary was cold despite the rum. Cyril struggled into his pea jacket with his bare feet still brushing the crests of the swells. Cleary put on his sport jacket, positioned one foot carefully an inch off the fat man's back, and push-kicked hard, toppling one more piece of garbage into the cesspool they called a harbor.

As he left, he could hear Cyril splashing below. He hoped that not knowing how to swim was a family tradition.

THE WIND at his back, Cleary lumbered out of the village, the movement making him abruptly aware of the liquor he had drunk. He wrapped the collar of his jacket around his neck and made himself hurry, intent on reaching the Island. It was later than he thought. The sky already shimmered in the east, its anemic light rendering the bridge forlorn, and he heard the dogs barking in the village. His mission was more than the confirming of Ransom's complicity. How do you tell your best friend that his daughter has been murdered and thrown to the sharks? The pale moon sank into the trees and made Cleary feel terribly alone.

He glanced at the foaming waters beneath the bridge where the ocean narrows to a river's width, and thought, *What would be so wrong with not telling him?* Grant's sorrow would fade through the years of uncertainty. Better for him not to know, to ease into the future unscathed. Transom, though, was another matter. He wished he had the fortitude and the means to kill that bastard himself.

When Cleary arrived at the marina, he remembered with the exaggerated care of the semi-drunk that his outboard motor tank was almost empty. The gasoline truck was locked and abandoned at three in the morning, but no lock secured the truck's own gas tank. He brought the empty fuel tank and a quart of outboard motor oil from the whaler to the truck, where he found a siphoning hose hanging from a hook. Remembering to add oil, he filled the portable tank. He also filled a gallon bottle with drinking water from one of the spigots at the series of boat slips. Placing the water and gasoline in the boat with his four pints of rum, he congratulated himself that even after drinking he had followed basic safety rules.

The boat battery was completely dead; the starter wouldn't turn over. Opening the utility compartment, he saw tied there the "Cleary paddle," the red wooden marker that was supposed to inform Shark that the battery needed charging. Bahamian maintenance, he thought with a shrug. He yanked the starter rope, and let out a sigh of relief when the engine kicked over on the first pull.

Once out of the marina and free of the boats in their slips, he gunned the engine, then throttled back to a steady plane. Beyond the inlet the waves picked up and he saw from the rocky coastline that the tide was high enough so he could run straight across the flats. He made it halfway before the first tank ran out of gas.

Cleary unfastened the engine-to-tank hose and tried to insert it into the connection on the other fuel can. The hose latch didn't fit the spare tank. Bahamian symmetry. There was no other fuel line in the whaler, and no funnel. He poured gasoline awkwardly out of the opening located in the top center of the can, but only a quart or two made it into the bottom tank before a wave knocked him off his feet and dumped the gas can into the ocean, upside down and out of reach. He started the engine and retrieved the can.

Two miles later the engine quit again.

Jack Cleary's years at sea taught him never to use contaminated fuel, but he had no choice. Pouring the gas into the connected tank, he prayed to St. Jude and pulled the starter rope. He fiddled with the choke, and pulled again. The engine coughed. Bitter wind frothed the waves, pushing him southwest.

On hands and knees, Cleary searched the compartments of the boat. No flares. No power for the radio. No anchor. And no ELT—emergency locator transmitter—because the whaler was meant only for quick trips to Great Snake where the water normally was so shallow you could get out and wade. Except tonight, because you were too far west and it was too deep to wade and too cold to swim, even if you weren't tired as hell.

The only rescue device aboard was a flashlight, coated with dew. Cleary spent long minutes sending the *dot-dot-dot, dash-dash-dash, dot-dot-dot* of the SOS toward the Island, knowing he was a good five miles off Scuba Beach and that the attenuated beam wouldn't be noticed from the east end even if anyone were awake. In desperation, he attacked the starter rope again, steadying himself by holding onto the engine with one hand. The outboard only sputtered.

Pulling until his arms felt like they were leaving their sockets, he toiled until the seas quickened and made standing difficult. The sky was lightening beyond the stern, turning Great Snake into a silhouette and the Island for Science into a shadow on the sky. The wind blew cold, perhaps as cold as the 1976 record the Bahamians talked about when snow flakes actually fell in one of the northern islands for the first time. If he had some Tums, or even a piece of chalk, or a radio that worked . . .

Only when he stopped wishing for things and decided that there was absolutely nothing he could do, did he calm down. Like most alcoholics, Jack Cleary had some understanding of his own complexity. Compared to himself, though, he saw his colleagues and his gods composed of simpler motives and a greater consistency. One or both of his patrons, St. Jude or Grant North, would get him out of this mess. They always had. Hopeful, cold, bone-tired, he sat on the center thwart with his jacket collar around his neck listening to the waves, plangent and fateful like Father Christie's church bells tolling for dead souls on a forsaken island.

Cleary had to stay warm. He opened the first of his remaining four pints of rum.

52 *Beyond There Be Dragons*

THE SUN that once had blessed the Island for Science, the same sun of Coby's disappearance almost a year ago, rose over the Wracking Islands on its daily journey to Florida and blasted Jack Cleary's sotted brain into wakefulness. He rubbed his mop of sandy hair and looked around in a complete circle. Against the blue-over-blue horizon he could barely make out the dark line of the Island in the direction opposite his path. There were no boats or airplanes.

Cleary, who hadn't had a hangover since the time North rescued him in Nassau, now listened to his pounding head and felt the surge of nausea. He wished he had some antacid to neutralize the chemical warfare going on in his stomach. Remembering something from long ago, he opened his wallet and in an inner slot found four Maalox tablets wrapped in a dollar bill. They were old and discolored, but he chewed them gratefully and drank a pint of his water supply at one long life-giving gulp, remembering how in that former, kinder life, staying at North's Lake Michigan home after the fires of a night's heavy drinking, he would soak his desiccated membranes in the lake and open his mouth to illimitable cool water.

He lit a cigarette and shook himself back to reality. This pathetic boat trip was a goddamn melodrama, not even a tragedy, one of life's time-wasting little interruptions. Now North, who expected him back this morning, would have to take time away from his work, track his movements on Great Snake Cay, and organize a search. Please, St. Jude, let him find me before dark.

He took inventory knowing that out-island boatmen never bother with survival kits in these deceptively benign seas. He had one gallon of water. One sport coat. Three books of matches, one cigarette, a plastic flashlight, and some useless coins and bills in a useless wallet. And only one pint of rum, the last of the six-pack, which meant he had consumed the other three. He wanted a drink right now but knew he had to save it to ward off the cold nights. In the aft compartment he found only the dead battery and the Cleary-paddle. Crouching to lower the boat's center of gravity, he moved to the bow thwart, opened the glove compartment, and added to his itemization two rusty screwdrivers, a half-full bottle of aspirin, a couple of Oris Fisher's fishhooks, some long wood screws, and a spare diode for the powerless radio, along with instructions on how to install it. No fishline, and no shoelaces either— compliments of Gucci loafers. He probably could use the painter rope for a line; what he desperately needed was bait.

Last night's alcohol and the rising sun sucked the water from his tissues leaving him feeling mummified, and he clung to the whaler with hands on opposite gunwales, head bent, trying to keep his stomach in one place. He swallowed four aspirin. They should call these boats turtles, not whalers, he thought; this one was closer in size to a tortoise shell than a vessel from which to harpoon whales, and while it wasn't supposed to sink, it certainly could flip over.

As if the pitching and rolling and his thirst weren't bad enough, he was plagued by the images of Coby's mutilated body. He tried focusing on her father, imagining North searching for him, remembering when he and Grant first met during the "Eichmann" Obedience Experiments at Yale. Christ Almighty, that was twenty-two years ago!

"Boat," North said.

"Drift," answered Cleary.

"Thirst."

"Water."

"North."

"Rescue?"

"Wrong! The correct answer is 'south,' said North's apparition. "Prepare for shock."

"Sure Grant, but you'll never turn it higher than a hundred volts!"

Cyril Christie's wretched confession joined his memory of the Obedience Experiments. A slug of guilt is standard for Bible Bahamians, exacerbated by having a clergyman for a father. The path from Adam and Eve losing paradise, through God telling Abraham to murder his own son, had lengthened to atrocities ordered by St. Gregory. It was the stuff of Auschwitz.

Flying fish, silver in the sunshine, skimmed the white crests. Ten miles up a jet streaked to Nassau or Europe, oblivious of a man adrift. At sunset a plum and watermelon sky colored the horizon, and only minutes later a quarter moon sat on the horizon like a slice of cantaloupe. Christ, he was hungry. He told himself he needed to lose weight and could live for months without food, although he knew he could live only eight days without a good supply of water—more than he had. Lifting the jerry jug, a plastic gallon bottle with a narrow neck, he permitted himself a few ounces, thinking of the long night ahead, then of Cyril Christie and of the dusty village where feckless boys grew up not knowing how to swim, quitting school after the third grade, drinking, snorting, sometimes injecting, mumbling through life and dying at sixty with crusted arteries, brown lungs, and empty heads. Except for the exceptions: Father Christie, Sidney Rolle, the owner of the Grave Yard Inn, Cuda the electrician, and a few others. How had these escaped their heritage?

That night the seas and winds clashed like a thousand swords in battle. Cleary fended them off by drinking the rest of his rum but it was not nearly enough. In the dark confessional of the night, he drifted in and out of visions of jellyfish with voices like Jelly Belly's. *"Ah doan know nuthin 'cept sorrow. Cap'n say de Prime Minister hisself order de raid!"* With his foot centered on Cyril's back, Cleary struggled awake. The sun was high, his thirst intolerable. Without thinking, he gulped his water. He looked at the bottle. Half empty.

Maybe he could catch rainwater or find something wet to eat. The Sargasso Sea had enough free-floating seaweed to feed an army, but that was a long way to the south. He imagined the Island workers sitting down to Naomi's greased grouper, atoning with corroded stomachs for their national sins. As much as he had maligned the Island cooking, he felt now an overwhelming desire for onion and grouper, and could smell them frying in a primordial gravy of lime juice and hot sauce, rich enough to spawn life. If he had just the peel of one potato! With sudden impulse he grabbed the neck of the empty rum bottle at his feet and smashed it against the top of the engine, producing a jagged cutting edge. It wasn't a machete and there were no needlefish here, but small fish sometimes sought the shade of a boat. If he could snare one, he could cut it up for bait.

He untied the painter from the bow, and unfurled a few strands to make leaders for two hooks, attaching them to the main body of the rope and tying a heavy screwdriver beneath for a weight. Holding one end firmly he threw the line with unbaited hooks over the gunwale. At least he was doing something. He took out his last cigarette, flattened and bent, and sat there staring at it. Eventually instead of lighting the cigarette, he ate it, paper and all. A few minutes later indigestion struck. The antacid was gone and his body felt like a shell abandoned by a molting crustacean. He forced his thoughts away from himself.

In the Eichmann Experiments, psychologically normal people hated what they were doing. They sweated, shook, stammered, snickered nervously, bit their lips until they bled, dug fingernails into their palms, agonized over the victim's pain, and begged to quit—anything but say no. When Authority said "press the button," the vast majority of ordinary men and women—people far more normal than that self-mortifying blob of Cyril Christie—administered shocks which if real would have killed their subjects.

Cleary gathered the sport coat around his head against the sun, letting it trail down his back Arab-style. He sat motionless, holding the painter in the water, conserving his strength. The green water turned blue—not the purple of deep water but not the pastel of the shallows either. No land in sight, not even the mountain mirages of low clouds. Ever since Columbus, mariners both arrived and departed the Spanish Main on sea and air currents of the North Atlantic basin that rotate in a clockwise direction. Fortunately he was too far south to be swept up in the currents headed for Europe, but unfortunately, he was too far north to drift toward Florida. He saw no sign of land, feeling like an ancient mariner reading the warning at the border of his map:

BEYOND THERE BE DRAGONS.

The fish came then. Squadrons of yellow jacks and triggerfish flapped up toward the side of the boat, dove, appeared again, and wheeled around each other in a submarine parade. His chance of snaring a reef fish was greater here on the Great Bahama Bank than waiting until he drifted into water hundreds of fathoms deep. He threw the stiff painter with its assembly of hooks and weight over the side, pushing it straight down six or seven feet where he could see clearly. Each time a fish came to investigate, he'd jerk the rope trying to snare one.

Please, God, one fish! Only one did he need in order to catch as many more as it would take to keep him alive until he was found. But after scores of attempts, he realized that trying to snare a living fish without bait was futile. From the back of his mind he dredged up a survival technique learned years ago in the Merchant Marine, and he forced himself to consider it seriously. After a time, he took off his trousers and sat there looking at his thigh, anticipating the pain. What the hell, it was better than dying of thirst. He grabbed the broken bottle. And stopped. What if the bleeding wouldn't stop? What if he got tetanus?

The waves calmed, replaced by the rhythmic suck of low swells. *Do it now while you're still on the bank! The fish won't stay forever.* The ragged edge of the brown bottle intimidated him—and gave birth to a better method. Taking the otherwise-useless flashlight, he unscrewed the lens assembly and removed the reflector cone that was sharp as a knife. With one quick movement, he sliced off a thick strip of skin about an inch long, stemming the flow of blood with his handkerchief. To make absolutely sure that his human and rather-limited bait wouldn't wash off the hook, he impaled it in several folds past the barb.

Eventually a yellow fish smaller than the others, no more than eight inches long, nibbled at the bait, and he wiggled the line enticingly. Size didn't matter; even the smallest would provide bait for catching more.

The fish bit. Cleary yanked the rope to set the hook. As he pulled it out of the water, the fish struck the gunwale, came loose of the hook, and arched in the air. Cleary lunged after it, missed, and toppled into the ocean where he felt the searing of the saltwater on his thigh and a profound despair in his heart.

He swam to the whaler, pulled himself in, and searched the area deep into the water. The fish were nowhere to be seen, and he had lost his fishline and flashlight reflector. For a long time he sat there shivering and gazing blankly out to sea, until the sun produced its mauve and golden routine. Where the colors smoothed into the indigo of the western horizon, a trawler hung in the sky, its diagonal mast clearly visible. A new shape, big as the trawler but closer, rose on the sea and disappeared—probably a whale or a submarine playing war games from the U.S. base on the other side of Andros. Whatever it was, it ran deep; he had to be close to the edge of the bank. Moving lights appeared every couple of hours, but the airplanes were flying toward destinations, not circling the ocean in some methodical search pattern.

Without rum, the third night was even more miserable than the second. His muscles stiffened under his wet clothes, his throat burned, his empty stomach craved anything—mostly a drink.

A new inspiration came to him. Propping the can of contaminated gasoline on the bow thwart, he unfastened the cap in the center, and threw into it a lighted book of matches. The mixture went up like a blowtorch, lighting the sky in a yellow beacon that surely could be seen by the yachts and cruise ships on the horizon. The fire burned in the tank for a quarter hour, warming him and drying his clothes, while he watched for any signal, any change in direction of the lights on those ships.

No one came.

The wind strengthened, breaking the swells, and the moon cut an ugly gash across the chop of the sea. The breakers sounded like cymbals, forming short vertical cliffs whose tops tumbled into the boat. He used the engine cowling to bail while mumbling prayers to St. Jude—and to unseen sentries of distant ships.

Every hellish annoyance mocked his labor: the lack of a real bailing bucket, the breaking waves, the rocking boat that made him seasick, the heckling lights of far-off yachts, and especially the winds that whipped the seas into liquid avalanches. For a while he couldn't tell which was out of level, the boat or himself. Their two destinies were linked, benthic creatures beyond redemption. He was not exactly afraid to die; he simply did not want to give up living. He bailed furiously. Unfulfilled goals—wife, children, some monument to his life, like the Island for Science—stood before him in accusation. He would be mourned only by a few girlfriends and by one close friend in jeopardy, for whom he had vital information.

In case . . . just in case he didn't make it, maybe he should leave a message confirming his proof that Ransom had been directing St. Gregory. A message isn't much to credit the meaning of a human life, he thought, but it was the only monument left to him. It would have to be a secret message, one that only North could decipher, in case someone found the whaler and turned it over to the Defence Force. As he bailed through the night, he contemplated ways to encode the most important cryptogram of his life.

THE SKY was a burning blur when Cleary awoke one moring, exhausted and feverish. Was this the third or fourth day? He couldn't tell from his water supply. There was less than a quart left, and he couldn't remember how much he had allowed himself to drink each day. The stubble on his chin felt as if it were a week old.

He spent the next few days on the bottom of the boat, sliding into watery dreams of a watery life. The dreams would subside only to emerge with force, as the ocean current is lost in a swell before it picks up again to propel the boat to unknown destinations.

Coby, his godchild, recurred in those dreams a schoolgirl in white blouse and flowered dress, playing with her friends. She had been more alive, more curious and less shy than the others, willing to guide her own destiny, telling life where it could take her. When he'd given her the J.C. medallion, she had reached up and pulled him down to her and kissed him full on the lips as she'd seen her mother do to her father, and had said, "C.N. loves you too, J.C." At age ten.

The sunsets brought company to the salesman who had always hated being alone. Delilah Mae would appear where the shadows of clouds played on the waves, silhouetted by streams of surreal sunlight, the sequins of her lamé dress sparkling as if she'd just finished a song and stepped off the stage.

"Christ Almighty, Delilah, you some kind of angel?"

She giggled lasciviously and crossed silken legs under the skirt that ended at her knees, shaping a conical conduit wide enough for his hand. Hardly an angel, she quoted from her private repertoire:

> Tricks and stunts,
> Unknown to common cunts

Steve, Eve, and Xaviera competed for his memory too, their hair falling in careless coils over bronze shoulders, drinking Cleary Coladas while swinging on the hammocks of the coconut grove. The girls hadn't understood that he and Grant had known the Island as more than the sum of its trees and beaches, in the same way that their own bodies were more than the sum of its cells and organs, and in a strange passage those organs had blended, Island and human. Grant had spoken of it to him only that one time, and Cleary wished he had told North that he had felt it too.

The seas savaged him back to his boat and his dwindling supply of water as the sun died with an almost audible sputter. He reached a hand overboard and wet his lips, drinking a few drops of saltwater, hoping to extend his remaining quart of liquid life. He willed the girls back again and for a moment he could smell their female scents, glorious and tropical. But a wave crashed over the gunwales and swept them away.

The night boiled, bucking the little whaler in the immense sea

416

and stinging his flesh like ice. He breathed in gasps between bouts of shivering and bailing, and implored St. Jude and the Virgin Mary, the mother of God, to pray for this sinner now at this hour of his death.

ON WHAT may have been the fifth or sixth day since he was lost at sea, Cleary awoke in eight inches of water with his head bouncing against the fuel tank. He could feel the Gulf Stream dragging the whaler along the longitudinal grids of the planet through purple-deep water, heading north. Raising his body painfully, he looked around. Far off to his stern lay a land mass, probably Cuba. Andros, unseen, must be somewhere to the east. Soon little blips broke the horizon like toy boats. He stared until he could identify them as tankers, which gave him no joy, for he had served on tankers and knew that all hands work to maintain the vessel, not to see where it goes.

Compared to the Bahama Bank, the Gulf Stream was littered with garbage, and he drifted past gumbos of splintered wood tangled into seaweed, pieces of plastic bottles, clotted clumps of oil, broken crates, frayed ropes . . . a boulevard of flotsam that stretched sporadically the length of the Florida Straights. When he came close enough to one of the patches, he grabbed a mass of gulfweed entwined around a piece of wood, and untangled the berrylike bladders. He chewed the viscid berries and nubby leaves for the water in them, but they tasted so bitter they made him retch.

By late afternoon the jerry jug was empty and the water in the boat, a mixture of rain and sea, was too salty to drink. He doubted whether he could live anywhere near eight days without water, for the sun already had dehydrated his tissues. With the rusty screwdriver, he hacked away the top third of the plastic jug to make a bailing bucket. As he bailed, the face of an old man stared up at him from the bilge—eyes swollen almost shut, skin dry and tight over glossy cheekbones—and his thigh throbbed where the infection had begun. He was no longer hungry; nature's way, he knew. And yet he dared to hope, even while knowing that hope is the worst of misfortunes because it prolongs agony.

Night brought calm skies and spasms of angina that left him

choking and suffocating. He searched the heavens, finding the Little Dipper and under it the jewels of Cassiopeia, and flicked his eyes back and forth to where the soul of Jude might be watching from some rogue star, for a long time focusing on the moon and thinking what a shame it was that Grant North had not been allowed to go there. The thought of North reminded him that his salvation, either in this world or in the next, depended upon delivering his message. When the end came, he would wedge himself between the bottom and the thwarts and hang on, and maybe his death grip would keep him from falling overboard. He didn't want his body to be eaten by sharks. He forced his mind back to the problem of the message. Using the screwdriver as a chisel, he etched by starlight onto the center thwart:

GRANT, FIND MESSAGE. . . .

Never before had there been dark meanings in Cleary's crypto-hobby, only a visceral recognition of life's vast humor, feigned or stated, surrounded by ripe wine and sunshine. Wrapping the night around his brutalized body like a blanket, he slid into himself until he reached the base of his soul where nothing was left except this single task. He knew he had a day, two at the most, to decide how to leave North a message the Defenders couldn't read, before succumbing to the final practical joke of his life.

Or for St. Jude or Grant North to intercede.

53 *The Tail of a Nightmare*

WHEN CLEARY FAILED to arrive at the Island that Thursday morning, North had a hunch his friend might be on the ocean and in trouble. The seas were galloping, too rough for the workers to make it to the Island, and anyone but Cleary would have stayed overnight in the village. The weather was creating so much static North couldn't reach Great Snake by radio. He made an hourly log of wind velocity and direction, and at night turned on the lights in all the buildings.

Friday morning the waves subsided enough for the workers to come over in the jollyboat, but none of them remembered seeing Cleary since the night before last. North and Rolle went looking for him in the Mako. As they sped past the seafarm, millions of tons of water were riding the tide, invoking the clean caviar smell of live shrimp and seaweed. A bevy of sand sharks patrolled the perimeter fencing looking for a way in. North ran the Mako straight across the banks to Great Snake Cay.

Father Josh was at the village wharf waiting for the mailboat, leaning against the community pile of conch shells that looked like broken pieces of pottery. In old shoes and torn shirt he seemed more an ordinary merchant than the priest of this island parish for fifty years. No, he had not seen Cleary. Nor had the few men on the street who ambled around like stray dogs. At this end of the island, only the owner of the Grave Yard Inn had noticed Cleary last night talking to the Christie boy and buying a six-pack of rum when he left, and he averted his eyes in a curious way when he told that to North. No one at the marina remembered Cleary buying gas.

North was certain that Cleary was lost at sea, and deep inside he embraced the Cleary maxim, that to travel with hope is better than to arrive. Rolle stayed on Great Snake to search from the inlets and coves and bayou-like back country of the creek, and to telephone BASRA in Nassau to request an aerial search. North headed the Mako across a storm-freshened sea to the bays and narrows of the other Wracking Islands, where he hailed boatmen to ask if they'd seen a white whaler. The wind could not have pushed Cleary southeast to these cays, but there was the possibility that he had gotten drunk and landed on one of them before running out of gas, or that he was hung up on a sandbar. North tried to visualize the Wracking chain, remembering how the islands appeared from the air, strung tail to nose along the edges of triangular sand flats like green paramecia in a microscope. The deep-water approaches to these cays are those coves where pirates once hid their masts from royal navies or went ashore to bury treasure. Behind them, the feathered tops of palms floated on the sky. At the end of the chain, North talked to vacationers on Fat Cay who were barbecuing fish on the beach. No one had seen the white whaler.

The day passed on the cobalt ocean with no sign of Cleary. Turning back along the deep side of the islands into the low sun, the rim of the ocean turned blood-red and streaked the sky in purples, browns, and blacks. Drawn to the infinity of colors, North's attention was caught time and again by a jumping dolphin, or stingrays, or seabirds diving beneath the mirrored surface. Once he saw the thin column of a whale's blow rising sixty feet in the air. The rolling waves tailed rainbow dust from their crests, now with beauty, at other times with violence. Tourists think there is but one season in the Caribbean. But those who live here know summers windless as the moon, autumns calm with mild breezes (when there are no hurricanes), winters of scud and chop, and springs treacherous with storms brought by rising temperatures. Yesterday the seas had been wild as any on the North Sea. Today they were calm.

Only an hour of daylight remained when North arrived at Great Snake, so he followed the creek from the mouth of the harbor. This was the first time he'd been in the river-like passageway between Great Snake and Water Cay since he and Cleary escaped from the thunderboat, and now he motored through the backwaters going the other way. The sun dropped behind the trees, bringing a swarm of Mesozoic insects like starving demons. As North slapped and scratched, he wondered with the detachment of a scientist whether the mosquitos in the swarm could be the *Aedes aegypti* that carry dengue or malaria. With some effort, he probably could eliminate all genera of mosquitos here as he had done on the Island for Science, by using synthetic pheromones to confuse them and prevent mating. A good-neighbor gesture for the future, he thought.

Slowing to avoid fallen logs, North saw against the sun three writhing figures covered with a luminous mist and hovering like serpents over black water, their shapes lengthened in a cold-air temperature inversion. As he drew closer, his engine at bare idle, the serpents turned into men—two black, one white—wearing dungarees and work shirts. The white man was poking a stick at something in the water, reluctantly, as if afraid to snag a corpse. One of the black men, thick torso, arms like a wrestler and wearing a leather vest, was heaping a body-sized load onto a pile of similar shapes in the middle of the skiff, while his partner reached over the gunwales for another. They worked fast, talking quietly.

North cut the engine, letting the Mako drift into a thicket of branches. He couldn't make out what they were saying but he recognized them from their features and voices. The blond Afro could belong to none other than Lionel Sweeting. The strongman in the vest was Purple Martin. The third, Cuda Colebrook. And they were retrieving dozens of big black plastic bags from a hiding place beneath the surface of the water.

It required no leap of intuitive thought for North to come to a conclusion. Black plastic garbage bags had become almost standard packaging in the Bahamas for marijuana; there had been a marijuana farm on his Island; and these men worked on the Island.

They were piling the skiff dangerously high, two men bracing the bags with their arms, the third starting the outboard motor, which coughed once, caught, and buzzed them slowly toward Goat Cay. North waited, then followed at idle until he saw the object of their rendezvous: a schooner burnished red against the darkening skies, its sails drooping like clothes on a line. No reason to linger further in this troposphere of mosquitos and sandflies. That much marijuana could have but one destination.

The moon rose like a bowl of milk, spilling light into the creek. North motored back to the marina, feeling he was navigating a river of falsehoods. Rolle was right: nothing is as it seems in the Bahamas. Cuda and Lionel could have slipped away for an odd hour to tend their marijuana crop, bringing it here at night and stowing it underwater until the mother ship arrived. They may have supplemented their harvest with additional quantities landed on the private airstrip alongside the creek. You could see where at least two such planes had missed, for their wrecks were visible underwater not far from the village. Who would have guessed that Cuda, the repentant smuggler, happy in electronics and his new freedom, would return to that once-abandoned world of crime?

If Cuda and the others were the marijuana farmers, his suspicions of Rolle had been unfounded! Sidney Rolle had befriended him, had worked selflessly for him, had come to his aid more than once, and North chided himself for having doubted his loyalty.

One Sidney Rolle, he realized, was worth more than the whole damn village.

THE BRIEF TWILIGHT blinked out as North motored under the bridge. He tied up at the marina and hiked to the airport where a dozen private planes ranging from Learjets to Bonanzas were parked. It was Friday night, and he knew the pilots would be with their employers at the weekly Great Snake party.

Unshaved, in dirty dungarees, North might have been mistaken for the janitor among the plush surroundings and middle-aged revelers in sport coats or long gowns. He crossed the dance floor to the radio room, and placed a radiophone call to the U.S. Coast Guard in Miami.

"I copy, Dr. North, but your data don't coincide with ours for the region around Andros. Over."

"The Island for Science is fifty miles from Andros. Wind direction and velocity could be different. Will you search?"

"That's an affirmative for the search. But we'll have to use our data for Andros weather that day. We will begin in the morning east of Bimini—between Freeport and Andros."

"Hypothetically, captain, where would a drifting boat be by tomorrow morning if the wind *had* blown through the entire region the way I recorded it at the Island?"

"*Hypothetically,* the boat would be blown toward south Andros, and if it missed Andros, it would head toward Cuba. It would never get there, of course. The Gulf Stream would pick it up and turn it north up the coast of Florida."

Then that's where he would search. He signed off.

North knew none of the wealthy homeowners or their pilots, yet every hour could be crucial. Feeling like a World War I commander asking for volunteers, he commandeered the microphone, and as the music stopped, described the emergency. He requested all pilots to meet with him at the entrance hall under a sprawling wall map of the Bahamas.

No one showed up.

In disgust, North sped the Mako back to the village, where he asked some boys lounging on the wharf if they'd seen Sidney Rolle.

"Sid-ney?" said one.

"Oh, never mind."

Entering the Grave Yard Inn, an unaccustomed silence met his ears, and when his eyes adapted to the darkness he saw the place was empty. Half-full glasses studded the horseshoe bar, uneaten dinners were abandoned on tables, cues rested on the pool table. He hurried through the dining room and out the back door, unnerved by what he saw. The cemetery was teeming with people, as if the drinkers and their families had gotten the urge *en masse* to be close to their departed friends. Moonlight glistened on the gold worn by some of the men and on the African amulets of the women, and the air smelled festive, like coconut rum. Most of the two hundred villagers were here, standing quietly in groups of twos or threes, facing in the same direction, their lips moving in prayer the way they do at wakes.

Father Joshua Christie leaned against a tombstone a little apart from his wife, his head downcast, looking older than his body. Two young women supported Mrs. Joshua Christie. Her hair acrawl with plastic rollers, apron loose across her ample waist, the stiffness had gone out of her. You could smell the sweet Bahama bread she had been baking at her home across the street, and it mingled with the ambient odor of rum. She was staring to the left of the flagpole that flew the Bahamian tricolors, where the trunk of the gum elemi parted the two headstones of her dead girls and branched over them, and she couldn't take her eyes away from her only son hanging motionless from the rope attached to the highest limb.

The crowd must have formed only moments ago, for no one seemed reconciled to the reality of the scene. Cyril Christie's skull, diminished by the huge knot of the rope, lolled over his flaccid neck, which widened into the moonlit mound of flesh beneath and cast a shadow on the gravestones like a question mark. These villagers had known privation, murder, and the devastation of hurricanes, but they were not prepared for suicide. They had never seen one. Most of them had never seen Cyril in his dress uniform either, which he had worn for the occasion. His noncom stripes pointed like arrows toward his bare feet.

"Why he do dot. . . ?"

"Ah dunno. I dunno. . . ."

"De coward way."

A boy climbed the tree and cut the rope to the corpse, which crumpled to the ground. Cuda, Lionel Sweeting, and Purple lingered like aliens in their own hometown, as if they'd come to this moment of out-island history straight from some desert on the opposite side of the planet. The three were heavy with jewelry. Cuda wore a thick chain around his neck and a diamond-encrusted Rolex on his wrist. A gold cross that might have weighed a pound hung on Purple's broad chest. Sweeting flaunted a watch like Cuda's.

Sidney Rolle arrived looking disgusted, and the four gathered around North. "This place was a two-bit settlement when my family came here," Rolle said, "and it looks to me like it's lost twenty-four cents since then."

They watched as the stretcher carrying Cyril's body was borne across the road and past the Christie shack to the church, trailing the rope behind it like the tail of a nightmare. Two constables worked the crowd, taking notes.

"Terrible ting," said Cuda, "All dese people . . . it like de air itself be hottin' up." Purple mumbled something unintelligible, and the others nodded.

A demonic moan made them shudder, their eyes following the sound to Mrs. Christie. Starting low and gathering volume, her moan rose to a crescendo unheard in the modern world, and ended in an explosion of vocal cords and tears. The villagers reacted in a curious way. As the body was carried past them, they tossed pennies onto it to express their disgust. One man poked a half-dollar bill into the corpse's mouth.

North felt nothing for the dead man, but everything for Cuda. It was time to strike and he seized it. He looked straight into the eyes of his former protégé and friend. "All right, Cuda, tell me about the marijuana. I want to understand your betrayal a little more clearly."

"What you talkin 'bout, mon?"

"I'll try to be clearer. Where did you motherfuckers get the Smoke you stowed in the creek?"

Cuda, Purple, and Sweeting looked at North with something like awe, their heads in unison, mouths ajar. "De creek . . . ?" said Cuda, their spokesman, buying time as it registered on him that they were being accused. "Aw, Doctuh Grant, suh . . ." He stopped, perhaps thinking of how North had befriended and taught him. "You our frien'. Yer de only white man we'd ever work for. So we do feels mos' terrible, you know, 'bout dot. But we all gotta mek our livin'. We got 'sponsibil*ities*! You understand?"

"I understand that you aren't dead." They'd heard often enough North's admonition against going back on your word. "You guys, especially Cuda and Lionel, earn about three times as much as the average worker. This isn't about making a living. It's about greed.

Tell me, Cuda, why you went back into smuggling."

Cuda jerked to attention as if eager to clear up a terrible mis-understanding. He wrinkled his forehead with a hurt look on his face and poured his sorrowful brown eyes into North's. "We ain't no smugglers, Mr. Grant. We *farmers!* We grow de Smoke wid our own honest labor, wid our own six hands. We gets de idea from dose Defenders who come lookin' fer de farm."

"On my Island?"

Cuda unlocked his eyes from North's and mumbled, "Yessuh."

Lionel's and Purple's interest in the episode dwindled, as toward the successful culmination of any argument. Their cavalier attitude flared North's anger, but he had said enough. Great Snake village is a small place where everybody knows everyone else. You fire three men at an emotional time like this and you attack the whole community. Without a word, he clutched Rolle's arm and moved him back toward the wharf.

"What was that all about?" Rolle asked.

But before North could answer, a constable came over with another man and said, "Doctuh Nort?"

"Yes."

"You know dis man, Mr. Davis? He de owner a de Grave Yard Inn."

"Of course," North said, extending a hand.

Davis, a man of property and more education than his patrons, smiled beneath a mournful face.

"Tell de doctor wot you tells me in de inter*view*, Mr. Davis," the constable said.

"Well, Dr. North, this boy Cyril come into the bar this mornin' while I cleanin' up. He wearin' his uni*form.* He all shook, an' say to tell you . . . thot he been confessin' to your man Cleary. . . ." Davis cast his eyes to the ground as if he were the proprietor of the graveyard instead of the Grave Yard Inn. "Cyril say . . . well, he say . . . he real sorry for killin' your daughter an' throwin' her body overboard. Cyril was in the Defenders, you know. He say he didn't know she be in the cabin when his captain order him to shoot up the barge with his machine gun. I try to get him to talk to the constables or to his daddy, Father Josh. He say no, he'll 'pay for it on de tree.' I didn't know what he meant at the time. I never thought he'd do nothin' like this!" Mr. Davis shot a glance toward the death tree. "I am truly sorry about your daughter, Dr. North."

Having unloaded his unwelcomed burden, Davis leaned in the direction of his inn, then turned back with an expression of sorrow on his face. "Oh yes. Cyril give me this for you." He fished in his pocket and came out with a thin gold chain which he puddled into North's palm.

Stunned, North stared blankly at the light chain that was broken in the middle, the two strands coming together at a small medallion bearing the inscription:

J.C. Loves You.

Rolle put an arm around North and led him away from Mr. Davis and the constable who were huddled together talking in soft tones. A few steps later, North's legs gelated and he collapsed under the tragedy of two hundred and fifty pounds of secrets swinging from a gum elemi branch. Clutching his stomach, he writhed on the asphalt road and choked with waves of horror. When he could breathe again, a strangled cry escaped his mouth, not a primitive wail like Mrs. Christie's, but a sharp blasphemy hurled into the mindlessness of the universe.

In the village you get the feeling that the twentieth century has not yet arrived. At any moment you expect to see horse-drawn carts and friars wearing sackcloth, or corpulent bodies hanging from trees. North lowered his head and vomited. Rolle knelt beside him and clasped his skull between two cool hands.

The cortege was inside the church now, and you could hear the villagers singing a hymn for Cyril. What did North care about their jellied slob of a Defender? He closed his mouth, his ears, his heart, fighting the images flooding his brain. The deaths of Knowles and the Zellers, the sins of St. Gregory and Ransom—these were the merest trivia compared to the overwhelming disaster of Coby's death. The references to "being thrown to the sharks" made sense to him now; it was an efficient and obvious way of disposing of a dead body in this water country. So mightily had he believed in Coby's survival, now he saw her life as a brief spark in the

427

cosmos, and understood the arrogance with which he'd searched for her. The mind of *Homo sapiens* has evolved as far as it has by shielding from itself the terror of death. He felt the plunder of hope dressed desperately in delusion, of an ego having completed its transformation into depression, of Grant North becoming something other than the intuitive he had believed himself to be.

The villagers who had not gone into the church were murmuring on the street. A cluster of them near North speculated as people do after some sporting event, about how Cyril must have taken off his shoes and used his sisters' tombstones as a stepladder to the first branch. North felt stranded in the wrong dream. We all are plunging to our deaths one way or another, he thought, from the top branch of our birth to the grime of the pavement, marveling on the way down at the intricacies of the passing bark.

He rose, inching toward the wharf, tasting the vomit in his mouth. "There's only one thing left for me," he whispered.

It was an ominous voice that Rolle had never heard before, but he answered, "St. Gregory, I suppose you mean."

"And Ransom!"

"You sure of that?"

North fought the paralysis that came from knowing too much and too little. Nothing had changed, he told himself, only his knowledge of it. Coby had been dead for a year. He dwelled on her last words to him, thinking of how certain he had been all this time that she was alive. ". . . *your plans, your ideas. You can't seem to understand that I am not you!*"

Now he understood.

The slice of moon rode a misty sky, bleak and distant, forming a halo several times its diameter and reddened at the outer circle. Rain tomorrow. It was hard to believe this was the same moon he'd dreamed of exploring, harder still to endure when hope was gone. He had lived these past twelve months for the hope of her.

And now?

Now he would live for the ruin of her assassins.

54 *Most Grievous Fault*

NORTH SPENT the night on the Island and returned to the Great Snake marina in the morning drizzle, avoiding the village and meeting Jo at the airport. She jumped out of the cockpit looking haggard and holding a jacket over her head. North had called her last night in Bimini about Coby and Jack Cleary. He held her, but he could do nothing to console her. Or himself. The only thing he could think of saying was what he knew he dare not say, that despite the evidence of Coby's death there remained a residual hope in a tired intuition that his rational mind told him never again to trust. Logic once had told him that if he did X, then Y would result. But reason and intuition both had failed him, and his best friend and his daughter were dead.

They entered the upper earth, fighting the terrors of their minds with the anesthetic of droning engines, flying low and sad, their plane a speck in the immensity of a gray chaos. North worked out a grid pattern designed to supplement the BASRA search, using the Gulf Stream locations suggested by his own wind data. Even straight down, visibility was bad, the seascape thickened by rain. Strong winds buffeted them like a penance. The Cessna clawed higher and dipped the port wing to turn around for another sweep.

Their silence settled back like the gray clouds. "When I awoke this morning," said Jo, "I looked outside at the rain and felt numb as if nothing were alive, not me, not the trees, not the sea. I blamed it on the cold, the March rain. For a moment, I wasn't even sure which island I was on. It turned out to be Alice Town, where I kept returning because I had been everywhere else. After we find Jack—or don't find him—I'm going back to the Turks & Caicos and pick up my life again. I don't make a hell of a lot of money at the station—"

"Jo, I'm sorry. I should have given—"

"The hell with the money. I'm telling you something. I was desperate to find Coby. I wanted things to be like they were . . . to protect her. I wanted my joy to be her joy, my knowledge to be her knowledge."

Tears had come to them both. She pulled out a man-sized handkerchief and dried her eyes. "Well, we can't bring Coby back," she said, "but we sure as hell can find Jack."

"Jo . . . maybe Coby—"

"*No, Grant. No!*" as if he were still her baby brother. "Don't start that intuition crap again. Let it die. With Coby."

MARIANNE joined them the next morning. It had been almost a week since her father's mysterious granting of the permits, and during that time she had turned over the management of REHAB to an associate. The blue of the sky reaffirmed itself, and by flying high the three of them commanded a wide vista of the sea. Every time one of them saw what could be a shimmering white whaler, Jo would head the plane downward only to discover a wave cresting over a reef. Their altitude thus was effectively restricted to two thousand feet, and when you fly that low you realize how vast is the sea. The Straits of Florida alone measure forty-five hundred square miles.

The rest of the weekend and into the following week they searched the Straits between the Florida peninsula and the Bahama islands. On the eighth day of their search, the news came to the Island by radio. Ten days after Cleary had departed from the marina, a commercial fisherman discovered his whaler drifting north with the Stream thirty miles off Cape Canaveral. Wedged under the thwarts, his sport coat wrapped around his head against the cold or the sun, Cleary had been dead of dehydration for forty-eight hours.

At the lodge, bent over now-useless charts, the man who once had felt blessed on this Island stood gaunt, unshaved, exhausted, his neck muscles strained like those of a fighter thrown out of the ring. The heart had gone out of Grant North—for the seafarm, for the Island, for anything except action against his tormentors.

The Coast Guard had called by radio and wanted someone to pick up the whaler—and to see on it a message Cleary had carved.

The LCM was not quite unloaded from having recently carried plywood and other lumber to the Island, but North and Rolle pre-empted the vessel from Andy. They piloted all night, without reference to navigation charts or direction finder, and the next morning arrived at the Ft. Pierce Coast Guard station where Cleary's body and the whaler were held. The station commander showed them the words etched on the center thwart:

> GRANT, FIND MESSAGE
> —YOUR BEST FRIEND IN THIS LIFE
> AND IN THE NEXT, JACK

"What the hell. . . ?" said Rolle.

"Jack is telling us he's left a cryptogram here somewhere." North was tinged in guilt for having made Cleary a soldier in a war he didn't understand; the least he could do was give meaning to Jack's death by decoding the message. He pushed the words around. "Jack in this life," he tried. "Jack in the next . . ."

CLEARY AVOIDED funerals. He used to say the dead had nothing but time on their hands and could damn well come to you if they felt the need. But this was one funeral he would find hard to avoid. The service, held at the Hillcrest Cemetery chapel, was meant both for Cleary who would be buried there and for Coby who would not be. Jo had flown Andy and Marianne to Ft. Pierce for the day, leaving the workers to manage themselves. Ernie and Lorraine Garbarino attended, bringing with them a wreath of yellow roses. Cleary's last audience consisted of seven mourners and one old priest who hadn't even known him.

Cleary had traveled alone, waited in reception rooms alone, made his presentations alone, died the death of a salesman alone. But society's design for a salesman is not the salesman's design for himself. He craved company so much he used to arrange mega-meetings and superlunches in New York, playing the court jester who plucked the chords on his lute and sang story songs that brought vast orders for North Detectors and other instruments of science. North remembered how Cleary could enter a bar and an hour later know everyone in it, how he would look a new friend straight in the eye, claiming you could read a man's heart through his eyes. He remembered the day Cleary had given Coby the medallion and how her face glowed with the prize. She was wearing a new pink dress her mother had given her, laughing and jumping, delighted to be having a birthday, to be wearing her own gold necklace at age ten, and she had flung her arms around her Uncle Jack and kissed him, and said later, "I'll wear it forever, all the way to heaven."

If he could, his friend of twenty-three years would crack his latest joke, make you feel glad it was you who had survived, and try to get you drunk at his own funeral. A best friend is someone you choose and who chooses you, to walk the corridors at three in the morning, to become a true godfather for your daughter, to be there when your wife dies of cancer. A best friend is someone who takes time away from his own survival to carve a vital message for your eyes only. And who wills you his wealth; Jo had sold Cleary's miniature Rubens and deposited more than two hundred thousand dollars in the Island for Science bank account.

The funeral mass was the usual Latin litany he remembered from when his father died. The universal church that reigned in Ireland also reigned in Croatia, and the sons of these lands, the scientist and the salesman, had grown up in unified traditions. The mass brought him back to his childhood, wedged between mother and sister, sitting, standing, kneeling, and tapping his breast in accusation: "*Mea culpa, mea maxima culpa*—my maximum fault." Had he not let his pride drive him to the Island, Coby and Cleary would be alive. The ancient ritual, the smell of incense, the taste of God dispensing hope—all these memories of two lives he had risked and lost, flooded him like a river. Now the round Eucharist quivering above the chalice in the fingers of the old priest brought no resurrection, no promise. For him, the Host had become a librating and featureless moon, inundated in vacuum and fury.

When the mass ended, the Islanders remembered Coby with tears and took one last look in the casket at Jack Cleary, whose cavalier humor endured after death. As requested, he had been dressed in baseball cap, polo shirt, and sneakers, and his eyes were closed as if he were enjoying the bright Florida sunshine.

Rolle placed a medal of St. Jude in Cleary's left palm. "Isn't it supposed to rain at funerals?" he said.

"Not at Cleary's."

North and Marianne laid Coby's medallion on his right hand, and the coffin shut forever on the silent conspiracy of death.

NORTH HELD the *Half Fast* close to shore to avoid the northward flow of the Gulf Stream, planning to travel south before crossing the Straits and return to the Island. He glanced at the wreath of roses Rolle had placed against the windshield, and turned over in his mind various combinations of Cleary's etched words.

Rolle fished from the afterdeck. Off Stuart, he landed a kingfish, and they turned into the first cove they saw for dinner, anchoring against a mud bank lined with flowering bushes and tall cedars. Rolle broiled the kingfish on the foredeck and brought cold bottles of German beer from the landing craft's cooler to the boxed-in water tank, where they sat with their backs against the cabin's forward window. It was North's favorite meal, but he nibbled absently and poked his fork around. He couldn't take his eyes off the whaler, which the Coast Guard had placed stern to bow on the long expanse of deck. His best friend had spent the last eight days of his life on that piece of fiberglass, withered by burning sun, drifting some four hundred miles, placing his trust in fallen saints.

Something at the edge of his vision lifted North from his dark thoughts. Something incongruous. He stepped over to the boat where a piece of red-painted wood had been partially hidden by the whaler's hull. Moving closer, he saw the red piece had been screwed to the inside of the transom. Rolle came over, curious.

"Isn't that a 'Cleary paddle?'" North said.

Rolle nodded. They both recognized the paddle as coming from the battery compartment.

"What's it doing there?"

"Who knows? Maybe the Coast Guard found it and put it there for safekeeping."

"Sid, the Coast Guard wouldn't have *screwed* it onto the transom just to keep it safe."

"It do not make a whole lot of sense, my mon. No matter how you look at it."

"I think it does." North smiled for the first time this week. "We use those red paddles on our boats to indicate which battery needs charging. Or which is *being* charged. Right?"

"Well there's only one battery in a whaler," said Rolle. "That paddle means *the transom* is in charge. As if Jack was delirious and trying to charge the transom instead of the batteries. . . !" Rolle's face lit up. "You mean that *is* his cryptogram?"

"Of course! Jack was charging T. Ransom—not the batteries. He's telling us that *'Transom is in charge!'* Why else would he have etched into the seat the fact that there *is* a message here for us to look for? Why else would he have screwed the paddle into the transom so it couldn't fall off?"

Rolle pondered that. "The only tool aboard was a screwdriver. It must have taken him days to work a hole in the paddle, screw it into the transom, and carve a message."

"He wasn't taking any chances."

Rolle's eyes grew serious as he imagined Cleary's final days fending off thirst and fear and exhaustion to deliver this hidden message. "I was dead wrong about him, Grant. He had more guts, more loyalty than I gave him credit for." He lowered his voice, and added, "More guts than Sidney Rolle."

North had been interpreting Cleary cryptograms for decades, and he was certain of its meaning. But why did North need to be told that Ransom was in charge when he already suspected it? The only conceivable answer: *Because Jelly Belly had confirmed to him that it was true.*

"Jack knew me better than I know myself," he said to Rolle. "He didn't want Coby's murderers to go unpunished, but he knew I wouldn't move against Marianne's father unless I had positive proof of his complicity."

"And now? He's still Marianne's father."

"The hell with that." North thought for a moment, and came to an irreversible decision. "Let's go get them both. Ransom and St. Gregory."

"Sure," said Rolle. "But how?"

They finished their meal in silence, separately devising battle plans in their minds. Along the shore of the cove, gnarled cedars as imperious as any human tyrant vanquished pine shoots and lesser plants in their quiet expansion. The raucous voices of spider monkeys surprised them, and the western side of the Florida Straits sounded as foreign to North as it was to Rolle. They entered each other's thoughts, digesting the events of the past year in the light of Ransom's complicity.

"'Transom in charge' explains the Cleary enigma," said Rolle. "First Ransom refuses the permits hoping we'll go home before we penetrate his secrets. When that doesn't work, he gives us permission to operate so he can keep watch on us, to make sure we don't find out that he himself is in charge of piracy, smuggling, and God knows what else."

"When we were in jail, Coby already was dead," said North in a low voice. "She was killed by St. Gregory, condoned by Ransom."

"So how do we grab them without gettin' ourselves killed? The state you're in . . . Jesus, Grant, no suicide mission!"

"The only suicides I'm interested in are theirs. We're not going back to the Island yet. We're going to Miami."

North ascended inside to the wheelhouse, radioed WOM, and placed a phone call to a number Rolle didn't recognize. He asked the voice that answered for directions to their warehouse on the Miami River. They plowed the LCM southward, Rolle piloting and avoiding the inland waterway with its armadas of pleasure craft and countless bridges to be opened. Night came with a half moon rising off the land, but North remained on deck, preferring it out here with Coby. He sat with his legs over the square ramp, the wreath in his lap, looking down at the bioluminescent foam. Coby used to sit like this watching for dolphins who sometimes paced the vessel at the foam of the bow.

At least Cleary left a body to bury. At that thought, North's damaged intuition made a last vain cry for Coby being alive: *No body, no death!* Parents of soldiers cling to notions like that when their sons are lost in combat. He took a deep breath of sea air and told himself it was time to abandon futile feelings, like the pulse of an island beating in the bloodstream of a man, or like his daughter's resurrection. He pulled the first rose from the wreath, remembered Coby at age one, and cast it into the sea, repeating the ritual through each year of her life until the eighteenth. At the last rose he lingered for a moment under the starlight. The molecules at the base of the petals released their bonds reluctantly, and flowed on the wind like yellow hair until they merged with the luminous waves.

At midnight the lights of Lauderdale dimmed the stars, and it was North's turn at the wheel. A breeze brought the smell of brine. High in the poop, he felt the gigantic power of the Atlantic, and knew that the oceans far from the West Indies would be the only sanctuary left to him after his private war was over. He loved Marianne, but his feelings for her were dulled by his torment and by his desperate logic. She would never accept what he was planning now. If he told her, she would warn her father; if he did not, she would resent him for the rest of her life.

As he steered he made order out of entropy, creating harmony from the flute sounds of the diesels and the cymbals of the steel hull striking the waves. A tranquil Brahms came first, but the wind picked up and amplified it into a raucous Bach of crashing mirrors. When your life smashes into shards of glass, he told himself, you've got to substitute something else, something like vengeance. Or else the jagged fragments of memory will slash you to pieces.

He revved the engines, synching one with the other, and the LCM reared her bow, rushing into the night. He felt himself plunging headlong into vengeance as fiercely as had his ancestors on the bridge over the River Drina. For centuries the old country had been the scene of atrocities committed by the Yugo, or southern,

Slavs who revenged themselves against the Turks. Captured soldiers on both sides were impaled on sharpened saplings from anus to shoulder, the stake pounded in carefully to miss heart and lungs so their screams would last the night. Propped against the staging above the milkstone bridge, they became living gargoyles for all to see.

Vengeance like that was new to North. Yet it flowed to him as exquisitely and naturally as it had to his forebears, becoming the only antidote for the fire that raged within him. Nothing but revenge could satisfy him now. The Drina tortures had ceased long ago, but for him the milkstone bridge still dripped blood and venom.

55 *Miami Hypermarket*

LITTLE HAVANA. Deep-throated engines and the mournful sounds of foghorns fused with electrically amplified warnings in Spanish as North and Rolle weaved between traffic on the Miami River and docked before a warehouse.

Inside, a grungy crew worked forklift trucks or climbed twenty-foot steel racks to retrieve weapons or ammunition. Rock music played from a radio, and once in a while one of the workers would roll a little, hinting at dance steps. A man with a greasy red bandana around his head and a nickel-plated Colt strapped to his thigh grinned at them. Another character, with hair as long as Marianne's, had a knife strapped to his lower leg scuba-style, except that it was big as a bolo. Belts of machine-gun ammo crossed his chest like a general in the Mexican revolution. Cleary would have loved it: these were the salesmen.

Mr. Novac, the proprietor Jo had told North about, ushered them into his office wearing a Slavic solemnity on his face. *"Hladno je danas, zar ne? Kako ste, Doktor Severe?"* he said, and from his accent North knew he was a Serb.

Jo had told him that Novac was arming both the Croatians and the Serbians for their next struggle, but he seemed to harbor only feelings of brotherhood. *"Dobro, hvala,"* North answered to

Novac's rather involved "How do you do?"

Novac stood with his stomach bulging and both thumbs stuck into his Eisenhower jacket, looking more like a veteran supply sergeant than the boss of this three acres of high technology. In the old days Novac had peddled Kalashnikov assault rifles and Saturday-night specials, but now in his huge warehouse he carried everything from cannons to rockets. Jo, who had met Novac years ago while doing a story on the arms buildup in the Caribbean, had told her brother she wouldn't be surprised to find a "Little Boy" stashed in the back room. Novac had that Slavic zest for immortality and sudden death, and seemed to be pursuing them both with an absolute absence of morality. Yet he was exceedingly cordial.

"They call me *Gotov*." He said in Serbo-Croatian, and North got the joke of his nickname: *Gotov* meant Ready; *Novac* meant Money.

North knew he was being tested, so he said in Novac's language that he had come "to buy artillery to fire a mile or two from a reasonably stable boat."

Satisfied that he was dealing with an authentic *zemljak*, or countryman, Novac switched to English, the language of warfare technology. "You say you want artillery to blow up . . . something on the water, from a long distance? Three kilometers or so? None of my business why or where, but I take it you're going to fire from. . . that?" He waved an arm at the window, through which the LCM *Half Fast* could be seen at the pier.

"Da" came to North, but he said, "Yes," thinking he was lucky to find a Slavic arms merchant in Miami. Dealers don't deal cannons to just anybody.

Novac pondered the problem of firing from an unstable platform and said with a certain intimacy, as though discussing a sex object, "What you really oughta have is an AAWS-M missile."

"Anti-armor weapons system?"

"Right. We got a proto here. Only one. This baby's got enough explosive power to destroy a tank, yet she's light enough to be carried by one man. She was used for the first time in Iraq. An air-cooled mid-infrared focal-plane array seeker in the missile nose. In-flight imagery passed by fiber-optic cable to the gunner's command and launch unit. Laser-beam rider. Aim her anywhere near the target and she'll track automatically to impact."

"What's wrong with . . . her?"

"*Gotov novac* is what's wrong," said Ready Money seriously. "I gotta have a hundred and fifty Gs for her. I got customers who buy prototypes so they can build more of them themselves. And this is the only one we're likely to get in for a while."

North glanced at Rolle, and said, "I don't think the shareholders would go for that."

The guy with the bandana wandered over. "How about a British Claribel? Uses Doppler techniques to tell you where shots are coming from." He spoke with an inner-city accent that said he was equally fluent in Spanish.

"We don't expect anybody to shoot back."

"Well, we got a shithouse full of Uzis, Haley & Weller riot guns, fléschette cartridges, AK-47s, CS grenades, Smith & Wesson fog-smoke generators, Striker automatic shotguns. . . . I don't want no details of your game, of course, but gimme a hint of the parameters."

Novac interrupted to introduce them. "Dr. North, this is my son-in-law, Melchior Marín." Novac chuckled. "He feels his, ah, 'uniform' adds authenticity." He turned to Marín. "Dr. North was in armor during the war. He wants something effective for a range of three or four kilometers—to be used at sea."

Marín glanced out the window and said, "Three or four klicks? Wow! A vessel on the water ain't exactly stable like a tank, you know."

Novac led North and Rolle into the main body of the enormous warehouse, where he motioned toward the heavily-ladened steel shelving that soared as high as the quonset roof. "Feel free to look around."

Marín and at least a half-dozen other salesmen were coming and going from one buyer to another. They were acting their roles in stringy hair, Pancho Villa mustaches, camouflage fatigues, and weapons worn like ornaments. Their customers, short Hispanic men in dark suits, spoke softly in South American accents.

Exploring the medley was like groping down a ten-page menu.

Hot hors d'oeuvres included hand guns, automatic rifles, revolving-drum shotguns, bazookas, mortars, rockets, cannons, and hundreds of crates of ammunition. There were salads of flak jackets, fatigues, berets in various colors, bulletproof vests, combat boots, cartridge belts, canteens, and olive-drab and khaki uniforms. For the main course you could have laser-guided missiles by LTV, or Teledyne Ryan Firebolts that cruise at Mach 4, or ramjet hypervelocity missiles. Chef Novac's choice for dessert was an MBB Penguin mine-hunter, which is a honey of a miniature robotic submarine equipped with camera and sonar, capable of demolishing anything on the ocean.

"I take it we're going to hoist the black flag and go after the bastards directly," Rolle whispered. "You sure you want to do this?"

"I'm sure," North said.

Novac left as Marín wandered over and said to North, "You goin' use an airborne spotter?"

"Yes."

Stroking his unctuous locks, Marín glanced around until he spotted Novac back in his office, then said in a conspirative voice, "Look fellas, forget about all these laser-fucking-directed missiles. The old man's got hypervelocity ramjets squirting out his asshole. Who needs 'em? What you want is the old reliable M40A2. That's a standard M206 one-oh-six-millimeter recoilless rifle with a 7.62-mm spotting machine gun mounted on top. You can buy the whole schmear for under ten Gs."

"Rifle?" said Rolle. "Our . . . *target* is rather large for a rifle."

Marín smiled condescendingly. "Tell him," he said to North.

"'Rifle' means only that the barrel is rifled," North said to Rolle. "It's really a recoilless cannon he's talking about. We used clusters of six of them aboard our tanks in Nam."

"Course, if your target has an engine," Marín said, warming to his subject, "you could use a heat-seeker like a Stinger for under a hundred gees. But you got a spotter, so who needs the high-tech shit?"

"You're right," said North. High tech was fine for going to the moon, but he wanted something simple and reliable. The weapon

Marín recommended was a compromise between the fire power of a tank and lack of recoil. "But the round is so short. Maybe we should have a 90-mm tank cannon."

"A 90-mm would bounce the boat and screw up the second shot. To say nothing of the forty-foot muzzle blast that might give you away. Don't worry about the round being too short. It comes with a 7.62-mm machine gun attached to the barrel. Just fire tracers until you get the range and your air guy says 'fire.' You can't miss."

"From where? Two miles? Three?"

Marín held up a finger, putting them on hold, and led them into the office where he edged toward a filing cabinet between his father-in-law and a dumpster of grenades. He emerged with a field manual on the recoilless weapon, opened it to the appropriate page, and said, "Range is seventy-seven hundred meters—or seven point seven klicks—almost five miles. But I'd get closer, no more than three klicks to be really effective. Even more important than distance is to pick a calm day for that moving platform of yours."

North caught Novac's eye and said to them both, "The hell with the machine gun. Trajectories would be too dissimilar, and 7.62-mm fire could kill someone other than the target. I'd rather use shells with marker-dye."

"*Oprezan*, aren't you?" Novac said, glancing at the others and translating, "Cautious." His dark face broke into a smile. "We can make some up. Right, Mel? What kind of ammo, *Doktor*? And how many?"

"Twenty markers shells and four incendiaries, Howitzer type," North said. "Plus the cannon, mount, and rangefinder. And a flak jacket for my friend here."

Hearing that, Rolle shot North a curious look.

"The jacket," said Marín. "You want bioengineered spider silk? State of the art—ten times stronger than steel. Two grand each."

"No."

"For fifty bucks you can buy a 'second-chance' jacket made of DuPont Kevlar. They'll stop secondary fragments or a pistol round, but not AR fire."

"We'll take one."

"Just one?"

"One."

Novac, who had been scribbling on his clipboard, peered at North over his half-glasses. "Okay Doktor Severe. Anything for a *zemljak*!" Fingering his adding machine, he said, "That'll be thirteen thousand six hundred and fifty bucks for the M-forty-A-one, which is the cannon, the M-seventy-nine mount, the handheld rangefinder, the four live shells, and the twenty dye jobs. Cash, of course; we don't keep very good records." He grinned. "I'll throw in the jacket and the manual. What color marker dye? Something that'll show up on the water, I suppose. Red, yellow—?"

"Orange," said North.

"Orange is for trees and foliage."

"Make it orange anyway."

After they paid, North and Rolle shook hands with Novac, walked out the dockside door, and climbed aboard the LCM, while Marín and his helpers assembled the marker shells. Rolle plugged an extension cord into the a.c. shore outlet for a power saw he removed from a locker, and started toward the stacks of plywood in the hold.

"What are you doing, Sid?"

"I've got it all figured out so the Coast Guard won't find this stuff."

"They don't check going *out*," said North.

"They might with me aboard." Rolle made a caricature of a smile. "They think all us darkies are druggies because we been so victimized by you honky slumlords."

Rolle sawed large rectangles out of the centers of two stacks of plywood sheets piled end to end, and North helped him sandwich the weapons and shells inside. They rebanded the plywood, and cast off with North at the wheel.

On the Miami River, the most-chaotic waterway of the hemisphere, it helps to have an armor commander at the helm, for the LCM drives like a tank. Its twin screws allow you to turn on a dime by backing one engine while shifting the other forward. North weaved around Haitian freighters piled high with bicycles, old tires, and mattresses; barges carrying used cars to Central America; floating lumber, animal corpses, and various slimy things of plastic. Halfway to the Atlantic, he pulled up to a marina where they bought five thousand feet of half-inch manila line, two heavy anchors, and a gasoline-engine powered winch with a huge drum. After stowing the equipment, they continued their serpentine route through the garbage of the river.

At last the expanse of uncluttered ocean opened before them like a gigantic field of wheat, and the waves fell in soft wings behind the square bow. Stratus clouds parted and flooded the wheel-house with a majestic light.

Rolle broke the silence. "You gonna tell Marianne you're gunning for her father, or just that we're out to convert St. Gregory into dog food?"

"Marianne doesn't trust Ransom any more than we do," North whispered, realizing as he spoke that it was a prayer, not a fact. How could he tell Marianne he loved her but wanted to retaliate against her father? He might as well say, *Here's a little love and no more!* Love to Marianne was an ardent ship that harbored no "buts," that sailed unbounded if it sailed at all.

Rolle shrugged. "Daughters always side with their fathers."

North thought about his impending marriage and contemplated that strange winding line between respect and love, between compulsion and a man's integrity. What would the normal response be for someone in his position? What would Cleary do? And he could hear Cleary saying, as he'd said after the hurricane, "Leave, Grant. Take Marianne on the first plane to someplace where you might want to start a new life."

Rejecting Cleary's advice from the grave, he turned to Rolle with the essence of his plan. "Maybe Marianne won't side with her father. Not if we let him live, but deprive him of what means just as much to him as his life."

"His money?"

"And his mansion."

56 *Bonfire at Scuba Beach*

NEVER HAD MARIANNE seen North so preoccupied, so intensely elsewhere. At the dock she watched him confront the handful of employees who had arrived on the jollyboat. Less than twenty men out of the usual fifty had shown up for work. In the light of a dreary March sun, the crags of North's face were angled in unfamiliar lines that made him look older. The stubble on his chin had lost its color and the whites of his eyes glistened like ice. He was glaring at Cuda, Purple, and Lionel Sweeting.

"What the hell are you guys doing here? You know I don't hire smugglers." He spoke from under a heavy burden, each word an effort.

"You ain't got no evidence ta call us smugglers, Mr. Grant," said Cuda.

Rolle tried to lighten things. "It like de cat and de canary, Cuda. He don't need no sworn testimony from de birds to interpret blood and feathers."

"Wha . . . ?" said Purple.

"You fire us, man," Sweeting said with uncharacteristic hostility, "and no one'll work here."

The other workers were nodding agreement, gaining strength from exchanged glances. Marianne realized they were seeking excuses to leave the Island. Cyril's suicide and the belief that Coby had been killed had shaken the villagers, and they were afraid of what North might do. Didn't he know that?

"These three are fired," North said to the crowd. "The rest of you can work if you want, or go home."

In other times, Marianne thought, North would have convinced the men to stay, told them they were needed to harvest the seaweed and feed the shrimp. He would have allayed their fears and appealed to their pride.

Most of the workers cast their eyes to the deckboards and climbed slowly back into the jollyboat where Cuda, Sweeting, and Purple sat defiant. Six men remained on the dock, among them Razor, devoid of his black coral and gold, and cousin Rahming in beard and sweater. The Rastafarian took quick glances at the sky as if anxious to return to his home planet. But Razor rested a foot on a piling and said, "Now see here, Doctuh Nort, if me an' jus' dese chaps are goin' ta keep all dese shrimp alive, we needs more *pay*—"

"Get back in the boat, Razor. You too, Louie."

Shark, who was one of the few still employed, revved the engine.

"But—"

"That's all there is to it," North said.

After the jollyboat left, North trudged toward the seafarm with the four men, hardly noticing Marianne who hurried to keep up with him.

"Freud was right," she said. "The opposite of love is not hate. It's indifference."

North didn't respond. Out on the flats, the overcast sun cast broad shadows over wide swells that rolled in toward the corrals. The mosaic of reddish-brown seaweed looked like angled squares of Martian farmland transposed onto the sea.

"Now that Father has given permission," she said as they arrived at the seaweed-drying racks, "why are you getting rid of your workers? How can you keep two million shrimp alive with only Andy, Rolle, Shark, and these four men?"

"Seven men are enough to feed the shrimp."

"Grant, what's going on? I've never seen you like this."

He sank back into silence and looked out toward the corrals, ragged and red. The ocean rollers had entered the barriers and were mounding the floating seaweed to look like rows of graves.

AT LUNCH the next day Jo and Marianne approached North while he was poking listlessly at his food. "It's over now, Grant," Jo said. "You're not helping the rest of us—or yourself—by becoming sullen."

"It's *not* over."

"What do you mean?"

A sudden memory of when he first came to the Island, a fleeting figment brushed his mind. The recurring sensation left him with a dreamy feeling, not at all unpleasant, and in an instant it was gone. "I mean . . . we still have the Island," he said obscurely.

Rolle came over with a letter he'd gotten at the village post office. It was from Sterling Hanna, and he read it aloud. The case against him had been dropped. Ransom had fired and deported Magistrate Margaret Amin for dishonesty after discovering she had been pocketing portions of enormous bail deposits paid in cash by indicted drug smugglers. Rolle's bail of thirty thousand dollars had been returned out of the fifty thousand Cleary had paid to the magistrate. It happened to be precisely the same amount as Hanna's legal fee. Hanna had ended the letter by congratulating them on having won their case.

"Who gives a shit," Rolle said. "Things are still broken in the Bahamas." But his grin betrayed his relief.

North nodded as though it were of no consequence.

Jo said, "I think we ought to get together and talk over what we're going to do."

"About what?" said Andy.

"About everything. About the seafarm, about where we're headed."

"Good idea," said Marianne.

"Let's do it away from the east end where the workers might hear us," Rolle said. He had told Shark and the other four remaining workers they could work a few hours overtime each evening. "Scuba

Beach—at sundown. Coming Grant?"

JO AND MARIANNE arrived first at the rocky flukes of west beach.

"The Grant North I thought I knew," began Marianne, "would rather talk than fight, reason instead of use force. What's happening to him?"

"Tragedy changes people," said Jo. "I guess I haven't known my brother all his life without realizing he's planning something—to solve the problem as he sees it."

Rolle and Andy came up wearing tails of gold dust against the setting sun. "Planning something?" said Rolle.

"Revenge," said Marianne with an expression of revulsion.

Rolle's steady gaze said nothing of the 106-mm recoilless cannon hidden inside the bundles of plywood on the LCM.

Jo shrugged. "I've been wanting to leave and pick up my life, but I'm worried about Grant, about all of you."

The others leaned against the coral boulders or knelt on the sand, uncomfortable, leaderless. Rolle lit a pile of driftwood he and Andy had gathered, and the flames shot into the darkening sky.

"Grant can take shit like permit problems and Knowles being killed," Jo said. "But when it comes to Coby and Cleary, that's something else. He's at the break point."

Jo didn't look good herself. For days now whenever anyone mentioned Coby, tears welled in her eyes. It was March already, the bleak month, and in Chicago the snow would be turning to slush. It had been a full year since the murders on the LCM.

Fidgeting with the fire, Rolle listened more intently than he let on. Marianne was sitting on the sand, feeling hypnotized by the wild flames, listening to the breeze and the sparks it brought. Her hair, charged by the static electricity in the night wind, wouldn't stay slung over one shoulder.

"We've got to stop him from doing something terrible," Jo said.

The brief twilight had ended and the rising moon burned orange through gray haze as if to compete with the bonfire. A rustling came from behind them, not the wind.

"You can't stop me," North said. His sudden appearance gave him an alien quality, like an exhausted space traveler who had wandered into an unfamiliar dimension. Bareheaded, wearing a white shirt, he seemed to give off light.

Marianne stood with her eyes lowered. The year-long search for Coby had pressed upon them all like a terminal disease. Now they were free of it and everyone but Marianne started talking at once.

"Grant," said Jo. "I hope you know you can't take on the whole Defence Force. . . ."

North positioned himself aside a coral formation that jutted chest high and separated him from the others by a short stretch of beach. Luminous in the dark, he spoke in a one-two-three monotone that let you feel his controlled rage. "We know the P.M. directs St. Gregory who ordered Coby's death. We know, according to Hanna and the opposition, that the P.M. has something like fifty million stashed away. Drug money. He doesn't travel much, so his wealth is mostly likely in cash, probably hidden in his mansion. Money and his *things* are what the P.M. values most in life. I mean to deprive him of them."

North's avoidance of the name "Ransom" did nothing to lessen the impact on Marianne, who looked ready to cry. He focused not on Marianne but on a point in space an inch beyond the eyes of his captive audience, directly into their skulls. "We've got a long-range cannon on the LCM. Jo will act as spotter in her Cessna. When Ransom and his colleagues are having one of their Thursday-night meetings at his mansion, Sidney will go there dressed as a cop to announce over a loudspeaker that a bomb will go off and that they'll have to get out."

Jo looked bitter, most likely considering whether to stay and be part of her brother's plan.

"Where's Sidney gonna get a cop uniform?" Andy asked.

"Rolle's got more relatives than a rabbit. Surely one of them is a cop."

Rolle smiled.

North allowed no further levity. He returned to commanding, reducing his closest friends to henchmen, allowing no dissention, no argument, making it clear from his tone that you never make a threat you don't intend to carry out. They could do nothing short of breaking off completely and going home.

"Buy the uniform from someone, Sid, so you don't have to return it." In a laconic voice, he discussed weather contingencies, radio frequencies, altering the identification numbers on Jo's Cessna, anchoring the LCM in deep water. Details unraveled from his tongue, baring layer after layer of anguish.

At last he came to the raw core. "Andy and I will be offshore in the *Half Fast.* We'll fire markers, and when everyone's out of the mansion, we'll—"

Marianne's face, desperate with despair, was on the edge of some violent emotion. She ran toward North. "Grant, you can't be serious! That's my *father* you're talking about. That's the house I *live* in . . . !"

"We'll fire a live shell," he said.

The group fell silent. The high cheekbones of Marianne's dusky face gave her protest a hopeless, Indian-like nobility. How could the man she would marry conceive of such a plan? No matter how culpable her father, no matter how much pain Grant suffered over Coby's death, nothing would be remedied by vengeance. The smoke of the bonfire thickened, dismal and diffuse, concealing the Islanders from the stars, and from each other.

"When are you going to *commit* this act?" she asked him through the smoke, fighting for control.

"Early in the morning after his 'board meeting.' Two and a half days from now."

The smoke, sweet with burning driftwood, filled the shadows with suspended conversation. Marianne was reduced to a silhouette, the light from the fire spilling out around the wind-blown strands of her hair. She rose, sobbing softly, and faded into the darkness up the rocky beach. Rain fell in a soft drizzle, smoking the bonfire.

Infected with North's fury, Rolle moved out of the smoke and said, "I've got only one question. Why do it with the mansion empty?"

"*Sidney,* for godsake!" said Jo. "This is Marianne's *father,* the Prime Minister!"

North's voice, clear and decisive, penetrated the near darkness. "She's right, Sid. Besides, if we kill the bastard, he'll feel pain only briefly. If we take his money away from him, he'll suffer for the rest of his life."

"Sure." said Rolle. "But remember this—if we don't kill them, we get to play the revenge game exactly once. After that, it's their turn."

IN THE VILLA that night Marianne lay curled into herself on the bed, facing away from North and watching a diffuse moon through the wall of glass. It was the kind of abysmal night when doubt haunts even loyal disciples, when you dread the man you love, and disarm your circular calculations only with exhaustion. North's prolonged silences, his brooding seemed to transcend normal grief over Coby's death. She resented his and Rolle's obsession with their Plan, their surreptitious nodding at each other. The two had grown closer since Cleary's death, and had entered a world where compulsion and clear thinking, paranoia and mental health no longer were opposites. No matter what her father may have done, she couldn't leave the decision of his life or death to Sidney Rolle. Marianne knew the male Bahamian mind too well for that.

She got up and went to the bathroom. In the mirror her face appeared unfamiliar, like the mask the Greeks wore in their plays. Her complexion was too dark, her lips too red, her eyes too hollow, her stare too intractable, her hair too unruly. Impulsively she took a scissors from the cabinet and cut a foot off of her hair, leaving it bobbed in a pageboy, brash and uncluttered—better to hear the black sounds within her heart.

When she returned to the bedroom, North was absently petting Sugar and Spice. The yellow bedlight cast long shadows against the watery black window.

"What did you do to your hair? Why . . . ? He looked disappointed.

"Maybe I'm changing too."

She sat on the bed holding her knees to her body with both arms like a defenseless child. But there was nothing childish about her look. "You seem to love cats, dogs, and octopi, but not people."

He sat up as if he'd been listening not to her but to the rain. "I was dreaming of Coby. She was telling me . . . something."

She knew him well enough to know that his feelings were escaping into his dreams, the only realm open to them where he could cling to irrational hopes for his daughter. Or was it simple revenge? Jo intimated he had a higher purpose. Does anyone ever understand the dimensions of another's thoughts? Grant, what are you really like inside your private place, your impregnable, armored skull where you create your lavish intuitions? But she said, "Grant, you can't *do* this thing. What if you kill someone?"

"I'm not going to kill your father, Marianne, though God knows he deserves it. He loves his possessions more than people, more even than he loves you. I want to destroy that revolting palace of his and all his opulent garbage. I want him to stand in his meadow and watch his mansion burn and his paintings burn and his money burn, and realize that no matter what he does he can never get them back."

She was close to tears. "Doesn't it bother you that you're committing a crime? You think two wrongs make a right?"

"Sometimes the only way to get justice is to break the law. The Prime Minister is about to learn that the outside world doesn't hold him in quivering reverence like all you Bahamians."

She choked back here tears. "When I offer my help, I'm a woman, but when I oppose you I'm a Bahamian."

"Don't deny the facts. Everything I said about your father is true. The only difference between Charles Ransom and Saddam Hussein is the size of his country, not his impact on his own population, or the country next door. Bahamian drugs do more damage than Scud missiles."

His words hurt her ears, for she was cursed by seeing both sides of every argument. She had been aware for some time that her father was involved in something pernicious, and perhaps Grant was right when he said it had to do with drugs. Maybe her father did deserve to lose his wealth, but not like *this!* Yellow light from the lamp blazed the body of the man to whom she had pledged her devotion, and his strength gave her a hope that outpaced rationality.

"What about us?" she said quietly.

"We'll talk about it afterwards."

She found utterly devastating his avoidance of her eyes, whose every movement he once had delighted in watching. She felt a sudden urge, and if at this moment she had crack, she'd smoke it to gain the feeling of being in control over what was happening. But she fought back the impulse and the tears, and came to a decision.

"Look at me," she said.

He looked at her, and she saw him watching the turbulence of her lips. Her voice broke but when the words came they fell hard as steel.

"I'm going to Nassau the day you leave in your barge, to confront my father. And to make sure Sidney Rolle clears the people out of the house before you start your bombardment. Before I go, I'll tell Jo and Sid that I'll be in the house with the rest of them. I won't tell Father about your . . . artillery. But if it's your intention—or Sidney's—to kill my father and his friends, then understand one thing."

His eyes met hers strangely as though he'd never seen her before, and silently they asked what she meant.

"That you'll be killing me too," she said.

57 *Board Meeting*

WHEN the speeding Ferrari skidded to a halt before the guard post, the two sentries had the spotlights on and their 9-mm SMGs clicked off safety before they saw it was Marianne. Abandoning the car at the gate, she sped past them without breaking stride. Ransom was wary of car-bombs, and no vehicle was allowed closer without an exhausting search. She ran in a straight line a half-mile across the maddening curves of the drive, opened the front door with her key, and plunged across an immensity of carpet to the tusk-flanked entrance of the conference room.

Wright, the burly bodyguard, stopped her. "No one's allowed inside, Miss Marianne, not even you."

She might be able to wrench past him and jerk open one of the heavy doors and yell, *Get out of the house; it's going to blow up!* But she resisted the urge. She trusted North not to start the bombardment until morning—and only after everyone was out of the house. Her urgency had a different target. She wanted to ask her father why he retained as the captain of the MOP a known pirate, Coby's murderer.

Instead she settled into a massive chair near the fireplace where she and Grant had welcomed in the new year, and waited. The heads of decapitated animals, the sculptures of dead monarchs, the rococo paintings, the imbui wood imported from Brazil—the heavy opulence turned her stomach. If her father had paid for this needless glut with drug money, he deserved to see it blown to hell. Her feelings were in a whirlpool, her decision imprisoned like the voice in the convoluted corridors of a conch shell.

An hour passed and the double doors swung open. Through a cloud of smoke she could see the conference table: papers awry, ashtrays full, the conferees with jackets off, ties loosened. They were taking a break to make phone calls, go to the bathroom, or retrieve papers from their guest rooms where they would stay the night. Benjamin Franklin, in a rumpled pinstriped suit, left the room carrying an overnight bag. He must have arrived as the meeting started and had no time to take it to his room.

"Marianne!" Ransom said when he spotted her waiting in the library. "What a nice surprise. You cut your hair."

She jumped up. "Father, we've got to talk!"

"Like that, is it? It'll be a couple of hours. . . . It can wait that long, can't it?"

"No!" But she knew she had to talk to him at length, and alone. "Oh, I suppose so."

He did an abrupt aboutface into the conference room.

Marianne sat where she wouldn't be seen easily by the conferees, beneath a blood-red oil painting of some nineteenth-century war. It seemed an appropriate place from which to study her father's emissaries to the people, ripe with their intrigues and their secrets. Cora Carstairs, carrying her globular body with characteristic energy, reclaimed her place at the table. Benjamin Franklin, the yellowish spineless conformist, returned followed by Malcolm Pyfrom, the one Marianne liked the most, her "Uncle Mal." She hadn't seen him for some time and was appalled that his mottled and papery skin looked even thinner than usual.

As she expected the doors to close, Wilson and another man came striding down the sea of carpet. Eyes straight ahead, his bearing military, the man was a Goliath next to the diminutive Wilson, and then she saw who it was. Captain St. Gregory.

The doors closed abruptly with a faint whoosh, as though compressing the air inside the room. She recalled an adage: individual men could become saints, but collective men are always corrupt.

THE ROOM was airless and sad, filled with the intimidators and the intimidated. At the head of the table Ransom frowned, saying nothing, reserving his enmity for St. Gregory. The Defender captain, impeccably dressed in his white uniform, dominated one long side of the table. Edged by the light of the chandelier, the face above the captain's beard made you think of a fortress ready for siege.

The gasoline rumor of a year ago, Marianne's pirate story, and Ambassador Armitage, who had called the Prime Minister from the hospital to tell him what the Americans suspected, had deposed any lingering doubt in the minds of the conferees. The Defender captain had been—and still was—conducting a reign of terror. The fact that Ransom and colleagues themselves had birthed this malignity only made things worse, and had culminated in a phone conversation last night between Ransom and the vice-premier of Cuba.

Armed with the result of that conversation, Ransom opened the proceedings. "Captain St. Gregory," he said.

"Yes, sir."

Malcolm Pyfrom glanced at the chandelier above the Defender officer as if willing it to fall.

"Two years ago, as you know," said Ransom, "this board decided to stop taking commissions from drug runners, an activity we had unwisely instituted in an attempt to control narcotics in the Bahamas. We have evidence that *you* are still in the drug business." Ransom chose his next words carefully. "And now, you son of a bitch, you're into *piracy!*" There would be no holds barred tonight.

The parody of a smile faded from St. Gregory's eyes, replaced by a look of surprise. "It takes a cluttered mind to undertake the analysis of the obvious," said the Defender, an aristocrat from Bay Street in the face of Ransom's disintegration into a Chicago street fighter. "Where did you get this so-called 'evidence?'"

"You deny it?" Ransom said.

Benjamin Franklin, smiling reasonably, said, "Now captain, at least abandon these . . . piracies. We might, that is, my colleagues here might look the other way now and then if you took a commission or two." He glanced around the table nervously, saw only stony faces, and started to ramble. "I'm not speaking for them, you understand . . . after all, they have their own ideas about this, as I know you realize, but my God—"

At one piercing look from St. Gregory, Franklin shut up and mopped his forehead with a handkerchief.

Ignoring Franklin, St. Gregory answered the Prime Minister. "Why should I deny it? Remember those Cuban pals you disowned back when you decided you had all the drug money you could spend? You *can* remember two years back?"

"Are you trying to say you're still working with the Cubans?" Pyfrom said.

A flame came to St. Gregory's eyes, hot as fire. He dropped his patrician manner, hardening his voice. "Yes, Mr. Deputy. Why do you think the Cuban smugglers have left you alone? *Because of me!* That's why. I alone have been taking the risk." He glanced toward Franklin. "Unless you include this whining turd who helped me with a few radio transmissions."

Benjamin Franklin, shirt and tie drenched in sweat, was waging his head back and forth. His right eye kept twitching but it was glazed, like the living dead.

"Benjamin. . . ?" Ransom asked.

"Listen, Charles," said Franklin, avoiding St. Gregory's eyes, "he's talking about a time right after we decided to get out of the business. I transmitted a couple of messages for him. He intimidated me. I thought it was . . . well, his way of tapering off. Afterwards he stopped bothering me, so I thought he'd quit like the rest of us."

Ransom believed his explanation. Franklin would be too frightened to lie to him in St. Gregory's presence.

Ignoring Franklin, who seemed to have dissolved into the varnish of the table, St. Gregory said, "The Cubans need transfer ships—motor vessels, pleasure craft. Just like always. Where the devil do you think they get them, at the Havana Yacht Club?"

"It's none of your fucking business where the Cubans get their boats," said Pyfrom. He hadn't used language like this in three decades. His voice, lowered by years of heavy drinking and the intensity of his feeling, resounded over the drumlike conference table and made heads swivel. "Your criminal activities put us all at risk—and for what? A lousy couple of hundred thousand bucks or whatever. You must be a millionaire many times over by now. Why don't you just quit?"

Just quit! mused Ransom. The words made it sound so easy. But you're never in it alone. Your lieutenants and *their* lieutenants all down the line grow accustomed to the big money. They don't *let* you quit. What was unique about his operation, what had saved him and Pyfrom and Franklin from a lifetime of corruption, was that they had apportioned most of the drug commissions to help addicts. He should have realized that their renouncement of further drug money had not been unanimous, and that they should not have allowed the captain to continue running a patrol boat.

St. Gregory rose slowly to his full stature. Turning a heavy chair around with one hand, he placed a foot on the upholstered seat, displaying the razor-sharp press of his trousers. "Do you for one moment believe that the American press will be any less forgiving of your activities just because you've been clean for a couple of years—?"

"Stop right there, mister," said Ransom. "You know those funds went for a good purp—"

"Don't give me that Robin Hood bullshit about helping the addicts! They *like* living in hovels with their rats and their hypodermics. If the Bahamian people can't kick their filthy habits, *they don't deserve to live!*"

Ransom jumped to his feet, his words like cannon balls. "No more, Captain! You will get your white ass out of the drug business!" Heads jerked toward him. If this wasn't the way a prime minister was supposed to talk, it nevertheless was the way you talked to a common criminal.

St. Gregory smiled in his predatory way. "And what if my white ass won't quit?"

Ransom lowered his voice almost to a whisper, enunciating each word. "First, you will find that you no longer have access to your Cuban friends. You ought to know there's no free enterprise in Cuba, that when you talk about smugglers in a communist state, you are talking about the government itself. Second, if you choose to do business with freelancers, we have been assured by the vice-chairman that our mutual assistance in your case will *not* take the form of legal process."

St. Gregory jerked his foot off the chair. "Are you threatening me?"

"Yes. I am threatening you. And when you're at sea, Captain, every time you see a Cuban MiG overhead, I want you to remember my threat."

St. Gregory looked at Ransom the way a taxidermist examines his work. He righted the chair, squared his shoulders, and saluted his commander-in-chief in a maneuver as smooth as sliding his gunboat alongside a dock. Turning on his heels, he marched out of the house.

THE MINUTE St. Gregory left, the room seemed to soften. The light from the chandelier grew warmer and a circle of silence spread across the room.

Cora Carstairs long had suspected some sort of shady activity, but these brawls, this animal behavior of men she thought she knew, were new to her. She could imagine Ransom at that decisive meeting two years ago: pale, gaunt, perhaps wearing something like the cream-white suit of his youth, eyes willfully myopic, voice trembling, as he told the others of Marianne's addiction. And none of them in their collective arrogance considering that their agenda for themselves was not St. Gregory's agenda for himself. Had she been a member of the inner circle from the beginning, she would have found some alternative to doing business with the sinister captain.

She flicked a hand, indicating that their past transgressions were of no consequence now. "How did all this happen?" she wanted to know.

In the back of the room Pyfrom opened the concealed lid of a credenza, revealing a liquor service. He poured himself a straight Scotch.

"Before we knew about the piracies," said Ransom in a weary monotone, "I went along with St. Gregory because I thought North might discover something of our past as he looked for his missing daughter. We simply refused to act on his project one way or the other, to dissuade him by bureaucratic inaction, as it were."

"And by more direct means, I might add," said Pyfrom. "It was St. Gregory's *provocateur*—William Symes—who tried to scare North off."

A head of state gone bad usually stays bad, thought Carstairs. Somosa, Trujillo, Papa Doc Duvalier, Noriega—these and countless others who raped their countries had one thing in common. They never quit. Charles *had* quit, only to live with the consequences.

"Apparently Dr. North doesn't scare easily," she said. "And apparently I was left in the dark as usual. Here toiled I, innocently trying to unravel the red tape so North could get his permits. Why didn't you let me know?"

"Because, Dame Cora," said Ransom, "you couldn't have pulled it off otherwise. North thought you were helping him. *You* thought you were helping him. And through you, we kept track of the tenacious scientist."

"It seems to me," said Franklin, recovering his statesman-like style, "that Captain St. Gregory is encumbered by a zealot's paucity of judgment. Every time he has sought to dissuade North and induce him to leave the country, it has backfired."

Pyfrom looked at Ransom accusingly. "You should have known he wouldn't go home with his daughter missing."

"Listen, you two," said Carstairs, "let's not pick pepper out of fly shit. The girl, Grant North, none of that matters anymore. The only thing that matters right now is what St. Gregory is likely to do to us. Or do you believe he's going to do nothing just because he saluted and clicked his heels?"

She twisted her bulk toward Ransom, keeping her voice low as if the captain were still in the room. "When I first met that man he only scared me. Now that I know him better he terrifies the livin' bejesus out of me. You look into those blazing eyes of his, you get voids, like he's seeing right through you. I got this gut feeling he's going to come after us."

"So do I," said Franklin, looking as if his carotid artery had become blocked.

Ransom refilled his pipe. Pyfrom got up and poured himself another Scotch, sipping it as he paced the room.

Carstairs said, "Maybe—just maybe—Charles, we ought to alert your buddies in the Cuban government *before* St. Gregory decides to retaliate. After all, he had Ambassador Armitage killed, didn't he?"

Franklin nodded his head.

Ransom shrugged. "Why wait for something to happen? Maybe we should give him to the Cubans first."

"Maybe we ought to give North to the Cubans too," Franklin said. "We can't have foreigners linking us to St. Gregory and to *pirates* for godsake! Let alone to our past . . ."

The air had soured from trepidation, lack of oxygen, and enough tobacco smoke to be immediately carcinogenic instead of taking the usual forty years. Pyfrom rose and flung open a window, letting the damp night air compete with the recycled air conditioning. He was drinking but was far from drunk.

"What have we become? Are we the super police who keep the secret police in check?" He focused his reptilian eyes directly on Ransom. "What is it about North you hate so much?"

"He's using my daughter. He's got an island full of dope. And I'm sick of foreigners in our country. I'll reduce the Family Islands to rubble before I see them in the hands of people like North!" He got up and slammed the window shut.

"He's got rights too," Pyfrom said.

"Nobody has rights in this country. Only obligations!"

"Pardon my ignorance, Charles," Carstairs broke in, "but why then did you all of a sudden grant Dr. North his permits?"

Ransom steepled his fingers, considering the question, deciding ultimately on the truth. "Because, if I did not, I would have lost Marianne forever."

"And now you're changing back again!" Pyfrom said. "Why? Because a corrupt magistrate couldn't put him away for you? Because he wants to marry Marianne?" His fractured voice rose an octave higher. "Or is it because he's white?"

"Yes, damn it! It's because he's white! Every time I trust a white man it turns out bad—like St. Gregory. I've spent a lifetime

shoving whites out of this country, and I don't want Marianne to marry another one of them."

"Charles, the man is a distinguished scientist," Pyfrom said. "God knows we need help in achieving self-sufficiency in food and energy. Without that we are a failed experiment in nationhood. We're nothing but a cocaine republic."

"We don't need his kind."

"Maybe we do. His science island could have taught our people new skills, elevated the country beyond tourism. Take a good look at our people, Charles. Lousy work habits, undereducation, addiction, the most expensive labor in the world—"

"So what?" said Ransom.

"So what happens to the country? Poverty as usual? Okay, we 'give' North to the Cubans. Why? For them to murder him? Is that the meaning of your euphemism, Charles?"

Malcom Pyfrom, who had been repressing these views for a long time, looked naked in his attack, like a chameleon who forgot how to change color. "You people think you're invincible. I suppose one day you'll 'give me' to someone too."

Violent arguments sometimes bring out the best in a man, sometimes the worst, but always the unexpected. Pyfrom seized a potted African violet from the windowsill and smashed it on the floor. For a horticultural hobbyist to do that was like a sculptor wrecking his statue. The crash of the pot became the crescendo of frustrations that had been building in him from his years under Ransom, a graduation from the passive antagonisms that once had driven him to blank out his mentor's photograph.

"All of you, listen carefully." Pyfrom shuffled awkwardly in the dirt of the spilled violets, searching for strong words that, instead, came out squeaky and mechanical. "If you ever try to 'give me to the Cubans'—I have arranged a retaliation that will survive my death. And ensure yours."

Carstairs's view of Pyfrom went back a long way, to Chicago where she'd regarded him as a sniveler. Although she agreed with his assessment of their country's problems, his new independence did nothing to change her view of his courage. She dangled a fresh cigarette from the corner of her mouth, lit it, and grinned.

"Malcolm, my whole life flashes before me when you frighten us like that. The way you pack genuine emotion into your threats penetrates the soul and reminds me of my God-fearing daddy with a switch in his hand."

Pyfrom clung to a belligerent silence. He finished his drink and gathered his papers while she talked.

"Malcolm belongs to an aer-o-plane club, don't let us forget," Dame Cora homilied, addressing the others as if he'd already left the room. "Maybe he plans to have a bomb dropped on our heads."

58 *Half-Castes*

THE DOUBLE DOORS opened between the vertical elephant tusks, venting enough tobacco smoke to vanquish a colony
of termites. Marianne looked at her watch. One in the morning.

In the portal stood her father, pipe in hand, imparting good-
nights in his deep public voice. Dame Cora and Benjamin Franklin
went to their rooms, as Marianne supposed Uncle Mal would have
done had he not left in a huff. A moment later her father came
toward her smiling, and she led him toward a private nook off the
library. The carrel was as far away as she could find from the
decapitated heads of the rare and beautiful African animals slaughtered by this man from whom she would try to learn the truth.

"What's it all about, Father? St. Gregory, pirates, drugs. Are
you involved?" Her total energy was concentrated in her eyes.

Ransom was bone tired of accusations, tired of explaining himself, but he knew from her look he could not put her off any
longer. "You've asked me that several times over the years."

"I know."

"Marianne, let's sit down," and he pressed her into a high-
backed chair, a solid Spanish monstrosity big enough for two. Drawing up another chair with an effort, he glanced around to make
sure Wilson or Wright or anyone else couldn't hear them.

"When the Cubans stopped being supplied by the Soviets, they had only one way to gain hard currency. They still had their MiGs, so they used them to chaperon drug shipments across the Caribbean to the States. We allowed them safe passage in return for not pushing their drugs in the Bahamas . . . and, I admit, for commissions." He sucked on his pipe and expelled a bluish veil through nose and mouth.

Marianne felt a cold sweat at the base of her neck. "If you were so motivated to keep the Bahamas pure, then why is the Plague still so epidemic here?"

"Because, Marianne, we quit. Two years ago. You remember what happened two years ago?"

She whispered. "That's when I . . . became addicted."

"Yes. I knew about it. I told Gérard, and he began to concentrate on addiction therapies, waiting for you to come to him."

The revelation made her love Geedee even more, but she would not be deterred. "How could you take *drug money* in the first place?"

"For someone who used to ingest cocaine into her body, you're being awfully pious, Marianne. The answer is that at the time it seemed a pragmatic solution to a lousy problem. How do you think REHAB got started?"

"Drug money?"

"Stop saying 'drug money.' We simply imposed a tax to set up clinics, retraining programs, antidrug literature. . . . What the hell, it's the same as Grant North's idea. Tax drugs to get the funds needed to fight them! That's why I was so intrigued by his book about ending the drug war."

Marianne stood up, speechless. Was she hearing the sclerosis of a regime unable to stop drugs any other way? An otherwise honest government funding rehabilitation in its own country by creating addicts in another?

"Look, it's not as though we did it for our own gain. We used most of the funds to fight drugs."

"'Most of the funds?' I suppose a few million here and there slipped through the cracks."

He shrugged, looking up at her from his chair. "Well-ll, you have to be practical."

She knew that "well" of his, an oiled and seductive antidote to the words that followed. It's not every man who can tell the truth and lie at the same time. But what must he have seen as his alternative to the Cuban problem? To rule as others rule, slowly, dully, safely grinding the days into microscopic decay, with no stunning leaps forward against the problems of the nation, no personal exhilarations from operating outside the mainstream, no fiery joys to stir the blood? And no millions for his safe. Always the pragmatist, he had accepted the money and salved his conscience by establishing REHAB. And quit while he was ahead.

"If we've learned anything from Hitler," she said, "it's that the end doesn't justify the means."

"Marianne, if the end doesn't justify the actions we take, then what does? We would be forever doing things without a reason."

You can't change the mind of an autocrat, she knew. The best you can hope for is to learn the truth. "Father, I forgive your sins, as you forgave mine. But why have you shown so much animosity toward the man I plan to marry?"

"Look at that crackhead of a husband you had. Look at St. Gregory! Every time either of us trusts a white man, it ends in disaster."

"You trusted the wrong white man," she said with no smile. "Funny, you and I. You're half white and you think of yourself as black. I'm half white and I think of myself as white, when I think of it at all. This is *Nassau*, Father, not Chicago! I grew up in this town when people never noticed your skin color. *You're* the one who's leading the country back to the dark ages."

"Marianne, being white isn't just a matter of skin color. It's an attitude. I've fought my whole life achieving majority government, sending those people back—"

"*Those people?* There's already enough hate here without race hatred. The out-islanders hate the Nassauvians who hate the Bay Street Boys who hate the Conchy Joes. We've got a quarter of a million people hating each other. Is that the future you see for our country?"

First St. Gregory, then Pyfrom, and now Marianne. Would the

night never end? "Say what you will, Marianne, but Grant North will destroy you."

"Father . . ." she started slowly, tears flooding her eyes, yet weighting each expression of her face with objective reason. But prejudice is beyond reason. Nothing she could say would make him see that his bigotry was killing the country, killing her, killing himself. Her admission of defeat, a raindrop at first, became a cloud of overwhelming sorrow drifting up from her damaged past, her abandoned childhood, her tortured marriage. Both of them, father and daughter, were half-castes, mulattoes, castoffs from the world and from each other. Life can do worse than make a daughter both love and hate her father. But not by much.

In those hidden corners of the secret mind where sadness comes and stays and infiltrates every thought, she found what she had to do. It would be the others who would end the absolute power of her father's crushing bigotry. All she had to do was . . . nothing.

59 *The Many Ways You Can Lose*

THEY HAD SWITCHED OFF the running lights, illegally, and the lamps inside were extinguished except for the compass in its binnacle. The engines murmured below, playing their music through the steel hull as the LCM sliced a flat ocean. Overhead the clouds raced across the moon, swarming with electricity and spreading a nimbus veil that blanked out a few million cubic light-years of the Milky Way. You could feel it and you could imagine the islands feeling it as they brushed against low clouds pregnant with unrained rain and unfulfilled promise. In the Bahamas, nights like this occur most often in March when the temperature changes from winter to summer and the clouds crackle in lucid purity, equalizing their potential with the sea and shimmering like pewter in the moonlight. North hoped for rain. Rain flattened the seas.

The *Half Fast* looked unfamiliar in the brassy moonlight with her upper deck gone, her slim tube of the gun mounted in the middle of the open well deck and merging into darkness. Andy's footsteps echoed on the hull. He was checking to make sure nothing had worked loose, and he ran his hand over the sleek barrel as if to befriend it.

After North and Rolle returned to the Island from Miami, they had unlatched and slung the LCM's massive foredeck onto the dock, using the ship's gin pole, as they used to do when preparing to haul a bulldozer. They'd welded the mount of the recoilless cannon to the steel plates of the well deck, keeping the cannon itself hidden within the stacks of plywood. The night following the meeting at Scuba Beach, between midnight and dawn when the seas were soft and the other Islanders were asleep, Andy and North labored like machines: speeding into position a few miles offshore, anchoring methodically in the deep water, fixing the cannon to its mount, and firing a half-dozen shells filled with orange marker dye. The unarmed shells that missed their practice target—Harbour Rock—sent waterspouts high into the air as though they were living cetaceans clearing their blowholes. North was unconcerned about the noise of the artillery; although the cannon was louder than their torpedoes had been, anyone on the Island or across the shallows in the village would hear it as thunder. At dawn, North and Andy once again hid the cannon before anchoring the LCM in the harbor.

The next night, North was hitting Harbour Rock at will, the dye splashing on the barren islet like an egg laid broken by some giant seabird. But the new exercise wasn't the sport that torpedo practice had been. This time no Cleary clowned around, no Garbarino joined the game of low-tech innovation, no team of Islanders responded to a common threat. The new practice was a systematic, precisely calibrated and lonely rehearsal for destruction.

And yet, the few who were left still followed. Why? To satisfy their own needs for vengeance? For adventure? Sidney Rolle in particular acted as though he couldn't wait for retaliation against Ransom. In an earlier time his unorthodox reverence for nature and hatred of authoritarian institutions would have gotten him burned at the stake. North realized the penalty for losing the battle at hand would be equally brutal, but he couldn't make himself care much one way or the other. There is only one worthwhile concern when you're planning aggression: how best to fire and get the hell out.

After the second predawn excursion, North slept into the afternoon and awoke to find Marianne packed and dressed in her town clothes. He walked with her to the dock where Rolle was waiting in the Mako.

"I'm taking the Bahamasair flight to Nassau," she had said, looking like she'd been up all night.

He had known she would say that and that she would cry saying it, and when the tears came he held her while Rolle revved up the engines. It was a light, passionless embrace that spoke of how things might have been different, should have been different, but were not different. Then she was gone.

And he had left too, sent by events to this floating tank under this racing moon, ready to wreck chaos on the property of another man, contemplating the responsibility of accuracy and that the human brain must be the most worthless adaptation ever to appear in the evolution of life because it so easily threatens self-destruction of the species.

Andy came up to the poop. "I know you're planning to get everyone out of the target house first, but couldn't we find a way to drop just one live shell on St. Greg? He's probably in his country estate pulling the legs off kittens and puppies."

"Or sharpening his pitchfork," said North, avoiding answering the question.

After a minute, Andy said thoughtfully, "Grant, I feel like I started all this. I was the guy who sawed off the shotgun barrel . . . because it was bent."

"Doesn't matter Andy. The shotgun had nothing to do with it."

About two in the morning, the hoped-for rain fell soft and settled on the ocean like dust. North slowed to a crawl, taking constant readings with his rangefinder, aiming at coastal lights that broke through the mist. When the *Half Fast* arrived at a point two miles offshore, directly opposite the yellow sodium-vapor glow he recognized as coming from the Ransom mansion, he hove to, slid the transmissions into neutral, and pulled the lever that opened the bow door. He climbed down to the well deck where he joined Andy in the drizzle. The diesel exhaust from the idling engines was caustic in their nostrils.

Shirtless and wearing his Gauguin hat to keep the hair out of his eyes, he operated the electric winch. Andy, also barechested against the soggy night, kept the lines from tangling, as together they payed out sixteen hundred feet of manila rope that followed the first anchor into the black sea. Slithering off the bow ramp, the heavy line sent a groan throughout the hull like an animal straining under a burden.

An hour later, North took the helm and shifted into forward, running dead slow, setting the anchor and tightening the first line to almost its breaking point. He slipped into neutral and helped Andy drop the second anchor, then the third, each time winching the lines as taut as possible. In the absence of high waves, the LCM had become as stable a platform as you can have on the ocean, short of a drilling rig whose feet reach to the bottom.

They loaded the 106-mm recoilless cannon with the first marker shell. Returning to the cabin, they dried themselves with a towel, and waited for dawn.

Andy came up from the galley carrying mugs of coffee and suffering second thoughts. "It's not too late to turn back," he said, avoiding eye contact by staring at the crescent on his mentor's left wrist.

North felt the humid breath of the tropics steaming out of the south. The seas couldn't be expected to stay calm every day, even before dawn. They might have no second chance. "I thought you wanted revenge?"

"Damn it, Grant, that was just talk. Actually killing somebody is . . . different."

"We're not killing anybody, Andy. Rolle's going to get them out of the house, and if he doesn't, Marianne will."

"Yeah . . . well, I hope so."

"You doubt it?"

"Shit happens, Grant. An overeager Sidney Rolle. An accident. Who knows? You sure you want to blow up your future father-in-law's house? Won't it make Christmases and birthdays a little strained?" His quiet chuckle wasn't returned. "I thought Ransom was some sort of benevolent despot or something."

"Despots are never benevolent." North rubbed the stubble on his chin.

"Couldn't we just capture Ransom, tie him up, and feed him

to the newspapers?"

"Sure we could, but then what? Ransom is no Noriega who rubbed a U.S. president the wrong way. Besides, Armitage was just about to try that and it got him killed."

Andy lit a cigarette and looked outside as the ship creaked against the taut anchor lines. The clouds still scudded, although the sky was lightening perceptibly. The poor visibility of night was giving way to the poor visibility of morning fog, and you could barely see the shore lights. The chronometer struck four. Andy's eyes traversed the open hold, gathering strength for a gigantic tele- pathic alarm. The cannon reared up from the well deck like a preying mantis on a paper boat, and he screamed in silence, *This weapon is no toy!*

Aloud, he said, "You're going to blow up the bastard, aren't you?"

A quiet filled the cabin, thick as the fog. Andy's cigarette glowed like an exclamation point in the semidarkness. All North had to do was hold Coby in his mind and the affirmation would come shrieking from his lungs. He wanted to say, *There is no way this corrupt dictator can get away with his life after murdering my Coby and murdering my Island!* But he said nothing because, he realized, he had not decided.

North squinted toward the horizon, and his squint held the pain of his Slavic forebears. The fury that had lain hermetic in him and in Jo since Coby's murder, a bloodlust as ancient and as violent as those that pillaged the Drina bridge, would come alive with the dawn and leap from that gleaming eleven-foot barrel. He would live with the result.

Soon they heard Jo's Cessna, unseen in the mist with its run- ning lights switched off, beginning the characteristic droning of an aircraft flying in tight circles. They had installed a VHF aircraft radio on the well deck of the *Half Fast* next to the gun. North could talk to and hear Jo, but not Rolle. Jo and Rolle were linked together by industrial walkie-talkies operating on a frequency North could not access on the LCM.

The radio crackled, and North hurried down the steps to the roofless well deck. Andy assumed the loader's position beside the cannon.

"*Mesece, ova je Zmaj. Završena.* Moon, this is Kite. Over."

"Moon here," said North in the language of their ancestors, the secret language of their childhood. "Where are you?"

"A thousand feet over object. Man is in position."

"With uniform?"

"Roger that, and with bullhorn. The yellow yardlights are coming through loud and clear."

"Where is the woman?"

"Man says he sees her, that she is waving at him. He says people are coming out of the building and wants you to begin operations. Repeat, woman is still inside. Confirm. *Završena.*"

Jo was taking no chances with an itchy trigger finger. "Moon confirms. *Završena.*"

Serbo-Croatian was not exactly a popular language in the Bahamas, and even if a listener could understand them it would make little sense.

Pink fingers of dawn touched the rim of the ocean to the east. The scientist who could tell the species of a shrimp or design the convolutions of a desalinator now used that discerning mind for calculating azimuth and differentiating the gestalt of the target.

"Moon to Kite," he said, still in Croatian. "We're about to send the first empty package. When you're directly over the object, switch your strobe on for a count of three. *Završena.*"

The top of the sun swam blood-red on the horizon, lighting a diffuse path to the ship. Still the Cessna remained invisible in the fog. North was thinking like a tank commander again. Conditions couldn't be better for a hidden barrage: misty-drizzle weather that would be confused with lightning-thunder weather. *Come on, Sidney, get Marianne out!*

Once he fired the first marker shell, North knew the process would segue automatically. Jo would relay the distances from the orange-dye splotches to the mansion. Rolle, wearing his police uniform, would give Jo the signal that everyone was out of the mansion. They would slide imperceptibly from the fourth or fifth marker shell to the final incendiary round. The first few unarmed shots, filled only with marker dye, were the important ones. After that, any further delusions of free will would be merely the prisoner of events banging his metal cup against the bars of his cell.

He saw Jo's lights blink on and off, and adjusted the trajectory. It wasn't like the old days when he had tank radar and an onboard computer to calculate wind speed, air density, humidity, and movement of the gun platform itself. His blood rose. His heart beat in tumult.

He squeezed the trigger.

The shell whooshed out of the long barrel, its aluminum casing clanging on the steel deck. Andy began the process of loading the next round.

"Kite to Moon." In their secret language. "I see oranges on the green one thousand feet too far west. Woman still inside. Even a marker might hurt someone. Wait for my signal. Confirm."

"Roger, Kite. I'll wait."

They had rehearsed this, and she knew he couldn't wait long. Even anchored as firmly as it was on a glass sea, the LCM could shift slightly, enough to make the second trajectory diverge. North computed the correction and cranked the gun slightly east. He settled back to wait. It seemed to him that he'd spent a good part of his time in the Bahamas waiting, or asking questions—waiting for permits, questioning the search for news of Cleary, questioning people about Coby, now waiting again on the *Half Fast* at his own instigation to deliver his blunt answer across an invisible sky.

The barest breeze rippled the water against the hull. The stress of metals emitted a sigh as the plates of the ship strained and the mounting of the big gun shuddered imperceptibly, like muted cymbals. He held his breath.

Jo's strobe blinked on again and she radioed, "Man says okay for second marker, but woman still inside. Repeat, *marker* only. Confirm."

North confirmed.

"*Tri, dva, jedan. Meta!*" she said. "Three, two, one. Mark!"

The novice sees only the one way he can win and ignores the many ways he can lose. Until after he makes the wrong decision.

Pucaj! Fire!

North squeezed the electric trigger for the second time, feeling

474

a strange sensation, a cry from his injured intuition. Why is it, he wondered after he fired, that we always think the decision we have just made is wrong?

The LCM didn't budge an inch on the flat sea. Judging from the first marker shell, he felt the second marker might be a direct hit. Dazzling and irrevocable, the shell steamed from Grant North's 106-mm recoilless cannon with a muzzle velocity of one thousand six hundred fifty feet per second, its white trail vanishing into the mist.

It would land in six point four seconds.

60 *Obedience Experiment*

FROM BEHIND a cluster of traveler palms trees on the Prime Minister's estate, Sidney Rolle saw the first marker shell flash out of the fog. He could hear Jo overhead, and a few minutes ago had told her via his mobile radio that, yes, he had made the evacuation announcement. In truth, he had not yet used his bullhorn. He was trying to hide from everyone in the compound except Marianne, whom he planned to abduct if necessary.

It had been easy for Rolle to get past the guardhouse in the uniform he'd bought from an uncle who had retired from the police force. The uncle had told him that Ransom eschewed the elaborate precautions adopted by most heads of state on the assumption that the more men with guns around you, the more risk of a shot in the back. Rolle then had told Ransom's sentry that he'd been ordered here at daybreak to help with security in view of the important meetings in progress. At four-thirty in the morning, the sentry was not about to awaken the P.M.'s bodyguards to clear this black cop who, after all, passed the body search for a gun and carried only a battery-powered megaphone.

Rolle suffered in the high humidity, made worse by the flak jacket under his uniform. But that wasn't the only reason he sweated. If anyone in authority discovered him, they'd ask questions more pointed than the sentry's. He breathed a little easier when, through the arched windows, he caught sight of Marianne. Wearing a light-colored blouse and skirt, she was rushing around the house turning on lights. After losing valuable minutes motioning her onto the veranda, he grew anxious again. Didn't she see him? Why didn't she come?

Rolle studied the building's cruciform shape, seeking a way in without being seen. Concentrated by the fog, the yellow glow of yardlights and the incessant drone of Jo's Cessna saturated the compound. No deserted castle on the Scottish moors could look or sound more ghostlike than this yellowish stone fortress blanketed by black branches of willows and drenched with the wailing of aircraft engines.

Suddenly Marianne appeared at a French door and waved to let Rolle know she saw him. He dashed across the ivy lawn onto the veranda and lunged through the door she held open.

"Use your bullhorn!" she whispered hoarsely.

"No, not until I get you out of here," he said, grabbing her arm, desperate to bring her to safety.

She shook herself free. And at exactly the wrong moment, Ransom appeared flanked by Wilson and Wright.

Rolle had no alternative now. He raised the electric bullhorn and barked, *"Everybody out! A bomb is ready to go off!"*

"The hell. . . !" said Ransom, wearing only trousers and bedroom slippers, his left eye wandering under a bushy, crawling eyebrow, his leathery torso that of an outdoorsman. He addressed the man in the police uniform, "Is that Pyfrom up there in the plane?"

"Yes sir," Rolle said.

The mansion was awake now, and its guests in various stages of dress were dashing around for their belongings. Rolle recognized Benjamin Franklin and Cora Carstairs. Taking advantage of the confusion, he tried again to seize Marianne's arm, but she moved too fast.

"No, Sid!" Her emerald eyes flashed. "Not until everyone is out of the house."

He switched on the bullhorn again. "Repeat, a bomb is about

to explode. *You have two minutes to evacuate!"*

Hearing the amplified warning, one of the guardhouse sentries darted into the mansion, saw two maids running, and followed them outside and across the ivy lawn toward the servants' quarters.

Ransom disappeared deeper into the bowels of his opulence, flanked by his bodyguards. Rolle and Marianne followed through the great hall, past the fireplace, and into the west arm of the crucifix where the master bedroom was located. Per square foot of wall space, the bedroom suite contained even more things of worth than the rest of the mansion. An enormous oval bed was surrounded by statues of plump Venetian nudes and a profusion of angular angels in gilded frames that overflowed into an adjoining sitting room. The bathroom door was open, and he could see gold-plated faucets and towel bars.

Ransom threw open a closet door and pushed aside a row of suits with one heavy swipe of his arm. He quickly dialed a combination, spun the lock, and opened a thick second door of steel, stepping into a vault larger than the closet that hid it.

"There's really no hurry," he said over his shoulder, nervous and hurrying. "I'm doing this only as a precaution. Pyfrom is just making his point for future reference. He would never drop a bomb with us inside."

Rolle fidgeted, lost for ideas, his tongue a stone in his mouth. Finally he pointed the megaphone out of the closet toward the open door of the bedroom and yelled, "Come on now, everybody, don't take foolish chances with your lives." His voice was loud but flat, emotion ground out by anxiety. He tried again with more authority. *"That flash you saw was a warning! Get out of the house, right now!"*

"No!" said Ransom, mostly to Marianne. "You know Malcolm is no murderer. He *wants* us to leave so he can destroy the house!" While he talked he was stuffing packets of currency into a suitcase. Wilson and Wright came in, and with rehearsed movements, pulled down five more empty cases and started packing cash into them with no apparent sense of crisis, as if this were a fire drill.

Rolle had never seen so much money. The safe's walls of stainless steel were lined from floor to ceiling with shelves containing green, brown, and gray bills denominated in hundreds and thousands—dollars, yen, pounds, marks, francs. One shelf held nothing but gold and silver ingots. Rolle estimated the six pieces of luggage could hold only a few million dollars in cash or precious metals, leaving at least forty or fifty million more in the vault.

Franklin and Carstairs, dressed now, came toward the others crowded around the closet doorway. "Come on now, gentlemen," said Carstairs, "do as the Prime Minister says. That flash was lightning, pure and simple. Old Malcolm Pyfrom up there wouldn't hurt a sandfly."

Rolle was obsessed with forcing Marianne out of the house without her father. Seeking any advantage in time or space, and knowing he was running out of both, he pulled her toward the far end of the bedroom and rasped in her ear, *"A live shell is next! Come with me, and your father will follow. Now!"*

Instead, Marianne grabbed Rolle's megaphone and aimed it in the direction of the vault. "That is *not* Malcolm Pyfrom up there! A shell *is* going to fall!"

Her amplified words kindled Ransom's adrenal glands. His ritual preliminaries to an emergency were cut short, and he staggered out of the room followed by Wilson and Wright, all three carrying suitcases.

Franklin, not knowing whether to believe Marianne or Carstairs, peered over the tops of his half-glasses at the senator. Dame Cora, with a smirk on her face, slowly shook her head no while casting a lustrous gaze through the open door at the shelves of currency and bullion. Franklin smiled back, and they entered the vault together.

Rolle, Marianne, and the bodyguards followed Ransom into the great hall. You could see the leader of his country oscillating between fear and greed as he slowed his escape before the gilded paintings, the antique chairs, the rococo statuary. He plainly wanted to take them all, but paused only seconds before lunging through the nearest French door. Outside, he trampled the morning glory vines and golden trumpets planted so fastidiously around the mansion by Malcolm Pyfrom, and led his entourage across the ivy meadow. Rolle had nowhere to go but after them, frantic to get the P.M. back into the building.

A hundred yards more and Ransom stopped suddenly. He turned toward Rolle and Marianne, his weathered body, bare from the waist, shimmering in the mist as if seen in mirage or fever. He studied the face above the police uniform for a moment before exploding in a thunder of recognition.

"You're North's man!"

When in trouble, complicate the issue, thought Rolle. "That was a long time ago, Mr. Prime Minister, before I joined the force." The ruse worked long enough for him to flee into a copse of rare shrubs and vines.

Wilson and Wright, who had been trained to protect the Prime Minister, with their bodies if necessary, could give no chase. They dropped their bags, knelt, and fired at the place where Rolle had entered the bushes.

Ransom's eyes drilled into Marianne's like a laser. "So it's you behind all this! You and your white lover. And you dare accuse me of wrongdoing! You've betrayed your own father, your own country. You're nothing but the slut of one more white colonialist. Can't you see what's going on? *Your white man is using you to ruin me!* You rotten dirty bitch—"

Marianne turned and ran in humiliation and fury, her short hair flying, her skirt stretched tight, her legs eating up the ground between her father and the mansion.

"Stop!" Ransom called as she entered the east wing. He bellowed to his bodyguards, *"Go after her!"*

Having been indoctrinated with the single vital responsibility of preserving the life of the Prime Minister—and not his money or his daughter—Wilson and Wright abandoned the suitcases and forcibly escorted Ransom across the meadow. Only when they reached the edge of the compound eight hundred yards from the house, did they release their grips on his arms. Breathing hard, he leaned against the high fence of casuarinas that bordered his estate.

A sudden flash blinded them! Chaos. Flames sucked air upward from the ground, creating a firestorm of gale force that bludgeoned Ransom and his bodyguards. The vortex pitched them headlong, igniting their clothes and their hair, leaving them gasping for breath.

Screams went unheard in the roar that followed. A series of secondary explosions, microseconds apart, numbed their ears but clapped out the flames on their bodies. Ransom hugged the ground and watched from behind a screen of foliage as billowing smoke and a white fireball collided like suns, freezing time for a long moment before releasing from the sky chimney stones, structural steel, jagged sheets of glass, the mutilated limbs of antique furniture, paintings, and ingots of gold and silver. All these artifacts of his life mingled or melted in a cataclysmic conversion of trea-sure to junk.

A shard of glass had gashed the thigh of the smaller bodyguard, Wilson. Spurting blood, he sat on the lawn and pressed both hands against the wound. In back of where the mansion had stood, a colonnade of black willows and royal palms burst into flame and burned like torches.

Struggling to one knee, the terrible truth reverberated in Ransom's skull without mercy. He searched the conflagration until his eyes were raw from heat and smoke.

"My God!" he said, "was Marianne . . . *in there?*"

THE IDEAL hiding place for a man not trying to cross the razor wire was in the middle of the casuarinas barrier at the edge of the compound. The bushy trees also gave cover from flying shrapnel. From there Sidney Rolle had watched the ordeal of his enemies, then crawled on elbows and knees along the base of the thicket until he was out of their sight. He rose and doubled back toward the entrance, hugging the treeline and keeping wide of the debris that had been the ten-million dollar mansion. The iron-hard imbuia beams, charred skeletons now, jabbed the sky like the fingers of a corpse. With the stench of burning treasure in his nostrils, Rolle sprinted across the serpentine drive, observing as he went the scorched fragments of millions of dollars worth of currencies scattered like confetti across the grounds. Nothing was alive, he realized. No one. Marianne had been killed with the rest of them.

Jo's voice squawked in the radio on his belt, but Rolle heard only the end of a sentence over the crackling of the fire. ". . . *happened?*"

When he was a mile from Wilson, Wright, or anyone else, he stopped to catch his breath and raised his radio antenna. His words tumbled into the microphone. "That wasn't a single shell, not even a live one. It was a whole *chain* of explosions around the perimeter of the house. The only thing I can figure is that the damn place was mined and the second marker shell set it off."

"Oh, Sidney."

"That's only conjecture. The facts are that Marianne is dead, along with all of them except Ransom and his bodyguards. I don't know how it really happened."

Jo's voice was so faint and her pause so long, he thought she might have flown out of range. His radio sputtered and Jo's voice came on one last time. "*I* know how it really happened," she said, her words expressing Rolle's former dread. "We followed orders blindly. We were our own Obedience Experiment."

61 *At the Ends of Space*

THE WATER PLANET was coming alive with low swells as Sidney Rolle rode the Mako like a steed. His pulse and respiration slowed, leaving him drained and sick at the thought of telling North about Marianne. Heading toward the LCM, he held the wheel with one hand and then the other as he removed his police uniform and flak jacket, throwing each article into the sea and dressing in clothes he had stowed previously. The breeze soothed his bruised body and the burns of his face, but he was unaware of pain. In a fury of rage and disbelief, he fought down an overwhelming urge to turn back and deprive Ransom not only of his possessions but of his life.

He glanced at his watch. It seemed impossible that it was only nine o'clock, he'd been awake so long. The fog was lifting with the climb of the sun, and the nimbus clouds that had lain like a gray blanket through the night coalesced into cotton shapes, tinged in copper. One of the clouds on the horizon lost its amorphous shape and slowly became the LCM. He could see two figures sep-arating out of the mist, North and Andy; they were sliding the big gun and its mount over the edge of the bow ramp. The mount went in first. The cannon hung suspended as one of them cut the line from the winch. From a distance the long silver barrel looked like a giant barracuda slipping beneath the surface. Artillery shells and two casings that had been ejected from the breech were rolling around the steel deck like smaller fish. The anchors already had been hauled, and the *Half Fast* floated free on the swells. Rolle slowed the Mako as he coasted around to the stern, threw his painter to Andy, and pulled himself up by the taffrail.

"Jesus!" Andy said. "Your hair's all burnt and your eye-brows are singed. You okay?"

"Yeah. How's Grant?"

Andy shrugged toward the front of the vessel, shaking his head slowly from side to side.

"Sid. That you?" The voice from the forward well deck was low and mechanical, a voice Rolle hardly recognized as belonging to Grant North.

They descended the seven-foot bulkhead in front of the cabin and came up behind North. He was bent over, his bronzed back bared, intent on keeping the lines from tangling as he wound them onto the winch drum. When he straightened, his face looked exhausted and bloodless, his neck muscles strained to the breaking point like those of a fighter thrown out of the ring.

The sky gleamed in Rolle's saddened eyes. He raised his voice over the noise of the winch. "Grant, there's no good way to tell you this. Marianne is dead. Ransom is still alive."

Andy flinched at the confirmation of what he'd suspected. North acted as if he had not heard. His eyes were stoic, the stubble on his chin dry and brittle, breath shallow, shoulders arched like a man with a vast past and no future. "You two get the rest of those shells overboard," he said.

"Grant! Talk to me," Rolle said. "It's not your fault. How the hell could anyone have known that there were explosives buried around the mansion?"

North continued to feed the endless lengths of rope coming up from three hundred fathoms.

"Who mined the place?" Andy asked Rolle.

"Probably Ransom's buddy, Malcolm Pyfrom. Politicians define friendship in more intriguing ways than the rest of us."

North snapped, "What difference does that make? Let's get

the fuck out of here." He said it in that new voice, quiet and raw with authority, lacking resonance, a voice Rolle couldn't place.

Man's capacity for guilt is inexorable, thought Rolle: the woman North loved is dead, and he has killed her. Having spent a lifetime listening to sea and sky, he finally recognized the voice stabbing up from the depths of his friend's anguish. It was the sound you wait for in the eye of the hurricane, before it explodes into a new direction.

THE SKY cleared, and from the poop North could smell ozone in the air, an odor that once seemed fresh to him and now brought painful memories, quickly rejected. You can mourn the dead later. First you plan.

He focused on Ransom, a man who lived his life untouched by human emotions, who would calculate the optimum method and retaliate. North could envision further use for the cannon, but he'd had to scuttle it. If the U.S. Coast Guard, which patrolled these waters regularly, found the gun or even one of the shells, they would be arrested and extradited to Nassau. The best place to hide and rearm with some undetectable weapon was in the Bahamas itself. North turned the wheel over to Andy and spread the charts over the console, setting a course for Bimini.

The *Half Fast* ran easily before a fair sea, a high and lonely rectangle on the cobalt surface that reflected the clouds. Late in the afternoon, they picked up the smell of the land, and for an hour more followed the coast that zigzagged into the distance like a continent. It was turning dark when the little ship, her running lights off, gave a wide berth to the lagoon between South and North Bimini, and pulled into a secluded cove a few miles from Alice Town. No point in advertising their presence, for Ransom would have alerted the police throughout the archipelago. Working the controls from the wheelhouse, Andy lowered the bow door for North and Rolle, then closed the ramp and waded ashore. The three hiked like spent troops over the narrow, dusty King's Highway until they arrived at an inn on the edge of the hamlet.

Alice Town had the rich wild smell of marsh water about it, as though it had reverted to its pristine state after Junkanoo Christmas. This far from town, the glow of the tourist district in the distance gave the shuttered stores and homes a desolate, abandoned feeling. They arrived at a place called the Marlin Inn, and banged on the door until lights blinked on inside and an old man came.

"Hello," said Rolle to the innkeeper. "How about rentin' us three rooms?"

The proprietor looked astonished at these men who had sprung from nowhere, but he nodded yes and switched on more lights. In the lobby, which was the barroom, a ceiling fan slowly turned and rearranged the dust that coated the mounted billfish on the walls. Soul music, almost inaudible, leaked from a radio on a shelf above the bar. You could picture Hemingway coming in here to drink after a day on the deep sea.

They took a table in the rear. The proprietor's boy came over for their order and Rolle said, "What are you drinking, you guys?"

"Anything except a Cleary Colada," Andy said.

"Bring a bottle of rum, ice, and three glasses," Rolle said.

The bottle arrived, showing on its label a light-skinned Bahama girl with enticing breasts, lusty lips, and earrings in great gold loops. Andy went to the bar to buy cigarettes.

"You want Rothman's, Sid?"

"Yeah."

"Get me a pack too," said North.

The three of them drank and smoked one after another. On their third drink, the news came on the radio and they craned their necks to hear. Andy reached up over the bar to turn the volume higher as a female voice repeated a news story that apparently had been aired throughout the day:

> The aerial bombing early this morning that killed the Prime Minister's daughter Marianne Price, Minister Benjamin Franklin, and Senate president Cora Carstairs is now thought to be the work of terrorists. Prime Minister Ransom told CID investigators that he suspected the assassins were drug lords who recently had been making anonymous threatening phone calls for him to relent on his crackdown against smugglers. Mr. Ransom said they were foreigners, apparently from the United States or

Canada, for he has requested that Nassau Radio broadcast this single sentence. We quote:

"The terrorists from the north will pay for this massacre." The P.M. said his daughter and the others had been holding a REHAB meeting at his home the night before, and he had left the house for his morning exercise.

Speculation that this morning's violence might be an attempted *coup d'état* was fueled by the arrest of Malcolm Pyfrom. The Deputy Prime Minister is being held for questioning, but has not yet been charged. The Prime Minister has authorized a full investigation by the Criminal Inves—

"Neat," said Rolle as the radio droned on. "Rewriting history makes the Bahamas one of those countries with an unpredictable past."

"That 'terrorists-from-the-North' bit shows creativity," said Andy.

"I guess Pyfrom's arrest proves he planted the explosives along with his violets all around the mansion."

"They won't be looking for the LCM," Andy said. "Ransom must think we dropped a bomb from the air that set off Pyfrom's present."

To North, the voices of Andy, Rolle, and the radio announcer were unrecognizable, as if they came from different species in a zoo. The burden of his deeds was upon him with brutal force, and each word of the broadcast was a drop of blood. He wanted desperately to wake up from this nightmare, or failing that, to sleep and cease thinking. But he could no more stop his mind than an alcoholic could decline a drink.

How does a prime minister settle a score? If Ransom had been willing to admit his own complicity and involve the U.S. authorities, the broadcast surely would have mentioned Grant North by name. The fact that he chose to disguise North's name meant he was arranging something else. Something more Machiavellian.

They drank into the night, alcohol diluting their anxiety. Life used to seem so indestructible, thought North. It goes on in the depths of the ocean, in the Arctic, and even in water droplets at the edge of space. In Vietnam after each massive bombing, the little people had shaken themselves off like ants and rebuilt their roads and fortifications. Yet in these dazzling islands where a man feels blessed and sucks happiness out of the sunshine, where girls have been known to fling themselves into the exotic colors of the sea, life is strangely fragile, curiously ephemeral.

As they drank, they navigated the sea of tyranny and the randomness of death, knowing that their action had released the violence that lives sequestered in civilized man. Ransom lived, and that meant all barriers on both sides had been dropped. Time was running out second by second, but still they drank, together yet alone, plowing parallel paths under the circle of destiny where each of them knew no danger except the fury of their obsessions.

Late that night they staggered to their upstairs rooms. North lay on the bed, fully dressed. He would sleep for an hour and come half-awake for two, as if on guard duty. In the middle of the night when the alcohol wore off, he jerked fully awake to the thumping of his heart and a piercing sorrow. His wife, his daughter, and now Marianne had achieved an immortality in his mind. Heather, sweet, pallid, ravished by disease, seemed an ethereal creature under her chestnut hair. Coby smiled up from her pert nose and passion for life, flung her arms around him and asked why he had no time for her. He had no answer now as he'd had none before. He dwelled on Marianne's face the longest, imagining in the dim light the silky touch of her tongue, the mysterious tilt of her brows. But then her eyes sank deeper into their sockets and she warned him, *You'll be killing me too!* Rolle had told her that a live shell was coming. Had she had gone back to the mansion for Carstairs and Franklin? For something else?

Or had she made a different choice between father and lover, between black and white, between the Bahamas and the rest of the world? That sudden, final choice that resolved all conflict. Suicide.

Pulling himself out of bed, North sat by the window and watched the moon set in an amber blaze, while he forced himself to forget Marianne for now and prowl in the brain of his adversary. The essence of Charles T. Ransom rose in him like a welcome fever, threatening panic, threatening pain.

What would it be like to be the Bahamian Prime Minister right now? Anguished, bitter, certainly. Still despotic? Perhaps. North felt through Ransom's ego the end of living in splendor, the loss of his hoards of cash, his walls of paintings, his marble busts. He would be deploring the lack of weapons and the inadequacy of the guards at his palace, fighting now to retain his glory, his Senate of acolytes, his foreign magistrates hired one year at a time, his Royal Defence Force, and all the perks: chauffeured limousine, plush office, gilded ceremonies of state, prestige of the United Nations, and the allegiance of the seven hundred Family Islands, especially the sweet jewel of New Providence where he reigned like a sultan. All threatened, if not already destroyed. And not by some natural calamity, but by the murderer of his daughter.

How would Ransom make his move? As a lawyer, seeking Bahamian indictment or extradition through U.S. authorities? No. Ransom would respond in kind. He would send St. Gregory after them. But where? The coveted land, of course, the place controlled by the enemy, the Island. If North knew this man at all, his odd mix of patrician arrogance and working-class pride, he knew Ransom would find it impossible to stay behind.

North rose well after noon in the half-death of hangover. He couldn't adapt his eyes to the light, his head ached, and his mouth, devoid of saliva, tasted metallic. Hot and nauseated, he felt as if his bones were broken, symptoms beyond an overdose of alcohol. With a shock, he knew he had breakbone fever, or dengue, and counted the days since his exposure to the mosquitos in the creek. Nineteen. Incubation usually took less than fifteen days; perhaps the extra time meant his would be a relatively mild case.

Rolle took one look at him, went downstairs, and returned with a thermometer. North's temperature was a hundred and two.

Sleep helped North escape his pain and sorrow, but his dreams were burdened with broken bodies burning in a fire of palms and pastel waters. At three in the afternoon, his fever subsided. Shaky and chilled, warmed only by his resolve, he met Rolle and Andy in the lounge where they were having a late breakfast.

"Ransom and St. Gregory will be on the Island," he announced to Rolle as if he'd read it somewhere. "If I'm wrong, we'll go on from there to Nassau."

"Why not," said Rolle. "Maybe we can get ammonium nitrate here at some farm. Three parts powder to one part kerosene makes one hell of a bomb, remember?"

"Too hard to detonate. We'll use gasoline alone, no nitrate."

Andy interrupted. "What is it with you guys? You're already out on a limb and now you want to try hanging from the twigs."

North looked at him sadly. What's left to say to your young protégé who would argue all day but if asked would follow you straight to hell? Or to Rolle who didn't deserve to die, but probably would? Or to a sister who has been reading your mind since you were four? But the parallel didn't hold that far. Rolle had told him that Jo already had flown out of the Bahamas.

Placing a hand on Andy's shoulder, Rolle smiled in an uncomfortable way. "Look, Andy, I won't hand you any crap about how we've got to get Ransom and St. Gregory before they ruin the country or kill anyone else with their drugs and pirating. The hell with the country. It's *them* I want! The way I look at it, they're using up oxygen we could be breathing."

Andy regarded this man he knew as if he'd turned out to be from another planet. He took short puffs of his cigarette and stubbornly went on talking about their plans being against the law, failing to understand that mere words never pervade emotional deafness.

North, drifting in and out of his fever, heard Rolle say, "I don't believe in the law. I believe in justice."

"But you could *die!*" Andy said.

"You live your life, you do things you think ought to done, and you die. Or you don't live your life, you don't do what you think ought be done. And you die anyway."

"So what happens next?" Andy said, tired of philosophy.

"What happens next," North said, "is that you go home to Chicago, and we take off in the LCM."

"Aw, Grant. Just because I think you're crazy is no reason to kick me out. What the hell am I supposed to do after being an LCM captain, get a job somewhere pumping gas? You are my family. I—"

"Listen, Andy. We feel the same way about you and that's why you're not going. You haven't lived much of your life yet. You don't want to end it . . . or spend the rest of it in Fox Hill."

Andy laughed. "If I die, I'll come back and fix the broken Bahamas."

North had led men to their deaths before, but they had been soldiers. The shelling of the compound and even the battle with the pirates had been mere Sunday walks in the park compared to what they faced now. "You are going home, Andy."

Taking money from a cupboard on the ship, he sent Andy into town to buy his airplane ticket while he and Rolle paid the proprietor to borrow his pickup truck, drove to a gas station, and bought two fifty-five gallon drums of gasoline, which they loaded aboard the landing craft. By the time they finished, it was dusk.

Andy came up to the vessel on a rented motorbike. His eyes grew moist when he said, "Take care of yourselves."

They knew he meant it, that he would be thinking he might never see them again.

Out past the tangled mangroves where the seagrass gives way to deep water, North came up to the wheelhouse and sat beside his sole remaining comrade-in-arms. The binnacle lit Rolle's skin with a purple sheen, making him look fierce as an African tribesman. An almost-full moon raced across scudding clouds, its craters and mares clearly visible, but the promise it once held for North was as dead as its surface. He lit a cigarette, remembering a line from a verse Marianne had shared with him one night, *"Brilliant at the ends of space."*

A calm descended upon the sea. Fish jumped. The *Half Fast* plowed evenly eastward toward a rising Libra who stretched her faint balance across seventy-five light-years. North was relieved that Andy would miss the finale. It was different with himself, different with Rolle too in an anomalous way. Rolle had a faith, a religion of tides and sky that lit his night-passage through life. If Rolle died in this battle, his molecules would return as drops of seawater or sargasso weed or rocks of coral.

And if North himself were killed? He would be mourned only by the dead.

62 *Contingency Plan*

WHEN HE HEARD the news, Captain Carlos St. Gregory, wearing his dress uniform and feeling elated, drove out to the Prime Minister's oceanside estate. White-clad mortuary attendants were placing the last of the charred bodies into the ambulances that double in Nassau as hearses. Despite the drizzle, scattered pockets of smoke lay over the moist earth. The swimming pool water, muddy and choked with burned wood, no longer cascaded over the side. Pieces of torn paintings littered the ivy lawn. Nothing remained of the mansion itself but ash and blackened stone smoldering in the rain.

St. Gregory had never seen the Prime Minister cry before but there he was, standing before the hearse, head low, mumbling three syllables like a mourning dove. *"Mar-i-anne!"*

The servants poked listlessly in the rubble, occasionally finding things of value, while the two bodyguards searched exclusively for gold and silver bullion. Wilson, his leg bulking where it was bandaged under his trousers, limped around helping Wright make a pile of the blackened bars that had hardened into deformed shapes. St. Gregory saw that nothing but ashes remained of the countless millions in currency he knew Ransom had hoarded in the house instead of risking detection and wiring it to Luxembourg as had he.

492

The odor of burned possessions and charred bodies left him feeling secure, firmly in control, and his father came to mind for a moment as he considered this opportunity of a lifetime to reposition himself, to become the Prime Minister's commander. He linked his arm in Ransom's and led him away from the hearse to a clump of date palms that had survived the fire.

"Let's take your cruiser and your bodyguards," he whispered in his guttural voice, "and go get the son of a bitch who did this."

Ransom coughed, coming out of his sorrow with narrowed eyes. His face was raw with burns, and his hair smelled singed. "*My* boat? Why don't we send the RBDF after him?"

St. Gregory snorted sardonically and made a show of glancing at the piles of gold and silver bricks on the lawn. "Don't you think you're going to have enough explaining to do?"

Too often we fear what we should face, only to end up facing what we should fear, Ransom told himself. He wanted North to pay with his life, for Marianne, for his mansion. But going off impulsively with St. Gregory violated every prudent standard of a lifetime. This was the same St. Gregory who had lied to him about the piracies, who doubtless lied about the raid on the LCM that started the whole mess. Yet . . . maybe he could use the son-of-a-Baystreeter one more time. Perhaps he could combine revenge for North and for St. Gregory in a single strike.

He mustered the proper inflection of susceptibility, and said, "Where is the bastard?"

St. Gregory deliberately delayed his answer to build his dominance. He craved a partnership of unequals, himself in command, the opposite of what he'd had with his father. Aloud, he scoffed, "Where else would the self-righteous American turd go to lick his wounds?"

"His Island, I suppose." Ransom spat the words, no mock emotion this time. "*His* Island!" It had been the overriding goal of each of his five-year terms to rid the country of its foreign masters, precisely to prevent island dukedoms like North's.

Concern for the prime ministerial office, for propriety, or for the appointments he must have had scheduled had dropped astern like garbage cut adrift. The Bahamas could run on empty for all he cared, thought St. Gregory. Yet the Defender captain had been around violence long enough to know that heated reactions often beget second thoughts.

"What if he isn't there?" said Ransom.

St. Gregory couldn't let him back out, not when he was this close. "If he's not on his fucking Island, I have a way of *getting* him there."

"How?"

"I can't tell you. Except that it is absolutely foolproof."

"That's not good enough, St. Gregory."

"There's no *time. . . !*" he barked, and immediately softened his tone. "Mr. Prime Minister, with all respect, I know the military mind better than you, and North was once a combat officer. It is essential that we get him before he has time to plan his defense. I, on the other hand, have had my contingency plan in place for a long time. Trust me. You'll be glad you did."

"If you think I'm going to let you take me and my boat to confront North on his Island without even knowing what you've got in mind—"

St. Gregory held up a hand. "Meet me at your cruiser in an hour. I'll present my plan, and if you don't like the looks of it, we won't leave your pier."

ST. GREGORY raced his armored Mercedes down Carmichael Road past the Bacardi rum distillery to the experimental agricultural station, that sprawling and abandoned gift of the U.S. government. At the far end of the grounds he opened a gate that led to a region of New Providence unknown to tourists and to most residents as well. Plumes of dust rose high into the air as he drove down the empty road, veering off at his private drive where he pulled up to his farmhouse. Not much larger than the cracker boxes in the slums of Bain Town, it had none of their cheerful garish colors. The building, weathered and unpainted, was surrounded not by crops but by a sea of brush like a field gone to seed. He could afford better, much better, even a palace like Ransom's, but then he would have to put up with prying servants as he did, in effect, aboard ship. In the farmhouse he could be alone to enjoy the isolation, despite the litter of paper and broken bottles which lent an air of decadence to the property, thereby assuring its invisibility.

He parked and entered through the kitchen door. From the refrigerator he took a bottle of milk, poured it with a double shot of rum into a glass, and drank it down. Only then did he go below.

The basement, like others in rural areas, was trisected into a rainwater cistern and two rooms: cool, damp, musty, with no windows, a cracked concrete floor, and overhead wooden joists. But here there were few of the family possessions normally found in basements the world over. No bicycles or toys, no old sewing machines, no garden implements. What distinguished St. Gregory's below-decks recreation area were the rusty bars that separated the rooms. One side opened into a gym with mats, dumbbells, weights and pulleys, hand grips, and a bench press. The opposite side was a cell containing the tools of the jailor's trade—shelves of canned food and toilet paper, and a cot, commode, sink, and clothesline— probably the only self-feeding jail in the world.

St. Gregory bent his head under the low ceiling and edged toward the bars, careful not to get rust on his uniform. He sat on the bench press and observed his hostage pretending to read a book, one of the musty novels or travel guides he had provided. Nothing like Velma, she was pale and weary, dressed in frayed denim shorts and a man's shirt, and had dirty yellow hair that hung lifeless around her ears. They were good ears, coupled with fast reflexes, and he knew she had heard him the moment he entered the house. She turned a page, but of course she knew he was there. It was a game they played. The other part of the game was the way she held her hands under the book so he couldn't see how calloused were her fingers, how broken and dirty her nails, the hands of a prisoner who worked at escape.

Coby North put down her book. "Jesus, Captain, you seem to crystallize in front of those bars every so often. What do you do, crawl out of the septic tank?"

St. Gregory lifted a nostril, leaving the rest of his face immobile. He had killed for less than that, and wanted to tell this rancid bitch that even after keeping her alive for so long he would kill her on the spot if she said anything more. But you never make a threat you aren't prepared to carry out, and he needed her to fulfill the purpose for which he had spared her life. He would stick to the plan.

"Today is your day," he said, screwing his face into a semblance of a smile. "Your sentence is over."

Coby's eyes widened. "You mean you're going to let me go?" In spite of her distrust, the depression of a year's incarceration lifted for a moment from her lithe body. Her shoulders straightened and her voice took on a new timbre. "Why?" she said, suspicion setting in. "This supposed to be a one-year sentence or something?"

He studied her in majestic silence. *One-year sentence indeed!* Let her have hope, the worst of maladies, for it prolongs torment which she deserved. More than once she had burned out the pump by letting the water run all night, had smashed light bulbs and thrown garbage out of her cell. Her constant demands for more books and fresh food, her crying jags, screams, endless questions about her father, her petty pretenses at being sick—these disruptions had worn on him every time he stayed in the farmhouse, and made something inside of him scream to control her with death. At the outset he had thought of letting her die by withholding the penicillin for her leg, or inducing a slower death by starvation.

A year ago when they raided the LCM, some hours after Cecil had machine-gunned the stateroom, St. Gregory had found Coby hiding in a crew cupboard with two 9-mm slugs in her right thigh. He had brought her to a Nassau hospital where he was known, and after the slugs were removed, had carried her here. The girl Cecil killed that night was a nameless drifter brought aboard at Bimini by one of the LCM crew members. St. Gregory had let Cyril believe it was Coby's body, leaving only himself knowing the truth, and he had hoarded her like the valuable secret she was.

Coby had been his captive longer than any of the others over the years, and she had been the quickest to dislodge the concrete blocks at the base of the wall. Sooner or later they all thought of that, and would spend weeks prying them out and months burrowing in the rock-hard soil. They had such ingenious ways of disposing of their diggings, flushing the sand down the toilet or stowing the stones on the cross braces of the ceiling joists. One enterprising hostage had managed to burrow eight feet up until he came to the concrete walk that bordered the house. For St. Gregory it was a sport like deep-sea fishing, in which you test your will against the will of the fish. You let it run to a precise limit, maneuver it to the surface, give it a measured taste of freedom, and when it is quiet in the net you gently remove the hook . . . and gut it for the fire.

Like any sportsman, he saw the action as only part of the sport, for the fish itself was a commodity of value. Over time Coby's value had grown in the currency of power, the loss of which he would do anything to avoid, and he would spend it now to lure North to the Island. If power corrupts, he thought wryly, it is the loss of power that corrupts absolutely.

Taking a baseball cap from his pocket, he pushed it through the bars. "Put this on and shove your hair up inside it."

When she finished, he unlocked the barred door, handcuffed and blindfolded her, and led her outside to the deserted area of scrubby trees and fields of weeds. When he had her stowed inside the trunk, he sped off toward Lyford Cay. On the way, the circular route of the Norths appealed to his sense of symmetry—Grant North from Island to jail, and Coby North from jail to Island.

CHARLES RANSOM leaned on the port rail of his yacht with a hang-dog expression, no longer the self-assured autocrat in jaunty captain's cap. Bareheaded, dressed in a wrinkled business suit, he looked like a salesman who had nothing to show for his week on the road.

When St. Gregory lifted Coby North from the trunk, the Prime Minister let out a muffled gasp and glanced around to see if anyone was watching. St. Gregory moved the girl aboard the cruiser, thankful that the Lyford Cay harbor was deserted at the moment. He placed a massive hand on her head, and pushed her police-style through the entryway and down into the cabin where he handcuffed her to a post.

"Who the hell is *that?*" Ransom said when St. Gregory came out on deck.

The captain studied Ransom's eyes and saw a betraying flicker of comprehension. The Prime Minister knew who she was all right, and feigned disgust at the delayed answer as he ascended to the flying bridge. At the helm, he nodded down to the burly figure of Wright, his one uninjured bodyguard and the only crewman he had said he wanted on this secret expedition. Wright stood on the foredeck ready to cast off.

Amid the rumble of the deep-throated diesels, the Defender captain came up the ladder behind Ransom, feeling contempt for men who don't want to know the details, who hang onto their illusions of virtue, even when their illusions smash themselves to pieces against the iron engine of reality.

"*That*, Mr. Prime Minister," he said in the P.M.'s ear, "is the contingency plan I told you about."

63 *Dragon's Breath*

WHITE FOAM sputtered past the steel hull, producing a plaintive sound that carried to the poop where North had the helm. A swath of moonlight like a river in the sea drew them east toward the Wracking Islands.

"It's oh one hundred hours," he said.

"We should take turns sleeping," Rolle said. "You especially need sleep with that fever coming and going."

"Who the hell can sleep?"

Out the starboard window, lights of villages crowned brooding shapes of distant islands. They were entering the dark country of revenge where no landmarks could guide them. Since leaving Bimini, they had been refining the plan, going over tactical details. Their strategy allowed for ceaseless provocation, but for killing only in self-defense. All the intricate steps to be taken seemed to fit, and now Rolle said, "Okay, let's suppose this works. What do we do afterwards?"

"Afterwards?" It was an alien concept to North. Rolle knew as well as he that if they failed they'd either be gunned down, put on trial and executed, or end up in prison for the rest of their lives. In the Third World only crimes of passion, like the Knowles murder, go relatively unpunished. And if they succeeded? "I don't know," he said.

"Well, we oughta have a plan for afterwards. Maybe we can chain Ransom to a poisonwood tree and tell the Nassau newspapers where they can find their dope king."

"If we dispose of him, or if we expose him, we don't have to worry about what happens later," North said.

"How's that?"

"With the demise of the Prime Minister, the Deputy Prime Minister takes over. That's Malcolm Pyfrom, the guy who mined Ransom's estate. Pyfrom couldn't have us arrested without implicating himself. No doubt he'd blame Ransom for everything." All this North said academically, in a monotone, knowing that the real purpose of a plan is to shield the planner from the terrors of the future.

"Yeah," said Rolle, smiling faintly. "All we have to do is plant drugs next to their chained or dead bodies."

"Where would we get the drugs?"

"What the hell, Grant, it's four days since we left the place! That's about three days longer that it takes for our so-called caretakers to start partying."

Instead of focusing on wiping out dope, societies need to channel the energy their citizens invest in such illegal enterprises, thought North, but no one makes the connection. He felt isolated from the rest of humanity but close to Rolle, and thought about their self-imposed restriction on killing the enemy, wondering whether in the end the intent of your actions matters. A year ago when Rolle, in a flippant mood, had asked him whether it mattered if he had thrown Rahming off the roof, North wanted to say something about integrity and invisible virtue, subjects difficult to express between men, and he had solemnly attempted the incommunicable. He had answered simply but with feeling, *Yes, it matters!* Invisible virtue like Rolle's is best glimpsed in actions where, after an incident such as the one on the roof, the virtue goes on breeding under the shingles and soon lights the entire edifice with its blazing radiance.

Yes, your intent matters!

As the night wore on, North became feverish again, and turned the wheel over to Rolle so he could rest his head against the back of the wide cushion. He fell into a fitful sleep. Cleary had been right when he'd said the dead could just as easily come to the living, for he arose out of North's delirium and said as he used to say, *Walk away from it, Grant!* And North answered, *I can't, any more than could you!* Half-awake, he summoned the other dead, Coby and Marianne, and he realized they had been opposites in many ways. Coby: blonde, mathematical, tomboyish, American. Marianne: dark, literary, feminine, citizen of a tiny island nation. Yet both were biophiles who had lived their lives intensely. And who had distrusted their fathers.

"Island, dead ahead," Rolle said quietly. He throttled down the engines to loitering speed while they still were too far out to be seen.

North jerked upright and glanced at his watch, surprised that it was after five. The moon sagged behind them and the oily sea heaved like a man getting out of bed with insufficient sleep. As the eastern sky lightened, they watched the miracle of an Island shimmering weightless in the pastel sky and rising out of the sea like the ascent of a whale, and it made North feel alive yet strangely jealous. Except for the shadows cast upon it from the outside world, the Island still was hallowed ground, still his.

They crept closer at idle, engines muted, making a wide sweep to starboard so they would approach the Island from the east. A half hour passed, and they could distinguish Harbour Rock from the main body of land. Above it a layer of nimbus hovered over the trees, broken into small patches like dirty cotton. Soon those dark shapes turned into something evil, and to his horror North realized they weren't rain clouds at all, but smoke. As he watched, the horizon boiled into black airborne soot along the length of the southern shore. The Island was dying, its living flesh afire.

"Shit, they torched the jungle," said Rolle. He searched through the binoculars and a smile of satisfaction spread over his face. "They're still there!" He handed the glasses to North.

At the dock, a white yacht jumped out against the dark band of smoke like a shaft of light. Ransom's no-name cruiser. Antennae bulged from her flying bridge like enormous insects. No one was on deck but it was evident she was manned, for her radar aerial was turning steadily, searching the horizon.

"So what do we do, charge right in?" That *was* the basic plan they'd discussed half the night, but Rolle added, "If I were St. Greg, I'd be salivating over that decision. They obviously set the fires as bait for us."

Upwind of the Island, they couldn't smell the smoke but could see it seething low over the treeline in a dozen or more patches. Random thoughts repulsed North's fever, registering reversely in his mind, like the sun's circle turning green on the retina against closed eyelids, each image a single frame of past goals and lost hope. It came to him superfluously that he could never live here now with Coby or Cleary or Marianne, could never bring his scientists to improve the characteristics of shrimp or windmills. The enemy had captured the territory.

North shook his head to clear it. "Steady as you go, Sid. Heading one-zero-five degrees. Keep Harbour Rock between us and the dock. I want to creep in as close as possible before their radar distinguishes us from this little island."

"We're going straight in then?"

"As planned."

With the engines barely turning over, they slid to the eastern tip of Harbour Rock. Reaching the low corner of the islet with the sun behind them, North saw through the binoculars across Slaughter Harbour with an amazing clarity. A Bahamian ensign flapped at the cruiser's sternmast. The wide windows of the saloon reflected the clouds, and over the cabin the radar revolved relentlessly. They'd be found soon after they moved out from under the electromagnetic shadow of Harbour Rock, but for the moment they were invisible.

"Let's get to work," said North, and Rolle shifted into neutral. They descended to the main cabin where they lifted the floor hatch and scurried down the ladder to the engine room. Crammed with machinery, the low-ceilinged space was stifling hot and noisy. North wedged himself between the port engine and forward bulkhead to disconnect the governor, then repeated the process on the starboard engine. Now the heavy diesels would rev up to more than twice their cruising speeds of seventeen hundred revolutions per minute.

Meanwhile, Rolle disengaged the automatic bilge pumps that eject seawater entering the well deck.

When they finished, they climbed back up the steel rungs and down on the other side of the bulkhead into the open cargo well. Without hesitation, they tipped over one of the fifty-five-gallon drums, sending its contents sloshing over the steel plates of the inner hull. The smell of it filled the ship with a raw fragrance of impending catastrophe. North opened a crew locker and took out three bedsheets. He stuffed the ends of each of them into the drum that was full, splaying the remainder of the fabric in different directions so it would soak in the river of gasoline. Then he filled a wine bottle halfway up with gas and stuffed a rag into it.

On the way back to the poop deck, they stopped in the cabin to fix snorkels to masks, arranging them tactically on the cabin floor between the two side doors. They brought their Molotov cocktail to the wheelhouse, and watched the cruiser through binoculars.

Two men in bush clothes appeared on the cruiser's deck forward of the cabin. One was Wright, the bigger of the P.M.'s bodyguards, brandishing an automatic rifle. The other was St. Gregory. No mistaking that black beard, mirrored sunglasses, and towering height. Out of uniform, the Defender captain seemed to have taken on the dimensions of wealth; he looked wider around his waist than North had remembered him, but that could be the cartridge belt he wore. His sleeves were rolled back to show forearms like a blacksmith's, in which he cradled an enormous weapon. No mere sidearm for this captain. Vlado Novac had shown them revolving shotguns, and even at this distance North recognized the South African Striker from its huge drum hanging between double pistol grips. More frightening than a machine gun, it had been designed for the Rhodesian bush wars, and could fire tear gas, tiny grenades, a mass of fléchettes—which were arrows of spring steel an inch and a half long—or rounds of "Dragon's Breath," flaming metal designed to set buildings or ships on fire. St. Gregory carried the gun with a robotic resolve, as if his genes had been insufficiently spliced for a more human look.

"He be one big son of a bitch, all right," said Rolle, seeing through the binoculars that St. Gregory was a head taller than the six-foot bodyguard as he edged past him to enter the cabin.

"Doesn't matter," North said in that hollow voice he'd used yesterday. "He can't drink burning gasoline better than anyone else." He eased the transmissions into gear, and the *Half Fast* crept forward unseen, still in the radar shadow of Harbour Rock. North and Rolle kept their eyes glued to the cruiser.

Charles Ransom and someone in long sleeves and baseball cap, who North assumed was the diminutive bodyguard, scrambled off the aft deck of the cruiser and ran toward the Island. The small one carried a canvas bag, and Ransom a rifle; their legs, shimmering on the beach, were thin as herons. As they headed toward an area of jungle so far uninjured by fire, it seemed they mimed the hypocrisy of Ransom's reign: heads low, backs bent in subjugation, steps labored, leading each other into oblivion. Too bad the taller of the two hadn't died nailed to that crucifix of his he called a ranch.

Thirty seconds passed, during which time North had crept the landing craft around the edge of Harbour Rock. Rolle watched intently through the binoculars. A minute. Eighty seconds. St. Gregory must have picked up their moving blip because he rushed back up on deck where he and Wright, their hands held in a salute over their brows, were looking straight into the sun at the LCM.

North rammed both throttles forward, experiencing the phenomenal strength of one who is willing to die. The vessel roared into Slaughter Harbour like a tank, North's heart pounding under the fiery flow of adrenaline. Aiming directly at the cruiser, he brought the engines to full, screaming power. The three-bladed bronze propellers clutched the ocean and spit it out behind in a boiling froth. Empty and light, full-fast at last, the LCM lifted onto a plane with her head held high like a stallion, and North smashed the hull against the waves as if they were St. Gregory and Ransom. Cascades of frothing water flew overhead like body parts. The props began to cavitate. In five or ten minutes the engines would overheat and seize.

They needed less than two of those minutes.

St. Gregory and Wright knelt on the foredeck of the cruiser

and fired on automatic, trying to lob rounds over the LCM's high bow, but the square steel ramp protected the wheelhouse at the stern as effectively as the armor of a tank. Seeing that, St. Gregory and Wright dashed off the yacht onto the dock where they lay prone and resumed firing.

Rolle yanked the long lever at the right of the control pylon, which through a series of chains, lowered the steel bow ramp. The LCM raced headlong toward the soft starboard belly of Ransom's yacht, yawing her fourteen-foot horizontal cleaver from side to side like a hammerhead in frenzy. Gasoline almost never blows up on impact, and North had no illusions about his ability to throw the Molotov into the fuel-soaked well deck at the precise moment required. If not, there was always the hope that the enemy gunfire would set it off, and if all else failed, the collision would create one hell of a diversion. He felt a final tinge of remorse for destroying the ship that had served him so well.

Two hundred yards. One hundred. Sixty. They were across the harbor, the LCM's big diesels screaming like Saturn rockets, tearing themselves up at forty knots.

A dozen rounds ripped through a cabin window below the poop and shattered the far wall.

Less than a half minute from collision, North eased the throttles without diminishing his speed appreciably in order to bring down the clever of the bow ramp to horizontal. At the same time, he turned slightly to port as if aiming at the two men firing from the dock.

The maneuver gave St. Gregory a field of fire over the open ramp. North could see the Defender clearly as he stood to gain height, his feet planted well apart on the dock, knees bent like a skier's, pointing the big shotgun up at the poop, his hands fore and aft of the rotating drum. For a brief instant their eyes locked on each other. North lit the rag wick stuffed into the bottle of gasoline, but it hadn't been soaked enough and went out.

There was no time to try again. The drum of the Striker began its rotation as North yanked the wheel to starboard and bounded down to the cabin with Rolle. They grabbed their masks, and at the last second, flung open the starboard door and leapt overboard.

Falling toward the water, they heard Wright's automatic rifle and the *THUMPH-thummph-THUMMMPP* of St. Gregory's shotgun hammering the cabin walls.

Dozens of darts stung Rolle's right thigh like wasps, and his head whirled in a red fog as pain flooded his brain. He dove deep, leveling off six feet below the surface, feeling the saltwater ignite each sting like a match in his flesh. He swam wildly after North in a three-limbed underwater scissors stroke. For as long as his breath allowed.

EVERY THIRTY or forty seconds when a swimmer's snorkel broke the surface to blow like a dolphin, Wright sprayed the area with his automatic rifle. St. Gregory had emptied his drum of fléchettes. Reloading with Dragon's Breath, he pumped a half-dozen rounds toward the snorkel at three hundred yards. A futile effort at that range, perhaps, but he enjoyed the feel of the gun in his arms, like working a lightweight jackhammer. Just as St. Gregory was afraid the swimmers were getting away, one or both snorkels broke the water, and Wright fired a long burst that emptied a full thirty-round clip.

St. Gregory stared at his watch for two full minutes, then three. The calm surface of Slaughter Harbour stayed unbroken. To make sure of the kill, he strode back toward the wrecks of the vessels; if North or Rolle somehow had survived, the wreckage would provide the only possible cover in the harbor. Wright followed, ramming another clip into his rifle.

The landing craft had struck the cruiser diagonally at the port beam with such force that both hulls were twisted into each other. You could see into the yacht's saloon where the horizontal bow ramp of the LCM, having severed the cabin at its base, protruded into the galley and dining area like a cleaver through a piece of meat.

"You see both snorkels before your blast?" St. Gregory asked Wright.

"I dunno."

"We might have gotten only one of 'em. North or the other guy might have doubled back and be hiding inside, or in the speedboat." The Mako, still tethered, was swinging free behind the hulk of the landing craft.

St. Gregory and Wright climbed onto the afterdeck of the listing cruiser, the odor of gunpowder and the burning Island sharp in their nostrils. Like one of Edward Teach's crew trying to tolerate the smoke, Wright let out a series of coughs. He stifled the next one, crouched behind the still-standing outdoor bar, and used his rifle to nudge open the swinging door to the cabin. St. Gregory bent gingerly over the low entryway, anticipating gunfire, his finger tense on the Striker's trigger. Inside, broken windows and dishes, pieces of fiberglass, and smashed radios made a slurry of litter where the steel ramp of the landing craft stuck into the belly of the cruiser. He saw he had a clear shot over the ramp into the guts of the LCM.

Something moved in that steel ship, maybe a falling object, maybe the stressed metal itself—maybe, he thought, North or Rolle. His finger squeezed the trigger, sliding a micron beyond the point of no return, a light-year beyond the edge of prudence. In his final signature, St. Gregory smelled the fumes too late and recalled a statistic known to those who use explosives, that a gallon of vaporized gasoline is equal to the blasting power of a hundred pounds of dynamite. A flame of Dragon's Breath, superheated by its nitro-based oxygenated propellant, shot out of the Striker and streamed beyond the wreckage into the LCM.

The hot breath of molten magnesium lapped at the gas-air mix, and slammed against the sides of the steel hull in a blinding fireball. At the atomic level, where the concepts of electrons and justice are diffuse and seem to merge, the two metals collided at a thousand feet per second. They tried to meld into a single brilliant alloy, but could not, because the history of the ship was life, and the history of the dragon was death.

64 *Definition of Murder*

THIRTY FEET deep, North heard a gurgling noise and realized it was himself gulping air. He had made it to one of the hemispheric airdomes, remnants of his underwater garden. Through the plexiglass he could see the crusty sides of Harbour Rock, coral protrusions like giant brains, swaying sea anemones, and the darting shadows of fish. Rolle's head broke the surface of the three-foot hemisphere, and abruptly they were face to face in the air of the dome.

Rolle shuddered, his mouth contorted. "My leg!"

Greenish-gray blood swirled below them in the blue water. Filling his lungs, North pulled his mask back over his face and submerged by gripping one of the stainless-steel cables that anchored the domes to the seabed. From knee to groin, Rolle's thigh was a mass of raw meat stuck with dozens of fléchettes. North found that by pushing deep into the flesh he could grip the steel barbs with his fingernails and jerk them out one at a time. With each extraction, Rolle gave an involuntary kick and spilled more of his weird-looking greenish blood into the ocean.

"Oxygen's depleted," said Rolle on one of North's ascents into the dome. "Let's move."

They swam along the bottom and were pulling themselves by

the guy wires toward the next airdome when they heard the explosion. Sound travels four times faster in water than air, and the vibrations from the blast came from all directions at once, bathing them in a lightning-like discharge. By the time they surfaced into the plexiglass mantle of another two-man dome, it was quiet again. These domes were resonate places where you could hear your own internal sounds, the ringing in your ears, your pounding heart, the gasps of your breathing.

"They must have fired their weapons into the gasoline," North said in an echo of relief.

"Nobody could live through that," said Rolle with a grimace, repressing his pain.

"Ransom could. He and the other guy ran off into the jungle before the shooting started."

The domes provided a phenomenal asylum, isolated and alien as the moon, and North found the underwater environment a practical operating theater. The water swept away the blood as he worked and the mask magnified his vision. The fléchettes were little arrows with barbed points, shafts like finishing nails, and ends of steel feathers. He removed about thirty of them, and wondered how many more were too deep to find, estimating that a single shotgun cartridge held about a hundred. The injury was dangerous, not because the blood would attract sharks—the explosion would have sent them racing out to sea—but because of the loss of blood. North ripped out the sleeves of his shirt, tied them together, and looped a tourniquet above the wound. Rolle kept the loop tight with his fingers.

As the oxygen became exhausted in one air station they made their way to the next, progressing dome by dome along the nine-hundred-foot Harbour Rock. At the last hemisphere they hyperventilated and swam underwater to the beach. They had been submerged for a half hour, and they were shivering.

On the beach North helped Rolle toward a nest of boulders, canvassing the area as they went. Directly ahead and atop the steep bank, he saw that two of the villas were burned to the ground and the windows of the others had been smashed. The Island beyond the buildings writhed in smoke. Across the harbor to his left, the dock lay tangled in the wreckage of Ransom's cruiser and the LCM. Nothing moved. Rolle settled into the rock alcove, the blood vessels of his face bulging in pain. Soon the warmth of the sun stopped his shivering and he could talk again.

"Going somewhere?"

"To reconnoiter."

"I think I've got some penicillin in my villa. You better give me a shot."

"After I get back, Sid. We don't want some other kind of shot from St. Greg and friends."

"I don't want to die on this Island, Grant."

"I'll be back soon. And don't worry about where you die. Only where you live."

Rolle let out a weak chuckle. "I don't want to *live* here either."

North had never seen Rolle so ashen, so hurt. He might bleed to death if they weren't careful. But there was little he could do for him now, and it was imperative to determine the strength of the enemy. Creeping low up the incline to the villas, he entered the side of the duplex that had been his. He opened the closet where he kept a spare plantation hat and two spearguns. The hat was on the shelf. One of the spearguns was gone, and the other was . . . below. It took him a moment to comprehend what he saw, and when he did, it was like an explosion in his heart. The spear had entered Bruiser near his stingray scar and emerged at his back. The dog's corpse had been positioned with the head facing straight ahead so you couldn't miss seeing the ends of the shaft jutting out of both sides.

North remembered Coby's definition of murder. The savage and needless killing had to be the work of a psychopath—had to be St. Gregory. But why? Obviously to enrage him, to bring him into the open, for the dog's death could serve no other purpose.

He looked for the cats, hoping they were hiding and not dead. Breathing deeply in an attempt to slow his respiration, he unscrewed the spearpoint and pulled the shaft, still tethered to its gun, back through Bruiser's body. With flint blades something like this spear tip, Aztec priests had ripped the beating hearts from animals and children to feed their gods, believing it would gain them heaven.

What did St. Gregory believe?

He wiped the blood off the shaft, loaded the gun, and reattached the point. Making his way through the woods paralleling the shore of the harbor, he emerged onto the beach at a point where the seafarm lay to the right, the dock to the left. The fires in the jungle were sucking air from the area of the corrals, and he could smell the unmistakable odor of rotting seaweed and shrimp. Shrouded by the brown biomass that had been starved of nutrients, tons of the underlying shrimp had died from oxygen depletion. The carnage hadn't happened today or yesterday with the arrival of Ransom's yacht. His five caretakers must have quit working the moment North and friends had left on their ill-fated venture.

Waiving the cover of forest, he sped to the battle-strewn dock. Like a living creature thrown to sharks, the *Half Fast* lay torn and ravaged. Borne up, flung down, ripped apart, her twisted hull floated perpendicular to the burned carcass of the cruiser like the inverted carapace of an enormous turtle. Little could be identified except two hulks of metal that had been the cruiser's engines; still veiled in lingering flames fed by motor oil, they resembled boulders of coal. The Mako, torn free of her halter, was beached a hundred yards up the shore of the harbor.

North saw the enemy then. In pieces.

One was Wright, recognizable even without his head which lay beside him like a coconut opened with a sledgehammer.

The other was St. Gregory, who had been flipped around like a pancake, his torso bent so far backwards his spine had cracked. The surprise frozen in the muscles surrounding his open eyes and the off-center set of his beard made his face seem more alive than it ever had been in life, as if in the instant before his death he had witnessed the ghost of his annihilation. But his eyes had lost their color, and were dull and glassy like those of a fish hauled up from the bottom. As in the olden days of Slaughter Harbour, blood ran purple against the tide.

Seeing his nemesis as a corpse, North felt dissociated, as if his other self were asleep in the forest waiting for the sun to wake him to find the ferns and trees green again. He indulged that sensation for a moment, looking at the necrophiliac one last time, recording a final fusion of the death lover with the dead.

North shook himself, took a deep breath, and calculated his tactical gain. He was ahead one knight. But his own knight was out of action.

Returning to the boulder where he'd left Rolle, he found him tightening his tourniquet with a stick. Beads of sweat appeared on his forehead. "What happened out there?" Rolle said with an effort.

"St. Gregory and Wright are dead."

"Phase one completed. I guess I feel like we've accomplished something, like we've killed Hitler before he slaughtered millions."

"Sure," said North.

"It was something our generation had to do. Even if—" Rolle stopped, thinking silent thoughts. "Even if Marianne was right and the 'horrendous demon' pops up again in some other century."

Lightheaded from loss of blood, Rolle leaned on North and they climbed the bank of beach to Rolle's room, which had not been touched by fire. Inside North found a needlenose pliers, which he sterilized in alcohol and used to poke around in the big thigh muscle, pulling out fléchettes that had penetrated too deep to grasp with his bare fingers.

"A few inches farther west, and it would have ended your sex life," said North, attempting distraction. He didn't know how Rolle could stand the pain. His thigh was leaking blood and swelling fast.

Rolle managed to turn his expression of suffering into a grin. "People have been trying to end my sex life for some time now, Grant. But I always rise again."

North found sulfa powder and aspirin in Rolle's medicine chest. There also was a hypodermic syringe with vials of sterile water and one small penicillin ampule, and he diluted the penicillin in the water. In the bedroom, he sprinkled sulfa over the wound, binding it with gauze and an elastic bandage. Applying a tourniquet to Rolle's arm, he tapped for a vein.

"We mainlining the stuff?"

"There's not enough of it to do you much good otherwise," North said. North injected the penicillin slowly and gave him a batch of aspirin, the only painkiller they had.

North turned to his own affliction then, knowing there was no antiviral treatment for dengue. He swallowed some aspirin, forced down as much water as he could drink to prevent dehydration, and borrowed one of Rolle's long-sleeved shirts and a pair of work pants. He found a fishing line in Rolle's tackle box and put it in his pocket; there were things you could do in a jungle with an invisible line.

"Look, Sid, you probably lost a quart of blood or more. If you can keep the infection down, you'll be okay. In the morning you'll feel stronger because your body will have manufactured more blood. The Mako wasn't damaged. Take it whenever you feel strong enough, and get the hell to a hospital. You can't be of help to me anyway with that leg, and for all I know there are another dozen fléchettes in there too deep to see without x-rays. Take this." He handed Rolle the speargun. "Just in case."

Sugar and Spice ran into the open door and jumped on Rolle's bed carrying their tails upright like small masts. They looked thin and dirty. North was glad to see them alive, but hunters had no time for affection. He told Rolle about Bruiser, then opened the door.

"Sid," he said from the doorway with a rolled-up blanket under his arm, "thanks."

Outside, a reddish mist sagged into a milky substance like a Chicago smog. It was suspended smoke particles settling over the Island. North began his march across the land, encountering a devastation worse than Sherman's to the sea, a total transformation of the Island's anatomy. The utility building had been burned to the ground. The lodge, so laboriously repaired after the hurricane, was gutted; nothing remained of it except stone rubble and beams turned to coal. Acres of charred berry trees and thatch palms sickened him, their once-fragrant turrets saturated with the stench of smoke. These were trees that would take twenty years to grow back. Pressing westward along a path cleared by the fire, he became aware of the biological process of the jungle, the wood soon to rot, the fertilizer of the ash, and the waxy spires of bromeliads already jutting through the forest litter, the only green in a monotony of charcoal.

COBY NORTH hadn't seen the LCM crash into the yacht, but she'd heard the machine-gun fire, roaring engines, and the screech of metal. A long silence followed, shattered by gun blasts and a fierce explosion, like worlds in collision. And while Ransom watched intently, his face a mask of fear and anxiety, she slipped the submachine gun away from where he'd leaned it against a tree, and dashed headlong down the road away from the harbor.

She turned off the road at the tower and weaved through the jungle. The acid-sweet odor of the smoldering trees pervaded the Island, but the fires hadn't destroyed this western half of the land, and the jungle remained lush and moist. Frightened, thirsty, and tired, she limped from unaccustomed running and the year-old wound in her right leg. She felt an immense relief to be back here with the hermit crabs, the lizards the color of dust, the verdant hills rising like humpback whales, where the woods were cool and smelled of chlorophyll against the distant smoke. She made herself pay attention to safety and look for water and food, postponing what she yearned to do, to find out whether her father was still alive. St. Gregory had told her he was dead, but then St. Greg had been lying to her for a year about everything from the location of the basement jail to his intentions toward her.

Slipping through the woods to the western edge of the palm grove, she picked up a coconut and moved back inside the cover of the forest, avoiding clearings. A fragrance of pines and pigeon plumb lay heavy on the air like perfumed sweat. Hidden by fronds of thatch and tamarind, she stopped to rest and to examine the gun in the filtered light, knowing she should familiarize herself with it in case she had to defend herself. Less than three feet long, the evil-looking thing had a short barrel within a metal sleeve full of holes, and a long perpendicular arm she supposed was the bullet cartridge. The first thing she did was locate the trigger. Holding the gun in both hands, she sighted down the barrel, wondering how many bullets the cartridge held and whether she could afford to waste any testing it.

What if St. Gregory and Ransom were not alone on the island? Some of their soldiers could have come in another boat. Awakening the tempo of fear, she glanced nervously around, half expecting to see grisly Defenders marching mindlessly out of her St. Gregory nightmare.

An idea burst in her mind, the kind of idea that accomplishes two goals at once. Placing a coconut in the crook of a tree, she took careful aim from a distance of a few feet, and pulled the trigger. Nothing happened. She discovered a small lever that kept the trigger from moving, flipped it, aimed again, and fired a short burst. The barrel rode up, giving her the temper of the thing, and the bullets shattered the top half of the coconut. She held it to her lips, and the milky water trickling into her mouth brought Island memories from her former life. She picked up the pieces of the white coconut meat that had scattered over the brittle fronds of the forest floor, and slumped down against a tree to eat her dinner. As the sun set she prepared for a long night, the submachine gun resting in her lap.

HIDDEN in the brush at the edge of the beach until dark, Charles Ransom ventured forth to behold the ruin that had been his yacht. The bright moonlight revealed the mangled corpses and the shapes of gulls and crows circling them like the buzzards of Andros. So much for St. Gregory's ideas. Like the raid on the barge that had started this chain of horror, his "insurance policy" and "foolproof" plans had achieved nothing but destruction.

What if Wright's bullets had not found North and his helper when they were in the water? Neither had surfaced during the shooting, and yet Ransom was too much a political realist to believe things happen just because you want them to. He knew that if North were alive, he and Rolle would be spending the night hunting. For him.

He hadn't felt so helpless since he was a student in Chicago waylaid by the police. To make things worse, the North girl had stolen his gun and had run off into the bush so that now he had to worry about her shooting him.

The sounds of his labored breathing made him remember Marianne as an adolescent and how he'd taught her to scuba dive, the submarine gardens they'd explored together, the reef fish, the pure tones of her conch flute piercing the afternoon calm, the rank perfumes of their beach fires. He used to think of her as a slender palm, the kind that doubles back in a hurricane and springs up at the right time, a creature of the light, fronds lashing as she leaps for the sky. With her streak of independence and adventure, she should have been the boy and Dean Gérard the girl. Then he imagined her body in the rubble of what had been his ranch house, and he felt empty, and cried for her. Only once before had he wept as an adult, and that was yesterday when she died.

The smoke drained the moonlight out of the sky. With the movements of an old man, Ransom lurched into the jungle carrying only his canvas bag. As he made his way to the vicinity of the wind tower, he heard from the west a short burst from a submachine gun. That could mean the North girl was not waiting in ambush after all, was probably using the gun to keep him away. He breathed easier. Physical fighting was the most primitive way of making war on your enemies, not the way he'd fought in Parliament or in the countless conference rooms of his career.

Deep in the jungle, his eyes dark-adapted, he came to a glade untouched by fire. Vines grew here, putting forth yellow blossoms, and the leaves shimmered with moisture, a sanctuary in a land of death. He laid down the speargun St. Gregory had stolen for him, and took a bottle of Scotch from the bag. Holding the bottle to his lips for a long time, he tasted the pungent sorrow of Marianne's death and of his own survival. His breath failed him and he fell against a tree. His heart was beating too fast. Hideous wisps of smoke tendrilled up from the ash around the glade.

Calming himself, he managed to slow his pulse, but he could do nothing to stem the feeling of isolation. You strive all your life only to find yourself shunned by your wife, your son, your daughter, your best friend, vanquished at the end, your enemies picking flesh from your bones. Then he realized that nothing had changed: he had always been alone.

The thought fortified him and he indulged the old timbre of independence, recalling scrapes as bad or worse than this one. The gulf between flight and fight, between vulnerability and rugged self-reliance, closed on his resolve. He threw away the bottle of Scotch. The wind had shifted, blowing the overhead smoke away, and a fiery energy from the moon lit the trees, cleansing his mind. In who else's blood, he thought, pulsed both the strength of the master and the fury of the slave?

Ransom plunged deeper into the woods, heading in the direction of the gunfire. When he came to the wind tower, he circled it, then cautiously climbed the spiral staircase to the platform at the top. Soldiers always tried to command the high ground, didn't they? At any rate, it seemed a good place to spend the night.

GRANT NORTH had known soldiers who could move through a landscape without disrupting it, but he had not been one of them. He plowed through the dead world of blackened trunks, making noise, snagging his clothing, wrenching his spirit. In the moonlight even the patches of forest untouched by fire seemed diseased, swarming with albino funguses and mildew. The worst part was forcing himself to accept the mortality of the Island and to believe that he no longer needed to be a part of it, or it a part of him. Too mightily could he feel the injured, dormant victim rising against its tormentor, and he knew he could travel far but never so far that he could renounce the soul of his Island.

Shapes arose at the edge of his vision, the jungle in pain. Head down and crouching close to the scorched thatch, he became one with the fallen trunks and the new green shoots of the bromeliads. He forced himself to think as his enemy would think in this alien place. Where would he go? Ransom had never been to the Island, had never been in the military. He wouldn't know how to deploy Wilson to outflank his foe or to set up a field of fire. He wouldn't know the subtleties of brush reconnaissance, the countless places where North and the Island, working together, could establish an ambush. Ransom and colleague would see only the obvious: the tower from which they could dominate the landscape, the open beach to be avoided, the laboratory building to give them shelter.

Earlier, a brief burst from a submachine gun far to the west had stabbed the trees, haunting the forest, but he'd heard no more bursts. He pictured Ransom, no longer armed with plenary power, playing the black pieces, and felt the frustration of that messianic man on the defensive.

The sky was bright with moonlit clouds, and its light widened the open spaces of the jungle. He felt a presence, and froze. Wedged into a hole eroded out of the coral ground was a crude nest, and in it the owl, North's old symbol of warning, stealth, and retaliation. North and the bird stared at each other for a moment, and then the owl flapped up above the woods on its wide wingspan, gliding toward the tower.

He stayed to listen, rejecting fear, concentrating intently. In the echoes of dying trees he conjured those who had helped the Island fulfill itself. There shimmering in the moonlight was Godfrey Knowles, that rock-solid lignum vitae. There Marianne, the curving sapling. Cleary the staunch gum elemi. And Cuda and Sweeting, Shark, Purple, Garlic, Oris, and all the rest, withered, blackened, gone. He slept an hour, and in his dreams held Marianne. He asked her to find her father for him but though she kissed him, she would lead him nowhere.

He awoke sweating in his blanket, wrapped in the fatigue of his fever, but he rose and followed a swatch of moonlight to the road. He stood in silent reconnaissance, listening to the breezes, and imagined descending upon him the faint, scuffling sounds of leather shoes against wood. Turning his gaze upward to the top of the wind tower, he was certain that Ransom was there, keeping watch through the night. Too exhausted to understand he was living again in the dynamic domain of raw intuition, Grant North knew simply that he did not need to see his enemies to know where they were hiding.

As he plodded back through the trees he thought about Rolle, and wondered whether he would see him again. We use a man for a time without questioning how our goals are different from his goals, and when he's hurt and in the way, we push him out of our lives. Rolle could go home now.

SIDNEY ROLLE had tried to stay vigilant, but the next thing he knew the first rays of the sun were streaking across Slaughter Harbour and rimming his window in a feathered halo. His thigh churned in pain and he was so haggard his skull felt carved of stone. North was gone. The fires, fermenting in the morning mist, had spread the decaying odors of blackened leaves, and when he hobbled out-side he thought the slavers had come again to wash the Island in blood. He shook his head. Civilization, the stars, the gods are not at fault, he knew. You blame slavers for slavery, and killers for killing.

North had been right that his body had manufactured more blood, and though his leg hurt, Rolle could feel his vitality returning like an old friend. Checking that his speargun safety was on, he turned the gun point down and used it as a crutch, taking strength from it. He found Bruiser's body in the closet, feeling a sense of loss for an old friend. The carcasses of St. Gregory and Wright could rot for all he cared, but he took a shovel and buried Bruiser beneath a coconut palm.

Rolle understood better than most men that in the world of nature there are no mourners, only survivors. The latter included himself—and, he hoped, Coby. Without telling North, for fear he could be wrong, he had been nursing the hunch that she, and not the bodyguard Wilson, was the bantam figure they saw running off the yacht with Ransom. Rolle had his intuitions too, and because of them he would not scurry back to the village with his *ravo partido*, his tail between his legs. Perhaps, he thought, the story of Slaughter Harbour would be different this time.

Rolle entered the jungle forest to search for Coby.

65 *The Cave, March 15*

SO MANY TIMES had North trod this hallowed ground, cherishing wild gardens of berry trees and orchids, or conjuring improvements for his Island. Now he moved as a destroyer through the bitter monochrome of gutted forest, the mold of decay, the fungi that sprouted through the ash, the dearth of animals. Long ago the rock iguanas, those miniature dinosaurs that once had grown to six feet, and the green parrots with their white helmets and sunny breasts had been shot into near extinction for their meat. Now the forest fires had caused their descendants, the lizards and the wood ducks who wintered here on the freshwater lake, to flee, refugees deserting a war zone. Yet North could sense the lifeblood of the Island stirring beneath the surface, emerging from coral-strewn caverns, cool and deep.

He had been out all night, alternately sleeping and searching, and his face burned with fever and fury. The horizontal rays of the sun shot an orange light across the central lake, transforming the dappled gloom into a mirror that reflected the windmill tower. He circled to higher ground, hunting with the determination of a Carib. When he reached the road he stood motionless in the tree line, hearing only the wind. He pressed a stud on his watch: six in the morning on the ides of March, a full year since Coby's death.

The turbine controls at the base of the wind tower were lit by the rising sun. Using a screwdriver stowed there, North removed the cover plate of the rotor controller and deliberately skewed the synchronizer mechanism, then detached the circuit boards from their fail-safe governors.

He lumbered downhill along the slave walls looking for the pothole entrance to the cave he had discovered after the hurricane. Finding it near the lake, a short distance off the path, he bent over the edge to peer down. The vertical tunnel widened as it descended to the quiet, atavistic cave he remembered, a place where he had wanted to go to lick his wounds. The pain of dengue ringing in his ears sounded like rippling water whispering from the nearby lake. As he listened for signs of the enemy, the winds seemed to sleep and the fronds and twigs on the forest floor withheld their crackling sounds when he stepped on them.

Something even stranger occurred. The hole in the ground, the entrance to the vertical tunnel of the cave, had moved. His gaze shifted from where the opening had been to where it was now, and he realized it had pulled away from the edge of the path to the center, a better location for the ambush he planned. The slope of the land descended slightly at the point of entry, and a cluster of tamarinds grew to the right of the opening, providing a place where he could hide. Could you expect less of this Island against the forces that had burned it alive?

North's fever had been waxing and waning all morning. On its next decline, he told himself that nothing so permanent as the tunnel to a cave could have moved, that he must surrender this notion of the Island incarnate as he had relinquished Coby and Cleary and Marianne, for there could be no future in loving the dying.

Moving methodically, he arranged thin branches in rows across the top of the pothole, and scattered dead fronds over them. At the precise forward edge of the opening, he stretched his fishline a foot above the ground between a gum elemi and the largest of the tamarinds. He tightened the line so you could see it only if you looked in the right place.

How could he bait the trap? He had left the blanket somewhere, and the only object remaining that might attract Ransom's attention was his Panama hat, the kind they sell in Nassau by the thousands. Inanely he turned it around and looked at the label: WOVEN IN ECUADOR. He placed it beyond the fishline at the far border of the frond-covered opening, and came around to the front to regard his work. Preparation for this trap had been unique, consisting of wind-rotor electronics, instinct, and the primitive art of misdirection.

North moved mechanically, his legs setting their own direction around wide-leafed bushes, feeling through his shoes for broken branches the way his recon scouts used to do. He crouched at the road and scanned both directions. One of those mysterious coral rocks that rest in Bahamian trees, as if they are lifted as the tree grows, lay suspended in the crook of a buttonwood. A grenade? The ambusher ambushed?

Expecting at any moment to hear automatic rifle fire or the whistle of a speargun, North forced himself to dash across the open space of the road. Nothing came. He skirted the scorched forest and emerged onto the upper beach. The three familiar coconut palms, two of them billowing fronds like long hair, the third standing guard over the others, reminded him of his former family. Fighting down dizziness, he used his belt and the foot-holds carved out of the trunk to climb the tallest of the trees. At the top he clung to the vines that supported the clustered coconuts, the bushy fronds camouflaging him from all sides. Filigreed clouds stretched gray and pink to the other islands of the Wracking chain, developing horizontal bands of palms and white beaches. Looking down on the laboratory roof, he could see the solar panels and the glass vent pipes from the distillation unit. Over the roof and across the road, the wind tower rose on a series of trusses to the four dough-nut-shaped wind augmenters and, above them, the observation plat-form.

North noticed a glint at the center of the platform that had not been there before. It was Ransom, as he'd expected. The P.M. had accepted North's bait, had taken the high ground, and now was at the railing scanning the horizon as the sun crept higher. The man *looked* like a Prime Minister, standing aloof in his charcoal suit, surveying the lands below. Except that his collar, tieless and unfolded around his neck, flapped in the breeze, and there were no bodyguards, aides, or servants in evidence.

North didn't press against time as he usually did, but let it flow, taking long minutes to make sure that Ransom's missing bodyguard was not down there somewhere stalking the stalker. The sun caught the western half of the Island in a moment of gold, shimmering the unburned hills. Wide green and blue horizons flowed before him in a limitless arc. Why had he entered into this strange partnership with this land? The Island, he answered, had become his life, his dream of truth. He had planted it, watered it, built on it, lit it with electricity, repaired it when it was sick, and now was protecting it against enemies who wanted to destroy it.

The March wind picked up, releasing sounds like the far-off rush of a waterfall. The wind became entrained within the four toroids of the wind machine, creating vortices in which the eight propellers spun with the speed of airplane propellers. With the sabotaged controllers telling the rotors to work against each other, the assembly vibrated, then shuddered.

A brief *brRRat!* sounded from the west, the automatic rifle North had heard yesterday spitting four rounds, five at the most. It had to be Wilson, he thought. But what could the bodyguard possibly be doing halfway to Scuba Beach? If there were more of Ransom's men on the Island, they could be signalling to each other, having abandoned their radios on the cruiser.

Ransom stared in the direction of the burst as if he too were puzzled. He was holding the rail with both hands as the wind gusted, became amplified, and torqued the propellers against each other. The tower shook violently. With a now-or-never burst, Ransom grabbed his speargun and bounded down the spiral stairwell.

North slid out of the tree and ran across the road well ahead of Ransom, who was still struggling through the brush. Circumventing the tower, he made it downhill to his ambush where he concealed himself in the foliage of the tamarinds. It was quiet inside this copse, sound-insulated along the bottom by a layer of decayed thatch fronds matted with broken spider webs. North listened, and waited.

In the distance he heard the rotors knocking against their toroidal housings, making a terrible racket as they spun wildly in different directions, tore themselves free, and flew off into the jungle. From the sound of it, they must have taken the sheet-metal housings with them. The loss of the top of the structure would set up stresses and crack the timber trusses, he knew, and then the tower collapsed. It felt to North as if the bones in his own legs were fracturing. After the crash, a vacuum of silence descended on the jungle, still as the moon.

Seconds later his ears picked up a rustle of footfalls from the frond-covered path. Through the lacy ferns and hanging cigar pods of the tamarinds, he heard then saw Ransom yawing down the slope like a Neanderthal, too dumb to move silently, too smart to go on the defensive. Half monarch, half hunter, he was thrusting his speargun ahead of him like a blind man probing danger. The steel spear gave off pale flickers where it was struck by rays of the sun sifting through the forest.

In his hiding place, stiff fronds creased North's face. He tried not to breathe.

Ransom stopped inches before the fishline, a few feet in front of the hat. There was fatigue in the lines of his face, and fear in his eyes. Suddenly he spun around with a savage glance, trying to see through the jungle. For a long moment the two opponents, equals before the lawlessness of the land, came face to face through the thick screen of ferns. North could see Ransom who could not see him. The Prime Minister stood absolutely still, brows quivering, drenched in sweat. He had taken off his suit coat and shirt. His trousers, torn and whitened with ash, hung beneath his navel and accented the sheen of his torso. His fingernails, pressed into the weapon, were shards of ice against the brown of his hands. North could sense in that intense concentration the competitiveness that had guided this politician's life and had grown into an instinct as fierce as survival. Ransom was the chessplayer examining the offered sacrifice, looking for the trap. And he found himself in *zugswang*.

Slowly, crouching to minimize the target of his body, Ransom switched off the safety and jabbed the speargun in front of him like an animal pawing at shadows. Then he saw the fishline.

North trembled in anticipation. If the trap didn't work, he knew the attack was bound to shift, for only Ransom was armed.

At the edge of the invisible brink, his arms extended, the long shaft of his spear pointing straight ahead, Ransom carefully lifted his left foot high over the almost-invisible nylon line. His foot came down and crashed through the thatch, sending him sliding legs-first into the hole.

Ransom immediately aborted his descent by clawing at the side of the tunnel near the top and using the speargun as an anchor to stab an outcropping. At the same time, North sprang from his hiding place and threw a kick into Ransom's shoulder. Ransom twisted, one hand on the weapon, the other clamped on North's ankle. His own weight and North's momentum sent them plunging together ten feet down the vertical tunnel. The rocky sides tore at their flesh; thatch floated under and over them.

At the bottom, both men came to their feet in semidarkness with Ransom holding the speargun vertically like a scepter. At the edge of North's vision insects crawled in the dampness. He could smell his own sweat. It seemed to him that he had arrived in a different place in a different time, somewhere behind enemy lines where he was soft and vulnerable with no tank of armor, no weapon of any kind. He wanted not to return to that place or that time as badly as he wanted not to be here in this bowel of the Island.

Ransom aimed at North's midsection, and fired.

The pain seared his side. For a moment North thought he'd been shot all the way through, like Bruiser. The sting of it, and then the lack of follow-through agony, jarred him back to reality: the spear had only split the skin above his belt, and the shaft had passed between his arm and body.

Turning around, his back to Ransom, North slid his fingers toward the end of the shaft where he found by touch that the point was imbedded in the rocky wall. North had shot too many spears into submarine coral heads to waste time saving the point. He grasped the rod with both hands and unscrewed it, like a chess-player emphasizing his opponent's blunder.

Now that he commanded the spear, a lethal weapon even without the point, he aimed it toward the Prime Minister. "I was a builder, Ransom. Before you changed me into a destroyer."

"And now, North? Now what are you?" Ransom asked no

quarter, defiant to the end. "A mirror of what you hate?"

Without answering, North thrust the blunt spear into Ransom's belly. Ransom gasped but did not scream. North's eyes had adapted enough to the dim light to see that the rod penetrated almost two inches into his abdomen. As he yanked it out of Ransom's flesh, the ragged puncture bubbled black against dark skin.

Stepping back, leveraging his arms for a second thrust, North felt through his fever the passion of the kill, the sanctity of retribution, a crushing hatred of this man responsible for Coby's death and his ruin.

"Stop! I've got your daughter!"

Ransom's words echoed with empty aspirations that made North crave again the touch of steel ripping flesh. A dry frond fluttered down to the rocky floor. Insects buzzed. He turned and saw under those caterpillar brows that ageless cinnamon face and suave mustache that had served this man so well in politics, now deformed in desperation. Coming close, he poured his eyes into Ransom's, staring through those windows to the soul. He still held the spear, but hesitated. Perhaps he had seen something in Ransom's mind. Perhaps a trace of his former morality repealed the bloodlust of his ancestry and made him understand that he was on the brink of mutating into the essence of what he despised.

Ransom's left eye skipped out of synch as it had done at the United Nations in those distant days of innocence, and the humbled, walleyed man slumped to the ground holding his abdomen. Here was the former man-god who had replaced the law in his country, who would kill him in an instant if it were he who held the spear, who to save himself had lied that he could produce Coby. . . .

Ransom tried to stand and doubled over in pain, but not cringing, not crying. Blood splattered his trousers and colored the cave floor. He lifted his eyes to North's and said in an oily echo:

"You want me to suffer, not to die. Isn't that why you bombed my estate, why you killed Marianne?"

"You must know Marianne's death was an accident," North whispered, his words barely audible. But Ransom was right about wanting him to suffer. He fondled the cold metal of the spear, trying to summon the barbarism of his forebears.

"Don't you want to see your daughter?"

The Prime Minister would know how to invest a lie with the ring of surprise, the avoidance of excessive zeal, the exact nuance of sincerity. North's brain swam with the certainty that it was a lie, even while hope clawed at his heart, probing his mind for fragments of truth.

The P.M. was breathing heavily, trying to stem the flow of blood with his hands and a saturated handkerchief. The discharged speargun at his feet reminded North he was unarmed and that there was Wilson to worry about too, and he made himself take the time to look around. He could see nothing of the world above; an anemic light seeped through the break in the matt of fronds that still partially covered the opening. At the bottom, the cave flared horizontally for a dozen paces or so, ending in the puddles of lesser potholes that wound deep into the intestines of the Island. There was no way out except straight up.

Ransom started to say something, but North had one more thing to do before he was ready to listen. He ripped the loading handle from Ransom's wrist, and used it to ram the spear into the barrel of the gun against the compressed air. The air-selector switch now was on full power, the setting you use when shooting sizable fish out in the open and didn't worry about the point getting stuck in rock. Even without the spearpoint, the airgun would propel the shaft right through Ransom's body, bone and all, and would pin him to the wall where he would bleed to death.

As if sensing this thought, the Prime Minister moved away from the damp walls and the scorpions, and tried sitting on a boulder in the middle of the area. The cave was quiet as the ocean floor. The only sound was the man on the boulder shaking with the fury of a head of state who has nothing left to lose. There was more light here away from the shadows, and North could see the bright red on the handkerchief and the darker blood that seeped around it and through Ransom's fingers.

"Help me," he said in a low voice, eyes bright with pain.

"Help *you!* Why?"

"Because, North, your daughter is here, because you're not a murderer, because you had it all wrong."

North was hearing what he longed to hear, the kind of blatant lie Cleary used to tell to make him feel better, a lie he knew he should not heed. But his finger relaxed on the trigger; he knew he wasn't fooling anybody.

Ransom was watching the scorpions clinging to the shadows. "A hell of a place for a final clash of cultures," he said. "It was your prejudice that brought us to this place, you know."

"*My* prejudice?"

"You prejudged me. You thought what St. Gregory did to your daughter was done at my instigation. Your prejudgment drove your actions, not the other way around."

The innuendos, the lies were beginning to reproduce like *E. coli* in Ransom's wound. North felt a curious indifference, but wished the man would stop saying "daughter." Didn't he even know her name?

"When St. Gregory discovered who she was," Ransom said, "he realized your daughter would be more valuable to him alive than dead. If I were to indict him, he could claim I had ordered her kidnapping. If you came after him, he could trade her for his freedom. St. Gregory was as much my enemy as yours. He wanted to be the power behind my office."

The breakbone fever of dengue swelled over North like a tide, and he smelled the beach-mud of his own hot skin mixing in the stagnant air with the odor of blood. Time passed, seconds or hours, he couldn't tell which, until he became aware of his ascent up the tunnel, the speargun slung over one shoulder, using protruding rocks as toeholds. Shuddering with pain and exertion, he extended a hand downward to Ransom whose fingers were soaked in the blood of his waist. The blood made it too slippery for a handhold so they clasped each others' wrists. It took time to reach the top, but they managed to climb out without falling back into the cave.

Together they struggled up the trail toward the lab and the infirmary with North holding his captive's wrist. He could feel the rapid throb of the enemy pulse, and in his ears the too-fast cadence of his own heart. The dengue clogged North's throat and raised his temperature. He didn't know what to think or what to believe.

He hadn't expected to live.

66 *Justify the Means*

THE LABORATORY floor was littered with palmetto bugs, and when they walked on them the shells crackled like the building was on fire. Smoke from the forest fires had sucked oxygen out of the air and made it hard to breathe. North helped Ransom to the infirmary bed where he reclined on one elbow and unfastened his belt, stemming the blood flow by pressing a towel to his wound. He had lost a lot of blood and his face was twisted in pain and fatigue. There was the smell of infection about him. But he wanted to talk, to purge himself and North of their delusions, as if to end the ordeal so they could go home and pick up their lives.

"The fact that you advocated legalization made me your collaborator, as well as your enemy," Ransom said, obsessed with explanations, his thick eyebrows lowered a millimeter. In the glow of the sun through the window, he radiated light as he spoke of his dark franchise. "At first, the problem was simple. You have a nation of addicts; we have a nation of businessmen. But when I discovered Marianne was an addict, everything changed."

North's thoughts drifted, then focused. You could no more blame the Plague for the tragedies of the nineties than you could blame rum-running for the poverty of the twenties. He knew the real problem was prejudice, then and now, the hot engine that still

529

drives relationships between rich countries and the Third World.

"We've changed places on the chessboard, you and I," said the P.M. "And not just on the legalization of drugs. In your mind you were the great builder, and I the terrible destroyer. But look at what I've built in this country. And what you've destroyed."

There was truth in Ransom's words, and North remembered Rolle's rule of the bizarre: *Nothing in this country is as it seems.* Having failed as a warrior, the Prime Minister was reverting to his more familiar role of politician, master of the end game.

"Who is the demon now, North? I may have spawned the monster in St. Gregory, but you, North, *you killed him!* Just like you killed everything around you." His voice trailed off. ". . . including the person I loved most in the world." Ransom gasped and asked for water.

North said nothing, bringing the water and taking the P.M.'s pulse. Ransom's heart was fibrillating as he sank back on the bed. The vast gulf between them, of race and nationality, of ambitions and ways to fix the broken world, had widened into an ocean.

"You don't believe in God, do you?" said Ransom.

North looked down and saw the worst of mankind's gods, the Christian god who burned witches, the Muslim god who promises heaven to killers, and all the rest.

"Well. . . ?" said Ransom. Even in his agony, pierced by a spear in his side and spread-eagled on the cross of this bed, that intimidating "well" of his came through sharp as a church bell.

North would not dignify this would-be god of the Indies with an answer bound to be complex. He took a deep breath to clear his head, and swallowed some aspirin from a bottle next to the bed. Logic told him he had to feed antibiotics to Ransom, to keep him alive for more questions about Coby. How far he had fallen, he thought, to where he valued a man's life only for its utility.

North trudged to the medicine closet. On the adjacent counter lay a box of sodium bicarbonate next to the solar desalinator, the base of which had been altered into a crucible. Golden globules of glass connected by curving tubes and spires shot through the ceiling like stems of exotic plants. North traced his finger against the side of the distillation unit, and tasted the residue. These were not the salts of seawater but of cocaine hydrochloride: crack.

Rolle had been right about drugs materializing the moment they left. *The hell with them all!* With a sweep of his arm, he sent the glassware crashing onto the floor, and stamped on the broken pieces, crunching his outrage into the concrete and scattering the evidence of the cocaine.

Afterwards he sat on a stool to slow his heartbeat. It was obvious by the modification of his desalinator and the condition of the seafarm that the five villagers they'd left to maintain the Island had been the ones who had converted the apparatus in order to make crack, choosing narco-solace instead of seafarming, perhaps nodding through the hours of their watch until Ransom and St. Gregory arrived and scared them off. His workers, yes, and his fault for leaving the Island, but he kept coming back to the one man who bore the ultimate responsibility. Charles T. Ransom. The man who played god from the heights of the Churchill building, whose toys were human lives, whose past actions had encouraged St. Gregory's piracies and had turned this idyllic nation into a dung heap of dope and racism. Transom in charge.

The lock on the closet door was broken. Inside, North found gauze, bandages, and bottles of pharmaceuticals, and picked up a bottle marked, SULFADIAZOL (POWDER). Acting on a hunch, he opened it and tasted a sample of the contents. Cocaine. He opened another bottle that read, BORIC ACID CRYSTALS. It tasted like phencyclidine, angel dust. IODINE, TERPIN HYDRATE, VITAMIN-C, PAREGORIC, QUININE—whatever the labels read, the bottles contained cocaine, crack, meth, amphetamines, and God knows what else. There were enough alkaloids here, enough uppers and downers and rocket fuel for blastoff and reentry. It didn't take genetic engineering to process dope, he realized; it took only a knowledge of bush medicine, a supply of imported drugs, and the use of a centrifuge and distillation unit. There was too much here for the consumption of five casual junkies; they must have been selling the stuff. His Island for Science had become a front for drugs after all, just as St. Gregory and the Commodore had suspected. The thought left him empty.

Abandoning the bottles of powders and crystals, and dizzy

from fever, North filled a hypodermic syringe with water and inserted the needle into an ampule he took from a box labeled: PENICILLIN-G POTASSIUM FOR INJECTION, USP. He shook the ampule to dissolve the powder, and aspirated the liquid back into the syringe barrel. *What am I doing?* he thought suddenly, and examined the rubber stoppers in a half-dozen of the ampules. They were firmly in place and seemed ordinary enough, but that could be the point of it all—if this were some leftover package of dope meant for shipment to the States.

Inflamed with dengue, the pain in his joints hit him all at once and he reeled from a surge of fever. He tossed the syringe on the counter and started painfully for the door, squashing palmetto bugs under foot. As he passed the bed on which Ransom lay propped on an elbow, the wounded man raised a hand to stop him from going outside. North half sat on the end table next to the bed and listened, remembering . . . something about Coby, something Ransom had said in the cave . . .

"Remember those arguments we had about the end justifying the means?" Ransom said. No longer liquid, his voice was a dry rasp, but it still was a weapon he could use to distract his opponent. "You know why I believe the end justified the means? Because Christ himself believed it."

"Forget it, Ransom. Where's Coby?"

"She'll be coming." He was having difficulty holding up his head, the head of a pundit on the body of an old and broken street fighter. "I'll make a deal with you, North. You find *her* alive, you keep *me* alive."

A man will do anything to prolong life, thought North, even for a few hours, or minutes.

Ransom was going on about Christ. "It was suicide, you know."

A gush of fever washed over North, but all he could think of was Marianne. Her death was suicide too.

"Whether you believe that Christ was the son of God, surely you accept that *he believed he was God,* and therefore sufficiently powerful to stop his own execution. Why didn't he try? The only possible answer is that he believed the desired end—his martyrdom and the subsequent inauguration of Christianity—justified the means, which was his suicide."

Ransom's face was a mask of agony, his voice a whisper. "Christ should have saved himself, as I should have saved Marianne."

North could carry the weight of his skeleton no longer. His bones felt like they were breaking, and his brain boiled in a fog of delirium. He thought he heard Sidney Rolle calling to him from a distance, and went outside to look. A vision of Jack Cleary swaggered up the slope of beach, sport coat slung over a shoulder, and in his hands were two green coconuts sliced off at the top, spiked with rum. He was wearing a baseball cap, sneakers, and a playful grin as though his funeral had been an immense practical joke.

Outside in the shade, the cool air entrained Ransom's desperate whispers. *Should have saved Marianne . . .* North tried to concentrate. He'd had nothing to eat since Bimini, and he was thirsty and hot. *Saved her from what. . . ?* Somebody called his name again, and he tried to see against the sun. Something at the water's edge slithered in the brownish haze of the seafarm, but he could not distinguish the shapes from their shadows. Halfway up the beach the two figures materialized in patterns distinctly human. They had their arms around each other, one limping slightly, one hobbling with the aid of a makeshift crutch. North slid to the ground, his head against the gum elemi. He had lost his Panama hat somewhere, and the reddish peel of bark flaked onto his head.

Mirage waves undulated from the fevered Island of North, and tried to break whatever of his bones were still intact. Knowing firsthand the pain of the crippled jungle, he burned with fury against this year of death and his own deeds. He wanted to talk, but his head was seized in the vice of dengue and it hurt too much to use his voice. Against the sun, the water glistened black. A small thin figure in bleached shirt raced up the slope of the beach waving a baseball cap.

Coby!

She had a submachine gun slung over her shoulder like a female revolutionary from some Liberation organization.

North felt he had entered into a fugue, but could do nothing to stop it. Suddenly she stood in front of him at the gum elemi tree, a silhouette with the aura of a young animal, her hair a golden candle against the sun. She knelt at his side, her face no longer in shadow, and he saw puffy eyes, arms full of sores, hair tangled, body ragged and thin, and her thigh as if it had been mauled by a shark. But her hands were white doves and they unfolded to him, flaring like open wings.

Rolle came next smiling from ear to ear. North sat erect as Rolle bent over and clasped his shoulders, the way men do to brothers or to those with whom they have survived a battle. "You're not the only guy who gets hunches, Grant!" He kneaded North's neck muscles as if to impress the meaning of his words.

"Dad!" said the vision of Coby who placed a cool hand on his forehead. "You're burning up."

Coby's illusion merged into that of the Nassau street girl, a clone from his nightmare seeping out of the sky where it met the sea. Fables came tumbling from the apparition through his fever: of a basement jail, of a year spent digging a tunnel, of her wound that had been attended at the same Rassin Hospital he had passed so often in Nassau. Curious that her scars were in the same place as Rolle's! But what about Cyril Christie's last message. . . ? "The Defender noncom—Cyril—said he killed you. . . ."

"He killed the girl that Basil had picked up," she said.

"What was her name?" he asked, testing reality. If the hypothesis were true, he could do nothing for the girl who had been machine-gunned and thrown to the sharks except remember her name.

"Ann," said Coby. "She was from New York."

Every detail had to fit his bleary hypothesis or else he could not allow himself to accept Coby's survival, even in a dream.

"How did Cyril get your necklace?"

"He must have found it on the floor. The chain had broken."
"Dad, I'm *home* now!" She kissed her father with salty lips, bitterer than tears, and wrapped thin arms around his neck.

North said nothing, wanting nothing to deny the miracle. The miracle was that Coby's spirit had stopped scintillating and was dancing around him in solid living happiness, stopping only long enough to answer his questions. The reality was that if Coby wasn't dead she must be dying, for everyone on earth was dying and waiting to be buried. Coby would have been nineteen now. He held her hand lightly, a calloused hand he was afraid to squeeze for fear the illusion might vanish.

Voices from inside the lab grew louder, struggling to expose some secret. Through the doorway North could see Rolle leaning over Ransom.

"Dad. . . ?"

He said nothing, for nothing need be said.

Coby looked into his eyes, only inches away. "You're terribly sick," she said. "You're dreaming, you know."

She nuzzled into his arms, as Coby had done so often in life before that fateful quarrel. He felt her kissing him, her tears mingling with his own in an illimitable delight, like horizons at the edge of space, or an Island all your own.

His delirium was a rolling fog that parted, and he came fully awake, his pulse racing across the ashes of a waiting heart. *Coby!* Alive, vigorous, responsive. Brushed by the sun, her face was a smile of love and forgiveness. She was his daughter, and she had come to him.

The icy thought assaulted him that if Coby had not been killed, then Ransom did not deserve to die. North came to his feet with Coby's help, and staggered into the laboratory amid sounds of Rolle's ministrations and Ransom's murmurs for water.

Ransom opened his mouth to say something, but his eyes went out of focus and rotated upward, showing white.

Rolle was holding a bottle marked sulfa in his left hand, and with his right was pressing a cotton compress over the two-inch puncture in Ransom's abdomen.

"Sidney, *NO! That's cocaine!*"

He lunged at Rolle's hand and tore the compress from the throbbing red meat of the wound. The white powder had turned into a pink paste, like puss, and had the smell of death on it. He tried to wipe it away in an action that lasted an eternity.

"*Water!*" he yelled.

Coby brought water and he flooded the mangled flesh as Ransom's muscles contracted violently. He was going into convulsions.

North saw the hypodermic syringe lying on the table. It was empty. He stopped abruptly with a sense of utter futility, knowing that the powder in the wound was relatively harmless, that it was the contents of the syringe that was doing the damage.

Rolle saw North looking at the empty hypodermic, and said, "Jesus, I didn't think he could be allergic to penicillin. He *asked* me for it. The infection was really bad, so I shot it in his vein."

"The stuff in the ampule," North said with sudden comprehension. "It was cocaine."

It is the consequences of our acts, he thought, not our intent, that count in the end.

Ransom stiffened under the paroxysmal rush that had found its way to his brain, where a billion axons leapt with the speed of lightning across a billion dendrites, exploding the synaptic cells throughout his nervous system, and shuddering his body as the massive overdose seized an already overburdened heart. The Prime Minister breathed out the rest of his life in grating gasps.

North was stunned. He draped an arm around Coby as if to make sure she didn't slide into his mirage again. Like most wars, there are only losers. Marianne, Cleary, and the other innocents. St. Gregory who deserved it. And Ransom who did not.

"My God but that stuff works fast!" Rolle said. "Did you know it was White Lady when you loaded the syringe?"

"Does it matter?" North said. "He's dead."

Sidney Rolle took a long and thoughtful look into the soul of this white man who had become his best friend. "Yes," he said, deadly serious. "It matters."

About the Author

NEIL RUZIC moves freely in both literary and scientific worlds. The founder of the world's leading magazine for research scientists and engineers (now called *R&D*), oceanographic, and other magazines, Ruzic was awarded the first U.S. patent for a device to be used exclusively on the moon. This is his tenth book. He is a journalism and science graduate of Northwestern University, served in the Army as a tank leader, and is a tournament chess player, scuba diver, and private pilot.

Ruzic incorporated Island for Science Inc. and bought the Bahamian island of Little Stirrup Cay where he spent many years developing wind generators, a seafarm, and other technologies to benefit the region. The government ultimately refused to let him operate, so he recast the Island into a cruise-ship port of call, now called "CocoCay."